Praise for Harlan Coben

'It is always satisfying to discover a new crime writer
– and this is the business . . . this book will keep you
up until 2 a.m.' *The Times*

'Harlan Coben. He's smart, he's funny, and he has
something to say' Michael Connelly

'An increasingly frightening conspiracy with an
unguessable ending . . . hard to put down'
Sunday Telegraph

'At last a British publisher has given British readers
the chance to discover something every US mystery
fan already knows – that Harlan Coben is one of the
most entertaining and intriguing crime writers
around'
Val McDermid, *Manchester Evening Guardian*

'What sets Harlan Coben above the crowd are wit and
. . . an entertaining plot'
Los Angeles Times Book Review

'Fast action, snappy dialogue and plenty of insider
hoops material make this a fast, enjoyable read'
Toronto Star

'Coben . . . scores a hole in one! The characters are
deftly etched and the details keenly observed'
Publishers Weekly

D0180107

Harlan Coben is the author of the bestselling *Tell No One*, as well as six Myron Bolitar novels: *The Final Detail*, *One False Move*, *Back Spin*, the Edgar and Shamus Award-winning *Fade Away*, *Drop Shot* and *Deal Breaker*, which won an Anthony and received an Edgar Award nomination for Best Original Paperback. His latest novel, *Gone For Good*, is also published by Orion. Harlan Coben lives in New Jersey with his wife and four children. His email address is me@harlancoben.com, and his website can be visited at www.harlancoben.com.

Back Spin

———

Tell No One

HARLAN COBEN

ORION

Back Spin
First published in Great Britain by Orion Books Ltd in 2002

Tell No One
First published in Great Britain by Orion Books Ltd in 2001

This omnibus edition published in 2006
by Orion Books Ltd,
Orion House, 5 Upper St Martin's Lane,
London WC2H 9EA

Published by arrangement with Dell Publishing,
an imprint of The Bantam Dell Publishing Group,
a division of Random House, Inc.

A CIP catalogue record for this book is available from the British
Library.

ISBN 1 89880 195 9

Printed and bound in Great Britain by
Mackays of Chatham Ltd, Chatham Kent

ACKNOWLEDGMENTS

When an author is writing about an activity he enjoys about as much as sticking his tongue in a fan (golf), he needs help and lots of it. With that in mind the author wishes to thank the following: James Bradbeer, Jr., Peter Roisman, Maggie Griffin, Craig Coben, Larry Coben, Jacob Hoye, Lisa Erbach Vance, Frank Snyder, the rec.sports.golf board, Knitwit, Sparkle Hayter, Anita Meyer, the many golfers who regaled me with their scintillating tales (snore), and of course, Dave Bolt. While the U.S. Open is a real golf tournament and Merion is a real golf club, this book is a work of fiction. I took some liberties, combined locales and tournaments, that kind of thing. As always, any errors—factual or otherwise—are totally the fault of these people. The author is not to blame.

Myron and I tried. But we're still not sure we get it.

Chapter 1

Myron Bolitar used a cardboard periscope to look over the suffocating throngs of ridiculously clad spectators. He tried to recall the last time he'd actually used a toy periscope, and an image of sending in proof-of-purchase seals from a box of Cap'n Crunch cereal flickered in front him like headache-inducing sunspots.

Through the mirrored reflection, Myron watched a man dressed in knickers—knickers, for crying out loud—stand over a tiny white sphere. The ridiculously clad spectators mumbled excitedly. Myron stifled a yawn. The knickered man crouched. The ridiculously clad spectators jostled and then settled into an eerie silence. Sheer stillness followed, as if even the trees and shrubs and well-coiffed blades of grass were holding their collective breath.

Then the knickered man whacked the white sphere with a stick.

The crowd began to murmur in the indistinguishable syllables of backstage banter. As the ball ascended, so did the volume of the murmurs. Words could be made out. Then phrases. "Lovely golf stroke." "Super golf shot." "Beautiful golf shot." "Truly fine golf stroke." They always said *golf* stroke, like someone might mistake it for a *swim* stroke, or—as Myron was currently contemplating in this blazing heat—a *sun*stroke.

"Mr. Bolitar?"

Myron took the periscope away from his eyes. He was

tempted to yell "Up periscope," but feared some at
stately, snooty Merion Golf Club would view the act as
immature. Especially during the U.S. Open. He looked
down at a ruddy-faced man of about seventy.

"Your pants," Myron said.

"Pardon me?"

"You're afraid of getting hit by a golf cart, right?"

They were orange and yellow in a hue slightly more
luminous than a bursting supernova. To be fair, the man's
clothing hardly stood out. Most in the crowd seemed to
have woken up wondering what apparel they possessed
that would clash with, say, the free world. Orange and
green tints found exclusively in several of your tackiest
neon signs adorned many. Yellow and some strange
shades of purple were also quite big—usually together—
like a color scheme rejected by a Midwest high school
cheerleading squad. It was as if being surrounded by all
this God-given natural beauty made one want to do all in
his power to offset it. Or maybe there was something else
at work here. Maybe the ugly clothes had a more functional origin. Maybe in the old days, when animals
roamed free, golfers dressed this way to ward off dangerous wildlife.

Good theory.

"I need to speak with you," the elderly man whispered. "It's urgent."

The rounded, jovial cheeks belied his pleading eyes.
He suddenly gripped Myron's forearm. "Please," he
added.

"What's this about?" Myron asked.

The man made a movement with his neck, like his
collar was on too tight. "You're a sports agent, right?"

"Yes."

"You're here to find clients?"

Myron narrowed his eyes. "How do you know I'm not

here to witness the enthralling spectacle of grown men taking a walk?''

The old man did not smile, but then again, golfers were not known for their sense of humor. He craned his neck again and moved closer. His whisper was hoarse. ''Do you know the name Jack Coldren?'' he asked.

''Sure,'' Myron said.

If the old man had asked the same question yesterday, Myron wouldn't have had a clue. He didn't follow golf that closely (or at all), and Jack Coldren had been little more than a journeyman over the past twenty years or so. But Coldren had been the surprise leader after the U.S. Open's first day, and now, with just a few holes remaining in the second round, Coldren was up by a commanding eight strokes. ''What about him?''

''And Linda Coldren?'' the man asked. ''Do you know who she is?''

This one was easier. Linda Coldren was Jack's wife and far and away the top female golfer of the past decade. ''Yeah, I know who she is,'' Myron said.

The man leaned in closer and did the neck thing again. Seriously annoying—not to mention contagious. Myron found himself fighting off the desire to mimic the movement. ''They're in deep trouble,'' the old man whispered. ''If you help them, you'll have two new clients.''

''What sort of trouble?''

The old man looked around. ''Please,'' he said. ''There are too many people. Come with me.''

Myron shrugged. No reason not to go. The old man was the only lead he'd unearthed since his friend and business associate Windsor Horne Lockwood III—Win, for short—had dragged his sorry butt down here. Being that the U.S. Open was at Merion—home course of the Lockwood family for something like a billion years—Win had felt it would be a great opportunity for Myron to land

a few choice clients. Myron wasn't quite so sure. As near
as he could tell, the major component separating him
from the hordes of other locust-like agents swarming the
green meadows of Merion Golf Club was his naked aversion for golf. Probably not a key selling point to the faith-
ful.

Myron Bolitar ran MB SportsReps, a sports representation firm located on Park Avenue in New York City. He
rented the space from his former college roommate, Win,
a Waspy, old-money, big-time investment banker whose
family owned Lock-Horne Securities on the same Park
Avenue in New York. Myron handled the negotiations
while Win, one of the country's most respected brokers,
handled the investments and finances. The other member
of the MB team, Esperanza Diaz, handled everything
else. Three branches with checks and balances. Just like
the American government. Very patriotic.

Slogan: *MB SportsReps—the other guys are commie
pinkos.*

As the old man ushered Myron through the crowd,
several men in green blazers—another look sported
mostly at golf courses, perhaps to camouflage oneself
against the grass—greeted him with whispered, "How
do, Bucky," or "Looking good, Buckster," or "Fine day
for golf, Buckaroo." They all had the accent of the rich
and preppy, the kind of inflection where *mommy* is pronounced "mummy" and summer and winter are verbs.
Myron was about to comment on a grown man being
called Bucky, but when your name is Myron, well, glass
houses and stones and all that.

Like every other sporting event in the free world, the
actual playing area looked more like a giant billboard
than a field of competition. The leader board was sponsored by IBM. Canon handed out the periscopes. American Airlines employees worked the food stands (an airline

handling food—what think tank came up with that one?).
Corporate Row was jam-packed with companies who
shelled out over one hundred grand a pop to set up a tent
for a few days, mostly so that company executives had an
excuse to go. Travelers Group, Mass Mutual, Aetna (golfers must like insurance), Canon, Heublein. Heublein.
What the hell was a Heublein? They looked like a nice
company. Myron would probably buy a Heublein if he
knew what one was.

The funny thing was, the U.S. Open was actually less
commercialized than most tourneys. At least they hadn't
sold their name yet. Other tournaments were named for
sponsors and the names had gotten a little silly. Who
could get up for winning the JC Penney Open or the
Michelob Open or even the Wendy's Three-Tour Challenge?

The old man led him to a primo parking lot.
Mercedeses, Caddies, limos. Myron spotted Win's Jag-
uar. The USGA had recently put up a sign that read MEM-
BERS PARKING ONLY.

Myron said, "You're a member of Merion." Dr. Deduction.

The old man twisted the neck thing into something
approaching a nod. "My family dates back to Merion's
inception," he said, the snooty accent now more pronounced. "Just like your friend Win."

Myron stopped and looked at the man. "You know
Win?"

The old man sort of smiled and shrugged. No commitment.

"You haven't told me your name yet," Myron said.

"Stone Buckwell," he said, hand extended. "Everyone calls me Bucky."

Myron shook the hand.

"I'm also Linda Coldren's father," he added.

Bucky unlocked a sky-blue Cadillac and they slid inside. He put the key in the ignition. The radio played Muzak—worse, the Muzak version of "Raindrops Keep Falling on My Head." Myron quickly opened the window for air, not to mention noise.

Only members were allowed to park on the Merion grounds, so it wasn't too much of a hassle getting out. They made a right at the end of the driveway and then another right. Bucky mercifully flipped off the radio. Myron stuck his head back in the car.

"What do you know about my daughter and her husband?" Bucky asked.

"Not much."

"You are not a golf fan, are you, Mr. Bolitar?"

"Not really."

"Golf is truly a magnificent sport," he said. Then he added, "Though the word *sport* does not begin to do it justice."

"Uh-huh," Myron said.

"It's the game of princes." Buckwell's ruddy face glowed a bit now, the eyes wide with the same type of rapture one saw in the very religious. His voice was low and awed. "There is nothing quite like it, you know. You alone against the course. No excuses. No teammate. No bad calls. It's the purest of activities."

"Uh-huh," Myron said again. "Look, I don't want to appear rude, Mr. Buckwell, but what's this all about?"

"Please call me Bucky."

"Okay. Bucky."

He nodded his approval. "I understand that you and Windsor Lockwood are more than business associates," he said.

"Meaning?"

"I understand you two go back a long way. College roommates, am I correct?"

"Why do you keep asking about Win?"

"I actually came to the club to find him," Bucky said. "But I think it's better this way."

"What way?"

"Talking to you first. Maybe after . . . well, we'll see. Shouldn't hope for too much."

Myron nodded. "I have no idea what you're talking about."

Bucky turned onto a road adjacent to the course called Golf House Road. Golfers were so creative.

The course was on the right, imposing mansions on the left. A minute later, Bucky pulled into a circular driveway. The house was fairly big and made of something called river rock. River rock was big in this area, though Win always referred to it as "Mainline Stone." There was a white fence and lots of tulips and two maple trees, one on each side of the front walk. A large porch was enclosed on the right side. The car came to a stop, and for a moment neither of them moved.

"What's this all about, Mr. Buckwell?"

"We have a situation here," he said.

"What kind of situation?"

"I'd rather let my daughter explain it to you." He grabbed the key out of the ignition and reached for the door.

"Why come to me?" Myron asked.

"We were told you could possibly help."

"Who told you that?"

Buckwell started rolling his neck with greater fervor. His head looked like it'd been attached by a loose ball socket. When he finally got it under control, he managed to look Myron in the eyes.

"Win's mother," he said.

Myron stiffened. His heart plummeted down a dark shaft. He opened his mouth, closed it, waited. Buckwell got out of the car and headed for the door. Ten seconds later, Myron followed.

"Win won't help," Myron said.

Buckwell nodded. "That's why I came to you first."

They followed a brick path to a door slightly ajar. Buckwell pushed it open. "Linda?"

Linda Coldren stood before a television in the den. Her white shorts and sleeveless yellow blouse revealed the lithe, toned limbs of an athlete. She was tall with short spunky black hair and a tan that accentuated the smooth, long muscles. The lines around her eyes and mouth placed her in her late thirties, and he could see instantly why she was a commercial darling. There was a fierce splendor to this woman, a beauty derived from a sense of strength rather than delicacy.

She was watching the tournament on the television. On top of the set were framed family photographs. Big, pillowy couches formed a V in one corner. Tactfully furnished, for a golfer. No putting green, AstroTurf carpet. None of that golf artwork that seemed a step or two below the aesthetic class of, say, paintings of dogs playing poker. No cap with a tee and ball on the brim hanging from a moose head.

Linda Coldren suddenly swung her line of vision toward them, firing a glare past Myron before settling on her father. "I thought you were going to get Jack," she snapped.

"He hasn't finished the round yet."

She motioned to the television. "He's on eighteen now. I thought you were going to wait for him."

"I got Mr. Bolitar instead."

"Who?"

Myron stepped forward and smiled. "I'm Myron Bolitar."

Linda Coldren flicked her eyes at him, then back to her father. "Who the hell is he?"

"He's the man Cissy told me about," Buckwell said.

"Who's Cissy?" Myron asked.

"Win's mother."

"Oh," Myron said. "Right."

Linda Coldren said, "I don't want him here. Get rid of him."

"Linda, listen to me. We need help."

"Not from him."

"He and Win have experience with this type of thing."

"Win," she said slowly, "is psychotic."

"Ah," Myron said. "Then you know him well?"

Linda Coldren finally turned her attention to Myron. Her eyes, deep and brown, met his. "I haven't spoken to Win since he was eight years old," she said. "But you don't have to leap into a pit of flames to know it's hot."

Myron nodded. "Nice analogy."

She shook her head and looked back at her father. "I told you before: no police. We do what they say."

"But he's not police," her father said.

"And you shouldn't be telling anyone."

"I only told my sister," Bucky protested. "She'd never say anything."

Myron felt his body stiffen again. "Wait a second," he said to Bucky. "Your sister is Win's mother?"

"Yes."

"You're Win's uncle." He looked at Linda Coldren. "And you're Win's first cousin."

Linda Coldren looked at him like he'd just peed on the floor. "With smarts like that," she said, "I'm glad you're on our side."

Everyone's a wiseass.

"If it's still unclear, Mr. Bolitar, I could break out some poster board and sketch a family tree for you."

"Could you use lots of pretty colors?" Myron said. "I like pretty colors."

She made a face and turned away. On the television, Jack Coldren lined up a twelve-foot putt. Linda stopped and watched. He tapped it; the ball took off and arched right into the hole. The gallery applauded with modest enthusiasm. Jack picked up the ball with two fingers and then tipped his hat. The IBM leader board flashed on the screen. Jack Coldren was up by a whopping nine strokes.

Linda Coldren shook her head. "Poor bastard."

Myron kept still. So did Bucky.

"He's waited twenty-three years for this moment," she continued. "And he picks now."

Myron glanced at Bucky. Bucky glanced back, shaking his head.

Linda Coldren stared at the television until her husband exited to the clubhouse. Then she took a deep breath and looked at Myron. "You see, Mr. Bolitar, Jack has never won a professional tournament. The closest he ever came was in his rookie year twenty-three years ago, when he was only nineteen. It was the last time the U.S. Open was held at Merion. You may remember the headlines."

They were not altogether unfamiliar. This morning's papers had rehashed it a bit. "He lost a lead, right?"

Linda Coldren made a scoffing sound. "That's a bit of an understatement, but yes. Since then, his career has been completely unspectacular. There were years he didn't even make the tour."

"He picked a hell of a time to snap his streak," Myron said. "The U.S. Open."

She gave him a funny look and folded her arms under her chest. "Your name rings a bell," she said. "You used to play basketball, right?"

"Right."

"In the ACC. North Carolina?"

"Duke," he corrected.

"Right, Duke. I remember now. You blew out your knee after the draft."

Myron nodded slowly.

"That was the end of your career, right?"

Myron nodded again.

"It must have been tough," she said.

Myron said nothing.

She made a waving motion with her hand. "What happened to you is nothing compared to what happened to Jack."

"Why do you say that?"

"You had an injury. It may have been tough, but at least you weren't at fault. Jack had a six-stroke lead at the U.S. Open with only eight holes left. Do you know what that's like? That's like having a ten-point lead with a minute left in the seventh game of the NBA finals. It's like missing a wide-open slam dunk in the final seconds to lose the championship. Jack was never the same man after that. He never recovered. He has spent his whole life since, just waiting for the chance of redemption." She turned back to the television. The leader board was back up. Jack Coldren was still up by nine strokes.

"If he loses again . . ."

She did not bother finishing the thought. They all stood in silence. Linda staring at the television. Bucky craning his neck, his eyes moist, his face quivering near tears.

"So what's wrong, Linda?" Myron asked.

"Our son," she said. "Somebody has kidnapped our son."

Chapter 2

"I shouldn't be telling you this," Linda Coldren said. "He said he'd kill him."

"Who said?"

Linda Coldren took several deep breaths, like a child atop the high board. Myron waited. It took some time, but she finally took the plunge.

"I got a call this morning," she said. Her large indigo eyes were wide and everywhere now, settling down on no one spot for more than a second. "A man said he had my son. He said if I called the police, he would kill him."

"Did he say anything else?"

"Just that he'd call back with instructions."

"That's it?"

She nodded.

"What time was this?" Myron asked.

"Nine, nine-thirty."

Myron walked over to the television and picked up one of the framed photographs. "Is this a recent photograph of your son?"

"Yes."

"How old is he?"

"Sixteen. His name is Chad."

Myron studied the photograph. The smiling adolescent had the fleshy features of his father. He wore a baseball cap with the brim curled the way kids like to nowadays. A golf club rested proudly on his shoulder like a minuteman with a bayonet. His eyes were squinted as though he were looking into the sun. Myron looked over Chad's face, as if it might give him a clue or some rare insight. It didn't.

"When did you first notice that your son was missing?"

Linda Coldren gave her father a quick glance, then straightened up, holding her head high as if she were readying himself for a blow. Her words came slow. "Chad had been gone for two days."

"Gone?" Myron Bolitar, Grand Inquisitor.

"Yes."

"When you say gone—"

"I mean just that," she interrupted. "I haven't seen him since Wednesday."

"But the kidnapper just called today?"

"Yes."

Myron started to speak, stopped himself, softened his voice. Tread gently, fair Myron. Ever gently. "Did you have any idea where he was?"

"I assumed he was staying with his friend Matthew," Linda Coldren replied.

Myron nodded, as if this statement showed brilliant insight. Then nodded again. "Chad told you that?"

"No."

"So," he said, aiming for casual, "for the past two days, you didn't know where your son was."

"I just told you: I thought he was staying with Matthew."

"You didn't call the police."

"Of course not."

Myron was about to ask another follow-up question, but her posture made him rethink his words. Linda took advantage of his indecisiveness. She walked to the kitchen with an upright, fluid grace. Myron followed. Bucky seemed to snap out of a trance and trailed.

"Let me make sure I'm following you," Myron said, approaching from a different angle now. "Chad vanished before the tournament?"

"Correct," she said. "The Open started Thursday." Linda Coldren pulled the refrigerator handle. The door opened with a sucking pop. "Why? Is that important?"

"It eliminates a motive," Myron said.

"What motive?"

"Tampering with the tournament," Myron said. "If Chad had vanished today—with your husband holding such a big lead—I might think that someone was out to sabotage his chances of winning the Open. But two days ago, before the tournament had begun . . ."

"No one would have given Jack a snowball's chance in hell," she finished for him. "Oddsmakers would have put him at one in five thousand. At best." She nodded as she spoke, seeing the logic. "Would you like some lemonade?" she asked.

"No, thanks."

"Dad?"

Bucky shook his head. Linda Coldren bent down into the refrigerator.

"Okay," Myron said, clapping his hand together, trying his best to sound casual. "We've ruled out one possibility. Let's try another."

Linda Coldren stopped and watched him. A gallon glass pitcher was gripped in her hand, her forearm bunching easily with the weight. Myron debated how to approach this. There was no easy way.

"Could your son be behind this?" Myron asked.

"What?"

"It's an obvious question," Myron said, "under the circumstances."

She put the pitcher down on a wooden center block.

"What the hell are you talking about? You think Chad faked his own kidnapping?"

"I didn't say that. I said I wanted to check out the possibility."

"Get out."

"He was gone two days, and you didn't call the police," Myron said. "One possible conclusion is that there was some sort of tension here. That Chad had run away before."

"Or," Linda Coldren countered, her hands tightening into fists, "you could conclude that we trusted our son. That we gave him a level of freedom compatible with his level of maturity and responsibility."

Myron looked over at Bucky. Bucky's head was lowered. "If that's the case—"

"That's the case."

"But don't responsible kids tell their parents where they're going? I mean, just to make sure they don't worry."

Linda Coldren took out a glass with too much care. She set it on the counter and slowly poured herself some lemonade. "Chad has learned to be very independent," she said as the glass filled. "His father and I are both professional golfers. That means, quite frankly, that neither one of us is home very often."

"Your being away so much," Myron said. "Has it led to tension?"

Linda Coldren shook her head. "This is useless."

"I'm just trying—"

"Look, Mr. Bolitar, Chad did not fake this. Yes, he's a teenager. No, he's not perfect, and neither are his parents. But he did not fake his own kidnapping. And if he did—I know he didn't, but let's just pretend for the sake of argument that he did—then he is safe and we do not need you. If this is some kind of cruel deception, we'll learn it soon enough. But if my son is in danger, then following this line of thought is a waste of time I can ill afford.''

Myron nodded. She had a point. ''I understand,'' he said.

''Good.''

''Have you called his friend since you heard from the kidnapper? The one you thought he might've been staying with?''

''Matthew Squires, yes.''

''Did Matthew have any idea where he was?''

''None.''

''They're close friends, right?''

''Yes.''

''Very close?''

She frowned. ''Yes, very.''

''Does Matthew call here a lot?''

''Yes. Or they talk by E-mail.''

''I'll need Matthew's phone number,'' Myron said.

''But I just told you I spoke to him already.''

''Humor me,'' Myron said. ''Okay, now let's back up a second. When was the last time you saw Chad?''

''The day he disappeared.''

''What happened?''

She frowned again. ''What do you mean, what happened? He left for summer school. I haven't seen him since.''

Myron studied her. She stopped and looked back at him a little too steadily. Something here was not adding up. ''Have you called the school,'' he asked, ''to see if he was there that day?''

''I didn't think of it.''

Myron checked his watch. Friday. Five P.M. ''I doubt anyone will still be there, but give it a shot. Do you have more than one phone line?''

''Yes.''

"Don't call on the line the kidnapper called in on. I don't want the line tied up in case he calls back."

She nodded. "Okay."

"Does your son have any credit cards or ATM cards or anything like that?"

"Yes."

"I'll need a list. And the numbers, if you have them."

She nodded again.

Myron said, "I'm going to call a friend, see if I can get an override Caller ID put in on this line. For when he calls back. I assume Chad has a computer?"

"Yes," she said.

"Where is it?"

"Up in his room."

"I'm going to download everything on it to my office via his modem. I have an assistant named Esperanza. She'll comb through it and see what she can find."

"Like what?"

"Frankly I have no idea. E-mails. Correspondence. Bulletin boards he participates in. Anything that might give us a clue. It's not a very scientific process. You check out enough stuff and maybe something will click."

Linda thought about it for a moment. "Okay," she said.

"How about you, Mrs. Coldren? Do you have any enemies?"

She sort of smiled. "I'm the number one-rated woman golfer in the world," she said. "That gives me a lot of enemies."

"Anyone you can imagine doing this?"

"No," she said. "No one."

"How about your husband? Anybody who hates your husband enough?"

"Jack?" She forced out a chuckle. "Everyone loves Jack."

"What's that supposed to mean?"

She just shook her head and waved him off.

Myron asked a few more questions, but there was little left for him to excavate. He asked if he could go up to Chad's room and she led him up the stairs.

The first thing Myron saw when he opened Chad's door were the trophies. Lots of them. All golf trophies. The bronze figure on the top was always a man coiled in postswing position, the golf club over his shoulder, his head held high. Sometimes the little man wore a golf cap. Other times he had short, wavy hair like Paul Hornung in old football reels. There were two leather golf bags in the right corner, both jammed past capacity with clubs. Photographs of Jack Nicklaus, Arnold Palmer, Sam Snead, Tom Watson blanketed the walls. Issues of *Golf Digest* littered the floor.

"Does Chad play golf?" Myron asked.

Linda Coldren just looked at him. Myron met her gaze and nodded sagely.

"My powers of deduction," he said. "They intimidate some people."

She almost smiled. Myron the Alleviator, Master Tension-Easer. "I'll try to still treat you the same," she said.

Myron stepped toward the trophies. "Is he any good?"

"Very good." She turned away suddenly and stood with her back to the room. "Do you need anything else?"

"Not right now."

"I'll be downstairs."

She didn't wait for his blessing.

Myron walked in. He checked the answering machine on Chad's phone. Three messages. Two from a girl named Becky. From the sound of it, she was a pretty good friend. Just calling to say, like, hi, see if he wanted to, like, do anything this weekend, you know? She and Millie and

Suze were going to, like, hang out at the Heritage, okay, and if he wanted to come, well, you know, whatever. Myron smiled. Times they might be a-changin', but her words could have come from a girl Myron had gone to high school with or his father or his father's father. Generations cycle in. The music, the movies, the language, the fashion—they change. But that's just outside stimuli. Beneath the baggy pants or the message-cropped hair, the same adolescent fears and needs and feelings of inadequacy remained frighteningly constant.

The last call was from a guy named Glen. He wanted to know if Chad wanted to play golf at "the Pine" this weekend, being that Merion was off-limits because of the Open. "Daddy," Glen's preppy taped voice assured Chad, "can get us a tee time, no prob."

No messages from Chad's close buddy Matthew Squires.

He snapped on the computer. Windows 95. Cool. Myron used it too. Chad Coldren, Myron immediately saw, used America Online to get his E-mail. Perfect. Myron hit FLASHSESSION. The modem hooked on and screeched for a few seconds. A voice said, "Welcome. You have mail." Dozens of messages were automatically downloaded. The same voice said, "Good-bye." Myron checked Chad's E-mail address book and found Matthew Squires's E-mail address. He skimmed the downloaded messages. None were from Matthew.

Interesting.

It was, of course, entirely possible that Matthew and Chad were not as close as Linda Coldren thought. It was also entirely possible that even if they were, Matthew had not contacted his friend since Wednesday—even though his friend had supposedly vanished without warning. It happens.

Still, it was interesting.

Myron picked up Chad's phone and hit the redial button. Four rings later a taped voice came on. "You've reached Matthew. Leave a message or don't. Up to you."

Myron hung up without leaving a message (it was, after all, "up to him"). Hmm. Chad's last call was to Matthew. That could be significant. Or it could have nothing to do with anything. Either way, Myron was quickly getting nowhere.

He picked up Chad's phone and dialed his office. Esperanza answered on the second ring.

"MB SportsReps."

"It's me." He filled her in. She listened without interrupting.

Esperanza Diaz had worked for MB SportReps since its inception. Ten years ago, when Esperanza was only eighteen years old, she was the Queen of Sunday Morning Cable TV. No, she wasn't on any infomercial, though her show ran opposite plenty of them, especially that one with the abdominal exerciser that bore a striking resemblance to a medieval instrument of torture; rather, Esperanza had been a professional wrestler named Little Pocahontas, the Sensual Indian Princess. With her petite, lithe figure bedecked in only a suede bikini, Esperanza had been voted FLOW's (Fabulous Ladies Of Wrestling) most popular wrestler three years running—or, as the award was officially known, the Babe You'd Most Like to Get in a Full Nelson. Despite this, Esperanza remained humble.

When he finished telling her about the kidnapping, Esperanza's first words were an incredulous, "Win has a mother?"

"Yep."

Pause. "There goes my spawned-from-a-satanic-egg theory."

"Ha-ha."

"Or my hatched-in-an-experiment-gone-very-wrong theory."

"You're not helping."

"What's to help?" Esperanza replied. "I like Win, you know that. But the boy is—what's the official psychiatric term again?—cuckoo."

"That cuckoo saved your life once," Myron said.

"Yeah, but you remember how," she countered.

Myron did. A dark alley. Win's doctored bullets. Brain matter tossed about like parade confetti. Classic Win. Effective but excessive. Like squashing a bug with a wrecking ball.

Esperanza broke the long silence. "Like I said before," she began softly, "cuckoo."

Myron wanted to change the subject. "Any messages?"

"About a million. Nothing that can't wait, though." Then she asked, "Have you ever met her?"

"Who?"

"Madonna," she snapped. "Who do you think? Win's mother."

"Once," Myron said, remembering. More than ten years ago. He and Win had been having dinner at Merion, in fact. Win hadn't spoken to her on that occasion. But she had spoken to him. The memory made Myron cringe anew.

"Have you told Win about this yet?" she asked.

"Nope. Any advice?"

Esperanza thought a moment. "Do it over the phone," she said. "At a very safe distance."

Chapter 3

They got a quick break.

Myron was still sitting in the Coldrens' den with Linda when Esperanza called back. Bucky had gone back to Merion to get Jack.

"The kid's ATM card was accessed yesterday at 6:18 P.M.," Esperanza said. "He took out $180. A First Philadelphia branch on Porter Street in South Philly."

"Thanks."

Information like that was not difficult to obtain. Anybody with an account number could pretty much do it with a phone by pretending they were the account holder. Even without one, any semi-human who had ever worked in law enforcement had the contacts or the access numbers or at least the wherewithal to pay off the right person. It didn't take much anymore, not with today's overabundance of user-friendly technology. Technology did more than depersonalize; it ripped your life wide open, gutted you, stripped away any pretense of privacy.

A few keystrokes revealed all.

"What is it?" Linda Coldren asked.

He told her.

"It doesn't necessarily mean what you think," she said. "The kidnapper could have gotten the PIN number from Chad."

"Could have," Myron said.

"But you don't believe it, do you?"

He shrugged. "Let's just say I'm more than a little skeptical."

"Why?"

"The amount, for one thing. What was Chad's max?"

"Five hundred dollars a day."

"So why would a kidnapper only take $180?"

Linda Coldren thought a moment. "If he took too much, someone might get suspicious."

Myron sort of frowned. "But if the kidnapper was that careful," he began, "why risk so much for $180? Everyone knows that ATMs are equipped with security cameras. Everyone also knows that even the simplest computer check can yield a location."

She looked at him evenly. "You don't think my son is in danger."

"I didn't say that. This whole thing may look like one thing and be another. You were right before. It's safest to assume that the kidnapping is real."

"So what's your next step?"

"I'm not sure. The ATM machine was on Porter Street in South Philadelphia. Is that someplace Chad likes to hang out?"

"No," Linda Coldren said slowly. "In fact, it's a place I would never imagine him going."

"Why do you say that?"

"It's a dive. One of the sleaziest parts of the city."

Myron stood. "You got a street map?"

"In my glove compartment."

"Good. I'll need to borrow your car for a little while."

"Where are you going?"

"I'm going to drive around this ATM."

She frowned. "What for?"

"I don't know," Myron admitted. "Like I said before, investigating is not very scientific. You do some legwork and you push some buttons and you hope something happens.''

Linda Coldren reached into a pocket for her keys. "Maybe the kidnappers grabbed him there," she said. "Maybe you'll see his car or something."

Myron almost slapped himself in the head. A car. He had forgotten something so basic. In his mind, a kid disappearing on his way to or from school conjured up images of yellow buses or strolling sprightly with a book bag. How could he have missed something as obvious as a car trace?

He asked her the make and model. Gray Honda Accord. Hardly a car that stands out in a crowd. Pennsylvania license plate 567-AHJ. He called it in to Esperanza. Then he gave Linda Coldren his cellular phone number.

"Call me if anything happens."

"Okay."

"I'll be back soon," he said.

The ride wasn't far. He traveled, it seemed, from green splendor to concrete crap instantaneously—like on *Star Trek* where they step through one of those time portals.

The ATM was a drive-through located in what would generously be labeled a business district. Tons of cameras. No human tellers. Would a kidnapper really risk this? Very doubtful. Myron wondered where he could get a copy of the bank's videotape without alerting the police. Win might know somebody. Financial institutions were usually anxious to cooperate with the Lockwood family. The question was, would Win be willing to cooperate?

Abandoned warehouses—or at least, they looked abandoned—lined the road. Eighteen-wheelers hurried by like something out of an old convoy movie. They reminded Myron of the CB craze from his childhood. Like everyone else, his dad had bought one—a man born in the

Flatbush section of Brooklyn who grew up to own an undergarment factory in Newark, barking "breaker one nine" with an accent he had picked up watching the movie *Deliverance*. Dad would be driving on Hobart Gap Road between their house and the Livingston Mall—maybe a one-mile drive—asking his "good buddies" if there was any sign of "smokeys." Myron smiled at the memory. Ah, CBs. He was sure that his father still had his someplace. Probably next to the eight-track player.

On one side of the ATM was a gas station so generic that it didn't even bother having a name. Rusted cars stood upon crumbling cinder blocks. On the other side, a dirt-bag, no-tell motel called the Court Manor Inn greeted customers with green lettering that read: $19.99 PER HOUR.

Myron Bolitar Traveling Tip #83: You may not be dealing with a five-star deluxe property when they prominently advertise hourly rates.

Under the price, in smaller black print, the sign read, MIRRORED CEILINGS AND THEME ROOMS SLIGHTLY EXTRA. Theme rooms. Myron didn't even want to know. The last line, back in the green big print: ASK ABOUT OUR FREQUENT VISITORS CLUB. Jesus.

Myron wondered if it was worth a shot and decided, why not? It probably wouldn't lead to anything, but if Chad was hiding out—or even if he'd been kidnapped—a no-tell was as good a place as any to disappear.

He parked in the lot. The Court Manor was a textbook two-level dump. The outer stairs and walkway terraces were made of rotting wood. The cement walls had that unfinished, swirling look that could cut your hand if you leaned against it wrong. Small chunks of concrete lay on the ground. An unplugged Pepsi machine guarded the door like one of the Queen's guards. Myron passed it and entered.

He'd expected to find the standard no-tell lobby interior—that is, an unshaven Neanderthal in a sleeveless,
too-short undershirt chewing on a toothpick while sitting
behind bullet-proof glass burping up a beer. Or something like that. But that was not the case. The Court
Manor Inn had a high wooden desk with a bronze sign
reading CONCIERGE on top of it. Myron tried not to
snicker. Behind the desk, a well-groomed, baby-faced
man in his late twenties stood at attention. He wore a
pressed shirt, starched collar, dark tie tied in a perfect
Windsor knot. He smiled at Myron.

"Good afternoon, sir!" he exclaimed. He looked and
sounded like a John Tesh substitute on *Entertainment
Weekly*. "Welcome to the Court Manor Inn!"

"Yeah," Myron said. "Hi."

"May I be of some service to you today, sir?"

"I hope so."

"Great! My name is Stuart Lipwitz. I'm the new manager of the Court Manor Inn." He looked at Myron ex-
pectantly.

Myron said, "Congrats."

"Well, thank you, sir, that's very kind. If there are any
problems—if anything at the Court Manor does not meet
your expectations—please let me know immediately. I
will handle it personally." Big smile, puffed-out chest.
"At the Court Manor, we guarantee your satisfaction."

Myron just looked at him for a minute, waiting for the
full-wattage smile to dim a bit. It didn't. Myron took out
the photograph of Chad Coldren.

"Have you seen this young man?"

Stuart Lipwitz did not even look down. Still smiling,
he said, "I'm sorry, sir. But are you with the police?"

"No."

"Then I'm afraid I can't help you. I'm very sorry."

"Pardon me?"

"I'm sorry, sir, but here at the Court Manor Inn we pride ourselves on our discretion."

"He's not in any trouble," Myron said. "I'm not a private eye trying to catch a cheating husband or anything like that."

The smile did not falter or sway. "I'm sorry, sir, but this is the Court Manor Inn. Our clientele use our services for a variety of activities and often crave anonymity. We at the Court Manor Inn must respect that."

Myron studied the man's face, searching for some signal that this was a put-on. Nothing. His whole persona glowed like a performer in an *Up with People* halftime show. Myron leaned over the desk and checked out the shoes. Polished like twin mirrors. The hair was slicked back. The sparkle in the eye looked real.

It took Myron some time, but he finally saw where this was leading. He took out his wallet and plucked a twenty from the billfold. He slid it across the counter. Stuart Lipwitz looked at it but made no move.

"What's this for, sir?"

"It's a present," Myron said.

Stuart Lipwitz did not touch it.

"It's for one piece of information," Myron continued. He plucked out another and held it in the air. "I have another, if you'd like."

"Sir, we have a credo here at the Court Manor Inn: The guest must come first."

"Isn't that a prostitute's credo?"

"Pardon me, sir?"

"Never mind," Myron said.

"I am the new manager of the Court Manor Inn, sir."

"So I've heard."

"I also own ten percent."

"Your mom must be the envy of her mah-jongg group."

Still the smile. "In other words, sir, I am in it for the long term. That's how I look at this business. Long term. Not just today. Not just tomorrow. But into the future. For the long term. You see?"

"Oh," Myron said flatly. "You mean long term?"

Stuart Lipwitz snapped his fingers. "Precisely. And our motto is this: There are many places you can spend your adultery dollar. We want it to be here."

Myron waited a moment. Then he said, "Noble."

"We at the Court Manor Inn are working hard to earn your trust, and trust has no price. When I wake up in the morning, I have to look at myself in the mirror."

"Would that mirror be on the ceiling?"

Still smiling. "Let me explain it another way," he said. "If the client knows that the Court Manor Inn is a place he can feel safe to commit an indiscretion, he or she will be more likely to return." He leaned forward, his eyes wet with excitement. "Do you see?"

Myron nodded. "Repeat business."

"Precisely."

"Referrals too," Myron added. "Like, 'Hey, Bob, I know a great place to get some ass on the side.' "

A nod added to the smile. "So you understand."

"That's all very nice, Stuart, but this kid is fifteen years old. Fifteen." Actually, Chad was sixteen, but what the hey. "That's against the law."

The smile stayed, but now it signaled disappointment in the favorite pupil. "I hate to disagree with you, sir, but the statutory rape law in this state is fourteen. And secondly, there is no law against a fifteen-year-old renting a motel room."

The guy was dancing too much, Myron thought. No reason to go through this rigmarole if the kid had never been here. Then again, let's face facts. Stuart Lipwitz was probably enjoying this. The guy was several french fries short of a Happy Meal. Either way, Myron thought, it was time to shake the tree a bit.

"It is when he is assaulted in your motel," Myron said. "It is when he claims that someone got an extra key from the front desk and used it to break into the room." Mr. Bluff Goes to Philadelphia.

"We don't have extra keys," Lipwitz said.

"Well, he got in somehow."

Still the smile. Still the polite tone. "If that were the case, sir, the police would be here."

"That's my next stop," Myron said, "if you don't cooperate."

"And you want to know if this young man"—Lipwitz gestured to the photograph of Chad—"stayed here?"

"Yes."

The smile actually brightened a bit. Myron almost shaded his eyes. "But, sir, if you are telling the truth, then this young man would be able to tell if he was here. You wouldn't need me for that, correct?"

Myron's face remained neutral. Mr. Bluff had just been outsmarted by the new manager of the Court Manor Inn. "That's right," he said, changing tactics on the fly. "I already know he was here. It was just an opening question. Like when the police ask you to state your name even though they already know it. Just to get the ball rolling." Mr. Improvision Takes Over for Mr. Bluff.

Stuart Lipwitz took out a piece of paper and began to scribble. "This is the name and telephone number of the Court Manor Inn's attorney. He will be able to help you with any problems you may have."

"But what about that handling it personally stuff? What about the satisfaction guarantee?"

"Sir." He leaned forward, maintaining eye contact. Not a hint of impatience had crept into his voice or face. "May I be bold?"

"Go for it."

"I don't believe a word you're saying."

"Thanks for the boldness," Myron said.

"No, thank you, sir. And do come again."

"Another prostitution credo."

"Pardon me?"

"Nothing," Myron said. "May I too be bold?"

"Yes."

"I may punch you in the face very hard if you don't tell me if you've seen this kid." Mr. Improvisation Loses His Cool.

The door swung open hard. A couple entwined about one another stumbled in. The woman was openly rubbing the man's crotch. "We need a room pronto," the man said.

Myron turned to them and said, "Do you have your frequent visitor card?"

"What?"

Still the smile from Stuart Lipwitz. "Good-bye, sir. And have a nice day." Then he rejuvenated the smile and moved toward the writhing mound. "Welcome to the Court Manor Inn. My name is Stuart Lipwitz. I'm the new manager."

Myron headed out to his car. He took a deep breath in the parking lot and looked back behind him. The whole visit already had an unreal feeling, like one of those descriptions of alien abductions *sans* the anal probe. He got in the car and dialed Win's cellular. He just wanted to leave him a message on the machine. But to Myron's surprise, Win answered.

"Articulate," he drolled.

Myron was momentarily taken aback. "It's me," he said.

Silence. Win hated the obvious. "It's me," was both questionable grammar (at best) and a complete waste.

Win would know who it was by the voice. If he didn't, hearing "It's me" would undeniably not help.

"I thought you didn't answer the phone on the course," Myron said.

"I'm driving home to change," Win said. "Then I'm dining at Merion." Mainliners never ate; they dined. "Care to join me?"

"Sounds good," Myron said.

"Wait a second."

"What?"

"Are you properly attired?"

"I don't clash," Myron said. "Will they still let me in?"

"My, my, that was very funny, Myron. I must write that one down. As soon as I stop laughing, I plan on locating a pen. However, I am so filled with mirth that I may wrap my precious Jag around an upcoming telephone pole. Alas, at least I will die with jocularity in my heart."

Win.

"We have a case," Myron said.

Silence. Win made this so easy.

"I'll tell you about it at dinner."

"Until then," Win said, "it'll be all I can do to douse my mounting excitement and anticipation with a snifter of cognac."

Click. Gotta love that Win.

Myron hadn't driven a mile when the cellular phone rang. Myron switched it on.

It was Bucky. "The kidnapper called again."

Chapter 4

"What did he say?" Myron asked.

"They want money," Bucky said.

"How much?"

"I don't know."

Myron was confused. "What do you mean, you don't know? Didn't they say?"

"I don't think so," the old man said.

There was noise in the background. "Where are you?" Myron asked.

"I'm at Merion. Look, Jack answered the phone. He's still in shock."

"Jack answered?"

"Yes."

Doubly confused. "The kidnapper called Jack at Merion?"

"Yes. Please, Myron, can you get back over here? It'll be easier to explain."

"On my way."

He drove from the seedy motel to a highway and then into green. Lots of green. The Philadelphia suburbs were lush lawns and high bushes and shady trees. Amazing how close it was—at least in a geographic sense—to the meaner streets of Philly. Like most cities, there was tremendous segregation in Philadelphia. Myron remembered driving with Win to Veterans Stadium for an Eagles game a couple of years back. They'd gone through an Italian block, a Polish block, an African American block; it was as if some powerful, invisible force field—again, like on *Star Trek*—isolated each ethnicity. The City of Brotherly Love could almost be called Little Yugoslavia.

Myron turned down Ardmore Avenue. Merion was about a mile away. His thoughts turned to Win. How, he wondered, would his old friend react to the maternal connection in this case?

Probably not well.

In all the years they had been friends, Myron had heard Win mention his mother on only one occasion.

It had been during their junior year at Duke. They were college roommates, just back from a wild frat party. The beer had flowed. Myron was not what you'd call a good drinker. Two drinks and he'd usually end up trying to French-kiss a toaster. He blamed this on his ancestry—his people had never handled spirits well.

Win, on the other hand, seemed to have been weaned on schnapps. Liquor never really affected him much. But at this particular party, the grain alcohol–laced punch made even his steps wobble a bit. It took Win three tries to unlock their dorm room door.

Myron quickly collapsed on his bed. The ceiling spun counterclockwise at a seemingly death-defying speed. He closed his eyes. His hands gripped the bed and held on in terror. His face had no color. Nausea clamped down painfully on his stomach. Myron wondered when he would vomit and prayed it would be soon.

Ah, the glamour of college drinking.

For a while neither of them said anything. Myron wondered if Win had fallen asleep. Or maybe Win was gone. Vanished into the night. Maybe he hadn't held on to his spinning bed tightly enough and the centrifugal force had hurled him out the window and into the great beyond.

Then Win's voice cut through the darkness. "Take a look at this."

A hand reached out and dropped something on Myron's chest. Myron risked letting go of the bed with one hand. So far, so good. He fumbled for whatever it was, found it, lifted it into view. A streetlight from outside—campuses are lit up like Christmas trees—cast enough illumination to make out a photograph. The color was grainy and faded, but Myron could still make out what looked to be an expensive car.

"Is that a Rolls-Royce?" Myron asked. He knew nothing about cars.

"A Bentley S Three Continental Flying Spur," Win corrected, "1962. A classic."

"Is it yours?"

"Yes."

The bed spun silently.

"How did you get it?" Myron asked.

"A man who was fucking my mother gave it to me."

The end. Win had shut down after that. The wall he put up was not only impenetrable but unapproachable, filled with land mines and a moat and lots of high-voltage electric wires. Over the ensuing decade and a half, Win had never again mentioned his mother. Not when the packages came to the dorm room every semester. Not when the packages came to Win's office on his birthday even now. Not even when they saw her in person ten years ago.

"Well, as I told you earlier, golf is very special." F scrambled to rewind; ahead the hammer over wild and the state of will ancu

The plain dark wood sign merely read MERION GOLF CLUB. Nothing else. No "For Members Only." No "We're Elitist and We Don't Want You." No "Ethnics Use Service Entrance." No need. It was just a given.

The last U.S. Open threesome had finished a while back and the crowd was mostly gone now. Merion could hold only seventeen thousand for a tournament—less than half the capacity of most courses—but parking was still a chore. Most spectators were forced to park at nearby Haverford College. Shuttle buses ran constantly.

At the top of the driveway a guard signaled him to stop.

"I'm here to meet Windsor Lockwood," Myron said.

Instant recognition. Instant wave-through.

Bucky ran over to him before he had the car in park. The rounded face was more jowly now, as if he were packing wet sand in his cheeks.

"Where is Jack?" Myron asked.

"The western course."

"The what?"

"Merion has two courses," the older man explained, stretching his neck again. "The east, which is the more famous one, and the west. During the Open, the western course is used as a driving range."

"And your son-in-law is there?"

"Yes."

"Driving balls?"

"Of course." Bucky looked at him, surprised. "You always do that after a round. Every golfer on the tour knows that. You played basketball. Didn't you used to practice your shot after a game?"

"No."

"Well, as I told you earlier, golf is very special. Players need to review their play immediately after a round. Even if they've played well. They focus in on their good strokes, see if they can figure out what went wrong with the bad strokes. They recap the day."

"Uh-huh," Myron said. "So tell me about the kidnapper's call."

"I'll take you to Jack," he said. "This way."

They walked across the eighteen fairway and then down sixteen. The air smelled of freshly cut grass and pollen. It'd been a big year for pollen on the East Coast; nearby allergists swooned with greedy delight.

Bucky shook his head. "Look at these roughs," he said. "Impossible."

He pointed to long grass. Myron had no idea what he was talking about so he nodded and kept walking.

"Damn USGA wants this course to bring the golfers to their knees," Bucky ranted on. "So they grow the rough way out. Like playing in a rice paddy, for chrissake. Then they cut the greens so close, the golfers might as well be putting on a hockey rink."

Myron remained silent. They two men kept walking.

"This is one of the famed stone-quarry holes," Bucky said, calmer now.

"Uh-huh." The man was babbling. People do that when they're nervous.

"When the original builders reached sixteen, seventeen, and eighteen," Bucky continued, sounding not unlike a tour guide in the Sistine Chapel, "they ran across a stone quarry. Rather than giving up then and there, they plowed ahead, incorporating the quarry into the hole."

"Gosh," Myron said softly, "they were so brave back then."

Some babble when nervous. Some grow sarcastic.

They reached the tee and made a right, walking along Golf House Road. Though the last group had finished playing more than an hour ago, there were still at least a dozen golfers hitting balls. The driving range. Yes, professional golfers hit balls here—practicing with a wide array of woods and irons and big clubs, nay, warheads, they called Bertha and Cathy and the like—but that was only part of what went on. Most touring pros used the range to work out strategies with their caddies, check on equipment with their sponsors, network, socialize with fellow golfers, smoke a cigarette (a surprising amount of pros chain-smoke), even talk to agents.

In golf circles, the driving range was called the office.

Myron recognized Greg Norman and Nick Faldo. He also spotted Tad Crispin, the new kid on the block, the latest next Jack Nicklaus—in a phrase, the dream client. The kid was twenty-three, good-looking, quiet, engaged to an equally attractive, happy-just-to-be-here woman. He also did not yet have an agent. Myron tried not to salivate. Hey, he was as human as the next guy. He was, after all, a sports agent. Cut him some slack.

"Where is Jack?" Myron asked.

"Down this way," Bucky said. "He wanted to hit alone."

"How did the kidnapper reach him?"

"He called the Merion switchboard and said it was an emergency."

"And that worked?"

"Yes," Bucky said slowly. "Actually, it was Chad on the phone. He identified himself as Jack's son."

Curious. "What time did the call come in?"

"Maybe ten minutes before I called you." Bucky stopped, gestured with his chin. "There."

Jack Coldren was a touch pudgy and soft in the middle, but he had forearms like Popeye's. His flyaway hair did just that in the breeze, revealing bald spots that had started off the day better covered. He whacked the ball with a wood club and an uncommon fury. To some this might all seem very strange. You have just learned your son is missing and you go out and hit golf balls. But Myron understood. Hitting balls was comfort food. The more stress Myron was under, the more he wanted to go in his driveway and shoot baskets. We all have something. Some drink. Some do drugs. Some like to take a long drive or play a computer game. When Win needed to unwind, he often watched videotapes of his own sexual exploits. But that was Win.

"Who's that with him?" Myron asked.

"Diane Hoffman," Bucky said. "Jack's caddie."

Myron knew that female caddies were not uncommon on the men's pro tour. Some players even hired their wives. Saves money. "Does she know what's going on?"

"Yes. Diane was there when the call came in. They're pretty close."

"Have you told Linda?"

Bucky nodded. "I called her right away. Do you mind introducing yourself? I'd like to go back to the house and check up on her."

"No problem."

"How will I reach you if something comes up?"

"Call my cellular."

Bucky nearly gasped. "Cellular phones are forbidden at Merion." Like it was a papal command.

"I walk on the wild side," Myron said. "Just call."

Myron approached them. Diane Hoffman stood with her feet shoulder-width apart, her arms folded, her face intent on Coldren's backswing. A cigarette dangled from her lips almost vertically. She didn't even glance at Myron. Jack Coldren coiled his body and then let go, snapping like a released spring. The ball rocketed over the distant hills.

Jack Coldren turned, looked at Myron, smiled tightly, nodded a hello. "You're Myron Bolitar, right?"

"Right."

He shook Myron's hand. Diane Hoffman continued to study her player's every move, frowning as if she'd spotted a flaw in his hand-shaking technique. "I appreciate your helping us out," he said.

Face-to-face now—no more than a few feet away—Myron could see the devastation on the man's face. The jubilant glow after nailing the putt on eighteen had been snuffed out by something more pasty and sickly. His eyes had the surprised, uncomprehending look of a man who'd just been sucker punched in the stomach.

"You tried making a comeback recently," Jack said. "With New Jersey."

Myron nodded.

"I saw you on the news. Gutsy move, after all these years."

Stalling. Not sure how to begin. Myron decided to help. "Tell me about the call."

Jack Coldren's eyes swerved over the expanse of green. "Are you sure it's safe?" he asked. "The guy on the phone told me no police. To just act normal."

"I'm an agent seeking clients," Myron said. "Talking to me is about as normal as it gets."

Coldren thought about that for a moment then nodded. He still hadn't introduced Diane Hoffman. Hoffman didn't seem to mind. She remained about ten feet away, rock-still. Her eyes remained narrow and suspicious, her face weathered and pinched. The cigarette ash was incredibly long now, almost defying gravity. She wore a cap and one of those caddie vests that looked like a jogger's night reflector.

"The club president came up to me and whispered that there was an emergency call from my son. So I went inside the clubhouse and picked it up."

He stopped suddenly and blinked several times. His breathing became heavier. He was wearing a tad-too-tight, yellow V-necked golf shirt. You could see his body expand against the cotton blend with each inhale. Myron waited.

"It was Chad," he finally spat out. "All he could say was 'Dad,' before someone grabbed the phone away from him. Then a man with a deep voice came on the line."

"How deep?" Myron asked.

"Pardon?"

"How deep was the voice?"

"Very."

"Did it sound funny to you? A little robotic?"

"Now that you mention it, yes, it did."

Electronic altering, Myron guessed. Those machines could make Barry White sound like a four-year-old girl. Or vice versa. They weren't hard to get. Even Radio Shack sold them now. The kidnapper or kidnappers could be any sex. Linda and Jack Coldren's description of a "male voice" was irrelevant. "What did he say?"

"That he had my son. He told me that if I called the police or anybody like that, Chad would pay. He told me that someone would be watching me all the time." Jack Coldren accentuated the point by looking around again. No one suspicious lurked about, though Greg Norman waved and gave them a smiling thumbs-up. G'day, mate.

"What else?" Myron asked.

"He said he wanted money," Coldren said.

"How much?"

"He just said a lot. He wasn't sure yet how much, but he wanted me to get it ready. He said he'd call back."

Myron made a face. "But he didn't tell you how much?"

"No. Just that it would be a lot."

"And that you should get it ready."

"Right."

This made no sense. A kidnapper who wasn't sure how much ransom to extort? "May I be blunt, Jack?"

Coldren stood a little taller, tucked in his shirt. He was what some would call boyishly and disarmingly handsome. His face was big and unthreatening with cottony, malleable features. "Don't sugarcoat anything for me," he said. "I want the truth."

"Could this be a hoax?"

Jack shot a quick glance at Diane Hoffman. She moved slightly. Might have been a nod. He turned back to Myron. "What do you mean?"

"Could Chad be behind this?"

The longer flyaway hairs got caught up in a cross-breeze and fell down into his eyes. He pushed them away with his fingers. Something came across his face. Rumination, maybe? Unlike Linda Coldren, the idea had not snapped him into a defensive stance. He was pondering the possibility, or perhaps merely grasping at an option that meant safety for his son.

"There were two different voices," Coldren said. "On the phone."

"It could be a voice changer." Myron explained what that was.

More rumination. Coldren's face scrunched up. "I really don't know."

"Is it something you can imagine Chad doing?"

"No," Coldren replied. "But who can imagine anyone's kid doing something like this? I'm trying to remain objective here, hard as that is. Do I think my boy could do something like this? Of course not. But then again, I wouldn't be the first parent to be wrong about my kid; now, would I?"

Fair enough, Myron thought. "Has Chad ever run away?"

"No."

"Any trouble in the family? Anything that might make him want to do something like this?"

"Something like fake his own kidnapping?"

"It doesn't have to be that extreme," Myron said. "Maybe something you or your wife did that got him upset."

"No," he said, his voice suddenly faraway. "I can't

think of anything." He looked up. The sun was low and not very strong anymore, but he still sort of squinted up at Myron, the side of his hand resting on his forehead in an eye-shading salute. The posture reminded Myron of the photograph of Chad he'd seen at the house.

Jack said, "You have a thought, Myron, don't you?"

"Barely."

"I'd still like to hear it," Coldren said.

"How badly do you want to win this tournament, Jack?"

Coldren gave a half-smile. "You were an athlete, Myron. You know how badly."

"Yes," Myron said, "I do."

"So what's your point?"

"Your son is an athlete. He probably knows too."

"Yes," Coldren said. Then: "I'm still waiting for the point."

"If someone wanted to hurt you," Myron said, "what better way than to mess up your chance of winning the Open?"

Jack Coldren's eyes had that sucker punched look again. He took a step back.

"I'm only theorizing," Myron added quickly. "I'm not saying your son is doing that. . . ."

"But you need to explore every avenue," Jack Coldren finished for him.

"Yes."

Coldren recovered, but it took him a little time. "Even if what you're saying is true, it doesn't have to be Chad. Someone else could have done this to get at me." Again he glanced over at his caddie. Still looking at her, he said, "Wouldn't be the first time."

"What do you mean?"

Jack Coldren didn't answer right away. He turned away from both of them and squinted out toward where he'd been hitting balls. There was nothing to see. His back was to Myron. "You probably know I lost the Open a long time ago."

"Yes."

He didn't elaborate.

"Did something happen back then?" Myron asked.

"Maybe," Jack Coldren said slowly. "I don't know anymore. The point is, someone else might be out to get me. It doesn't have to be my son."

"Maybe," Myron agreed. He didn't go into the fact that he'd pretty much dismissed this possibility because Chad had vanished before Coldren had his lead. No reason to go into it now.

Coldren turned back to Myron. "Bucky mentioned something about an ATM card," he said.

"Your son's ATM card was accessed last night. At Porter Street."

Something crossed his face. Not for long. Not for more than a second. A flash and then it was gone. "On Porter Street?" he repeated.

"Yep. A First Philadelphia Bank on Porter Street in South Philadelphia."

Silence.

"Are you familiar with that part of town?"

"No," Coldren said. He looked over at his caddie. Diane Hoffman remained the statue. Arms still folded. Feet still shoulder-width apart. Ash finally gone.

"Are you sure?"

"Of course I am."

"I visited there today," Myron said.

His face remained steady. "Did you learn anything?"

"No."

Silence.

Jack Coldren gestured behind him. "You mind if I take a few more swings while we talk?"

"Not at all."

He put on his glove. "Do you think I should play tomorrow?"

"That's up to you," Myron said. "The kidnapper said to act normal. Your not playing would certainly draw suspicion."

Coldren bent down to put a ball on the tee. "Can I ask you something, Myron?"

"Sure."

"When you played basketball, how important was winning to you?"

Odd question. "Very."

Jack nodded like he'd been expecting that. "You won the NCAA championship one year, right?"

"Yes."

Coldren shook his head. "Must have been something."

Myron did not reply.

Jack Coldren picked up a club and flexed his fingers around the grip. He lined up next to the ball. Again the smooth coil-and-release movement. Myron watched the ball sail away. For a moment no one spoke. They just looked off into the distance and watched the final streaks of sun color the sky purple.

When Coldren finally spoke, his voice was thick. "You want to hear something awful?"

Myron moved closer to him. Coldren's eyes were wet.

"I still care about winning this thing," Coldren said. He looked at Myron. The pain on his face was so naked, Myron almost reached out and hugged him. He imagined that he could see the reflection of the man's past in his eyes, the years of torment, of thinking of what might have been, of finally having the chance at redemption, of having that chance suddenly snatched away.

"What kind of man still thinks about winning at a time like this?" Coldren asked.

Myron didn't say anything. He didn't know the answer. Or maybe he feared that he did.

Chapter 5

Merion's clubhouse was an expanded white farm-house with black shutters. The only splash of color came from the green awnings shading the famed back porch and even that was muted by the surrounding green of the golf course. You expected something more awe-inspiring or intimidating at one of the country's most exclusive clubs, and yet the simplicity seemed to say, "We're Merion. We don't need more."

Myron walked past the pro shop. Golf bags were lined up on a metal stand. The men's locker room door was on his right. A bronze sign read that Merion had been designated a historic landmark. A bulletin board listed members' handicaps. Myron skimmed the names for Win's. Three handicap. Myron didn't know much about golfing, but he knew that was pretty damn good.

The outside porch had a stone floor and about two dozen tables. The legendary dining area did more than overlook the first tee—it actually seemed perched right over it. From here, members watched golfers tee off with the practiced glares of Roman senators at the Colosseum. Powerful businessmen and community leaders often crumbled under such century-old scrutiny. Even professionals were not immune—the porch's dining facility was kept open during the Open. Jack Nicklaus and Arnold Palmer and Ben Hogan and Bobby Jones and Sam Snead had all been subjected to the small restaurant noises, the grating tinkling of glass and silverware blending most disharmoniously with golf's hushed crowds and distant cheers.

The porch was packed with members. Most were men —elderly and red-faced and well fed. They wore blue or green blazers with different crests on them. Their ties were loud and usually striped. Many had floppy white or yellow hats on their heads. Floppy hats. And Win had been worried about Myron's "attire."

Myron spotted Win at a corner table with six chairs. He sat alone. His expression was both glacial and serene, his body completely at ease. A mountain lion patiently waiting for prey. One would think that the blond hair and patrician good looks would be life assets for Win. In many ways, they were; in many more ways, they branded him. His entire appearance reeked of arrogance, old money, and elitism. Most people did not respond well to that. A specific, seething hostility frothed and boiled over when people looked at Win. To look at such a person was to hate him. Win was used to it. People who judged purely on looks did not concern him. People who judged purely on looks were oft surprised.

Myron greeted his old friend and sat down.

"Would you care for a drink?" Win said.

"Sure."

"If you ask for a Yoo-Hoo," Win said, "I'll shoot you in the right eye."

"Right eye," Myron repeated with a nod. "Very specific."

A waiter who must have been a hundred years old materialized. He wore a green jacket and pants—green, Myron surmised, so that even the help would blend into the famed milieu. Didn't work, though. The old waiter looked like the Riddler's grandfather. "Henry," Win said, "I'll have an iced tea."

Myron was tempted to ask for a "Colt 45, like Billy Dee," but decided against it. "I'll have the same."

"Very good, Mr. Lockwood."

Henry left. Win looked over at Myron. "So tell me."

"It's a kidnapping," Myron said.

Win arched an eyebrow.

"One of the players' sons is missing. The parents have gotten two calls." Myron quickly told him about them. Win listened in silence.

When Myron finished, Win said, "You left something out."

"What?"

"The name of the player."

Myron kept his voice steady. "Jack Coldren."

Win's face betrayed nothing, but Myron still felt a cold gust blow across his heart.

Win said, "And you've met Linda."

"Yes."

"And you know that she is related to me."

"Yes."

"Then you must have realized that I will not help."

"No."

Win sat back, steepled his fingers. "Then you realize it now."

"A boy might be in real danger," Myron said. "We have to help."

"No," Win said. "I do not."

"You want me to drop it?"

"What you do is your affair," Win said.

"Do you want me to drop it?" Myron repeated.

The iced teas came. Win took a gentle sip. He looked off and tapped his chin with his index finger. His signal to end the topic. Myron knew better than to push it.

"So who are the other seats for?" Myron asked.

"I am mining a major lead."

"A new client?"

"For me, almost definitely. For you, a barely remote possibility."

"Who?"

"Tad Crispin."

Myron's chin dropped. "We're having dinner with Tad Crispin?"

"As well as our old friend Norman Zuckerman and his latest rather attractive ingenue."

Norm Zuckerman was the owner of Zoom, one of the largest sneaker and sporting apparel companies in the country. He was also one of Myron's favorite people. "How did you get to Crispin? I heard he was agenting himself."

"He is," Win said, "but he still wants a financial adviser." Barely in his mid-thirties, Win was already something of a Wall Street legend. Reaching out to Win made sense. "Crispin is quite a shrewd young man, actually," he went on. "Unfortunately, he believes that all agents are thieves. That they have the morals of a prostitute practicing politics."

"He said that? A prostitute practicing politics?"

"No, I came up with that one myself." Win smiled. "Pretty good, no?"

Myron nodded. "No."

"Anyway, the Zoom folks here are tailing him like a lapdog. They're introducing a whole new line of men's clubs and clothing on the back of young Mr. Crispin."

Tad Crispin was in second place, a goodly distance behind Jack Coldren. Myron wondered how happy Zoom was about Coldren possibly stealing their thunder. Not very, he supposed.

"So what do you make of Jack Coldren's good showing?" Myron asked. "You surprised?"

Win shrugged. "Winning was always very important to Jack."

"Have you known him long?"

Flat eyes. "Yes."

"Did you know him when he lost here as a rookie?"

"Yes."

Myron calculated the years. Win would have been in elementary school. "Jack Coldren hinted that he thought someone tried to sabotage his chances back then."

Win made a noise. "Guff," he said.

"Guff?"

"You don't recall what happened?"

"No."

"Coldren claims his caddie gave him the wrong club on sixteen," Win said. "He asked for a six iron and supposedly his caddie handed him an eight. His shot landed short. More specifically, in one of the rock quarry bunkers. He never recovered."

"Did the caddie admit the error?"

"He never commented, as far as I know."

"What did Jack do?"

"He fired him."

Myron chewed on that tidbit. "Where is the caddie now?"

"I do not have the slightest idea," Win said. "He wasn't a young man at the time and this was more than twenty years ago."

"Do you remember his name?"

"No. And this conversation is officially terminated."

Before Myron could ask why, a pair of hands covered his eyes. "Guess who?" came a familiar sing-song. "I'll give you a couple of hints: I'm smart, good-looking, and loaded with talent."

"Gee," Myron said, "before that hint, I would have thought you were Norm Zuckerman."

"And with the hint?"

Myron shrugged. "If you add 'adored by women of all ages,' I'd think it was me."

Norman Zuckerman laughed heartily. He bent down and gave Myron a big, loud smack on the cheek. "How are you, meshuggener?"

"Good, Norm. You?"

"I'm cooler than Superfly in a new Coupe de Ville."

Zuckerman greeted Win with a loud hello and an enthusiastic handshake. Diners stared in distaste. The stares did not quiet Norman Zuckerman. An elephant gun could not quiet Norman Zuckerman. Myron liked the man. Sure, a lot of it was an act. But it was a genuine act. Norm's zest for everything around him was contagious. He was pure energy; the kind of person who made you examine yourself and left you feeling just a little wanting.

Norm brought forward a young woman who'd been standing behind him. "Let me introduce you to Esme Fong," he said. "She's one of my marketing vee-pees. In charge of the new golf line. Brilliant. The woman is absolutely brilliant."

The attractive ingenue. Early-to-mid twenties, Myron guessed. Esme Fong was Asian with perhaps a hint of Caucasian. She was petite with almond eyes. Her hair was long and silky, a black fan with an earthy auburn tinge. She wore a beige business suit and white stockings. Esme nodded a hello and stepped closer. She wore the serious face of an attractive young woman who was afraid of not being taken seriously because she was an attractive young woman.

She stuck out her hand. "A pleasure to meet you, Mr. Bolitar," she said crisply. "Mr. Lockwood."

"Doesn't she have a firm handshake?" Zuckerman asked. Then turning to her: "What's with all the *mister*s? This is Myron and Win. They're practically family, for crying out loud. Okay, Win's a little goyish to be in my family. I mean, his people came over on the *Mayflower,* while most of mine fled a czar pogrom in a cargo ship. But we're still family, right, Win?''

"As rain," Win said.

"Sit down already, Esme. You're making me nervous with all the seriousness. Try a smile, okay?" Zuckerman demonstrated, pointing at his teeth. Then he turned to Myron, spread his hands. "The truth, Myron. How do I look?''

Norman was over sixty. His customary loud clothing, matching the man's personality, hardly stood out after what Myron had seen today. His skin was dark and rough; his eyes dropped inside black circles; his features jutted out in classical Semitism; his beard and hair were too long and somewhat unkempt.

"You look like Jerry Rubin at the Chicago Seven trial," Myron said.

"Just the look I wanted," Norm said. "Retro. Hip. Attitude. That's what's in nowadays."

"Hardly Tad Crispin's look," Myron said.

"I'm talking about the real world, not golf. Golfers don't know from hip or attitude. Hasidim are more open to change than golfers, you know what I'm saying? I'll give you an example: Dennis Rodman is not a golfer. You know what golfers want? The same thing they've wanted since the dawn of sports marketing: Arnold Palmer. That's what they want. They wanted Palmer, then Nicklaus, then Watson—always good ol' boys." He pointed a thumb at Esme Fong. "Esme is the one who signed Crispin. He's her boy."

Myron looked at her. "Quite a coup," he said.

"Thank you," she said.

"We'll see how big a coup it is," Zuckerman said.

"Zoom is moving into golf in a very big way. Huge. Humongous. Gigantic."

"Enormous," Myron said.

"Mammoth," Win added.

"Colossal."

"Titanic."

"Bunyanesque."

Win smiled. "Brobdingnagian," he said.

"Oooo," Myron said. "Good one."

Zuckerman shook his head. "You guys are funnier than the Three Stooges without Curly. Anyway, it's a helluva campaign. Esme is running it for me. Male and female lines. Not only have we got Crispin, but Esme's landed the numero uno female golfer in the world."

"Linda Coldren?" Myron asked.

"Whoa!" Norm clapped his hands once. "The Hebrew hoopster knows his golf! By the way, Myron, what kind of name is *Bolitar* for a member of the tribe?"

"It's a long story," Myron said.

"Good, I wasn't interested anyway. I was just being polite. Where was I?" Zuckerman threw one leg over the other, leaned back, smiled, looked about. A ruddy-faced man at a neighboring table glared. "Hi, there," Norm said with a little wave. "Looking good."

The man made a huffing noise and looked away.

Norm shrugged. "You'd think he never saw a Jew before."

"He probably hasn't," Win said.

Norm looked back over at the ruddy-faced man. "Look!" Zuckerman said, pointing to his head. "No horns!"

Even Win smiled.

Zuckerman turned his attention back to Myron. "So tell me, you trying to sign Crispin?"

"I haven't even met him yet," Myron said.

Zuckerman put his hand to his chest, feigning surprise. "Well then, Myron, this is some eerie coincidence. You being here when we're about to break bread with him —what are the odds? Wait." Norm stopped, put his hand to his ear. "I think I hear *Twilight Zone* music."

"Ha-ha," Myron said.

"Oh, relax, Myron. I'm teasing you. Lighten up, for crying out loud. But let me be honest for a second, okay? I don't think Cripsin needs you, Myron. Nothing personal, but the kid signed the deal with me himself. No agent. No lawyer. Handled it all on his own."

"And got robbed," Win added.

Zuckerman put a hand to his chest. "You wound me, Win."

"Crispin told me the numbers," Win said. "Myron would have gotten him a far better deal."

"With all due respect to your centuries of upper-crust inbreeding, you don't know what the hell you're talking about. The kid left a little money in the till for me, that's all. Is that a crime nowadays—for a man to make a profit? Myron's a shark, for crying out loud. He rips off my clothes when we talk. He leaves my office, I don't even have undies left. I don't even have furniture. I don't even have an office. I start out with this beautiful office and Myron comes in and I end up naked in some soup kitchen someplace."

Myron looked at Win. "Touching."

"He's breaking my heart," Win said.

Myron turned his attention to Esme Fong. "Are you happy with how Crispin's been playing?"

"Of course," she said quickly. "This is his first major, and he's in second place."

Norm Zuckerman put a hand on her arm. "Save the spinning for those morons in the media. These two guys are family."

Esme Fong shifted in her seat. She cleared her throat. "Linda Coldren won the U.S. Open a few weeks ago," she said. "We're running dual television, radio, and print ads—they'll both be in every spot. It's a new line, completely unknown to golf enthusiasts. Naturally, if we could introduce Zoom's new line with two U.S. Open winners, it would be helpful."

Norm pointed his thumb again. "Ain't she something? *Helpful*. Nice word. Vague. Look, Myron, you read the sports section, am I right?"

"As rain."

"How many articles did you see on Crispin before the tournament began?"

"A lot."

"How much coverage has he gotten in the past two days?"

"Not much."

"Try none. All anybody is talking about is Jack Coldren. In two days that poor son of a bitch is either going to be a miracle man of messianic proportions or the most pitiful loser in the history of the world. Think about it for a second. A man's entire life—both his past and his future—will be shaped by a few swings of a stick. Nuts, when you think about it. And you know what the worst part is?"

Myron shook his head.

"I hope like hell he messes up! I feel like a major son of a bitch, but that's the truth. My guy comes back and wins, you wait and see the way Esme spins it. The brilliant play of newcomer Tad Crispin forces a veteran to crack. The new kid stares down the pressure like Palmer and Nicklaus combined. You know what it'll mean to the launch of the new line?" Zuckerman looked over at Win and pointed. "God, I wish I looked like you. Look at him, for crying out loud. He's beautiful."

Win, in spite of himself, laughed. Several ruddy-faced men turned and stared. Norman waved at them, friendly-like. "Next time I come," Norm said to Win, "I'm wearing a yarmulke."

Win laughed harder. Myron tried to remember the last time he'd seen his friend laugh so openly. It'd been a while. Norm had that effect on people.

Esme Fong glanced at her watch and rose. "I only stopped by to say hello," she explained. "I really must be going."

All three men stood. Norm bussed her cheek. "Take care, Esme, okay? I'll see you tomorrow morning."

"Yes, Norm." She gave Myron and Win demure smiles accompanied by a shy lowering of the head. "Nice meeting you, Myron. Win."

She left. The three men sat. Win steepled his fingers. "How old is she?" Win asked.

"Twenty-five. Phi Beta Kappa from Yale."

"Impressive."

Norm said, "Don't even think it, Win."

Win shook his head. He wouldn't. She was in the business. Harder to disentangle. When it came to the opposite sex, Win liked quick and absolute closure.

"I stole her from those sons of bitches at Nike," Norm said. "She was a bigwig in their basketball department. Don't get me wrong. She was making a ton of dough, but she smartened up. Hey, it's like I told her: There's more to life than money. You know what I'm saying?"

Myron refrained from rolling his eyes.

"Anyway, she works like a dog. Always checking and rechecking. In fact, she's on her way to Linda Coldren's right now. They're going to have a late-night tea party or something girly-girl."

Myron and Win exchanged a glance. "She's going to Linda Coldren's house?"

"Yeah, why?"

"When did she call her?"

"What do you mean?"

"Was this appointment made a long time ago?"

"What, now, I look like a receptionist?"

"Forget it."

"Forgotten."

"Excuse me a second," Myron said. "Do you mind if I go make a call?"

"Am I your mother?" Zuckerman made a shooing motion. "Go already."

Myron debated using his cellular phone but decided not to piss off the Merion gods. He found a phone booth in the men's locker room foyer and dialed the Coldrens' house. He used Chad's line. Linda Coldren answered.

"Hello?"

"Just checking in," Myron said. "Anything new?"

"No," Linda said.

"Are you aware that Esme Fong is coming over?"

"I didn't want to cancel," Linda Coldren explained. "I didn't want to do anything that would draw attention."

"You'll be okay, then?"

"Yes," she said.

Myron watched Tad Crispin walk by in the direction of Win's table. "Were you able to reach the school?"

"No; nobody was there," she said. "So what do we do next?"

"I don't know," Myron said. "I have the override Caller ID on your phone. If he calls again, we should be able to get the number."

"What else?"

"I'll try to speak to Matthew Squires. See what he can tell me."

"I already spoke to Matthew," Linda said impatiently. "He doesn't know anything. What else?"

"I could get the police involved. Discreetly. There's not much else I can do on my own."

"No," she said firmly. "No police. Jack and I are both adamant on that point."

"I have friends in the FBI—"

"No."

He thought about his conversation with Win. "When Jack lost at Merion, who was his caddie?"

She hesitated. "Why would you want to know that?"

"I understand Jack blamed his caddie for the loss."

"In part, yes."

"And that he fired him."

"So?"

"So I asked about enemies. How did the caddie feel about what happened?"

"You're talking about something that happened over twenty years ago," Linda Coldren said. "Even if he did harbor a deep hatred for Jack, why would he wait so long?"

"This is the first time the Open has been at Merion since then. Maybe that's reawakened dormant anger. I don't know. Chances are there's nothing to this, but it might be worth checking out."

He could hear talking on the other end of the line. Jack's voice. She asked Myron to hold on a moment.

A few moments later, Jack Coldren came on the line. Without preamble, he said, "You think there's a connection between what happened to me twenty-three years ago and Chad's disappearance?"

"I don't know," Myron said.

His tone was insistent. "But you think—"

"I don't know what I think," he interrupted. "I'm just checking out every angle."

There was a stony silence. Then: "His name was Lloyd Rennart," Jack Coldren said.

"Do you know where he lives?"

"No. I haven't seen him since the day the Open ended."

"The day you fired him."

"Yes."

"You never bumped into him again? At the club or a tournament or something?"

"No," Jack Coldren said slowly. "Never."

"Where did Rennart live back then?"

"In Wayne. It's the neighboring town."

"How old would he be now?"

"Sixty-eight." No hesitation.

"Before this happened, were you two close?"

Jack Coldren's voice, when he finally spoke, was very soft. "I thought so," he said. "Not on a personal level. We didn't socialize. I never met his family or visited his home or anything like that. But on the golf course"—he paused—"I thought we were very close."

Silence.

"Why would he do it?" Myron asked. "Why would he purposely ruin your chances of winning?"

Myron could hear him breathing. When he spoke again, his voice was hoarse and scratchy. "I've wanted to know the answer to that for twenty-three years."

Chapter 6

Myron called in Lloyd Rennart's name to Esperanza. It probably wouldn't take much. Again modern technology would simplify the feat. Anyone with a modem could type in the address www.switchboard.com—a Web site that was virtually a telephone directory of the entire country. If that site didn't work, there were others. It probably wouldn't take long, if Lloyd Rennart was still among the living. If not, well, there were sites for that too.

"Did you tell Win?" Esperanza asked.

"Yes."

"How did he react?"

"He won't help."

"Not surprising," she said.

"No," he agreed.

Esperanza said, "You don't work well alone, Myron."

"I'll be fine," he said. "You looking forward to graduation?"

Esperanza had been going to NYU Law School at night for the past six years. She graduated on Monday.

"I probably won't go."

"Why not?"

"I'm not big on ceremony," she said.

Esperanza's only close relative, her mother, had died a few months back. Myron suspected that her death had more to do with Esperanza's decision than not being big on ceremony.

"Well, I'm going," Myron said. "Sitting front row center. I want to see it all."

Silence.

Esperanza broke it. "Is this the part where I choke back tears because someone cares?"

Myron shook his head. "Forget I said anything."

"No, really, I want to get it right. Should I break down in loud sobs or just sniffle a little? Or better yet, I could get a little teary, like Michael Landon on *Little House on the Prairie*."

"You're such a wiseass."

"Only when you're being patronizing."

"I'm not being patronizing. I care. Sue me."

"Whatever," she said.

"Any messages?"

"About a million, but nothing that I can't handle until Monday," she said. "Oh, one thing."

"What?"

"The bitch asked me out to lunch."

"The bitch" was Jessica, the love of Myron's life. Putting it kindly, Esperanza did not like Jessica. Many assumed that this had something to do with jealousy, with some sort of latent attraction between Esperanza and Myron. Nope. For one thing, Esperanza liked, er, flexibility in her love life. For a while she had dated a guy named Max, then a woman named Lucy, and now another woman named Hester. "How many times have I asked you not to call her that?" Myron said.

"About a million."

"So are you going?"

"Probably," she said. "I mean, it's a free meal. Even if I do have to look at her face."

They hung up. Myron smiled. He was a bit surprised. While Jessica did not reciprocate Esperanza's animosity, a lunch date to thaw out their personal cold war was not something Myron would have anticipated. Perhaps now that they were living together, Jess figured it was time to offer an olive branch. What the hell. Myron dialed Jessica.

The machine picked up. He heard her voice. When the beep came on, he said, "Jess? Pick up."

She did. "God, I wish you were here right now." Jessica had a way with openings.

"Oh?" He could see her lying on the couch, the phone cord twisted in her fingers. "Why's that?"

"I'm about to take a ten-minute break."

"A full ten minutes?"

"Yup."

"Then you'd be expecting extended foreplay?"

She laughed. "Up for it, big guy?"

"I will be," he said, "if you don't stop talking about it."

"Maybe we should change the subject," she said.

Myron had moved into Jessica's Soho loft a few months ago. For most people, this would be a somewhat dramatic change—moving from a suburb in New Jersey to a trendy section of New York, moving in with a woman you love, etc.—but for Myron, the change rivaled puberty. He had spent his entire life living with his mom and dad in the classic suburban town of Livingston, New Jersey. Entire life. Age zero to six in the upstairs bedroom on the right. Age six to thirteen in the upstairs bedroom on the left. Age thirteen to thirty-something in the basement.

After that long, the apron strings become steel bands.

"I hear you're taking Esperanza out for lunch," he said.

"Yup."

"How come?"

"No reason."

"No reason?"

"I think she's cool. I want to go to lunch. Stop being so nosy."

"You realize, of course, that she hates you."

"I can handle it," Jessica said. "So how's the golf tournament?"

"Very strange," he said.

"How so?"

"Too long a story to tell now, sweetcakes. Can I call you later?"

"Sure." Then: "Did you say 'sweetcakes'?"

When they hung up, Myron frowned. Something was amiss. He and Jessica had never been closer, their relationship never stronger. Moving in together had been the right move, and a lot of their past demons had been exorcised away of late. They were loving toward each other, considerate of each other's feelings and needs, and almost never fought.

So why did Myron feel like they were standing on the cusp of some deep abyss?

He shook it off. All of this was just the by-product of an overstimulated imagination. Just because a ship is sailing upon smooth waters, he surmised, does not mean it is heading for an iceberg.

Wow, that was deep.

By the time he got back to the table, Tad Crispin was sipping an iced tea too. Win made the introductions. Crispin was dressed in yellows, lots of yellows, kind of like the man with the yellow hat from the Curious George books. Everything was yellow. Even his golf shoes. Myron tried not to make a face.

As if reading his mind, Norm Zuckerman said, "This isn't our line."

"Good to hear," Myron said.

Tad Crispin stood. "Nice to meet you, sir."

Myron offered up a great big smile. "It's a true honor to meet you, Tad." His voice reeked with the sincerity of, say, a chain-store appliance salesman. The two men shook hands. Myron kept on smiling. Crispin began to look wary.

Zuckerman pointed a thumb at Myron and leaned toward Win. "Is he always this smooth?"

Win nodded. "You should see him with the ladies."

Everyone sat.

"I can't stay long," Crispin said.

"We understand, Tad," Zuckerman said, doing the shooing thing again with both hands. "You're tired, you need to concentrate on tomorrow. Go already, get some sleep."

Crispin sort of smiled a little and looked at Win. "I want you to have my account," he said.

"I don't 'have' accounts," Win corrected. "I advise on them."

"There's a difference?"

"Most definitely," Win said. "You are in control of your money at all times. I will make recommendations. I will make them to you directly. No one else. We will discuss them. You will then make a final decision. I will not buy or sell or trade anything without you being fully aware of what is going on."

Crispin nodded. "That sounds good."

"I thought it might," Win said. "From what I see, you plan on watching your money carefully."

"Yes."

"Savvy," Win said with a nod. "You've read about too many athletes retiring broke. Of being taken advantage of by unscrupulous money managers and the like."

"Yes."

"And it will be my job to help you maximize your return, correct?"

Crispin leaned forward a bit. "Correct."

"Very well, then. It will be my task to help maximize your investment opportunities *after* you earn it. But I would not be serving your best interests if I did not also tell you how to make more."

Crispin's eyes narrowed. "I'm not sure I follow."

Zuckerman said, "Win."

Win ignored him. "As your financial consultant, I would be remiss if I did not make the following recommendation: You need a good agent."

Crispin's line of vision slid toward Myron. Myron remained still, looking back at him steadily. He turned back to Win. "I know you work with Mr. Bolitar," Crispin said.

"Yes and no," Win said. "If you decide to use his services I do not make one penny more. Well, that's not exactly true. If you choose to use Myron's services, you will make more money and subsequently I will have more of your money to invest. So in that way, I will make more."

"Thanks," Crispin said, "but I'm not interested."

"That's up to you," Win said, "but let me just explain a little further what I meant by yes and no. I manage assets worth approximately four hundred million dollars. Myron's clients represent less than three percent of that total. I am not employed by MB SportsReps. Myron Bolitar is not employed by Lock-Horne Securities. We do not have a partnership. I have not invested in his enterprise and he is not invested in mine. Myron has never looked at, asked about, or in any way discussed the financial situation of any of my clients. We are totally separate. Except for one thing."

All eyes were on Win. Myron, not famous for knowing when to keep his mouth shut, knew now.

"I am the financial consultant for every one of his clients," Win said. "Do you know why?"

Crispin shook his head.

"Because Myron insists upon it."

Crispin looked confused. "I don't understand. If he gets nothing out of it—"

"I didn't say that. He gets plenty out of it."

"But you said—"

"He, too, was an athlete; did you know that?"

"I heard something about it."

"He knows what happens to athletes. How they get cheated. How they squander their earnings, never fully accepting the fact that their careers can be over in a heartbeat. So he insists—insists, mind you—that he does not handle their finances. I've seen him refuse clients because of this. He further insists that I handle them. Why? For the same reason you sought me out. He knows I am the best. Immodest but true. Myron further insists that they see me in person at least once every quarter. Not just phone calls. Not just faxes or E-mails or letters. He insists that I go over every item in the account personally with them."

Win leaned farther back and steepled his fingers. The man loved to steeple his fingers. It looked good on him. Gave him an air of wisdom. "Myron Bolitar is my best friend. I know he'd give his life for me and I for him. But if he ever thought that I was not doing what was in a client's best interest, he would take away their portfolios without a second thought."

Norm said, "Beautiful speech, Win. Got me right there." He pointed to his stomach.

Win gave him the look. Norm stopped smiling.

"I made the deal with Mr. Zuckerman on my own," Crispin said. "I could make others."

"I won't comment on the Zoom deal," Win said.

"But I will tell you this. You are a bright young man. A bright man knows not only his strengths but equally important, he knows his weaknesses. I do not, for example, know how to negotiate an endorsement contract. I may know the basics, but it is not my business. I'm not a plumber. If a pipe in my house broke, I would not be able to fix it. You are a golfer. You are one of the greatest talents I have ever seen. You should concentrate on that."

Tad Crispin took a sip of iced tea. He crossed his ankle on his knee. Even his socks were yellow. "You are making a hard sale for your friend," he said.

"Wrong," Win said. "I would kill for my friend, but financially I owe him nothing. You, on the other hand, are my client, and thus I have a very serious fiscal responsibility with regard to you. Stripping it bare, you have asked me to increase your portfolio. I will suggest several investment sources to you. But this is the best recommendation I can make."

Crispin turned to Myron. He looked him up and down, studying him hard. Myron almost brayed so he could examine his teeth. "He makes you sound awfully good," Crispin said to Myron.

"I am good," Myron said. "But I don't want him to give you the wrong impression. I'm not quite as altruistic as Win might have made me sound. I don't insist clients use him because I'm a swell guy. I know that having him handle my clients is a major plus. He improves the value of my services. He helps keep my clients happy. That's what I get out of it. Yes, I insist on having clients heavily involved in the decision-making on money matters, but that's as much to protect me as them."

"How so?"

"Obviously you know something about managers or agents robbing athletes."

"Yes."

"Do you know why so much of that occurs?"

Crispin shrugged. "Greed, I suppose."

Myron tilted his head in a yes-and-no gesture. "The main culprit is apathy. An athlete's lack of involvement. They get lazy. They decide it's easier to fully trust their agent, and that's bad. Let the agent pay the bills, they say. Let the agent invest the money. That kind of thing. But that won't ever happen at MB SportsReps. Not because I'm watching. Not because Win's watching. But because you are watching."

"I'm watching now," Crispin said.

"You're watching your money, true. I doubt you're watching everything else."

Crispin considered that for a moment. "I appreciate the talk," he said, "but I think I'm okay on my own."

Myron pointed at Tad Crispin's head. "How much are you getting for that hat?" he asked.

"Excuse me?"

"You're wearing a hat with no company logo on it," Myron explained. "For a player of your ilk, that's a loss of at least a quarter of a million dollars."

Silence.

"But I'm going to be working with Zoom," Crispin said.

"Did they purchase hat rights from you?"

He thought about it. "I don't think so."

"The front of the hat is a quarter million. We can also sell the sides if you want. They'll go for less. Maybe we'll total four hundred grand. Your shirt is another matter."

"Now just wait one minute here," Zuckerman interjected. "He's going to be wearing Zoom shirts."

"Fine, Norm," Myron said. "But he's allowed to wear logos. One on the chest, one on either sleeve."

"Logos?"

"Anything. Coca-Cola maybe. IBM. Even Home Depot."

"Logos on my shirt?"

"Yep. And what do you drink out there?"

"Drink? When I play?"

"Sure. I can probably get you a deal with Powerade or one of the soda companies. How about Poland Spring water? They might be good. And your golf bag. You have to negotiate a deal for your golf bag."

"I don't understand."

"You're a billboard, Tad. You're on television. Lots of fans see you. Your hat, your shirt, your golf bag—those are all places to post ads."

Zuckerman said, "Now hold on a second. He can't just—"

A cell phone began to sound, but it never made it past the first ring. Myron's finger reached the ringer and turned it off with a speed that would have made Wyatt Earp retire. Fast reflexes. They came in handy every once in a while.

Still, the brief sound had drawn the ire of nearby club members. Myron looked around. He was on the receiving end of several dagger-glares, including one from Win.

"Hurry around behind the clubhouse," Win said pointedly. "Let no one see you."

Myron gave a flippant salute and rushed out like a man with a suddenly collapsing bladder. When he reached a safe area near the parking lot, he answered the call.

"Hello."

"Oh, God . . ." It was Linda Coldren. Her tone struck the marrow of his bone.

"What's wrong?"

"He called again," she said.

"Do you have it on tape?"

"Yes."

"I'll be right ov—"

"No!" she shouted. "He's watching the house."

"You saw him?"

"No. But . . . Don't come here. Please."

"Where are you calling from?"

"The fax line in the basement. Oh God, Myron, you should have heard him."

"Did the number come up on the Caller ID?"

"Yes."

"Give it to me."

She did. Myron took out a pen from his wallet and wrote the number down on an old Visa receipt.

"Are you alone?"

"Jack is right here with me."

"Anybody else? What about Esme Fong?"

"She's upstairs in the living room."

"Okay," Myron said. "I'll need to hear the call."

"Hold on. Jack is plugging the machine in now. I'll put you on the speaker so you can hear."

Chapter 7

The tape player was snapped on. Myron heard the phone ringing first. The sound was surprisingly clear. Then he heard Jack Coldren: "Hello?"

"Who's the chink bitch?"

The voice was very deep, very menacing, and definitely machine-altered. Male or female, young or old, it was anyone's guess.

"I don't know what—"

"You trying to fuck with me, you dumb son of a bitch? I'll start sending you the fucking brat in little pieces."

Jack Coldren said, "Please—"

"I told you not to contact anyone."

"We haven't."

"Then tell me who that chink bitch is who just walked into your house."

Silence.

"You think we're stupid, Jack?"

"Of course not."

"So who the fuck is she?"

"Her name is Esme Fong," Coldren said quickly. "She works for a clothing company. She's just here to set up an endorsement deal with my wife, that's all."

"Bullshit."

"It's the truth, I swear."

"I don't know, Jack. . . ."

"I wouldn't lie to you."

"Well, Jack, we'll just see about that. This is gonna cost you."

"What do you mean?"

"One hundred grand. Call it a penalty price."

"For what?"

"Never you fucking mind. You want the kid alive? It's gonna cost you one hundred grand now. That's in—"

"Now hold on a second." Coldren cleared his throat. Trying to gain some footing, some degree of control.

"Jack?"

"Yes?"

"You interrupt me again and I'm going to stick your kid's dick in a vise."

Silence.

"You get the money ready, Jack. One hundred grand. I'll call you back and let you know what to do. Do you understand?"

"Yes."

"Don't fuck up, Jack. I enjoy hurting people."

The brief silence was shattered by a sharp, sudden scream, a scream that jangled nerve endings and raised hackles. Myron's hand tightened on the receiver.

The phone disconnected. Then a dial tone. Then nothing.

Linda Coldren took him off the speaker. "What are we going to do?"

"Call the FBI," Myron said.

"Are you out of your mind?"

"I think it's your best move."

Jack Coldren said something in the background. Linda came back on the line. "Absolutely not. We just want to pay the ransom and get our son back."

No point in arguing with them. "Sit tight. I'll call you back as soon as I can."

Myron disconnected the call and dialed another number. Lisa at New York Bell. She'd been a contact of theirs since the days he and Win had worked for the government.

"A Caller ID came up with a number in Philadelphia," he said. "Can you find an address for me?"

"No problem," Lisa said.

He gave her the number. People who watch too much television think this sort of thing takes a long time. Not anymore. Traces are instantaneous now. No "keep him on a little longer" or any of that stuff. The same is true when it comes to finding the location of a phone number. Any operator almost anywhere can plug the number into her computer or use one of those reverse directories, and whammo. Heck, you don't even need an operator. Computer programs on CD-ROM and Web sites did the same thing.

"It's a pay phone," she said.

Not good news, but not unexpected either. "Do you know where?"

"The Grand Mercado Mall in Bala-Cynwyd."

"A mall?"

"Yes."

"You're sure?"

"That's what it says."

"Where in the mall?"

"I have no idea. You think they list it 'between Sears and Victoria's Secret'?"

This made no sense. A mall? The kidnapper had dragged Chad Coldren to a mall and made him scream into a phone?

"Thanks, Lisa."

He hung up and turned back toward the porch. Win was standing directly behind him. His arms were folded, his body, as always, completely relaxed.

"The kidnapper called," Myron said.

"So I overheard."

"I could use your help tracking this down."

"No," Win said.

"This isn't about your mother, Win."

Win's face did not change, but something happened to his eyes. "Careful," was all he said.

Myron shook his head. "I have to go. Please make my excuses."

"You came here to recruit clients," Win said. "You claimed earlier that you agreed to help the Coldrens in the hopes of representing them."

"So?"

"So you are excruciatingly close to landing the world's top golf protégé. Reason dictates that you stay."

"I can't."

Win unfolded his arms, shook his head.

"Will you do one thing for me? To let me know if I'm wasting time or not?"

Win remained still.

"You know how I told you about Chad using his ATM card?"

"Yes."

"Get me the security videotape of the transaction," he said. "It may tell me if this whole thing is just a hoax on Chad's part."

Win turned back to the porch. "I'll see you at the house tonight."

Chapter 8

Myron parked at the mall and checked his watch. Seven forty-five. It had been a very long day and it was still relatively early. He entered through a Macy's and immediately located one of those big table blueprints of the mall. Public telephones were marked with blue locators. Eleven altogether. Two at the south entrance downstairs. Two at the north entrance upstairs. Seven at the food court.

Malls were the great American geographical equalizer. Between shiny anchor stores and beneath excessively floodlit ceilings, Kansas equaled California, New Jersey equaled Nevada. No place was truly more Americana. Some of the stores inside might be different, but not by much. Athlete's Foot or Foot Locker, Rite Aid or CVS, Williams-Sonoma or Pottery Barn, the Gap or Banana Republic or Old Navy (all, coincidentally, owned by the same people), Waldenbooks or B. Dalton, several anonymous shoe stores, a Radio Shack, a Victoria's Secret, an art gallery with Gorman, McKnight, and Behrens, a museum store of some kind, two record stores—all wrapped up in some Orwellian, sleek-chrome neo–Roman Forum with chintzy fountains and overstated marble and dentist-office sculptures and unmanned information booths and fake ferns.

In front of a store selling electric organs and pianos sat an employee dressed in an ill-fitting navy suit and a sailor's cap. He played "Muskrat Love" on an organ.

Myron was tempted to ask him where Tenille was, but he refrained. Too obvious. Organ stores in malls. Who goes to the mall to buy an organ?

He hurried past the Limited or the Unlimited or the Severely Challenged or something like that. Then Jeans Plus or Jeans Minus or Shirts Only or Pants Only or Tank Top City or something like that. They all looked pretty much the same. They all employed lots of skinny, bored teenagers who stocked shelves with the enthusiasm of a eunuch at an orgy.

There were lots of high school kids draped about— just hanging, man—and looking very, er, rad. At the risk of sounding like a reverse racist, all the white boys looked the same to him. Baggie shorts. White T-shirts. Unlaced black hundred-dollar high-top sneakers. Baseball cap pulled low with the brim worked into a nifty curve, covering a summer buzzcut. Thin. Lanky. Long-limbed. Pale as a Goya portrait, even in the summer. Poor posture. Eyes that never looked directly at another human being. Uncomfortable eyes. Slightly scared eyes.

He passed a hair salon called Snip Away, which sounded more like a vasectomy clinic than a beauty parlor. The Snip Away beauticians were either reformed mall girls or guys named Mario whose fathers were named Sal. Two patrons sat in a window—one getting a perm, the other a bleach job. Who wanted that? Who wanted to sit in a window and have the whole world watch you get your hair done?

He took an escalator up past a plastic garden complete with plastic vines to the crowned jewel of the mall: the food court. It was fairly empty now, the dinner crowd long since gone. Food courts were the final outpost of the great American melting pot. Italian, Chinese, Japanese, Mexican, Middle Eastern (or Greek), a deli, a chicken place, one fast food chain like McDonald's (which had the biggest crowd), a frozen yogurt place, and then a few strange offshoots—the ones started by people who dream of franchising themselves into becoming the next Ray Kroc. Ethiopian Ecstasy. Sven's Swedish Meatballs. Curry Up and Eat.

Myron checked for numbers on the seven phones. All had been whited out. Not surprising, the way people abused them nowadays. No problemo either. He took out his cellular phone and punched in the number from the Caller ID. A phone starting ringing immediately.

Bingo.

The one on the far right. Myron picked it up to make sure. "Hello?" he said. He heard the hello in his cellular phone. Then he said to himself through the cellular, "Hello, Myron, nice to hear from you." He decided to stop talking to himself. Too early in the evening to be this goofy.

He hung up the phone and looked around. A group of mall girls inhabited a table not far away. They sat in a closed circle with the protectiveness of coyotes during mating season.

Of the food stands, Sven's Swedish Meatballs had the best view of the phone. Myron approached. Two men worked the booth. They both had dark hair and dark skin and Saddam Hussein mustaches. One's name tag read Mustafa. The other Achmed.

"Which one of you is Sven?" he asked.

No smiles.

Myron asked about the phone. Mustafa and Achmed were less than helpful. Mustafa snapped that he worked for a living, and didn't watch phones. Achmed gestured and cursed him in a foreign tongue.

"I'm not much of a linguist," Myron said, "but that didn't sound like Swedish."

Death glares.

"Bye now. I'll be sure to tell all my friends."

Myron turned toward the table of mall girls. They all quickly looked down, like rats scurrying in the glare of a flashlight. He stepped toward them. Their eyes darted to and fro with what they must have thought were surreptitious glances. He heard a low cacophony of "ohmygod!ohmygod!ohmygod!he'scomingover!"

Myron stopped directly at their table. There were four girls. Or maybe five or even six. Hard to say. They all seemed to blend into one another, into one hazy, indistinct mesh of hair and black lipstick and Fu Manchu–length fingernails and earrings and nose rings and cigarette smoke and too-tight halter tops and bare midriffs and popping gum.

The one sitting in the middle looked up first. She had hair like Elsa Lancaster in *The Bride of Frankenstein* and what looked like a studded dog collar around her neck. The other faces followed suit.

"Like, hi," Elsa said.

Myron tried his most gentle, crooked smile. Harrison Ford in *Regarding Henry*. "Do you mind if I ask you a few questions?"

The girls all looked at one another. A few giggles escaped. Myron felt his face redden, though he wasn't sure why. They elbowed one another. No one answered. Myron proceeded.

"How long have you been sitting here?" he asked.

"Is this, like, one of those mall surveys?"

"No," Myron said.

"Good. Those are, like, so lame, you know?"

"Uh-huh."

"It's like, get away from me already, Mr. Polyester Pants, you know?"

Myron said "uh-huh" again. "Do you remember how long you've been sitting here?"

"Nah. Amber, you know?"

"Like, we went to the Gap at four."

"Right, the Gap. Fab sale."

"Ultra sale. Love that blouse you bought, Trish."

"Isn't it, like, the total package, Mindy?"

"Totally. Ultra."

Myron said, "It's almost eight now. Have you been here for the past hour?"

"Like, hello, anybody home? At least."

"This is, like, our spot, you know?"

"No one else, like, sits here."

"Except that one time when those gross lame-os tried to move in."

"But, like, whoa, don't even go there, 'kay?"

They stopped and looked at Myron. He figured the answer to his prior question was yes, so he plowed ahead. "Have you seen anybody use that pay phone?"

"Are you, like, a cop or something?"

"As if."

"No way."

"Way."

"He's too cute to be a cop."

"Oh, right, like Jimmy Smits isn't cute."

"That's, like, TV, dumb wad. This is real life. Cops aren't cute in real life."

"Oh, right, like Brad isn't totally cute? You, like, love him, remember?"

"As if. And he's not a cop. He's, like, some rent-a-uniform at Florsheim."

"But he's so hot."

"Totally."

"Ultra buff."

"He likes Shari."

"Eeeuw. Shari?"

"I, like, hate her, you know?"

"Me too. Like, does she only shop at Sluts 'R' Us, or what?"

"Totally."

"It's, like, 'Hello, Dial-a-Disease, this is Shari speaking.'"

Giggles.

Myron looked for an interpreter. "I'm not a cop," he said.

"Told you."

"As if."

"But," Myron said, "I am dealing with something very important. Life-and-death. I need to know if you remember anyone using that phone—the one on the far right—forty-five minutes ago."

"Whoa!" The one called Amber pushed her chair back. "Clear out, because I'm, like, gonna barf for days, you know?"

"Like, Crusty the Clown."

"He was, like, so gross!"

"Totally gross."

"Totally."

"He, like, winked at Amber!"

"As if!"

"Totally eeeuw!"

"Gag city."

"Bet that slut Shari would have Frenched him."

"At least."

Giggles.

Myron said, "You saw somebody?"

"Serious groatie."

"Totally crusty."

"He was, like, hello, ever wash your hair?"

"Like, hello, buy your cologne at the local Gas-N-Go?"

More giggles.

Myron said, "Can you describe him to me?"

"Blue jeans from, like, 'Attention, Kmart shoppers.' "

"Work boots. Definitely not Timberland."

"He was, like, so skinhead wanna-be, you know?"

Myron said, "Skinhead wanna-be?"

"Like, a shaved head. Skanky beard. Tattoo of that thing on his arm."

"That thing?" Myron tried.

"You know, that tattoo." She kind of drew something in the air with her finger. "It kinda looks like a funny cross from, like, the old days."

Myron said, "You mean a swastika?"

"Like, whatever. Do I look like a history major?"

"Like, how old was he?" Like. He'd said *like*. If he stayed here much longer, he'd end up getting some part of him pierced. Way.

"Old."

"Grampa-ville."

"Like, at least twenty."

"Height?" Myron asked. "Weight?"

"Six feet."

"Yeah, like six feet."

"Bony."

"Very."

"Like, no ass at all."

"None."

"Was anybody with him?" Myron asked.

"As if."

"Him?"

"No way."

"Who would be with a skank like that?"

"Just him by that phone for like half an hour."

"He wanted Mindy."

"Did not!"

"Wait a second," Myron said. "He was there for half an hour?"

"Not that long."

"Seemed a long time."

"Maybe like fifteen minutes. Amber, like, always exaggerates."

"Like, fuck you, Trish, all right? Just fuck you."

"Anything else?" Myron asked.

"Beeper."

"Right, beeper. Like anybody would ever call that skank."

"Held it right up to the phone, too."

Probably not a beeper. Probably a microcassette player. That would explain the scream. Or a voice changer. They also came in a small box.

He thanked the girls and handed out business cards that listed his cellular phone number. One of the girls actually read it. She made a face.

"Like, your name is really Myron?"

"Yes."

They all just stopped and looked at him.

"I know," Myron said. "Like, ultra lame-o."

He was heading back to his car when a nagging thought suddenly resurfaced. The kidnapper on the phone had mentioned a "chink bitch." Somehow he had known about Esme Fong arriving at the house. The question was, how?

There were two possibilities. One, they had a bug in the house.

Not likely. If the Coldren residence was bugged or under some kind of electronic surveillance, the kidnapper would also have known about Myron's involvement.

Two, one of them was watching the house.

That seemed most logical. Myron thought a moment. If someone had been watching the house only an hour or so ago, it was fair to assume that they were still there, still hiding behind a bush or up a tree or something. If Myron could locate the person surreptitiously, he might be able to follow them back to Chad Coldren.

Was it worth the risk?

Like, totally.

Chapter 9

Ten o'clock.

Myron used Win's name again and parked in Merion's
lot. He checked for Win's Jaguar, but it was nowhere to
be seen. He parked and checked for guards. No one.
They'd all been stationed at the front entrance. Made
things easier.

He quickly stepped over the white rope used to hold
back the galley and started crossing the golf course. It
was dark now, but the lights from the houses across the
way provided enough illumination to cross. For all its
fame, Merion was a tiny course. From the parking lot to
Golf House Road, across two fairways, was less than a
hundred yards.

Myron trudged forward. Humidity hung in the air in a
heavy blanket of beads. Myron's shirt began to feel
sticky. The crickets were incessant and plenteous, their
swarming tune as monotonous as a Mariah Carey CD,
though not quite as grating. The grass tickled Myron's
sockless ankles.

Despite his natural aversion to golf, Myron still felt
the appropriate sense of awe, as if he were trespassing
over sacred ground. Ghosts breathed in the night, the
same way they breathed at any sight that had borne legends. Myron remembered once standing on the parquet
floor at Boston Garden when no one else was there. It was
a week after he had been picked by the Celtics in the first
round of the NBA draft. Clip Arnstein, the Celtics' fabled

general manager, had introduced him to the press earlier that day. It had been enormous fun. Everybody had been laughing and smiling and calling Myron the next Larry Bird. That night, as he stood alone in the famed halls of the Garden, the championship flags hanging from the rafters actually seemed to sway in the still air, beckoning him forward and whispering tales of the past and promises of what was to come.

Myron never played a game on that parquet floor.

He slowed as he reached Golf House Road and stepped over the white rope. Then he ducked behind a tree. This would not be easy. Then again, it would not be easy for his quarry either. Neighborhoods like this noted anything suspicious. Like a parked car where it didn't belong. That had been why Myron had parked in the Merion lot. Had the kidnapper done likewise? Or was his car out on the street? Or had someone dropped him off?

He kept low and darted to another tree. He looked, he assumed, rather doofy—a guy six-feet four inches tall and comfortably over two hundred pounds darting between bushes like something left on the cutting room floor of *The Dirty Dozen*.

But what choice did he have?

He couldn't just casually walk down the street. The kidnapper might spot him. His whole plan relied on the fact that he could spot the kidnapper before the kidnapper spotted him. How to do this? He really did not have a clue. The best he could come up with was to keep circling closer and closer to the Coldren house, looking out for, er, uh, something.

He scanned the surroundings—for what, he wasn't sure. Someplace for a kidnapper to use as a lookout spot, he guessed. A safe place to hide, maybe, or a perch where a man with binoculars could survey the scene. Nothing. The night was absolutely windless and still.

He circled the block, dashing haphazardly from one bush to another, feeling now very much like John Belushi breaking into Dean Wormer's office in *Animal House*.

Animal House and *The Dirty Dozen*. Myron watched too many movies.

As he continued to spiral closer to the Coldrens' residence, Myron realized that there was probably a good chance that he'd be the "spottee" rather than the "spotter." He tried to hide himself better, to concentrate on making himself become part of the night, to blend in to the background and become invisible.

Myron Bolitar, Mutant Ninja Warrior.

Lights twinkled from spacious homes of stone and black shutters. They were all imposing and rather beautiful with a tutelary, stay-away coziness about them. Solid homes. The third-little-piggie homes. Settled and staying and proud homes.

He was getting very close to the Coldren house now. Still nothing—not even a single car parked on the roads. Sweat coated him like syrup on a stack of pancakes. God, he wanted to take a shower. He hunched down and watched the house.

Now what?

Wait. Be on the lookout for movement of some kind. Surveillance and the like was not Myron's forte. Win usually handled that kind of stuff. He had the body control and the patience. Myron was already getting fidgety. He wished he'd brought a magazine or something to read.

The three minutes of monotony was broken when the front door opened. Myron sat up. Esme Fong and Linda Coldren appeared in the door frame. They said their good-byes. Esme gave Linda the firm handshake and headed to her car. Linda Coldren shut the front door. Esme Fong started her car and left.

A thrill a second, this surveillance stuff.

Myron settled back behind a shrub. There were lots of shrubs around here. Everywhere one looked, there were shrubs of various sizes and shapes and purposes. Rich blue bloods must really like shrubs, Myron decided. He wondered if they had had any on the *Mayflower*.

His legs were beginning to cramp from all this crouching. He straightened them out one at a time. His bad knee, the one that ended his basketball career, began to throb. Enough. He was hot and sticky and in pain. Time to get out of here.

Then he heard a sound.

It seemed to be coming from the back door. He sighed, creaked to his feet, and circled. He found yet another comfy shrub and hid behind it. He peered out.

Jack Coldren was in the backyard with his caddie, Diane Hoffman. Jack held a golf club in his hands, but he wasn't hitting. He was talking with Diane Hoffman. Animatedly. Diane Hoffman was talking back. Equally animated. Neither one of them seemed very pleased. Myron could not hear them, but they were both gesturing like mad.

An argument. A rather heated argument.

Hmm.

Of course, there probably was an innocent explanation. Caddies and players argue all the time, Myron guessed. He remembered reading how Seve Ballesteros, the Spanish former wunderkind, was always fighting with his caddie. Bound to happen. Routine stuff, a caddie and a pro having a little tiff, especially during such a pressure-filled tournament as the U.S. Open.

But the timing was curious.

Think about it a second. A man gets a terrifying call from a kidnapper. He hears his son scream in apparent fright or pain. Then, a couple of hours later, he is in his backyard arguing about his backswing with his caddie.

Did that make sense?

Myron decided to move closer, but there was no straight path. Shrubs again, like tackle dummies at a football practice. He'd have to move to the side of the house and circle in behind them. He made a quick bolt to his left and risked another glance. The heated argument continued. Diane Hoffman took a step closer to Jack.

Then she slapped him in the face.

The sound sliced through the night like a scythe. Myron froze. Diane Hoffman shouted something. Myron heard the word *bastard,* but nothing else. Diane flicked her cigarette at Jack's feet and stormed off. Jack looked down, shook his head slowly, and went back inside.

Well, well, Myron thought. Must have been some trouble with that backswing.

Myron stayed behind the shrub. He heard a car start in the driveway. Diane Hoffman's, he assumed. For a moment, he wondered if she had a role in this. Obviously she had been in the house. Could she be the mysterious lookout? He leaned back and considered the possibility. The idea was just starting to soak in and settle when Myron spotted the man.

Or at least he assumed it was a man. It was hard to tell from where he was crouched. Myron could not believe what he was seeing. He had been wrong. Dead wrong. The perpetrator hadn't been hiding in the bushes or anything like that. Myron watched now in silence as someone dressed completely in black climbed out an upper-floor window. More specifically—if memory didn't fail him—Chad Coldren's bedroom window.

Hello there.

Myron ducked down. Now what? He needed a plan. Yes, a plan. Good thinking. But what plan? Did he grab the perp now? No. Better to follow him. Maybe he'd lead him back to Chad Coldren. That would be nice.

He took another peek out. The black-clad figure had scaled down a white lattice fence with entwined ivy. He jumped the last few feet. As soon as he hit the ground, he sprinted away.

Great.

Myron followed, trying to stay as far behind the figure as possible. The figure, however, was running. This made following silently rather difficult. But Myron kept back. Didn't want to risk being seen. Besides, chances were good that the perpetrator had brought a car or was getting picked up by someone. These streets barely had any traffic. Myron would be bound to hear an engine.

But then what?

What would Myron do when the perp got to the car? Run back to get his own? No, that wouldn't work. Follow a car on foot? Er, not likely. So what exactly was he going to do?

Good question.

He wished Win were here.

The perp kept running. And running. Myron was starting to suck air. Jesus, who the hell was he chasing anyway, Frank Shorter? Another quarter mile passed before the perp abruptly veered to the right and out of view. The turn was so sudden that for a moment Myron wondered if he'd been spotted. Impossible. He was too far back and his quarry had not so much as glanced over his shoulder.

Myron tried to hurry a bit, but the road was gravelly. Running silently would be impossible. Still, he had to make up ground. He ran high atop his tiptoes, looking not unlike Baryshnikov with dysentery. He prayed nobody would see him.

He reached the turn. The name of the street was Green Acres Road. Green Acres. The old TV show theme song started in his head, like someone had pressed buttons on a jukebox. He couldn't stop it. Eddie Albert rode a tractor.

Eva Gabor opened boxes in a Manhattan penthouse. Sam Drucker waved from behind the counter of his general store. Mr. Haney pulled his suspenders with both thumbs. Arnold the pig snorted.

Man, the humidity was definitely getting to him.

Myron wheeled to the right and looked ahead.

Nothing.

Green Acres was a short cul-de-sac with maybe five homes. Fabulous homes, or so Myron assumed. Towering shrub walls—again with the shrubs—lined either side of the street. Locked gates were on the driveways, the kind that worked by remote control or by pushing a combination in a keypad. Myron stopped and looked down the road.

So where was our boy?

He felt his pulse quicken. No sign of him. The only escape route was through the woods between two houses in the cul-de-sac. He must have gone in there, Myron surmised—if, that is, he was trying to escape and not, say, hide in the bushes. He might, after all, have spotted Myron. He might have decided to duck down somewhere and hide. Hide and then pounce when Myron walked by.

These were not comforting thoughts.

Now what?

He licked the sweat off his upper lip. His mouth felt terribly dry. He could almost hear himself sweat.

Suck it up, Myron, he told himself. He was six-four and two hundred and twenty pounds. A big guy. He was also a black belt in tae kwon do and a well-trained fighter. He could fend off any attack.

Unless the guy was armed.

True. Let's face it. Fight training and experience were helpful, but they did not make one bullet-proof. Not even Win. Of course, Win wouldn't have been stupid enough to get himself into this mess. Myron carried a weapon only when he thought it was absolutely necessary. Win, on the other hand, carried at least two guns and one bladed instrument at all times. Third world countries should be as well armed as Win.

So what to do?

He looked left and right, but there was no place much for anybody to hide. The shrub walls were thick and fully impenetrable. That left only the woods at the end of the road. But there were no lights down that way and the woods looked dense and forbidding.

Should he go in?

No. That would be pointless at best. He had no idea how big the woods were, what direction to head in, nothing. The odds of finding the perpetrator were frighteningly remote. Myron's best hope was that the perp was just hiding for a while, waiting for Myron to clear out.

Clear out. That sounded like a plan.

Myron moved back to the end of Green Acres. He turned left, traveled a couple of hundred yards, and settled behind yet another shrub. He and shrubs were on a first-name basis by now. This one he named Frank.

He waited an hour. No one appeared.

Great.

He finally stood up, said good-bye to Frank, and headed back to the car. The perpetrator must have escaped through the woods. That meant that he had planned an escape route or, more probably, he knew the area well. Could mean that it was Chad Coldren. Or it could mean that the kidnappers knew what they were doing. And if that was so, it meant there was a good chance that they now knew about Myron's involvement and the fact that the Coldrens had disobeyed them.

Myron hoped like hell it was just a hoax. But if it wasn't, if this was indeed a real kidnapping, he wondered about repercussions. He wondered how the kidnappers would react to what he had done. And as he continued on his way, Myron remembered their previous phone call and the harrowing, flesh-creeping sound of Chad Coldren's scream.

Chapter 10

"Meanwhile, back at stately Wayne Manor . . ."

That voice-over from the TV *Batman* always came to Myron when he reached the steely gates of the Lockwood estate. In reality, Win's family home looked very little like Bruce Wayne's house, though it did offer up the same aura. A tremendous serpentine driveway wound to an imposing stone mansion on the hill. There was grass, lots of it, all the blades kept at a consistently ideal length, like a politician's hair in an election year. There were also lush gardens and hills and a swimming pool, a pond, a tennis court, horse stables, and a horse obstacle course of some kind.

All in all, the Lockwood estate was very "stately" and worthy of the term "manor," whatever that meant.

Myron and Win were staying at the guest house—or as Win's father liked to call it, "the cottage." Exposed beams, hardwood floors, fireplace, new kitchen with a big island in the middle, pool room—not to mention five bedrooms, four and half baths. Some cottage.

Myron tried to sort through what was happening, but all he came up with was a series of paradoxes, a whole lot of "which came first, the chicken or the egg?" Motive, for example. On the one hand, it might make sense to kidnap Chad Coldren to throw off Jack Coldren. But Chad had been missing since *before* the tournament, which meant the kidnapper was either very cautious or very prophetic. On the other hand, the kidnapper had asked for one hundred grand, which pointed to a simple case of kidnapping for money. A hundred grand was a nice, tidy sum—a little low for a kidnapping, but not bad for a few days' work.

But if this was merely a kidnapping to extort mucho dinero, the timing was curious. Why now? Why during the one time a year the U.S. Open was played? More than that, why kidnap Chad during the one time in the last twenty-three years the Open was being played at Merion —the one time in almost a quarter of a century that Jack Coldren had a chance to revisit and redeem his greatest failing?

Seemed like a hell of a coincidence.

That brought it back to a hoax and a scenario that went something like this: Chad Coldren disappears before the tournament to screw around with his dad's mind. When that doesn't work—when, to the contrary, Dad starts winning—he ups the ante and fakes his own kidnapping. Taking it a step further, one could assume that it had been Chad Coldren who had been climbing out of his own window. Who better? Chad Coldren knew the area. Chad Coldren probably knew how to go through those woods. Or maybe he was hiding out at a friend's house who lived on Green Acres Road. Whatever.

It added up. It made sense.

All of this assumed, of course, that Chad truly disliked his father. Was there evidence of that? Myron thought so. Start off with the fact that Chad was sixteen years old. Not an easy age. Weak evidence for sure, but worth keeping in mind. Second—and far, far more important—Jack Coldren was an absent father. No athlete is away from home as much as a golfer. Not basketball players or football players or baseball players or hockey players. The only ones who come close are tennis players. In both tennis and golf, tournaments are taking place almost all year—there is little so-called off season—and there is no such thing as a home game. If you were lucky, you hit your home course once a year.

Lastly—and perhaps most crucial of all—Chad had been gone for *two* days without raising eyebrows. Forget Linda Coldren's discourse on responsible children and open child-raising. The only rational explanation for their nonchalance was that this had happened before, or at the very least, was not unexpected.

But there were problems with the hoax scenario too.

For example, how did Mr. Total Grunge from the mall fit in?

There was indeed the rub. What role was the Crusty Nazi playing in all this? Did Chad Coldren have an accomplice? Possibly, but that really didn't fit in well with a revenge scenario. If Chad was indeed behind all this, Myron doubted that the preppy golfer would join forces with a "skinhead wanna-be," complete with a swastika tattoo.

So where did that leave Myron?

Baffled.

As Myron pulled up to the guest house, he felt his heart constrict. Win's Jag was there. But so was a green Chevy Nova.

Oh, Christ.

Myron got out of the car slowly. He checked the license plate on the Nova. Unfamiliar. As he expected. He swallowed and moved away.

He opened the cottage's front door and welcomed the sudden onslaught of air-conditioning. The lights were out. For a moment he just stood in the foyer, eyes closed, the cool air tingling his skin. An enormous grandfather clock ticked.

Myron opened his eyes and flicked on a light.

"Good evening."

He pivoted to his right. Win was seated in a high-back

leather chair by the fireplace. He cupped a brandy snifter in his hand.

"You were sitting in the dark?" Myron asked.

"Yes."

Myron frowned. "A bit theatrical, don't you think?"

Win switched on a nearby lamp. His face was a tad rosy from the brandy. "Care to join me?"

"Sure. I'll be right back."

Myron grabbed a cold Yoo-Hoo from the refrigerator and sat on the couch across from his friend. He shook the can and popped it open. They drank in silence for several minutes. The clock ticked. Long shadows snaked across the floor in thin, almost smoky tendrils. Too bad it was summertime. This was the kind of setting that begged for a roaring fire and maybe some howling wind. An air conditioner just didn't cut it.

Myron was just getting comfortable when he heard a toilet flush. He looked a question at Win.

"I am not alone," Win said.

"Oh." Myron adjusted himself on the couch. "A woman?"

"Your gifts," Win said. "They never cease to amaze."

"Anybody I know?" Myron asked.

Win shook his head. "Not even somebody I know."

The norm. Myron looked steadily at his friend. "You want to talk about this?"

"No."

"I'm here if you do."

"Yes, I see that." Win swished around the drink in the snifter. He finished it in one gulp and reached for the crystal decanter. There was a slight slur in his speech. Myron tried to remember the last time he had seen Win the vegetarian, the master of several martial arts, the transcendental meditator, the man so at ease and in focus with his surroundings, have too much to drink.

It had been a very long time.

"I have a golf question for you," Myron said.

Win nodded for him to proceed.

"Do you think Jack Coldren can hang on to this lead?"

Win poured the brandy. "Jack will win," he said.

"You sound pretty sure."

"I am sure."

"Why?"

Win raised the glass to his mouth and looked over the rim. "I saw his eyes."

Myron made a face. "What's that supposed to mean?"

"He has it back. The look in the eyes."

"You're kidding, right?"

"Perhaps I am. But let me ask you something."

"Go ahead."

"What separates the great athletes from the very good? The legend from the journeyman? Simply put, what makes winners?"

"Talent," Myron said. "Practice. Skill."

Win gave a slight shake of the head. "You know better than that."

"I do?"

"Yes. Many have talent. Many practice. There is more to the art of creating a true winner."

"This look-in-the-eye thing?"

"Yes."

Myron winced. "You're not going to start singing 'Eye of the Tiger,' are you?"

Win cocked his head. "Who sang that song?"

The continuing trivia game. Win knew the answer, of course. "It was in *Rocky II*, right?"

"*Rocky III*," Win corrected.

"That the one with Mr. T?"

Win nodded. "Who played . . . ?" he prompted.

"Clubber Lange."

"Very good. Now who sang the song?"

"I don't remember."

"The name of the group was Survivor," Win said. "Ironic name when you think of how quickly they vanished, no?"

"Uh-huh," Myron said. "So what is this great divider, Win? What makes a winner?"

Win took another swish and sip. "Wanting," he said.

"Wanting?"

"Hunger."

"Uh-huh."

"The answer isn't surprising," Win said. "Look in Joe DiMaggio's eyes. Or Larry Bird's. Or Michael Jordan's. Look at pictures of John McEnroe in his prime, or Chris Evert. Look at Linda Coldren." He stopped. "Look in the mirror."

"The mirror? I have this?"

"When you were on the court," Win said slowly, "your eyes were barely sane."

They fell into silence. Myron took a swig of Yoo-Hoo. The cold aluminum felt good in his hand. "You make the whole 'wanting' thing sound like it's all foreign to you," Myron said.

"It is."

"Bull."

"I am a good golfer," Win said. "Correction: I am a very good golfer. I practiced quite a bit in my youth. I have even won my share of tournaments. But I never wanted it bad enough to move up to that next level."

"I've seen you in the ring," Myron countered. "In

martial arts tournaments. You seemed plenty 'wanting' to me.''

"That is very different,'' Win said.

"How so?''

"I do not view a martial arts tournaments as a sporting contest, whereby the winner brings home a chintzy trophy and brags to colleagues and friends—nor do I view it as a competition that will lead to some sort of empty emotion that the insecure among us perceive as glory. Fighting is not a sport to me. It's about survival. If I could lose in there''—he motioned to an imaginary ring—"I could lose in the real world.'' Win looked up in the air. "But . . .'' His voice drifted off.

"But?'' Myron repeated.

"But you may be on to something.''

"Oh?''

Win steepled his fingers. "You see, fighting is life-and-death to me. That's how I treat it. But the athletes we've been talking about take it a step further. Every competition, even the most banal, is viewed by them as life-and-death—and losing is death.''

Myron nodded. He didn't buy it, but what the hell. Keep him talking. "I don't get something,'' he said. "If Jack has this special 'wanting,' why hasn't he ever won a professional tournament?''

"He lost it.''

"The wanting?''

"Yes.''

"When?''

"Twenty-three years ago.''

"During the Open?''

"Yes,'' Win said again. "Most athletes lose it in a slow burnout. They grow weary or they win enough to quench whatever inferno rages in their bellies. But that was not the case with Jack. His fire was extinguished in one crisp, cold gust. You could almost see it. Twenty-three years ago. The sixteenth hole. The ball landing in the stone quarry. His eyes have never been the same.''

"Until now," Myron added.

"Until now," Win agreed. "It took him twenty-three years, but he stoked the flames back to life."

They both drank. Win sipped. Myron guzzled. The chocolaty coldness felt wonderful sliding down his throat. "How long have you known Jack?" Myron asked.

"I met him when I was six years old. He was fifteen."

"Did he have the 'wanting' back then?"

Win smiled at the ceiling. "He would sooner carve out his own kidney with a grapefruit spoon than lose to someone on the golf course." He lowered his gaze to Myron. "Did Jack Coldren have the 'wanting'? He was the pure definition."

"Sounds like you admired him."

"I did."

"You don't anymore?"

"No."

"What made you change?"

"I grew up."

"Wow." Myron took another swig of Yoo-Hoo. "That's heavy."

Win chuckled. "You wouldn't understand."

"Try me."

Win put down the brandy snifter. He leaned forward very slowly. "What is so great about winning?"

"Pardon?"

"People love a winner. They look up to him. They admire—nay, revere—him. They use terms like *hero* and *courage* and *perseverance* to describe him. They want to be near him and touch him. They want to be like him."

Win spread his hands. "But why? What about the winner do we want to emulate? His ability to blind himself to anything but the pursuit of empty aggrandizement? His ego-inflating obsession with wearing a hunk of metal around his neck? His willingness to sacrifice anything, including people, in order to best another human being on a lump of AstroTurf for a cheesy statuette?'' He looked up at Myron, his always serene face suddenly lost. ''Why do we applaud this selfishness, this self-love?''

''Competitive drive isn't a bad thing, Win. You're talking about extremes.''

''But it is the extremists we admire most. By its nature, what you call 'competitive drive' leads to extremism and destroys all in its path.''

''You're being simplistic, Win.''

''It is simple, my friend.''

They both settled back. Myron stared up at the exposed beams. After some time, he said, ''You have it wrong.''

''How so?''

Myron wondered how to explain it. ''When I played basketball,'' he began, ''I mean, when I really got into it and reached these levels you're talking about—I barely thought about the score. I barely thought about my opponent or about beating somebody. I was alone. I was in the zone. This is going to sound stupid, but playing at the top of my game was almost Zen-like.''

Win nodded. ''And when did you feel this way?''

''Pardon?''

''When did you feel your most—to use your word—Zen?''

''I don't follow.''

''Was it at practice? No. Was it during an unimportant game or when your team was up by thirty points? No. What brought you to this sweat-drenched state of Nirvana, my friend, was competition. The desire—the naked need—to defeat a top-level opponent.''

Myron opened his mouth to counter. Then he stopped. Exhaustion was starting to take over. "I'm not sure I have an answer to that," he said. "At the end of the day, I like to win. I don't know why. I like ice cream too. I don't know why either."

Win frowned. "Impressive simile," he said flatly.

"Hey, it's late."

Myron heard a car pull up front. A young blond entered the room and smiled. Win smiled back. She bent down and kissed him. Win had no problem with that. Win was never outwardly rude to his dates. He was not the type to rush them out. He had no problem with them staying the night, if it made them happier. Some might mistake this for kindness or a tender spot in the soul. They'd be wrong. Win let them stay because they meant so little to him. They could never reach him. They could never touch him. So why not let them stay?

"That's my taxi," the blonde said.

Win's smile was blank.

"I had fun," she said.

Not even a blink.

"You can reach me through Amanda if you want"— she looked at Myron, then back at Win—"well, you know."

"Yes," Win said. "I know."

The young woman offered up an uncomfortable smile and left.

Myron watched, trying to keep his face from registering shock. A prostitute! Christ, she was a prostitute! He knew that Win had used them in the past—in the mid-eighties, he used to order in Chinese food from Hunan Grill and Asian prostitutes from the Noble House bordello for what he called "Chinese Night"—but to still partake, in this day and age?

Then Myron remembered the Chevy Nova and his whole body went cold.

He turned to his friend. They looked at each other. Neither one of them said anything.

"Moralizing," Win said. "How nice."

"I didn't say anything."

"Indeed." Win stood.

"Where are you going?"

"Out."

Myron felt his heart pound. "Mind if I go with you?"

"Yes."

"What car are you taking?"

Win did not bother responding. "Good night, Myron."

Myron's mind raced for solutions, but he knew it was hopeless. Win was going. There was no way to stop him.

Win stopped at the door and turned back to him. "One question, if I may."

Myron nodded, unable to speak.

"Was Linda Coldren the one who first contacted you?" Win asked.

"No," Myron said.

"Then who?"

"Your uncle Bucky."

Win arched an eyebrow. "And who suggested us to Bucky?"

Myron looked back at Win steadily, but he couldn't stop shaking. Win nodded and turned back to the door.

"Win?"

"Go to sleep, Myron."

Chapter 11

Myron did not go to sleep. He didn't even bother trying.

He sat in Win's chair and tried to read, but the words never registered. He was exhausted. He leaned back against the rich leather and waited. Hours passed. Disjointed images of Win's potential handiwork wrested free in a heavy spray of dark crimson. Myron closed his eyes and tried to ride it out.

At 3:30 A.M., Myron heard a car pull up. The ignition died. A key clicked in the door and then it swung open. Win stepped inside and looked at Myron with nary a trace of emotion.

"Good night," Win said.

He walked away. Myron heard the bedroom door close and let loose a held breath. Fine, he thought. He lifted himself into a standing position and made his way to his bedroom. He crawled under the sheets, but sleep still would not come. Black, opaque fear fluttered in his stomach. He had just begun to slide into true REM sleep when the bedroom door flew open.

"You're still asleep?" a familiar voice asked.

Myron managed to tear his eyes open. He was used to Esperanza Diaz barging into his office without knocking; he wasn't used to her doing it where he slept.

"What time is it?" he croaked.

"Six-thirty."

"In the morning?"

Esperanza gave him one of her patented glares, the one road crews tried to hire out to raze large rock formations. With one finger she tucked a few spare strands of her raven locks behind her ear. Her shimmering dark skin made you think of a Mediterranean cruise by moonlight, of clear waters and puffy-sleeved peasant blouses and olive groves.

"How did you get here?" he asked.

"Amtrak red-eye," she said.

Myron was still groggy. "Then what did you do? Catch a cab?"

"What are you, a travel agent? Yes, I took a cab."

"Just asking."

"The idiot driver asked me for the address three times. Guess he's not used to taking Hispanics into this neighborhood."

Myron shrugged. "Probably thought you were a domestic," he said.

"In *these* shoes?" She lifted her foot so he could see.

"Very nice." Myron adjusted himself in the bed, his body still craving sleep. "Not to belabor the point, but what exactly are you doing here?"

"I got some information on the old caddie."

"Lloyd Rennart?"

Esperanza nodded. "He's dead."

"Oh." Dead. As in dead end. Not that it had been much of a beginning. "You could have just called."

"There's more."

"Oh?"

"The circumstances surrounding his death are"—she stopped, bit her lower lip—"fuzzy."

Myron sat up a bit. "Fuzzy?"

"Lloyd Rennart apparently committed suicide eight months ago."

"How?"

"That's the fuzzy part. He and his wife were on vacation in a mountain range in Peru. He woke up one morning, wrote a brief note, then he jumped off a cliff of some kind."

"You're kidding."

"Nope. I haven't been able to get too many details yet. The *Philadelphia Daily News* just had a brief story on it." There was a hint of a smile. "But according to the article, the body had not yet been located."

Myron was starting to wake up in a big hurry. "What?"

"Apparently Lloyd Rennart took the plunge in a remote crevasse with no access. They may have located the body by now, but I couldn't find a follow-up article. None of the local papers carried an obituary."

Myron shook his head. No body. The questions that sprang to mind were obvious: could Lloyd Rennart still be alive? Did he fake his own death in order to plot out his revenge? Seemed a tad out there, but you never know. If he had, why would he have waited twenty-three years? True, the U.S. Open was back at Merion. True, that could make old wounds resurface. But still. "Weird," he said. He looked up at her. "You could have told me all this on the phone. You didn't have to come all the way down here."

"What the hell is the big deal?" Esperanza snapped. "I wanted to get out of the city for the weekend. I thought seeing the Open would be fun. You mind?"

"I was just asking."

"You're so nosy sometimes."

"Okay, okay." He held up his hands in mock surrender. "Forget I asked."

"Forgotten," she said. "You want to fill me in on what's going on?"

He told her about the Crusty Nazi at the mall and about losing the black-clad perpetrator.

When he finished, Esperanza shook her head. "Jesus," she said. "Without Win, you're hopeless."

Ms. Morale Booster.

"Speaking of Win," Myron said, "don't talk to him about the case."

"Why?"

"He's reacting badly."

She watched him closely. "How badly?"

"He went night visiting."

Silence.

"I thought he stopped doing that," she said.

"I thought so too."

"Are you sure?"

"There was a Chevy parked in the driveway," Myron said. "He took it out of here last night and didn't get back till three-thirty."

Silence. Win stored a bunch of old, unregistered Chevys. Disposable cars, he called them. Completely untraceable.

Esperanza's voice was soft. "You can't have it both ways, Myron."

"What are you talking about?"

"You can't ask Win to do it when it suits you, then get pissed off when he does it on his own."

"I never ask him to play vigilante."

"Yeah, you do. You involve him in violence. When it suits your needs, you unleash him. Like he's a weapon of some kind."

"It's not like that."

"It is like that," she said. "It is exactly like that. When Win goes out on these night errands, he doesn't hurt the innocent, does he?"

Myron considered the question. "No," he said.

"So what's the problem? He is just attacking a different type of guilty. He picks out the guilty instead of you."

Myron shook his head. "It's not the same thing."

"Because you judge?"

"I don't send him out to hurt people. I send him out to watch people or to back me up."

"I'm not sure I see the difference."

"Do you know what he does when he night visits, Esperanza? He walks through the worst neighborhoods he can find in the middle of the night. Old FBI buddies tell him where drug dealers or child pornographers or street gangs hang out—alleyways, abandoned buildings, whatever—and he goes strolling through those hellholes no cop would dare tread."

"Sounds like Batman," Esperanza countered.

"You don't think it's wrong?"

"Oh, I think it's wrong," she replied steadily. "But I'm not sure you do."

"What the hell is that supposed to mean?"

"Think about it," she said. "About why you're really upset."

Footsteps approached. Win stuck his head in the doorway. He was smiling like a guest star on the opening credits of the *Love Boat*. "Good morning, all," he said with far too much cheer. He bussed Esperanza's cheek. He was decked out in classic, though fairly understated, golf clothes. Ashworth shirt. Plain golf cap. Sky-blue pants with pleats.

"Will you be staying with us, Esperanza?" he asked in his most solicitous tone.

Esperanza looked at him, looked at Myron. Nodded.

"Wonderful. You can use the bedroom down the hall on the left." Win turned to Myron. "Guess what?"

"I'm all ears, Mr. Happy Face," Myron said.

"Crispin still wants to meet with you. It appears that

your walking out last night actually made something of an impression on him.'' Big smile, spread hands. ''The reluctant suitor approach. I must try it sometime.''

Esperanza said, ''Tad Crispin? *The* Tad Crispin?''

''The very,'' Win replied.

She gave Myron an approving look. ''Wow.''

''Indeed,'' Win said. ''Well, I must be going. I'll see you at Merion. I'll be at the Lock-Horne tent most of the day.'' Renewing the smile. ''Ta-ta.''

Win started to leave, stopped, snapped his fingers. ''I almost forgot.'' He tossed Myron a videotape. ''Maybe this will save you some time.''

The videotape landed on the bed. ''Is this . . . ?''

''The bank security tape from First Philadelphia,'' Win said. ''Six-eighteen on Thursday afternoon. As per your request.'' One more smile, one more wave. ''Have a great day.''

Esperanza watched him go. '' 'Have a great day'?'' she repeated.

Myron shrugged.

''Who the hell was that guy?'' she asked.

''Wink Martindale,'' Myron said. ''Come on. Let's go downstairs and watch this.''

Chapter 12

Linda Coldren opened the door before Myron knocked.

"What is it?" she asked.

Linda's face was drawn, accentuating the already high cheekbones. Her eyes had a lost and hollow look. She hadn't slept. The pressure was growing unbearable. The worrying. The not knowing. She was strong. She was trying to stand up to it. But her son's disappearance was beginning to gnaw away at her core.

Myron held up the videotape. "Do you have a VCR?" he asked.

In something of a daze, Linda Coldren led him to the same television he had seen her watching yesterday when they first met. Jack Coldren appeared from a back room, his golf bag on his shoulder. He, too, looked worn. There were sacks under his eyes, fleshy pouches like soft cocoons. Jack tried to toss up a welcoming smile, but it sputtered up like a lighter low on fluid.

"Hey, Myron."

"Hey, Jack."

"What's going on?"

Myron slid the tape into the opening. "Do you know anybody who lives on Green Acres Road?" he asked.

Jack and Linda looked each other.

"Why do you want to know that?" Linda asked.

"Because last night I watched your house. I saw somebody crawl out a window."

"A window?" It was Jack. He lowered his eyebrows. "What window?"

"Your son's."

Silence.

Then Linda asked, "What does that have to do with Green Acres Road?"

"I followed whoever it was. He turned down Green Acres Road and disappeared—either into a house or into the woods."

Linda lowered her head. Jack stepped forward and spoke. "The Squires live on Green Acres Road," he said. "Chad's best friend Matthew."

Myron nodded. He was not surprised. He flicked on the television. "This is a bank security tape from First Philadelphia."

"How did you get it?" Jack asked.

"It's not important."

The front door opened and Bucky entered. The older man, dressed today in checked pants with a yellow-and-green top, stepped into the den doing his customary neck craning bit. "What's going on here?" he demanded.

Nobody replied.

"I said—"

"Just watch the screen, Dad," Linda interrupted.

"Oh," Bucky said softly, moving in closer.

Myron turned the channel to Three and hit the PLAY button. All eyes were on the screen. Myron had already seen the tape. He studied their faces instead, watching for reactions.

On the television, a black-and-white image appeared. The bank's driveway. The view was from up high and a bit distorted, a concave fish-eye effect to capture as much space as possible. There was no sound. Myron had the tape all cued up on the right spot. Almost immediately a car pulled into view. The camera was on the driver's side.

"It's Chad's car," Jack Coldren announced.

They watched in rapt silence as the car window lowered. The angle was a bit odd—above the car and from the machine's point of view—but there was no doubt. Chad Coldren was the driver. He leaned out the window and put his card in the ATM machine slot. His fingers tripped across the buttons like an experienced stenographer's.

Young Chad Coldren's smile was bright and happy.

When his fingers finished their little rumba, Chad settled back into the car to wait. He turned away from the camera for a moment. To the passenger seat. Someone was sitting next to Chad. Again Myron watched for a reaction. Linda, Jack, and Bucky all squinted, all trying to make out a face, but it was impossible. When Chad finally turned back to the camera, he was laughing. He pulled the money out, grabbed his card, leaned back into the car, closed the window, and drove off.

Myron switched off the VCR and waited. Silence flooded the room. Linda Coldren slowly lifted her head. She kept her expression steady, but her jaw trembled from being so set.

"There was another person in the car," Linda offered. "He could have had a gun on Chad or—"

"Stop it!" Jack shouted. "Look at his face, Linda! For crying out loud, just look at his goddamn smirking face!"

"I know my son. He wouldn't do this."

"You don't know him," Jack countered. "Face it, Linda. Neither one of us knows him."

"It's not what it looks like," Linda insisted, speaking more to herself than anyone in the room.

"No?" Jack gestured at the television, his face reddening. "Then how the hell do you explain what we just saw? Huh? He was laughing, Linda. He's having the time of his life at our expense." He stopped, struggled with something. "At my expense," he corrected himself.

Linda gave him a long look. "Go play, Jack."

"That's exactly what I am going to do."

He lifted his bag. His eyes met Bucky's. Bucky remained silent. A tear slid down the older man's cheek. Jack tore his gaze away and started for the door.

Myron called out, "Jack?"

Coldren stopped.

"It still might not be what it looks like," Myron said.

Again with the eyebrows. "What do you mean?"

"I traced the call you got last night," Myron explained. "It was made from a mall pay phone." He briefly filled them in on his visit to the Grand Mercado Mall and the Crusty Nazi. Linda's face kept slipping from hope to heartbreak and mostly confusion. Myron understood. She wanted her son to be safe. But at the same time, she did not want this to be some cruel joke. Tough mix.

"He is in trouble," Linda said as soon as he'd finished. "That proves it."

"That proves nothing," Jack replied in tired exasperation. "Rich kids hang out at malls and dress like punks too. He's probably a friend of Chad's."

Again Linda looked at her husband hard. Again she said in a measured tone, "Go play, Jack."

Jack opened his mouth to say something, then stopped. He shook his head, adjusted the bag on his shoulder, and left. Bucky crossed the room. He tried to hold his daughter, but she stiffened at his touch. She moved away, studying Myron's face.

"You think he's faking too," she said.

"Jack's explanation makes sense."

"So you're going to stop looking?"

"I don't know," Myron said.

She straightened her back. "Stay with it," she began, "and I promise to sign with you."

"Linda . . ."

"That's why you're here in the first place, right? You want my business. Well, here's the deal. You stay with me and I'll sign whatever you want. Hoax or no hoax. It'll be quite a coup, no? Signing the number one–ranked female golfer in the world?"

"Yes," Myron admitted. "It would be."

"So there you go." She stuck out her hand. "Do we have a deal?"

Myron kept his hands by his side. "Let me ask you something."

"What?"

"Why are you so sure it's not a hoax, Linda?"

"You think I'm being naive?"

"Not really," he said. "I just want to know what makes you so certain."

She lowered her hand and turned away from him. "Dad?"

Bucky seemed to snap out of a daze. "Hmm?"

"Would you mind leaving us alone for a minute?"

"Oh," Bucky said. Neck crane. Then another. Two of them back-to-back. Good thing he wasn't a giraffe. "Yes, well, I wanted to get to Merion anyway."

"You go ahead, Dad. I'll meet you there."

When they were alone, Linda Coldren began to pace the room. Myron was again awed by her looks—the paradoxical combination of beauty, strength and now delicacy. The strong, toned arms, yet the long, slender neck. The harsh, pointed features, yet the soft indigo eyes. Myron had heard beauty described as "seamless"; hers was quite the opposite.

"I'm not big on"—Linda Coldren made quote marks in the air with her fingers—"woman's intuition or any of

that mother-knows-her-boy-best crap. But I know that my
son is in danger. He wouldn't just disappear like this. No
matter how it looks, that's not what happened.''

Myron remained silent.

"I don't like asking for help. It's not my way—to
depend on someone else. But this is a situation. . . . I'm
scared. I've never felt fear like this in all of my life. It's
all-consuming. It's suffocating. My son is in trouble and I
can't do anything to help him. You want proof that this is
not a hoax. I can't provide that. I just know. And I'm
asking you to please help me.''

Myron wasn't sure how to respond. Her argument
came straight from the heart, *sans* facts or evidence. But
that didn't make her suffering any less real. "I'll check
out Matthew's house," he said finally. "Let's see what
happens after that.''

Chapter 13

In the light of day, Green Acres Road was even more imposing. Both sides of the street were lined with ten-foot-high shrubs so thick that Myron couldn't tell how thick. He parked his car outside a wrought iron gate and approached an intercom. He pressed a button and waited. There were several surveillance cameras. Some remained steady. Some whirred slowly from side to side. Myron spotted motion detectors, barbed wire, Dobermans.

A rather elaborate fortress, he thought.

A voice as impenetrable as the shrubs came through the speaker. "May I help you?"

"Good morning," Myron said, offering up a friendly-but-not-a-salesman smile to the nearest camera. Talking to a camera. He felt like he was on *Nightline*. "I'm looking for Matthew Squires."

Pause. "Your name, sir?"

"Myron Bolitar."

"Is Master Squires expecting you?"

"No." *Master* Squires?

"Then you do not have an appointment?"

An appointment to see a sixteen-year-old? Who is this kid, Doogie Howser? "No, I'm afraid I don't."

"May I ask the purpose of your visit?"

"To speak to Matthew Squires." Mr. Vague.

"I am afraid that will not be possible at this time," the voice said.

"Will you tell him it involves Chad Coldren?"

Another pause. Cameras pirouetted. Myron looked around. All the lenses were aiming down from up high, glaring at him like hostile space aliens or lunchroom monitors.

"In what way does it involve Master Coldren?" the voice asked.

Myron squinted into a camera. "May I ask with whom I am speaking?"

No reply.

Myron waited a beat, then said, "You're supposed to say, 'I am the great and powerful Oz.'"

"I am sorry, sir. No one is admitted without an appointment. Please have a nice day."

"Wait a second. Hello? Hello?" Myron pressed the button again. No reply. He leaned on it for several seconds. Still nothing. He looked up into the camera and gave his best caring-homespun-family-guy smile. Very Tom Brokaw. He tried a small wave. Nothing. He took a small step backward and gave a great big Jack Kemp fake-throwing-a-football wave. Nada.

He stood there for another minute. This was indeed odd. A sixteen-year-old with this kind of security? Something was not quite kosher. He pressed the button one more time. When no one responded he looked into the camera, put a thumb in either ear, wiggled his fingers and stuck out his tongue.

When in doubt, be mature.

Back at his car, Myron picked up the car phone and dialed his friend Sheriff Jake Courter.

"Sheriff's office."

"Hey, Jake. It's Myron."

"Fuck. I knew I shouldn't have come in on Saturday."

"Ooo, I'm wounded. Seriously, Jake, do they still call you the Henny Youngman of law enforcement?"

Heavy sigh. "What the fuck do you want, Myron? I just came in to get a little paperwork done."

"No rest for those vigilantly pursuing peace and justice for the common man."

"Right," Jake said. "This week, I went out on a whole twelve calls. Guess how many of them were for false burglar alarms?"

"Thirteen."

"Pretty close."

For more than twenty years, Jake Courter had been a cop in several of the country's meanest cities. He'd hated it and craved a quieter life. So Jake, a rather large black man, resigned from the force and moved to the picturesque (read: lily-white) town of Reston, New Jersey. Looking for a cushy job, he ran for sheriff. Reston was a college (read: liberal) town, and thus Jake played up his— as he put it—"blackness" and won easily. The white man's guilt, Jake had told Myron. The best vote-getter this side of Willie Horton.

"Miss the excitement of the big city?" Myron asked.

"Like a case of herpes," Jake countered. "Okay, Myron, you've done the charm thing on me. I'm like Play-Doh in your paws now. What do you want?"

"I'm in Philly for the U.S. Open."

"That's golf, right?"

"Yeah, golf. And I wanted to know if you've heard of a guy name Squires."

Pause. Then: "Oh, shit."

"What?"

"What the fuck are you involved in now?"

"Nothing. It's just that he's got all this weird security around his house—"

"What the fuck are you doing by his house?"

"Nothing."

"Right," Jake said. "Guess you were just strolling by."

"Something like that."

"Nothing like that." Jake sighed. Then: "Ah what the hell, it ain't on my beat anymore. Squires. Reginald Squires aka Big Blue."

Myron made a face. "Big Blue?"

"Hey, all gangsters need a nickname. Squires is known as Big Blue. Blue, as in blue blood."

"Those gangsters," Myron said. "Pity they don't channel their creativity into honest marketing."

" 'Honest marketing,' " Jake repeated. "Talk about your basic oxymoron. Anyway Squires got a kiloton of family dough and all this blue-blood breeding and schooling and shit."

"So what's he doing keeping such bad company?"

"You want the simple answer? The son of a bitch is a serious wacko. Gets his jollies hurting people. Kinda like Win."

"Win doesn't get his jollies hurting people."

"If you say so."

"If Win hurts someone, there's a reason. To prevent them from doing it again or to punish or something."

"Sure, whatever," Jake said. "Kinda touchy though, aren't we, Myron?"

"It's been a long day."

"It's only nine in the morning."

Myron said, "For what breeds time but two hands on a clock?"

"Who said that?"

"No one. I just made it up."

"You should consider writing greeting cards."

"So what is Squires into, Jake?"

"Want to hear something funny? I'm not sure. Nobody is. Drugs and prostitution. Shit like that. But very

upscale. Nothing very well organized or anything. It's
more like he plays at it, you know? Like he gets involved
in whatever he thinks will give him a thrill, then dumps
it.''

"How about kidnapping?"

Brief pause. "Oh shit, you are involved in something
again, aren't you?"

"I just asked you if Squires was into kidnapping."

"Oh. Right. Like it's a hypothetical question. Kinda
like, 'If a bear shits in the forest and no one is around,
does it still reek'?''

"Precisely. Does kidnapping reek like his kind of
thing?"

"Hell if I know. The guy is a major league loon, no
question. He blends right into all that snobbish bullshit—
the boring parties, the shitty food, the laughing at jokes
that aren't remotely funny, the talking with the same boring people about the same boring worthless bullshit—"

"It sounds like you really admire them."

"Just my point, my friend. They got it all, right? On
the outside. Money, big homes, fancy clubs. But they're
all so fucking boring—shit, I'd kill myself. Makes me
wonder if maybe Squires feels that way too, you know?"

"Uh-huh," Myron said. "And Win is the scary one
here, right?"

Jake laughed. "Touché. But to answer your question, I
don't know if Squires would be into kidnapping.
Wouldn't surprise me though."

Myron thanked him and hung up. He looked up. At
least a dozen security cameras lined the top of the shrubs
like tiny sentinels.

What now?

For all he knew, Chad Coldren was laughing his ass
off, watching him on one of those security cameras. This
whole thing could be an exercise in pure futility. Of

course, Linda Coldren had promised to be a client. Much as he didn't want to admit it to himself, the idea was not wholly unpleasant. He considered the possibility and started to smile. If he could also somehow land Tad Crispin . . .

Yo, Myron, a kid may be in serious trouble.

Or, more likely, a spoiled brat or neglected adolescent —take your pick—is playing hooky and having some fun at his parents' expense.

So the question remained: What now?

He thought again about the videotape of Chad at the ATM machine. He didn't go into details with the Coldrens, but it bothered him. Why there? Why that particular ATM machine? If the kid was running away or hiding out, he might have to pick up money. Fine and dandy, that made sense.

But why would he do it at Porter Street?

Why not do it at a bank closer to home? And equally important, what was Chad Coldren doing in that area in the first place? There was nothing there. It wasn't a stop between highways or anything like that. The only thing in that neighborhood that would require cash was the Court Manor Inn. Myron again remembered *motelier extraordinaire* Stuart Lipwitz's attitude and wondered.

He started the car. It might be something. Worth looking into, at any rate.

Of course, Stuart Lipwitz had made it abundantly clear that he would not talk. But Myron thought he had just the tool to make him change his mind.

Chapter 14

"Smile!"

The man did not smile. He quickly shifted the car in reverse and backed out. Myron shrugged and lowered the camera. It was on a neck strap and bounced lightly against his chest. Another car approached. Myron lifted the camera again.

"Smile!" Myron repeated.

Another man. Another no smile. This guy managed to duck down before shifting his car into reverse.

"Camera shy," Myron called out to him. "Nice to see in this age of paparazzi overkill."

It didn't take long. Myron had been on the sidewalk in front of the Court Manor Inn for less than five minutes when he spotted Stuart Lipwitz sprinting toward him. Big Stu was in full custom—gray tails, wide tie, a concierge key pin in the suit's lapel. Gray tails at a no-tell motel. Like a maître d' at Burger King. Watching Stu move closer, a Pink Floyd song came to mind: *Hello, hello, hello, is there anybody out there?* David Bowie joined in: *Ground control to Major Tom.*

Ah, the seventies.

"You there," he called out.

"Hi, Stu."

No smile this time. "This is private property," Stuart Lipwitz said, a little out of breath. "I must ask you to remove yourself immediately."

"I hate to disagree with you, Stu, but I am on a public sidewalk. I got every right to be here."

Stuart Lipwitz stammered, then flapped his arms in frustration. With the tails, the movement kind of reminded Myron of a bat. "But you can't just stand there and take pictures of my clientele," he semi-whined.

" 'Clientele,' " Myron repeated. "Is that a new euphemism for *john*?"

"I'll call the police."

"Ooooo. Stop scaring me like that."

"You are interfering with my business."

"And you are interfering with mine."

Stuart Lipwitz put his hands on his hips and tried to look threatening. "This is the last time I'll ask you nicely. Leave the premises."

"That wasn't nice."

"Excuse me?"

"You said it was the last time you'd ask me nicely," Myron explained. "Then you said, 'Leave the premises.' You didn't say *please*. You didn't say, 'Kindly leave the premises.' Where's the nice in that?"

"I see," Lipwitz said. Beads of sweat dotted his face. It was hot and the man was, after all, in tails. "Please kindly leave the premises."

"Nope. But now, at least, you're a man of your word."

Stuart Lipwitz took several deep breaths. "You want to know about the boy, don't you? The one in the picture."

"You bet."

"And if I tell you if he was here, will you leave?"

"Much as it would pain me to leave this quaint locale, I would somehow tear myself away."

"That, sir, is blackmail."

Myron looked at him. "I would say '*blackmail* is such

an ugly word,' but that would be too cliché. So instead I'll just say 'Yup.' "

"But"—Lipwitz started stammering—"that's against the law!"

"As opposed to, say, prostitution and drug dealing and whatever other sleazy activity goes on in this fleabag?"

Stuart Lipwitz's eyes widened. "Fleabag? This is the Court Manor Inn, sir. We are a respectable—"

"Stuff it, Stu. I got pictures to take." Another car pulled up. Gray Volvo station wagon. Nice family car. A man about fifty years old was neatly attired in a business suit. The young girl in the passenger seat must have shopped—as the mall girls had recently taught him—at Sluts "R" Us.

Myron smiled and leaned toward the window. "Whoa, sir, vacationing with your daughter?"

The man splashed on a classic deer-caught-in-the-headlights look. The young prostitute whooped with laughter. "Hey, Mel, he thinks I'm your daughter!" She whooped again.

Myron raised the camera. Stuart Lipwitz tried to step in his way, but Myron swept him away with his free hand. "It's Souvenir Day at the Court Manor," Myron said. "I can put the picture on a coffee mug if you'd like. Or maybe a decorative plate?"

The man in the business suit reversed the car. They were gone several seconds later.

Stuart Lipwitz's face reddened. He made two fists. Myron looked at him. "Now Stuart . . ."

"I have powerful friends," he said.

"Ooooo. I'm getting scared again."

"Fine. Be that way." Stuart turned away and stormed up the drive. Myron smiled. The kid was a tougher nut to crack than he'd anticipated, and he really didn't want to do this all day. But let's face it: There were no other leads and besides, playing with Big Stu was fun.

Myron waited for more customers. He wondered what Stu was up to. Something frantic, no doubt. Ten minutes later, a canary yellow Audi pulled up and a large black man slid out. The black man was maybe an inch shorter than Myron, but he was built. His chest could double as a jai alai wall and his legs resembled the trunks of red-woods. He glided when he moved—not the bulky moves one usually associated with the overmuscled.

Myron did not like that.

The black man had sunglasses on and wore a red Ha-waiian shirt with blue jean shorts. His most noticeable feature was his hair. The kinks had been slicked straight and parted on the side, like old photographs of Nat King Cole.

Myron pointed at the top of the man's head. "Is that hard to do?" he asked.

"What?" the black man said. "You mean the hair?"

Myron nodded. "Keeping it straight like that."

"Nah, not really. Once a week I go to a guy named Ray. In an old-fashioned barbershop, as a matter of fact. The kind with the pole in front and everything." His smile was almost wistful. "Ray takes care of it for me. Also gives me a great shave. With hot towels and every-thing." The man stroked his face for emphasis.

"Looks smooth," Myron said.

"Hey, thanks. Nice of you to say. I find it relaxing, you know? Doing something just for me. I think it's im-portant. To relieve the stress."

Myron nodded. "I hear you."

"Maybe I'll give you Ray's number. You could stop by and check it out."

"Ray," Myron repeated. "I'd like that."

The black man stepped closer. "Seems we have a little situation here, Mr. Bolitar."

"How did you know my name?"

He shrugged. Behind the sunglasses, Myron sensed that he was being sized up. Myron was doing the same. Both were trying to be subtle. Both knew exactly what the other was doing.

"I'd really appreciate it if you would leave," he said very politely.

"I'm afraid I can't do that," Myron said. "Even though you did ask nicely."

The black man nodded. He kept his distance. "Let's see if we can work something out here, okay?"

"Okeydokey."

"I got a job to do here, Myron. You can appreciate that, can't you?"

"Sure can," Myron said.

"And so do you."

"That's right."

The black man took off his sunglasses and put them in his shirt pocket. "Look, I know you won't be easy. And you know I won't be easy. If push comes to shove, I don't know which one of us will win."

"I will," Myron said. "Good always triumphs over evil."

The man smiled. "Not in this neighborhood."

"Good point."

"I'm also not sure it's worth it to either one of us to find out. I think we're both probably past the proving-himself, macho-bullshit stage."

Myron nodded. "We're too mature."

"Right."

"It seems then," Myron continued, "that we've hit an impasse."

"Guess so," the black man agreed. "Of course, I could always take out a gun and shoot you."

Myron shook his head. "Not over something this small. Too many repercussions involved."

"Yeah. I didn't think you'd go for it, but I had to give it a whirl. You never know."

"You're a pro," Myron agreed. "You'd feel remiss if you didn't at least try. Hell, I'd have felt cheated."

"Glad you understand."

"Speaking of which," Myron said, "aren't you a tad high-level to be dealing with this situation?"

"Can't say I disagree." The black man walked closer to Myron. Myron felt his muscles tighten; a not-unpleasant anticipatory chill steeled him.

"You look like a guy who can keep his mouth shut," the man said.

Myron said nothing. Proving the point.

"The kid you had in that picture, the one that got Leona Helmsley's panties in a bunch? He was here."

"When?"

The black man shook his head. "That's all you get. I'm being very generous. You wanted to know if the kid was here. The answer is yes."

"Nice of you," Myron said.

"I'm just trying to make it simple. Look, we both know that Lipwitz is a dumb kid. Acts like this urinal is the Beverly Wilshire. But the people who come here, they don't want that. They want to be invisible. They don't even want to look at themselves, you know what I'm saying?"

Myron nodded.

"So I gave you a freebie. The kid in the picture was here."

"Is he still here?"

"You're pushing me, Myron."

"Just tell me that."

"No. He only stayed that one night." He spread his hands. "Now you tell me, Myron. Am I being fair with you?"

"Very."

He nodded. "Your turn."

"I guess there's no way you'll tell me who you're working for."

The black man made a face. "Nice meeting you, Myron."

"Same here."

They shook hands. Myron got into his car and drove away.

He had almost reached Merion when the cellular rang. He picked up and said hello.

"Is this, like, Myron?"

Mall girl. "Hi, yes. Actually this is Myron, not just like him."

"Huh?"

"Never mind. What's up?"

"That skank you were, like, looking for last night?"

"Right."

"He's, like, back at the mall."

"Where at the mall?"

"The food court. He's on line at the McDonald's."

Myron spun the car around and hit the gas pedal.

Chapter 15

The Crusty Nazi was still there.

He sat at a corner table by himself, downing a burger of some sort like it had personally offended him. The girls were right. *Skank* was the only word to describe him, even though Myron didn't know what the word meant or if it even existed. The punk's face was aiming for tough-guy-unshaven, but a lack of testosterone made it land far closer to upkempt-adolescent-Hasid. He wore a black baseball cap with a skull and crossbones decal. His ripped white T-shirt was rolled all the way up to reveal milky, reedy arms, one with a swastika tattoo. Myron shook his head. Swastika. The kid was too old to be so utterly clueless.

The Crusty Nazi took another vicious bite, clearly furious with his burger now. The mall girls were there, pointing toward Crusty like Myron might not know which guy they'd been talking about. Myron signaled them to stop with a shushing finger at his lips. They obeyed, overcompensating by engaging in a too-loud, too-casual conversation, sliding furtive-to-the-point-of-totally-obvious glances in his direction. Myron looked away.

The Crusty Nazi finished his burger and stood. Good timing. As advertised, Crusty was very skinny. The girls were right—the boy had no ass. None at all. Myron couldn't tell if the kid was going for that too-big-jeans look or if it was because he lacked a true backside, but

every few steps, Crusty paused to hitch up the pants. Myron suspected a bit of both.

He followed him outside into the blazing sun. Hot.
Damn hot. Myron felt almost a nostalgic longing for the
omnipresent mall air-conditioning. Crusty strutted cool-
like into the lot. Going to his car, no doubt. Myron veered
to the right so as to get ready to follow. He slid into his
Ford Taurus (read: Chick Trawler) and started up the engine.

He slowly cruised the lot and spotted Crusty heading
way out to the last row of cars. Only two vehicles were
parked out there. One was a silver Cadillac Seville. The
other was a pickup truck with those semi-monster wheels,
a Confederate flag decal, and the words BAD TO THE BONE
painted on the side. Using his years of investigative know-
how, Myron deduced that the pickup truck was probably
Crusty's vehicle. Sure enough, Crusty opened the door
and hopped up and in. Amazing. Sometimes Myron's
powers of deduction bordered on the psychic. Maybe he
should get a 900 line like Jackie Stallone.

Tailing the pickup truck was hardly a challenge. The
vehicle stuck out like a golfer's clothing in a monastery,
and El Crust-ola wasn't heavy on the gas pedal. They
drove for about half an hour. Myron had no idea where
they were going, but up ahead he recognized Veterans
Stadium. He'd gone with Win to several Eagles games
there. Win always had seats on the fifty-yard line, lower
tier. Being an old stadium, the ''luxury'' skyboxes at the
Vet were too high up; Win did not care for them. So he
chose instead to sit with the masses. Big of him.

About three blocks before the stadium, Crusty pulled
down a side road. He threw his pickup into park and got
out running. Myron once again debated calling Win for
backup, but it was pointless. Win was at Merion. His
phone would be off. He wondered again about last night

and about Esperanza's accusations this morning. Maybe she was right. Maybe he was, at least partially, responsible for what Win did. But that wasn't the point. He knew that now. The truth, the one that scared Esperanza too, was far clearer:

Maybe Myron didn't care so much.

You read the papers and you watch the news and you see what Myron has seen and your humanity, your basic faith in human beings, begins to look frighteningly Pollyanna. That was what was really eating away at him—not that he was repulsed by what Win did, but that it really didn't bother him that much.

Win had an eerie way of seeing the world in black and white; lately, Myron had found his own gray areas blackening. He didn't like that. He did not like the change that experience—seeing the cruelty man inflicts on man—was forcing upon him. He tried to hold on to his old values, but the rope was getting awfully slick. And why was he holding on, anyway? Was it because he truly believed in these values, or because he liked himself more as a person who believed?

He didn't know anymore.

He should have brought a gun. Stupid. Still he was only following some grunge-ball. Of course, even a grunge-ball could fire a gun and kill him. But what choice did he have? Should he call the police? Well, that would appear a bit extreme based on what he had. Come back later with a firearm of some sort? By that time, Crusty could be gone—along with Chad Coldren maybe.

Nope, he had to follow. He'd just be careful.

Myron was not sure what to do. He stopped the car at the end of the block and got out. The street was crowded with low-rise brick dwellings that all looked the same. At one time, this might have been a nice area, but now the neighborhood looked like a man who'd lost his job and stopped bathing. There was an overgrown, faded quality to it, like a garden that no one bothered to tend anymore.

Crusty turned down an alleyway. Myron followed. Lots of plastic garbage bags. Lots of rusted fire escapes. Four legs stuck out of a refrigerator box. Myron heard snoring. At the end of the alley, Crusty turned right. Myron trailed slowly. Crusty had gone into what looked like an abandoned building through a fire door. There was no knob or anything, but the door was slightly ajar. Myron reached in with his fingers and pried it open.

As soon as he crossed the musty threshold, Myron heard a primal scream. Crusty. Right in front of him. Something swung toward Myron's face. Fast reflexes paid off. Myron managed to duck enough so that the iron bar only clipped his shoulder blade. A quick flash of pain bolted down his arm. Myron dropped to the ground. He rolled across the cement floor and stood back up.

There were three of them now. All armed with crowbars or tire irons. All with shaved heads and tattooed swastikas. They were like sequels to the same awful movie. The Crusty Nazi was the original. Beneath the Planet of Crusty Nazi—the one on his left—was smiling with idiotic glee. The one on his right—Escape from the Planet of Crusty Nazi—looked a bit more frightened. The weak link, Myron thought.

"Changing a tire?" Myron asked.

The Crusty Nazi slapped the tire iron against his palm for emphasis. "Gonna flatten yours."

Myron raised his hand in front of him with the palm facing down. He shook it back and forth and said, "Eh."

"Why the fuck you following me, asshole?"

"Me?"

"Yeah, you. Why the fuck you following me?"

"Who says I'm following you?"

There was momentary confusion on Crusty's face. Then: "You think I'm fucking stupid or something?"

"No, I think you're Mr. Mensa."

"Mister what?"

Beneath the Planet of Crusty Nazi said, "He's just fucking with you, man."

"Yeah," Escape chimed in. "Fucking with you."

Crusty's wet eyes bulged out. "Yeah? Is that what you're doing, asshole? You fucking with me, huh? Is that what you're doing? Fucking with me?"

Myron looked at him. "Can we move on please?"

Beneath said, "Let's fuck him up a little. Soften his ass up."

Myron knew that three of them were probably not experienced fighters, but he also knew that three armed men beat one good man on almost any given day. They were also a bit too jittery, their eyes as glazed as morning doughnuts. They were constantly sniffing and rubbing their noses.

Two words: Coked up. Or Nose Candy. Or Toot Sweet. Take your pick.

Myron's best chance was to confuse and strike. Risky. You wanted to piss them off, to upset their already-tipsy equilibrium. But at the same time, you wanted to control it, to know when to back off a bit. A delicate balance requiring Myron Bolitar, darling of the high wire, to perform high above the crowd without the benefit of a safety net.

Once again Crusty asked, "Why the fuck you following me, asshole?"

"Maybe I'm just attracted to you," Myron said. "Even if you don't have an ass."

Beneath started cackling. "Oh man, oh man, let's fuck him up. Let's fuck him up good."

Myron tried to give them the tough-guy look. Some

mistook this for constipation, but he was getting better at it. Practice. "I wouldn't do that if I were you."

"Oh no?" It was Crusty. "Give me one good reason why we don't just fuck you up. Give me one good reason why I don't break every fucking rib in your body with this." He raised the tire iron. In case Myron thought he was being too subtle.

"You asked before if I thought you were stupid," Myron said.

"Yeah, so?"

"So do you think I'm stupid? Do you think somebody who meant you harm would be dumb enough to follow you in here—knowing what was about to go down?"

That made all three of them pause.

"I followed you," Myron continued, "as a test."

"What the fuck you talking about?"

"I work for certain people. We won't mention names." Mostly, Myron thought, because he didn't know what the hell he was talking about. "Let's just say they are in a business you guys frequent."

"Frequent?" More nose rubbing. Toot, sweet, toot, sweet.

"Frequent," Myron repeated. "As in occurring or appearing quite often or at close intervals. Frequent."

"What?"

Jesus. "My employer," Myron said, "he needs someone to handle certain territory. Somebody new. Somebody who wants to make ten percent on sales and get all the free blow they can."

Eyes went buggy.

Beneath turned to Crusty. "You hear that, man?"

"Yeah, I hear him."

"Shit, we don't get no commission from Eddie," Beneath went on. "The fucker is so small-time." He gestured at Myron with the tire iron. "This guy, man, look

how fucking old he is. He's gotta be working for somebody with juice.''

"Got to be," Escape added.

The Crusty One hesitated, squinted suspicion. "How
did you find out about us?"

Myron shrugged. "Word gets around." Shovel,
shovel.

"So you was just following me for some kinda fucking test?"

"Right."

"Just came to the mall and decided to follow me?"

"Something like that."

Crusty smiled. He looked at Escape and at Beneath.
His grip on the tire iron tightened. Uh-oh. "Then how the
fuck come you were asking about me last night, huh?
How come you want to know about a call I made?"

Uh-oh.

Crusty stepped closer, eyes aglow.

Myron raised his hand. "The answer is simple." They
all hesitated. Myron took advantage. His foot moved like
a piston, shooting out and landing squarely on the knee of
the unprepared Escape. Escape fell. Myron was already
running.

"Get the fucker!"

They chased, but Myron had already slammed his
shoulder into the fire door. The "macho-bullshit" part of
him, as his friend at the Court Manor Inn had described it,
wanted to try to take them on, but he knew that would be
foolhardy. They were armed. He wasn't.

By the time Myron reached the end of the alley, his
lead was only about ten yards. He wondered if he'd have
enough time to open his car door and get in. No choice.
He'd have to try.

He grabbed the handle and swung the door open. He
was sliding in when a tire iron whacked his shoulder.

Pain erupted. He kept rolling, closing the door. A hand grabbed it, offered resistance. Myron used his weight and leaned into the pull.

His window exploded.

Glass tinkled down into his face. Myron kicked his heel through the open window and hit face. The grip on the door released. He already had the key out and in the ignition. He turned it as the other car window exploded. Crusty leaned into the car, his eyes blazing with fury.

"Motherfucker, you're gonna die!"

The tire iron was heading toward his face again. Myron blocked it. From behind him, he felt a sharp blow connect with his lower neck. Numbness ensued. Myron shifted into reverse and flew out of the spot, tires squealing. Crusty tried to leap into the car through the broken window. Myron elbowed him in the nose and Crusty's grip eased. He fell hard to the pavement, but then he jumped right back up. That was the problem with fighting cokeheads. Pain often does not register.

All three men ran for the pickup, but Myron already had too big a lead. The battle was over. For now.

Chapter 16

Myron called in the pickup truck's license plate number, but that was a dead end. The plate had expired four years ago. Crusty must have taken it off a car in a dump or something. Not uncommon. Even petty crooks knew enough not to use their real plates when committing a traceable crime.

He circled back and checked the inside of the building for clues. Bent syringes and broken vials and empty bags of Doritos lay scattered about the cement. There was also an empty garbage can. Myron shook his head. Bad enough being a drug dealer. But a litterbug?

He looked around a bit more. The building was abandoned and half–burned out. There was no one inside. And no clues.

Okay, so what did this all mean? Were the three cokeheads the kidnappers? Myron had a hard time picturing it. Cokeheads break into houses. Cokeheads jump people in alleyways. Cokeheads attack with tire irons. Cokeheads, by and large, do not plan elaborate kidnappings.

But on the other hand, how elaborate was this kidnapping? The first two times the kidnapper called, he didn't even know how much money to extort. Wasn't that a little odd? Could it be that all this was merely the work of some out-of-their-league crusty cokeheads?

Myron got into his car and headed toward Win's house. Win had plenty of vehicles. He'd switch for a car

without smashed windows. The residual damage to his
body seemed to be clearing up. A bruise or two but nothing broken. None of the blows had landed flush, except
the ones to his car windows.

He ran several possibilities through his head and eventually managed to come up with a pretty decent scenario.
Let's say that for some reason Chad Coldren decided to
check into the Court Manor Inn. Maybe to spend some
time with a girl. Maybe to buy some drugs. Maybe because he enjoyed the friendly service. Whatever. As per
the bank surveillance camera, Chad grabbed some dough
at a local ATM. Then he checked in for the night. Or the
hour. Or whatever.

Once at the Court Manor Inn, something went awry.
Stu Lipwitz's denials notwithstanding, the Court Manor
is a sleazy joint patronized by sleazy people. It wouldn't
be hard to get in trouble there. Maybe Chad Coldren tried
to buy drugs from Crusty. Maybe he witnessed a crime.
Maybe the kid just talked too much and some nasty people realized that he came from money. Whatever. The life
orbits of Chad Coldren and the Crusty Nazi's crew
dovetailed. The end result was a kidnapping.

It kinda fit.

The key word here: *kinda*.

On the road toward Merion, Myron helped deflate his
own scenario with several well-placed puncture holes.
First of all, the timing. Myron had been convinced that
the kidnapping had something to do with Jack's return to
playing the U.S. Open at Merion. But in his Crusty-orbit
scenario, the nagging timing question had to be written
off as mere coincidence. Okay, maybe Myron could live
with that. But then how, for example, had the Crusty Nazi
—stationed at a mall pay phone—known that Esme Fong
was in the Coldren house? How did the man who climbed
out the window and disappeared on Green Acres Road—a

person Myron had been sure was either Matthew Squires or Chad Coldren—fit into all this? Was the well-shielded Matthew Squires in cahoots with the Crusties? Or was it just a coincidence that the window man disappeared down Green Acres Road?

The scenario balloon was going *ssssss* in a very big way.

By the time Myron got to Merion, Jack Coldren was on the fourteenth hole. His partner for today's round was none other than Tad Crispin. No surprise there. First place and second place were normally the final twosome of the day.

Jack was still playing well, though not spectacularly. He'd lost only one stroke off his lead, remaining a very comfortable eight strokes ahead of Tad Crispin. Myron trudged toward the fourteenth green. Green—that word again. Everything was so dang green. The grass and trees, naturally, but also tents, overhangs, scoreboards, the many television towers and scaffolds—everything was lush green to blend in with the picturesque natural surroundings, except, of course, for the sponsors' boards, which drew the eye with all the subtlety of Vegas hotel signs. But hey, the sponsors paid Myron's salary. Be kinda hypocritical to complain.

"Myron, sweetheart, get your wiggly ass over here."

Norm Zuckerman beckoned Myron forward with a big wave. Esme Fong stood next to him. "Over here," he said.

"Hey, Norm," Myron said. "Hi, Esme."

"Hi, Myron," Esme said. She was dressed a bit more casual today, but she still clutched at her briefcase like it was a favorite stuffed animal.

Norm threw his arm around Myron's back, draping the hand over the sore shoulder. "Myron, tell me the truth here. The absolute truth. I want the truth, okay?"

"The truth?"

"Very funny. Just tell me this. Nothing more, just this. Am I not a fair man? The truth, now. Am I a fair man?"

"Fair," Myron said.

"Very fair, am I right? I am a very fair man."

"Let's not push it, Norm."

Norm put up both hands, palms out. "Fine, be that way. I'm fair. Good enough, I'll take it." He looked over toward Esme Fong. "Keep in mind, Myron is my adversary. My worst enemy. We're always on opposite sides. Yet he is willing to admit that I'm a fair man. We straight on that?"

Esme rolled her eyes. "Yes, Norm, but you're preaching to the converted. I already told you that I agreed with you on this—"

"Whoa," Norm said, as though reining in a frisky pony. "Just hold the phone a sec, because I want Myron's opinion too. Myron, here's the deal. I bought a golf bag. Just one. I wanted to test it out. Cost me fifteen grand for the year."

Buying a golf bag meant pretty much what it said. Norm Zuckerman had bought the rights to advertise on a golf bag. In other words, he put a Zoom logo on it. Most of the golf bags were bought by the big golf companies— Ping, Titleist, Golden Bear, that kind of thing. But more and more often, companies that had nothing to do with golf advertised on the bags. McDonald's, for example. Spring-Air mattresses. Even Pennzoil oil. Pennzoil. Like someone goes to a golf tournament, sees the Pennzoil logo, and buys a can of oil.

"So?" Myron said.

"So, look at it!" Norm pointed at a caddie. "I mean, just look at it!"

"Okay, I'm looking."

"Tell me, Myron, do you see a Zoom logo?"

The caddie held the golf bag. Like on every golf bag, there were towels draped over the top in order to clean off the clubs.

Norm Zuckerman spoke in a first-grade–teacher singsong. "You can answer orally, Myron, by uttering the syllable 'no.' Or if that's too taxing on your limited vocabulary, you can merely shake your head from side to side like this." Norm demonstrated.

"It's under the towel," Myron said.

Norm dramatically put his hand to his ear. "Pardon?"

"The logo is under the towel."

"No shit it's under the towel!" Norm railed. Spectators turned and glared at the crazy man with the long hair and heavy beard. "What good does that do me, huh? When I film an advertisement for TV, what good would it do me if they stick a towel in front of the camera? When I pay all those schmucks a zillion dollars to wear my sneakers, what good would it do me if they wrapped their feet in towels? If every billboard I had was covered with a great big towel—"

"I get the picture, Norm."

"Good. I'm not paying fifteen grand for some idiot caddie to cover my logo. So I go over to the idiot caddie and I kindly tell him to move the towel away from my logo and the son of a bitch gives me this look. This look, Myron. Like I'm some brown stain he couldn't rinse out of the toilet. Like I'm this little ghetto Jew who's gonna take his goy crap."

Myron looked over at Esme. Esme smiled and shrugged.

"Nice talking to you, Norm," Myron said.

"What? You don't think I'm right?"

"I see your point."

"So if it was your client, what would you do?"

"Make sure the caddie kept the logo in plain view."

"Exactamundo." He swung his arm back around Myron's shoulder and lowered his head conspiratorially. "So what's going on with you and golf, Myron?" he whispered.

"What do you mean?"

"You're not a golfer. You don't have any golf clients. All of a sudden I see you with my very own eyes closing in on Tad Crispin—and now I hear you're hanging out with the Coldrens."

"Who told you that?"

"Word gets around. I'm a man with tremendous sources. So what's the deal? Why the sudden interest in golf?"

"I'm a sports agent, Norm. I try to represent athletes. Golfers are athletes. Sort of."

"Okay, but what's up with the Coldrens?"

"What do you mean?"

"Look, Jack and Linda are lovely people. Connected, if you know what I mean."

"I don't know what you mean."

"LBA represents Linda Coldren. Nobody leaves LBA. You know that. They're too big. Jack, well, Jack hasn't done anything in so long, he hasn't even bothered with an agent. So what I'm trying to figure out is, why are the Coldrens suddenly hot to trot with you?"

"Why do you want to figure that out?"

Norm put his hand on his chest. "Why?"

"Yeah, why would you care?"

"Why?" Norm repeated, incredulous now. "I'll tell you why. Because of you, Myron. I love you, you know that. We're brothers. Tribe members. I want nothing but the best for you. Hand to God, I mean that. You ever need a recommendation, I'll give it to you, you know that."

"Uh-huh." Myron was less than convinced. "So what's the problem?"

Norm threw up both hands. "Who said there's a problem? Did I say there was a problem? Did I even use the word *problem*? I'm just curious, that's all. It's part of my nature. I'm a curious guy. A modern-day *yenta*. I ask a lot of questions. I stick my nose in where it doesn't belong. It's part of my makeup."

"Uh-huh," Myron said again. He looked over at Esme Fong, who was now comfortably out of earshot. She shrugged at him. Working for Norm Zuckerman probably meant you did a lot of shrugging. But that was part of Norm's technique, his own version of good-cop, bad-cop. He came across as erratic, if not totally irrational, while his assistant—always young, bright, attractive—was the calming influence you grabbed on to like a life preserver.

Norm elbowed him and nodded toward Esme. "She's a looker, huh? Especially for a broad from Yale. You ever see what that school matriculates? No wonder they're known as the Bulldogs."

"You're so progressive, Norm."

"Ah, screw progressive. I'm an old man, Myron. I'm allowed to be insensitive. On an old man, insensitive is cute. A cute curmudgeon, that's what they call it. By the way, I think Esme is only half."

"Half?"

"Chinese," Norm said. "Or Japanese. Or whatever. I think she's half white too. What do you think?"

"Good-bye, Norm."

"Fine, be that way. See if I care. So tell me, Myron, how did you hook up with the Coldrens? Win introduce you?"

"Good-bye, Norm."

Myron walked off a bit, stopping for a moment to watch a golfer hit a drive. He tried to follow the ball's route. No go. He lost sight of it almost immediately. This shouldn't be a surprise really—it is, after all, a tiny white sphere traveling at a rate of over one hundred miles per hour for a distance of several hundred yards—except that Myron was the only person in attendance who couldn't achieve this ophthalmic feat of hawklike proportions. Golfers. Most of them can't read an exit sign on an interstate, but they can follow the trajectory of a golf ball through several solar systems.

No question about it. Golf is a weird sport.

The course was packed with silent fans, though *fan* didn't exactly feel like the right word to Myron. *Parishioners* was a hell of a lot closer. There was a constant reverie on a golf course, a hushed, wide-eyed respect. Every time the ball was hit, the crowd release was nearly orgasmic. People cried sweet bliss and urged the ball with the ardor of *Price Is Right* contestants: Run! Sit! Bite! Grab! Grow teeth! Roll! Hurry! Get down! Get up!— almost like an aggressive mambo instructor. They lamented over a snap hook and a wicked slice and a babied putt and goofy greens and soft greens and waxed greens and the rub of the green and the pursuit of a snowman and being stymied and when the ball traveled off the fairway and on the fringe and in the rough and deep lies and rough lies and bad lies and good lies. They showed admiration when a player got all of that one or ripped a drive or banged it home and gave dirty looks when someone loudly suggested that a certain tee-shot made a certain player "da man." They accused a putter who did not reach the hole of hitting the ball "with your purse, Alice." Players were constantly playing shots that were "unplayable."

Myron shook his head. All sports have their own lexicons, but speaking golfese was tantamount to mastering Swahili. It was like rich people's rap.

But on a day like today—the sun shining, the blue sky unblemished, the summer air smelling like a lover's hair

—Myron felt closer to the chalice of golf. He could imagine the course free of spectators, the peace and tranquillity, the same aura that drew Buddhist monks to mountaintop retreats, the double-cut grass so rich and green that God Himself would want to run barefoot. This did not mean Myron got it—he was still a nonbeliever of heretic proportions—but for a brief moment he could at least envision what it was about this game that ensnared and swallowed so many whole.

When he reached the fourteenth green, Jack Coldren was lining up for a fifteen-foot putt. Diane Hoffman took the pin out of the hole. At almost every course in the world, the "pin" had a flag on the top. But that would just not do at Merion. Instead, the pole was topped with a wicker basket. No one seemed to know why. Win came up with this story about how the old Scots who invented golf used to carry their lunch in baskets on sticks, which could then double as hole markers, but Myron smelled the pungent odor of lore in Win's rationale rather than fact. Either way, Merion's members made a big fuss over these wicker baskets on the end of a big stick. Golfers.

Myron tried to move in closer to Jack Coldren, looking for Win's "eye of the tiger." Despite his protestations, Myron knew very well what Win had meant the previous night, the intangibles that separated raw talent from on-field greatness. Desire. Heart. Perseverance. Win spoke about these things as though they were evil. They were not. Quite the opposite, in fact. Win, of all people, should know better. To paraphrase and completely abuse a famous political quote: Extremism in the pursuit of excellence is no vice.

Jack Coldren's expression was smooth and unworried and distant. Only one explanation for that: the zone. Jack had managed to squeeze his way into the hallowed zone, that tranquil room in which no crowd or big payday or famous course or next hole or knee-bending pressure or hostile opponent or successful wife or kidnapped son may reside. Jack's zone was a small place, comprising only his club, a small dimpled ball, and a hole. All else faded away now like the dream sequence in a movie.

This, Myron knew, was Jack Coldren stripped to his purest state. He was a golfer. A man who wanted to win. Needed to. Myron understood. He had been there—his zone consisting of a large orange ball and a metallic cylinder—and a part of him would always be enmeshed in that world. It was a fine place to be—in many ways, the best place to be. Win was wrong. Winning was not a worthless goal. It was noble. Jack had taken life's hits. He had striven and battled. He had been battered and bloodied. Yet here he stood, head high, on the road to redemption. How many people are awarded this opportunity? How many people truly get the chance to feel this vibrant, to reside for even a short time on such a plateau, to have their hearts and dreams stirred with such unquenchable inner passion?

Jack Coldren stroked the putt. Myron found himself watching the ball slowly arc toward the hole, lost in that vicarious rush that so fiercely drew spectators to sports. He held his breath and felt something like a tear well up in his eye when the ball dropped in. A birdie. Diane Hoffman made a fist and pumped it. The lead was back up to nine strokes.

Jack looked up at the applauding galley. He acknowledged them with a tip of his hat, but he saw nothing. Still in the zone. Fighting to stay there. For a moment, his eyes locked on Myron's. Myron nodded back, not wanting to nudge him back to reality. Stay in that zone, Myron thought. In that zone, a man can win a tournament. In that zone, a son does not purposely sabotage a father's life-long dream.

Myron walked past the many portable toilets—they'd been provided by a company with the semiaccurate name Royal Flush—and headed toward Corporate Row. Golf matches had an unprecedented hierarchy for ticket holders. True, at most sporting arenas there was a grading of one sort or another—some had better seats, obviously, while some had access to skyboxes or even courtside seats. But in those cases, you handed a ticket to an usher or ticket collector and took your place. In golf, you displayed your entrance pass all day. The general-admission folk (read: serfs) usually had a sticker plastered on their shirt, not unlike, say, a scarlet letter. Others wore a plastic card that dangled from a metal chain wrapped around their neck. Sponsors (read: feudal lords) wore either red, silver, or gold cards, depending on how much money they spent. There were also different passes for players' family and friends, Merion club members, Merion club officers, even steady sports agents. And the different cards gave you different access to different places. For example, you had to have a colored card to enter Corporate Row. Or you needed a gold card if you wanted to enter one of those exclusive tents—the ones strategically perched on hills like generals' quarters in an old war movie.

Corporate Row was merely a row of tents, each sponsored by one enormous company or another. The theoretical intention of spending at least one hundred grand for a four-day tent rental was to impress corporate clients and gain exposure. The truth, however, was that the tents were a way for the corporate bigwigs to go to the tournament for free. Yes, a few important clients were invited, but Myron also noticed that the company's major officers always managed to show too. And the hundred grand rental fee was just a start. It didn't include the food, the drinks, the employees—not to mention the first-class flights, the deluxe hotel suites, the stretch limos, et cetera, for the bigwigs and their guests.

Boys and girls, can you say, "Chu-ching goes the cash register"? I thought you could.

Myron gave his name to the pretty young woman at the Lock-Horne tent. Win was not there yet, but Esperanza was sitting at a table in the corner.

"You look like shit," Esperanza said.

"Maybe. But at least I feel awful."

"So what happened?"

"Three crackheads adorned with Nazi memorabilia and crowbars jumped me."

She arched an eyebrow. "Only three?"

The woman was constant chuckles. He told her about his run-in and narrow escape. When he was finished, Esperanza shook her head and said, "Hopeless. Absolutely hopeless."

"Don't get all dewy-eyed on me. I'll be fine."

"I found Lloyd Rennart's wife. She's an artist of some kind, lives on the Jersey shore."

"Any word on Lloyd Rennart's body?"

Esperanza shook her head. "I checked the NVI and Treemaker Web sites. No death certificate has been issued."

Myron looked at her. "You're kidding."

"Nope. But it might not be on the Web yet. The other offices are closed until Monday. And even if one hasn't been issued, it might not mean anything."

"Why not?" he asked.

"A body is supposed to be missing for a certain amount of time before the person can be declared dead," Esperanza explained. "I don't know—five years or something. But what often happens is that the next of kin files a motion in order to settle insurance claims and the estate. But Lloyd Rennart committed suicide."

"So there'd be no insurance," Myron said.

"Right. And assuming everything was held jointly between Rennart and his wife, then there would be no need for her to press it."

Myron nodded. It made sense. Still it was yet another nagging hangnail that needed to be clipped. "You want something to drink?" he asked.

She shook her head.

"I'll be right back." Myron grabbed a Yoo-Hoo. Win had made sure the Lock-Horne tent stocked them. What a pal. A television monitor in the upper corner had a scoreboard. Jack had just finished the fifteenth hole. Both he and Crispin had parred it. Barring a sudden collapse, Jack was going to take a huge lead into tomorrow's final round.

When Myron got settled again, Esperanza said, "I want to talk to you about something."

"Shoot."

"It's about my graduating law school."

"Okay," Myron said, dragging out the word.

"You've been avoiding the subject," she said.

"What are you talking about? I'm the one who wants to go to your graduation, remember?"

"That's not what I mean." Her fingers found and began to fiddle with a straw wrapper. "I'm talking about what happens *after* I graduate. I'm going to be a full-fledged attorney soon. My role in the company should change."

Myron nodded. "Agreed."

"For one thing, I'd like an office."

"We don't have the space."

"The conference room is too large," she countered. "You can slice a little out of there and a little out of the waiting room. It won't be a huge office, but it'll be good enough."

Myron nodded slowly. "We can look into that."

"It's important to me, Myron."

"Okay, it sounds possible."

"Second, I don't want a raise."

"Don't?"

"That's right."

"Odd negotiating technique, Esperanza, but you convinced me. Much as I might like to give you a raise, you will not receive one penny more. I surrender."

"You're doing it again."

"Doing what?"

"Joking around when I'm serious. You don't like change, Myron. I know that. It's why you lived with your parents until a few months ago. It's why you still keep Jessica around when you should have forgotten about her years ago."

"Do me a favor," he said wearily. "Spare me the amateur analysis, okay?"

"Just stating the facts. You don't like change."

"Who does? And I love Jessica. You know that."

"Fine, you love her," Esperanza said dismissively. "You're right, I shouldn't have brought it up."

"Good. Are we done?"

"No." Esperanza stopped playing with the straw wrapper. She crossed her legs and folded her hands in her lap. "This isn't easy for me to talk about," she said.

"Do you want to do it another time?"

She rolled her eyes. "No, I don't want to do it another time. I want you to listen to me. Really listen."

Myron stayed silent, leaned forward a little.

"The reason I don't want a raise is because I don't want to work for someone. My father worked his whole life doing menial jobs for a variety of assholes. My mother spent hers cleaning other people's houses." Esperanza stopped, swallowed, took a breath. "I don't want to do that. I don't want to spend my life working for anyone.''

"Including me?''

"I said *anyone,* didn't I?'' She shook her head. "Jesus, you just don't listen sometimes.''

Myron opened his mouth, closed it. "Then I don't see where you're going with this.''

"I want to be a part owner,'' she said.

He made a face. "Of MB SportsReps?''

"No, of AT&T. Of course MB.''

"But the name is MB,'' Myron said "The M is for Myron. B for Bolitar. Your name is Esperanza Diaz. I can't make it MBED. What kind of name is that?''

She just looked at him. "You're doing it again. I'm trying to have a serious conversation.''

"Now? You pick now when I just got hit over the head with a tire iron—''

"Shoulder.''

"Whatever. Look, you know how much you mean to me—''

"This isn't about our friendship,'' she interrupted. "I don't care what I mean to you right now. I care about what I mean to MB SportsReps.''

"You mean a lot to MB. A hell of a lot.'' He stopped. "But?''

"But nothing. You just caught me a little off balance, that's all. I was just jumped by a group of neo-Nazis. That does funny things to the psyche of people of my persuasion. I'm also trying to solve a possible kidnapping. I know things have to change. I planned on giving you more to do, letting you handle more negotiations, hiring someone new. But a partnership . . . that's a different kettle of gefilte.''

Her voice was unyielding. "Meaning?''

"Meaning I'd like to think about it, okay? How do

you plan on becoming a partner? What percentage do you want? Do you want to buy in or work your way in or what? These are things we'll have to go over, and I don't think now is the time.''

''Fine.'' She stood up. ''I'm going to hang around the players' lounge. See if I can strike up a conversation with one of the wives.''

''Good idea.''

''I'll see you later.'' She turned to leave.

''Esperanza?''

She looked at him.

''You're not mad, right?''

''Not mad,'' she repeated.

''We'll work something out,'' he said.

She nodded. ''Right.''

''Don't forget. We're meeting with Tad Crispin an hour after they finish. By the pro shop.''

''You want me there?''

''Yes.''

She shrugged. ''Okay.'' Then she left.

Myron leaned back and watched her go. Great. Just what he needed. His best friend in the world as a business partner. It never worked. Money screwed up relationships; it was simply one of life's givens. His father and his uncle —two closer brothers you never saw—had tried it. The outcome had been disastrous. Dad finally bought Uncle Morris out, but the two men didn't speak to each other for four years. Myron and Win had labored painstakingly to keep their businesses separate while maintaining the same interests and goals. It worked because there was no cross-interference or money to divide up. With Esperanza things had been great, but that was because the relationship had always been boss and employee. Their roles were well defined. But at the same time, he understood. Esperanza deserved this chance. She had earned it. She was

more than an important employee to MB. She was a part
of it.

So what to do?

He sat back and chugged the Yoo-Hoo, waiting for an
idea. Fortunately, his thoughts were waylaid when someone tapped his shoulder.

Chapter 17

"Hello."

Myron turned around. It was Linda Coldren. Her head was wrapped in a semi-babushka and she wore dark sunglasses. Greta Garbo circa 1984. She opened her purse. "I forwarded the home phone here," she whispered, pointing to a cellular phone in the purse. "Mind if I sit down?"

"Please do," Myron said.

She sat facing him. The sunglasses were big, but Myron could still see a hint of redness around the rims of her eyes. Her nose, too, looked like it had been rubbed raw by a Kleenex overdose. "Anything new?" she asked.

He told her about the Crusty Nazis jumping him. Linda asked several follow-up questions. Again the internal paradox tore at her: she wanted her son to be safe, yet she did not want it all to be a hoax. Myron finished by saying, "I still think we should get in touch with the feds. I can do it quietly."

She shook her head. "Too risky."

"So is going on like this."

Linda Coldren shook her head again and leaned back. For several moments they sat in silence. Her gaze was cast somewhere over his shoulder. Then she said, "When Chad was born, I took off nearly two years. Did you know that?"

"No," Myron said.

"Women's golf," she muttered. "I was at the height

of my game, the top female golfer in the world, and yet you never read about it."

"I don't follow golf much," Myron said.

"Yeah, right," she snorted. "If Jack Nicklaus took two years off, you would have heard about it."

Myron nodded. She had a point. "Was it tough coming back?" he asked.

"You mean in terms of playing or leaving my son?"

"Both."

She took a breath and considered the question. "I missed playing," she said. "You have no idea how much. I regained the number one spot in a couple of months. As for Chad, well, he was still an infant. I hired a nanny to travel with us."

"How long did that last?"

"Until Chad was three. That's when I realized that I couldn't drag him around anymore. It wasn't fair to him. A child needs some sort of stability. So I had to make a choice."

They fell into silence.

"Don't get me wrong," she said. "I'm not into the self-pity thing and I'm glad women are given choices. But what they don't tell you is that when you have choices, you have guilt."

"What kind of guilt?"

"A mother's guilt, the worst kind there is. The pangs are constant and ceaseless. They haunt your sleep. They point accusatory fingers. Every joyous swing of the golf club made me feel like I was forsaking my own child. I flew home as often as I could. I missed some tournaments that I really wanted to play in. I tried damn hard to balance career and motherhood. And every step of the way, I felt like a selfish louse." She looked at him. "Do you understand that?"

"Yes, I think so."

"But you don't really sympathize," she added.

"Of course I do."

Linda Coldren gave him a skeptical glance. "If I had been a stay-at-home mother, would you have been so quick to suspect that Chad was behind this? Didn't the fact that I was an absent mother sway your thinking?"

"Not an absent mother," Myron corrected. "Absent parents."

"Same thing."

"No. You were making more money. You were by far the more successful parent business-wise. If anyone should have stayed home, it was Jack."

She smiled. "Aren't we politically correct?"

"Nope. Just practical."

"But it's not that simple, Myron. Jack loves his son. And during the years he didn't qualify for the tour, he did stay home with him. But let's face facts: Like it or not, it's the mother who bears that burden."

"Doesn't make it right."

"Nor does it let me off the hook. Like I said, I made my choices. If I had to do it all over again, I still would have toured."

"And you still would have felt guilty."

She nodded. "With choice comes guilt. No escaping it."

Myron took a sip of his Yoo-Hoo. "You said that Jack stayed home some of the time."

"Yes," she said. "When he failed Q school."

"Q school?"

"Qualifying school," she said. "Every year the top 125 moneymakers get their PGA Tour card automatically. A couple of other players get sponsor exemptions. The rest are forced to go to Q school. Qualifying school. If you don't do well there, you don't play for the year."

"One tournament decides all that?"

She tilted the glass at him as though making a toast.
"That's right."

Talk about pressure. "So when Jack failed Q school,
he'd stay home for the year?"

She nodded.

"How did Jack and Chad get along?"

"Chad used to worship his father," Linda said.

"And now?"

She looked off, her face vaguely pained. "Now Chad
is old enough to wonder why his father keeps losing. I
don't know what he thinks anymore. But Jack is a good
man. He tries very hard. You have to understand what
happened to him. Losing the Open that way—it might
sound overly melodramatic, but it killed something inside
him. Not even having a son could make him whole."

"It shouldn't matter so much," Myron said, hearing
the echo of Win in his words. "It was just one tournament."

"You were involved in a lot of big games," she said.
"Ever choke away a victory like Jack did?"

"No."

"Neither have I."

Two gray-haired men sporting matching green ascots
made their way down the buffet table. They leaned over
each food selection and frowned like it had ants. Their
plates were still piled high enough to cause the occasional
avalanche.

"There's something else," Linda said.

Myron waited.

She adjusted the sunglasses and put her hands on the
table palms down. "Jack and I are not close. We've
haven't been close in many years."

When she didn't continue, Myron said, "But you've
stayed married."

"Yes."

He wanted to ask why, but the question was so obvious, just hanging out there within easy view, that to voice it would be redundant.

"I am a constant reminder of his failures," she continued. "It's not easy for a man to live with that. We're supposed to be life partners, but I have what Jack longs for most." Linda tilted her head. "It's funny."

"What?"

"I never allow mediocrity on the golf course. Yet I allowed it to dominate my personal life. Don't you find that odd?"

Myron made a noncommittal motion with his head. He could feel Linda's unhappiness radiating off her like a breaking fever. She looked up now and smiled at him. The smile was intoxicating, nearly breaking his heart. He found himself wanting to lean over and hold Linda Coldren. He felt this almost uncontrollable urge to press her against him and feel the sheen of her hair in his face. He tried to remember the last time he had held such thought for any woman but Jessica; no answer came to him.

"Tell me about you," Linda suddenly said.

The change of subject caught him off guard. He sort of shook his head. "Boring stuff."

"Oh, I doubt that," she said, almost playfully. "Come on now. It'll distract me."

Myron shook his head again.

"I know you almost played pro basketball. I know you hurt your knee. I know you went to law school at Harvard. And I know you tried to make a comeback a few months ago. Want to fill in the blanks?"

"That's pretty much it."

"No, I don't think so, Myron. Aunt Cissy didn't say that you could help us because you were good at basketball."

"I worked a bit for the government."

"With Win?"

"Yes."

"Doing what?"

Again he shook his head.

"Top secret, huh?"

"Something like that."

"And you date Jessica Culver?"

"Yes."

"I like her books."

He nodded.

"Do you love her?"

"Very much."

"So what do you want?"

"Want?"

"Out of life. What are your dreams?"

He smiled. "You're kidding, right?"

"Just getting to the heart of the matter," Linda said. "Humor me. What do you want, Myron?" She looked at him with keen interest. Myron felt flushed.

"I want to marry Jessica. I want to move to the suburbs. I want to raise a family."

She leaned back as though satisfied. "For real?"

"Yes."

"Like your parents?"

"Yes."

She smiled. "I think that's nice."

"It's simple," he said.

"Not all of us are built for the simple life," she said, "even if it's what we want."

Myron nodded. "Deep, Linda. I don't know what it means, but it sounded deep."

"Me neither." She laughed. It was deep and throaty and Myron liked the sound of it. "Tell me where you met Win."

"At college," Myron said. "Freshman year."

"I haven't seen him since he was eight years old."
Linda Coldren took a swallow of her seltzer. "I was fifteen then. Jack and I had already been dating a year,
believe it or not. Win loved Jack, by the way. Did you
know that?"

"No," Myron said.

"It's true. He followed Jack everywhere. And Jack
could be such a prick back then. He bullied other kids. He
was mischievous as all hell. At times he was downright
cruel."

"But you fell for him?"

"I was fifteen," she said, as if that explained everything. And maybe it did.

"What was Win like as a kid?" Myron asked.

She smiled again, the lines in the corners of her eyes
and lips deepening. "Trying to figure him out, eh?"

"Just curious," Myron said, but the truth in her words
stung. He suddenly wanted to withdraw the question, but
it was too late.

"Win was never a happy kid. He was always"—Linda
stopped, searching for the word—"off. I don't know how
else to put it. He wasn't crazy or flaky or aggressive or
anything like that. But something was not right with him.
Always. Even as a child, he had this strange ability to
detach."

Myron nodded. He knew what she meant.

"Aunt Cissy is like that too."

"Win's mother?"

Linda nodded. "The woman can be pure ice when she
wants to be. Even when it comes to Win. She acts as
though he doesn't exist."

"She must talk about him," Myron said. "To your
father, at least."

Linda shook her head. "When Aunt Cissy told my

father to contact Win, it was the first time she'd mentioned his name to him in years.''

Myron said nothing. Again the obvious question hung in the air unasked: What had happened between Win and his mother? But Myron would never voice it. This conversation had already gone too far. Asking would be an unforgivable betrayal; if Win wanted him to know, he'd tell him.

Time passed, but neither one of them noticed. They talked, mostly about Chad and the kind of son he was. Jack had held on and still led by eight strokes. A gigantic lead. If he blew it this time, it would be worse than twenty-three years ago.

The tent began to empty out, but Myron and Linda stayed and talked some more. A feeling of intimacy began to warm him; he found it hard to breathe when he looked at her. For a moment he closed his eyes. Nothing, he realized, was really going on here. If there was an attraction of some sort, it was simply a classic case of damsel-in-distress syndrome—and there was nothing less politically correct (not to mention Neanderthal) than that.

The crowd was gone now. For a long time nobody came into view. At one point, Win stuck his head into the tent. Seeing them together, he arched an eyebrow and then slipped back out.

Myron checked his watch. "I have to go. I have an appointment."

"With whom?"

"Tad Crispin."

"Here at Merion?"

"Yes."

"Do you think you'll be long?"

"No."

She started fiddling with her engagement ring, studying it as though making an appraisal. "Do you mind if I wait?'' she asked. "We can catch dinner together." She took off her glasses. The eyes were puffy, but they were also strong and focused.

"Okay."

He met up with Esperanza at the clubhouse. She made a face at him.

"What?" he said.

"You thinking about Jessica?" Esperanza asked suspiciously.

"No, why?"

"Because you're making your nauseating, lovesick-puppy face. You know. The one that makes me want to throw up on your shoes."

"Come on," he said. "Tad Crispin is waiting."

The meeting ended with no deal. But they were getting close.

"That contract he signed with Zoom," Esperanza said. "A major turkey."

"I know."

"Crispin likes you."

"We'll see what happens," Myron said.

He excused himself and walked quickly back to the tent. Linda Coldren was in the same seat, her back to him, her posture still queenlike.

"Linda?"

"It's dark now," she said softly. "Chad doesn't like the dark. I know he's sixteen, but I still leave the hall light on. Just in case."

Myron remained still. When she turned toward him—when he first saw her smile—it was like something corkscrewed into his heart. "When Chad was little," she began, "he always carried around this red plastic golf club and Wiffle ball. It's funny. When I think about him now, that's how I see him. With that little red club. For a long time I hadn't been able to picture him like that. He's so much like a man now. But since he's been gone, all I see is that little, happy kid in the backyard hitting golf balls.''

Myron nodded. He stretched out his hand toward hers. ''Let's go, Linda,'' he said gently.

She stood. They walked together in silence. The night sky was so bright it looked wet. Myron wanted to reach out and hold her hand. But he didn't. When they got to her car, Linda unlocked it with a remote control. Then she opened the door as Myron began circling for the passenger side. He stopped suddenly.

The envelope was on her seat.

For several seconds, neither of them moved. The envelope was manila, big enough for an eight-by-ten photograph. It was flat except for an area in the middle that puffed up a bit.

Linda Coldren looked up at Myron. Myron reached down, and using his palms, he picked up the envelope by the edges. There was writing on the back. Block letters:

I WARNED YOU NOT SEEK HELP

NOW CHAD PAYS THE PRICE

CROSS US AGAIN AND IT WILL GET MUCH WORSE.

Dread wrapped Myron's chest in tight steel bands. He slowly reached out and tentatively touched the puffy part with just a knuckle. It felt claylike. Carefully, Myron slit the seal open. He turned the envelope upside down and let the contents fall to the car seat.

The severed finger bounced once and then settled onto the leather.

Chapter 18

Myron stared, unable to speak.

Ohmygodohmygodohmygodohmygod . . .

Raw terror engulfed him. He started shivering, and his body went numb. He looked down at the note in his hand. A voice inside his head said, *Your fault, Myron. Your fault.*

He turned to Linda Coldren. Her hand fluttered near her mouth, her eyes wide.

Myron tried to step toward her, but he staggered like a boxer who didn't take advantage of a standing eight count. "We have to call someone," he managed, his voice sounding distant even to him. "The FBI. I have friends—"

"No." Her tone was strong.

"Linda, listen to me. . . ."

"Read the note," she said.

"But—"

"Read the note," she repeated. She lowered her head grimly. "You're out of this now, Myron."

"You don't know what you're dealing with."

"Oh no?" Her head snapped up. Her hands tightened into fists. "I'm dealing with a sick monster," she said. "The kind of monster who maims at the slightest provocation." She stepped closer to the car. "He cut off my son's finger just because I talked to you. What do you think he'd do if I went directly against his orders?"

Myron's head swirled. "Linda, paying off the ransom doesn't guarantee—"

"I know that," she interrupted.

"But . . ." His mind flailed about helplessly and then said something exceedingly dumb. "You don't even know if it's his finger."

She looked down now. With one hand, she held back a sob. With the other, she caressed the finger lovingly, without a trace of repulsion on her face. "Yes," Linda said softly. "I do."

"He may already be dead."

"Then it makes no difference what I do, does it?"

Myron stopped himself from saying any more. He had sounded asinine enough. He just needed a moment or two to gather himself, to figure out what the next step should be.

Your fault, Myron. Your fault.

He shook it off. He had, after all, been in worse scrapes. He had seen dead bodies, taken on some very bad people, caught and brought killers to justice. He just needed—

All with Win's help, Myron. Never on your own.

Linda Coldren lifted the finger into view. Tears streamed down her cheeks, but her face remained a placid pool.

"Good-bye, Myron."

"Linda . . ."

"I'm not going to disobey him again."

"We have to think this through—"

She shook her head. "We should never have contacted you."

Cupping her son's severed finger like a baby chick, Linda Coldren slid into the car. She put the finger down carefully and started the car. Then she shifted it into gear and drove away.

* * *

Myron made his way to his car. For several minutes he sat and took deep breaths, willing himself to calm down. He had studied martial arts since Win had first introduced him to tae kwon do when they were college freshmen. Meditation was a big part of what they'd learned, yet Myron never quite grasped the critical nuances. His mind had a habit of drifting. Now he tried to practice the simple rules. He closed his eyes. He breathed in through the nose slowly, forcing it down low, letting only his stomach, not his chest, expand. He released it through the mouth, even slower, draining his lungs fully.

Okay, he thought, what is your next step?

The first answer to float to the surface was the most basic: Give up. Cut your losses. Realize that you are very much out of your element. You never really worked for the feds. You only accompanied Win. You were way out of your league on this and it cost a sixteen-year-old boy his finger and maybe more. As Esperanza had said, "Without Win, you're hopeless." Learn your lesson and walk away.

And then what? Let the Coldrens face this crisis alone?

If he had, maybe Chad Coldren would still have ten fingers.

The thought made something inside of him crumble. He opened his eyes. His heart started trip-hammering again. He couldn't call the Coldrens. He couldn't call the feds. If he pursued this on his own, he would be risking Chad Coldren's life.

He started up the car, still trying to regain his balance. It was time to be analytical. It was time to be cold. He had to look at this latest development as a clue for a moment.

Forget the horror. Forget the fact that he might have screwed up. The finger was just a clue.

One: The placement of the envelope was curious—inside Linda Coldren's locked (yes, it had been locked—Linda had used the remote control to open it) car. How had it gotten there? Had the kidnapper simply broken into the vehicle? Good possibility, but would he have had time in Merion's parking lot? Wouldn't someone have reported it? Probably. Did Chad Coldren have a key that the kidnapper could have used? Hmm. Very good possibility, but one he couldn't confirm unless he spoke to Linda, which was out of the question.

Dead end. For now.

Two: More than one person was involved in this kidnapping. This hardly took brilliant detective work. First off, you have the Crusty Nazi. The phone call at the mall proved that he had something to do with this—not to mention his subsequent behavior. But there was no way a guy like Crusty could sneak into Merion and plant the envelope in Linda Coldren's car. Not without drawing suspicion. Not during the U.S. Open. And the note had warned the Coldrens not to ''cross'' them again. Cross. Did that sound like a Crusty word?

Okay, good. What else?

Three: The kidnappers were both vicious and dumb. Vicious was again obvious—the dumb part maybe less so. But look at the facts. For example, making a large ransom demand over a weekend when you know that the banks won't be open until Monday—was that bright? Not knowing how much to ask for the first two times they called—didn't that say ding-a-ling? And lastly, was it really prudent to cut off a kid's finger just because his parents happened to talk to a sports agent? Did that even make sense?

No.

Unless, of course, the kidnappers knew that Myron was more than a sports agent.

But how?

Myron pulled into Win's long driveway. Unfamiliar people were taking horses out of the stable. As he approached the guest house, Win appeared in the doorway. Myron pulled into a spot and got out.

"How did your meeting with Tad Crispin go?" Win asked.

Myron hurried over to him. "They chopped off his finger," he managed, breathy to the point of almost hyperventilating. "The kidnappers. They cut off Chad's finger. Left it in Linda's car."

Win's expression did not change. "Did you discover this before or after your meeting with Tad Crispin?"

Myron was puzzled by the question. "After."

Win nodded slowly. "Then my original question remains: How did your meeting go with Tad Crispin?"

Myron stepped back as though slapped. "Jesus Christ," he said in an almost reverent tone. "You can't be serious."

"What happens to that family does not concern me. What happens to your business dealings with Tad Crispin does."

Myron shook his head, stunned. "Not even you could be that cold."

"Oh please."

"Please what?"

"There are far greater tragedies in this world than a sixteen-year-old boy losing his finger. People die, Myron. Floods wipe out entire villages. Men do horrible things to children every day." He paused. "Did you, for example, read this afternoon's paper?"

"What are you rambling about?"

"I'm just trying to make you understand," Win continued in too slow, too measured a voice. "The Coldrens mean nothing to me—no more than any other stranger and perhaps less. The newspaper is filled with tragedies that hit me on a more personal level. For example . . ."

Win stopped and looked at Myron very steadily.

"For example what?" Myron asked.

"There was a new development in the Kevin Morris case," Win replied. "Are you familiar with that one?"

Myron shook his head.

"Two seven-year-old boys—Billy Waters and Tyrone Duffy—have been missing for nearly three weeks. They disappeared while riding their bikes home from school. The police questioned one Kevin Morris, a man with a long record of perversion, including molestation, who had been hanging around the school. But Mr. Morris had a very sharp attorney. There was no physical evidence and despite a fairly convincing circumstantial case—they found the boys' bikes in a Dumpster not far from his home—Mr. Morris was set free."

Myron felt something cold press against his heart. "So what was the new development, Win?"

"The police received a tip late last night."

"How late?"

Again Win looked at him steadily. "Very late."

Silence.

"It seems," Win went on, "that someone had witnessed Kevin Morris burying the bodies off a road in the woods near Lancaster. The police dug them up last night. Do you know what they found?"

Myron shook his head again, afraid to even open his mouth.

"Billy Waters and Tyrone Duffy were both dead. They'd been sexually molested and mutilated in ways that even the media couldn't report. The police also found enough evidence at the burial site to arrest Kevin Morris.

Fingerprints on a medical scalpel. Plastic bags that matched ones in his kitchen. Semen samples that offer a preliminary match in both boys."

Myron flinched.

"Everyone seems quite confident that Mr. Morris will be convicted," Win finished.

"What about the person who called in the tip? Will he be a witness?"

"Funny thing," Win said. "The man called from a pay phone and never gave his name. No one, it seems, knows who he was."

"But the police captured Kevin Morris?"

"Yes."

The two men stared at each other.

"I'm surprised you didn't kill him," Myron said.

"Then you really don't know me."

A horse whinnied. Win turned and looked at the magnificent animal. Something strange came across his face, a look of loss.

"What did she do to you, Win?"

Win kept staring. They both knew whom Myron was talking about.

"What did she do to make you hate so much?"

"Don't engage in too much hyperbole, Myron. I am not that simple. My mother is not solely responsible for shaping me. A man is not made up of one incident, and I am a far cry from crazy, as you suggested earlier. Like any other human being, I choose my battles. I battle quite a bit—more than most—and usually on the right side. I battled for Billy Waters and Tyrone Duffy. But I do not wish to battle for the Coldrens. That is my choice. You, as my closest friend, should respect that. You should not try to prod or guilt me into a battle I do not wish to fight."

Myron was not sure what to say. It was scary when he could understand Win's cold logic. "Win?"

Win wrested his gaze from the horse. He looked at Myron.

"I'm in trouble," Myron said, hearing the desperation in his tone. "I need your help."

Win's voice was suddenly soft, his face almost pained. "If that were true, I'd be there. You know that. But you are not in any trouble from which you cannot easily disentangle. Just back away, Myron. You have the option of ending your involvement. To draw me into this against my will—using our friendship in that way—is wrong. Walk away this time."

"You know I can't do that."

Win nodded and headed toward his car. "Like I said, we all choose our battles."

When he entered the guest house, Esperanza was screaming, "Bankrupt! Lose a turn! Bankrupt!"

Myron came up behind her. She was watching *Wheel of Fortune*.

"This woman is so greedy," Esperanza said, gesturing at the screen. "She's got over six thousand dollars and she keeps spinning. I hate that."

The wheel stopped, landing on the glittery $1,000. The woman asked for a *B*. There were two of them. Esperanza groaned. "You're back early," she said. "I thought you were going out to dinner with Linda Coldren."

"It didn't work out."

Esperanza finally turned around and looked at his face. "What happened?"

He told her. Her dark complexion lost a bit of color along the way. When he finished, Esperanza said, "You need Win."

"He won't help."

"Time to swallow your macho pride and ask him. Beg him if you have to."

"Been there, done that. He's out." On the television, the greedy woman bought a vowel. This always baffled Myron. Why do contestants who clearly know the puzzle's solution still buy vowels? To waste money? To make sure their opponents know the answer too?

"But," he said, "you're here."

Esperanza looked at him. "So?"

It was, he knew, the real reason she had come down in the first place. On the phone she had told him that he didn't work well alone. The words spoke volumes about her true motivation for fleeing the Big Apple.

"Do you want to help?" he asked.

The greedy woman leaned forward, spun the wheel, and then started clapping and shouting, "Come on, a thousand!" Her opponents clapped too. Like they wanted her to do well. Right.

"What do you want me to do?" Esperanza asked.

"I'll explain on the way. If you want to come."

They both watched the wheel decelerate. The camera moved in for a close-up. The arrow slowed and slowed before settling on the word BANKRUPT. The audience groaned. The greedy woman kept the smile, but now she looked like someone had just punched her hard in the stomach.

"That's an omen," Esperanza said.

"Good or bad?" Myron asked.

"Yes."

Chapter 19

The girls were still at the mall. Still at the food court. Still at the same table. It was amazing, when you thought about it. The long summer days beckoned with sunny skies and chirping birds. School was out, and yet so many teenagers spent all their time inside a glorified school cafeteria, probably lamenting the day they would have to return to school.

Myron shook his head. He was complaining about teenagers. A sure sign of lost youth. Soon he'd be screaming at someone for turning up the thermostat.

As soon as he entered the food court, the girls all turned in his direction. It was like they had people-we-know detectors at every entrance. Myron did not hesitate. Making his expression as stern as possible, he rushed toward them. He studied each face as he approached. These were, after all, just teenagers. The guilty one, Myron was sure, would show it.

And she did. Almost instantly.

She was the one that had been teased yesterday, the one they taunted for being the recipient of a Crusty smile. Missy or Messy or something. It all made sense now. Crusty hadn't spotted Myron's tail. He'd been tipped off. In fact, the whole thing had been arranged. That was how Crusty had known that Myron had been asking questions about him. That explained the seemingly fortuitous timing—that is, Crusty hanging around the food court just long enough for Myron to arrive.

It had all been a big setup.

The one with Elsa Lancaster hair screwed up her face and said, "Like, what's the matter?"

"That guy tried to kill me," Myron said.

Lots of gasps. Faces lit up with excitement. To most of them, this was like a television show come to life. Only Missy or Messy or some name with an *M* remained rock-still.

"Not to worry though," Myron continued. "We've just about got him. In an hour or two, he'll be under arrest. The police are on their way to find him right now. I just wanted to thank you all for your cooperation."

The *M* girl spoke: "I thought you weren't a cop."

A sentence without the word *like*. Hmm. "I'm undercover," Myron said.

"Oh. My. God."

"Get out!"

"Whoa!"

"You mean like on *New York Undercover*?"

Myron, no stranger to TV, had no idea what she was talking about. "Exactly," he said.

"This is *so* cool."

"Are we, like, going to be on TV?"

"The six o'clock news?"

"That guy on Channel Four is *so* cute, you know?"

"My hair totally sucks."

"No way, Amber. But mine is like a total rat nest."

Myron cleared his throat. "We have this pretty much all wrapped up. Except for one thing. The accomplice."

Myron waited for one of them to say, "Accomplice?" No one did. Myron elaborated. "Someone in this very mall helped that creep set me up."

"In, like, here?

"In *our* mall?"

"Not *our* mall. No way."

They said the word *mall* like some people said the word *synagogue*.

"Someone helped that skank?"

"*Our* mall?"

"Eeeuw."

"I can't, like, believe it."

"Believe it," Myron said. "In fact, he or she is probably here right now. Watching us."

Heads swirled about. Even *M* managed to get into the act, though it was an uninspired display.

Myron had shown the stick. Now the carrot. "Look, I want you ladies to keep your eyes and ears open. We'll catch the accomplice. No question about it. Guys like that always talk. But if the accomplice was just a hapless dupe . . ."

Blank faces.

"If she, like, didn't really know the score"—not exactly hip-hop lingo, but they nodded now—"and she came to me right away, before the cops nail her, well, then I'd probably be able to help her out. Otherwise, she could be charged with attempted murder."

Nothing. Myron had expected that. *M* would never admit this in front of her friends. Jail was a great fear-inducer, but it was little more than a wet match next to the bonfire that was teenage peer pressure.

"Good-bye, ladies."

Myron moved to the other side of the food court. He leaned against a pillar, putting himself in the path between the girls' table and the bathroom. He waited, hoping she'd make an excuse and come over. After about five minutes, *M* stood up and began walking toward Myron. Just as he planned. Myron almost smiled. Maybe he should have been a high school guidance counselor. Mold young minds, change lives for the better.

The *M* girl veered away from him and toward the exit.

Damn.

Myron quickly trotted over, the smile on full blast. "Mindy?" He had suddenly remembered her name.

She turned to him but said nothing.

He put on the soft voice and the understanding eyes. A male Oprah. A kinder, gentler Regis. "Whatever you say to me is confidential," he said. "If you're involved in this—"

"Just stay away from me, okay? I'm not, like, involved in anything."

She pushed past him and hurried past Foot Locker and the Athlete's Foot—two stores Myron had always assumed were the same, alter egos if you will, like you never saw Batman and Bruce Wayne in the same room.

Myron watched her go. She hadn't cracked, which was a bit of a surprise. He nodded and his backup plan went into action. Mindy kept hurrying away, glancing behind her every few steps to make sure Myron wasn't following her. He wasn't.

Mindy, however, did not notice the attractive, jean-clad Hispanic woman just a few feet to her left.

Mindy found a pay phone by the record store that looked exactly like every other mall record store. She glanced about, put a quarter into the slot, and dialed a number. Her finger had just pressed the seventh digit when a small hand reached over her shoulder and hung up the phone.

She spun toward Esperanza. "Hey!"

Esperanza said, "Put down the phone."

"Hey!"

"Right, hey. Now put down the phone."

"Like, who the fuck are you?"

"Put down the phone," Esperanza repeated, "or I'll shove it up a nostril."

Wide-eyed with confusion, Mindy obeyed. Several seconds later, Myron appeared. He looked at Esperanza. "Up a nostril?"

She shrugged.

Mindy shouted, "You can't, like, do that."

"Do what?" Myron said.

"Like"—Mindy stopped, struggled with the thought —"like, make me hang up a phone?"

"No law against that," Myron said. He turned to Esperanza. "You know any law against that?"

"Against hanging up a phone?" Esperanza emphatically shook her head. "No, señor."

"See, no law against it. On the other hand, there is a law against aiding and abetting a criminal. It's called a felony. It means jail time."

"I didn't aid nothing. And I don't bet."

Myron turned to Esperanza. "You get the number?"

She nodded and gave it to him.

"Let's trace it."

Again, the cyber-age made this task frightening easy. Anybody can buy a computer program at their local software store or hop on certain Web sites like Biz, type in the number, and voilà, you have a name and address.

Esperanza used a cellular phone to dial the home number of MB SportsReps' new receptionist. Her name was, fittingly, Big Cyndi. Six-five and over three hundred pounds, Big Cyndi had wrestled professionally under the moniker Big Chief Mama, tag-team partner of Esperanza "Little Pocahontas" Diaz. In the ring, Big Cyndi wore makeup like Tammy Faye on steroids; spiked hair that would have been the envy of Sid and Nancy; ripped muscle-displaying T-shirts; and an awful, sneering glare complete with a ready growl. In real life, well, she was exactly the same.

Speaking Spanish, Esperanza gave Cyndi the number.

Mindy said, "Hey, I'm, like, outta here."

Myron grabbed her arm. " 'Fraid not."

"Hey! You can't, like, hold me here."

Myron maintained his grip.

"I'll scream rape."

Myron rolled his eyes. "At a mall pay phone. In broad fluorescent light. When I'm standing here with my girl-friend."

Mindy looked at Esperanza. "She's your girlfriend?"

"Yes."

Esperanza began whistling "Dream Weaver."

"But you can't, like, make me stay with you."

"I don't get it, Mindy. You look like a nice girl." Actually, she was wearing black leggings, too-high pumps, a red halter top, and what looked like a dog choker around her neck. "Are you trying to tell me that this guy is worth going to jail over? He deals drugs, Mindy. He tried to kill me."

Esperanza hung up. "It's a bar called the Parker Inn."

"You know where it is?" he asked Mindy.

"Yeah."

"Come on."

Mindy pulled away. "Let go," she said, stretching out the last word.

"Mindy, this isn't fun and games here. You helped someone try to kill me."

"So you say."

"What?"

Mindy put her hands on her hips, chewed gum. "So, like, how do I know that you're not the bad one, huh?"

"Excuse me?"

"You, like, come up to us yesterday, right, all mysteri-ous and stuff, right? You don't, like, have a badge or nothing. How do I know that you aren't, like, after Tito?

How do I know that you aren't another drug dealer trying to take over his turf?''

'' 'Tito?' '' Myron repeated, looking at Esperanza. "A neo-Nazi named Tito?''

Esperanza shrugged.

"None of his friends, like, call him Tito,'' Mindy went on. "It's way too long, you know? So they call him Tit.''

Myron and Esperanza exchanged a glance, shook their heads. Too easy.

"Mindy,'' Myron said slowly, "I wasn't kidding back there. Tito is not a nice fellow. He may, in fact, be involved in kidnapping and maiming a boy about your age. Somebody cut off the boy's finger and sent it to his mother.''

Her face pinched up. "Oh, that's, like, so gross.''

"Help me, Mindy.''

"You a cop?''

"No,'' Myron said. "I'm just trying to save a boy.''

She waved her hands dismissively. "Then, like, go. You don't need me.''

"I'd like you to come with us.''

"Why?''

"So you don't try to warn Tito.''

"I won't.''

Myron shook his head. "You also know how to get to Parker Inn. It'll save us time.''

"Uh-uh, no way. I'm not going with you.''

"If you don't,'' Myron said, "I'll tell Amber and Trish and the gang all about your new boyfriend.''

That snared her attention. "He's not my boyfriend,'' she insisted. "We just, like, hung out a couple of times.''

Myron smiled. "So I'll lie,'' he said. "I'll tell them you slept with him.''

"I did not!'' she screamed. "That's, like, so unfair.''

Myron shrugged helplessly.

She crossed her arms and chewed her gum. Her version of defiance. It didn't last long. "Okay, okay, I'll go." She pointed a finger at Myron. "But I don't want Tit to see me, okay? I stay in the car."

"Deal," Myron said. He shook his head. Now they were after a man named Tit. What next?

The Parker Inn was a total redneck, biker, skeezer bar. The parking lot was packed with pickup trucks and motorcycles. Country music blared from the constantly opening door. Several men in John Deere baseball caps were using the side of the building as a urinal. Every once in a while one would turn and piss on another. Curses and laughter spewed forward. Fun city.

From his car parked across the street, Myron looked at Mindy and said, "You used to hang out here?"

She shrugged. "I, like, came here a couple of times," she said. "For excitement, you know?"

Myron nodded. "Why didn't you just douse yourself with gasoline and light matches?"

"Fuck you, all right? You my father now?"

He held his hands up. She was right. None of his business. "Do you see Tito's truck?" Myron just couldn't call him Tit. Maybe if he got to know him better.

Mindy scanned the lot. "No."

Neither did Myron. "Do you know where he lives?"
"No."

Myron shook his head. "He deals drugs. He wears a swastika tattoo. And he has no ass. But don't tell me . . . underneath all that, Tito is really sweet."

Mindy shouted, "Fuck you, all right? Just fuck you."

"Myron," Esperanza said by way of warning.

Again Myron put his hands up. They all sat back and watched. Nothing happened.

Mindy sighed as audibly as possible. "So, like, can I go home now?"

Esperanza said, "I have a thought."

"What?" Myron asked.

Esperanza pulled the tail of her blouse out of her jeans. She tied it up, making a knot under her rib cage and revealing plenty of flat, dark stomach. Then she unbuttoned her top to a daring low. A black bra was now visible, Myron noticed, trained detective that he was. She pulled down the visor mirror and began to apply makeup. Lots of makeup. Far too much makeup. She mussed up her hair a bit and rolled up her jeans cuffs. When she finished she smiled at Myron.

"How do I look?" she asked.

Even Myron felt a little weak at the knees. "You're going to walk in there looking like that?"

"That's how everyone in there dresses."

"But everyone doesn't look like you," he said.

"Oh, my, my," Esperanza said. "A compliment."

"I meant, like a chorus dancer in *West Side Story*."

" 'A boy like that,' " Esperanza sang, " 'he keel your brother, forget that boy, go find another—' "

"If I do make you a partner," Myron said, "don't dress like this at board meetings."

"Deal," Esperanza said. "Can I go now?"

"First call me on the cellular now. I want to make sure I can hear everything that goes on."

She nodded, dialed the phone. He picked it up. They tested the connection.

"Don't go playing hero," he said. "Just find out if he's there. Something gets out of hand, you get out of there pronto."

"Okay."

"And we should have a code word. Something you say if you need me."

Esperanza nodded, feigning seriousness. "If I say the words premature ejaculation, it means I want you to come."

"So to speak."

Esperanza and even Mindy groaned.

Myron reached into his glove compartment. He snapped it open and pulled out a gun. He was not going to be caught unprepared again. "Go," he said.

Esperanza hopped out of the car and crossed the street. A black Corvette with flame decals on the hood and an extra-*vrooming* engine pulled up. A gold-chain-enmeshed primate raced the engine and leaned his head out the window. He smiled greasily at Esperanza. He hit the gas again, giving off a few more deep *vroom*s. Esperanza looked at the car, then at the driver. "Sorry to hear about your penis," she deadpanned.

The car drove off. Esperanza shrugged and waved at Myron. It wasn't an original line, but it never failed her.

"God, I love that woman," Myron said.

"She's, like, totally hot," Mindy agreed. "I wish I looked like her."

"You should wish to be like her," he corrected.

"What's the difference? She must, like, really work out, right?"

Esperanza entered the Parker Inn. The first thing that hit her was the smell—a pungent combination of dried vomit and body odor, only less olfactorily pleasing. She wrinkled her nose and continued inside. The floor was hardwood with lots of sawdust. The light was dingy, coming off the pool table ceiling fixtures that were supposed to look like imitation Tiffany lamps. The crowd was probably two-to-one men over women. Everyone was dressed —in a word—cheesy.

Esperanza looked around the room. Then she spoke out loud so that Myron would hear her through the phone. "About a hundred guys in here fit your description," she said. "It's like asking me to find an implant in a strip club."

Myron's phone was on mute, but she'd bet he was laughing. An implant at a strip club. Not bad, she thought. Not bad at all.

So now what?

People were staring at her, but she was used to that. Three seconds passed before a man approached her. He had a long, kinky beard; bits of coagulated food were lodged in it. He smiled toothlessly, looked her up and down unapologetically.

"I've got a great tongue," he said to her.

"Now all you need is some teeth."

She pushed past him and made her way to the bar. Two seconds later, a guy jumped toward her. He wore a cowboy hat. Cowboy hat. Philadelphia. What's wrong with this picture?

"Hey, sweetheart, don't I know you?"

Esperanza nodded. "Another line that smooth," she said, "and I may start to undress."

The cowboy whooped it up like it was the funniest thing he had ever heard. "No, little darling, I'm not handing you a line. I'm serious here. . . ." His voice sort of drifted off. "Holy shit!" the man cried. "It's Little Pocahontas! The Indian Princess! You're Little Pocahontas, right? Don't deny it now, darling. It's you! I can't believe it!"

Myron was probably laughing his ass off right now.

"Nice to see you," Esperanza said. "Thank you very much for remembering."

"Shit, Bobby, take a lookie here. It's Little Pocahontas! Remember? That hot little vixen on FLOW?"

FLOW, of course, stood for the "Fabulous Ladies Of Wrestling." The organization's original name had been the "Beautiful Ladies Of Wrestling," but once they became popular enough for television, the networks insisted on a new acronym.

"Where?" Another man approached, eyes wide and drunk and happy. "Holy shit, you're right! It's her! It's really her!"

"Hey, thanks for the memories, fellas, but—"

"I remember this one time, you were fighting Tatiana the Siberian Husky? Remember that one? Shit, my hard-on nearly poked a hole clean through my bedroom window."

Esperanza hoped to file that little tidbit under Too Much Information.

An enormous bartender came over. He looked like the pullout centerfold for *Leather Biker Monthly*. Extra big and extra scary. He had long hair, a long scar, and tattoos of snakes slithering up both arms. He shot the two men a glare and—poof—they were gone. Like the glare had evaporated them. Then he turned his eyes toward Esperanza. She met the glare and gave him one back. Neither backed down.

"Lady, what the fuck are you?" he asked.

"Is that a new way of asking what I'm drinking?"

"No." The mutual glaring continued. He leaned two massive snake-arms on the bar. "You're too good-looking to be a cop," he said. "And you're too good-looking to be hanging out in this toilet."

"Thanks, I guess," Esperanza said. "And you are?"

"Hal," he said. "I own this toilet."

"Hi, Hal."

"Hi back. Now what the fuck do you want?"

"I'm trying to score some blow," she said.

"Nah," Hal said with a shake of his head. "You'd go

to Spic City for that. Buy it from one of your own kind, no offense.'' He leaned even closer now. Esperanza couldn't help but wonder if Hal would be a good match for Big Cyndi. She liked big biker guys. ''Let's cut the crap, sweetheart. What do you want?''

Esperanza decided to try the direct approach. ''I'm looking for a sliver of scum named Tito. People call him Tit. Skinny, shaved head—''

''Yeah, yeah, I *might* know him. How much?''

''Fifty bucks.''

Hal made a scoffing sound. ''You want me to sell out a customer for fifty bucks?''

''A hundred.''

''Hundred and fifty. The deadbeat sack of shit owes me money.''

''Deal,'' she said.

''Show me the money.''

Esperanza took the bills out of her wallet. Hal reached it for it, but she pulled back. ''You first,'' she said.

''I don't know where he lives,'' Hal said. ''He and his goose-stepping faggots come in every night except Wednesdays and Saturdays.''

''Why not Wednesdays and Saturdays?'' she asked.

''How the fuck am I supposed to know? Bingo night and Saturday night mass maybe. Or maybe they all do a circle jerk crying 'Heil, Hitler' when they shoot off. How the fuck do I know?''

''What's his real name?''

''I don't know.''

She looked around the bar. ''Any of the boys here know?''

''Nah,'' Hal said. ''Tit always comes in with the same limp-dicked crew and they leave together. They don't talk to no one else. It's *verboten*.''

''Sounds like you don't like him.''

"He's a stupid punk. They all are. Assholes who blame the fact that they're genetic mutations on other people."

"So why do you let them hang out here?"

"Because unlike them, I know that this is the U.S. of A. You can do what you want. Anyone is welcome here. Black, white, Spic, Jap, whatever. Even stupid punks."

Esperanza almost smiled. Sometimes you find tolerance in the strangest places. "What else?"

"That's all I know. It's Saturday night. They'll be here tomorrow."

"Fine," Esperanza said. She ripped the bills in half. "I'll give you the other half of the bills tomorrow."

Hal reached out his big hand and closed it over her forearm. His glare grew a little meaner. "Don't be too smart, hot legs," he said slowly. "I can yell *gang bang* and have you on your back on a pool table in five seconds. You give the hundred and fifty now. Then you rip another hundred in half to keep my mouth shut. You got it?"

Her heart was beating wildly in her chest. "Got it," she said. She handed him the other half of the bills. Then she took out another hundred, ripped it, and handed it to him.

"Get out, sweet buns. Like now."

He didn't have to tell her twice.

Chapter 20

There was nothing else they could do tonight. To approach the Squires estate would be foolhardy, at best. He couldn't call or contact the Coldrens. It was too late to try to reach Lloyd Rennart's widow. And lastly—and perhaps most important—Myron was bone-tired.

So he spent the evening at the guest house with his two best friends in the world. Myron, Win, and Esperanza lay sprawled on separate couches like Dalí clocks. They wore T-shirts and shorts and buried themselves deep within puffy pillows. Myron drank too much Yoo-Hoo; Esperanza drank too much diet Coke; Win drank almost enough Brooklyn Lager (Win drank only lager, never beer). There were pretzels and Fritos and Ruffles and freshly delivered pizza. The lights were out. The big-screen television was on. Win had recently taped a whole bunch of *Odd Couple* episodes. They were on the fourth in a row. The best thing about the *Odd Couple*, Myron surmised, was the consistency. They never had a weak episode—how many shows could say that?

Myron bit into a slice of pizza. He needed this. He had barely slept in the millennium since he'd first encountered the Coldrens (in reality, it only had been yesterday). His brain was fried; his nerves were fraying like overused floss. Sitting with Win and Esperanza, their faces blue-lit by the picture tube, Myron felt true contentment.

"It's simply not true," Win insisted.

"No way," Esperanza agreed, tossing down a Ring-Ding.

"I'm telling you," Myron said. "Jack Klugman is wearing a hairpiece."

Win's voice was firm. "Oscar Madison would never wear a rug. Never, I say. Felix, maybe. But Oscar? It simply cannot be."

"It is," Myron said. "That's a hairpiece."

"You're still thinking of the last episode," Esperanza said. "The one with Howard Cosell."

"Yes, that's it," Win agreed with a snap of his fingers. "Howard Cosell. He wore a hairpiece."

Myron looked up the ceiling, exasperated. "I'm not thinking of Howard Cosell. I know the difference between Howard Cosell and Jack Klugman. I'm telling you. Klugman is sporting a rug."

"Where's the line?" Win challenged, pointing at the screen. "I cannot see a break or a line or a discoloration. And I'm usually quite good at spotting lines."

"I don't see it either," Esperanza added, squinting.

"That's two against one," Win said.

"Fine," Myron said. "Don't believe me."

"He had his own hair on *Quincy*," Esperanza said.

"No," Myron said, "he didn't."

"Two against one," Win repeated. "Majority rules."

"Fine," Myron repeated. "Wallow in ignorance."

On the screen, Felix fronted for a band called Felix Unger and the Sophisticatos. They rambled through an up-tempo number with the repeated phrase "Stumbling all around." Kinda catchy.

"What makes you so sure it's a rug?" Esperanza asked.

"*The Twilight Zone*," Myron said.

"Come again?"

"*The Twilight Zone.* Jack Klugman was in at least two episodes."

"Ah, yes," Win said. "Now, don't tell me, let me see if I remember." He paused, tapping his lip with his index finger. "The one with the little boy Pip. Played by . . . ?" Win knew the answer. Life with his friends was an ever-continuing game of Useless Trivia.

"Bill Mumy." It was Esperanza.

Win nodded. "Whose most famous role was . . . ?"

"Will Robinson," Esperanza said. "*Lost in Space.*"

"Remember Judy Robinson?" Win sighed. "Quite the Earth babe, no?"

"Except," Esperanza interjected, "what was up with her clothes? Kmart velour sweaters for space travel? Who came up with that one?"

"And we cannot forget the effervescent Dr. Zachery Smith," Win added. "The first gay character on series TV."

"Scheming, conniving, gutless—with a hint of pedophilia," Esperanza said with a shake of her head. "He set back the movement twenty years."

Win grabbed another slice of pizza. The pizza box was white with red-and-green lettering and had the classic caricature of a heavy-set chef twirling a thin mustache with his finger. The box read—and this is absolutely true:

> *Whether it's a pizza or submarine,*
> *We buy the best,*
> *To prepare the best,*
> *And leave it to you for the rest.*

Wordsworth.

"I don't recall Mr. Klugman's second *Twilight Zone*," Win said.

"The one with the pool player," Myron answered. "Jonathan Winters was in it too."

"Ah, yes," Win said with a serious nod. "Now I remember. Jonathan Winters's ghost shoots pool against Mr. Klugman's character. For bragging rights or some such thing."

"Correct answer."

"So what do those two *Twilight Zone* episodes have to do with Mr. Klugman's hair?"

"You got them on tape?"

Win paused. "I believe that I do. I taped the last *Twilight Zone* marathon. One of those episodes is bound to be on it."

"Let's find it," Myron said.

It took the three of them almost twenty minutes of sifting through his vast video collection before they finally found the episode with Bill Mumy. Win put it in the VCR and reclaimed his couch. They watched in silence.

Several minutes later, Esperanza said, "I'll be damned."

A black-and-white Jack Klugman was calling out "Pip," the name of his dead son, his tormented cries chasing a tender apparition from his past. The scene was quite moving, but also very much beside the point. The key factor, of course, was that even though this episode predated the *Odd Couple* by some ten years, Jack Klugman's hairline was in a serious state of retreat.

Win shook his head. "You are good," he said in a hushed voice. "So very good." He looked at Myron. "I am truly humbled to be in your presence."

"Don't feel bad," Myron said. "You're special in your own way."

This was about as heavy as the conversation got.

They laughed. They joked. They made fun of one another. No one talked about a kidnapping or the Coldrens or business or money matters or landing Tad Crispin or the severed finger of a sixteen-year-old boy.

Win dozed off first. Then Esperanza. Myron tried to call Jessica again, but there was no answer. No surprise. Jessica often didn't sleep well. Taking walks, she claimed, inspired her. He heard her voice on the machine and felt something inside him plunge. When the beep came on, he left a message:

"I love you," he said. "I will always love you."

He hung up. He crawled back onto the couch and pulled the cover up to his neck.

Chapter 21

When Myron arrived at Merion Golf Club the next morning, he wondered briefly if Linda Coldren had told Jack about the severed finger. She had. By the third hole, Jack had already dropped three strokes off his lead. His complexion was cartoon Casper. His eyes were as vacant as the Bates Motel, his shoulders slumped like bags of wet peat moss.

Win frowned. "Guess that finger thing is bothering him."

Mr. Insight.

"That sensitivity workshop," Myron said, "it's really starting to pay off."

"I did not expect Jack's collapse to be so total."

"Win, his son's finger was chopped off by a kidnapper. That's the kind of thing that could distract someone."

"I guess." Win didn't sound convinced. He turned away and started heading up the fairway. "Did Crispin show you the numbers in his Zoom deal?"

"Yes," Myron said.

"And?"

"And he got robbed."

Win nodded. "Not much you can do about it now."

"Plenty I can do about it," Myron said. "It's called renegotiate."

"Crispin signed a deal," Win said.

"So?"

"Please do not tell me that you want him to back out of it."

"I didn't say I wanted him to back out. I said I wanted to renegotiate."

" 'Renegotiate,' " Win repeated as though the word tasted vinegary. He continued trudging up the fairway. "How come an athlete who performs poorly never renegotiates? How come you never see a player who has a terrible season restructure his deal downward?"

"Good point," Myron said. "But, you see, I have this job description. It reads something like this: Get the most money I can for a client."

"And ethics be damned."

"Whoa, where did that come from? I may search for legal loopholes, but I always play by the rules."

"You sound like a criminal defense attorney," Win said.

"Ooo, now that's a low blow," Myron said.

The crowd was getting caught up in the unfolding drama in an almost disturbing way. The whole experience was like watching a car crash in super slow motion. You were horrified; you stared; and part of you almost cheered the misfortune of a fellow human being. You gaped, wondering about the outcome, almost hoping the crash would be fatal. Jack Coldren was slowly dying. His heart was crumbling like brown leaves caught in a closed fist. You saw it all happening. And you wanted it to continue.

On the fifth hole Myron and Win met up with Norm Zuckerman and Esme Fong. They were both on edge, especially Esme, but then again she had a hell of a lot riding on this round. On the eighth hole they watched Jack miss an easy putt. Stroke by stroke, the lead shrank from insurmountable to comfortable to nail-biting.

On the back nine Jack managed to control the hemorrhaging a bit. He continued to play poorly, but with only three holes left to play, Jack was still hanging on to a two-stroke lead. Tad Crispin was applying pressure, but it would still take a fairly major gaffe on Jack Coldren's part for Tad to win.

Then it happened.

The sixteenth hole. The same hazard that had laid waste to Jack's dream twenty-three years ago. Both men started off fine. They hit good tee-shots to what Win called "a slightly offset fairway." Uh-huh. But on Jack's second shot, disaster struck. He came over the top and left the sucker short. Way short.

The ball landed in the stone quarry.

The crowd gasped. Myron watched in horror. Jack had done the unthinkable. Again.

Norm Zuckerman nudged Myron. "I'm moist," he said giddily. "Swear to God, I'm moist in my nether regions. Go ahead, feel for yourself."

"I'll take your word for it, Norm."

Myron turned to Esme Fong. Her face lit up. "Me too," she said.

A more intriguing proposal but still no sale.

Jack Coldren barely reacted, as if some internal wiring had shorted out. He was not waving a white flag, but it looked like he should have been.

Tad Crispin took advantage. He hit a fine approach shot and was left with an eight-foot putt that would give him the lead. As young Tad stood over the ball, the silence in the gallery was overwhelming—not just the crowd, but it was as if the nearby traffic and overhead planes and even the grass, the trees, the very course had all aligned themselves against Jack Coldren.

This was big-time pressure. And Tad Crispin responded in a big way.

When the putt dropped into the cup, there was no polite golf clap. The crowd erupted like Vesuvius in the last days. The sound spilled forward in a powerful wave, warming the young newcomer and sweeping aside the dying warhorse. Everyone seemed to want this. Everyone wanted to crown Tad Crispin and behead Jack Coldren. The young handsome man against the ruffled veteran—it was like the golf equivalent of the Nixon-Kennedy debates.

"What a yip master," someone said.

"A major case of the yips," another agreed.

Myron looked a question at Win.

"Yip," Win said. "The latest euphemism for *choke*."

Myron nodded. There was nothing worse you could call an athlete. It was okay to be untalented or to screw up or to have an off day—but not to choke. Never to choke. Chokers were gutless. Chokers had their very manhood questioned. Being called a choker was tantamount to standing naked in front of a beautiful woman while she pointed and laughed.

Er, or so Myron imagined.

He spotted Linda Coldren in a private grandstand tent overlooking the eighteenth hole. She wore sunglasses and a baseball cap pulled low. Myron looked up at her. She did not look back. Her expression was one of mild confusion, like she was working on a math word problem or trying to recall the name behind a familiar face. For some reason, the expression troubled Myron. He stayed in her line of vision, hoping she'd signal to him. She didn't.

Tad Crispin took a one-stroke lead into the final hole. The other golfers were finished for the day, many coming out and standing around the eighteenth green to watch the final act of golf's greatest collapse.

Win started playing Mr. Merion. "The eighteenth hole is a four hundred and sixty-five yard, par four," he began. "The tee is in the stone quarry. You need to hit it up the hill—a two-hundred yard carry."

"I see," Myron said. Huh?

Tad was up first. He hit what looked like a good, solid drive. The gallery did that polite golf-clap thing. Jack Coldren took his turn. His shot climbed higher, seemingly pulling itself against the elements.

"Very nice golf shot," Win said. "Super."

Myron turned to Esme Fong. "What happens if it ends in a tie? Sudden death?"

Esme shook her head. "Other tournaments, yes. But not at the Open. They make both players come back to-morrow and play a whole round."

"All eighteen holes?"

"Yes."

Tad's second shot left him just short of the green.

"A solid golf shot," Win informed him. "Sets him up nicely for the par."

Jack took out an iron and approached the ball.

Win smiled at Myron. "Recognize this?"

Myron squinted. Déjà vu swarmed in. He was no golf fan, but from this angle even he recognized the spot. Win kept the picture on his credenza at the office. Almost every golf book or golf pub or golf whatever had the photograph. Ben Hogan had stood exactly where Jack Coldren now stood. In 1950 or thereabouts. Hogan had stroked the famous one-iron that had made him the U.S. Open champion. It was the golf equivalent of "Havlicek stole the ball!"

As Jack took his practice swing, Myron could not help but wonder about old ghosts and strange possibilities.

"He has an almost impossible task," Win said.

"Why's that?"

"The pin placement is brutal today. Behind that yawn-ing bunker."

A yawning bunker? Myron did not bother asking.

Jack fired a long iron at the green. He reached it, but

as Win had predicted, he still left himself a good twenty-plus feet away. Tad Crispin took his third shot, a beautiful little chip that came to rest within six inches of the hole. Tad tapped it in for par. That meant that Jack had no chance of winning in regulation. The best he could do was force a tie. If he made this putt.

"A twenty-two-foot putt," Win said with a grim shake of the head. "No chance."

He had said twenty-two feet—not twenty-one feet or twenty-three feet. Twenty-two feet. Win could tell from a quick glance from over fifty yards away. Golfers. Go figure.

Jack Coldren strolled to the green. He bent down, picked up his ball, put down a marker, picked up the marker, put down the ball again in the exact same spot. Myron shook his head. Golfers.

Jack looked very far away, like he was putting from New Jersey. Think about it. He was twenty-two feet away from a hole four-and-a-quarter inches in diameter. Break out a calculator. Do the math.

Myron, Win, Esme, and Norm waited. This was it. The coup de grâce. The part where the matador finally drives the long, thin blade home.

But as Jack studied the break in the green, some sort of transformation seemed to take place. The fleshy features hardened. The eyes became focused and steely and —though it was probably Myron's imagination—a hint of yesterday's "eye" seemed to flint up in them. Myron looked behind him. Linda Coldren had spotted the change too. For a brief moment she let her attention slip and her eyes sought out Myron's, as if for confirmation. Before Myron could do more than meet her gaze, she looked away.

Jack Coldren took his time. He read the green from several angles. He squatted down, his club pointing in

front of him the way golfers do. He talked to Diane Hoffman at some length. But once he addressed the ball, there
was no hesitation. The club went back like a metronome
and kissed the ball hard on the way down.

The tiny white sphere carrying all of Jack Coldren's
dreams circled toward the hole like an eagle seeking its
prey. There was no question in Myron's mind. The pull
was almost magnetic. Several seemingly infinite seconds
later, the tiny white sphere dropped to the bottom of the
hole with an audible clink. For a moment there was silence and then another eruption, this one more from surprise than exhilaration. Myron found himself applauding
wildly.

Jack had done it. He'd tied the score.

Over the crowd's cacophony, Norm Zuckerman said,
"This is beautiful, Esme. The whole world will be watching tomorrow. The exposure will be incredible."

Esme looked stunned. "Only if Tad wins."

"What do you mean?"

"What if Tad loses?"

"Hey, second place at the U.S. Open?" Norm said,
palms up to the sky. "Not bad, Esme. Not bad at all.
That's where we were this morning. Before all this happened. Nothing lost, nothing gained."

Esme Fong shook her head. "If Tad loses now, he
doesn't come in second place. He's just a loser. He would
have gone one-on-one with a famed choke-artist and lost.
Outchoked the ultimate choker. It'll be worse than the
Buffalo Bills."

Norm made a scoffing noise. "You worry too much,
Esme," he said, but his usual bluster had tapered off.

The crowd began to dissipate, but Jack Coldren just
stood in the same position, still holding his putter. He did
not celebrate. He did not move, even when Diane Hoffman began to pound his back. His features seemed to lose

their tone again, his eyes suddenly more glazed than ever. It was as if the effort of that one stroke had drained every ounce of energy, karma, strength, life force right out of him.

Or maybe, Myron wondered, there was something else at work here. Something deeper. Maybe that last moment of magic had given Jack some new insight—some new life clarity—as to the relative, long-term importance of this tournament. Everyone else saw a man who had just sunk the most important putt of his life. But maybe Jack Coldren saw a man standing alone wondering what the big deal was and if his only son was still alive.

Linda Coldren appeared on the fringe of the green. She tried to look enthusiastic as she approached her husband and dutifully kissed him. A television crew followed her. Long-lensed cameras clicked and their flashes strobed. A sportscaster came up to them, microphone at the ready. Linda and Jack both managed to smile.

But behind the smiles, Linda looked almost wary. And Jack looked positively terrified.

Chapter 22

Esperanza had come up with a plan. "Lloyd Rennart's widow's name is Francine. She's an artist."

"What kind?"

"I don't know. Painting, sculpture—what's the difference?"

"Just curious. Go ahead."

"I called her up and said that you were a reporter for the *Coastal Star*. It's a local paper in the Spring Lake area. You are doing a lifestyle piece on several local artists."

Myron nodded. It was a good plan. People rarely refuse the chance to be interviewed for self-promoting puff pieces.

Win had already gotten Myron's car windows fixed. How, Myron had no idea. The rich. They're different.

The ride took about two hours. It was eight o'clock Sunday night. Tomorrow Linda and Jack Coldren would drop off the ransom money. How would it be done? A meeting in a public place? A go-between? For the umpteenth time, he wondered how Linda and Jack and Chad were faring. He took out the photograph of Chad. He imagined what Chad's young, carefree face must have looked like when his finger was being severed off. He wondered if the kidnapper had used a sharp knife or a cleaver or an axe or a saw or what.

He wondered what it felt like.

Francine Rennart lived in Spring Lake Heights, not

Spring Lake. There was a big difference. Spring Lake was on the Atlantic Ocean and about as beautiful a shore town as you could hope to find. There was plenty of sun, very little crime, and almost no ethnics. It was a problem, actually. The wealthy town was nicknamed the Irish Riviera. That meant no good restaurants. None. The town's idea of *haute cuisine* was food served on a plate rather than in a basket. If you craved exotic, you drove to a Chinese take-out place whose eclectic menu included such rare delicacies as chicken chow mein, and for the especially adventurous, chicken *lo* mein. This was the problem with some of these towns. They needed some Jews or gays or something to spice things up, to add a bit of theater and a couple of interesting bistros.

One man's opinion.

If Spring Lake was an old movie, then Spring Lake Heights would be the other side of the tracks. There weren't slums or anything like that. The area where the Rennarts lived was a sort of tract-house suburbia—the middle ground between a trailer park and circa 1967 split-level colonials. Solid Americana.

Myron knocked on the door. A woman he guessed was Francine Rennart pushed open the screen. Her ready smile was shadowed by a daunting beak of a nose. Her burnt-auburn hair was wavy and undisciplined, like she'd just taken out her curlers but hadn't had time to comb it out.

"Hi," Myron said.

"You must be from the *Coastal Star*."

"That's right." Myron stuck out his hand. "I'm Bernie Worley." Scoop Bolitar uses a disguise.

"Your timing is perfect," Francine said. "I've just started a new exhibit."

The living room furniture didn't have plastic on it, but it should have. The couch was off-green. The Bar-

caLounger—a real, live BarcaLounger—was maroon
with duct tape mending rips. The console television had
rabbit ears on top. Collectors plates Myron had seen advertised in *Parade* were neatly hung on a wall.

"My studio's in the back," she said.

Francine Rennart led him to a big addition off the
kitchen. It was a sparsely furnished room with white
walls. A couch with a spring sticking out of it sat in the
middle of the room. A kitchen chair leaned against it. So
did a rolled-up carpet. There was something that looked
like a blanket draped over the top in a triangular pattern.
Four bathroom wastepaper baskets lined the back wall.
Myron guessed that she must have a leak.

Myron waited for Francine Rennart to ask him to sit
down. She didn't. She stood with him in the entranceway
and said, "Well?"

He smiled, his brain stuck in a cusp where he was not
dumb enough to say, "Well what?" but not smart enough
to know what the hell she was talking about. So Myron
froze there with his anchorman-waiting-to-go-to-com-
mercial grin.

"You like it?" Francine Rennart asked.

Still the grin. "Uh-huh."

"I know it's not for everybody."

"Hmm." Scoop Bolitar engages in sparkling repartee.

She watched his face for a moment. He kept up the
idiot grin. "You don't know anything about installation
art, do you?"

He shrugged. "Got me." Myron shifted gears on the
fly. "Thing is, I don't do features normally. I'm a sports
writer. That's my beat." Beat. Note the authentic reporter
lingo. "But Tanya—she's my boss—she needed somebody to handle a lifestyle piece. And when Jennifer called
in sick, well, the job fell to me. It's a story on a variety of
local artists—painters, sculptors . . ." He couldn't think

of any other kind of artist, so he stopped. "Anyway, maybe you could explain a little bit about what it is you do."

"My art is about space and concepts. It's about creating a mood."

Myron nodded. "I see."

"It's not art, per se, in the classic sense. It goes beyond that. It's the next step in the artistic evolutionary process."

More nods. "I see."

"Everything in this exhibit has a purpose. Where I place the couch. The texture of the carpeting. The color of the walls. The way the sunlight shines in through the windows. The blend creates a specific ambience."

Oh, boy.

Myron motioned at the, uh, art. "So how do you sell something like this?"

She frowned. "You don't sell it."

"Pardon?"

"Art is not about money, Mr. Worley. True artists do not put a monetary value on their work. Only hacks do that."

Yeah, like Michelangelo and Da Vinci, those hacks. "But what do you do with this?" he asked. "I mean, do you just keep the room like this?"

"No. I change it around. I bring in other pieces. I create something new."

"And what happens to this?"

She shook her head. "Art is not about permanence. Life is temporary. Why shouldn't art be the same?"

Oooookay.

"Is there a name for this art?"

"Installation art. But we do not like labels."

"How long have you been an, uh, installation artist?"

"I've been working on my masters at the New York Art Institute for two years."

He tried not to look shocked. "You go to school for this?"

"Yes. It's a very competitive program."

Yeah, Myron thought, like a TV/VCR repair course advertised by Sally Struthers.

They finally moved back into the living room. Myron sat on the couch. Gently. Might be art. He waited to be offered a cookie. Might be art too.

"You still don't get it, do you?"

Myron shrugged. "Maybe if you threw in a poker table and some dogs."

She laughed. Mr. Self-Deprecation strikes again. "Fair enough," she said.

"Let me shift gears for a moment, if I may," Myron said. "How about a little something on Francine Rennart, the person?" Scoop Bolitar mines the personal angle.

She looked a bit wary, but she said, "Okay, ask away."

"Are you married?"

"No." Her voice was like a slamming door.

"Divorced?"

"No."

Scoop Bolitar loves an garrulous interviewee. "I see," he said. "Then I guess you have no children."

"I have a son."

"How old is he?"

"Seventeen. His name is Larry."

A year older than Chad Coldren. Interesting. "Larry Rennart?"

"Yes."

"Where does he go to school?"

"Right here at Manasquan High. He's going to be a senior."

"How nice." Myron risked it, nibbled on a cookie. "Maybe I could interview him too."

"My son?"

"Sure. I'd love a quote from the prodigal son on how proud he is of his mom, of how he supports what she's doing, that kinda thing." Scoop Bolitar grows pathetic.

"He's not home."

"Oh?"

He waited for her to elaborate. Nothing.

"Where is Larry?" Myron tried. "Is he staying with his father?"

"His father is dead."

Finally. Myron put on the big act. "Oh, sheesh, I'm sorry. I didn't . . . I mean, you being so young and all. I just didn't consider the possibility that . . ." Scoop Bolitar as Robert DeNiro.

"It's okay," Francine Rennart said.

"I feel awful."

"No need to."

"Have you been widowed long?"

She tilted her head. "Why do you ask?"

"Background," he said.

"Background?"

"Yes. I think it's crucial to understanding Francine Rennart the artist. I want to explore how being widowed affected you and your art." Scoop Bolitar shovels it good.

"I've only been a widow a short time."

Myron motioned toward the, uh, studio. "So when you created this work, did your husband's death have any bearing on the outcome? On the color of the wastebaskets maybe. Or the way you rolled up that rug."

"No, not really."

"How did your husband die?"

"Why would you—"

"Again, I think it's important for digesting the entire

artistic statement. Was it an accident, for example? The kind of death that makes you ponder fickle fate. Was it a long illness? Seeing a loved one suffer—''

"He committed suicide."

Myron feigned aghast. "I'm so sorry," he said.

Her breathing was funny now, her chest giving off short hitches. As Myron watched her, an awful pang struck him deep in the chest. Slow down, he told himself. Stop focusing solely on Chad Coldren and remember that this woman, too, has suffered. She had been married to this man. She had loved him and lived with him and built a life with him and had a child with him.

And after all that, he had chosen to end his life rather than spend it with her.

Myron swallowed. Fiddling with her pathos like this was, at best, unfair. Belittling her artistic expression because he did not understand it was cruel. Myron did not like himself much right now. For a moment he debated just going away—the odds that any of this had anything to do with the case were so remote—but then again, he couldn't simply forget a sixteen-year-old boy with a missing finger, either.

"Were you married long?"

"Almost twenty years," she said softly.

"I don't mean to intrude, but may I ask you his name?"

"Lloyd," she said. "Lloyd Rennart."

Myron narrowed his eyes as though scanning for a memory. "Why does that name ring a bell?"

Francine Rennart shrugged. "He co-owned a tavern in Neptune City. The Rusty Nail."

"Of course," Myron said. "Now I remember. He hung out there a lot, right?"

"Yes."

"My God, I met the man. Lloyd Rennart. Now I remember. He used to teach golf, right? Was in the big time for a while.''

Francine Rennart's face slid closed like a car window. ''How do you know that?''

''The Rusty Nail. And I'm a huge golf fan. A real duffer, but I follow it like some people follow the Bible.'' He was flailing, but maybe he was getting somewhere. ''Your husband caddied Jack Coldren, right? A long time ago. We talked about it a bit.''

She swallowed hard. ''What did he say?''

''Say?''

''About being a caddie.''

''Oh, not much. We mostly talked about some of our favorite golfers. Nicklaus, Trevino, Palmer. Some great courses. Merion mostly.''

''No,'' she said.

''Ma'am?''

Her voice was firm. ''Lloyd never talked about golf.''

Scoop Bolitar steps in it in a big way.

Francine Rennart skewered him with her eyes. ''You can't be from the insurance company. I didn't even try to make a claim.'' She pondered that for a moment. Then: ''Wait a second. You said you're a sports writer. That's why you're here. Jack Coldren is making a comeback, so you want to do a where-are-they-now story.''

Myron shook his head. Shame flushed his face. Enough, he thought. He took a few deep breaths and said, ''No.''

''Then who are you?''

''My name is Myron Bolitar. I'm a sports agent.''

She was confused now. ''What do you want with me?''

He searched for the words, but they all sounded lame. ''I'm not sure. It's probably nothing, a complete waste of time. You're right. Jack Coldren is making a comeback.

But it's like . . . it's like the past is haunting him. Terrible things are happening to him and his family. And I just thought—''

"Thought what?" she snapped. "That Lloyd came back from the dead to claim vengeance?"

"Did he want vengeance?"

"What happened at Merion," she said. "It was a long time ago. Before I met him."

"Was he over it?"

Francine Rennart thought about that for a while. "It took a long time," she said at last. "Lloyd couldn't get any golf work after what happened. Jack Coldren was still the fair-haired boy and no one wanted to cross him. Lloyd lost all his friends. He started drinking too much." She hesitated. "There was an accident."

Myron stayed still, watching Francine Rennart draw breaths.

"He lost control of his car." Her voice was robot-like now. "It slammed into another car. In Narberth. Near where he used to live." She stopped and then looked at him. "His first wife died on impact."

Myron felt a chill rush through him. "I didn't know," he said softly.

"It was a long time ago, Mr. Bolitar. We met not long after that. We fell in love. He stopped drinking. He bought the tavern right away—I know, I know, it sounds weird. An alcoholic owning a bar. But for him, it worked. We bought this house too. I—I thought everything was okay."

Myron waited a beat. Then he asked, "Did your husband give Jack Coldren the wrong club on purpose?"

The question did not seem to surprise her. She plucked at the buttons on her blouse and took her time before answering. "The truth is, I don't know. He never talked about this incident. Not even with me. But there was something there. It may have been guilt, I don't know." She smoothed her skirt with both hands. "But all of this is irrelevant, Mr. Bolitar. Even if Lloyd did harbor ill feelings toward Jack, he's dead."

Myron tried to think of a tactful way of asking, but none came to him. "Did they find his body, Mrs. Rennart?"

His words landed like a heavyweight's hook. "It-it was a deep crevasse," Francine Rennart stammered. "There was no way . . . the police said they couldn't send anyone down there. It was too dangerous. But Lloyd couldn't have survived. He wrote a note. He left his clothes there. I still have his passport. . . ." Her voice faded away.

Myron nodded. "Of course," he said. "I understand."

But as he showed himself out, he was pretty sure that he understood nothing.

Chapter 23

Tito the Crusty Nazi never showed at the Parker Inn.

Myron sat in a car across the street. As usual, he hated surveillance. Boredom didn't set in this time, but the devastated face of Francine Rennart kept haunting him. He wondered about the long-term effects of his visit. The woman had been privately dealing with her grief, locking her private demons in a back closet, and then Myron had gone and blown the hinges off the door. He had tried to comfort her. But in the end what could he say?

Closing time. Still no sign of Tito. His two buddies—Beneath and Escape—were another matter. They'd arrived at ten-thirty. At one A.M. they both exited. Escape was on crutches—the aftertaste, Myron was sure, of the nasty side kick to the knee. Myron smiled. It was a small victory, but you take them where you can.

Beneath had his arm slung around a woman's neck. She had a dye job from the planet Bad Bottle and basically looked like the type of woman who might go for a tattoo-infested skinhead—or to say the same thing in a slightly different way, she looked like a regular on the *Jerry Springer* show.

Both men stopped to urinate on the outside wall. Beneath actually kept his arm around the girl while emptying his bladder. Jesus. So many men peed on that wall that Myron wondered if there was a bathroom inside. The two men broke off. Beneath got into the passenger side of a Ford Mustang. Bad Bleach drove. Escape hobbled onto his own chariot, a motorcycle of some kind. He strapped the crutches onto the side. The two vehicles drove off in separate directions.

Myron decided to follow Escape. When in doubt, tail the one that's lame.

He kept far back and remained extra careful. Better to lose him than risk in the slightest way the possibility of being spotted. But the tail didn't last long. Three blocks down the road, Escape parked and headed into a shabby excuse for a house. The paint was peeling off in flakes the size of manhole covers. One of the support columns on the front porch had completely given way, so the front lip of the roof looked like it'd been ripped in half by some giant. The two upstairs windows were shattered like a drunk's eyes. The only possible reason that this dump hadn't been condemned was that the building inspector had not been able to stop laughing long enough to write up a summons.

Okay, so now what?

He waited an hour for something to happen. Nothing did. He had seen a bedroom light go on and off. That was it. The whole night was fast turning into a complete waste of time.

So what should he do?

He had no answer. So he changed the question around a bit.

What would Win do?

Win would weigh the risks. Win would realize that the situation was desperate, that a sixteen-year-old boy's finger had been chopped off like a bothersome thread. Rescuing him imminently was paramount.

Myron nodded to himself. Time to play Win.

He got out of the car. Making sure he kept out of sight, Myron circled around to the back of the dump. The yard was bathed in darkness. He trampled through grass long enough to hide Viet Cong, occasionally stumbling across a cement block or rake or a garbage can top. His shin got whacked twice; Myron had to bite down expletives.

The back door was boarded up with plywood. The window to its left, however, was open. Myron looked inside. Dark. He carefully climbed into the kitchen.

The smell of spoilage assaulted his nostrils. Flies buzzed about. For a moment, Myron feared that he might find a dead body, but this stink was different, more like the odor of a Dumpster at a 7-Eleven than anything in the rotting flesh family. He checked the other rooms, walking on tiptoes, avoiding the several spots on the floor where there was no floor. No sign of a kidnap victim. No sixteen-year-old boy tied up. No one at all. Myron followed the snoring to the room he had seen the light in earlier. Escape was on his back. Asleep. Without a care.

That was about to change.

Myron leapt into the air and landed hard on Escape's bad knee. Escape's eyes widened. His mouth opened in a scream that Myron cut off with a snap punch in the mouth. He moved quickly, straddling Escape's chest with his knees. He put his gun against the punk's cheek.

"Scream and die," Myron said.

Escape's eyes stayed wide. Blood trickled out of his mouth. He did not scream. Still, Myron was disappointed in himself. Scream and die? He couldn't come up with anything better than scream and die?

"Where is Chad Coldren?"

"Who?"

Myron jammed the gun barrel into the bleeding mouth. It hit teeth and nearly gagged the man. "Wrong answer."

Escape stayed silent. The punk was brave. Or maybe, just maybe, he couldn't talk because Myron had stuck a gun in his mouth. Smooth move, Bolitar. Keeping his face firm, Myron slowly slid the barrel out.

"Where is Chad Coldren?"

Escape gasped, caught his breath. "I swear to God, I don't know what you're talking about."

"Give me your hand."

"What?"

"Give me your hand."

Escape lifted his hand into view. Myron grabbed the wrist, turned it, and plucked out the middle finger. He curled it inward and flattened the folded digit against the palm. The kid bucked in pain. "I don't need a knife," Myron said. "I can just grind it into splinters."

"I don't know what you're talking about," the kid managed. "I swear!"

Myron squeezed a little harder. He did not want the bone to snap. Escape bucked some more. Smile a little, Myron thought. That's how Win does it. He has just a hint of a smile. Not much. You want your victim to think you are capable of anything, that you are completely cold, that you might even enjoy it. But you don't want him thinking you are a complete lunatic, out of control, a nut who would hurt you no matter what. Mine that middle ground.

"Please . . ."

"Where is Chad Coldren?"

"Look, I was there, okay? When he jumped you. Tit said he'd give me a hundred bucks. But I don't know no Chad Coldren."

"Where is Tit?" That name again.

"At his crib, I guess. I don't know."

Crib? The neo-Nazi was using dated urban street lingo. Life's ironies. "Doesn't Tito usually hang out with you guys at the Parker Inn?"

"Yeah, but he never showed."

"Was he supposed to?"

"I guess. It's not like we talk about it."

Myron nodded. "Where does he live?"

"Mountainside Drive. Right down the street. Third house on the left after you make the turn."

"If you're lying to me, I will come back here and slice your eyes out."

"I ain't lying. Mountainside Drive."

Myron pointed at the swastika tattoo with the barrel of the gun. "Why do you have this?"

"What?"

"The swastika, moron."

"I'm proud of my race, that's why."

"You want to put all the 'kikes' in gas chambers? Kill all the 'niggers'?"

"That ain't what we're about," he said. More confidence in his voice now that he was on well-rehearsed ground. "We're for the white man. We're tired of being overrun by niggers. We're sick of being trampled on by the Jews."

Myron nodded. "Well, by this Jew anyway," he said. In life, you take satisfaction where you can. "You know what duct tape is."

"Yeah."

"Gee, and I thought all neo-Nazis were dumb. Where is yours?"

Escape's eyes kinda narrowed. Like he was actually thinking. You could almost hear rusty gears churning. Then: "I don't have none."

"Too bad. I was going to use it to tie you up, so you couldn't warn Tito. But if you don't have any, I'll just have to shoot both your kneecaps."

"Wait!"

Myron used up almost the entire roll.

* * *

Tito was in the driver's seat of his pickup truck with the monster wheels.

He was also dead.

Two shots in the head, probably from very close range. Very bloody. There wasn't much of a head left anymore. Poor Tito. No head to match his no ass. Myron didn't laugh. Then again, gallows humor was not his forte.

Myron remained calm, probably because he was still in Win mode. No lights were on in the house. Tito's keys were still in the ignition. Myron took them and unlocked the front door. His search confirmed what he'd already guessed: no one was there.

Now what?

Ignoring the blood and brain matter, Myron went back to the truck and did a thorough search. Talk about not his forte. Myron reclicked the Win icon. Just protoplasm, he told himself. Just hemoglobin and platelets and enzymes and other stuff he'd forgotten since ninth-grade biology. The blocking worked enough to allow him to dig his hands under the seats and into the cushion crevices. His fingers located lots of crud. Old sandwiches. Wrappers from Wendy's. Crumbs of various shapes and sizes.

Fingernail clippings.

Myron looked at the dead body and shook his head. A little late for a scolding, but what the hell.

Then he hit pay dirt.

It was gold. It had a golf insignia on it. The initials *C.B.C.* were engraved lightly on the inside—Chad Buckwell Coldren.

It was a ring.

Myron's first thought was that Chad Coldren had cleverly taken it off and left it behind as a clue. Like in a movie. The young man was sending a message. If Myron was playing his part correctly, he would shake his head, toss the ring in the air, and mutter admiringly, "Smart kid."

Myron's second thought, however, was far more sobering.

The severed finger in Linda Coldren's car had been the ring finger.

Chapter 24

What to do?

Should he contact the police? Just leave? Make an anonymous call? What?

Myron had no idea. He had to think first and foremost of Chad Coldren. What risk would calling the police put the kid in?

No idea.

Christ, what a mess. He wasn't even supposed to be involved in this anymore. He was supposed to have—should have—stayed out. But now the proverbial doo-doo was hitting a plethora of proverbial fans. What should he do about finding a dead body? And what about Escape? Myron couldn't just leave him tied and gagged indefinitely. Suppose he vomited into the duct tape, for chrissake?

Okay, Myron, think. First, you should not—repeat, not —call the police. Someone else will discover the body. Or maybe he should make an anonymous call from a pay phone. That might work. But don't the police tape all incoming calls nowadays? They'd have his voice on tape. He could change it maybe. The rhythm and tempo. Make the tone a little deeper. Add an accent or something. Oh, right, like Meryl Streep. Tell the dispatcher to hurry because "the dingo's got ma baby."

Wait, hold the phone.

Think about what had just happened. Rewind to about an hour ago and see how it looks. Without provocation,

Myron had broken into a man's house. He had physically assaulted the man, threatened him in terrible ways, left him tied and gagged—all in the pursuit of Tito. Not long after this incident, the police get an anonymous call. They find Tito dead in his pickup.

Who is going to be the obvious suspect?

Myron Bolitar, sports agent of the terminally troubled. Damn.

So now what? No matter what Myron did at this stage —call or not call—he was going to be a suspect. Escape would be questioned. He would tell about Myron, and then Myron would look like the killer. Very simple equation when you thought about it.

So the question remained: What to do?

He couldn't worry about what conclusions the police might leap upon. He also couldn't worry about himself. The focus must be on Chad Coldren. What would be best for him? Hard to say. The safest bet, of course, would be to upset the apple cart as little as possible. Try not to make his presence in all this known.

Okay, good, that made sense.

So the answer was: Don't report it. Let the body lay where it was. Put the ring back in the seat cushion in case the police need it as evidence later. Good, this looked like a plan—a plan that seemed the best way of keeping the kid safe and also obeying the Coldrens' wishes.

Now, what about Escape?

Myron drove back to Escape's shack. He found Escape right where he left him—on his bed, hog-tied and gagged with gray duct tape. He looked half dead. Myron shook him. The punk started to, his face the green of seaweed. Myron ripped off the gag.

Escape retched and did a few dry heaves.

"I have a man outside," Myron said, removing more duct tape. "If he sees you move from this window, you will experience an agony very few have been forced to endure. Do you understand?''

Escape nodded quickly.

Experience an agony very few have been forced to endure. Jesus.

There was no phone in the house, so he didn't have to worry about that. With a few more harsh warnings lightly sprinkled with torture clichés—including Myron's personal favorite, "Before I'm finished, you'll beg me to kill you"—he left the neo-Nazi alone to quake in his goose-stepping black boots.

No one was outside. The proverbial coast was clear. Myron got in the car, wondering yet again about the Coldrens. What was going on with them right now? Had the kidnapper already called? Had he given them instructions? How did Tito's death affect what was happening? Had Chad suffered more bloodshed or had he escaped? Maybe he'd gotten hold of the gun and shot someone.

Maybe. But doubtful. More likely, something had gone awry. Someone had lost control. Someone had gone nuts.

He stopped the car. He had to warn the Coldrens.

Yes, Linda Coldren had clearly instructed him to stay away. But that was before he'd found a dead body. How could he sit back now and leave them blind? Someone had chopped off their son's finger. Someone had murdered one of the kidnappers. A "simple" kidnapping—if there is such a thing—had spun off its axis. Blood had been splattered about freely.

He had to warn them. He had to contact the Coldrens and let them know what he had learned.

But how?

He pulled onto Golf House Road. It was very late now, almost two in the morning. Nobody would be up. Myron flicked off his lights and cruised silently. He glided the car into a spot on the property line between two houses—if by some chance one of the occupants was awake and looked out the window, he or she might believe the car belonged to someone visiting a neighbor. He stepped out and slowly made his way on foot toward the Coldren house.

Keeping out of sight, Myron moved closer. He knew, of course, that there was no chance the Coldrens would be asleep. Jack might give it a token effort; Linda wouldn't even sit down. But right now, that didn't much matter.

How was he going to contact them?

He couldn't call on the phone. He couldn't walk up and knock on the door. And he couldn't throw pebbles at the window, like some clumsy suitor in a bad romantic comedy. So where did that leave him?

Lost.

He moved from shrub to shrub. Some of the shrubs were familiar from his last sojourn into these parts. He said hello to them, chatted, offered up his best cocktail-party banter. One shrub gave him a stock tip. Myron ignored it. He circled closer to the Coldren house, slowly, still careful not to be seen. He had no idea what he was going to do, but when he got close enough to see a light on in the den, an idea came to him.

A note.

He would write a note, telling them of his discovery, warning them to be extra careful, offering up his services. How to get the note close to the house? Hmm. He could fold the note into a paper airplane and fly it in. Oh, sure, with Myron's mechanical skills, that would work. Myron Bolitar, the Jewish Wright Brother. What else? Tie the note to a rock maybe? And then what? Smash a window?

As it happened, he didn't have to do any of that.

He heard a noise to his right. Footsteps. On the street. At two in the morning.

Myron quickly dove back down behind a shrub. The footsteps were moving closer. Faster. Someone approaching. Running.

He kept down, his heart beating wildly in his chest. The footsteps grew louder and then suddenly stopped. Myron peeked around the side of the shrub. His view was blocked by still more hedges.

He held his breath. And waited.

The footsteps started up again. Slower this time. Unhurried. Casual. Taking a walk now. Myron craned his neck around the other side of the shrub. Nothing. He moved into a crouch now. Slowly he raised himself, inch by inch, his bad knee protesting. He fought through the pain. His eyes reached the top of the shrub. Myron looked out and finally saw who it was.

Linda Coldren.

She was dressed in a blue sweat suit with running sneakers. Out for a jog? Seemed like a very strange time for it. But you never know. Jack drove golf balls. Myron shot baskets. Maybe Linda was into late-night jogging.

He didn't think so.

She neared the top of the driveway. Myron had to reach her. He clawed a rock out of the dirt and skimmed it toward her. Linda stopped and looked up sharply, like a deer interrupted while drinking. Myron threw another rock. She looked toward the bush. Myron waved a hand. Christ, this was subtle. But if she had felt safe enough to leave the house—if the kidnapper had not minded her taking a little night stroll—then walking toward a bush shouldn't cause a panic either. Bad rationale, but it was getting late.

If not out for a jog, why was Linda out so late?

Unless . . .

Unless she was paying off the ransom.

But no, it was still Sunday night. The banks wouldn't

be open. She couldn't raise one hundred grand without going to a bank. She had made that clear, hadn't she?

Linda Coldren slowly approached the bush. Myron was almost tempted to light the bush on fire, deepen his voice, and say, "Come forward, Moses." More gallows humor. More not-funny.

When she was about ten feet away, Myron raised his head into view. Linda's eyes nearly leaped out of their sockets.

"Get out of here!" Linda whispered.

Myron wasted no time. Whispering back, he said, "I found the guy from the pay phone dead. Shot twice in the head. Chad's ring was in his car. But no sign of Chad."

"Get out!"

"I just wanted to warn you. Be careful. They're playing for keeps."

Her eyes darted about the yard. She nodded and turned away.

"When's the drop-off?" Myron tried. "And where's Jack? Make sure you see Chad with your own eyes before you hand over anything."

But if Linda heard him, she gave no indication. She hurried down the driveway, opened the door, and disappeared from sight.

Chapter 25

Win opened the bedroom door. "You have visitors."

Myron kept his head on the pillow. Friends not knocking hardly fazed him anymore. "Who is it?"

"Law enforcement officials," Win said.

"Cops?"

"Yes."

"Uniformed?"

"Yes."

"Any idea what it's about?"

"Oooo, sorry. That would be a no. Let's move on to Kitty Carlisle."

Myron picked the sleep out of his eyes and threw on some clothes. He slipped into a pair of Top-Siders without socks. Very Win-like. A quick brush of the teeth, for the sake of breath rather than long-term dental health. He opted for a baseball cap rather than taking the time to wet his hair. The baseball cap was red and said TRIX CEREAL in the front and SILLY RABBIT on the back. Jessica had bought it for him. Myron loved her for it.

The two uniforms waited with cop-patience in the living room. They were young and healthy-looking. The taller one said, "Mr. Bolitar?"

"Yes."

"We'd appreciate it if you would accompany us."

"Where?"

"Detective Corbett will explain when we arrive."

"How about a hint?"

Two faces of stone. ''We'd rather not, sir.''

Myron shrugged. ''Let's go then.''

Myron sat in the back of the squad car. The two uniforms sat in the front. They drove at a pretty good clip but kept their siren off. Myron's cell phone rang.

''Do you guys mind if I take a call?''

Taller said, ''Of course not, sir.''

''Polite of you.'' Myron hit the *on* switch. ''Hello.''

''Are you alone?'' It was Linda Coldren.

''Nope.''

''Don't tell anyone I'm calling. Can you please get here as soon as possible? It's urgent.''

''What do you mean you can't deliver it until Thursday?'' Mr. Throw Them Off Track.

''I can't talk right now either. Just get here as soon as you can. And don't say anything until you do. Please. Trust me on this.''

She hung up.

''Fine, but then I better get free bagels. You hear me?''

Myron turned off the cell phone. He looked out the window. The route the cops were taking was overly familiar. Myron had taken the same one to Merion. When they reached the club entranceway on Ardmore Avenue, Myron saw a plethora of media vans and cop cars.

''Dang,'' the taller cop said.

''You knew it wouldn't stay quiet for long,'' Shorter added.

''Too big a story,'' Taller agreed.

''You fellas want to clue me in?''

The shorter cop twisted his head toward Myron. ''No, sir.'' He turned back around.

''Okeydokey,'' Myron said. But he didn't have a good feeling about this.

The squad car drove steadily through the press gauntlet. Reporters pushed against the windows, peering in. Flashes popped in Myron's face. A policeman waved them through. The reporters slowly peeled off the car like dandruff flakes. They parked in the club lot. There were at least a dozen other police cars, both marked and unmarked, nearby.

"Please come along," Taller said.

Myron did so. They walked across the eighteenth fairway. Lots of uniformed officers were walking with their heads down, picking up pieces of lord-knows-what and putting them in evidence bags.

This was definitely not good.

When they reached the top of the hill, Myron could see dozens of officers making a perfect circle in the famed stone quarry. Some were taking photos. Crime scene photos. Others were bent down. When one stood up, Myron saw him.

He felt his knees buckle. "Oh no . . ."

In the middle of the quarry—sprawled in the famed hazard that had cost him the tournament twenty-three years ago—lay the still, lifeless body of Jack Coldren.

The uniforms watched him, gauging his reaction. Myron showed them nothing. "What happened?" he managed.

"Please wait here, sir."

The taller cop walked down the hill; the shorter stayed with Myron. Taller spoke briefly to a man in plainclothes Myron suspected was Detective Corbett. Corbett glanced up at Myron as the man spoke. He nodded to the shorter cop.

"Please follow me, sir."

Still dazed, Myron trudged down the hill into the stone quarry. He kept his eye on the corpse. Coagulated blood coated Jack's head like one of those spray-on toupees. The body was twisted into a position it was never supposed to achieve. Oh, Christ. Poor, sad bastard.

The plainclothes detective greeted him with an enthusiastic handshake. "Mr. Bolitar, thank you so much for coming. I'm Detective Corbett."

Myron nodded numbly. "What happened?"

"A groundskeeper found him this morning at six."

"Was he shot?"

Corbett smiled crookedly. He was around Myron's age and petite for a cop. Not just short. Plenty of cops were on the short side. But this guy was small-boned to the point of being almost sickly. Corbett covered up the small physique with a trench coat. Not a great summer look. Too many episodes of *Columbo,* Myron guessed.

"I don't want to be rude or anything," Corbett said, "but do you mind if I ask the questions?"

Myron glanced at the still body. He felt light-headed. Jack dead. Why? How did it happen? And why had the police decided to question him? "Where is Mrs. Coldren?" Myron asked.

Corbett glanced at the two officers, then at Myron. "Why would you want to know that?"

"I want to make sure she's safe."

"Well then," Corbett began, folding his arms under his chest, "if that's the case, you should have asked, 'How is Mrs. Coldren?' or 'Is Mrs. Coldren all right?'— not 'Where is Mrs. Coldren?' I mean, if you're really interested in how she is."

Myron looked at Corbett for several seconds. "God. You. Are. Good."

"No reason for sarcasm, Mr. Bolitar. You just seem very concerned about her."

"I am."

"You a friend?"

"Yes."

"A close friend?"

"Pardon me?"

"Again, I don't want to appear rude or anything," Corbett said, spreading his hands, "but have you been— you know—porking her?"

"Are you out of your mind?"

"Is that a yes?"

Calm down, Myron. Corbett was trying to keep him off balance. Myron knew the game. Dumb to let it get to him. "The answer is no. We've had no sexual contact whatsoever."

"Really? That's odd."

He wanted Myron to bite with a "What's odd?" Myron did not oblige him.

"You see, a couple of witnesses saw you two together several times over the past few days. At a tent in Corporate Row, mostly. You sat alone for several hours. Very snuggly. Are you sure you weren't playing a little kissy-face?"

Myron said, "No."

"No, you weren't playing a little kissy-face, or no—"

"No, we weren't playing kissy-face or anything like that."

"Uh-huh, I see." Corbett feigned chewing over this little tidbit. "Where were you last night, Mr. Bolitar?"

"Am I a suspect, Detective?"

"We're just chatting amicably, Mr. Bolitar. That's all."

"Do you have an estimated time of death?" Myron asked.

Corbett offered up another cop-polite smile. "Once again, far be it from me to be obtuse or rude, but I would rather concentrate on you right now." His voice gathered a little more muster. "Where were you last night?"

Myron remembered Linda's call on the cell phone.

Undeniably the police had already questioned her. Had she told them about the kidnapping? Probably not. Either way, it was not his place to mention it. He didn't know where things stood. Speaking out of turn could jeopardize Chad's safety. Best to get out of here pronto.

"I'd like to see Mrs. Coldren."

"Why?"

"To make sure she's okay."

"That's sweet, Mr. Bolitar. And very noble. But I'd like you to answer my question."

"I'd like to see Mrs. Coldren first."

Corbett gave him the narrow cop-eyes. "Are you refusing to answer my questions?"

"No. But right now my priority is my potential client's welfare."

"Client?"

"Mrs. Coldren and I have been discussing the possibility of her signing on with MB SportsReps."

"I see," Corbett said, rubbing his chin. "So that explains your sitting together in the tent."

"I'll answer your questions later, Detective. Right now I'd like to check up on Mrs. Coldren."

"She's fine, Mr. Bolitar."

"I'd like to see for myself."

"You don't trust me?"

"It's not that. But if I am going to be her agent, then I must be at her disposal first and foremost."

Corbett shook his head and raised his eyebrows. "That's some crock of shit you're peddling, Bolitar."

"May I go now?"

Corbett gave the big hand spread again. "You're not under arrest. In fact"—he turned to the two officers—"please escort Mr. Bolitar to the Coldren residence. Make sure nobody bothers him on the way."

Myron smiled. "Thank you, Detective."

"Think nothing of it." As Myron began to walk away, Corbett called out, "Oh, one more thing." The man had definitely watched too much *Columbo*. "That call you got in the squad car just now. Was that from Mrs. Coldren?"

Myron said nothing.

"No matter. We can check the phone records." He gave the Columbo wave. "Have a special day."

Chapter 26

There were four more cop cars outside the Coldren house. Myron walked to the door on his own and knocked. A black woman Myron did not recognize opened it.

Her eyes flicked at the top of his head. "Nice hat," she said without inflection. "Come on in."

The woman was about fifty years old and wore a nicely tailored suit. Her coffee skin looked leathery and worn. Her face was kind of sleepy, her eyes half-closed, her expression perpetually bored. "I'm Victoria Wilson," she said.

"Myron Bolitar."

"Yes, I know." Bored voice too.

"Is anybody else here?"

"Just Linda."

"Can I see her?"

Victoria Wilson nodded slowly; Myron half expected her to stifle a yawn. "Maybe we should talk first."

"Are you with the police?" Myron asked.

"The opposite," she said. "I'm Mrs. Coldren's attorney."

"That was fast."

"Let me put this plainly," she ho-hummed, sounding like a diner waitress reading off the specials in the last hour of a double shift. "The police believe that Mrs. Coldren killed her husband. They also think that you're involved in some way."

Myron looked at her. "You're kidding, right?"

The same sleepy expression. "Do I look like a prankster, Mr. Bolitar?"

Rhetorical question.

"Linda does not have a solid alibi for late last night," she went on, still with the flat tone. "Do you?"

"Not really."

"Well, let me tell you what the police already know." The woman took blasé and raised it to an art form. "First"—raising a finger in the air seemed to take great effort—"they have a witness, a groundskeeper, who saw Jack Coldren enter Merion at approximately one in the morning. The same witness also saw Linda Coldren do likewise thirty minutes later. He also saw Linda Coldren leave the grounds not long after that. He never saw Jack Coldren leave."

"That doesn't mean—"

"Second"—another finger in the air, making a peace sign—"the police received a report last night at approximately two in the morning that your car, Mr. Bolitar, was parked on Golf House Road. The police will want to know what you were doing parking in such a strange spot at such a strange time."

"How do you know all this?" Myron asked.

"I have good connections with the police," she said. Again bored. "May I continue?"

"Please."

"Third"—yep, another finger—"Jack Coldren had been seeing a divorce attorney. He had, in fact, begun the process of filing papers."

"Did Linda know this?"

"No. But one of the allegations Mr. Coldren made concerned his wife's recent infidelity."

Myron put both hands to his chest. "Don't look at me."

"Mr. Bolitar?"

"What?"

"I am just stating facts. And I'd appreciate it if you didn't interrupt. Fourth"—final finger—"on Saturday, at the U.S. Open golf tournament, several witnesses described you and Mrs. Coldren as being a bit more than chummy."

Myron waited. Victoria Wilson lowered the hand, never showing the thumb.

"Is that it?" Myron asked.

"No. But that's all we'll discuss for now."

"I met Linda for the first time on Friday."

"And you can prove that?"

"Bucky can testify to it. He introduced us."

Another big sigh. "Linda Coldren's father. What a perfect, unbiased witness."

"I live in New York."

"Which is less than two hours by Amtrak from Philadelphia. Go on."

"I have a girlfriend. Jessica Culver. I live with her."

"And no man has ever cheated on his girlfriend before. Stunning testimony."

Myron shook his head. "So you're suggesting—"

"Nothing," Victoria Wilson interrupted him with the monotone. "I am suggesting absolutely nothing. I am telling you what the police believe—that Linda killed Jack. The reason why there are so many police officers surrounding this house is because they want to make sure that we do not remove anything before a search warrant is issued. They have made it crystal clear that they want no Kardashians on this one."

Kardashian. As in O.J. The man had changed law lexicon forever. "But . . ." Myron stopped. "This is ridiculous. Where is Linda?"

"Upstairs. I've informed the police that she is too grief-stricken to speak to them at this time."

"You don't understand. Linda shouldn't even be a suspect. Once she tells you the whole story, you'll see what I mean."

Another near yawn. "She has told me the whole story."

"Even about . . . ?"

"The kidnapping," Victoria Wilson finished for him. "Yes."

"Well, don't you think that kind of exonerates her?"

"No."

Myron was confused. "Do the police know about the kidnapping?"

"Of course not. We are saying nothing at this time."

Myron made a face. "But once they hear about the kidnapping, they'll focus on that. They'll know Linda couldn't be involved."

Victoria Wilson turned away. "Let's go upstairs."

"You don't agree?"

She didn't respond. They began to climb the staircase. Victoria said, "You are an attorney."

It didn't sound like a question, but Myron still said, "I don't practice."

"But you passed the bar."

"In New York."

"Good enough. I want you to be co-counsel in this case. I can get you an immediate dispensation."

"I don't do criminal law," Myron said.

"You don't have to. I just want you to be an attorney of record for Mrs. Coldren."

Myron nodded. "So I can't testify," he said. "So everything I hear falls under privilege."

Still bored. "You are a smart one." She stopped next

to a bedroom door and leaned against a wall. "Go in. I'm
going to wait out here."

Myron knocked. Linda Coldren told him to come in.
He opened the door. Linda stood by the far window looking out onto her backyard.

"Linda?"

Her back still faced him. "I'm having a bad week,
Myron." She laughed. It was not a happy sound.

"Are you okay?" he asked.

"Me? Never better. Thanks for asking."

He stepped toward her, unsure what to say. "Did the
kidnappers call about the ransom?"

"Last night," Linda said. "Jack spoke to them."

"What did they say?"

"I don't know. He stormed out after the call. He never
told me."

Myron tried to picture this scene. A call comes in.
Jack answers it. He runs out without saying anything. It
didn't exactly mesh.

"Have you heard from them again?" he tried.

"No, not yet."

Myron nodded, even though she wasn't facing him.
"So what did you do?"

"Do?"

"Last night. After Jack stormed out."

Linda Coldren folded her arms across her chest. "I
waited a few minutes for him to calm down," she said.
"When he didn't come back, I went out looking for
him."

"You went to Merion," Myron said.

"Yes. Jack likes to stroll the grounds. To think and be
alone."

"Did you see him there?"

"No. I looked around for a while. Then I came back
here. That's when I ran into you."

"And Jack never came back," Myron said.

With her back still to him, Linda Coldren shook her head. "What tipped you off, Myron? The dead body in the stone quarry?"

"Just trying to help."

She turned to him. Her eyes were red. Her face was drawn. She was still incredibly beautiful. "I just need someone to take it out on." She shrugged, tried a smile. "You're here."

Myron wanted to step closer. He refrained. "You've been up all night?"

She nodded. "I've been standing right here, waiting for Jack to come home. When the police knocked on the door, I thought it was about Chad. This is going to sound awful, but when they told me about Jack, I was almost relieved."

The phone rang.

Linda spun around with enough speed to start up a wind tunnel. She looked at Myron. He looked at her.

"It's probably the media," he said.

Linda shook her head. "Not on that line." She reached for the phone, pressed the lit-up button, picked up the receiver.

"Hello," she said.

A voice replied. Linda gasped and bit down in mid-scream. Her hand flew to her mouth. Tears pushed their way out of her eyes. The door flew open. Victoria Wilson stepped into the room, looking like a bear stirred from a power nap.

Linda looked up at them both. "It's Chad," she said. "He's free."

Chapter 27

Victoria Wilson took control. "We'll go pick him up," she said. "You stay on the line with him."

Linda started shaking her head. "But I want—"

"Trust me on this, honey. If you go, every cop and news reporter will follow. Myron and I can lose them if we have to. I don't want the police talking to your son until I have. You just stay here. You say nothing. If the police come in with a warrant, you let them in. You don't say a word. No matter what. Do you understand?"

Linda nodded.

"So where is he?"

"On Porter Street."

"Okay, tell him Aunt Victoria is on the way. We'll take care of him."

Linda grabbed her arm, her face pleading. "Will you bring him back here?"

"Not right away, hon." The voice was still matter-of-fact. "The police will see. I can't have that. It'll raise too many questions. You'll see him soon enough."

Victoria Wilson turned away. There was no debate with this woman.

In the car, Myron asked, "How do you know Linda?"

"My mother and father were servants for the Buckwells and Lockwoods," she replied. "I grew up on their estates."

"But somewhere along the line you went to law school?"

She frowned. "You writing my biography?"

"I'm just asking."

"Why? You surprised that a middle-aged black woman is the attorney for rich WASPs?"

"Frankly," Myron said, "yes."

"Don't blame you. But we don't have time for that now. You got any important questions?"

"Yes," Myron said. He was doing the driving. "What aren't you telling me?"

"Nothing that you need to know."

"I'm an attorney of record on the case. I need to know everything."

"Later. Let's concentrate on the boy first."

Again the no-argument monotone.

"Are you sure we're doing the right thing?" Myron continued. "Not telling the police about the kidnapping?"

"We can always tell them later," Victoria Wilson replied. "That's the mistake most defendants make. They think they have to talk their way out of it right away. But that's dangerous. There is always time to talk later."

"I'm not sure I agree."

"Tell you what, Myron. If we need some expertise on negotiating a sneaker deal, I'll put you in charge. But while this thing is still a criminal case, let me take the lead, okay?"

"The police want to question me."

"You say nothing. That is your right. You don't have to say a word to the police."

"Unless they subpoena me."

"Even then. You are Linda Coldren's attorney. You don't say anything."

Myron shook his head. "That only works for what was said *after* you asked me to be co-counsel. They can ask me about anything that happened before."

"Wrong." Victoria Wilson gave a distracted sigh. "When Linda Coldren first asked you to help, she knew you were a bar-appointed attorney. Therefore everything she told you fell under attorney-client."

Myron had to smile. "That's reaching."

"But that's the way it is." He could feel her eyes on him now. "No matter what you might want to do, morally and legally you are not allowed to talk to anyone."

She was good.

Myron drove a bit faster. No one was tailing them; the police and the reporters had stuck to the house. The story was all over the radio. The anchorman kept repeating a one-line statement issued by Linda Coldren: "We are all saddened by this tragedy. Please allow us to grieve in peace."

"You issue that statement?" Myron asked.

"No. Linda did it before I got there."

"Why?"

"She thought it would keep the media off her back. She knows better now."

They pulled up on Porter Street. Myron scanned the sidewalks.

"Up there," Victoria Wilson said.

Myron saw him. Chad Coldren was huddled on the ground. The telephone receiver was still gripped in one hand, but he wasn't talking. The other hand was heavily bandaged. Myron felt a little queasy. He hit the gas pedal. The car jerked forward. They pulled up to the boy. Chad stared straight ahead.

Victoria Wilson's indifferent expression finally melted a bit. "Let me handle this," she said.

She got out of the car and walked over to the boy. She bent down and cradled him. She took the receiver away from him, talked into it, hung up. She helped Chad to his feet, stroking his hair, whispering comforts. They both got into the backseat. Chad leaned his head against her. She made soothing shushing noises. She nodded at Myron. Myron put the car in drive.

Chad did not speak during the drive. Nobody asked him to. Victoria gave Myron directions to her office building in Bryn Mawr. The Coldren family doctor—a gray-haired, old family friend named Henry Lane—had his office there too. He unwrapped Chad's bandage and examined the boy while Myron and Victoria waited in another room. Myron paced. Victoria read a magazine.

"We should take him to a hospital," Myron said.

"Dr. Lane will decide if that's necessary." Victoria yawned and flipped a page.

Myron tried to take it all in. With all the activity surrounding the police accusation and Chad's safe recovery, he had almost forgotten about Jack Coldren. Jack was dead. It was almost impossible for Myron to comprehend. The irony did not escape him: the man finally has the chance at redemption and he ends up dead in the same hazard that altered his life twenty-three years ago.

Dr. Lane appeared in the doorway. He was everything you wanted a doctor to look like—Marcus Welby without the receding hairline. "Chad is better now. He's talking. He's alert."

"How's his hand?" Myron asked.

"It'll need to be looked at by a specialist. But there's no infection or anything like that."

Victoria Wilson stood. "I'd like to talk to him."

Lane nodded. "I would warn you to go easy on him, Victoria, but I know you never listen."

Her mouth almost twitched. Not a smile. Not even close. But there was a sign of life. "You'll have to stay out here, Henry. The police may ask you what you heard."

The doctor nodded again. "I understand."

Victoria looked at Myron. "I'll do the talking."

"Okay."

When Myron and Victoria entered the room, Chad was staring down at his bandaged hand like he expected the missing finger to grow back.

"Chad?"

He slowly looked up. There were tears in his eyes. Myron remembered what Linda had said about the kid's love of golf. Another dream lay in ashes. The kid did not know it, but right now he and Myron were kindred spirits.

"Who are you?" Chad asked Myron.

"He's a friend," Victoria Wilson replied. Even with the boy, the tone was completely detached. "His name is Myron Bolitar."

"I want to see my parents, Aunt Vee."

Victoria sat across from him. "A lot has happened, Chad. I don't want to go into it all now. You'll have to trust me, okay?"

Chad nodded.

"I need to know what happened to you. Everything. From the beginning."

"A man car-jacked me," Chad said.

"Just one man?"

"Yeah."

"Go on. Tell me what happened."

"I was at a traffic light, and this guy just opens the passenger door and gets in. He's wearing a ski mask and sticks this gun in my face. He told me to keep driving."

"Okay. What day was this?"

"Thursday."

"Where were you Wednesday night?"

"At my friend Matt's house."

"Matthew Squires?"

"Yes."

"Okay, fine." Victoria Wilson's eyes did not wander

from the boy's face. "Now where were you when this man got into your car?"

"A couple of blocks from school."

"Did this happen before or after summer school?"

"After. I was on my way home."

Myron kept quiet. He wondered why the boy was lying.

"Where did the man take you?"

"He told me to drive around the block. We pulled into this parking lot. Then he put something over my head. A burlap bag or something. He made me lie down in the back. Then he started driving. I don't know where we went. I never saw anything. Next thing I knew I was in a room someplace. I had to keep the bag on my head all the time so I didn't see anything."

"You never saw the man's face?"

"Never."

"Are you sure it was a man? Could it have been a woman?"

"I heard his voice a few times. It was a man. At least, one of them was."

"There was more than one?"

Chad nodded. "The day he did this . . ." He lifted his bandaged hand into view. His face went totally blank. He looked straight ahead, his eyes unfocused. "I had that burlap bag over my head. My hands were handcuffed behind my back." His voice was as detached as Victoria's now. "That bag was so itchy. I used to rub my chin against my shoulder. Just for relief. Anyway, the man came in and unlocked the handcuffs. Then he grabbed my hand and put it flat on the table. He didn't say anything. He didn't warn me. The whole thing took less than ten seconds. He just put my hand on the table. I never saw a thing. I just heard a whack. Then I felt this weird sensation. Not even pain at first. I didn't know what it was.

Then I felt a warm wetness. From the blood, I guess. The pain came a few seconds later. I passed out. When I woke up, my hand was wrapped. The throbbing was awful. The burlap bag was back over my head. Someone came in. Gave me some pills. It dulled the pain a little. Then I heard voices. Two of them. It sounded like they were arguing.''

Chad Coldren stopped as though out of breath. Myron watched Victoria Wilson. She did not go over and comfort him.

"Were the voices both male?''

"Actually, one sounded like a female. But I was pretty out of it. I can't say for sure.''

Chad looked back down at his bandages. He moved his fingers a bit. Testing them out.

"What happened next, Chad?''

He kept his eyes on the bandages. "There's not a lot to tell, Aunt Vee. They kept me that way for a few days. I don't know how many. They fed me mostly pizza and soda. They brought a phone in one day. Made me call Merion and ask for my dad.''

The ransom call at Merion, Myron thought. The kidnapper's second call.

"They also made me scream.''

"Made you scream?''

"The guy came in. He told me to scream and to make it scary. Otherwise, he would make me scream for real. So I tried different screams for, like, ten minutes. Until he was satisfied.''

The scream from the call at the mall, Myron thought. The one where Tito demanded a hundred grand.

"That's about it, Aunt Vee.''

"How did you escape?'' Victoria asked.

"I didn't. They let me go. A little while ago someone led me to a car. I still had the burlap bag on my head. We drove a little. Then the car stopped. Someone opened the door and pulled me out. Next thing I knew, I was free.''

Victoria looked over at Myron. Myron looked back. Then she nodded slowly. Myron took that as his cue.

''He's lying.''

Chad said, ''What?''

Myron turned his attention to him. ''You're lying, Chad. And worse, the police will know you're lying.''

''What are you talking about?'' His eyes sought Victoria's. ''Who is this guy?''

''You used your ATM card at 6:18 P.M. on Thursday on Porter Street,'' Myron said.

Chad's eyes widened. ''That wasn't me. It was the asshole who grabbed me. He took my wallet—''

''It's on videotape, Chad.''

He opened his mouth, but nothing came out. Then: ''They made me.'' But his voice was weak.

''I saw the tape, Chad. You were smiling. You were happy. You were not alone. You also spent an evening at the sleazy motel next door.''

Chad lowered his head.

''Chad?'' It was Victoria. She did not sound pleased. ''Look at me, boy.''

Chad slowly raised his eyes.

''Why are you lying to me?''

''It has nothing to do with what happened, Aunt Vee.''

Her face was unyielding. ''Start talking, Chad. And now.''

He looked down again, studying the bandaged hand. ''It's just like I said—except the man didn't grab me in my car. He knocked on my door at that motel. He came in with a gun. Everything else I told you is the truth.''

''When was this?''

''Friday morning.''

''So why did you lie to me?''

"I promised," he said. "I just wanted to keep her out of this."

"Who?" she asked.

Chad looked surprised. "You don't know?"

"I have the tape," Myron said, giving a little bluff here. "I haven't shown it to her yet."

"Aunt Vee, you have to keep her out of it. This could really hurt her."

"Honey, listen to me now. I think it's sweet that you're trying to protect your girlfriend. But I don't have time for that."

Chad looked from Myron to Victoria. "I want to see my mom please."

"You will, honey. Soon. But first you have to tell me about this girl."

"I promised that I would keep her out of it."

"If I can keep her name out of this, I will."

"I can't, Aunt Vee."

"Forget it, Victoria," Myron said. "If he won't tell, we can all just watch the tape together. Then we can call the girl on her own. Or maybe the police will find her first. They'll have a copy of the tape too. They won't be so worried about her feelings."

"You don't understand," Chad said, looking from Victoria Wilson to Myron, then back at Victoria again. "I promised her. She can get in serious trouble."

"We'll talk to her parents, if need be," Victoria said. "We'll do what we can."

"Her parents?" Chad looked confused. "I'm not worried about her parents. She's old enough. . . ." His voice died away.

"Who were you with, Chad?"

"I swore I'd never say anything, Aunt Vee."

"Fine," Myron said. "We can't waste time on this, Victoria. Let the police track her down."

"No!" Chad looked down. "She had nothing to do with it, okay? We were together. She went out for a little while and that's when they grabbed me. It wasn't her fault."

Victoria shifted in her seat. "Who, Chad?"

His words came out slow and grudging. But they were also quite clear. "Her name is Esme Fong. She works for a company called Zoom."

Chapter 28

It was all starting to make awful, horrible sense.

Myron did not wait for permission. He stormed out of the office and down the corridor. It was time to confront Esme.

A scenario was fast taking shape in Myron's mind. Esme Fong meets Chad Coldren while negotiating the Zoom deal with his mother. She seduces him. Why? Hard to say. For kicks maybe. Not important.

Anyway, Chad spends Wednesday night with his buddy Matthew. Then on Thursday he meets up with Esme for a romantic tryst at the Court Manor Inn. They pick up some cash at an ATM. They have their fun. And then things get interesting.

Esme Fong has not only signed Linda Coldren, but she has managed to land wunderkind Tad Crispin. Tad is playing wonderfully well in his first U.S. Open. After one round, he is in second place. Amazing. Great publicity. But if Tad could somehow win—if he could catch the veteran with a gigantic lead—it would give Zoom's launch into the golf business a nuclear boost. It would be worth millions.

Millions.

And Esme had the leader's son right in front of her.

So what does the ambitious Esme Fong do? She hires Tito to grab the boy. Nothing complicated. She wants to distract Jack big-time. Make him lose that edge. What better way than kidnapping his kid?

It all kinda fit together.

Myron turned his attention to some of case's more bothersome aspects. First of all, the not demanding the ransom for so long suddenly made sense. Esme Fong is no expert at this and she doesn't want a payoff—that would just complicate manners—so the first few calls are awkward. She forgets to demand a ransom. Second, Myron remembered Tito's ''chink bitch'' call. How had he known Esme was there? Simple. Esme had told him when she would be there—to scare the hell out of the Coldrens and make them think they were being watched.

Yep. It fit. Everything had been going according to Esme Fong's plan. Except for one thing.

Jack continued to play well.

He maintained his insurmountable lead through the next round. The kidnapping may have stunned him a bit, but he had regained his footing. His lead was still huge. Drastic action was necessary.

Myron got into the elevator and headed down to the ground-floor lobby. He wondered how it had happened. Maybe it had been Tito's idea. Maybe that was why Chad had heard two voices arguing. Either way, someone decided to do something that was guaranteed to throw Jack off his game.

Cut off Chad's finger.

Like it or not—Tito's idea or hers—Esme Fong took advantage. She had Linda's car keys. She knew what her car looked like. It wouldn't take much. Just a turn of the key, a quick drop on the car seat. Easy for her. Nothing suspicious. Who would notice an attractive, well-dressed woman unlocking a car with a key?

The severed finger did the trick, too. Jack's game was left in shambles. Tad Crispin stormed back. It was everything she wanted. But, alas, Jack had one more trick up his sleeve. He managed to land a big putt on the eighteenth hole, forcing a tie. This was a nightmare for Esme. She could not take the risk of Tad Crispin losing to Jack, the ultimate choker, in a one-on-one situation.

A loss would be disastrous.

A loss would cost them millions. Maybe destroy her entire campaign.

Man, did it fit.

When Myron thought about it, hadn't he heard Esme voice that very viewpoint with Norm Zuckerman? Her Buffalo Bill analogy—hadn't he been standing right there when she said it? Now that she was trapped, was it so hard to believe that she'd go the extra mile? That she would call Jack on the phone last night? That she would set up a rendezvous at the course? That she would insist he come alone—right now—if he wanted to see his son alive?

Ka-bang.

And once Jack was dead, there was no reason to hold on to the kid anymore. She let him go.

The elevator slid open. Myron stepped out. Okay, there were holes. But maybe after confronting Esme, he would be able to plug a few of them up. Myron pushed open the glass door. He headed into the parking lot. There were taxis waiting near the street. He was midway through the lot when a voice reached out and pulled him to a stop.

"Myron?"

An icy nerve-jangle punctured a hole through his heart. He had heard the voice only once before. Ten years ago. At Merion.

Chapter 29

Myron froze.

"I see you've met Victoria," Cissy Lockwood said.

He tried a nod, but it wouldn't happen.

"I called her as soon as Bucky told me about the murder. I knew she'd be able to help. Victoria is the best lawyer I know. Ask Win about her."

He tried the nod again. Got a little motion going this time.

Win's mother stepped closer. "I'd like a word with you in private, Myron."

He found his voice. "It's not a good time, Ms. Lockwood."

"No, I imagine not. Still, this won't take long."

"Really, I should go."

She was a beautiful woman. Her ash-blond hair was streaked with gray, and she had the same regal bearing as her blood niece Linda. The porcelain face, however, she had given almost verbatim to Win. The resemblance was uncanny.

She took one more step forward, her eyes never off him. Her clothes were a bit odd. She wore a man's over-size shirt, untucked, and stretch pants. Annie Hall goes maternity shopping. It was not what he'd have expected, but then again, he had bigger worries than fashion right now.

"It's about Win," she said.

Myron shook his head. "Then it's none of my business."

"True enough. But that does not make you immune to responsibility, does it? Win is your friend. I count myself lucky that my son has a friend who cares like you do."

Myron said nothing.

"I know quite a bit about you, Myron. I've had private investigators keep tabs on Win for years now. It was my way of staying close. Of course, Win knew about it. He never said anything, but you can't keep something like that from Win, now can you?"

"No," Myron said. "You can't."

"You're staying at the Lockwood estate," she said. "In the guest cottage."

He nodded.

"You've been there before."

Another nod.

"Have you ever seen the horse stables?"

"Only from a distance," Myron said.

She smiled Win's smile. "You've never been inside?"

"No."

"I'm not surprised. Win doesn't ride anymore. He used to love horses. More than golf even."

"Ms. Lockwood—"

"Please call me Cissy."

"I really don't feel comfortable hearing this."

Her eyes hardened a bit. "And I do not feel comfortable telling you this. But it must be done."

"Win wouldn't want me to hear it," Myron said.

"That's too bad, but Win cannot always have what he wants. I should have learned that long ago. He did not want to see me as a child. I never forced it. I listened to the experts, who told me that my son would come around, that compelling him to see me would be counterproductive. But they did not know Win. By the time I stopped listening to them it was too late. Not that it mattered. I don't think ignoring them would have changed anything."

Silence.

She stood proud and tall, her slender neck high. But something was going on. Her fingers kept flexing, as if she were fighting off the desire to make fists. Myron's stomach knotted up. He knew what was coming next. He just didn't know what to do about it.

"The story is simple," she began, her voice almost wistful. She was no longer looking at Myron. Her gaze rose above his shoulder, but he had no idea what she was actually seeing. "Win was eight years old. I was twenty-seven at the time. I married young. I never went to college. It was not as though I had a choice. My father told me what to do. I had only one friend—one person I could confide in. That was Victoria. She is still my dearest friend, not unlike what you are to Win."

Cissy Lockwood winced. Her eyes closed.

"Ms. Lockwood?"

She shook her head. The eyes slowly opened. "I am getting off track," she said, catching her breath. "I apologize. I'm not here to tell you my life story. Just one incident in it. So let me just state it plainly."

A deep breath. Then another.

"Jack Coldren told me that he was taking Win out for a golf lesson. But it never happened. Or perhaps they had finished far earlier than expected. Either way, Jack was not with Win. His father was. Somehow Win and his father ended up going into the stables. I was there when they entered. I was not alone. More specifically, I was with Win's riding instructor."

She stopped. Myron waited.

"Do I need to spell this out for you?"

Myron shook his head.

"No child should see what Win saw that day," she said. "And worse, no child should ever see his father's face under those circumstances."

Myron felt tears sting his eyes.

"There is more to it, of course. I won't go into it now. But Win has never spoken to me since that moment. He also never forgave his father. Yes, his father. You think he hates only me and loves Windsor the Second. But it is not so. He blames his father, too. He thinks that his father is weak. That he allowed it to happen. Utter nonsense, but that is the way it is."

Myron shook his head. He didn't want to hear any more. He wanted to run and find Win. He wanted to hug his friend and shake him and somehow make him forget. He thought of the lost expression on Win's face as he watched the horse stables yesterday morning.

My God. Win.

When Myron spoke, his voice was sharper than he'd expected. "Why are you telling me this?"

"Because I am dying," she replied.

Myron slumped against a car. His heart ripped anew.

"Again, let me put this simply," she said in too calm a voice. "It has reached the liver. It is eleven centimeters long. My abdomen is swelling from liver and kidney failure." That explained the wardrobe—the untucked, oversize shirt and the stretch pants. "We are not talking months. We are talking perhaps weeks. Probably less."

"There are treatments," Myron tried lamely. "Procedures."

She simply dismissed this with a shake of her head. "I am not a foolish woman. I do not have delusions of engaging in a moving reunion with my son. I know Win. That will not happen. But there is still unfinished business here. Once I am dead, there will be no chance for him to disentangle himself again. It will be over. I do not know what he will do with this opportunity. Probably nothing. But I want him to know. So that he can decide. It is his last chance, Myron. I do not believe he will take it. But he should.''

With that, she turned away and left. Myron watched her walk away. When she was out of sight, Myron hailed a taxi. He got in the back.

''Where to, bud?''

He gave the man the address where Esme Fong was staying. Then he settled back in the seat. His eyes stared blankly out the window. The city passed by in a misty, silent blur.

Chapter 30

When he thought that his voice would not betray him, Myron called Win on the cell phone.

After a quick hello, Win said, "Bummer about Jack."

"From what I hear, he used to be your friend."

Win cleared his throat. "Myron?"

"What?"

"You know nothing. Remember that."

True enough. "Can we have dinner tonight?"

Win hesitated. "Of course."

"At the cottage. Six-thirty."

"Fine."

Win hung up. Myron tried to put it out of his mind. He had other things to worry about.

Esme Fong paced the sidewalk outside the entrance to the Omni Hotel on the corner of Chestnut Street and Fourth. She wore a white suit and white stockings. Killer legs. She kept wringing her hands.

Myron got out of the taxi. "Why are you waiting out here?" he asked.

"You insisted on talking privately," Esme answered. "Norm is upstairs."

"You two live in the same room?"

"No, we have adjoining suites."

Myron nodded. The no-tell motel was making more sense now. "Not much privacy, huh?"

"No, not really." She gave him a tentative smile. "But it's okay. I like Norm."

"I'm sure you do."

"What's this about, Myron?"

"You heard about Jack Coldren?"

"Of course. Norm and I were shocked. Absolutely shocked."

Myron nodded. "Come on," he said. "Let's walk."

They headed up Fourth Street. Myron was tempted to stay on Chestnut Street, but that would have meant strolling past Independence Hall and that would have been a tad too cliché for his liking. Still, Fourth Street was in the colonial section. Lots of brick. Brick sidewalk, brick walls and fence, brick buildings of tremendous historical significance that all looked the same. White ash trees lined the walk. They turned right into a park that held the Second Bank of the United States. There was a plaque with a portrait of the bank's first president. One of Win's ancestors. Myron looked for a resemblance but could not find one.

"I've tried to reach Linda," Esme said. "But the phone is busy."

"Did you try Chad's line?"

Something hit her face, then fled. "Chad's line?"

"He has his own phone in the house," he said. "You must have known that."

"Why would I know that?"

Myron shrugged. "I thought you knew Chad."

"I do," she said, but her voice was slow, careful. "I mean, I've been over to the house a number of times."

"Uh-huh. And when was the last time you saw Chad?"

She put her hand to her chin. "I don't think he was there when I went over Friday night," she said, the voice still slow. "I don't really know. I guess a few weeks ago."

Myron made a buzzing noise. "Incorrect answer."

"Excuse me?"

"I don't get it, Esme."

"What?"

Myron continued walking, Esme stayed in step. "You're what," he said, "twenty-four years old?"

"Twenty-five."

"You're smart. You're successful. You're attractive. But a teenage boy—what's up with that?"

She stopped. "What are you talking about?"

"You really don't know?"

"I don't have the slightest idea."

His eyes bore into hers. "You. Chad Coldren. The Court Manor Inn. That help?"

"No."

Myron gave her skeptical. "Please."

"Did Chad tell you that?"

"Esme . . ."

"He's lying, Myron. My God, you know how teenage boys are. How could you believe something like that?"

"Pictures, Esme."

Her face went slack. "What?"

"You two stopped at an ATM machine next door to the motel, remember? They have cameras. Your face was clear as day." It was a bluff. But it was a damn good one. She caved a little piece at a time. She looked around and then collapsed on a bench. She turned and faced a colonial building with a lot of scaffolding. Scaffolding, Myron thought, ruined the effect—like armpit hair on a beautiful woman. It shouldn't really matter, but it did.

"Please don't tell Norm," she said in a faraway voice. "Please don't."

Myron said nothing.

"It was dumb. I know that. But it shouldn't cost me my job."

Myron sat next to her. "Tell me what happened."

She looked back at him. "Why? What business is this of yours?"

"There are reasons."

"What reasons?" Her voice was a little sharper now. "Look, I'm not proud of myself. But who appointed you my conscience?"

"Fine. I'll go ask Norm then. Maybe he can help me."

Her mouth dropped. "Help you with what? I don't understand. Why are you doing this to me?"

"I need some answers. I don't have time to explain."

"What do you want me to say? That I was dumb? I was. I could tell you that I was lonely being in a nice place. That he seemed like a sweet, handsome kid and that at his age, I figured there'd be no fear of disease or attachments. But at the end of the day, that does not change much. I was wrong. I'm sorry, okay?"

"When was the last time you saw Chad?"

"Why do you keep asking me that?" Esme insisted.

"Just answer my questions or I'll go to Norm, I swear it."

She studied his face. He put on his most impermeable face, the one he'd learned from really tough cops and toll collectors on the New Jersey Turnpike. After a few seconds she said, "At that motel."

"The Court Manor Inn?"

"Whatever it was called. I don't remember the name."

"What day was that?" Myron asked.

She thought a moment. "Friday morning. Chad was still sleeping."

"You haven't seen or spoken to him since?"

"No."

"You didn't have any plans to rendezvous for another tryst?"

She made an unhappy face. "No, not really. I thought he was just out for some fun, but once we were there, I could see he was developing a crush. I didn't count on that. Frankly I was worried."

"Of what exactly?"

"That he'd tell his mother. Chad swore he wouldn't, but who knew what he'd do if I hurt him? When I didn't hear from him again, I was relieved."

Myron searched her face and her story for lies. He couldn't find one. Didn't mean they weren't there.

Esme shifted on the bench, crossing her legs. "I still don't understand why you're asking me all this." She thought about it a moment and then something seemed to spark in her eyes. She squared her shoulders toward Myron. "Does this have something to do with Jack's murder?"

Myron said nothing.

"My God." Her voice quaked. "You can't possibly think that Chad has something to do with it."

Myron waited a beat. All-or-nothing time. "No," he said. "But I'm not so sure about you."

Confusion set camp on her face. "What?"

"I think you kidnapped Chad."

She raised both hands. "Are you out of your mind? Kidnapped? It was completely consensual. Chad was more than willing, believe me. Okay, he was young. But do you think I took him to that motel at gunpoint?"

"That's not what I mean," Myron said.

Confusion again. "Then what the hell do you mean?"

"After you left the motel on Friday. Where did you go?"

"To Merion. I met you there that night, remember?"

"How about last night? Where were you?"

"Here."

"In your suite?"

"Yes."

"What time?"

"From eight o'clock on."

"Anybody who can verify that?"

"Why would I need someone to verify that?" she snapped. Myron put on the impermeable face again—not even gases could get through. Esme sighed. "I was with Norm until midnight. We were working."

"And after that?"

"I went to bed."

"Would the hotel's nightman be able to verify that you never left your suite after midnight?"

"I think so, yes. His name is Miguel. He's very nice."

Miguel. He'd have Esperanza track down that one. If her alibi stuck, his neat little scenario went down the toilet. "Who else knew about you and Chad Coldren?"

"No one," she said. "At least, I told no one."

"How about Chad? Did he tell anyone?"

"It sounds to me like he told you," she said pointedly. "He might have told someone else, I don't know."

Myron thought about it. The black-clad man crawling out Chad's bedroom window. Matthew Squires. Myron remembered his own teenage years. If he had somehow managed to bed an older woman who looked like Esme Fong, he would have been busting to tell someone—especially if he'd been staying at his best friend's house the night before.

Once again, things circled back to the Squires kid.

Myron asked, "Where will you be if I need to reach you?"

She reached into her pocket and pulled out a card. "My cell phone number is on the bottom."

"Good-bye, Esme."

"Myron?"

He turned to her.

"Are you going to tell Norm?"

She seemed only worried about her reputation and her job, not a murder rap. Or was this just a clever diversion? No way of knowing for sure.

"No," he said. "I won't tell."

At least, not yet.

Chapter 31

Episcopal Academy. Win's high school alma mater.

Esperanza had picked him up in front of Esme Fong's and driven him here. She parked across the street. She turned off the ignition and faced him.

"Now what?" she asked.

"I don't know. Matthew Squires is in there. We can wait for a lunch break. Try to get in then."

"Sounds like a plan," Esperanza said with a nod. "A really bad one."

"You have a better idea?"

"We can go in now. Pretend we're touring parents."

Myron thought about it. "You think that'll work?"

"Better than hanging out here doing nothing."

"Oh, before I forget. I want you to check out Esme's alibi. The hotel nightman named Miguel."

"Miguel," she repeated. "It's because I'm Hispanic, right?"

"Pretty much, yeah."

She had no problem with that. "I put a call in to Peru this morning."

"And?"

"I spoke to some local sheriff. He says Lloyd Rennart committed suicide."

"What about the body?"

"The cliff is called *El Garganta del Diablo*—in English, Throat of the Devil. No bodies are ever located. It's actually a fairly common suicide plunge."

"Great. Think you can do a little more background stuff on Rennart?"

"Like what?"

"How did he buy the bar in Neptune? How did he buy the house in Spring Lake Heights? Stuff like that."

"Why would you want know that?"

"Lloyd Rennart was a caddie for a rookie golfer. That isn't exactly loads of dough."

"So?"

"So maybe he had a windfall after Jack blew the U.S. Open."

Esperanza saw where he was going. "You think somebody paid Rennart off to throw the Open?"

"No," Myron said. "But I think it's a possibility."

"It's going to be hard to trace after all this time."

"Just give it a shot. Also, Rennart got into a serious car accident twenty years ago in Narberth. It's a small town right around here. His first wife was killed in the crash. See what you can find out about it."

Esperanza frowned. "Like what?"

"Like was he drunk. Was he charged with anything. Were there other fatalities."

"Why?"

"Maybe he pissed off someone. Maybe his first wife's family wants vengeance."

Esperanza kept the frown. "So they—what?—waited twenty years, followed Lloyd Rennart to Peru, pushed him off a cliff, came back, kidnapped Chad Coldren, killed Jack Coldren. . . . Are you getting my point?"

Myron nodded. "And you're right. But I still want you to run down everything you can on Lloyd Rennart. I think there's a connection somewhere. We just have to find what it is."

"I don't see it," Esperanza said. She tucked a curl of

black hair behind her ear. "Seems to me that Esme Fong is still a much better suspect."

"Agreed. But I'd still like you to look into it. Find out what you can. There's also a son. Larry Rennart. Seventeen years old. See if we can find out what he's been up to."

She shrugged. "A waste of time, but okay." She gestured toward the school. "You want to go in now?"

"Sure."

Before they moved, a giant set of knuckles gently tapped on Myron's window. The sound startled him. Myron looked out his window. The large black man with the Nat King Cole hair—the one from the Court Manor Inn —was smiling at him. "Nat" made a cranking motion with his hand, signaling Myron to lower the window. Myron complied.

"Hey, I'm glad we ran into you," Myron said. "I never got the number of your barber."

The black man chuckled. He made a frame with his large hands—thumbs touching, arms outstretched—and tilted it back and forth the way a movie director does. "You with my doo," he said with a shake of his head. "Somehow I just don't see it."

He leaned into the car and stuck his hand across Myron toward Esperanza. "My name is Carl."

"Esperanza." She shook his hand.

"Yes, I know."

Esperanza squinted at him. "I know you."

"Indeed you do."

She snapped her fingers. "Mosambo, the Kenyan Killer, the Safari Slasher."

Carl smiled. "Nice to see Little Pocahontas remembers."

Myron said, "The Safari Slasher?"

"Carl used to be a professional wrestler," Esperanza

explained. "We were in the ring together once. In Boston, right?"

Carl climbed into the backseat of the car. He leaned forward so his head was between Esperanza's right shoulder and Myron's left. "Hartford," he said. "At the Civic Center."

"Mixed tag-team," Esperanza said.

"That's right," Carl said with his easy smile. "Be a sweetheart, Esperanza, and start up the car. Head straight until the third traffic light."

Myron said, "You mind telling us what's going on?"

"Sure thing. See that car behind you?"

Myron used the passenger-side mirror. "The one with the two goons?"

"Yep. They're with me. And they are bad men, Myron. Young. Far too violent. You know how the kids are today. *Bam, bam,* no talk. The three of us are supposed to escort you to an unknown destination. In fact, I'm supposed to be holding a gun on you now. But hell, we're all friends here, right? No need, the way I see it. So just start heading straight. The goons will follow."

"Before we take off," Myron said, "do you mind if we let Esperanza go?"

Carl chuckled. "Kinda sexist, don't you think?"

"Excuse me?"

"If Esperanza were a man—like, say, your buddy Win —would you be making this gallant gesture?"

"I might," he said. But even Esperanza was shaking her head.

"Me thinks not, Myron. And trust me here: it would be the wrong move. The young goons back there, they'd want to know what's up. They'd see her get out of the car and they got those itchy fingers and those crazy eyes and they like hurting people. Especially women. And maybe, just maybe, Esperanza here is an insurance policy. Alone, you might try something dumb; with Esperanza right there, you might not be so inclined."

Esperanza glanced at Myron. Myron nodded. She started the car.

"Make a left at the third light," Carl said.

"Tell me something," Myron said. "Is Reginald Squires as big a nut-job as I hear?"

Still leaning forward, Carl turned to Esperanza. "Am I supposed to be wowed by his sharp deductive reasoning skills?"

"Yes," Esperanza replied. "He'll be terribly disappointed if you aren't."

"Figured that. And to answer your question, Squires is not that big a nut-job—when he stays on his medication."

"Very comforting," Myron said.

The young goons stayed right on their tail for the entire fifteen-minute drive. Myron was not surprised when Carl told Esperanza to turn down Green Acres Road. When they approached the ornate front entrance, the iron gates swung open like on the closing credits of *Get Smart*. They continued up a windy driveway through the heavily wooded property. After about a half mile, they hit a clearing with a building. The building was big and plain and rectangular, like a high school gym.

The only entrance Myron could see was a garage door. As if on cue, the door slid open. Carl told Esperanza to pull into it. Once far enough inside, he told her to park and kill the engine. The goon car came in behind them and did likewise.

The garage door came back down, slowly slicing out the sun. No lights were on inside; the room was submerged in total darkness.

"This is just like the haunted house at Six Flags," Myron said.

"Give me your gun, Myron."

Carl had his game face on. Myron handed him the gun.

"Step out of the car."

"But I'm afraid of the dark," Myron said.

"You too, Esperanza."

They all stepped out the car. So did the two goons behind them. Their movements echoed off the cement floor, hinting to Myron that they were in a very large room. The interior car lights provided a modicum of illumination, but that didn't last long. Myron made out nothing before the doors were closed.

Absolute blackness.

Myron made his way around the car and found Esperanza. She took his hand in hers. They remained still and waited.

A beacon, the kind used at a lighthouse or a movie premiere, snapped on in their faces. Myron's eyes slammed shut. He shaded them with his hand and slowly squinted them open. A man stepped in front of the bright light. His body cast a giant shadow on the wall behind Myron. The effect reminded Myron of the Bat Signal.

"No one will hear your screams," the man said.

"Isn't that a line from a movie?" Myron asked. "But I think the line was, 'No one will hear you scream.' I could be wrong about that."

"People have died in this room," the voice boomed. "My name is Reginald Squires. You will tell me everything I want to know. Or you and your friend will be next."

Oh, boy. Myron looked at Carl. Carl's face remained stoic. Myron turned back toward the light. "You're rich, right?"

"Very rich," Squires corrected.

"Then maybe you could afford a better scriptwriter."

Myron glanced back at Carl. Carl slowly shook his

head no. One of the two young goons stepped forward. In the harsh light, Myron could see the man's psychotic, happy smile. Myron tensed, waited.

The goon cocked a fist and threw it at Myron's head. Myron ducked, and the punch missed. As the fist flew by him, Myron grabbed the goon's wrist. He put his forearm against the back of the man's elbow and pulled the joint back in a way it was never intended to bend. The goon had no choice. He dropped to the ground. Myron added a bit more pressure. The goon tried to squirm free. Myron snapped his knee straight into the goon's nose. Something splattered. Myron could actually feel the nose cartilage give way and fan out.

The second goon took out his gun and pointed it at Myron.

"Stop," Squires shouted.

Myron let the goon go. He slid to the floor like wet sand through a torn bag.

"You will pay for that, Mr. Bolitar." Squires liked to project his voice. "Robert?"

The goon with the gun said, "Yes, Mr. Squires."

"Hit the girl. Hard."

"Yes, Mr. Squires."

Myron said, "Hey, hit me. I'm the one who smarted off."

"And this is your punishment," Squires said calmly. "Hit the girl, Robert. Now."

Goon Robert moved toward Esperanza.

"Mr. Squires?" It was Carl.

"Yes, Carl."

Carl stepped into the light. "Allow me to do it."

"I did not think you were the type, Carl."

"I'm not, Mr. Squires. But Robert might do serious damage to her."

"But that's my intent."

"No, I mean, he'll leave bruising or break something. You want her to feel pain. That's my area of expertise."

"I realize that, Carl. It's why I pay you what I do."

"So then let me do my job. I can hit her without leaving a mark or permanent injury. I know control. I know the right spots."

The shadowy Mr. Squires considered this a moment. "Will you make it painful?" he asked. "Very painful?"

"If you insist." Carl sounded reluctant but resolved.

"I do. Right now. I want it to hurt her a great deal."

Carl walked up to Esperanza. Myron start to move toward him, but Robert placed the gun against his head. There was nothing he could do. He tried fire-throwing a warning glare at Carl.

"Don't," Myron said.

Carl ignored him. He stood in front of Esperanza now. She looked at him defiantly. Without preamble he punched her deep in the stomach.

The power of the blow lifted Esperanza off her feet. She made an oofing noise and folded at the waist like an old wallet. Her body landed on the floor. She curled up into a protective ball, her eyes wide, her chest heaving for air. Carl looked down at her without emotion. Then he looked at Myron.

"You son of a bitch," Myron said.

"It's your fault," Carl said.

Esperanza continued to roll on the ground in obvious agony. She still couldn't get any air into her lungs. Myron's whole body felt hot and red. He moved toward her, but Robert again stopped him by pressing the gun hard against his neck.

Reginald Squires did the big voice-projection again. "You will listen now, won't you, Mr. Bolitar?"

Myron took deep breaths. His muscles bunched. Every part of him fumed. Every part of him craved vengeance. He watched in silence as Esperanza writhed on the floor. After a while she managed to get to all fours. Her head was down. Her body heaved. A retching noise came out of her. Then another retching noise.

The sound made Myron pause.

Something about the sound . . . Myron searched his memory banks. Something about the whole scenario, the way she doubled up, the way she rolled on the floor—it was strangely familiar. As though he'd seen it before. But that was impossible. When would he . . . ? He stopped as the answer came to him.

In the wrestling ring.

My God, Myron thought. She was faking it!

Myron looked over at Carl. There was a hint of a smile on his face.

Son of a bitch. It was an act!

Reginald Squires cleared his throat. "You have taken an unhealthy interest in my son, Mr. Bolitar," he continued, voice thundering. "Are you some sort of pervert?"

Myron almost flew off another wisecrack, but he bit it back. "No."

"Then tell me what you want with him."

Myron squinted into the light. He still couldn't see anything but the shadowy outline of Squires. What should he say? The guy was a major loony tune. No question about that. So how to play this . . . ?

"You've heard about Jack Coldren's murder," Myron said.

"Of course."

"I'm working on the case."

"You're trying to find out who murdered Jack Coldren?"

"Yes."

"But Jack was murdered last night," Squires countered. "You were asking about my son Saturday."

"It's a long story," Myron said.

The shadow's hands spread. "We have all the time in the world."

How did Myron know he was going to say that?

With nothing much to lose, Myron told Squires about the kidnapping. Most of it anyway. He emphasized several times that the actual abduction had happened at the Court Manor Inn. There was a reason for that. It had to do with the egocentricity. Reginald Squires—the ego in question—reacted in predictable fashion.

"Are you telling me," he shouted, "that Chad Coldren was kidnapped at *my* motel?"

His motel. Myron had figured that out by now. It was the only explanation for why Carl had run interference for Stuart Lipwitz.

"That's right," Myron said.

"Carl?"

"Yes, Mr. Squires?"

"Did you know anything about this kidnapping?"

"No, Mr. Squires."

"Well, something has to be done," Squires shouted. "No one does something like that on my turf. You hear me? No one."

This guy had seen waaaaaay too many gangster films.

"Whoever did this is dead," he ranted on. "Do you hear me? I want them dead. D-E-A-D. Do you understand what I'm saying, Mr. Bolitar?"

"Dead," Myron said with a nod.

The shadow pointed a long finger at Myron. "You find him for me. You find who did this and then you call me. You let me handle it. Do you understand, Mr. Bolitar?"

"Call you. You handle."

"Go then. Find the wretched bastard."

Myron said, "Sure thing, Mr. Squires. Sure thing."

Hey, two can play the Bad Movie Dialogue game. "But the thing is, I need some help."

"What sort of help?"

"With your permission, I'd like to speak with your son Matthew. Find out what he knows about all this."

"What makes you think he knows anything?"

"He's Chad's best friend. He may have heard or seen something. I don't know, Mr. Squires, but I'd like to check it out."

There was a brief silence. Then Squires snapped, "Do it. Carl will take you back to the school. Matthew will speak freely to you."

"Thank you, Mr. Squires."

The light went off, bathing them again in thick darkness. Myron felt his way to the car door. The "recovering" Esperanza managed to do likewise. So did Carl. The three of them got in.

Myron turned around and looked at Carl. Carl shrugged his shoulders and said, "Guess he forgot to take his medication."

Chapter 32

"Chad, like, told me he was hooking up with an older babe."

"Did he tell you her name?" Myron asked.

"Nah, man," Matthew Squires said. "Just that she was take-out."

"Take-out?"

"You know. Chinese."

Jesus.

Myron sat facing Matthew Squires. The kid was pure Yah Dude. His long, stringy hair was parted in the middle and hung past his shoulders. The coloring and texture reminded Myron of Cousin It from the *Addams Family*. He had acne, a fair amount of it. He was over six feet and weighed maybe one hundred twenty pounds. Myron wondered what it had been like for this kid growing up with Mr. Spotlight as a father.

Carl was on his right. Esperanza had taken a taxi to check out Esme Fong's alibi and look into Lloyd Rennart's past.

"Did Chad tell you where he was meeting her?"

"Sure, dude. That hot sheet is, like, my dad's haunt, you know."

"Did Chad know your father owned the Court Manor?"

"Nah. We don't, like, talk daddy's dinero or anything. Not righteous, you know what I'm saying?"

Myron and Carl exchanged a glance. The glance be-
moaned today's youth.

"Did you go with him to the Court Manor?"

"Nah. I went later, you know. I figured the dude
would want to party after getting a little, you know. Kinda
celebrate and shit."

"So what time did you go to the Court Manor?"

"Ten-thirty, eleven, something like that."

"Did you see Chad?"

"Nah. Things got, like, so weird right away. Never got
the chance."

"What do you mean, weird?"

Matthew Squires hesitated a bit. Carl leaned forward.
"It's okay, Matthew. Your father wants you to tell him
the whole story."

The kid nodded. When the chin went down, the
stringy hair slid across the face. It was like a tasseled
curtain opening and closing in rapid succession. "Okay,
like, here's the deal: When I pulled my Benz into the
parking lot, I saw Chad's old man."

Myron felt a queasy surge. "Jack Coldren? You saw
Jack Coldren? At the Court Manor Inn?"

Squires nodded. "He was just, like, sitting in his car,"
he said. "Next to Chad's Honda. He looked really pissed
off, man. I wanted no part of it, you know? So I took a
hike."

Myron tried not to look too stunned. Jack Coldren at
the Court Manor Inn. His son inside a room screwing
Esme Fong. The next morning Chad Coldren would be
kidnapped.

What the hell was going on?

"Friday night," Myron continued, "I saw someone
climb out the window of Chad's room. Was that you?"

"Yeah."

"You want to tell me what you were doing?"

"Seeing if Chad was home. That's what we do. I climb through his window. Like Vinny used to do with Doogie Howser. Remember that show?"

Myron nodded. He did know. Kinda sad when you thought about it.

There was not much more to extract from young Matthew. When they finished up, Carl walked Myron to his car.

"Strange shit," Carl said.

"Yep."

"You'll call when you learn something?"

"Yep." Myron didn't bother telling him that Tito was already dead. No point. "Nice move, by the way. The fake punch with Esperanza."

Carl smiled. "We're professionals. I'm disappointed you spotted it."

"If I hadn't seen Esperanza in the ring, I wouldn't have. It was very nice work. You should be proud."

"Thanks." Carl stuck out his hand. Myron shook it. He got in the car and drove away. Now where?

Back to the Coldren house, he guessed.

His mind still reeled from this latest revelation: Jack Coldren had been at the Court Manor Inn. He had seen his son's car there. How the heck did that fit into this? Was Jack Coldren following Chad? Maybe. Was he just there by coincidence? Doubtful. So what other options were there? Why would Jack Coldren be following his own son? And where had he followed him from—Matthew Squires's house? Did that make sense? The man plays in the U.S. Open, has a great opening round, and then goes parking in front of the Squires estate waiting for his kid to pull out?

Nope.

Hold the phone.

Suppose Jack Coldren had not been following his son. Suppose he had been following Esme Fong.

Something in his brain went "click."

Maybe Jack Coldren had been having an affair with Esme Fong too. His marriage was on the rocks. Esme Fong was probably a bit of a kinkster. She had seduced a teenage boy—what would have stopped her from seducing his father? But did this make sense either? Was Jack stalking her? Had he somehow found out about the tryst? What?

And the larger question: What does any of this have to do with Chad Coldren's kidnapping and Jack Coldren's murder?

He pulled up to the Coldren house. The media had been kept back, but there were now at least a dozen cops on hand. They were hauling out cardboard boxes. As Victoria Wilson had feared, the police had gotten a search warrant.

Myron parked around the corner and walked toward the house. Jack's caddie, Diane Hoffman, sat alone on the curb across the street. He remembered the last time he had seen her at the Coldren house: in the backyard, fighting with Jack. He also realized that she had been one of the very few people who knew about the kidnapping—hadn't she been standing right there when Myron first talked about it with Jack at the driving range?

She was worth a conversation.

Diane Hoffman was smoking a cigarette. The several stubs by her feet indicated that she had been there for more than a few minutes. Myron approached.

"Hi," he said. "We met the other day."

Diane Hoffman looked up at him, took a deep drag of the cigarette, released it into the still air. "I remember." Her hoarse voice sounded like old tires on rough pavement.

"My condolences," Myron said. "You and Jack must have been very close."

Another deep drag. "Yeah."

"Caddy and golfer. Must be a tight relationship."

She looked up at him, squinting suspiciously. "Yeah."

"Almost like husband and wife. Or business partners."

"Uh-huh. Something like that."

"Did you two ever fight?"

She glared at him for a second, then she broke into a laugh that ended in a hacking cough. When she could talk again, she asked, "Why the hell do you want to know that?"

"Because I saw you two fighting."

"What?"

"Friday night. You two were in the backyard. You called him names. You threw down your cigarette in disgust."

Diane Hoffman crushed out the cigarette. There was the smallest smile on her face. "You some kinda Sherlock Holmes, Mr. Bolitar?"

"No. I'm just asking you a question."

"And I can tell you to go mind your own fucking business, right?"

"Right."

"Good. Then you go do that." The smile became fuller now. It was not a particularly pretty smile. "But first—to save you some time—I'll tell you who killed Jack. And also who kidnapped the kid, if you like."

"I'm all ears."

"The bitch in there." She pointed to the house behind her with a thumb. "The one you got the hots for."

"I don't have the hots for her."

Diane Hoffman sneered. "Right."

"What makes you so sure it was Linda Coldren?"

"Because I know the bitch."

"That's not much of an answer."

"Tough luck, cowpoke. Your girlfriend did it. You want to know why Jack and me was fighting? I'll tell you. I told him he was being an asshole for not calling the police about the kidnapping. He said he and Linda thought it best." She sneered. "He and Linda, my ass."

Myron watched her. Something wasn't meshing again.

"You think it was Linda's idea not to call the police?"

"Damn straight. She's the one who grabbed the kid. The whole thing was a big setup."

"Why would she do that?"

"Ask her." An awful smile. "Maybe she'll tell you."

"I'm asking you."

She shook her head. "Not that easy, cowpoke. I told you who did it. That's enough, don't you think?"

Time to approach from another angle. "How long have you been Jack's caddie?" he asked.

"A year."

"What's your qualifications, if I may ask? Why did Jack choose you?"

She snorted a chuckle. "Don't matter none. Jack didn't listen to caddies. Not since ol' Lloyd Rennart."

"Did you know Lloyd Rennart?"

"Nope."

"So why did Jack hire you?"

She did not answer.

"Were you two sleeping together?"

Diane Hoffman gave another cough-laugh. A big one. "Not likely." More hacking laughter. "Not likely with ol' Jack."

Somebody called his name. Myron turned around. It was Victoria Wilson. Her face was still sleepy, but she beckoned him with some urgency. Bucky stood next to her. The old man looked like a window draft would send him skittering.

"Better head on down there, cowpoke," she mocked. "I think your girlfriend is gonna need some help."

He gave her a last look and turned toward the house. Before he moved three steps, Detective Corbett was on him. "Need a word with you, Mr. Bolitar."

Myron brushed past him. "In a minute."

When he reached Victoria Wilson, she made herself very clear: "Do not talk to the cops," she said. "In fact, go to Win's and stay put."

"I'm not crazy about taking orders," Myron said.

"Sorry if I'm bruising your male ego," she said in a tone that made it clear she was anything but. "But I know what I'm doing."

"Have the police found the finger?"

Victoria Wilson crossed her arms. "Yes."

"And?"

"And nothing."

Myron looked at Bucky. Bucky looked away. He turned his attention back to Victoria Wilson. "They didn't ask you about it?"

"They asked. We refused to answer."

"But the finger could exonerate her."

Victoria Wilson sighed and turned away. "Go home, Myron. I'll call you if anything new turns up."

Chapter 33

It was time to face Win.

Myron rehearsed several possible approaches in the car. None felt right, but that really did not matter much. Win was his friend. When the time came, Myron would deliver the message and Win would adhere to it or not.

The trickier question was, of course, should the message be delivered at all? Myron knew that repression was unhealthy and all that—but did anybody really want to risk unbottling Win's suppressed rage?

The cell phone rang. Myron picked it up. It was Tad Crispin.

"I need your help," Tad said.

"What's up?"

"The media keep hounding me for a comment. I'm not sure what to say."

"Nothing," Myron told him. "Say nothing."

"Yeah, okay, but it's not that easy. Learner Shelton—he's the Commissioner of the USGA—called me twice. He wants to have a big trophy ceremony tomorrow. Name me U.S. Open champion. I'm not sure what to do."

Smart kid, Myron thought. He knows that if this is handled poorly, it could seriously wound him. "Tad?"

"Yes?"

"Are you hiring me?" Business was still business. Agenting was not charity work.

"Yeah, Myron, you're hired."

"Okay then, listen up. There'll be details to work out

first. Percentages, that kinda thing. Most of it is fairly standard.'' Kidnapping, limb-severing, murder—nothing stopped the almighty agent from trying to turn a buck. ''In the meantime, say nothing. I'll have a car come by to pick you up in a couple of hours. The driver will call up to your room before he gets there. Go straight to the car and say nothing. No matter what the press yells at you, keep silent. Do not smile or wave. Look grim. A man has just been murdered. The driver will bring you to Win's estate. We'll discuss strategy then.''

''Thanks, Myron.''

''No, Tad, thank you.''

Profiting from a murder. Myron had never felt so much like a real agent in all his life.

The media had set up camp outside Win's estate.

''I've hired extra guards for the evening,'' Win explained, empty brandy snifter in hand. ''If anybody approaches the gate, they've been instructed to shoot to kill.''

''I appreciate that.''

Win gave a quick head bow. He poured some Grand Marnier into the snifter. Myron grabbed a Yoo-Hoo from the fridge. The two men sat.

''Jessica called,'' Win said.

''Here?''

''Yes.''

''Why didn't she call me on the cellular?''

''She wanted to speak with me,'' Win said.

''Oh.'' Myron shook his Yoo-Hoo, just like the side of the can said. SHAKE! IT'S GREAT! Life is poetry. ''What about?''

''She was worried about you,'' Win said.

''Why?''

"For one thing, Jessica claimed that you left a cryptic message on the answering machine."

"Did she tell you what I said?"

"No. Just that your voice sounded strained."

"I told her that I loved her. That I'd always love her."

Win took a sip and nodded as though that explained everything.

"What?"

"Nothing," Win said.

"No, tell me. What?"

Win put down the snifter and steepled his fingers. "Who were you trying to convince?" he asked. "Her or you?"

"What the hell does that mean?"

Bouncing the fingers now instead of steepling. "Nothing."

"You know how much I love Jessica."

"Indeed I do," Win said.

"You know what I've gone through to get her back."

"Indeed I do."

"I still don't get it," Myron said. "That's why Jess called you? Because my voice sounded strained?"

"Not entirely, no. She'd heard about Jack Coldren's murder. Naturally, she was upset. She asked me to watch your back."

"What did you tell her?"

"No."

Silence.

Win lifted the snifter in the air. He swirled around the liquid and inhaled deeply. "So what did you wish to discuss with me?"

"I met your mother today."

Win took a slow sip. He let the liquid roll over his tongue, his eyes studying the bottom of the glass. After he swallowed, he said, "Pretend I just gasped in surprise."

"She wanted me to give you a message."

A small smile came to Win's lips. "I assume that dear ma-ma told you what happened."

"Yes."

A bigger smile now. "So now you know it all, eh, Myron?"

"No."

"Oh come, come, don't make it so easy. Give me some of that pop psychology you're so fond of expounding. An eight-year-old boy witnessing his grunting mother on all fours with another man—surely that scarred me emotionally. Can we not trace back everything I've become to that one dastardly moment? Isn't this episode the reason why I treat women the way I do, why I build an emotional fortress around myself, why I choose fists where others choose words? Come now, Myron. You must have considered all this. Tell me all. I am sure it will all be oh-so-insightful."

Myron waited a beat. "I'm not here to analyze you, Win."

"No?"

"No."

Win's eyes hardened. "Then wipe that pity off your face."

"It's not pity," Myron said. "It's concern."

"Oh please."

"It may have happened twenty-five years ago, but it had to hurt. Maybe it didn't shape you. Maybe you would have ended up the exact same person you are today. But that doesn't mean it didn't hurt."

Win relaxed his jaw. He picked up the snifter. It was empty. He poured himself more. "I no longer wish to discuss this," he said. "You know now why I want nothing to do with Jack Coldren or my mother. Let us move on."

"There's still the matter of her message."

"Ah, yes, the message," Win repeated. "You are aware, are you not, that dear ma-ma still sends me presents on my birthday and assorted holidays?"

Myron nodded. They had never discussed it. But he knew.

"I return them unopened," Win said. He took another sip. "I think I will do the same with this message."

"She's dying, Win. Cancer. She has maybe a week or two."

"I know."

Myron sat back. His throat felt dry.

"Is that the entire message?"

"She wanted you to know that it's your last chance to talk to her," Myron said.

"Well, yes, that's true. It would be very difficult for us to chat after she's dead."

Myron was flailing now. "She's not expecting any kind of big reconciliation. But if there are any issues you want to resolve . . ." Myron stopped. He was being redundant and obvious now. Win hated that.

"That's it?" Win asked. "That's your big message?"

Myron nodded.

"Fine, then. I'm going to order some Chinese. I hope that will be suitable with you."

Win rose from his seat and strolled toward the kitchen.

"You claim it didn't change you," Myron said. "But before that day, did you love her?"

Win's face was a stone. "Who says I don't love her now?"

Chapter 34

The driver brought Tad Crispin in through the back entrance.

Win and Myron had been watching television. A commercial came on for Scope. A married couple in bed woke up and turned their heads in disgust. Morning breath, the voice-over informed them. You need Scope. Scope cures morning breath.

Myron said, "So would, say, brushing your teeth?"

Win nodded.

Myron opened the door and led Tad into the living room. Tad sat on a couch across from Myron and Win. He glanced about, his eyes searching for a spot to settle on but not having any luck. He smiled weakly.

"Would you care for a beverage?" Win asked. "A croissant or a Pop Tart perhaps?" The Host with the Most.

"No, thank you." Another weak smile.

Myron leaned forward. "Tad, tell us about Learner Shelton's call."

The kid dove right in. "He said that he wanted to congratulate me on my victory. That the USGA had officially declared me the U.S. Open champion." For a moment, Tad stopped. His eyes hazed over, the words hitting him anew. Tad Crispin, U.S. Open champion. The stuff of dreams.

"What else did he say?"

Crispin's eyes slowly cleared. "He's holding a press

conference tomorrow afternoon. At Merion. They'll give me the trophy and a check for $360,000.''

Myron did not waste time. "First of all, we tell the media that you do not consider yourself the U.S. Open champion. If they want to call you that, fine. If the USGA wants to call you that, fine. You, however, believe that the tournament ended in a tie. Death should not rob Jack Coldren of his magnificent accomplishment or his claim to the title. A tie it ended. A tie it is. From your vantage point, you two are co-winners. Do you understand?"

Tad was hesitant. "I think so."

"Now, about that check." Myron strummed the end table with his fingers. "If they insist on giving you the full winner's purse, you'll have to donate Jack's portion to charity."

"Victims' rights," Win said.

Myron nodded. "That would be good. Something against violence—"

"Wait a second," Tad interrupted. He rubbed the palms of his hands on his thighs. "You want me to give away $180,000?"

"It'll be a tax write-off," Win said. "That knocks the value down to half that."

"And it'll be chicken feed compared to the positive press you'll get," Myron added.

"But I was charging back," Tad insisted. "I had the momentum. I would have won."

Myron leaned in a little closer. "You're an athlete, Tad. You're competitive and confident. That's good— heck, that's great. But not in this situation. This murder story is huge. It transcends sports. For most of the world's population, this will be their first look at Tad Crispin. We want them to see someone likable. Someone decent and trustworthy and modest. If we brag now about what a great golfer you are—if we dwell on your comeback rather than this tragedy—people are going to see you as cold, as another example of what's wrong with today's athletes. Do you see what I'm saying?"

Tad nodded. "I guess so."

"We have to present you in a certain light. We have to control the story as much as possible."

"So we do interviews?" Tad asked.

"Very few."

"But if we want publicity—"

"We want carefully orchestrated publicity," Myron corrected. "This story is so big, the last thing we need to do is create more interest. I want you to be reclusive, Tad. Thoughtful. You see, we have to maintain the right balance. If we toot our horn, it looks like we're grandstanding. If we do a lot of interviews, it looks like we're taking advantage of a man's murder."

"Disastrous," Win added.

"Right. What we want to do is control the flow of information. Feed the press a few tiny morsels. No more."

"Perhaps one interview," Win said. "One where you will be at your most contrite."

"With Bob Costas maybe."

"Or even Barbara Walters."

"And we don't announce your big donation."

"Correct, no press conference. You are far too magnanimous for such bravado."

That confused Tad. "How are we supposed to get good press if we don't announce it?"

"We leak it," Myron said. "We get someone at the charity to tell a nosy reporter, maybe. Something like that. The key is, Tad Crispin must remain far too modest a fellow to publicize his own good deeds. Do you see what we're aiming for here?"

Tad's nod was more enthusiastic now. He was warming up. Myron felt like a heel. Spin-doctoring—just another hat today's sports representative must wear. Being an agent was not always pretty. You had to get dirty sometimes. Myron did not necessarily like it, but he was willing. The media would portray events one way; he would present them another. Still he felt like a grinning political strategist after a debate, and you cannot get much lower than that.

They discussed details for a few more minutes. Tad started to look off again. He was rubbing the famed palms against the pants again. When Win left the room for a minute, Tad whispered, "I saw on the news that you're Linda Coldren's attorney."

"I'm one of them."

"Are you her agent?"

"I might be," Myron said. "Why?"

"Then you're a lawyer too, right? You went to law school and everything?"

Myron was not sure he liked where this was going. "Yes."

"So I can hire you to be my lawyer too, right? Not just my agent?"

Myron really didn't like where this was going. "Why would you need a lawyer, Tad?"

"I'm not saying I do. But if I did—"

"Whatever you tell me is confidential," Myron said.

Tad Crispin stood. He put his arms out straight and gripped an imaginary golf club. He took a swing. Air golf. Win played it all the time. All golfers do. Basketball players don't do that. It's not like Myron stops at every store window and checks the reflection of his shot in the mirror.

Golfers.

"I'm surprised you don't know about this already," Tad said slowly.

But the creeping feeling in the pit of Myron's stomach told him that maybe he did. "Don't know about what, Tad?"

Tad took another swing. He stopped his movement to check his backswing. Then his expression changed to one of panic. He dropped the imaginary club to the floor. "It was only a couple of times," he said, his words pouring out like silver beads. "It was no big deal really. I mean, we met while we were filming those ads for Zoom." He looked at Myron, his eyes pleading. "You've seen her, Myron. I mean, I know she's twenty years older than me, but she's so good-looking and she said her marriage was dead. . . ."

Myron did not hear the rest of his words; the ocean was crashing in his ears. Tad Crispin and Linda Coldren. He could not believe it, yet it made perfect sense. A young guy obviously charmed by a stunning older woman. The mature beauty trapped in a loveless marriage finding escape in young, handsome arms. Nothing really wrong with it.

Yet Myron felt his cheeks go scarlet. Something inside of him began to fume.

Tad was still droning on. Myron interrupted him.

"Did Jack find out?"

Tad stopped. "I don't know," he said. "But I think maybe he did."

"What makes you say that?"

"It was just the way he acted. We played two rounds together. I know we were competitors and that he was trying to intimidate me. But I kind of got the impression he knew."

Myron lowered his head into his hands. He felt sick to his stomach.

Tad asked, "Do you think it'll get out?"

Myron held back a chuckle. This would be one of the biggest news stories of the year. The media would attack like old women at a Loehmann's clearance sale. "I don't know, Tad."

"What do we do?"

"We hope it doesn't get out."

Tad was scared. "And if it does?"

Myron faced him. Tad Crispin looked so damn young —check that, he was young. Most kids his age are happily pulling fraternity pranks. And when you thought about it, what had Tad really done that was so bad? Slept with an older woman who for some odd reason remained in a dead marriage. Hardly unnatural. Myron tried to picture himself at Tad's age. If a beautiful older woman like Linda Coldren had come on to him, would he have stood a chance?

Like, duh. He probably did not stand a chance now.

But what about Linda Coldren? Why did she stay in this dead marriage? Religion? Doubtful. For the sake of her son? The kid was sixteen years old. It might not be easy, but he'd survive.

"Myron, what'll happen if the media find out?"

But Myron was suddenly no longer thinking about the media. He was thinking about the police. He was thinking about Victoria Wilson and reasonable doubt. Linda Coldren had probably told her ace attorney about her affair with Tad Crispin. Victoria would have seen it too.

Who is declared U.S. Open champion now that Jack Coldren is dead?

Who doesn't have to worry about out-choking the choker in front of a massive audience?

Who has all the same motives to kill Jack Coldren that Myron had earlier assigned to Esme Fong?

Whose squeaky-clean image might get soiled by a

Coldren divorce, especially one where Jack Coldren
would name his wife's indiscretion?

Who was having an affair with the deceased's wife?

The answer to all the above was sitting in front of him.

Chapter 35

Tad Crispin left not long after that.

Myron and Win settled into the couch. They put on Woody Allen's *Broadway Danny Rose*, one of Woody's most underrated masterpieces. What a flick. Rent it sometime.

During the scene where Mia drags Woody to the fortune-teller, Esperanza arrived.

She coughed into her fist. "I, ahem, don't want to sound didactic or fictitious in any manner," she began, doing a great Woody impression. She had his timing, the speech delay tactics. She had the hand mannerisms. She had the New York accent. It was her best work. "But I may have some important information."

Myron looked up. Win kept his eyes on the screen.

"I located the man Lloyd Rennart bought the bar from twenty years ago," Esperanza said, returning to her own voice. "Rennart paid him in cash. Seven grand. I also checked on the house in Spring Lake Heights. Bought at the same time for $21,000. No mortgage."

"Lots of expenses," Myron said, "for a washed-up caddie."

"Sí, señor. And to make matters more interesting, I also found no indication that he worked or paid taxes from the time he was fired by Jack Coldren until he purchased the Rusty Nail bar."

"Could be an inheritance."

"I would doubt it," Esperanza said. "I managed to go

back to 1971 and found no record of him paying any inheritance tax.''

Myron looked at Win. "What do you think?"

Win's eyes were still on the screen. "I'm not listening."

"Right, I forgot.'' He looked back at Esperanza. ''Anything else?''

"Esme Fong's alibi checks out. I spoke to Miguel. She never left the hotel.''

"Is he solid?"

"Yeah, I think so.''

Strike one. "Anything else?"

"Not yet. But I found the office for the local paper in Narberth. They have the back editions in a storage room. I'll go through them tomorrow, see what I can dig up on the car accident.''

Esperanza grabbed a take-out container and a pair of chopsticks from the kitchen and then she plopped down on the open couch. A mafioso hit man was calling Woody a cheesehead. Woody commented that he had no idea what that meant, but he was confident it wasn't a good thing. Ah, the Woodman.

Ten minutes into *Love and Death*, not long after Woody wondered how old Nahampkin could be younger than young Nahampkin, exhaustion overtook Myron. He fell asleep on the couch. A deep sleep. No dreams. No stirring. Nothing but the long fall down the deep well.

He woke up at eight-thirty. The television was off. A clock ticked and then chimed. Someone had laid a comforter over Myron while he'd been sleeping. Win probably. He checked the other bedrooms. Win and Esperanza were both gone.

He showered and dressed and put on some coffee. The phone rang. Myron picked it up and said, "Hello.''

It was Victoria Wilson. She still sounded bored. "They arrested Linda."

Myron found Victoria Wilson in an attorney waiting area.

"How is she?"

"Fine," Victoria replied. "I brought Chad home last night. That made her happy."

"So where is Linda?"

"In a holding cell awaiting arraignment. We'll see her in a few minutes."

"What do they have?"

"Quite a bit, actually," Victoria said. She sounded almost impressed. "First, they have the guard who saw her entering and leaving an otherwise abandoned golf course at the time of the murder. With the exception of Jack, nobody else was seen going in or out all night."

"Doesn't mean nobody did. It's an awfully big area."

"Very true. But from their standpoint it gives Linda opportunity. Second, they found hairs and fibers on Jack's body and around the murder scene that preliminary tests link to Linda. Naturally, this one should be no problem to discredit. Jack is her husband; of course he'd have hair and fibers from her on his body. He could have spread them around the scene."

"Plus she told us she went to the course to look for Jack," Myron added.

"But we're not telling them that."

"Why not?"

"Because right now we are saying and admitting to nothing."

Myron shrugged. Not important. "What else?"

"Jack owned a twenty-two-caliber handgun. The police found it in a wooded area between the Coldren residence and Merion last night."

"It was just sitting out?"

"No. It was buried in fresh dirt. A metal detector picked it up."

"They're sure it's Jack's gun?"

She nodded. "The serial numbers match. The police ran an immediate ballistics test. It's the murder weapon."

Myron's veins iced up.

"Fingerprints?" he asked.

Victoria Wilson shook her head. "Wiped clean."

"Are they running a powder test on her?" The police run a test on the hands, see if there are any powder burns.

"It'll take a few days," Victoria said, "and it'll probably be negative."

"You had her scrub her hands?"

"And treat them, yes."

"Then you think she did it."

Her tone remained unruffled. "Please don't say that."

She was right. But it was starting to look bad. "Is there more?" he asked.

"The police found your tape machine still hooked up to the phone. They were obviously curious as to why the Coldrens found it necessary to tape all incoming calls."

"Did they find any tapes of the conversations with the kidnapper?"

"Just the one where the kidnapper refers to the Fong woman as a 'chink bitch' and demands one hundred grand. And to answer your next two questions, no, we did not elaborate on the kidnapping and yes, they are pissed off."

Myron pondered that for a moment. Something was not right. "That was the only tape they found?"

"That's it."

He frowned. "But if the machine was still hooked up, it should have taped the last call the kidnapper made to

Jack. The one that got him to storm out of the house and head to Merion.''

Victoria Wilson looked at him steadily. ''The police found no other tapes. Not in the house. Not on Jack's body. Nowhere.''

Again the ice in the veins. The implication was obvious: The most reasonable explanation for there being no tape was that there was no call. Linda Coldren had made it up. The lack of a tape would have been viewed as a major contradiction *if* she had said anything to the cops. Fortunately for Linda, Victoria Wilson had never let her tell her story in the first place.

The woman was good.

''Can you get me a copy of the tape the police found?'' he asked.

Victoria Wilson nodded. ''There is still more,'' she said.

Myron was almost afraid to hear it.

''Let's take the severed finger for a moment,'' she continued as though ordering it as an appetizer. ''You found it in Linda's car in a manila envelope.''

Myron nodded.

''The envelope is the type sold only at Staples—their brand, the number ten size. The writing was done by a red Flair pen, medium-point. Three weeks ago, Linda Coldren visited Staples. According to the receipt found at her house yesterday, she purchased numerous office supplies, including a box of Staples' number ten manila envelopes and a red Flair medium-point pen.''

Myron could not believe what he was hearing.

''On the positive side, their handwriting analyst could not tell if the writing on the envelope came from Linda.''

But something else was dawning on Myron. Linda had waited around for him at Merion. The two of them had gone to the car together. They had found the finger together. The district attorney would pounce upon that story. Why had she waited for Myron? The answer, the DA would claim, was obvious: she needed a witness. She had planted the finger in her own car—she could certainly do that without drawing suspicion—and she needed a hapless dupe to be with her when she found it.

Enter Myron Bolitar, the dupe du jour.

But of course, Victoria Wilson had neatly arranged it so that the DA would never hear that story. Myron was Linda's attorney. He could not tell. No one would ever know.

Yep, the woman was good—except for one thing.

"The severed finger," Myron said. "That has to be the kicker, Victoria. Who is going to believe that a mother would cut off her own son's finger?"

Victoria looked at her watch. "Let's go talk to Linda."

"No, hold up here. That's the second time you blew this off. What aren't you telling me?"

She slung her purse over her shoulder. "Come on."

"Hey, I'm getting a little tired of getting jerked around here."

Victoria Wilson nodded slowly, but she did not speak or stop walking. Myron followed her into a holding room. Linda Coldren was already there. She was decked out in a bright orange prison jumpsuit. Her hands were still manacled. She looked up at Myron through hollow eyes. There were no hellos or hugs or even pleasantries.

Without preamble, Victoria said, "Myron wants to know why I don't think the severed finger helps us."

Linda faced him. There was a sad smile on her face. "I guess that's understandable."

"What the hell is going on here?" Myron said. "I know you didn't cut off your own son's finger."

The sad smile remained. "I didn't do it," Linda said. "That part is true."

"What do you mean, that part?"

"You said I didn't cut off my son's finger," she continued. "But Chad is not my son."

Chapter 36

Something in Myron's head clicked again.

"I'm infertile," Linda explained. She said the words with great ease, but the pain in her eyes was so raw and naked that Myron almost flinched. "I have this condition where my ovaries cannot produce eggs. But Jack still wanted a biological child."

Myron spoke softly. "You hired a surrogate?"

Linda looked toward Victoria. "Yes," she said. "Though it was not quite so aboveboard."

"It was all done to the letter of the law," Victoria interjected.

"You handled it for them?" Myron asked.

"I did the paperwork, yes. The adoption was completely legal."

"We wanted to keep it a secret," Linda said. "That's why I took off from the tour so early. I went into seclusion. The birth mother was never even supposed to know who we were."

Something else in his head went click. "But she found out."

"Yes."

Another click. "It's Diane Hoffman, isn't it?"

Linda was too exhausted to look surprised. "How did you know?"

"Just an educated guess." Why else would Jack hire Diane Hoffman as his caddie? Why else would she have gotten upset at the way they were handling the kidnapping? "How did she find you?"

Victoria answered that one. "As I said, it was all done legally. With all the new disclosure laws, it wasn't that hard to do."

Another click. "That's why you couldn't divorce Jack. He was the biological parent. He'd have the upper hand in a custody battle."

Linda slumped her shoulders and nodded.

"Does Chad know about all this?"

"No," Linda said.

"At least, not to your knowledge," Myron said.

"What?"

"You don't know for sure. Maybe he found out. Maybe Jack told him. Or Diane. Maybe that's how this whole thing got started."

Victoria crossed her arms. "I don't see it, Myron. Suppose Chad did find out. How would that have led to his own kidnapping and his father's murder?"

Myron shook his head. It was a good question. "I don't know yet. I need time to think it through. Do the police know all this?"

"About the adoption? Yes."

It was beginning to make sense now. "This gives the DA their motive. They'll say that Jack's suing for divorce worried Linda. That she killed him to keep her son."

Victoria Wilson nodded. "And the fact that Linda is not the biological mother could play one of two ways: either she loved her son so much that she killed Jack to keep him—or because Chad was not her own flesh and blood, she could indeed be driven to cut off his finger."

"Either way, finding the finger doesn't help us."

Victoria nodded. She did not say "I told you so," but she might as well have.

"Can I say something?" It was Linda. They turned and looked at her.

"I didn't love Jack anymore. I told you that straight out, Myron. I doubt I would have, if I'd been planning on killing him."

Myron nodded. Made sense.

"But I do love my son—*my* son—more than life itself. The fact that it's more believable that I'd maim him because I'm an adoptive mother rather than a biological one is sick and grotesque in the extreme. I love Chad as much as any mother could love a child."

She stopped, her chest heaving. "I want you both to know that."

"We know," Victoria said. Then: "Let's all sit down."

When they were settled in their seats, Victoria continued to take charge. "I know it's early, but I want to start thinking about reasonable doubt. Their case will have holes. I'll be sure to exploit them. But I'd like to hear some alternative theories on what happened."

"In other words," Myron said, "some other suspects."

Victoria caught something in his tone. "That's exactly what I mean."

"Well, you already have one ace in the hole, don't you?"

Victoria nodded coolly. "I do."

"Tad Crispin, right?"

This time, Linda did indeed look surprised. Victoria remained unfazed. "Yes, he's a suspect."

"The kid hired me last night," Myron said. "Talking about him would be a conflict of interest."

"Then we won't talk about him."

"I'm not sure that's good enough."

"Then you'll have to dump him as a client," Victoria

said. "Linda hired you first. Your obligation must be to her. If you feel that there is a conflict, then you'll have to call Mr. Crispin and tell him that you cannot represent him."

Trapped. And she knew it.

"Let's talk about other suspects," Myron said.

Victoria nodded. Battle won. "Go ahead."

"First off, Esme Fong." Myron filled them in on all the reasons that she made a good suspect. Again Victoria looked sleepy; Linda looked semi-homicidal.

"She seduced my son?" Linda shouted. "The bitch came into my house and seduced my son?"

"Apparently so."

"I can't believe it. That's why Chad was at that sleazy motel?"

"Yup—"

"Okay," Victoria interrupted. "I like it. This Esme Fong has motive. She has means. She was one of the few people who knew where Chad was."

"She also has an alibi for the killing," Myron added.

"But not a great one. There must be other ways in and out of that hotel. She could have worn a disguise. She could have sneaked out when Miguel took a bathroom break. I like her. Who else?"

"Lloyd Rennart."

"Who?"

"Jack's former caddie," Myron explained. "The one who helped throw the Open."

Victoria frowned. "Why him?"

"Look at the timing. Jack returns to the site of his greatest failure and suddenly all this happens. It can't be a coincidence. Firing Rennart ruined his life. He became a drunk. He killed his own wife in a car crash."

"What?" It was Linda.

"Not long after the Open, Lloyd totaled his car while DWI. His wife was killed."

Victoria asked, "Did you know her?"

Linda shook her head. "We never met his family. In fact, I don't think I ever saw Lloyd outside of our home or the golf course."

Victoria crossed her arms and leaned back. "I still do not see what makes him a viable suspect."

"Rennart wanted vengeance. He waited twenty-three years to get it."

Victoria frowned again.

"I admit that it's a bit of a stretch."

"A bit? It's ridiculous. Do you know where Lloyd Rennart is now?"

"That's a little complicated."

"Oh?"

"He may have committed suicide."

Victoria looked at Linda, then at Myron. "Would you please elaborate?"

"The body was never found," Myron said. "But everyone thinks he jumped off a cliff in Peru."

Linda groaned. "Oh, no . . ."

"What is it?" Victoria asked.

"We got a postcard from Peru."

"Who did?"

"It was addressed to Jack, but it was unsigned. It arrived last fall or winter."

Myron's pulse raced. Last fall or winter. About the time Lloyd allegedly jumped. "What did it say?"

"It only had two words on it," Linda said. " 'Forgive me.' "

Silence.

Victoria broke it. "That doesn't sound like the words of a man out for revenge."

"No," Myron agreed. He remembered what Esperanza had learned about the money Rennart had used to buy his house and bar. This postcard now confirmed what he had already suspected: Jack had been sabotaged. "But it also means that what happened twenty-three years ago was no accident."

"So what good does that do us?" Victoria asked.

"Someone paid Rennart off to throw the U.S. Open. Whoever did that would have motive."

"To kill Rennart maybe," Victoria countered. "But not Jack."

Good point. Or was it? Somebody had hated Jack enough twenty-three years ago to destroy his chances of winning the Open. Maybe that hatred had not died. Or maybe Jack had learned the truth and thus had to be quieted. Either way, it was worth looking into.

"I do not want to go digging into the past," Victoria said. "It could make things very messy."

"I thought you liked messy. Messy is fertile land for reasonable doubt."

"Reasonable doubt, I like," she said. "But the unknown, I don't. Look into Esme Fong. Look into the Squires family. Look into whatever. But stay away from the past, Myron. You never know what you might find back there."

Chapter 37

On the car phone: "Mrs. Rennart? This is Myron Bolitar."

"Yes, Mr. Bolitar."

"I promised that I'd call you periodically. To keep you updated."

"Have you learned something new?"

How to proceed? "Not about your husband. So far, there is no evidence that suggests Lloyd's death was anything other than a suicide."

"I see."

Silence.

"So why are you calling me, Mr. Bolitar?"

"Have you heard about Jack Coldren's murder?"

"Of course," Francine Rennart said. "It's on every station." Then: "You don't suspect Lloyd—"

"No," Myron said quickly. "But according to Jack's wife, Lloyd sent Jack a postcard from Peru. Right before his death."

"I see," she said again. "What did it say?"

"It had only two words on it: 'Forgive me.' He didn't sign it."

There was a brief pause and then she said, "Lloyd is dead, Mr. Bolitar. So is Jack Coldren. Let it lie."

"I'm not out to damage your husband's reputation. But it is becoming clear that somebody either forced Lloyd to sabotage Jack or paid him to do it."

"And you want me to help you prove that?"

"Whoever it was may have murdered Jack and maimed his son. Your husband sent Jack a postcard asking for forgiveness. With all due respect, Mrs. Rennart, don't you think Lloyd would want you to help?"

More silence.

"What do you want from me, Mr. Bolitar? I don't know anything about what happened."

"I realize that. But do you have any old papers of Lloyd's? Did he keep a journal or a diary? Anything that might give us a clue?"

"He didn't keep a journal or a diary."

"But there might be something else." Gently, fair Myron. Tread gently. "If Lloyd did receive compensation"—a nice way of saying a bribe—"there may be bank receipts or letters or something."

"There are boxes in the basement," she said. "Old photos, some papers maybe. I don't think there are any bank statements." Francine Rennart stopped talking for a moment. Myron kept the receiver pushed against his ear. "Lloyd always did have a lot of cash," she said softly. "I never really asked where it came from."

Myron licked his lips. "Mrs. Rennart, can I look through those boxes?"

"Tonight," she said. "You can come by tonight."

Esperanza was not back at the cottage yet. But Myron had barely sat down when the intercom buzzed.

"Yes?"

The guard manning the front gate spoke with perfect diction. "Sir, a gentleman and a young lady are here to see you. They claim that they are not with the media."

"Did they give a name?"

"The gentleman said his name is Carl."

"Let them in."

Myron stepped outside and watched the canary-yellow Audi climb the drive. Carl pulled to a stop and got out. His flat hair looked freshly pressed, like he'd just gotten it "martinized," whatever that was. A young black woman who couldn't have been twenty years old came out of the passenger door. She looked around with eyes the size of satellite dishes.

Carl turned to the stables and cupped his big hand over his eyes. A female rider decked out in full gear was steering a horse through some sort of obstacle course.

"That what they call steeplechasing?" Carl asked.

"Got me," Myron said.

Carl continued to watch. The rider got off the horse. She unstrapped her black hat and patted the horse. Carl said, "You don't see a lot of brothers dressed like that."

"What about lawn jockeys?"

Carl laughed. "Not bad," he said. "Not great, but not bad."

Hard to argue. "You here to take riding lessons?"

"Not likely," Carl said. "This is Kiana. I think she may be of help to us."

"Us?"

"You and me together, bro." Carl smiled. "I get to play your likable black partner."

Myron shook his head. "No."

"Excuse me?"

"The likable black partner always ends up dead. Usually early on, too."

That stopped Carl a second. "Damn, I forgot about that."

Myron shrugged a what-can-you-do. "So who is she?"

"Kiana works as a maid at the Court Manor Inn."

Myron looked at her. She was still out of earshot.
"How old is she?"

"Why?"

Myron shrugged. "Just asking. She looks young."

"She's sixteen. And guess what, Myron? She's not an
unwed mother, she's not on welfare, and she's not a
junkie."

"I never said she was."

"Uh-huh. Guess none of that racist shit ever seeps
into your color-blind cranium."

"Hey, Carl, do me a favor. Save the racial-sensitivity
seminar for a less active day. What does she know?"

Carl beckoned her forward with a tight nod. Kiana
approached, all long limbs and big eyes. "I showed her
this photo"—he handed Myron a snapshot of Jack Coldren—"and she remembered seeing him at the Court
Manor."

Myron glanced at the photograph, and then at Kiana.
"You saw this man at the motel?"

"Yes." Her voice was firm and strong and belied her
years. Sixteen. She was the same age as Chad. Hard to
imagine.

"Do you remember when?"

"Last week. I saw him there twice."

"Twice?"

"Yes."

"Would that have been Thursday or Friday?"

"No." Kiana kept up with the poise. No ringing
hands or happy feet or darting eyes. "It was Monday or
Tuesday. Wednesday at the latest."

Myron tried to process this tidbit. Jack had been at the
Court Manor twice *before* his son. Why? The reason was
fairly obvious: If the marriage was dead for Linda, it was
probably dead for Jack. He, too, would be engaging in
extramarital liaisons. Maybe that was what Matthew

Squires witnessed. Maybe Jack had pulled in for his own affair and spotted his son's car. It kinda made sense. . . .

But it was also a hell of a coincidence. Father and son end up at the same hot sheets at the same time? Stranger things have happened, but what were the odds?

Myron gestured to Jack's photograph. "Was he alone?"

Kiana smiled. "The Court Manor doesn't rent out a lot of single rooms."

"Did you see who was with him?"

"Very briefly. The guy in the photograph checked them in. His partner stayed in the car."

"But you saw her? Briefly anyway."

Kiana glanced at Carl, then back at Myron. "It wasn't a her."

"Excuse me?"

"The guy in the photograph," she said. "He wasn't there with a woman."

A large boulder fell from the sky and landed on Myron's head. It was his turn now to glance at Carl. Carl nodded. Another click. A big click. The loveless marriage. He had known why Linda Coldren stayed in it—she was afraid of losing custody of her son. But what about Jack? Why hadn't he left? The answer was suddenly transparent: Being married to a beautiful, constantly traveling woman was the perfect cover. He remembered Diane Hoffman's reaction when he asked her if she'd been sleeping with Jack—the way she laughed and said, "Not likely with ol' Jack."

Because ol' Jack was gay.

Myron turned his focus back to Kiana. "Could you describe the man he was with?"

"Older—maybe fifty or sixty. White. He had this long dark hair and a bushy beard. That's about all I can tell you."

But Myron did not need more.

It was starting to come together now. It wasn't there. Not yet anyway. But he was suddenly a quantum leap closer.

Chapter 38

As Carl drove out, Esperanza drove in.

"Find anything?" Myron asked her.

Esperanza handed him a photocopy of an old newspaper clipping. "Read this."

The headline read: CRASH FATALITY

Economy of words. He read on:

Mr. Lloyd Rennart of 27 Darby Place crashed his automobile into a parked car on South Dean Street near the intersection of Coddington Terrace. Mr. Rennart was taken into police custody under suspicion of driving while intoxicated. The injured were rushed to St. Elizabeth's Medical Center, where Lucille Rennart, Mr. Lloyd Rennart's wife, was pronounced dead. Funeral services are to be arranged.

Myron reread the paragraph twice. " 'The injured were rushed,' " he read out loud. "As in more than one."

Esperanza nodded.

"So who else was hurt?"

"I don't know. There was no follow-up article."

"Nothing on the arrest or the arraignment or the court case?"

"Nothing. At least, nothing I could find. There was no further mention of any Rennarts. I also tried to get something from St. Elizabeth's, but they wouldn't help. Hospital-patient confidentiality, they claimed. I doubt their computers go back to the seventies anyway."

Myron shook his head. "This is too weird," he said.

"I saw Carl heading out," Esperanza said. "What did he want?"

"He came by with a maid from the Court Manor. Guess who Jack Coldren was linking up with for a little afternoon delight?"

"Tonya Harding?"

"Close. Norm Zuckerman."

Esperanza tilted her head back and forth, as though sizing up an abstract work at the Met. "I'm not surprised. About Norm anyway. Think about it. Never married. No family. In public, he always surrounds himself with young, beautiful women."

"For show," Myron said.

"Right. They're beards. Camouflage. Norm is the front man for a major sports fashion business. Being a known gay could destroy him."

"So," Myron said, "if it got out that he was gay . . ."

"It would hurt a lot," Esperanza said.

"Is that a motive for murder?"

"Sure," she said. "It's millions of dollars and a man's reputation. People kill for a lot less."

Myron thought about it. "But how did it happen? Let's say Chad and Jack meet up at the Court Manor by accident. Suppose Chad figures out what Daddy and Norm are up to. Maybe he mentions it to Esme, who works for Norm. Maybe she and Norm . . ."

"They what?" Esperanza finished. "They kidnap the kid, cut off his finger, and then let him go?"

"Yeah, it doesn't mesh," Myron agreed. "Not yet anyway. But we're getting close."

"Oh sure, we're really narrowing down the field. Let's

see. It could be Esme Fong. It could be Norm Zuckerman. It could be Tad Crispin. It could be a still-alive Lloyd Rennart. It could be his wife or his kid. It could be Matthew Squires or his father or both. Or it could be a combination plan of any of the above—the Rennart family perhaps, or Norm and Esme. And it could be Linda Coldren. How does she explain the gun from her house being the murder weapon? Or the envelopes and the pen she bought?"

"I don't know," Myron said slowly. Then: "But you may be on to something here."

"What?"

"Access. Whoever killed Jack and cut off Chad's finger had access to the Coldren house. Barring a break-in, who could have gotten hold of the gun and the stationery supplies?"

Esperanza barely hesitated. "Linda Coldren, Jack Coldren, maybe the Squires kid, since he liked to crawl in through the window." She paused. "I guess that's it."

"Okay, good. Now let's move on a little. Who knew that Chad Coldren was at the Court Manor Inn? I mean, whoever kidnapped him had to know where he was, right?"

"Right. Okay, Jack again, Esme Fong, Norm Zuckerman, Matthew Squires again. Boy, Myron, this is really helpful."

"So what names show up on both lists?"

"Jack and Matthew Squires. And I think we can leave Jack's name off—his being the victim and all."

But Myron stopped for a moment. He thought about his conversation with Win. About the naked desire to win. How far would Jack go to guarantee victory? Win had said that he would stop at nothing. Was he right?

Esperanza snapped her fingers in his face. "Yo, Myron?"

"What?"

"I said, we can eliminate Jack Coldren. Dead people rarely bury murder weapons in nearby woods."

That made sense. "So that leaves Matthew Squires," Myron said, "and I don't think he's our boy."

"Neither do I," Esperanza said. "But we're forgetting someone—someone who knew where Chad Coldren was and had complete access to the gun and stationery supplies."

"Who?"

"Chad Coldren."

"You think he cut off his own finger?"

Esperanza shrugged. "What about your old theory? The one where the kidnapping was a hoax that went out of control. Think about it. Maybe he and Tito had a falling-out. Maybe it was Chad who killed Tito."

Myron considered the possibility. He thought about Jack. He thought about Esme. He thought about Lloyd Rennart. Then he shook his head. "This is getting us nowhere. Sherlock Holmes warned that you should never theorize without all the facts because then you twist facts to suit theories rather than theories to suit facts."

"That never stopped us before," Esperanza said.

"Good point." Myron checked his watch. "I gotta go see Francine Rennart."

"The caddie's wife."

"Yup."

Esperanza went sniff, sniff.

"What?" Myron asked.

One more big sniff. "I smell a complete waste of time," she said.

She smelled wrong.

Chapter 39

Victoria Wilson called on the car phone. What, Myron wondered, did people do before the car phone, before the cell phone, before the beeper?

Probably had a lot more fun.

"The police found the body of your neo-Nazi friend," she said. "His last name is Marshall."

"Tito Marshall?" Myron frowned. "Please tell me you're joking."

"I don't joke, Myron."

Of that he had little doubt. "Do the police have any idea he's tied into this?" Myron asked.

"None whatsoever."

"And I assume he died of a gunshot wound."

"That's the preliminary finding, yes. Mr. Marshall was shot twice in the head at close range with a thirty-eight."

"A thirty-eight? But Jack was killed with a twenty-two."

"Yes, Myron, I know."

"So different guns killed Jack Coldren and Tito Marshall."

Victoria did the bored thing again. "Hard to believe you're not a professional ballistics expert."

Everyone's a smart-ass. But this new development threw a whole bunch of scenarios out of whack. If two different guns had killed Jack Coldren and Tito Marshall, did that mean there were two different killers? Or was the killer smart enough to use different weapons? Or had the killer disposed of the thirty-eight after killing Tito and was thus forced to use the twenty-two on Jack? And what kind of warped mind names a kid Tito Marshall? Bad enough to go through life with a moniker like Myron. But Tito Marshall? No wonder the kid had turned out as a neo-Nazi. Probably started out as a virulent anti-Communist.

Victoria interrupted his thoughts. "I called for another reason, Myron."

"Oh?"

"Did you pass on the message to Win?"

"You set that up, didn't you? You told her I'd be there."

"Please answer the question."

"Yes, I delivered the message."

"What did Win say?"

"I delivered the message," Myron said. "But that doesn't mean I'm giving out reports on my friend's reaction."

"She's getting worse, Myron."

"I'm sorry."

Silence.

"Where are you right now?" she asked.

"I just hit the New Jersey Turnpike. I'm on my way to Lloyd Rennart's house."

"I thought I told you to leave that path alone."

"So you did."

More silence.

"Good-bye, Myron."

She hung up. Myron sighed. He suddenly longed for the days before the car phone, the cell phone, the beeper. Reaching out and touching someone was getting to be a real pain in the ass.

An hour later, Myron parked again in front of the

Rennarts' modest home. He knocked on the door. Mrs. Rennart opened it immediately. She studied his face for a few long seconds. Neither of them spoke. Not even a greeting or salutation.

"You look tired," she said at last.

"I am."

"Did Lloyd really send that postcard?"

"Yes."

The answer had been automatic. But now he wondered —had Lloyd Rennart sent a postcard? For all he knew, Linda was simply sizing him for the title role in *Big Sap: The Musical.* Take the missing taped phone call, for example. If indeed the kidnapper had called Jack before his death, where was the tape of the call? Maybe the call had never occurred. Maybe Linda had lied about it. Maybe she was lying about the postcard too. Maybe she was lying about everything. Maybe Myron was simply being semi-seduced, like the hormone-driven male in one of those cheesy, unrated, direct-to-video, *Body Heat* rip-offs co-starring women with names like Shannon or Tawny.

Not a pleasant thought.

Francine Rennart silently led him into a dark basement. When they hit bottom, she reached up and switched on one of those swinging lightbulbs like something out of *Psycho.* The room was pure cement. There was a water heater, a gas heater, a washer and dryer, and storage containers of various sizes, shapes, and material. Four boxes lay on the floor in front of him.

"That's his old stuff," Francine Rennart said without looking down.

"Thank you."

She tried, but she could not make herself look at the boxes. "I'll be upstairs," she said. Myron watched her feet disappear from view. Then he turned to the boxes and squatted down. The boxes were taped shut. He took out his key-chain penknife and slit the packing tape.

The first box had golf memorabilia. There were certificates and trophies and old tees. A golf ball was mounted to a wooden base with a rusty plaque that read:

HOLE IN ONE—15TH HOLE AT HICKORY PARK
JANUARY 17, 1972

Myron wondered what life had been like for Lloyd on that clear, crisp golf afternoon. He wondered how often Lloyd had replayed the shot in his mind, how many times he'd sat alone in that BarcaLounger and tried to recapture that pure, cold rush. Had he remembered the feel of the club's grip, the tightness in his shoulders as he began the backswing, the clean, solid stroke of the ball, the floating follow-through.

In the second box, Myron found Lloyd's high school diploma. He found a yearbook from Penn State. There was a picture of the golf team. Lloyd Rennart had been captain. Myron's finger touched upon a large, felt *P*. Lloyd's varsity letter. There was a recommendation letter from his golf coach at Penn State. The words *bright future* jumped out at Myron. Bright future. The coach may have been a great motivator, but he made a lousy soothsayer.

The third box started off with a photograph of Lloyd in Korea. It was a casual group photo, a dozen or so boys/men in unbuttoned fatigues, arms dangling loosely around neighboring necks. Lots of smiles, seemingly happy smiles. Lloyd was thinner there, but he saw nothing gaunt or drawn in the eyes.

Myron put the picture down. In the background, Betty Buckley was not singing "Memory," but maybe she should have been. These boxes were a life—a life that in spite of these experiences and dreams and wants and hopes had chosen to terminate itself.

From the bottom of the box Myron pulled out a wedding album. The faded gold leaf read: *Lloyd and Lucille, November 17, 1968, Now and Forever*. More irony. The fake-leather cover was crusted with what looked like drink ringlets. Lloyd's first marriage, neatly wrapped and packed away in the bottom of a box.

Myron was about to put the album to the side when his curiosity got the better of him. He sat all the way down, his legs splayed like a kid with a new pack of baseball cards. He placed the photo album on the cement floor and began to open it. The binding made a cracking noise from the years of disuse.

The first photograph almost made Myron scream out loud.

Chapter 40

Myron's accelerator foot never eased.

Chestnut Street near Fourth is a no-parking zone, but that did not even make Myron pause. He was out of the car before it had come to a complete stop, ignoring the chorus of honking horns. He hurried through the Omni's lobby and into an open elevator. When he got off on the top floor, he found the right room number and knocked hard.

Norm Zuckerman opened the door. "*Bubbe*," he said with a big smile. "What a nice surprise."

"Can I come in?"

"You? Of course, sweetheart, anytime."

But Myron had already pushed by him. The suite's outer room was—to use hotel brochure lingo—spacious and elegantly appointed. Esme Fong sat on a couch. She looked up at him with the cornered-rabbit face. Posters and blueprints and advertisements and similar paraphernalia carpeted the floor and cascaded off the coffee table. Myron spotted blown-up images of Tad Crispin and Linda Coldren. Zoom logos were everywhere, inescapable, like vengeful ghosts or telemarketers.

"We were just doing a little strategizing," Norm said. "But hey, we can always take a break, right, Esme?"

Esme nodded.

Norm made his way behind a wet bar. "You want something, Myron? I don't think they have any Yoo-Hoo in here, but I'm sure—"

"Nothing," Myron interrupted.

Norm did the mock surrender thing with his hands. "Sheesh, Myron, relax," he said. "What's twisting your nipple?"

"I wanted to warn you, Norm."

"Warn me about what?"

"I don't want to do this. As far as I'm concerned, your love life should be personal. But it's not that easy. Not anymore. It's going to get out, Norm. I'm sorry."

Norm Zuckerman did not move. He opened his mouth as though readying to protest. Then he stopped. "How did you find out?"

"You were with Jack. At the Court Manor Inn. A maid saw you."

Norm looked at Esme, who kept her head high. He turned back to Myron. "Do you know what will happen if words gets out that I'm a *faygeleh*?"

"I can't help that, Norm."

"I am the company, Myron. Zoom is about fashion and image and sports—which just so happens to be the most blatantly homophobic entity on this planet. Perception is everything in this business. If they find out I'm an old queen, you know what happens? Zoom goes plop down the septic tank."

"I'm not sure I agree," Myron said, "but either way, it can't be helped."

"Do the police know?" Norm asked.

"No, not yet."

Norm threw up his hands. "So why does it have to come out? It was just a fling, for crying out loud. Okay, so I met Jack. So we were attracted to each other. So we both had a ton to lose if either of us opened our traps. No big whup. It's got nothing to do with his murder."

Myron stole a glance at Esme. She looked back at him

with eyes that urged him to keep silent. "Unfortunately," Myron said, "I think it does."

"You think? You're going to destroy me on an 'I think'?"

"I'm sorry."

"I can't talk you out of it?"

"I'm afraid not."

Norm moved away from the bar and half-collapsed into a chair. He put his face in the palms of his hands, his fingers sliding toward the back, meeting up in the hair, interweaving. "I've spent my entire life with lies, Myron," he began. "I spent my childhood in Poland pretending I wasn't a Jew. Can you believe that? Me, Norm Zuckerman, pretending I was some slack-jawed *goy*. But I survived. I came here. And then I spent my adult life pretending I was a real man, a Casanova, a guy who always had a beautiful girl on his arm. You get used to lying, Myron. It gets easier, you know what I mean? The lies become a sort of second reality."

"I'm sorry, Norm."

He breathed deeply and forced up a tired smile. "Maybe it's for the best," Norm said. "Look at Dennis Rodman. He cross-dresses, for crying out loud. Hasn't hurt him any, has it?"

"No. It hasn't."

Norm Zuckerman lifted his eyes toward Myron. "Hey, once I got to this country, I became the most in-your-face Jew you ever saw. Didn't I? Tell me the truth. Am I not the most in-your-face Jew you've ever met, or what?"

"In my face," Myron said.

"Bet your skinny *melinka* of a butt I am. And when I first started out, everyone told me to tone it down. Stop being so Jewish, they said. So ethnic. You'll never be accepted." His face had true hope now. "Maybe I can do the same for us closet *faygelehs*, Myron. Be in the world's face again, you know what I'm saying?''

"Yes, I do," Myron said softly. Then he asked, "Who else knew about you and Jack?"

"Knew?"

"Did you tell anybody?"

"No, of course not."

Myron gestured toward Esme. "How about one of those beautiful girlfriends on your arm? How about someone who practically lived with you? Wouldn't it have been easy for her to find out?"

Norm shrugged. "I suppose so. You get this close to someone, you trust them. You drop your guard. So maybe she knew. So what?"

Myron looked at Esme. "You want to tell him?"

Esme's voice was cool. "I don't know what you're talking about."

"Tell me what?"

Myron kept his eyes on hers. "I wondered why you'd seduce a sixteen-year-old boy. Don't get me wrong. You gave a bravo performance—all that talk about being lonely and Chad being sweet and disease-free. You waxed quite eloquent. But it still rang hollow."

Norm said, "What the hell are you talking about, Myron?"

Myron ignored him. "And then there was the matter of the bizarre coincidence—you and Chad showing up at the same motel at the same time as Jack and Norm. Too weird. I just couldn't buy it. But of course, we both know that it wasn't a coincidence. You planned it that way, Esme."

"What plan?" Norm interjected. "Myron, will you tell me what the hell is going on?"

"Norm, you mentioned that Esme used to work on

Nike's basketball campaign. That she quit that job to come to you."

"So?"

"Did she take a cut in salary?"

"A little." Norm shrugged. "Not much."

"When exactly did she hook up with you?"

"I don't know."

"Within the past eight months?"

Norm thought a moment. "Yeah, so?"

"Esme seduced Chad Coldren. She set up a liaison with him at the Court Manor Inn. But she wasn't bringing him there for sex or because she was lonely. She brought him there as part of a setup."

"What kind of setup?"

"She wanted Chad to see his father with another man."

"Huh?"

"She wanted to destroy Jack. It was no coincidence. Esme knew your routine. She learned about your affair with Jack. So she tried to set it up so Chad would see what his father was really about."

Esme remained silent.

"Tell me something, Norm. Were you and Jack supposed to meet Thursday night?"

"Yeah," Norm said.

"What happened?"

"Jack called it off. He pulled into the lot and got spooked. He said he saw a familiar car."

"Not just familiar," Myron said. "His son's. That's where Esme screwed up. Jack spotted the car. He left before Chad had a chance to see him."

Myron stood and walked toward Esme. She remained still. "I almost had it right from the beginning," he told her. "Jack took the lead at the Open. His son was there, right in front of you. So you kidnapped Chad to throw

Jack's game off. It was just like I thought. Except I missed your real motive. Why would you kidnap Chad? Why would you crave such vengeance against Jack Coldren? Yes, money was part of the motive. Yes, you wanted Zoom's new campaign to succeed. Yes, you knew that if Tad Crispin won the Open, you'd be heralded as the marketing genius of the world. All that played into it. But, of course, that never explained why you brought Chad to the Court Manor Inn in the first place—*before* Jack had the lead.''

Norm sighed. "So tell us, Myron. What possible reason could she have for wanting to hurt Jack?"

Myron reached into his pocket and pulled out a grainy photograph. The first page of the wedding album. Lloyd and Lucille Rennart. Smiling. Happy. Standing side by side. Lloyd in a tux. Lucille holding a bouquet of flowers. Lucille looking stunning in a long white gown. But that wasn't what had shocked Myron to the core. What shocked him had nothing to do with what Lucille wore or held; rather, it was what she was.

Lucille Rennart was Asian.

"Lloyd Rennart was your father," Myron said. "You were in the car that day when he crashed into a tree. Your mother died. You were rushed to the hospital too."

Esme's back was rod-straight, but her breathing was coming out in hitches.

"I'm not sure what happened next," he continued. "My guess would be that your father had hit rock bottom. He was a drunk. He had just killed his own wife. He felt washed-up, useless. So maybe he realized that he couldn't raise you. Or he didn't deserve to raise you. Or maybe an arrangement was reached with your mother's family. In return for not pressing charges, Lloyd would give Lucille's family custody of you. I don't know what happened. But you ended up being raised by your mother's family. By the time Lloyd straightened himself out, he probably felt it would be wrong to tear you out by the roots. Or maybe he was afraid that his daughter wouldn't take back the father who'd been responsible for killing her mother. Whatever, Lloyd kept quiet. He never even told his second wife about you."

Tears were streaming down Esme's cheeks now. Myron felt like crying too.

"How close am I, Esme?"

"I don't even know what you're talking about."

"There'll be records," Myron said. "Birth certificates, for certain. Probably adoption papers. It won't take the police long to trace." He held up the photograph, his voice soft.

"The resemblance between you and your mother is almost enough."

Tears continued to flow, but she was not crying. No sobs. No hitching. No quivering facial muscles. Just tears. "Maybe Lloyd Rennart was my father," Esme said. "But you still have nothing. The rest is pure conjecture."

"No, Esme. Once the police confirm your parentage, the rest will be easy. Chad will tell them that it was you who suggested you go to the Court Manor Inn. They'll look closely into Tito's death. There'll be a connection there. Fibers. Hairs. It'll all come together. But I have one question for you."

She remained still.

"Why did you cut off Chad's finger?"

Without warning, Esme broke into a run. Myron was caught off guard. He jumped over the couch to block her path. But he had misjudged her. She had not been heading for an exit; she was going into a bedroom. Her bedroom. Myron hurdled back over the couch. He reached her room, but he was a little late.

Esme Fong had a gun. She pointed it at Myron's chest.

He could see in her eyes that there'd be no confession, no explanations, no talk. She was ready to shoot.

"Don't bother," Myron said.

"What?"

He pulled out his cell phone and handed it to her. "This is for you."

Esme did not move for a moment. Then, with her hand still on the gun, she reached out and took the phone. She pressed it against her ear, but Myron could hear just fine.

A voice said, "This is Detective Alan Corbett from the Philadelphia Police Department. We are standing outside your door listening to every word that has been said. Put down the gun."

Esme looked back at Myron. She still had the gun aimed at his chest. Myron felt a bead of sweat run down his back. Looking into the barrel of a gun was like staring into the cavern of death. Your eyes saw the barrel, only the barrel, as though it were growing impossibly larger, preparing to swallow you whole.

"It would be dumb," he said.

She nodded then and lowered the gun. "And pointless."

The weapon dropped to the floor. Doors burst open. Police swarmed in.

Myron looked down at the gun. "A thirty-eight," he said to Esme. "That the gun you killed Tito with?"

Her expression gave him the answer. The ballistics tests would be conclusive. She would be prosecutorial toast.

"Tito was a lunatic," Esme said. "He chopped off the boy's finger. He started making money demands. You have to believe that."

Myron gave a noncommittal nod. She was testing out her defense, but it sort of sounded like the truth to Myron.

Corbett snapped handcuffs onto her wrists.

Her words were spilling out fast now. "Jack Coldren destroyed my entire family. He ruined my father and killed my mother. And for what? My father did nothing wrong."

"Yes," Myron said, "he did."

"He pulled the wrong club out of a golf bag, if you believe Jack Coldren. He made a mistake. An accident. Should it have cost him so much?"

Myron said nothing. It was no mistake, no accident. And Myron had no idea what it should have cost.

Chapter 41

The police cleaned up. Corbett had questions, but Myron was not in the mood. He left as soon as the detective
was distracted. He sped to the police station where Linda
Coldren was about to be released. He took the cement
steps three or four at a clip, looking like a spastic Olym-
pian timing the triple jump.

Victoria Wilson almost—the key word being *almost*—
smiled at him. "Linda will be out in a few minutes."

"Do you have that tape I asked you to get?"

"The phone call between Jack and the kidnapper?"

"Yes."

"I have it," she said. "But why—"

"Please give it to me," Myron said.

She heard something in his tone. Without argument,
she reached into her handbag and pulled it out. Myron
took it. "Do you mind if I drive Linda home?" he said.

Victoria Wilson regarded him. "I think maybe that
would be a good idea."

A policeman came out. "She's ready to leave," he
said.

Victoria was about to turn away, when Myron said, "I
guess you were wrong about digging into the past. The
past ended up saving our client."

Victoria held his eye. "It's like I said before," she
began. "You never know what you will find."

They both waited for the other to break the eye contact. Neither did until the door behind them opened.

Linda was back in civilian clothes. She stepped out tentatively, like she'd been in a dark room and wasn't sure her eyes could handle the sudden light. Her face broke into a wide smile when she saw Victoria. They hugged. Linda dug her face into Victoria's shoulder and rocked in her arms. When they released, Linda turned and hugged Myron. Myron closed his eyes and felt his muscles unbunch. He smelled her hair and felt the wondrous skin of her cheek against his neck. They embraced for a long time, almost like a slow dance, neither wanting to let go, both perhaps a little bit afraid.

Victoria coughed into her fist and made her excuses. With the police leading the way, Myron and Linda made it to the car with a minimum of press fuss. They strapped on their seat belts in silence.

"Thank you," she said.

Myron said nothing. He started the car. For a while neither of them spoke. Myron switched on the air-conditioning.

"We have something here, don't we?"

"I don't know," Myron said. "You were worried about your son. Maybe that's all it was."

Her face said that she was not buying. "How about you?" Linda asked. "Did you feel anything?"

"I think so," he said. "But part of that might be fear, too."

"Fear of what?"

"Of Jessica."

She gave a weary grin. "Don't tell me you're one of those guys who fears commitment."

"Just the opposite. I fear how much I love her. I fear how much I want to commit."

"So what's the problem?"

"Jessica left me once before. I don't want to be exposed like that again."

Linda nodded. "So you think that's what it was? Fear of abandonment?"

"I don't know."

"I felt something," she said. "For the first time in a very long time. Don't get me wrong. I've had affairs. Like with Tad. But that's not the same thing." She looked at him. "It felt nice."

Myron said nothing.

"You're not making this very easy," Linda said.

"We have other things to talk about."

"Like what?"

"Victoria filled you in on Esme Fong?"

"Yes."

"If you remember, she had a solid alibi for Jack's murder."

"A night clerk at a big hotel like the Omni? I doubt that will hold up on scrutiny."

"Don't be so sure," Myron said.

"Why do you say that?"

Myron did not answer. He turned right and said, "You know what always bothered me, Linda?"

"No, what?"

"The ransom calls."

"What about them?" she asked.

"The first one was made on the morning of the kidnapping. You answered. The kidnappers told you that they had your son. But they made no demands. I always found that odd, didn't you?"

She thought about it. "I guess so."

"Now I understand why they did that. But back then, we didn't know what the real motive for the kidnapping was."

"I don't understand."

"Esme Fong kidnapped Chad because she wanted revenge on Jack. She wanted to make him lose the tourna-

ment. How? Well, I'd thought that she'd kidnapped Chad
to fluster Jack. Make him lose his focus. But that was too
abstract. She wanted to make sure Jack lost. That was her
ransom demand right from the beginning. But you see,
the ransom call came in a little late. Jack was already at
the course. You answered the phone.''

Linda nodded. ''I think I see what you're saying. She
had to reach Jack directly.''

''She or Tito, but you're right. That's why she called
Jack at Merion. Remember the second call, the one Jack
got after he finished the round?''

''Of course.''

''That was when the ransom demand was made,'' Myron said. ''The kidnapper told Jack plain and simple—
you start losing or your son dies.''

''Hold up a second,'' Linda said. ''Jack said they
didn't make any demands. They told him to get some
money ready and they'd call back.''

''Jack lied.''

''But . . . ?'' She stopped, and then said, ''Why?''

''He didn't want us—or more specifically, you—to
know the truth.''

Linda shook her head. ''I don't understand.''

Myron took out the cassette Victoria had given him.
''Maybe this will help explain.'' He pushed the tape into
the cassette player. There were several seconds of silence
and then he heard Jack's voice like something from beyond the grave:

''Hello?''

''Who's the chink bitch?''

''I don't know what—''

*''You trying to fuck with me, you dumb son of a bitch?
I'll start sending you the fucking brat in little pieces.''*

''Please—''

"What's the point of this, Myron?" Linda sounded a little annoyed.

"Just hold on another second. The part I'm interested in is coming up."

"*Her name is Esme Fong. She works for a clothing company. She's just here to set up an endorsement deal with my wife, that's all.*"

"*Bullshit.*"

"*It's the truth, I swear.*"

"*I don't know, Jack. . . .*"

"*I wouldn't lie to you.*"

"*Well, Jack, we'll just see about that. This is gonna cost you.*"

"*What do you mean?*"

"*One hundred grand. Call it a penalty price.*"

"*For what?*"

Myron hit the STOP button. "Did you hear that?"

"What?"

" 'Call it a penalty price.' Clear as day."

"So?"

"It wasn't a ransom demand. It was a penalty."

"This is a kidnapper, Myron. He's probably not all that caught up in semantics."

" 'One hundred grand,' " Myron repeated. " 'Call it a penalty price.' As if a ransom demand had already been made. As if the hundred grand was something he'd just decided to tack on. And what about Jack's reaction? The kidnapper asks for one hundred grand. You would figure he would just tell him fine. But instead he says, 'For what?' Again, because it's in addition to what he's already been told. Now listen to this." Myron pushed the PLAY button.

"*Never you fucking mind. You want the kid alive? It's gonna cost you one hundred grand now. That's in—*"

"*Now hold on a second.*"

Myron hit the STOP button again. " 'It's gonna cost you one hundred grand *now*.' " Myron repeated. "*Now*. That's the key word. *Now*. Again as if it's something new. As if before this call there was another price. And then Jack interrupts him. The kidnapper says, 'That's in—' when Jack jumps in. Why? Because Jack doesn't want him to finish the thought. He knew that we were listening. 'That's in addition.' I'd bet anything that was the next word he was about to say. 'That's in addition to our original demand.' Or, 'that's in addition to losing the tournament.' "

Linda looked at him. "But I still don't get it. Why wouldn't Jack just tell us what they wanted?"

"Because Jack had no intention of complying with their demand."

That stopped her. "What?"

"He wanted to win too badly. More than that—he needed to win. Had to. But if you learned the truth—you who had won so often and so easily—you would never understand. This was his chance at redemption, Linda. His chance of going back twenty-three years and making his life worth living. How badly did he want to win, Linda? You tell me. What would he have sacrificed?"

"Not his own son," Linda countered. "Yes, Jack needed to win. But not badly enough to forfeit his own son's life."

"But Jack didn't see it that way. He was looking through his own rose-tinted prism of desire. A man sees what he wants to, Linda. What he has to. When I showed you and Jack the bank videotape, you both saw something different. You didn't want to believe your son could do something so hurtful. So you looked for explanations that would counter that evidence. Jack did just the opposite. He wanted to believe that his son was behind it. That it was only a big hoax. That way he could continue to try his hardest to win. And if by some chance he was wrong —if Chad had indeed been kidnapped—well, the kidnappers were probably bluffing anyway. They'd never really go through with it. In other words, Jack did what he had to do: he rationalized the danger away.''

"You think his desire to win clouded his thinking that much?''

"How much clouding did he need? We all had doubts after watching that bank tape. Even you. So how hard would it be for him to go the extra step?''

Linda sat back. "Okay,'' she said. "Maybe I buy it. But I still don't see what this has to do with anything.''

"Bear with me a little while longer, okay? Let's go back to when I showed you the bank videotape. We're at your house. I show the tape. Jack storms out. He is upset, of course, but he still plays well enough to keep the big lead. This angers Esme. He's ignoring her threat. She realizes that she has to up the ante.''

"By cutting off Chad's finger.''

"It was probably Tito, but that's not really relevant right now anyway. The key thing is, the finger is severed, and Esme wants to use it to show Jack she's serious.''

"So she plants it in my car and we find it.''

"No,'' Myron said.

"What?''

"Jack finds it first.''

"In my car?''

Myron shook his head. "Remember that Chad's key chain has Jack's car keys on it as well as yours. Esme wants to warn Jack, not you. So she puts the finger in Jack's car. He finds it. He's shocked, of course, but he's in the lie too deep now. If the truth came out, you'd never forgive him. Chad would never forgive him. And the tournament would be over for him. He has to get rid of the finger. So he puts the finger in an envelope and writes that note. Remember it? 'I warned you not to seek help.' Don't you see? It's the perfect distraction. It not only draws attention away from him, but it also gets rid of me.''

Linda chewed on her lower lip. "That would explain the envelope and pen,'' she said. "I bought all the office supplies. Jack would have had some in his briefcase.''

"Exactly. But here is where things get really interesting.''

She arched an eyebrow. "They're not interesting now?''

"Just hold on. It's Sunday morning. Jack is about to head into the final round with an insurmountable lead. Bigger than he had twenty-three years ago. If he loses now, it would be the greatest golf collapse in history. His name would forever be synonymous with choking—the one thing Jack hated more than anything else. But on the other hand, Jack was not a complete ogre. He loved his son. He knew now that the kidnapping was not a hoax. He was probably torn, not sure what to do. But in the end he made a decision. He was going to lose the tournament.''

Linda said nothing.

"Stroke by stroke, we watched him die. Win understands the destructive side of wanting to win far better than I. He also saw that Jack had the fire back, that old need to win. But despite all that, Jack still tried to lose. He didn't completely collapse. That would have looked too suspicious. But he started dropping strokes. He made it close. And then he purposely fumbled big-time in the stone quarry and lost his lead.

"But imagine what was going on in his head. Jack was fighting against everything that he was. They say a man can't drown himself. Even if it means saving his own child's life, a man cannot keep himself under water until his lungs burst. I'm not so sure that's any different than what Jack was trying to do. He was literally killing himself. His sanity was probably ripping away like divots on the course. On the eighteenth green, the survival instinct took over. Maybe he started rationalizing again—or more likely, he just couldn't help himself. But we both saw the transformation, Linda. We saw his face suddenly crystallize on eighteen. Jack stroked that putt home and tied the score.''

Linda's voice was barely audible. ''Yes,'' she said. ''I saw him change.'' She sat up in her seat and let loose a long breath. ''Esme Fong must have been in a panic by then.''

''Yes.''

''Jack had left her no choice. She had to kill him.''

Myron shook his head. ''No.''

She looked confused again. ''But it adds up. Esme was desperate. You said so yourself. She wanted vengeance for her father, and on top of that she was now worried about what would happen if Tad Crispin lost. She had to kill him.''

''One problem,'' Myron said.

''What?''

''She called your house that night.''

''Right,'' Linda said. ''To set up the meeting at the course. She probably told Jack to come alone. To not tell me anything.''

''No,'' Myron said. ''That's not what happened.''

''What?''

''If that was what happened,'' Myron continued, ''we'd have the call on tape.''

Linda shook her head. ''What are you talking about?''

''Esme Fong did call your house. That part is true. My bet is that she just threatened him some more. Let him know that she meant business. Jack probably begged forgiveness. I don't know. I'll probably never know. But I'd bet he ended the call by promising to lose the next day.''

"So?" Linda said. "What does that have to do with the call being taped?''

"Jack was going through hell," Myron went on. "The pressure was too much. He was probably close to a break- down. So he ran out of the house—just as you said—and ended up at his favorite place in the world. Merion. The golf course. Did he go out there just to think? I don't know. Did he bring the gun with him, maybe even con- templating suicide? Again, I don't know. But I do know that the tape machine was still hooked up to your phone. The police confirmed that. So where did the tape of that last conversation go?''

Linda's tone was suddenly more measured. "I don't know.''

"Yes, Linda, you do.''

She gave him a look.

"Jack might have forgotten the call was recorded,'' Myron continued. "But you didn't. When he ran out of the house, you went down to the basement. You played the tape. And you heard everything. What I'm telling you in this car is not new to you. You knew why the kidnap- pers had taken your child. You knew what Jack had done. You knew where he liked to go when he took his walks. And you knew you had to stop him.''

Myron waited. He missed the turnoff, took the next one, U-turned back onto the highway. He found the right exit and put on his blinker.

"Jack did bring the gun,'' Linda said too calmly. "I didn't even know where he kept it.''

Myron gave a slight nod, silently trying to encourage.

"You're right,'' she continued. "When I played back the tape, I realized that Jack couldn't be trusted. He knew it too. Even with the threat of his own son's death, he had nailed that putt on eighteen. I followed him out to the course. I confronted him. He started to cry. He said he would try to lose. But''—she hesitated, weighed her words—''that drowning man example you gave. That was Jack.''

Myron tried to swallow, but his throat was too dry.

''Jack wanted to kill himself. And I knew he had to. I'd listened to the tape. I'd heard the threats. And I had no doubts: If Jack won, Chad was dead. I also knew something else.''

She stopped and looked at Myron.

''What?'' he said.

''I knew Jack would win. Win was right—the fire was back in Jack's eyes. But it was a raging inferno now. One that even he couldn't control anymore.''

''So you shot him,'' Myron said.

''I struggled to get the gun from him. I wanted to injure him. Seriously injure him. If there was the possibility he could play again, I was afraid the kidnapper might just hold on to Chad indefinitely. The voice on the phone sounded that desperate. But Jack wouldn't surrender the gun—nor would he pull it away from me. It was weird. He just held on and looked at me. Almost like he was waiting. So I curled my finger around the trigger and pulled.'' Her voice was very clear now. ''It didn't go off accidentally. I had hoped to wound him seriously, not kill him. But I fired. I fired to save my son. And Jack ended up dead.''

More silence.

''Then you headed back to the house,'' Myron said. ''You buried the gun. You saw me in the bushes. When you got inside, you erased the tape.''

''Yes.''

''And that was why you released that press announcement so early. The police wanted to keep it quiet, but you needed the story to go public. You wanted the kidnappers to know that Jack was dead, so they'd let Chad go.''

''It was my son or my husband,'' Linda said. She turned her body to face him. ''What would you have done?''

''I don't know. But I don't think I would have shot him.''

'' 'Don't think'?'' she repeated with a laugh. ''You talk about Jack being under pressure, but what about me? I hadn't slept. I was stressed and I was confused and I was more scared than I had ever been in my entire life—and yes, I was enraged that Jack had sacrificed our son's chance of playing the game we all so loved. I didn't have the luxury of an I-don't-know, Myron. My son's life was hanging in the balance. I only had time to react.''

They turned up Ardmore Avenue and drove in silence past the Merion Golf Club. They both looked out the window at the course's gently sloping sea of green broken up only by the clean, white faces of sand. It was, Myron had to admit, a magnificent sight.

''Are you going to tell?'' she asked.

She already knew the answer. ''I'm your attorney,'' Myron said. ''I can't tell.''

''And if you weren't my attorney?''

''It wouldn't matter. Victoria would still be able to offer up enough reasonable doubt to win the case.''

''That's not what I meant.''

''I know,'' Myron said. He left it at that. She waited, but no answer was coming.

''I know you don't care,'' Linda continued, ''but I meant what I said before. My feelings for you were real.''

Neither of them spoke again. Myron pulled into the driveway. The police kept the media back. Chad was outside, waiting. He smiled at his mother and ran toward her. Linda opened the car door and got out. They might have embraced, but Myron did not see it. He was already backing out the drive.

Chapter 42

Victoria opened the door.

"In the bedroom. Follow me."

"How is she?" Myron asked.

"She's been sleeping a lot. But I don't think the pain is that bad yet. We have a nurse and a morphine drip ready if she needs it."

The decor was far simpler and less opulent than Myron had expected. Solid-colored furniture and pillows. Uncluttered white walls. Pine bookcases with artifacts gathered from vacations to Asia and Africa. Victoria had told him that Cissy Lockwood loved to travel.

They stopped in front of a doorway. Myron looked inside. Win's mother lay in bed. Exhaustion emanated from her. Her head was back on the pillow as though it were too heavy to lift. An IV bag was attached to her arm. She looked at Myron and mustered a gentle smile. Myron smiled back. With his peripheral vision, he saw Victoria signal to the nurse. The nurse stood and moved past him. Myron stepped inside. The door closed behind him.

Myron moved closer to the bed. Her breathing was labored and constricted, as though she was being slowly strangled from inside. Myron did not know what to say. He had seen people die before, but those had been quick, violent deaths, the life force snuffed out in one big, powerful gust. This was different. He was actually watching a human being die, her vitality dripping out of her like the liquid in her IV bag, the light in her eyes almost imperceptibly dimming, the grinding whir of tissues and sinews and organs eroding under the onslaught of whatever manic beast had lain claim to her.

She lifted a hand and put it on his. Her grip was surprisingly strong. She was not bony or pale. Her muscles were still toned, her summer tan only slightly faded.

"You know," she said.

Myron nodded.

She smiled. "How?"

"A lot of little things," he said. "Victoria not wanting me to dig into the past. Jack's mischievous past. Your too-casual comment about how Win was supposed to be playing golf with Jack that day. But mostly it was Win. When I told him about our conversation, he said that I now knew why he wanted nothing to do with you and Jack. You, I could understand. But why Jack?"

Her chest heaved a bit. She closed her eyes for a moment. "Jack destroyed my life," she said. "I realize that he was only a teenager pulling a prank. He apologized profusely. He told me that he had not realized that my husband was on the premises. He said that he was certain I would hear Win coming and hide. It was all a joke, he said. Nothing more. But none of that made him less liable. I lost my son forever because of what he did. He had to face the consequences."

Myron nodded. "So you paid off Lloyd Rennart to sabotage Jack at the Open."

"Yes. It was an inadequate punishment for what he had done to my family, but it was the best I could do."

The bedroom door opened, and Win stepped into the room. Myron felt the hand release his. A sob came out of Cissy Lockwood. Myron did not hesitate or say good-bye. He turned away and walked out the door.

* * *

She died three days later. Win never left her side. When the last pitiful breath was drawn, when the chest mercifully stopped rising and falling and her face froze in a final, bloodless death mask, Win appeared in the corridor.

Myron stood and waited. Win looked at him. His face was serene, untroubled.

"I did not want her to die alone," he said.

Myron nodded. He tried to stop shaking.

"I am going to take a walk."

"Is there anything I can do?" Myron asked.

Win stopped. "Actually," he said, "there is."

"Name it."

They played thirty-six holes at Merion that day. And thirty-six more the next. And by the third day, Myron was starting to get it.

TELL NO ONE

Small said, "But what about when we are dead and gone, will you love me then, does love go on?"

Large held Small snug as they looked out at the night, at the moon in the dark and the stars shining bright. "Small, look at the stars, how they shine and glow, some of the stars died a long time ago. Still they shine in the evening skies, for you see, Small, love like starlight never dies. . . ."

—Debi Gliori
No Matter What

Acknowledgments

Right then. Before we start, I'd like to introduce the band:

editor extraordinaire Beth de Guzman, as well as Susan Corcoran, Sharon Lulek, Nita Taublib, Irwyn Applebaum, and the rest of the prime-time players at Bantam Dell

Lisa Erbach Vance and Aaron Priest, my agents

Anne Armstrong-Coben, M.D., Gene Riehl, Jeffrey Bedford, Gwendolen Gross, Jon Wood, Linda Fairstein, Maggie Griffin, and Nils Lofgren for their insight and encouragement

and Joel Gotler, who pushed and prodded and inspired

There should have been a dark whisper in the wind. Or maybe a deep chill in the bone. Something. An ethereal song only Elizabeth or I could hear. A tightness in the air. Some textbook premonition. There are misfortunes we almost expect in life—what happened to my parents, for example—and then there are other dark moments, moments of sudden violence, that alter everything. There was my life before the tragedy. There is my life now. The two have painfully little in common.

Elizabeth was quiet for our anniversary drive, but that was hardly unusual. Even as a young girl, she'd possessed this unpredictable melancholy streak. She'd go quiet and drift into either deep contemplation or a deep funk, I never knew which. Part of the mystery, I guess, but for the first time, I could feel the chasm between us. Our relationship had survived so much. I wondered if it could survive the truth. Or for that matter, the unspoken lies.

The car's air-conditioning whirred at the blue MAX setting. The day was hot and sticky. Classically August. We crossed the Delaware Water Gap at the Milford Bridge and were welcomed to Pennsylvania by a friendly toll collector. Ten miles later, I spotted the stone sign that read Lake Charmaine—private. I turned onto the dirt road.

The tires bore down, kicking up dust like an Arabian stampede. Elizabeth flipped off the car stereo. Out of the corner of my eye, I could tell that she was studying my profile. I wondered what she saw, and my heart started fluttering. Two deer nibbled on some leaves on our right. They stopped, looked at us, saw we meant no harm, went back to nibbling. I kept driving and then the lake rose before us. The sun was now in its death throes, bruising the sky a coiling purple and orange. The tops of the trees seemed to be on fire.

"I can't believe we still do this," I said.

"You're the one who started it."

"Yeah, when I was twelve years old."

Elizabeth let the smile through. She didn't smile often, but when she did, *pow*, right to my heart.

"It's romantic," she insisted.

"It's goofy."

"I love romance."

"You love goofy."

"You get laid whenever we do this."

"Call me Mr. Romance," I said.

She laughed and took my hand. "Come on, Mr. Romance, it's getting dark."

Lake Charmaine. My grandfather had come up with that name, which pissed off my grandmother to no end. She wanted it named for her. Her name was Bertha. Lake Bertha. Grandpa wouldn't hear it. Two points for Grandpa.

Some fifty-odd years ago, Lake Charmaine had been the sight of a rich-kids summer camp. The owner had gone belly-up and Grandpa bought the entire lake and surrounding acreage on the cheap. He'd fixed up the camp director's house and tore down most of the lake-front buildings. But farther in the woods, where no one went anymore, he left the kids' bunks alone to rot. My sister, Linda, and I used to explore them, sifting through their ruins for old treasures, playing hide-and-seek, daring ourselves to seek the Boogeyman we were sure watched and waited. Elizabeth rarely joined us. She liked to know where everything was. Hiding scared her.

When we stepped out of the car, I heard the ghosts. Lots of them here, too many, swirling and battling for my attention. My father's won out. The lake was hold-your-breath still, but I swore I could still hear Dad's howl of delight as he cannonballed off the dock, his knees pressed tightly against his chest, his smile just south of sane, the upcoming splash a virtual tidal wave in the eyes of his only son. Dad liked to land near my sunbathing mother's raft. She'd scold him, but she couldn't hide the laugh.

I blinked and the images were gone. But I remembered how the laugh and the howl and the splash would ripple and echo in the stillness of our lake, and I wondered if ripples and echoes like those ever fully die away, if somewhere in the woods my father's joyful yelps still bounced quietly off the trees. Silly thought, but there you go.

Memories, you see, hurt. The good ones most of all.

"You okay, Beck?" Elizabeth asked me.

I turned to her. "I'm going to get laid, right?"

"Perv."

She started walking up the path, her head high, her back straight. I watched her for a second, remembering the first time I'd seen that walk. I was seven years old, taking my bike—the one with the banana seat and Batman decal—for a plunge down Goodhart Road. Goodhart Road was steep and windy, the perfect thoroughfare for the discriminating Stingray driver. I rode downhill with no hands, feeling pretty much as cool and hip as a seven-year-old possibly could. The wind

3

whipped back my hair and made my eyes water. I spotted the moving van in front of the Ruskins' old house, turned and—first pow—there she was, my Elizabeth, walking with that titanium spine, so poised, even then, even as a seven-year-old girl with Mary Janes and a friendship bracelet and too many freckles.

We met two weeks later in Miss Sobel's second-grade class, and from that moment on—please don't gag when I say this—we were soul mates. Adults found our relationship both cute and unhealthy—our inseparable tomboy-kickball friendship morphing into puppy love and adolescent preoccupation and hormonal high school dating. Everyone kept waiting for us to outgrow each other. Even us. We were both bright kids, especially Elizabeth, top students, rational even in the face of irrational love. We understood the odds.

But here we were, twenty-five-year-olds, married seven months now, back at the spot when at the age of twelve we'd shared our first real kiss.

Nauseating, I know.

We pushed past branches and through humidity thick enough to bind. The gummy smell of pine clawed the air. We trudged through high grass. Mosquitoes and the like buzzed upward in our wake. Trees cast long shadows that you could interpret any way you wanted, like trying to figure out what a cloud looked like or one of Rorschach's inkblots.

We ducked off the path and fought our way through thicker brush. Elizabeth led the way. I followed two paces back, an almost symbolic gesture when I think about it now. I always believed that nothing could drive us apart—certainly our history had proven that, hadn't it?—but now more than ever I could feel the guilt pushing her away.

4

My guilt.

Up ahead, Elizabeth made a right at the big semi-phallic rock and there, on the right, was our tree. Our initials were, yup, carved into the bark:

E.P.
+
D.B.

And yes, a heart surrounded it. Under the heart were twelve lines, one marking each anniversary of that first kiss. I was about to make a wisecrack about how nauseating we were, but when I saw Elizabeth's face, the freckles now either gone or darkened, the tilt of the chin, the long, graceful neck, the steady green eyes, the dark hair braided like thick rope down her back, I stopped. I almost told her right then and there, but something pulled me back.

"I love you," I said.

"You're already getting laid."

"Oh."

"I love you too."

"Okay, okay," I said, feigning being put out, "you'll get laid too."

She smiled, but I thought I saw hesitancy in it. I took her in my arms. When she was twelve and we finally worked up the courage to make out, she'd smelled wonderfully of clean hair and strawberry Pixie Stix. I'd been overwhelmed by the newness of it, of course, the excitement, the exploration. Today she smelled of lilacs and cinnamon. The kiss moved like a warm light from the center of my heart. When our tongues met, I still felt a jolt. Elizabeth pulled away, breathless.

"Do you want to do the honors?" she asked.

She handed me the knife, and I carved the thirteenth

line in the tree. Thirteen. In hindsight, maybe there had been a premonition.

It was dark when we got back to the lake. The pale moon broke through the black, a solo beacon. There were no sounds tonight, not even crickets. Elizabeth and I quickly stripped down. I looked at her in the moonlight and felt something catch in my throat. She dove in first, barely making a ripple. I clumsily followed. The lake was surprisingly warm. Elizabeth swam with clean, even strokes, slicing through the water as though it were making a path for her. I splashed after her. Our sounds skittered across the lake's surface like skipping stones. She turned into my arms. Her skin was warm and wet. I loved her skin. We held each other close. She pressed her breasts against my chest. I could feel her heart and I could hear her breathing. Life sounds. We kissed. My hand wandered down the delicious curve of her back.

When we finished—when everything felt so right again—I grabbed a raft and collapsed onto it. I panted, my legs splayed, my feet dangling in the water.

Elizabeth frowned. "What, you going to fall asleep now?"

"Snore."

"Such a man."

I put my hands behind my head and lay back. A cloud passed in front of the moon, turning the blue night into something pallid and gray. The air was still. I could hear Elizabeth getting out of the water and stepping onto the dock. My eyes tried to adjust. I could barely make out her naked silhouette. She was, quite simply, breathtaking. I watched her bend at the waist and wring the water out of her hair. Then she arched her spine and threw her head back.

My raft drifted farther away from shore. I tried to sift through what had happened to me, but even I didn't understand it all. The raft kept moving. I started losing sight of Elizabeth. As she faded into the dark, I made a decision: I would tell her. I would tell her everything.

I nodded to myself and closed my eyes. There was a lightness in my chest now. I listened to the water gently lap against my raft.

Then I heard a car door open.

I sat up.

"Elizabeth?"

Pure silence, except for my own breathing.

I looked for her silhouette again. It was hard to make out, but for a moment I saw it. Or I thought I saw it. I'm not sure anymore or even if it matters. Either way, Elizabeth was standing perfectly still, and maybe she was facing me.

I might have blinked—I'm really not sure about that either—and when I looked again, Elizabeth was gone.

My heart slammed into my throat. "Elizabeth!"

No answer.

The panic rose. I fell off the raft and started swimming toward the dock. But my strokes were loud, maddeningly loud, in my ears. I couldn't hear what, if anything, was happening. I stopped.

"Elizabeth!"

For a long while there was no sound. The cloud still blocked the moon. Maybe she had gone inside the cabin. Maybe she'd gotten something out of the car. I opened my mouth to call her name again.

That was when I heard her scream.

I lowered my head and swam, swam hard, my arms pumping, my legs kicking wildly. But I was still far from the dock. I tried to look as I swam, but it was too dark now, the moon offering just faint shafts of light, illuminating nothing.

I heard a scraping noise, like something being dragged.

Up ahead, I could see the dock. Twenty feet, no more. I swam harder. My lungs burned. I swallowed some water, my arms stretching forward, my hand fumbling blindly in the dark. Then I found it. The ladder. I grabbed hold, hoisted myself up, climbed out of the water. The dock was wet from Elizabeth. I looked toward the cabin. Too dark. I saw nothing.

"Elizabeth!"

Something like a baseball bat hit me square in the solar plexus. My eyes bulged. I folded at the waist, suffocating from within. No air. Another blow. This time it landed on the top of my skull. I heard a crack in my head, and it felt as though someone had hammered a nail through my temple. My legs buckled and I dropped to my knees. Totally disoriented now, I put my hands against the sides of my head and tried to cover up. The next blow—the final blow—hit me square in the face.

I toppled backward, back into the lake. My eyes closed. I heard Elizabeth scream again—she screamed my name this time—but the sound, all sound, gurgled away as I sank under the water.

1

Eight Years Later

Another girl was about to break my heart. She had brown eyes and kinky hair and a toothy smile. She also had braces and was fourteen years old and—

"Are you pregnant?" I asked.

"Yeah, Dr. Beck."

I managed not to close my eyes. This was not the first time I'd seen a pregnant teen. Not even the first time today. I've been a pediatrician at this Washington Heights clinic since I finished my residency at nearby Columbia-Presbyterian Medical Center five years ago. We serve a Medicaid (read: poor) population with general family health care, including obstetrics, internal medicine, and, of course, pediatrics. Many people believe this makes me a bleeding-heart do-gooder. It doesn't. I like being a pediatrician. I don't particularly like doing it out in the suburbs with soccer moms and manicured dads and, well, people like me.

"What do you plan on doing?" I asked.

"Me and Terrell. We're real happy, Dr. Beck."

"How old is Terrell?"

"Sixteen."

She looked up at me, happy and smiling. Again I managed not to close my eyes.

The thing that always surprises me—always—is that most of these pregnancies are not accidental. These babies want to have babies. No one gets that. They talk about birth control and abstinence and that's all fine and good, but the truth is, their cool friends are having babies and their friends are getting all kinds of attention and so, hey, Terrell, why not us?

"He loves me," this fourteen-year-old told me.

"Have you told your mother?"

"Not yet." She squirmed and looked almost all her fourteen years. "I was hoping you could tell her with me."

I nodded. "Sure."

I've learned not to judge. I listen. I empathize. When I was a resident, I would lecture. I would look down from on high and bestow upon patients the knowledge of how self-destructive their behavior was. But on a cold Manhattan afternoon, a weary seventeen-year-old girl who was having her third kid with a third father looked me straight in the eye and spoke an indisputable truth: "You don't know my life."

It shut me up. So I listen now. I stopped playing Benevolent White Man and became a better doctor. I will give this fourteen-year-old and her baby the absolute best care possible. I won't tell her that Terrell will never stay, that she's just cut her future off at the pass, that if she is like most of the patients here, she'll be in a similar state with at least two more men before she turns twenty.

Think about it too much and you'll go nuts.

We spoke for a while—or, at least, she spoke and I listened. The examining room, which doubled as my office, was about the size of a prison cell (not that I know this from firsthand experience) and painted an institutional green, like the color of a bathroom in an elementary school. An eye chart, the one where you point in the directions the Es are facing, hung on the back of the door. Faded Disney decals spotted one wall while another was covered with a giant food pyramid poster. My fourteen-year-old patient sat on an examining table with a roll of sanitary paper we pulled down fresh for each kid. For some reason, the way the paper rolled out reminded me of wrapping a sandwich at the Carnegie Deli.

The radiator heat was beyond stifling, but you needed that in a place where kids were frequently getting undressed. I wore my customary pediatrician garb: blue jeans, Chuck Taylor Cons, a button-down oxford, and a bright Save the Children tie that screamed 1994. I didn't wear the white coat. I think it scares the kids.

My fourteen-year-old—yes, I couldn't get past her age—was a really good kid. Funny thing is, they all are. I referred her to an obstetrician I liked. Then I spoke to her mother. Nothing new or surprising. As I said, I do this almost every day. We hugged when she left. Over her shoulder, her mother and I exchanged a glance. Approximately twenty-five moms take their children to see me each day; at the end of the week, I can count on one hand how many are married.

Like I said, I don't judge. But I do observe.

After they left, I started jotting notes in the girl's chart. I flipped back a few pages. I'd been following her since I was a resident. That meant she started with me when she was eight years old. I looked at her growth chart. I remembered her as an eight-year-old, and then I thought about what she'd just looked like. She hadn't changed much. I finally closed my eyes and rubbed them.

Homer Simpson interrupted me by shouting, "The mail! The mail is here! Oooo!"

I opened my eyes and turned toward the monitor. This was Homer Simpson as in the TV show *The*

Simpsons. Someone had replaced the computer's droning "You've got mail" with this Homer audio wave. I liked it. I liked it a lot.

I was about to check my email when the intercom's squawking stopped my hand. Wanda, a receptionist, said, "You're, uh, hmm, you're, uh . . . Shauna is on the phone."

I understood the confusion. I thanked her and hit the blinking button. "Hello, sweetums."

"Never mind," she said. "I'm here."

Shauna hung up her cellular. I stood and walked down the corridor as Shauna made her entrance from the street. Shauna stalks into a room as though it offends her. She was a plus-size model, one of the few known by one name. Shauna. Like Cher or Fabio. She stood six one and weighed one hundred ninety pounds. She was, as you might expect, a head-turner, and all heads in the waiting room obliged.

Shauna did not bother stopping at Reception and Reception knew better than to try to stop her. She pulled open the door and greeted me with the words "Lunch. Now."

"I told you. I'm going to be busy."

"Put on a coat," she said. "It's cold out."

"Look, I'm fine. The anniversary isn't until tomorrow anyway."

"You're buying."

I hesitated and she knew she had me.

"Come on, Beck, it'll be fun. Like in college. Remember how we used to go out and scope hot babes together?"

"I never scoped hot babes."

"Oh, right, that was me. Go get your coat."

On the way back to my office, one of the mothers

gave me a big smile and pulled me aside. "She's even more beautiful in person," she whispered.

"Eh," I said.

"Are you and she . . ." The mother made a together motion with her hands.

"No, she's already involved with someone," I said.

"Really? Who?"

"My sister."

We ate at a crummy Chinese restaurant with a Chinese waiter who spoke only Spanish. Shauna, dressed impeccably in a blue suit with a neckline that plunged like Black Monday, frowned. "Moo shu pork in a tortilla shell?"

"Be adventurous," I said.

We met our first day of college. Someone in the registrar's office had screwed up and thought her name was Shaun, and we thus ended up roommates. We were all set to report the mistake when we started chatting. She bought me a beer. I started to like her. A few hours later, we decided to give it a go because our real roommates might be assholes.

I went to Amherst College, an exclusive small-Ivy institution in western Massachusetts, and if there is a preppier place on the planet, I don't know it. Elizabeth, our high school valedictorian, chose Yale. We could have gone to the same college, but we discussed it and decided that this would be yet another excellent test for our relationship. Again, we were doing the mature thing. The result? We missed each other like mad. The separation deepened our commitment and gave our love a new distance-makes-the-heart-grow-fonder dimension.

Nauseating, I know.

Between bites, Shauna asked, "Can you baby-sit Mark tonight?"

Mark was my five-year-old nephew. Sometime during our senior year, Shauna started dating my older sister, Linda. They had a commitment ceremony seven years ago. Mark was the by-product of, well, their love, with a little help from artificial insemination. Linda carried him to term and Shauna adopted him. Being somewhat old-fashioned, they wanted their son to have a male role model in his life. Enter me.

Next to what I see at work, we're talking *Ozzie and Harriet*.

"No prob," I said. "I want to see the new Disney film anyway."

"The new Disney chick is a babe and a half," Shauna said. "Their hottest since Pocahontas."

"Good to know," I said. "So where are you and Linda going?"

"Beats the hell out of me. Now that lesbians are chic, our social calendar is ridiculous. I almost long for the days when we hid in closets."

I ordered a beer. Probably shouldn't have, but one wouldn't hurt.

Shauna ordered one too. "So you broke up with what's-her-name," she said.

"Brandy."

"Right. Nice name, by the way. She have a sister named Whiskey?"

"We only went out twice."

"Good. She was a skinny witch. Besides, I got someone perfect for you."

"No, thanks," I said.

"She's got a killer bod."

"Don't set me up, Shauna. Please."

"Why not?"

"Remember the last time you set me up?"

"With Cassandra."

"Right."

"So what was wrong with her?"

"For one thing, she was a lesbian."

"Christ, Beck, you're such a bigot."

Her cell phone rang. She leaned back and answered it, but her eyes never left my face. She barked something and flipped the mouthpiece up. "I have to go," she said.

I signaled for the check.

"You're coming over tomorrow night," she pronounced.

I feigned a gasp. "The lesbians have no plans?"

"I don't. Your sister does. She's going stag to the big Brandon Scope formal."

"You're not going with her?"

"Nah."

"Why not?"

"We don't want to leave Mark without us two nights in a row. Linda has to go. She's running the trust now. Me, I'm taking the night off. So come over tomorrow night, okay? I'll order in, we'll watch videos with Mark."

Tomorrow was the anniversary. Had Elizabeth lived, we'd be scratching our twenty-first line in that tree. Strange as this might sound, tomorrow would not be a particularly hard day for me. For anniversaries or holidays or Elizabeth's birthday, I get so geared up that I usually handle them with no problems. It's the "regular" days that are hard. When I flip with the remote and stumble across a classic episode of *The Mary Tyler Moore Show* or *Cheers*. When I walk through a bookstore and see a new title by Alice Hoffman or Anne Tyler. When I listen to the O'Jays or the Four Tops or Nina Simone. Regular stuff.

"I told Elizabeth's mother I'd stop by," I said.

"Ah, Beck . . ." She was about to argue but caught herself. "How about after?"

"Sure," I said.

Shauna grabbed my arm. "You're disappearing again, Beck."

I didn't reply.

"I love you, you know. I mean, if you had any sort of sexual appeal whatsoever, I probably would have gone for you instead of your sister."

"I'm flattered," I said. "Really."

"Don't shut me out. If you shut me out, you shut everyone out. Talk to me, okay?"

"Okay," I said. But I can't.

I almost erased the email.

I get so much junk email, spam, bulk emails, you know the drill, I've become quite handy with the delete button. I read the sender's address first. If it's someone I know or from the hospital, fine. If not, I enthusiastically click the delete button.

I sat at my desk and checked the afternoon schedule. Chock-full, which was no surprise. I spun around in my chair and readied my delete finger. One email only. The one that made Homer shriek before. I did the quick scan, and my eyes got snagged on the first two letters of the subject.

What the—?

The way the window screen was formatted, all I could see were those two letters and the sender's email address. The address was unfamiliar to me. A bunch of numbers @comparama.com.

I narrowed my eyes and hit the right scroll button. The subject appeared a character at a time. With each click, my pulse raced a bit more. My breathing grew funny. I kept my finger on the scroll button and waited.

When I was done, when all the letters showed themselves, I read the subject again and when I did, I felt a deep, hard thud in my heart.

"Dr. Beck?"

My mouth wouldn't work.

"Dr. Beck?"

"Give me a minute, Wanda."

She hesitated. I could still hear her on the intercom. Then I heard it click off.

I kept staring at the screen:

To: dbeckmd@nyhosp.com
From: 13943928@comparama.com
Subject: E.P.+ D.B ////////////////////

Twenty-one lines. I've counted four times already.

It was a cruel, sick joke. I knew that. My hands tightened into fists. I wondered what chicken-shitted son of a bitch had sent it. It was easy to be anonymous in emails—the best refuge of the techno-coward. But the thing was, very few people knew about the tree or our anniversary. The media never learned about it. Shauna knew, of course. And Linda. Elizabeth might have told her parents or uncle. But outside of that . . .

So who sent it?

I wanted to read the message, of course, but something held me back. The truth is, I think about Elizabeth more than I let on—I don't think I'm fooling anyone there—but I never talk about her or what happened. People think I'm being macho or brave, that I'm trying to spare my friends or shunning people's pity or some such nonsense. That's not it. Talking about Elizabeth hurts. A lot. It brings back her last scream. It brings back all the unanswered questions. It brings back the might-have-beens (few things, I assure you, will devastate like the might-have-beens). It brings back the guilt, the feelings, no matter how irrational, that a stronger man—a better man—might have saved her.

They say it takes a long time to comprehend a tragedy. You're numb. You can't adequately accept the grim reality. Again, that's not true. Not for me anyway. I understood the full implications the moment they found Elizabeth's body. I understood that I would never see her again, that I would never hold her again, that we would never have children or grow old together. I understood that this was final, that there was no reprieve, that nothing could be bartered or negotiated.

I started crying immediately. Sobbing uncontrollably. I sobbed like that for almost a week without letup. I sobbed through the funeral. I let no one touch me, not even Shauna or Linda. I slept alone in our bed, burying my head in Elizabeth's pillow, trying to smell her. I went through her closets and pressed her clothes against my face. None of this was comforting. It was weird and it hurt. But it was her smell, a part of her, and I did it anyway.

Well-meaning friends—often the worst kind—handed me the usual clichés, and so I feel in a pretty good position to warn you: Just offer your deepest condolences. Don't tell me I'm young. Don't tell me it'll get better. Don't tell me she's in a better place. Don't tell me it's part of some divine plan. Don't tell me that I was lucky to have known such a love. Every one of those platitudes pissed me off. They made me—and this is going to sound uncharitable—stare at the idiot and

18

wonder why he or she still breathed while my Elizabeth rotted.

I kept hearing that "better to have loved and lost" bullshit. Another falsehood. Trust me, it is not better. Don't show me paradise and then burn it down. That was part of it. The selfish part. What got to me more— what really hurt—was that Elizabeth was denied so much. I can't tell you how many times I see or do something and I think of how much Elizabeth would have loved it and the pang hits me anew.

People wonder if I have any regrets. The answer is, only one. I regret that there were moments I wasted doing something other than making Elizabeth happy.

"Dr. Beck?"

"One more second," I said.

I put my hand on the mouse and moved the cursor over the Read icon. I clicked it and the message came up:

To: dbeckmd@nyhosp.com
From: 13943928@comparama com
Subject: E.P.+ D.B ////////////////////
Message: Click on this hyperlink, kiss time, anniversary.

A lead block formed in my chest.

Kiss time?

It was a joke, had to be. I am not big on cryptic. I'm also not big on waiting.

I grabbed the mouse again and moved the arrow over the hyperlink. I clicked and heard the primordial modem screech the mating call of machinery. We have an old system at the clinic. It took a while for the Web browser to appear. I waited, thinking *kiss time, how do they know about kiss time?*

The browser came up. It read error.

I frowned. Who the hell sent this? I tried it a second time, and again the error message came up. It was a broken link.

Who the hell knew about kiss time?

I have never told anyone. Elizabeth and I didn't much discuss it, probably because it was no big deal. We were corny to the point of Pollyanna, so stuff like this we just kept to ourselves. It was embarrassing really, but when we kissed that first time twenty-one years ago, I noted the time. Just for fun. I pulled back and looked at my Casio watch and said, "Six-fifteen."

And Elizabeth said, *"Kiss time."*

I looked at the message yet again. I started getting pissed now. This was way beyond funny. It's one thing to send a cruel email, but . . .

Kiss time.

Well, kiss time was 6:15 p.m. tomorrow. I didn't have much choice. I'd have to wait until then.

So be it.

I saved the email onto a diskette just in case. I pulled down the print options and hit Print All. I don't know much about computers, but I know that you could sometimes trace the origin of a message from all that gobbledygook at the bottom. I heard the printer purr. I took another look at the subject. I counted the lines again. Still twenty-one.

I thought about that tree and that first kiss, and there in my tight, stifling office I started to smell the strawberry Pixie Stix.

2

At home, I found another shock from the past.

I live across the George Washington Bridge from Manhattan—in the typical American-dream suburb of Green River, New Jersey, a township with, despite the moniker, no river and shrinking amounts of green. Home is Grandpa's house. I moved in with him and a revolving door of foreign nurses when Nana died three years ago.

Grandpa has Alzheimer's. His mind is a bit like an old black-and-white TV with damaged rabbit-ear antennas. He goes in and out and some days are better than others and you have to hold the antennas a certain way and not move at all, and even then the picture does the intermittent vertical spin. At least, that was how it used to be. But lately—to keep within this metaphor—the TV barely flickers on.

I never really liked my grandfather. He was a domineering man, the kind of old-fashioned, lift-by-the-boot-straps type whose affection was meted out in direct proportion to your success. He was a gruff man of tough love and old-world machismo. A grandson who was both sensitive and unathletic, even with good grades, was easily dismissed.

The reason I agreed to move in with him was that I knew if I didn't, my sister would have taken him in. Linda was like that. When we sang at Brooklake summer camp that "He has the whole world in His hands," she took the meaning a little too much to heart. She would have felt obligated. But Linda had a son and a life partner and responsibilities. I did not. So I made a pre-emptive strike by moving in. I liked living here well enough, I guess. It was quiet.

Chloe, my dog, ran up to me, wagging her tail. I scratched her behind the floppy ears. She took it in for a moment or two and then started eyeing the leash.

"Give me a minute," I told her.

Chloe doesn't like this phrase. She gave me a look—no easy feat when your hair totally covers your eyes. Chloe is a bearded collie, a breed that appears far more like a sheepdog than any sort of collie I've ever seen. Elizabeth and I had bought Chloe right after we got married. Elizabeth had loved dogs. I hadn't. I do now.

Chloe leaned up against the front door. She looked at the door, then at me, then back at the door again. Hint, hint.

Grandpa was slumped in front of a TV game show. He didn't turn toward me, but then again, he didn't seem to be looking at the picture either. His face was stuck in what had become a steady, pallid death-freeze. The only time I saw the death-freeze melt was when he was having his diaper changed. When that happened, Grandpa's lips thinned and his face went slack. His eyes watered and sometimes a tear escaped. I think he is at his most lucid at the exact moment he craves senility.

God has some sense of humor.

The nurse had left the message on the kitchen table: CALL SHERIFF LOWELL.

There was a phone number scribbled under it.

My head began to pound. Since the attack, I suffer migraines. The blows cracked my skull. I was hospital-ized for five days, though one specialist, a classmate of mine at medical school, thinks the migraines are psychological rather than physiological in origin. Maybe he's right. Either way, both the pain and guilt remain. I should have ducked. I should have seen the blows coming. I shouldn't have fallen into the water. And finally, I somehow summoned up the strength to save myself—shouldn't I have been able to do the same to save Elizabeth?

Futile, I know.

I read the message again. Chloe started whining. I put up one finger. She stopped whining but started doing her glance-at-me-and-the-door again.

I hadn't heard from Sheriff Lowell in eight years, but I still remembered him looming over my hospital bed, his face etched with doubt and cynicism.

What could he want after all this time?

I picked up the phone and dialed. A voice answered on the first ring.

"Dr. Beck, thank you for calling me back."

I am not a big fan of caller ID—too Big Brother for my tastes. I cleared my throat and skipped the pleasantries. "What can I do for you, Sheriff?"

"I'm in the area," he said. "I'd very much like to stop by and see you, if that's okay."

"Is this a social call?" I asked.

"No, not really."

He waited for me to say something. I didn't.

"Would now be convenient?" Lowell asked.

"You mind telling me what it's about?"

"I'd rather wait until—"

"And I'd rather you didn't."

I could feel my grip on the receiver tighten.

"Okay, Dr. Beck, I understand." He cleared his throat in a way that indicated he was trying to buy some time. "Maybe you saw on the news that two bodies were found in Riley County."

I hadn't. "What about them?"

"They were found near your property."

"It's not my property. It's my grandfather's."

"But you're his legal custodian, right?"

"No," I said. "My sister is."

"Perhaps you could call her then. I'd like to speak with her too."

"The bodies were not found on Lake Charmaine, right?"

"That's correct. We found them on the western neighboring lot. County property actually."

"Then what do you want from us?"

There was a pause. "Look, I'll be there in an hour. Please see if you can get Linda to come by, will you?"

He hung up.

The eight years had not been kind to Sheriff Lowell, but then again, he hadn't been Mel Gibson to begin with. He was a mangy mutt of a man with features so extralong hangdog that he made Nixon look as though he'd gotten a nip and tuck. The end of his nose was bulbous to the nth degree. He kept taking out a much-used hanky, carefully unfolding it, rubbing his nose, carefully refolding it, jamming it deep into his back pocket.

Linda had arrived. She leaned forward on the couch, ready to shield me. This was how she often sat. She was one of those people who gave you their full, undivided attention. She fixed you with those big brown eyes and you could look nowhere else. I'm definitely biased, but Linda is the best person I know. Corny, yes, but the fact that she exists gives me hope for this world. The fact that she loves me gives me whatever else I have left.

We sat in my grandparents' formal living room, which I usually do my utmost to avoid. The room was stale, creepy, and still had that old-people's-sofa smell. I found it hard to breathe. Sheriff Lowell took his time getting situated. He gave his nose a few more swipes, took out a pocket pad, licked his finger, found his page. He offered us his friendliest smile and started.

"Do you mind telling me when you were last at the lake?"

"I was there last month," Linda said.

But his eyes were on me. "And you, Dr. Beck?"

"Eight years ago."

He nodded as though he'd expected that response. "As I explained on the phone, we found two bodies near Lake Charmaine."

"Have you identified them yet?" Linda asked.

"No."

"Isn't that odd?"

Lowell thought about that one while leaning forward to pull out the hanky again. "We know that they're both male, both full-grown, both white. We're now searching through missing persons to see what we can come up with. The bodies are rather old."

"How old?" I asked.

Sheriff Lowell again found my eyes. "Hard to say. Forensics is still running tests, but we figure they've been dead at least five years. They were buried pretty good too. We'd never have found them except there was a landslide from that record rainfall, and a bear came up with an arm."

My sister and I looked at each other.

"Excuse me?" Linda said.

Sheriff Lowell nodded. "A hunter shot a bear and found a bone next to the body. It'd been in the bear's mouth. Turned out to be a human arm. We traced it back. Took some time, I can tell you. We're still excavating the area."

"You think there may be more bodies?"

"Can't say for sure."

I sat back. Linda stayed focused. "So are you here to get our permission to dig on Lake Charmaine property?"

"In part."

We waited for him to say more. He cleared his throat and looked at me again. "Dr. Beck, you're blood type B positive, isn't that right?"

I opened my mouth, but Linda put a protective hand on my knee. "What does that have to do with anything?" she asked.

"We found other things," he said. "At the grave site."

"What other things?"

"I'm sorry. That's confidential."

"Then get the hell out," I said.

Lowell did not seem particularly surprised by my outburst. "I'm just trying to conduct—"

"I said, get out."

Sheriff Lowell didn't move. "I know that your wife's murderer has already been brought to justice," he said. "And I know it must hurt like hell to bring this all up again."

"Don't patronize me," I said.

"That's not my intent."

"Eight years ago you thought I killed her."

"That's not true. You were her husband. In such cases, the odds of a family member's involvement—"

"Maybe if you didn't waste time with that crap, you would have found her before—" I jerked back, feeling myself choking up. I turned away. Damn. Damn him.

Linda reached for me, but I moved away.

"My job was to explore every possibility," he droned on. "We had the federal authorities helping us. Even your father-in-law and his brother were kept informed of all developments. We did everything we could."

I couldn't bear to hear another word. "What the hell do you want here, Lowell?"

He rose and hoisted his pants onto his gut. I think he wanted the height advantage. To intimidate or something. "A blood sample," he said. "From you."

"Why?"

"When your wife was abducted, you were assaulted."

"So?"

"You were hit with a blunt instrument."

"You know all this."

"Yes," Lowell said. He gave his nose another wipe, tucked the hanky away, and started pacing. "When we found the bodies, we also found a baseball bat."

The pain in my head started throbbing again. "A bat?"

Lowell nodded. "Buried in the ground with the bodies. There was a wooden bat."

Linda said, "I don't understand. What does this have to do with my brother?"

"We found dried blood on it. We've typed it as B positive." He tilted his head toward me. "Your blood type, Dr. Beck."

We went over it again. The tree-carving anniversary, the swim in the lake, the sound of the car door, my pitifully frantic swim to shore.

"You remember falling back in the lake?" Lowell asked me.

"Yes."

"And you heard your wife scream?"

"Yes."

"And then you passed out? In the water?"

I nodded.

"How deep would you say the water was? Where you fell in, I mean?"

"Didn't you check this eight years ago?" I asked.

"Bear with me, Dr. Beck."

"I don't know. Deep."

"Over-your-head deep?"

"Yes."

"Right, okay. Then what do you remember?"

"The hospital," I said.

"Nothing between the time you hit the water and the time you woke up at the hospital?"

"That's right."

"You don't remember getting out of the water? You don't remember making your way to the cabin or calling for an ambulance? You did all that, you know. We found you on the floor of the cabin. The phone was still off the hook."

"I know, but I don't remember."

Linda spoke up. "Do you think these two men are more victims of"—she hesitated—"KillRoy?"

She said it in a hush. KillRoy. Just uttering his name chilled the room.

Lowell coughed into his fist. "We're not sure, ma'am. KillRoy's only known victims are women. He never hid a body before—at least, none that we know about. And the two men's skin had rotted so we can't tell if they'd been branded."

Branded. I felt my head spin. I closed my eyes and tried not to hear any more.

3

I rushed to my office early the next morning, arriving two hours before my first scheduled patient. I flipped on the computer, found the strange email, clicked the hyperlink. Again it came up an error. No surprise really. I stared at the message, reading it over and over as though I might find a deeper meaning. I didn't.

Last night, I gave blood. The DNA test would take weeks, but Sheriff Lowell thought they might be able to get a preliminary match earlier. I pushed him for more information, but he remained tight-lipped. He was keeping something from us. What, I had no idea.

As I sat in the examining room and waited for my first patient, I replayed Lowell's visit. I thought about the two bodies. I thought about the bloody wooden bat. And I let myself think about the branding.

Elizabeth's body was found off Route 80 five days after the abduction. The coroner estimated that she'd been dead for two days. That meant she spent three days alive with Elroy Kellerton, aka KillRoy. Three days. Alone with a monster. Three sunrises and sunsets, scared and in the dark and in immense agony. I try very hard not to think about it. There are some places the mind should not go; it gets steered there anyway.

KillRoy was caught three weeks later. He confessed to killing fourteen women on a spree that began with a coed in Ann Arbor and ended with a prostitute in the Bronx. All fourteen women were found dumped on the side of the road like so much refuse. All had also been branded with the letter K. Branded in the same way as cattle. In other words, Elroy Kellerton took a metal poker, stuck it in a blazing fire, put a protective mitt on his hand, waited until the poker turned molten red with heat, and then he seared my Elizabeth's beautiful skin with a sizzling hiss.

My mind took one of those wrong turns, and images started flooding in. I squeezed my eyes shut and wished them away. It didn't work. He was still alive, by the way. KillRoy, I mean. Our appeals process gives this monster the chance to breathe, to read, to talk, to be interviewed on CNN, to get visits from do-gooders, to smile. Meanwhile his victims rot. Like I said, God has some sense of humor.

I splashed cold water on my face and checked the mirror. I looked like hell. Patients started filing in at nine o'clock. I was distracted, of course. I kept one eye on the wall clock, waiting for "kiss time"—6:15 p.m. The clock's hands trudged forward as though bathed in thick syrup.

I immersed myself in patient care. I'd always had that ability. As a kid, I could study for hours. As a doctor, I can disappear into my work. I did that after Elizabeth died. Some people point out that I hide in my work, that I choose to work instead of live. To that cliché I respond with a simple "What's your point?"

At noon, I downed a ham sandwich and Diet Coke and then I saw more patients. One eight-year-old boy had visited a chiropractor for "spinal alignment" eighty times in the past year. He had no back pain. It was a con job perpetrated by several area chiropractors. They offer the parents a free TV or VCR if they bring their kids in. Then they bill Medicaid for the visit. Medicaid is a wonderful, necessary thing, but it gets abused like a Don King undercard. I once had a sixteen-year-old boy rushed to the hospital in an ambulance—for routine sunburn. Why an ambulance instead of a taxi or subway? His mother explained that she'd have to pay for those herself or wait for the government to reimburse. Medicaid pays for the ambulance right away.

At five o'clock, I said good-bye to my last patient. The support staff headed out at five-thirty. I waited until the office was empty before I sat and faced the computer. In the background I could hear the clinic's phones ringing. A machine picks them up after five-thirty and gives the caller several options, but for some reason, the machine doesn't pick up until the tenth ring. The sound was somewhat maddening.

I got online, found the email, and clicked on the hyperlink yet again. Still a no-go. I thought about this strange email and those dead bodies. There had to be a connection. My mind kept going back to that seemingly simple fact. I started sorting through the possibilities.

Possibility one: These two men were the work of KillRoy. True, his other victims were women and easily found, but did that rule out his killing others?

Possibility two: KillRoy had persuaded these men to help him abduct Elizabeth. That might explain a lot. The wooden bat, for one thing, if the blood on it was indeed mine. It also put to rest my one big question mark about the whole abduction. In theory, KillRoy, like all serial killers, worked alone. How, I'd always wondered, had he been able to drag Elizabeth to the car and at the same time lie in wait for me to get out of the water? Before her body surfaced, the authorities had assumed there had been more than one abductor. But once her corpse was found branded with the K, that hypothesis was finessed. KillRoy could have done it, it was theorized, if he'd cuffed or somehow subdued Elizabeth and then gone after me. It wasn't a perfect fit, but if you pushed hard enough, the piece went in.

Now we had another explanation. He had accomplices. And he killed them.

Possibility three was the simplest: The blood on the bat was not mine. B positive is not common, but it's not that rare either. In all likelihood, these bodies had nothing to do with Elizabeth's death.

I couldn't make myself buy it.

I checked the computer's clock. It was hooked into some satellite that gave the exact time.

6:04.42 p.m.

Ten minutes and eighteen seconds to go.

To go to what?

The phones kept ringing. I tuned them out and drummed my fingers. Under ten minutes now. Okay, if there was going to be a change in the hyperlink, it would have probably happened by now. I put my hand on the mouse and took a deep breath.

My beeper went off.

I wasn't on call tonight. That meant it was either a mistake—something made far too often by the clinic night operators—or a personal call. It beeped again. Double beep. That meant an emergency. I looked at the display.

It was a call from Sheriff Lowell. It was marked Urgent.

Eight minutes.

I thought about it but not for very long. Anything was better than stewing with my own thoughts. I decided to call him back.

Lowell again knew who it was before he picked up.

"Sorry to bother you, Doc." Doc, he called me now. As though we were chums. "But I just have a quick question."

I put my hand back on the mouse, moved the cursor over the hyperlink, and clicked. The Web browser stirred to life.

"I'm listening," I said.

The Web browser was taking longer this time. No error message appeared.

"Does the name Sarah Goodhart mean anything to you?"

I almost dropped the phone.

"Doc?"

I pulled the receiver away and looked at it as though it had just materialized in my hand. I gathered myself together a piece at a time. When I trusted my voice, I put the phone back to my ear. "Why do you ask?"

Something started coming up on the computer screen. I squinted. One of those sky cams. Or street cam, I guess you'd call this one. They had them all over the Web now. I sometimes used the traffic ones, especially to check out the morning delay on the Washington Bridge.

"It's a long story," Lowell said.

I needed to buy time. "Then I'll call you back."

I hung up. Sarah Goodhart. The name meant something to me. It meant a lot.

What the hell was going on here?

The browser stopped loading. On the monitor, I saw a street scene in black and white. The rest of the page was blank. No banners or titles. I knew you could set it up so that you grabbed only a certain feed. That was what we had here.

I checked the computer clock.

6:12.18 p.m.

The camera was pointing down at a fairly busy street corner, from maybe fifteen feet off the ground. I didn't know what corner it was or what city I was looking at. It was definitely a major city, though. Pedestrians flowed mostly from right to left, heads down, shoulders slumped, briefcases in hand, downtrodden at the end of a workday, probably heading for a train or bus. On the far right, I could see the curb. The foot traffic came in waves, probably coordinated with the changing of a traffic light.

I frowned. Why had someone sent me this feed?

The clock read 6:14.21 p.m. Less than a minute to go.

I kept my eyes glued to the screen and waited for the countdown as though it were New Year's Eve. My pulse started speeding up. Ten, nine, eight . . .

Another tidal wave of humanity passed from right to left. I took my eyes off the clock. Four, three, two. I held my breath and waited. When I glanced at the clock again, it read:

6:15.02 p.m.

Nothing had happened—but then again, what had I expected?

The human tidal wave ebbed and once again, for a second or two, there was nobody in the picture. I settled back, sucking in air. A joke, I figured. A weird joke, sure. Sick even. But nonetheless—

And that was when someone stepped out from directly under the camera. It was as though the person had been hiding there the whole time.

I leaned forward.

It was a woman. That much I could see even though her back was to me. Short hair, but definitely a woman. From my angle, I hadn't been able to make out any faces so far. This was no different. Not at first.

The woman stopped. I stared at the top of her head, almost willing her to look up. She took another step. She was in the middle of the screen now. Someone else walked by. The woman stayed still. Then she turned around and slowly lifted her chin until she looked straight up into the camera.

My heart stopped.

I stuck a fist in my mouth and smothered a scream. I couldn't breathe. I couldn't think. Tears filled my eyes and started spilling down my cheeks. I didn't wipe them away.

I stared at her. She stared at me.

Another mass of pedestrians crossed the screen. Some of them bumped into her, but the woman didn't move. Her gaze stayed locked on the camera. She lifted her hand as though reaching toward me. My head spun. It was as though whatever tethered me to reality had been severed.

I was left floating helplessly.

She kept her hand raised. Slowly I managed to lift my hand. My fingers brushed the warm screen, trying to meet her halfway. More tears came. I gently caressed the woman's face and felt my heart crumble and soar all at once.

"Elizabeth," I whispered.

She stayed there for another second or two. Then she said something into the camera. I couldn't hear her, but I could read her lips.

"I'm sorry," my dead wife mouthed.

And then she walked away.

4

Vic Letty looked both ways before he limped inside the strip mall's Mail Boxes Etc. His gaze slid across the room. Nobody was watching. Perfect. Vic couldn't help but smile. His scam was foolproof. There was no way to trace it back to him, and now it was going to make him big-time rich.

The key, Vic realized, was preparation. That was what separated the good from the great. The greats covered their tracks. The greats prepared for every eventuality.

The first thing Vic did was get a fake ID from that loser cousin of his, Tony. Then, using the fake ID, Vic rented a mailbox under the pseudonym UYS Enterprises. See the brilliance? Use a fake ID *and* a pseudonym. So even if someone bribed the bozo behind the desk, even if someone could find out who rented the UYS Enterprises box, all you'd come up with was the name Roscoe Taylor, the one on Vic's fake ID.

No way to trace it back to Vic himself.

From across the room, Vic tried to see in the little window for Box 417. Hard to make out much, but there was something there for sure. Beautiful. Vic accepted only cash or money orders. No checks, of course. Nothing that could be traced back to him. And whenever he picked up the money, he wore a disguise. Like right now. He had on a baseball cap and a fake mustache. He also pretended to have a limp. He read somewhere that people notice limps, so if a witness was asked to identify the guy using Box 417, what would the witness say? Simple. The man had a mustache and a limp. And if you bribed the dumb-ass clerk, you'd conclude some guy named Roscoe Taylor had a mustache and a limp.

And the real Vic Letty had neither.

But Vic took other precautions too. He never opened the box when other people were around. Never. If someone else was getting his mail or in the general vicinity, he'd act as though he was opening another box or pretend he was filling out a mailing form, something like that. When the coast was clear—and only when the coast was clear—would Vic go over to Box 417.

Vic knew that you could never, ever be too careful.

Even when it came to getting here, Vic took precautions. He'd parked his work truck—Vic handled repairs and installations for CableEye, the East Coast's biggest cable TV operator—four blocks away. He'd ducked through two alleys on his way here. He wore a black windbreaker over his uniform coverall so no one would be able to see the "Vic" sewn over the shirt's right pocket.

He thought now about the huge payday that was probably in Box 417, not ten feet from where he now stood. His fingers felt antsy. He checked the room again.

There were two women opening their boxes. One turned and smiled absently at him. Vic moved toward the boxes on the other side of the room and grabbed his key chain—he had one of those key chains that jangled off his belt—and pretended to be sorting through them. He kept his face down and away from them.

More caution.

Two minutes later, the two women had their mail and

were gone. Vic was alone. He quickly crossed the room and opened his box.

Oh wow.

One package addressed to UYS Enterprises. Wrapped in brown. No return address. And thick enough to hold some serious green.

Vic smiled and wondered: Is that what fifty grand looks like?

He reached out with trembling hands and picked up the package. It felt comfortably heavy in his hand. Vic's heart started jackhammering. Oh, sweet Jesus. He'd been running this scam for four months now. He'd been casting that net and landing some pretty decent fish. But oh lordy, now he'd landed a friggin' whale!

Checking his surroundings again, Vic stuffed the package into the pocket of his windbreaker and hurried outside. He took a different route back to his work truck and started for the plant. His fingers found the package and stroked it. Fifty grand. Fifty thousand dollars. The number totally blew his mind.

By the time Vic drove to the CableEye plant, night had fallen. He parked the truck in the back and walked across the footbridge to his own car, a rusted-out 1991 Honda Civic. He frowned at the car and thought, Not much longer.

The employee lot was quiet. The darkness started weighing against him. He could hear his footsteps, the weary slap of work boots against tar. The cold sliced through his windbreaker. Fifty grand. He had fifty grand in his pocket.

Vic hunched his shoulders and hurried his step.

The truth was, Vic was scared this time. The scam would have to stop. It was a good scam, no doubt about it. A great one even. But he was taking on some big boys now. He had questioned the intelligence of such a move, weighed the pros and cons, and decided that the great ones—the ones who really change their lives—go for it.

And Vic wanted to be a great one.

The scam was simple, which was what made it so extraordinary. Every house that had cable had a switch box on the telephone line. When you ordered some sort of premium channel like HBO or Showtime, your friendly neighborhood cable man came out and flicked a few switches. That switch box holds your cable life. And what holds your cable life holds all about the real you.

Cable companies and hotels with in-room movies always point out that your bill will not list the names of the movies you watch. That might be true, but that doesn't mean they don't know. Try fighting a charge sometime. They'll tell you titles until you're blue in the face.

What Vic had learned right away—and not to get too technical here—was that your cable choices worked by codes, relaying your order information via the cable switch box to the computers at the cable company's main station. Vic would climb the telephone poles, open the boxes, and read off the numbers. When he went back to the office, he'd plug in the codes and learn all.

He'd learn, for example, that at six p.m. on February 2, you and your family rented *The Lion King* on pay-per-view. Or for a much more telling example, that at ten-thirty p.m. on February 7, you ordered a double bill of *The Hunt for Miss October* and *On Golden Blonde* via Sizzle TV.

See the scam?

At first Vic would hit random houses. He'd write a letter to the male owner of the residence. The letter would be short and chilling. It would list what porno movies had been watched, at what time, on what day. It would make it clear that copies of this information would be disseminated to every member of the man's family, his neighbors, his employer. Then Vic would ask for $500 to keep his mouth shut. Not much money maybe, but Vic thought it was the perfect amount—high enough to give Vic some serious green yet low enough so that most marks wouldn't balk at the price.

Still—and this surprised Vic at first—only about ten percent responded. Vic wasn't sure why. Maybe watching porno films wasn't the stigma it used to be. Maybe the guy's wife already knew about it. Hell, maybe the guy's wife watched them with him. But the real problem was Vic's scam was too scattershot.

He had to be more focused. He had to cherry-pick his marks.

That was when he came up with the idea of concentrating on people in certain professions, ones who would have a lot to lose if the information came out. Again the cable computers had all the info he needed. He started hitting up schoolteachers. Day care workers. Gynecologists. Anyone who worked in jobs that would be sensitive to a scandal like this. Teachers panicked the most, but they had the least money. He also made his letters more specific. He would mention the wife by name. He would mention the employer by name. With teachers, he'd promise to flood the Board of Education and the parents of his students with "proof of perversion," a phrase Vic came up with on his own. With doctors, he'd threaten to send his "proof" to the specific licensing board, along with the local papers, neighbors, and patients.

Money started coming in faster.

To date, Vic's scams had netted him close to forty

thousand dollars. And now he had landed his biggest fish yet—such a big fish that at first Vic had considered dropping the matter altogether. But he couldn't. He couldn't just walk away from the juiciest score of his life.

Yes, he'd hit someone in the spotlight. A big, big bigtime spotlight. Randall Scope. Young, handsome, rich, hottie wife, 2.4 kids, political aspirations, the heir apparent to the Scope fortune. And Scope hadn't ordered just one movie. Or even two.

During a one-month stint, Randall Scope had ordered twenty-three pornographic films.

Ee-yow.

Vic had spent two nights drafting his demands, but in the end he stuck with the basics: short, chilling, and very specific. He asked Scope for fifty grand. He asked that it be in his box by today. And unless Vic was mistaken, that fifty grand was burning a hole in his windbreaker pocket.

Vic wanted to look. He wanted to look right now. But Vic was nothing if not disciplined. He'd wait until he got home. He'd lock his door and sit on the floor and slit open the package and let the green pour out.

Serious big-time.

Vic parked his car on the street and headed up the driveway. The sight of his living quarters—an apartment over a crappy garage—depressed him. But he wouldn't be there much longer. Take the fifty grand, add the almost forty grand he had hidden in the apartment, plus the ten grand in savings ...

The realization made him pause. One hundred thousand dollars. He had one hundred grand in cash. Hot damn.

He'd leave right away. Take this money and head out to Arizona. He had a friend out there, Sammy Viola. He and Sammy were going to start their own business, maybe open a restaurant or nightclub. Vic was tired of New Jersey.

It was time to move on. Start fresh.

Vic headed up the stairs toward his apartment. For the record, Vic had never carried out his threats. He never sent out any letters to anyone. If a mark didn't pay, that was the end of it. Harming them after the fact wouldn't do any good. Vic was a scam artist. He got by on his brains. He used threats, sure, but he'd never carry through with them. It would only make someone mad, and hell, it would probably expose him too.

He'd never really hurt anyone. What would be the point?

He reached the landing and stopped in front of his door. Pitch dark now. The damn lightbulb by his door was out again. He sighed and heaved up his big key chain. He squinted in the dark, trying to find the right key. He did it mostly through feel. He fumbled against the knob until the key found the lock. He pushed open the door and stepped inside and something felt wrong.

Something crinkled under his feet.

Vic frowned. Plastic, he thought to himself. He was stepping on plastic. As though a painter had laid it down to protect the floor or something. He flicked on the light switch, and that was when he saw the man with the gun.

"Hi, Vic."

Vic gasped and took a step back. The man in front of him looked to be in his forties. He was big and fat with a belly that battled against the buttons of his dress shirt and, in at least one place, won. His tie was loosened and he had the worst comb-over imaginable—eight braided strands pulled ear to ear and greased against the dome.

The man's features were soft, his chin sinking into folds of flab. He had his feet up on the trunk Vic used as a coffee table. Replace the gun with a TV remote and the man would be a weary dad just home from work.

The other man, the one who blocked the door, was the polar opposite of the big guy—in his twenties, Asian, squat, granite-muscular and cube-shaped with bleached-blond hair, a nose ring or two, and a yellow Walkman in his ears. The only place you might think to see the two of them together would be on a subway, the big man frowning behind his carefully folded newspaper, the Asian kid eyeing you as his head lightly bounced to the too-loud music on his headset.

Vic tried to think. Find out what they want. Reason with them. You're a scam artist, he reminded himself. You're smart. You'll find a way out of this. Vic straightened himself up.

"What do you want?" Vic asked.

The big man with the comb-over pulled the trigger.

Vic heard a pop and then his right knee exploded. His eyes went wide. He screamed and crumbled to the ground, holding his knee. Blood poured between his fingers.

"It's a twenty-two," the big man said, motioning toward the gun. "A small-caliber weapon. What I like about it, as you'll see, is that I can shoot you a lot and not kill you."

With his feet still up, the big man fired again. This time, Vic's shoulder took the hit. Vic could actually feel the bone shatter. His arm flopped away like a barn door with a busted hinge. Vic fell flat on his back and started breathing too fast. A terrible cocktail of fear and pain engulfed him. His eyes stayed wide and unblinking, and through the haze, he realized something.

The plastic on the ground.

He was lying on it. More than that, he was bleeding on it. That was what it was there for. The men had put it down for easy cleanup.

"Do you want to start telling me what I want to hear," the big man said, "or should I shoot again?"

Vic started talking. He told them everything. He told them where the rest of the money was. He told them where the evidence was. The big man asked him if he had any accomplices. He said no. The big man shot Vic's other knee. He asked him again if he had accomplices. Vic still said no. The big man shot him in the right ankle.

An hour later, Vic begged the big man to shoot him in the head.

Two hours after that, the big man obliged.

5

I stared unblinking at the computer screen.

I couldn't move. My senses were past overload. Every part of me was numb.

It couldn't be. I knew that. Elizabeth hadn't fallen off a yacht and assumed drowned, her body never found. She hadn't been burned beyond recognition or any of that. Her corpse had been found in a ditch off Route 80. Battered, perhaps, but she had been positively IDed.

Not by you ...

Maybe not, but by two close family members: her father and her uncle. In fact, Hoyt Parker, my father-in-law, was the one who told me that Elizabeth was dead. He came to my hospital room with his brother Ken not long after I regained consciousness. Hoyt and Ken were large and grizzled and stone-faced, one a New York City cop, the other a federal agent, both war veterans with beefy flesh and large, undefined muscles. They took off their hats and tried to tell me with the semidistant empathy of professionals, but I didn't buy it and they weren't selling too hard.

So what had I just seen?

On the monitor, flows of pedestrians still spurted by. I stared some more, willing her to come back. No dice. Where was this anyway? A bustling city, that was all I could tell. It could be New York for all I knew.

So look for clues, idiot.

I tried to concentrate. Clothes. Okay, let's check out

the clothes. Most people were wearing coats or jackets. Conclusion: We were probably somewhere up north or, at least, someplace not particularly warm today. Great. I could rule out Miami.

What else? I stared at the people. The hairstyles? That wouldn't help. I could see the corner of a brick building. I looked for identifiable characteristics, something to separate the building from the norm. Nothing. I searched the screen for something, anything, out of the ordinary.

Shopping bags.

A few people were carrying shopping bags. I tried to read them, but everyone was moving too fast. I willed them to slow down. They didn't. I kept looking, keeping my gaze at knee level. The camera angle wasn't helping here. I put my face so close to the screen, I could feel the heat.

Capital R.

That was the first letter on one bag. The rest was too squiggly to make out. It looked written in some fancy script. Okay, what else? What other clues could I—?

The camera feed went white.

Damn. I hit the reload button. The error screen returned. I went back to the original email and clicked the hyperlink. Another error.

My feed was gone.

I looked at the blank screen, and the truth struck me anew: I'd just seen Elizabeth.

I could try to rationalize it away. But this wasn't a dream. I'd had dreams where Elizabeth was alive. Too many of them. In most, I'd just accept her return from the grave, too thankful to question or doubt. I remember one dream in particular where we were together—I don't remember what we were doing or even where we were—and right then, in mid-laugh, I realized with breath-crushing certainty that I was dreaming, that very soon I'd wake up alone. I remember the dream—me reaching out at that moment and grabbing hold of her, pulling her in close, trying desperately to drag Elizabeth back with me.

I knew dreams. What I had seen on the computer wasn't one.

It wasn't a ghost either. Not that I believe in them, but when in doubt, you might as well keep an open mind. But ghosts don't age. The Elizabeth on the computer had. Not a lot, but it had been eight years. Ghosts don't cut their hair either. I thought of that long braid hanging down her back in the moonlight. I thought about the fashionably short cut I'd just seen. And I thought about those eyes, those eyes that I had looked into since I was seven years old.

It was Elizabeth. She was still alive.

I felt the tears come again, but this time I fought them back. Funny thing. I'd always cried easily, but after mourning for Elizabeth it was as though I couldn't cry anymore. Not that I had cried myself out or used up all my tears or any of that nonsense. Or that I'd grown numb from grief, though that might have been a tiny part of it. What I think happened was that I instinctively snapped into a defensive stance. When Elizabeth died, I threw open the doors and let the pain in. I let myself feel it all. And it hurt. It hurt so damn much that now something primordial wouldn't let it happen again.

I don't know how long I sat there. Half an hour maybe. I tried to slow my breath and calm my mind. I wanted to be rational. I needed to be rational. I was supposed to be at Elizabeth's parents' house already, but I couldn't imagine facing them right now.

Then I remembered something else.

Sarah Goodhart.

Sheriff Lowell had asked if I knew anything about the name. I did.

Elizabeth and I used to play a childhood game. Perhaps you did too. You take your middle name and make it your first, then you take your childhood street name and make it your last. For example, my full name is David Craig Beck and I grew up on Darby Road. I would thus be Craig Darby. And Elizabeth would be . . .

Sarah Goodhart.

What the hell was going on here?

I picked up the phone. First I called Elizabeth's parents. They still lived in that house on Goodhart Road. Her mother answered. I told her I was running late. People accept that from doctors. One of the fringe benefits of the job.

When I called Sheriff Lowell, his voice mail picked up. I told him to beep me when he had a chance. I don't have a cell phone. I realize that puts me in the minority, but my beeper leashes me to the outside world too much as it is.

I sat back, but Homer Simpson knocked me out of my trance with another "The mail is here!" I shot forward and gripped the mouse. The sender's address was unfamiliar, but the subject read Street Cam. Another thud in my chest.

I clicked the little icon and the email came up:

Tomorrow same time plus two hours at Bigfoot.com.
A message for you will be left under:
Your user name: Bat Street
Password: Teenage

48

Beneath this, clinging to the bottom of the screen, just five more words:

They're watching. Tell no one.

Larry Gandle, the man with the bad comb-over, watched Eric Wu quietly handle the cleanup.

Wu, a twenty-six-year-old Korean with a staggering assortment of body pierces and tattoos, was the deadliest man Gandle had ever known. Wu was built like a small army tank, but that alone didn't mean much. Gandle knew plenty of people who had the physique. Too often, show muscles meant useless muscles.

That was not the case with Eric Wu.

The rock brawn was nice, but the real secret of Wu's deadly strength lay in the man's callused hands—two cement blocks with steel-talon fingers. He spent hours on them, punching cinder blocks, exposing them to extreme heat and cold, performing sets of one-finger push-ups. When Wu put those fingers to use, the devastation to bone and tissue was unimaginable.

Dark rumors swirled around men like Wu, most of which were crap, but Larry Gandle had seen him kill a man by digging his fingers into the soft spots of the face and abdomen. He had seen Wu grab a man by both ears and rip them off in a smooth pluck. He had seen him kill four times in four very different ways, never using a weapon.

None of the deaths had been quick.

Nobody knew exactly where Wu came from, but the most accepted tale had something to do with a brutal childhood in North Korea. Gandle had never asked. There were some night paths the mind was better off not traversing; the dark side of Eric Wu—right, like

49

there might be a light side—was one of them.

When Wu finished wrapping up the protoplasm that had been Vic Letty in the drop cloth, he looked up at Gandle with those eyes of his. Dead eyes, Larry Gandle thought. The eyes of a child in a war newsreel.

Wu had not bothered taking off his headset. His personal stereo did not blare hip hop or rap or even rock 'n' roll. He listened pretty much nonstop to those soothing-sounds CDs you might find at Sharper Image, the ones with names like Ocean Breeze and Running Brook.

"Should I take him to Benny's?" Wu asked. His voice had a slow, odd cadence to it, like a character from a Peanuts cartoon.

Larry Gandle nodded. Benny ran a crematorium. Ashes to ashes. Or, in this case, scum to ashes. "And get rid of this."

Gandle handed Eric Wu the twenty-two. The weapon looked puny and useless in Wu's giant hand. Wu frowned at it, probably disappointed that Gandle had chosen it over Wu's own unique talents, and jammed it in his pocket. With a twenty-two, there were rarely exit wounds. That meant less evidence. The blood had been contained by a vinyl drop cloth. No muss, no fuss.

"Later," Wu said. He picked up the body with one hand as though it were a briefcase and carried it out.

Larry Gandle nodded a good-bye. He took little joy from Vic Letty's pain—but then again, he took little discomfort either. It was a simple matter really. Gandle had to know for absolute certain that Letty was working alone and that he hadn't left evidence around for someone else to find. That meant pushing the man past the breaking point. There was no other way.

In the end, it came down to a clear choice—the Scope

family or Vic Letty. The Scopes were good people. They had never done a damn thing to Vic Letty. Vic Letty, on the other hand, had gone out of his way to try to hurt the Scope family. Only one of them could get off unscathed—the innocent, well-meaning victim or the parasite who was trying to feed off another's misery. No choice when you thought about it.

Gandle's cell phone vibrated. He picked it up and said, "Yes."

"They identified the bodies at the lake."

"And?"

"It's them. Jesus Christ, it's Bob and Mel."

Gandle closed his eyes.

"What does it mean, Larry?"

"I don't know."

"So what are we going to do?"

Larry Gandle knew that there was no choice. He'd have to speak with Griffin Scope. It would unearth unpleasant memories. Eight years. After eight years. Gandle shook his head. It would break the old man's heart all over again.

"I'll handle it."

6

Kim Parker, my mother-in-law, is beautiful. She'd always looked so much like Elizabeth that her face had become for me the ultimate what-might-have-been. But Elizabeth's death had slowly sapped her. Her face was drawn now, her features almost brittle. Her eyes had that look of marbles shattered from within.

The Parkers' house had gone through very few changes since the seventies—adhesive wood paneling, wall-to-wall semi-shag carpet of light blue with flecks of white, a faux stone raised fireplace à la the Brady Bunch. Folded TV trays, the kind with white plastic tops and gold metal legs, lined one wall. There were clown paintings and Rockwell collector plates. The only noticeable update was the television. It had swelled over the years from a bouncing twelve-inch black-and-white to the monstrous full-color fifty-incher that now sat hunched in the corner.

My mother-in-law sat on the same couch where Elizabeth and I had so often made out and then some. I smiled for a moment and thought, ah, if that couch could talk. But then again, that hideous chunk of sitting space with the loud floral design held a lot more than lustful memories. Elizabeth and I had sat there to open our college acceptance letters. We cuddled to watch *One Flew Over the Cuckoo's Nest* and *The Deer Hunter* and all the old Hitchcock films. We did homework, me sitting upright and Elizabeth lying with her head on my lap. I told Elizabeth I wanted to be a doctor—a big-time surgeon, or so I thought. She told me she wanted to get a law degree and work with kids. Elizabeth couldn't bear the thought of children in pain.

I remember an internship she did during the summer break after our freshman year of college. She worked for Covenant House, rescuing runaway and homeless children from New York's worst streets. I went with her once in the Covenant House van, cruising up and down Forty-second Street pre-Giuliani, sifting through putrid pools of quasi-humanity for children who needed shelter. Elizabeth spotted a fourteen-year-old hooker who was so strung out that she'd soiled herself. I winced in disgust. I'm not proud of that. These people may have been human, but—I'm being honest here—the filth repulsed me. I helped. But I winced.

Elizabeth never winced. That was her gift. She took the children by the hand. She carried them. She cleaned off that girl and nursed her and talked to her all night. She looked them straight in the eye. Elizabeth truly believed that everyone was good and worthy; she was naïve in a way I wish I could be.

I'd always wondered if she'd died that same way—with that naïveté intact—still clinging through the pain to her faith in humanity and all that wonderful nonsense. I hope so, but I suspect that KillRoy probably broke her.

Kim Parker sat primly with her hands in her lap. She'd always liked me well enough, though during our youth both sets of parents had been concerned with our closeness. They wanted us to play with others. They wanted us to make more friends. Natural, I suppose.

Hoyt Parker, Elizabeth's father, wasn't home yet, so Kim and I chatted about nothing—or, to say the same thing a different way, we chatted about everything except Elizabeth. I kept my eyes focused on Kim because I knew that the mantel was chock-full of photographs of Elizabeth and her heart-splitting smile.

She's alive ...

I couldn't make myself believe it. The mind, I know from my psychiatric rotation in medical school (not to mention my family history), has incredible distortive powers. I didn't believe I was nuts enough to conjure up her image, but then again, crazy people never do. I thought about my mother and wondered what she realized about her mental health, if she was even capable of engaging in serious introspection.

Probably not.

Kim and I talked about the weather. We talked about my patients. We talked about her new part-time job at Macy's. And then Kim surprised the hell out of me.

"Are you seeing anyone?" she asked.

It was the first truly personal question she had ever asked me. It knocked me back a step. I wondered what she wanted to hear. "No," I said.

She nodded and looked as though she wanted to say something else. Her hand fluttered up to her face.

"I date," I said.

"Good," she replied with too hearty a nod. "You should."

I stared at my hands and surprised myself by saying, "I still miss her so much." I didn't plan on that. I planned on keeping quiet and following our usual safe track. I glanced up at her face. She looked pained and grateful.

"I know you do, Beck," Kim said. "But you should-n't feel guilty about seeing other people."

"I don't," I said. "I mean, it's not that."

She uncrossed her legs and leaned toward me. "Then what is it?"

I couldn't speak. I wanted to. For her sake. She looked at me with those shattered eyes, her need to talk about her daughter so surface, so raw. But I couldn't. I shook my head.

I heard a key in the door. We both turned suddenly, straightening up like caught lovers. Hoyt Parker shouldered open the door and called out his wife's name. He stepped into the den and with a hearty sigh, he put down a gym bag. His tie was loosened, his shirt wrinkled, his sleeves rolled up to the elbows. Hoyt had forearms like Popeye. When he saw us sitting on the couch, he let loose another sigh, this one deeper and with more than a hint of disapproval.

"How are you, David?" he said to me.

We shook hands. His grip, as always, was callous-scratchy and too firm. Kim excused herself and hurried out of the room. Hoyt and I exchanged pleasantries, and silence settled in. Hoyt Parker had never been comfortable with me. There might have been some Electra complex here, but I'd always felt that he saw me as a threat. I understood. His little girl had spent all her time with me. Over the years, we'd managed to fight through his resentment and forged something of a friendship. Until Elizabeth's death.

He blames me for what happened.

He has never said that, of course, but I see it in his eyes. Hoyt Parker is a burly, strong man. Rock-solid, honest Americana. He'd always made Elizabeth feel unconditionally safe. Hoyt had that kind of protective aura. No harm would come to his little girl as long as Big Hoyt was by her side.

I don't think I ever made Elizabeth feel safe like that.

"Work good?" Hoyt asked me.

"Fine," I said. "You?"

"A year away from retirement."

I nodded and we again fell into silence. On the ride over here, I decided not to say anything about what I'd seen on the computer. Forget the fact that it sounded loony. Forget the fact that it would open old wounds and hurt them both like all hell. The truth was, I didn't have a clue what was going on. The more time passed, the more the whole episode felt unreal. I also decided to take that last email to heart. *Tell no one.* I couldn't imagine why or what was going on, but whatever connection I'd made felt frighteningly tenuous.

Nonetheless I still found myself making sure Kim was out of earshot. Then I leaned closer to Hoyt and said softly, "Can I ask you something?"

He didn't reply, offering up instead one of his patented skeptical gazes.

"I want to know—" I stopped. "I want to know how you found her."

"Found her?"

"I mean when you first walked into the morgue. I want to know what you saw."

Something happened to his face, like tiny explosions collapsing the foundation. "For the love of Christ, why would you ask me that?"

"I've just been thinking about it," I said lamely. "With the anniversary and all."

He stood suddenly and wiped his palms on the legs of his pants. "You want a drink?"

"Sure."

"Bourbon okay?"

"That would be great."

He walked over to an old bar cart near the mantel

and thus the photographs. I kept my gaze on the floor.

"Hoyt?" I tried.

He twisted open a bottle. "You're a doctor," he said, pointing a glass at me. "You've seen dead bodies."

"Yes."

"Then you know."

I did know.

He brought over my drink. I grabbed it a little too quickly and downed a sip. He watched me and then brought his glass to his lips.

"I know I never asked you about the details," I began. More than that, I had studiously avoided them. Other "families of the victims," as the media referred to us, bathed in them. They showed up every day at KillRoy's trial and listened and cried. I didn't. I think it helped them channel their grief. I chose to channel mine back at myself.

"You don't want to know the details, Beck."

"She was beaten?"

Hoyt studied his drink. "Why are you doing this?"

"I need to know."

He peered at me over the glass. His eyes moved along my face. It felt as though they were prodding my skin. I kept my gaze steady.

"There were bruises, yes."

"Where?"

"David—"

"On her face?"

His eyes narrowed, as though he'd spotted something unexpected. "Yes."

"On her body too?"

"I didn't look at her body," he said. "But I know the answer is yes."

"Why didn't you look at her body?"

"I was there as her father, not an investigator—for the purposes of identification only."

"Was that easy?" I asked.

"Was what easy?"

"Making the identification. I mean, you said her face was bruised."

His body stiffened. He put down his drink, and with mounting dread, I realized I'd gone too far. I should have stuck to my plan. I should have just kept my mouth shut.

"You really want to hear all this?"

No, I thought. But I nodded my head.

Hoyt Parker put down his drink, crossed his arms, and leaned back on his heels. "Elizabeth's left eye was swollen closed. Her nose was broken and flattened like wet clay. There was a slash across her forehead, probably made with a box cutter. Her jaw had been ripped out of its hinges, snapping all the tendons." His voice was a total monotone. "The letter K was burnt into her right cheek. The smell of charred skin was still obvious."

My stomach knotted.

Hoyt's eyes settled onto mine hard. "Do you want to know what was the worst part, Beck?"

I looked at him and waited.

"It still took no time at all," he said. "I knew in an instant that it was Elizabeth."

7

Champagne flutes tinkled in harmony with the Mozart sonata. A harp underscored the subdued pitch of the party chatter. Griffin Scope moved serpentine through the black tuxedos and shimmering gowns. People always used the same word to describe Griffin Scope: billionaire. After that, they might call him businessman or power broker or mention that he was tall or a husband or a grandfather or that he was seventy years old. They might comment on his personality or his family tree or his work ethic. But the first word—in the papers, on television, on people's lists—was always the B word. Billionaire. Billionaire Griffin Scope.

Griffin had been born rich. His grandfather was an early industrialist; his father improved the fortune; Griffin multiplied it several-fold. Most family empires fall apart before the third generation. Not the Scopes'. A lot of that had to do with their upbringing. Griffin, for example, did not attend a prestigious prep school like Exeter or Lawrenceville, as so many of his peers did. His father insisted that Griffin not only attend public school but that he do so in the closest major city, Newark. His father had offices there, thus setting up a fake residence was no problem.

Newark's east side wasn't a bad neighborhood back then—not like now, when a sane person would barely want to drive through it. It was working class, blue collar—tough rather than dangerous.

Griffin loved it.

His best friends from those high school days were still his friends fifty years later. Loyalty was a rare quality; when Griffin found it, he made sure to reward it. Many of tonight's guests were from those Newark days. Some even worked for him, though he tried to make it a point to never be their day-to-day boss.

Tonight's gala celebrated the cause most dear to Griffin Scope's heart: the Brandon Scope Memorial Charity, named for Griffin's murdered son. Griffin had started the fund with a one-hundred-million-dollar contribution. Friends quickly added to the till. Griffin was not stupid. He knew that many donated to curry his favor. But there was more to it than that. During his too-brief life, Brandon Scope touched people. A boy born with so much luck and talent, Brandon had an almost supernatural charisma. People were drawn to him.

His other son, Randall, was a good boy who had grown up to be a good man. But Brandon ... Brandon had been magic.

The pain flooded in again. It was always there, of course. Through the shaking hands and slapping of the backs, the grief stayed by his side, tapping Griffin on the shoulder, whispering in his ear, reminding him that they were partners for life.

"Lovely party, Griff."

Griffin said thank you and moved on. The women were well coiffed and wore gowns that highlighted lovely bare shoulders; they fit in nicely with the many ice sculptures—a favorite of Griffin's wife Allison—that slowly melted atop imported linen tablecloths. The Mozart sonata changed over to one by Chopin. White-gloved servers made the rounds with silver trays of Malaysian shrimp and Omaha tenderloin and a potpourri of bizarre finger-food that always seemed to contain sun-dried tomatoes.

He reached Linda Beck, the young lady who headed up Brandon's charitable fund. Linda's father had been an old Newark classmate too, and she, so like so many others, had become entwined in the massive Scope holdings. She'd started working for various Scope enterprises while still in high school. Both she and her brother had paid for their education with Scope scholarship grants.

"You look smashing," he told her, though in truth he thought she looked tired.

Linda Beck smiled at him. "Thank you, Mr. Scope."

"How many times have I asked you to call me Griff?"

"Several hundred," she said.

"How's Shauna?"

"A little under the weather, I'm afraid."

"Give her my best."

"I will, thank you."

"We should probably meet next week."

"I'll call your secretary."

"Good."

Griffin gave her a peck on the cheek, and that was when he spotted Larry Gandle in the foyer. Larry looked bleary-eyed and disheveled, but then again, he always looked that way. You could slap a custom-cut Joseph Abboud on him, and an hour later he'd still look like someone who'd gotten into a tussle.

Larry Gandle was not supposed to be here.

The two men's eyes met. Larry nodded once and turned away. Griffin waited another moment or two and then followed his young friend down the corridor.

Larry's father, Edward, had also been one of Griffin's

61

classmates from the old Newark days. Edward Gandle died of a sudden heart attack twelve years ago. Damn shame. Edward had been a fine man. Since then, his son had taken over as the Scopes' closest confidant.

The two men entered Griffin's library. At one time, the library had been a wonderful room of oak and mahogany and floor-to-ceiling bookshelves and antique globes. Two years ago, Allison, in a postmodern mood, decided that the room needed a total updating. The old woodwork was torn out and now the room was white and sleek and functional and held all the warmth of a work cubicle. Allison had been so proud of the room that Griffin didn't have the heart to tell her how much he disliked it.

"Was there a problem tonight?" Griffin asked.

"No," Larry said.

Griffin offered Larry a seat. Larry shook him off and started pacing.

"Was it bad?" Griffin asked.

"We had to make certain there were no loose ends."

"Of course."

Someone had attacked Griffin's son Randall—ergo, Griffin attacked back. It was one lesson he never forgot. You don't sit back when you or a loved one is being assaulted. And you don't act like the government with their "proportional responses" and all that nonsense. If someone hurts you, mercy and pity must be put aside. You eliminate the enemy. You scorch the earth. Those who scoffed at this philosophy, who thought it unnecessarily Machiavellian, usually were the ones who caused excess destruction.

In the end, if you eliminate problems swiftly, less blood is shed.

"So what's wrong?" Griffin asked.

Larry kept pacing. He rubbed the front of his bald pate. Griffin didn't like what he was seeing. Larry was not one to get keyed up easily. "I've never lied to you, Griff," he said.

"I know that."

"But there are times for . . . insulation."

"Insulation?"

"Who I hire, for example. I never tell you names. I never tell them names either."

"Those are details."

"Yes."

"What is it, Larry?"

He stopped pacing. "Eight years ago, you'll recall that we hired two men to perform a certain task."

The color drained from Griffin's face. He swallowed. "And they performed admirably."

"Yes. Well, perhaps."

"I don't understand."

"They performed their task. Or, at least, part of it. The threat was apparently eliminated."

Even though the house was swept for listening devices on a weekly basis, the two men never used names. A Scope rule. Larry Gandle often wondered if the rule was for the sake of caution or because it helped depersonalize what they were occasionally forced to do. He suspected the latter.

Griffin finally collapsed into a chair, almost as though someone had pushed him. His voice was soft. "Why are you bringing this up now?"

"I know how painful this must be for you."

Griffin did not reply.

"I paid the two men well," Larry continued.

"As I'd have expected."

"Yes." He cleared his throat. "Well, after the incident,

they were supposed to lay low for a while. As a precaution."

"Go on."

"We never heard from them again."

"They'd already collected their money, correct?"

"Yes."

"So what's surprising about that? Perhaps they fled with their newfound wealth. Perhaps they moved across the country or changed identities."

"That," Larry said, "was what we'd always assumed."

"But?"

"Their bodies were found last week. They're dead."

"I still don't see the problem. They were violent men. They probably met a violent end."

"The bodies were old."

"Old?"

"They've been dead at least five years. And they were found buried by the lake where ... where the incident took place."

Griffin opened his mouth, closed it, tried again. "I don't understand."

"Frankly, neither do I."

Too much. It was all too much. Griffin had been fighting off the tears all night, what with the gala being in Brandon's honor and all. Now the tragedy of Brandon's murder was suddenly resurfacing. It was all he could do not to break down.

Griffin looked up at his confidant. "This can't come back."

"I know, Griff."

"We have to find out what happened. I mean everything."

"I've kept tabs on the men in her life. Especially her husband. Just in case. Now I've put all our resources on it."

"Good," Griffin said. "Whatever it takes, this gets buried. I don't care who gets buried with it."

"I understand."

"And, Larry?"

Gandle waited.

"I know the name of one man you hire." He meant Eric Wu. Griffin Scope wiped his eyes and started back toward his guests. "Use him."

8

Shauna and Linda rent a three-bedroom apartment on Riverside Drive and 116 Street, not far from Columbia University. I'd managed to find a spot within a block, an act that usually accompanies a parting sea or stone tablet.

Shauna buzzed me up. Linda was still out at her formal. Mark was asleep. I tiptoed into his room and kissed his forehead. Mark was still hanging on to the Pokémon craze and it showed. He had Pikachu sheets, and a stuffed Squirtle doll lay nestled in his arms. People criticize the trend, but it reminded me of my own childhood obsession with Batman and Captain America. I watched him a few more seconds. Cliché to say, yes, but it is indeed the little things.

Shauna stood in the doorway and waited. When we finally moved back into the den, I said, "Mind if I have a drink?"

Shauna shrugged. "Suit yourself."

I poured myself two fingers of bourbon. "You'll join me?"

She shook her head.

We settled onto the couch. "What time is Linda supposed to be home?" I asked.

"Got me," Shauna said slowly. I didn't like the way she did it.

"Damn," I said.

"It's temporary, Beck. I love Linda, you know that."

66

"Damn," I said again.

Last year, Linda and Shauna had separated for two months. It hadn't been good, especially for Mark.

"I'm not moving out or anything," Shauna said.

"So what's wrong, then?"

"Same ol' same ol'. I have this glamorous high-profile job. I'm surrounded by beautiful, interesting people all the time. Nothing new, right? We all know this. Anyway, Linda thinks I have a wandering eye."

"You do," I said.

"Yeah, sure, but that's nothing new, is it?"

I didn't reply.

"At the end of the day, Linda is the one I go home to."

"And you never take any detours on the way?"

"If I did, they'd be irrelevant. You know that. I don't do well locked in a cage, Beck. I need the stage."

"Nice mix of metaphors," I said.

"At least it rhymed."

I drank in silence for a few moments.

"Beck?"

"What?"

"Your turn now."

"Meaning?"

She shot me a look and waited.

I thought about the "Tell no one" warning at the end of the email. If the message were indeed from Elizabeth—my mind still had trouble even entertaining such a notion—she would know that I'd tell Shauna. Linda—maybe not. But Shauna? I tell her everything. It would be a given.

"There's a chance," I said, "that Elizabeth is still alive."

Shauna didn't break stride. "She ran off with Elvis,

right?" When she saw my face, she stopped and said, "Explain."

I did. I told her about the email. I told her about the street cam. And I told her about seeing Elizabeth on the computer monitor. Shauna kept her eyes on me the whole time. She didn't nod or interrupt. When I finished, she carefully extracted a cigarette from its carton and put it in her mouth. Shauna gave up smoking years ago, but she still liked to fiddle with them. She examined the cancer stick, turning it over in her hand as though she'd never seen one before. I could see the gears churning.

"Okay," she said. "So at eight-fifteen tomorrow night, the next message is supposed to come in, right?"

I nodded.

"So we wait until then."

She put the cigarette back in the pack.

"You don't think it's crazy?"

Shauna shrugged. "Irrelevant," she said.

"Meaning?"

"There are several possibilities that'd explain what you just said."

"Including insanity."

"Yeah, sure, that's a strong one. But what's the point of hypothesizing negatively right now? Let's just assume it's true. Let's just assume you saw what you saw and that Elizabeth is still alive. If we're wrong, hey, we'll learn that soon enough. If we're right ..." She knitted her eyebrows, thought about it, shook her head. "Christ, I hope like hell we're right."

I smiled at her. "I love you, you know."

"Yeah," she said. "Everyone does."

* * *

When I got home, I poured myself one last quick drink. I took a deep sip and let the warm liquor travel to destinations well known. Yes, I drink. But I'm not a drunk. That's not denial. I know I flirt with being an alcoholic. I also know that flirting with alcoholism is about as safe as flirting with a mobster's underage daughter. But so far, the flirting hasn't led to coupling. I'm smart enough to know that might not last.

Chloe sidled up to me with her customary expression that could be summed up thusly: "Food, walk, food, walk." Dogs are wonderfully consistent. I tossed her a treat and took her for a stroll around the block. The cold air felt good in my lungs, but walking never cleared my head. Walking is, in fact, a tremendous bore. But I liked watching Chloe walk. I know that sounds queer, but a dog derives such pleasure from this simple activity. It made me Zen-happy to watch her.

Back home I moved quietly toward my bedroom. Chloe followed me. Grandpa was asleep. So was his new nurse. She snored with a cartoonlike, high-pitched exhale. I flipped on my computer and wondered why Sheriff Lowell hadn't called me back. I thought about calling him, though the time was nearing midnight. Then I figured: tough.

I picked up the phone and dialed. Lowell had a cell phone. If he was sleeping, he could always turn it off, right?

He answered on the third ring. "Hello, Dr. Beck."

His voice was tight. I also noted that I was no longer Doc.

"Why didn't you call me back?" I asked.

"It was getting late," he said. "I figured I'd catch you in the morning."

"Why did you ask me about Sarah Goodhart?"

"Tomorrow," he said.

"Pardon me?"

"It's late, Dr. Beck. I'm off duty. Besides, I think I'd rather go over this with you in person."

"Can't you at least tell me—?"

"You'll be at your clinic in the morning?"

"Yes."

"I'll call you then."

He bade me a polite but firm good night and then he was gone. I stared at the phone and wondered what the hell that was all about.

Sleep was out of the question. I spent most of the night on the Web, surfing through various city street cams, hoping to stumble across the right one. Talk about the high-tech needle in the worldwide haystack.

At some point, I stopped and slipped under the covers. Part of being a doctor is patience. I constantly give children tests that have life-altering—if not life-ending—implications and tell them and their parents to wait for the results. They have no choice. Perhaps the same could be said for this situation. There were too many variables right now. Tomorrow, when I logged in at Bigfoot under the Bat Street user name and Teenage password, I might learn more.

I stared up at the ceiling for a while. Then I looked to my right—where Elizabeth had slept. I always fell asleep first. I used to lie like this and watch her with a book, her face in profile, totally focused on whatever she was reading. That was the last thing I saw before my eyes closed and I drifted off to sleep.

I rolled over and faced the other way.

At four in the morning, Larry Gandle looked over the bleached-blond locks of Eric Wu. Wu was incredibly disciplined. If he wasn't working on his physical prowess, he was in front of a computer screen. His complexion had turned a sickly blue-white several thousand Web surfs ago, but that physique remained serious cement.

"Well?" Gandle said.

Wu popped the headphones off. Then he folded his marble-column arms across his chest. "I'm confused."

"Tell me."

"Dr. Beck has barely saved any of his emails. Just a few involving patients. Nothing personal. But then he gets two bizarre ones in the last two days." Still not turning from the screen, Eric Wu handed two pieces of paper over his bowling ball of a shoulder. Larry Gandle looked at the emails and frowned.

"What do they mean?"

"I don't know."

Gandle skimmed the message that talked about clicking something at "kiss time." He didn't understand computers—nor did he want to understand them. His eyes traveled back up to the top of the sheet and he read the subject.

E.P.+ D.B. and a bunch of lines.

Gandle thought about it. D.B. David Beck maybe? And E.P. . . . .

The meaning landed on him like a dropped piano. He slowly handed the paper back to Wu.

"Who sent this?" Gandle asked.

"I don't know."

"Find out."

"Impossible," Wu said.

"Why?"

"The sender used an anonymous remailer." Wu spoke with a patient, almost unearthly monotone. He used that same tone while discussing a weather report or ripping off a man's cheek. "I won't go into the computer jargon, but there is no way to trace it back."

Gandle turned his attention to the other email, the one with the Bat Street and Teenage. He couldn't make head or tail out of it.

"How about this one? Can you trace it back?"

Wu shook his head. "Also an anonymous remailer."

"Did the same person send both?"

"Your guess would be as good as mine."

"How about the content? Do you understand what either one is talking about?"

Wu hit a few keys and the first email popped up on the monitor. He pointed a thick, veiny finger at the screen. "See that blue lettering there? It's a hyperlink. All Dr. Beck had to do was click it and it would take him someplace, probably a Web site."

"What Web site?"

"It's a broken link. Again, you can't trace it back."

"And Beck was supposed to do this at 'kiss time'?"

"That's what it says."

"Is kiss time some sort of computer term?"

Wu almost grinned. "No."

"So you don't know what time the email refers to?"

"That's correct."

"Or even if we've passed kiss time or not?"

"It's passed," Wu said.

"How do you know?"

"His Web browser is set up to show you the last twenty sites he visited. He clicked the link. Several times, in fact."

"But you can't, uh, follow him there?"

"No. The link is useless."

"What about this other email?"

Wu hit a more few keys. The screen changed and the other email appeared. "This one is easier to figure out. It's very basic, as a matter of fact."

"Okay, I'm listening."

"The anonymous emailer has set up an email account for Dr. Beck," Wu explained. "He's given Dr. Beck a user name and a password and again mentioned kiss time."

"So let me see if I understand," Gandle said. "Beck goes to some Web site. He types in that user name and that password and there'll be a message for him?"

"That's the theory, yes."

"Can we do it too?"

"Sign in using that user name and password?"

"Yes. And read the message."

"I tried it. The account doesn't exist yet."

"Why not?"

Eric Wu shrugged. "The anonymous sender might set up the account later. Closer to kiss time."

"So what can we conclude here?"

"Put simply"—the light from the monitor danced off Wu's blank eyes—"someone is going through a great deal of trouble to stay anonymous."

"So how do we find out who it is?"

Wu held up a small device that looked like something you might find in a transistor radio. "We've installed one of these on his home and work computers."

"What is it?"

"A digital network tracker. The tracker sends digital signals from his computers to mine. If Dr. Beck gets any emails or visits any Web sites or even if he just types up a letter, we'll be able to monitor it all in real time."

"So we wait and watch," Gandle said.

"Yes."

Gandle thought about what Wu had told him—about the lengths someone was going through to remain anonymous—and an awful suspicion started creeping into the pit of his belly.

I parked at the lot two blocks from the clinic. I never made it past block one.

Sheriff Lowell materialized with two men sporting buzz cuts and gray suits. The two men in suits leaned against a big brown Buick. Physical opposites. One was tall and thin and white, the other short and round and black; together they looked a little like a bowling ball trying to knock down the last pin. Both men smiled at me. Lowell did not.

"Dr. Beck?" the tall white pin said. He was impeccably groomed—gelled hair, folded hanky in the pocket, tie knotted with supernatural precision, tortoiseshell designer glasses, the kind actors wear when they want to look smart.

I looked at Lowell. He said nothing.

"Yes."

"I'm Special Agent Nick Carlson with the Federal Bureau of Investigation," the impeccably groomed one continued. "This is Special Agent Tom Stone."

They both flashed badges. Stone, the shorter and more rumpled of the two, hitched up his trousers and nodded at me. Then he opened the back door of the Buick.

"Would you mind coming with us?"

"I have patients in fifteen minutes," I said.

"We've already taken care of that." Carlson swept a long arm toward the car door, as though he were displaying a game show prize. "Please."

I got in the back. Carlson drove. Stone squeezed himself into the front passenger seat. Lowell didn't get in.
We stayed in Manhattan, but the ride still took close to
forty-five minutes. We ended up way downtown on
Broadway near Duane Street. Carlson stopped the car in
front of an office building marked 26 Federal Plaza.

The interior was basic office building. Men in suits,
surprisingly nice ones, moved about with cups of
designer coffee. There were women too, but they were
heavily in the minority. We moved into a conference
room. I was invited to sit, which I did. I tried crossing
my legs, but that didn't feel right.

"Can someone tell me what's going on?" I asked.

White-Pin Carlson took the lead. "Can we get you
something?" he asked. "We make the world's worst coffee, if you're interested."

That explained all the designer cups. He smiled at
me. I smiled back. "Tempting, but no thanks."

"How about a soft drink? We have soft drinks, Tom?"

"Sure, Nick. Coke, Diet Coke, Sprite, whatever the
doctor here wants."

They smiled some more. "I'm fine, thanks," I said.

"Snapple?" Stone tried. He once again hitched up his
pants. His stomach was the kind of round that made it
hard to find a spot where the waistband wouldn't slide.
"We got a bunch of different varieties here."

I almost said yes so that they'd get on with it, but I
just gently shook him off. The table, some sort of
Formica mix, was bare except for a large manila envelope. I wasn't sure what to do with my hands, so I put
them on the table. Stone waddled to the side and stood
there. Carlson, still taking the lead, sat on the corner of
the table and swiveled to look down at me.

"What can you tell us about Sarah Goodhart?" Carlson asked.

I wasn't sure how to answer. I kept trying to figure out the angles, but nothing was coming to me.

"Doc?"

I looked up at him. "Why do you want to know?"

Carlson and Stone exchanged a quick glance. "The name Sarah Goodhart has surfaced in connection with an ongoing investigation," Carlson said.

"What investigation?" I asked.

"We'd rather not say."

"I don't understand. How am I connected into this?"

Carlson let loose a sigh, taking his time on the exhale. He looked over at his rotund partner and suddenly all smiles were gone. "Am I asking a complicated question here, Tom?"

"No, Nick, I don't think so."

"Me neither." Carlson turned his eyes back at me. "Maybe you object to the form of the question, Doc. That it?"

"That's what they always do on *The Practice*, Nick," Stone chimed in. "Object to the form of the question."

"That they do, Tom, that they do. And then they say, 'I'll rephrase,' right? Something like that."

"Something like that, yeah."

Carlson looked me down. "So let me rephrase: Does the name Sarah Goodhart mean anything to you?"

I didn't like this. I didn't like their attitude or the fact that they had taken over for Lowell or the way I was getting grilled in this conference room. They had to know what the name meant. It wasn't that difficult. All you had to do was casually glance at Elizabeth's name and address. I decided to tread gently.

"My wife's middle name is Sarah," I said.

"My wife's middle name is Gertrude," Carlson said.

"Christ, Nick, that's awful."

"What's your wife's middle name, Tom?"

"McDowd. It's a family name."

"I like when they do that. Use a family name as a middle name. Honor the ancestors like that."

"Me too, Nick."

Both men swung their gazes back in my direction.

"What's your middle name, Doc?"

"Craig," I said.

"Craig," Carlson repeated. "Okay, so if I asked you if the name, say"—he waved his arms theatrically—"Craig Dipwad meant anything to you, would you chirp up, 'Hey, my middle name is Craig'?"

Carlson flashed me the hard eyes again.

"I guess not," I said.

"I guess not. So let's try it again: Have you heard the name Sarah Goodhart, yes or no?"

"You mean ever?"

Stone said, "Jesus Christ."

Carlson's face reddened. "You playing semantic games with us now, Doc?"

He was right. I was being stupid. I was flying blind, and that last line of the email—*Tell no one*—kept flashing in my head like something in neon. Confusion took over. They had to know about Sarah Goodhart. This was all a test to see if I was going to cooperate or not. That was it. Maybe. And cooperate about what?

"My wife grew up on Goodhart Road," I said. They both moved back a little, giving me room, folding their arms. They led me to a pool of silence and I foolishly dived in. "See, that's why I said Sarah was my wife's middle name. The Goodhart made me think of her."

"Because she grew up on Goodhart Road?" Carlson said.

"Yes."

"Like the word Goodhart was a catalyst or something?"

"Yes," I said again.

"That makes sense to me." Carlson looked at his partner. "That make sense to you, Tom?"

"Sure," Stone agreed, patting his stomach. "He wasn't being evasive or anything. The word Goodhart was a catalyst."

"Right. That's what got him thinking about his wife."

They both looked at me again. This time I forced myself to keep quiet.

"Did your wife ever use the name Sarah Goodhart?" Carlson asked.

"Use it how?"

"Did she ever say, 'Hi, I'm Sarah Goodhart,' or get an ID with that name or check into some hot-sheets under that name—"

"No," I said.

"You sure?"

"Yes."

"That the truth?"

"Yes."

"Don't need another catalyst?"

I straightened up in the chair and decided to show some resolve. "I don't much like your attitude, Agent Carlson."

His toothy, dentist-proud smile returned, but it was like some cruel hybrid of its earlier form. He held up his hand and said, "Excuse me, yeah, okay, that was rude." He looked around as though thinking about what to say next. I waited.

"You ever beat up your wife, Doc?"

The question hit me like a whiplash. "What?"

"That get you off? Smacking around a woman?"

"What . . . are you insane?"

"How much life insurance did you collect when your wife died?"

I froze. I looked at his face and then at Stone's. Totally opaque. I couldn't believe what I was hearing. "What's going on here?"

"Please just answer the question. Unless, of course, you got something you don't want to tell us."

"It's no secret," I said. "The policy was for two hundred thousand dollars."

Stone whistled. "Two hundred grand for a dead wife. Hey, Nick, where do I get in line?"

"That's a lot of life insurance for a twenty-five-year-old woman."

"Her cousin was starting out with State Farm," I said, my words stumbling over one another. The funny thing is, even though I knew I hadn't done anything wrong—at least not what they thought—I started feeling guilty. It was a weird sensation. Sweat started pouring down my armpits. "She wanted to help him out. So she bought this big policy."

"Nice of her," Carlson said.

"Real nice," Stone added. "Family is so important, don't you think?"

I said nothing. Carlson sat back down on the table's corner. The smile was gone again. "Look at me, Doc."

I did. His eyes bore into mine. I managed to maintain eye contact, but it was a struggle.

"Answer my question this time," he said slowly. "And don't give me shocked or insulted. Did you ever hit your wife?"

80

"Never," I said.

"Not once?"

"Not once."

"Ever push her?"

"Never."

"Or lash out in anger. Hell, we've all been there, Doc. A quick slap. No real crime in that. Natural when it comes to the affairs of the heart, you know what I mean?"

"I never hit my wife," I said. "I never pushed her or slapped her or lashed out in anger. Never."

Carlson looked over at Stone. "That clear it up for you, Tom?"

"Sure, Nick. He says he never hit her, that's good enough for me."

Carlson scratched his chin. "Unless."

"Unless what, Nick?"

"Well, unless I can provide Dr. Beck here with another one of those catalysts."

All eyes were on me again. My own breaths echoed in my ears, hitched and uneven. I felt light-headed. Carlson waited a beat before he snatched up the large manila envelope. He took his time untying the string flap with long, slender fingers and then he opened the slit. He lifted it high in the air and let the contents fall to the table.

"How's this for a catalyst, huh, Doc?"

They were photographs. Carlson pushed them toward me. I looked down and felt the hole in my heart expand.

"Dr. Beck?"

I stared. My fingers reached out tentatively and touched the surface.

Elizabeth.

They were photographs of Elizabeth. The first one was a close-up of her face. She was in profile, her right hand holding her hair back away from her ear. Her eye was purple and swollen. There was a deep cut and more bruising on her neck, below the ear.

It looked as though she'd been crying.

Another photo was shot from the waist up. Elizabeth stood wearing only a bra, and she was pointing to a large discoloration on her rib cage. Her eyes still had that red-tinged rim. The lighting was strangely harsh, as though the flash itself had sought out the bruise and pulled it closer to the lens.

There were three more photographs—all from various angles and of various body parts. All of them highlighted more cuts and bruises.

"Dr. Beck?"

My eyes jerked up. I was almost startled to see them in the room. Their expressions were neutral, patient. I faced Carlson, then Stone, then I went back to Carlson.

"You think I did this?"

Carlson shrugged. "You tell us."

"Of course not."

"Do you know how your wife got those bruises?"

"In a car accident."

They looked at each other as though I'd told them my dog ate my homework.

"She got into a bad fender-bender," I explained.

"When?"

"I'm not sure exactly. Three, four months before"—the words got stuck for a second—"before she died."

"Did she visit a hospital?"

"No, I don't think so."

"You don't think?"

"I wasn't around."

82

"Where were you?"

"I was doing a pediatric workshop in Chicago at the time. She told me about the accident when I got home."

"How long after did she tell you?"

"After the accident?"

"Yeah, Doc, after the accident."

"I don't know. Two, three days maybe."

"You two were married by then?"

"For just a few months."

"Why didn't she tell you right away?"

"She did. I mean, as soon as I got home. I guess she didn't want to worry me."

"I see," Carlson said. He looked at Stone. They didn't bother masking their skepticism. "So did you take these pictures, Doc?"

"No," I said. As soon as I did, I wished I hadn't. They exchanged another glance, smelling blood. Carlson tilted his head and moved closer.

"Have you ever seen these pictures before?"

I said nothing. They waited. I thought about the question. The answer was no, but ... where did they get them? Why didn't I know about them? Who took them? I looked at their faces, but they gave away nothing.

It's an amazing thing really, but when you think about it, we learn life's most important lessons from TV. The vast majority of our knowledge about interrogations, Miranda rights, self-incriminations, cross-examinations, witness lists, the jury system, we learn from *NYPD Blue* and *Law & Order* and the like. If I tossed you a gun right now and asked you to fire it, you'd do what you saw on TV. If I told you to look out for a "tail," you'd know what I'm talking about because you'd seen it done on *Mannix* or *Magnum PI*.

I looked up at them and asked the classic question:

"Am I a suspect?"

"Suspect for what?"

"For anything," I said. "Do you suspect that I committed any crime?"

"That's a pretty vague question, Doc."

And that was a pretty vague answer. I didn't like the way this was going. I decided to use another line I learned from television.

"I want to call my lawyer," I said.

10

I don't have a criminal lawyer—who does?—so I called Shauna from a pay phone in the corridor and explained the situation. She wasted no time.

"I got just the person," Shauna said. "Sit tight."

I waited in the interrogation room. Carlson and Stone were kind enough to wait with me. They spent the time whispering to each other. Half an hour passed. Again the silence was unnerving. I know that was what they wanted. But I couldn't stop myself. I was innocent, after all. How could I harm myself if I was careful?

"My wife was found branded with the letter K," I said to them.

They both looked up. "Pardon me," Carlson said, craning his long neck back in my direction. "You talking to us?"

"My wife was found branded with the letter K," I repeated. "I was in the hospital after the attack with a concussion. You can't possibly think ..." I let it hang.

"Think what?" Carlson said.

In for a penny, in for a pound. "That I had something to do with my wife's death."

That was when the door burst open, and a woman I recognized from television stamped into the room. Carlson jumped back when he saw her. I heard Stone mumble "Holy shit" under his breath.

Hester Crimstein didn't bother with intros. "Didn't my client ask for counsel?" she asked.

Count on Shauna. I had never met my attorney, but I recognized her from her stints as a "legal expert" on talk shows and from her own *Crimstein on Crime* program on Court TV. On the screen Hester Crimstein was quick and cutting and often left guests in tatters. In person, she had the most bizarre aura of power, the kind of person who looks at everyone as though she were a hungry tiger and they were limping gazelles.

"That's right," Carlson said.

"Yet here you are, all nice and cozy, still questioning him."

"He started talking to us."

"Oh, I see." Hester Crimstein snapped open her briefcase, dug out a pen and paper, and tossed them onto the table. "Write down your names."

"Pardon?"

"Your names, handsome. You know how to spell them, right?"

It was a rhetorical question, but Crimstein still waited for an answer.

"Yeah," Carlson said.

"Sure," Stone added.

"Good. Write them down. When I mention on my show how you two trampled my client's constitutional rights, I want to make sure I get the names right. Print plainly, please."

She finally looked at me. "Let's go."

"Hold up a second," Carlson said. "We'd like to ask your client a few questions."

"No."

"No? Just like that?"

"Exactly like that. You don't talk to him. He doesn't talk to you. Ever. You two understand?"

"Yes," Carlson said.

She turned her glare to Stone.

"Yes," Stone said.

"Swell, fellas. Now are you arresting Dr. Beck?"

"No."

She turned in my direction. "What are you waiting for?" she snapped at me. "We're out of here."

Hester Crimstein didn't say a word until we were safely ensconced in her limousine.

"Where do you want me to drop you off?" she asked.

I gave the driver the clinic's address.

"Tell me about the interrogation," Crimstein said. "Leave out nothing."

I recounted my conversation with Carlson and Stone as best I could. Hester Crimstein didn't so much as glance in my direction. She took out a day planner thicker than my waist and started leafing through it.

"So these pictures of your wife," she said when I finished. "You didn't take them?"

"No."

"And you told Tweedledee and Tweedledum that?"

I nodded.

She shook her head. "Doctors. They're always the worst clients." She pushed back a stand of hair. "Okay, that was dumb of you, but not crippling. You say you've never seen those pictures before?"

"Never."

"But when they asked you that, you finally shut up."

"Yes."

"Better," she said with a nod. "That story about her getting those bruises in a car accident. Is it the truth?"

"Pardon me?"

Crimstein closed her day planner. "Look ... Beck, is

it? Shauna says everyone calls you Beck, so you mind if I do the same?"

"No."

"Good. Look, Beck, you're a doctor, right?"

"Right."

"You good at bedside manner?"

"I try to be."

"I don't. Not even a little. You want coddling, go on a diet and hire Richard Simmons. So let's skip all the pardon-mes and excuse-mes and all that objectionable crap, okay? Just answer my questions. The car accident story you told them. Is it true?"

"Yes."

"Because the feds will check all the facts. You know that, right?"

"I know."

"Okay, fine, just so we're clear here." Crimstein took a breath. "So maybe your wife had a friend take these pictures," she said, trying it on for size. "For insurance reasons or something. In case she ever wanted to sue. That might make sense, if we need to peddle it."

It didn't make sense to me, but I kept that to myself.

"So question uno: Where have these pictures been, Beck?"

"I don't know."

"Dos and tres: How did the feds get them? Why are they surfacing now?"

I shook my head.

"And most important, what are they trying to nail you on? Your wife's been dead for eight years. It's a little late for a spousal battery charge." She sat back and thought about it a minute or two. Then she looked up and shrugged. "No matter. I'll make some calls, find out what's up. In the meantime, don't be a dimwit. Say nothing to anyone. You understand?"

"Yes."

She sat back and thought about it some more. "I don't like this," she said. "I don't like this even a little bit."

11

On May 12, 1970, Jeremiah Renway and three fellow radicals set off an explosion at Eastern State University's chemistry department. Rumor had it from the Weather Underground that military scientists were using the university labs to make a more powerful form of napalm. The four students, who in a fit of stark originality called themselves Freedom's Cry, decided to make a dramatic albeit showy stand.

At the time, Jeremiah Renway did not know if the rumor was true. Now, more than thirty years later, he doubted it. No matter. The explosion did not damage any of the labs. Two university security guards, however, stumbled across the suspicious package. When one picked it up, the package exploded, killing both men.

Both had children.

One of Jeremiah's fellow "freedom fighters" was captured two days later. He was still in jail. The second died of colon cancer in 1989. The third, Evelyn Cosmeer, was captured in 1996. She was currently serving a seven-year prison sentence.

Jeremiah disappeared into the woods that night and never ventured out. He had rarely seen fellow human beings or listened to the radio or watched television. He had used a telephone only once—and that was in an emergency. His only real connection to the outside world came from newspapers, though they had what happened here eight years ago all wrong.

Born and raised in the foothills of northwest Georgia, Jeremiah's father taught his son all kinds of survival techniques, though his overriding lesson was simply this: You could trust nature but not man. Jeremiah had forgotten that for a little while. Now he lived it.

Fearing they would search near his hometown, Jeremiah took to the woods in Pennsylvania. He hiked around for a while, changing camp every night or two, until he happened upon the relative comfort and security of Lake Charmaine. The lake had old camp bunks that could house a man when the outdoors got a little too nasty. Visitors rarely came to the lake—mostly in the summer, and even then, only on weekends. He could hunt deer here and eat the meat in relative peace. During the few times of the year when the lake was being used, he simply hid or took off for points farther west.

Or he watched.

To the children who used to come here, Jeremiah Renway had been the Boogeyman.

Jeremiah stayed still now and watched the officers move about in their dark windbreakers. FBI windbreakers. The sight of those three letters in big yellow caps still punctured his heart like an icicle.

No one had bothered to yellow-tape the area, probably because it was so remote. Renway had not been surprised when they found the bodies. Yes, the two men had been buried good and deep, but Renway knew better than most that secrets don't like to stay underground. His former partner in crime, Evelyn Cosmeer, who'd transformed herself into the perfect Ohio suburban mom before her capture, knew that. The irony did not escape Jeremiah.

He stayed hidden in the bush. He knew a lot about

camouflage. They would not see him.

He remembered the night eight years ago when the two men had died—the sudden gun blasts, the sounds of the shovels ripping into the earth, the grunts from the deep dig. He'd even debated telling the authorities what happened—all of it.

Anonymously, of course.

But in the end he couldn't risk it. No man, Jeremiah knew, was meant for a cage, though some could live through it. Jeremiah could not. He'd had a cousin named Perry who'd been serving eight years in a federal penitentiary. Perry was locked in a tiny cell for twenty-three hours a day. One morning, Perry tried to kill himself by running headfirst into the cement wall.

That would be Jeremiah.

So he kept his mouth shut and did nothing. For eight years anyway.

But he thought about that night a lot. He thought about the young woman in the nude. He thought about the men in wait. He thought about the scuffle near the car. He thought about the sickening, wet sound of wood against exposed flesh. He thought about the man left to die.

And he thought about the lies. The lies, most of all, haunted him.

12

By the time I returned to the clinic, the waiting room
was packed with the sniffing and impatient. A television
replayed a video of *The Little Mermaid*, automatically
rewinding at the end and starting over, the color frayed
and faded from overuse. After my hours with the FBI,
my mind sympathized with the tape. I kept rehashing
Carlson's words—he was definitely the lead guy—trying
to figure out what he was really after, but all that did
was make the picture murkier and more surreal. It also
gave me a whopping headache.

"Yo, Doc."

Tyrese Barton hopped up. He was wearing butt-
plunge baggy pants and what looked like an oversized
varsity jacket, all done by some designer I never heard
of but soon would.

"Hi, Tyrese," I said.

Tyrese gave me a complicated handshake, which was
a bit like a dance routine where he leads and I follow.
He and Latisha had a six-year-old son they called TJ. TJ
was a hemophiliac. He was also blind. I met him after
he was rushed in as an infant and Tyrese was seconds
away from being arrested. Tyrese claimed I saved his
son's life on that day. That was hyperbole.

But maybe I did save Tyrese.

He thought that made us friends—like he was this
lion and I was some mouse who pulled a thorn from his
paw. He was wrong.

Tyrese and Latisha were never married, but he was one of the few fathers I saw in here. He finished shaking my hands and slipped me two Ben Franklins as though I were a maître d' at Le Cirque.

He gave me the eye. "You take good care of my boy now."

"Right."

"You the best, Doc." He handed me his business card, which had no name, no address, no job title. Just a cell phone number. "You need anything, you call."

"I'll keep that in mind," I said.

Still with the eye. "*Anything*, Doc."

"Right."

I pocketed the bills. We've been going through this same routine for six years now. I knew a lot of drug dealers from working here; I knew none who survived six years.

I didn't keep the money, of course. I gave it to Linda for her charity. Legally debatable, I knew, but the way I figured it, better the money went to charity than to a drug dealer. I had no idea how much money Tyrese had. He always had a new car, though—he favored BMWs with tinted windows—and his kid's wardrobe was worth more than anything that inhabited my closet. But, alas, the child's mother was on Medicaid, so the visits were free.

Maddening, I know.

Tyrese's cell phone sounded something hip-hop.

"Got to take this, Doc. Bidness."

"Right," I said again.

I do get angry sometimes. Who wouldn't? But through that haze, there are real children here. They hurt. I don't claim that all children are wonderful. They are not. I sometimes treat ones that I know—*know*—

will amount to no good. But children are, if nothing else, helpless. They are weak and defenseless. Believe me, I've seen examples that would alter your definition of human beings.

So I concentrate on the children.

I was supposed to work only until noon, but to make up for my FBI detour, I saw patients until three. Naturally, I'd been thinking about the interrogation all day. Those pictures of Elizabeth, battered and defeated, kept popping through my brain like the most grotesque sort of strobe light.

Who would know about those pictures?

The answer, when I took the time to think about it, was somewhat obvious. I leaned forward and picked up the phone. I hadn't dialed this number in years, but I still remembered it.

"Schayes Photography," a woman answered.

"Hi, Rebecca."

"Son of a gun. How are you, Beck?"

"Good. How about yourself?"

"Not bad. Busy as all hell."

"You work too hard."

"Not anymore. I got married last year."

"I know. I'm sorry I couldn't make it."

"Bull."

"Yeah. But congrats anyway."

"So what's up?"

"I need to ask you a question," I said.

"Uh-huh."

"About the car accident."

I hear a tinny echo. Then silence.

"Do you remember the car accident? The one before Elizabeth was killed?"

Rebecca Schayes, my wife's closest friend, did not reply. I cleared my throat. "Who was driving?"

"What?" She did not say that into the phone. "Okay, hold on." Then back at me: "Look, Beck, something just came up here. Can I call you back in a little while?"

"Rebecca—"

But the line was dead.

Here is the truth about tragedy: It's good for the soul.

The fact is, I'm a better person because of the deaths. If every cloud has a silver lining, this one is admittedly pretty flimsy. But there it is. That doesn't mean it's worth it or an even trade or anything like that, but I know I'm a better man than I used to be. I have a finer sense of what's important. I have a keener understanding of people's pain.

There was a time—it's laughable now—when I used to worry about what clubs I belonged to, what car I drove, what college degree I stuck on my wall—all that status crap. I wanted to be a surgeon because that wowed people. I wanted to impress so-called friends. I wanted to be a big man.

Like I said, laughable.

Some might argue that my self-improvement is simply a question of maturity. In part, true. And much of the change is due to the fact I am now on my own. Elizabeth and I were a couple, a single entity. She was so good that I could afford to be not so good, as though her goodness raised us both, was a cosmic equalizer.

Still, death is a great teacher. It's just too harsh.

I wish I could tell you that through the tragedy I mined some undiscovered, life-altering absolute that I could pass on to you. I didn't. The clichés apply—people are what count, life is precious, materialism is overrated, the little things matter, live in the moment—and I can repeat them to you ad nauseam. You might listen, but you won't internalize. Tragedy hammers it home. Tragedy etches it onto your soul. You might not be happier. But you will be better.

What makes this all the more ironic is that I've often wished that Elizabeth could see me now. Much as I'd like to, I don't believe the dead watch over us or any similar comfort-fantasy we sell ourselves. I believe the dead are gone for good. But I can't help but think: Perhaps now I am worthy of her.

A more religious man might wonder if that is why she's returned.

Rebecca Schayes was a leading freelance photographer. Her work appeared in all the usual glossies, though strangely enough, she specialized in men. Professional athletes who agreed to appear on the cover of, for example, *GQ* often requested her to do the shoot. Rebecca liked to joke that she had a knack for male bodies due to "a lifetime of intense study."

I found her studio on West Thirty-second Street, not far from Penn Station. The building was a butt-ugly semi-warehouse that reeked from the Central Park horse and buggies housed on the ground floor. I skipped the freight elevator and took the stairs.

Rebecca was hurrying down the corridor. Trailing her, a gaunt, black-clad assistant with reedy arms and pencil-sketch facial hair dragged two aluminum suitcases. Rebecca still had the unruly sabra locks, her fiery hair curling angrily and flowing freely. Her eyes were wide apart and green, and if she'd changed in the past eight years, I couldn't see it.

She barely broke stride when she saw me. "It's a bad time, Beck."

"Tough," I said.

"I got a shoot. Can we do this later?"

"No."

She stopped, whispered something to the sulking black-clad assistant, and said, "Okay, follow me."

Her studio had high ceilings and cement walls painted white. There were lots of lighting umbrellas and black screens and extension cords snaking everywhere. Rebecca fiddled with a film cartridge and pretended to be busy.

"Tell me about the car accident," I said.

"I don't get this, Beck." She opened a canister, put it down, put the top back on, then opened it again. "We've barely spoken in, what, eight years? All of a sudden you get all obsessive about an old car accident?"

I crossed my arms and waited.

"Why, Beck? After all this time. Why do you want to know?"

"Tell me."

She kept her eyes averted. The unruly hair fell over half her face, but she didn't bother pushing it back. "I miss her," she said. "And I miss you too."

I didn't reply to that.

"I called," she said.

"I know."

"I tried to stay in touch. I wanted to be there."

"I'm sorry," I said. And I was. Rebecca had been Elizabeth's best friend. They'd shared an apartment near Washington Square Park before we got married. I should have returned her calls or invited her over or made some kind of effort. But I didn't.

Grief can be inordinately selfish.

"Elizabeth told me that you two were in a minor car crash," I went on. "It was her fault, she said. She took her eyes off the road. Is that true?"

"What possible difference does it make now?"

"It makes a difference."

"How?"

"What are you afraid of, Rebecca?"

Now it was her time for silence.

"Was there an accident or not?"

Her shoulders slumped as though something internal had been severed. She took a few deep breaths and kept her face down. "I don't know."

"What do you mean, you don't know?"

"She told me it was a car accident too."

"But you weren't there?"

"No. You were out of town, Beck. I came home one night, and Elizabeth was there. She was bruised up. I asked her what happened. She told me she'd been in a car accident and if anyone asked, we'd been in my car."

"If anyone asked?"

Rebecca finally looked up. "I think she meant you, Beck."

I tried to take this in. "So what really happened?"

"She wouldn't say."

"Did you take her to a doctor?"

"She wouldn't let me." Rebecca gave me a strange look. "I still don't get it. Why are you asking me about this now?"

Tell no one.

"I'm just trying to get a little closure."

She nodded, but she didn't believe me. Neither one of us was a particularly adept liar.

"Did you take any pictures of her?" I asked.

"Pictures?"

"Of her injuries. After the accident."

"God, no. Why would I do that?"

An awfully good question. I sat there and thought about it. I don't know how long.

"Beck?"

"Yeah."

"You look like hell."

"You don't," I said.

"I'm in love."

"It becomes you."

"Thanks."

"Is he a good guy?"

"The best."

"Maybe he deserves you, then."

"Maybe." She leaned forward and kissed my cheek. It felt good, comforting. "Something happened, didn't it?"

This time I opted for the truth. "I don't know."

13

Shauna and Hester Crimstein sat in Hester's swanky midtown law office. Hester finished up her phone call and put the receiver back in the cradle.

"No one's doing much talking," Hester said.

"But they didn't arrest him?"

"No. Not yet."

"So what's going on?" Shauna asked.

"Near as I can tell, they think Beck killed his wife."

"That's nuts," Shauna said. "He was in the hospital, for crying out loud. That KillRoy loony tune is on death row."

"Not for her murder," the attorney replied.

"What?"

"Kellerton's suspected of killing at least eighteen women. He confessed to fourteen, but they only had enough hard evidence to prosecute and convict him on twelve. That was enough. I mean, how many death sentences does one man need?"

"But everyone knows he killed Elizabeth."

"Correction: Everyone *knew*."

"I don't get it. How can they possibly think Beck had anything to do with it?"

"I don't know," Hester said. She threw her feet up on her desk and put her hands behind her head. "At least, not yet. But we'll have to be on our guard."

"How's that?"

"For one thing, we have to assume the feds are

watching his every step. Phone taps, surveillance, that kind of thing."

"So?"

"What do you mean, so?"

"He's innocent, Hester. Let them watch."

Hester looked up and shook her head. "Don't be naïve."

"What the hell does that mean?"

"It means that if they tape him having eggs for breakfast, it can be something. He has to be careful. But there's something else."

"What?"

"The feds are going to go after Beck."

"How?"

"Got me, but trust me, they will. They got a hard-on for your friend. And it's been eight years. That means they're desperate. Desperate feds are ugly, constitutional-rights-stamping feds."

Shauna sat back and thought about the strange emails from "Elizabeth."

"What?" Hester said.

"Nothing."

"Don't hold back on me, Shauna."

"I'm not the client here."

"You saying Beck isn't telling me everything?"

An idea struck Shauna with something approaching horror. She thought about it some more, ran the idea over some test tracks, let it bounce around for a few moments.

It made sense, and yet Shauna hoped—nay, prayed—that she was wrong. She stood and hurried toward the door. "I have to go."

"What's going on?"

"Ask your client."

* * *

Special agents Nick Carlson and Tom Stone positioned themselves on the same couch over which Beck had recently waxed nostalgic. Kim Parker, Elizabeth's mother, sat across from them with her hands primly in her lap. Her face was a frozen, waxy mask. Hoyt Parker paced.

"So what's so important that you couldn't say anything over the phone?" Hoyt asked.

"We want to ask you some questions," Carlson said.

"What about?"

"Your daughter."

That froze them both.

"More specifically, we'd like to ask you about her relationship with her husband, Dr. David Beck."

Hoyt and Kim exchanged a glance. "Why?" Hoyt asked.

"It involves a matter currently under investigation."

"What matter? She's been dead for eight years. Her killer is on death row."

"Please, Detective Parker. We're all on the same side here."

The room was still and dry. Kim Parker's lips thinned and trembled. Hoyt looked at his wife and then nodded at the two men.

Carlson kept his gaze on Kim. "Mrs. Parker, how would you describe the relationship between your daughter and her husband?"

"They were very close, very much in love."

"No problems?"

"No," she said. "None."

"Would you describe Dr. Beck as a violent man?"

She looked startled. "No, never."

They looked at Hoyt. Hoyt nodded his agreement.

"To your knowledge, did Dr. Beck ever hit your daughter?"

"What?"

Carlson tried a kind smile. "If you could just answer the question."

"Never," Hoyt said. "No one hit my daughter."

"You're certain?"

His voice was firm. "Very."

Carlson looked toward Kim. "Mrs. Parker?"

"He loved her so much."

"I understand that, ma'am. But many wife-beaters profess to loving their wives."

"He never hit her."

Hoyt stopped pacing. "What's going on here?"

Carlson looked at Stone for a moment. "I want to show you some photographs, if I may. They are a bit disturbing, but I think they're important."

Stone handed Carlson the manila envelope. Carlson opened it. One by one, he placed the photographs of the bruised Elizabeth on a coffee table. He watched for a reaction. Kim Parker, as expected, let out a small cry. Hoyt Parker's face seemed at odds with itself, settling into a distant blankness.

"Where did you get these?" Hoyt asked softly.

"Have you seen them before?"

"Never," he said. He looked at his wife. She shook her head.

"But I remember the bruises," Kim Parker offered.

"When?"

"I can't remember exactly. Not long before she died. But when I saw them, they were less"—she searched for the word—"pronounced."

"Did your daughter tell you how she got them?"

"She said she was in a car accident."

"Mrs. Parker, we've checked with your wife's insurance company. She never reported a car accident. We checked police files. No one ever made a claim against her. No policeman ever filled out a report."

"So what are you saying?" Hoyt came in.

"Simply this: If your daughter wasn't in a car accident, how did she get these bruises?"

"You think her husband gave them to her?"

"It's a theory we're working on."

"Based on what?"

The two men hesitated. The hesitation said one of two things: not in front of the lady or not in front of the civilian. Hoyt picked up on it. "Kim, do you mind if I talk to the agents alone for moment?"

"Not at all." She stood on wobbly legs and teetered toward the stairs. "I'll be in the bedroom."

When she was out of sight, Hoyt said, "Okay, I'm listening."

"We don't think Dr. Beck just beat your daughter," Carlson said. "We think he murdered her."

Hoyt looked from Carlson to Stone and back to Carlson, as though waiting for the punch line. When none came, he moved to the chair. "You better start explaining."

14

What else had Elizabeth been keeping from me?

As I headed down Tenth Avenue toward the Quick-n-Park, I again tried to dismiss those photographs as merely a record of her car accident injuries. I remembered how nonchalant Elizabeth had been about the whole thing at the time. Just a fender-bender, she said. No big deal. When I asked for details, she had pretty much brushed me off.

Now I knew that she'd lied to me about it.

I could tell you that Elizabeth never lied to me, but that would be, in light of this recent discovery, a pretty unconvincing argument. This was, however, the first lie I was aware of. I guess we both had our secrets.

When I reached the Quick-n-Park, I spotted something strange—or perhaps, I should say, someone strange. There, on the corner, was a man in a tan overcoat.

He was looking at me.

And he was oddly familiar. No one I knew, but there was still the unease of déjà vu. I'd seen this man before. This morning even. Where? I ran through my morning and spotted him in my mind's eye:

When I pulled over for coffee at eight a.m. The man with the tan overcoat had been there. In the parking lot of Starbucks.

Was I sure?

No, of course not. I diverted my eyes and hurried over to the attendant's booth. The parking attendant—

his name tag read Carlo—was watching television and eating a sandwich. He kept his eyes on the screen for half a minute before sliding his gaze toward me. Then he slowly brushed the crumbs off his hands, took my ticket, and stamped it. I quickly paid the man and he handed me my key.

The man in the tan overcoat was still there.

I tried very hard not to look in his direction as I walked to my car. I got in, started it up, and when I hit Tenth Avenue, I checked the rearview mirror.

The man with the tan overcoat didn't so much as glance at me. I kept watching him until I turned toward the West Side Highway. He never looked in my direction. Paranoid. I was going nutsy paranoid.

So why had Elizabeth lied to me?

I thought about it and came up with nothing.

There were still three hours until my Bat Street message came in. Three hours. Man, I needed to distract myself. Thinking too hard about what might be on the other end of that cyber-connection shredded my stomach lining.

I knew what I had to do. I was just trying to delay the inevitable.

When I got home, Grandpa was in his customary chair, alone. The television was off. The nurse was yakking on the phone in Russian. She wasn't going to work out. I'd have to call the agency and get her replaced.

Small particles of egg were stuck to the corners of Grandpa's mouth, so I took out a handkerchief and gently scraped them away. Our eyes met, but his gaze was locked on something far beyond me. I saw us all up at the lake. Grandpa would be doing his beloved weight-loss before-and-after pose. He'd turn profile, slump, let his elastic gut hang out, and shout "Before!" and then suck it up and flex and yell "After!" He did it brilliantly. My father would howl. Dad had the greatest, most infectious laugh. It was a total body release. I used to have it too. It died with him. I could never laugh like that again. Somehow it seemed obscene.

Hearing me, the nurse hurried off the phone and hightailed it into the room with a bright smile. I didn't return it.

I eyed the basement door. I was still delaying the inevitable.

No more stalling.

"Stay with him," I said.

The nurse bowed her head and sat down.

The basement had been finished in the days before people finished basements, and it showed. The once-brown shag carpet was pockmarked and water-buckled. Faux white brick made from some sort of bizarre synthetic had been glued to asphalt walls. Some sheets had fallen to the shag; others stopped mid-topple, like columns of the Acropolis.

In the center of the room, the Ping-Pong table's green had been washed to an almost in-vogue spearmint. The torn net looked like the barricades after the French troops stormed. The paddles were stripped down to the splintery wood.

Some cardboard boxes, many sprouting mold, sat on top of the Ping-Pong table. Others were piled in the corner. Old clothes were in wardrobe boxes. Not Elizabeth's. Shauna and Linda had cleared those out for me. Goodwill got them, I think. But some of the other boxes held old items. *Her* items. I couldn't throw them away, and I couldn't let other people have them. I'm not sure why. Some things we pack away, stick in the back of the closet, never expect to see again—but we can't quite make ourselves discard them. Like dreams, I guess.

I wasn't sure where I had put it, but I knew it was there. I started going through old photographs, once again averting my gaze. I was pretty good at that, though as time went on, the photographs hurt less and less. When I saw Elizabeth and me together in some greening Polaroid, it was as though I were looking at strangers.

I hated doing this.

I dug deeper into the box. My fingertips hit something made of felt, and I pulled out her tennis varsity letter from high school. With a sad smirk, I remembered her tan legs and the way her braid bounced as she hopped toward the net. On the court, her face was locked in pure concentration. That was how Elizabeth would beat you. She had decent enough ground strokes and a pretty good serve, but what lifted her above her classmates was that focus.

I put the letter down gingerly and started digging again. I found what I was looking for at the bottom.

Her daily planner.

The police had wanted it after the abduction. Or so I was told. Rebecca came by the apartment and helped them find it. I assume they searched for clues in it—the same thing I was about to do—but when the body popped up with the K branding, they probably stopped.

I thought about that some more—about how everything had been neatly pinned on KillRoy—and another thought scurried through my brain. I ran upstairs to my computer and got online. I found the Web site for the New York City Department of Correction. Tons of stuff on it, including the name and phone number I needed.

I signed off and called Briggs Penitentiary.

That's the prison that holds KillRoy.

When the recording came on, I pressed in the proper extension and was put through. Three rings later, a man said, "Deputy Superintendent Brown speaking."

I told him that I wanted to visit Elroy Kellerton.

"And you are?" he said.

"Dr. David Beck. My wife, Elizabeth Beck, was one of his victims."

"I see." Brown hesitated. "May I ask the purpose of your visit?"

"No."

There was more silence on the line.

"I have the right to visit him if he's willing to see me," I said.

"Yes, of course, but this is a highly unusual request."

"I'm still making it."

"The normal procedure is to have your attorney go through his—"

"But I don't have to," I interrupted. I learned this at a victim's rights Web site—that I could make the request myself. If Kellerton was willing to see me, I was in. "I just want to talk to Kellerton. You have visiting hours tomorrow, don't you?"

"Yes, we do."

"Then if Kellerton agrees, I'll be up tomorrow. Is there a problem with that?"

"No, sir. If he agrees, there's no problem."

I thanked him and hung up the phone. I was taking action. It felt damn good.

The day planner sat on the desk next to me. I was avoiding it again, because as painful as a photograph or recording might be, handwriting was somehow worse, somehow more personal. Elizabeth's soaring capital letters, the firmly crossed ts, the too many loops between letters, the way it all tilted to the right ...

I spent an hour going through it. Elizabeth was detailed. She didn't shorthand much. What surprised me was how well I'd known my wife. Everything was clear, and there were no surprises. In fact, there was only one appointment I couldn't account for.

Three weeks before her death, there was an entry that read simply: *PF*.

And a phone number without an area code.

In light of how specific she'd been elsewhere, I found this entry a little unsettling. I didn't have a clue what the area code would be. The call was made eight years ago. Area codes had split and changed several different ways since then.

I tried 201 and got a disconnect. I tried 973. An old lady answered. I told her she'd won a free subscription to the *New York Post*. She gave me her name. Neither initial matched. I tried 212, which was the city. And that was where I hit bingo.

"Peter Flannery, attorney-at-law," a woman said mid-yawn.

"May I speak to Mr. Flannery, please."

"He's in court."

She could have sounded more bored but not without a quality prescription. I heard a lot of noise in the background.

"I'd like to make an appointment to see Mr. Flannery."

"You answering the billboard ad?"

"Billboard ad?"

"You injured?"

"Yes," I said. "But I didn't see an ad. A friend recommended him. It's a medical malpractice case. I came in with a broken arm and now I can't move it. I lost my job. The pain is nonstop."

She set me up for an appointment tomorrow afternoon.

I put the phone back into the cradle and frowned. What would Elizabeth be doing with a probable ambulance-chaser like Flannery?

The sound of the phone made me jump. I snatched it up mid-ring.

"Hello," I said.

It was Shauna. "Where are you?" she asked.

"Home."

"You need to get over here right away," she said.

15

Agent Carlson looked Hoyt Parker straight in the eye. "As you know, we recently found two bodies in the vicinity of Lake Charmaine."

Hoyt nodded.

A cell phone chirped. Stone managed to hoist himself up and said "Excuse me" before lumbering into the kitchen. Hoyt turned back to Carlson and waited.

"We know the official account of your daughter's death," Carlson said. "She and her husband, David Beck, visited the lake for an annual ritual. They went swimming in the dark. KillRoy lay in wait. He assaulted Dr. Beck and kidnapped your daughter. End of story."

"And you don't think that's what happened?"

"No, Hoyt—can I call you Hoyt?"

Hoyt nodded.

"No, Hoyt, we don't."

"So how do you see it?"

"I think David Beck murdered your daughter and pinned it on a serial killer."

Hoyt, a twenty-eight-year veteran of the NYPD, knew how to keep a straight face, but he still leaned back as though the words were jabs at his chin. "Let's hear it."

"Okay, let's start from the beginning. Beck takes your daughter up to a secluded lake, right?"

"Right."

"You've been there?"

"Many times."

"Oh?"

"We were all friends. Kim and I were close to David's parents. We used to visit all the time."

"Then you know how secluded it is."

"Yes."

"Dirt road, a sign that you'd only see if you knew to look for it. It's as hidden as hidden can be. No signs of life."

"What's your point?"

"What are the odds of KillRoy pulling up that road?"

Hoyt raised his palms to the sky. "What are the odds of anyone meeting up with a serial killer?"

"True, okay, but in other cases, there was a logic to it. Kellerton abducted somebody off a city street, he car-jacked a victim, even broke into a house. But think about it. He sees this dirt road and somehow decides to search for a victim up there? I'm not saying it's impossible, but it's highly unlikely."

Hoyt said, "Go on."

"You'll admit that there are plenty of logic holes in the accepted scenario."

"All cases have logic holes."

"Right, okay, but let me try an alternate theory on you. Let's just say that Dr. Beck wanted to kill your daughter."

"Why?"

"For one thing, a two-hundred-thousand-dollar life insurance policy."

"He doesn't need money."

"Everyone needs money, Hoyt. You know that."

"I don't buy it."

"Look, we're still digging here. We don't know all the

motivations yet. But let me just go through our scenario, okay?"

Hoyt gave him a suit-yourself shrug.

"We have evidence here that Dr. Beck beat her."

"What evidence? You have some photographs. She told my wife she'd been in a car accident."

"Come on, Hoyt." Carlson swept his hand at the photographs. "Look at the expression on your daughter's face. That look like the face of a woman in a car accident?"

No, Hoyt thought, it didn't. "Where did you find these pictures?"

"I'll get to that in a second, but let's go back to my scenario, okay? Let's assume for the moment that Dr. Beck beat your daughter and that he had a hell of an inheritance coming his way."

"Lot of assuming."

"True, but stay with me. Think of the accepted scenario and all those holes. Now compare it with this one: Dr. Beck brings your daughter up to a secluded spot where he knows there will be no witnesses. He hires two thugs to grab her. He knows about KillRoy. It's in all the papers. Plus your brother worked on the case. Did he ever discuss it with you or Beck?"

Hoyt sat still for a moment. "Go on."

"The two hired thugs abduct and kill your daughter. Naturally, the first suspect will be the husband—always is in a case like this, right? But the two thugs brand her cheek with the letter K. Next thing we know, it's all blamed on KillRoy."

"But Beck was assaulted. His head injury was real."

"Sure, but we both know that's not inconsistent with him being behind it. How would Beck explain coming out of the abduction healthy? 'Hi, guess what, someone kidnapped my wife, but I'm fine'? It'd never play. Getting whacked on the head gave his story credibility."

"He took a hell of a shot."

"He was dealing with thugs, Hoyt. They probably miscalculated. And what about his injury anyway? He tells some bizarre story about miraculously crawling out of the water and dialing 911. I gave several doctors Beck's old medical chart. They claim his account of what he did defies medical logic. It would have been pretty much impossible, given his injuries."

Hoyt considered that. He had often wondered about that himself. How had Beck survived and called for help? "What else?" Hoyt said.

"There's strong evidence that suggests the two thugs, not KillRoy, assaulted Beck."

"What evidence?"

"Buried with the bodies, we found a baseball bat with blood on it. The full DNA match will take a while, but the preliminary results strongly suggest that the blood is Beck's."

Agent Stone plodded back in the room and sat down hard. Hoyt once again said, "Go on."

"The rest is pretty obvious. The two thugs do the job. They kill your daughter and pin it on KillRoy. Then they come back to get the rest of their payment—or maybe they decide to extort more money from Dr. Beck. I don't know. Whatever, Beck has to get rid of them. He sets up a meet in the secluded woods near Lake Charmaine. The two thugs probably thought they were dealing with a wimpy doctor or maybe he caught them unprepared. Either way Beck shoots them and buries the bodies along with the baseball bat and whatever evidence might haunt him later on. The perfect crime now. Nothing to tie him with the murder. Let's face it. If we didn't get enormously lucky, the bodies would have never been found."

Hoyt shook his head. "Hell of a theory."

"There's more."

"Like?"

Carlson looked at Stone. Stone pointed to his cell phone. "I just got a strange phone call from someone at Briggs Penitentiary," Stone said. "It seems your son-in-law called there today and demanded a meeting with KillRoy."

Hoyt now looked openly stunned. "Why the hell would he do that?"

"You tell us," Stone responded. "But keep in mind that Beck knows we're onto him. All of a sudden, he has this overwhelming desire to visit the man he set up as your daughter's killer."

"Hell of a coincidence," Carlson added.

"You think he's trying to cover his tracks?"

"You have a better explanation?"

Hoyt sat back and tried to let all of this settle. "You left something out."

"What?"

He pointed to the photographs on the table. "Who gave you those?"

"In a way," Carlson said, "I think your daughter did."

Hoyt's face looked drained.

"More specifically, her alias did. One Sarah Goodhart. Your daughter's middle name and the name of this street."

"I don't understand."

"At the crime scene," Carlson said. "One of the two thugs—Melvin Bartola—had a small key in his shoe." Carlson held up the key. Hoyt took it from his hand, peering at it as though it held some mystical answer. "See the *UCB* on the flip side?"

Hoyt nodded.

"That stands for United Central Bank. We finally traced this key down to their branch at 1772 Broadway in the city. The key opens Box 174, which is registered to one Sarah Goodhart. We got a search warrant for it."

Hoyt looked up. "The photographs were in there?"

Carlson and Stone glanced at each other. They had already made the decision not to tell Hoyt everything about that box—not until all the tests came back and they knew for sure—but both men nodded now.

"Think about it, Hoyt. Your daughter kept these pictures hidden in a safety-deposit box. The reasons are obvious. Want more? We questioned Dr. Beck. He admitted knowing nothing about the pictures. He'd never seen them before. Why would your daughter hide them from him?"

"You talked to Beck?"

"Yes."

"What else did he say?"

"Not much because he demanded a lawyer." Carlson waited a beat. Then he leaned forward. "He not only lawyered up, he called Hester Crimstein. That sound like the act of an innocent man to you?"

Hoyt actually gripped the sides of the chair, trying to steady himself. "You can't prove any of this."

"Not yet, no. But we know. That's half the battle sometimes."

"So what are you going to do?"

"Only one thing we can do." Carlson smiled at him. "Apply pressure until something breaks."

* * *

Larry Gandle looked over the day's developments and mumbled to himself, "Not good."

One, the FBI picks up Beck and questions him.

Two, Beck calls a photographer named Rebecca Schayes. He asks her about an old car accident involving his wife. Then he visits her studio.

A photographer no less.

Three, Beck calls Briggs Penitentiary and says he wants to meet Elroy Kellerton.

Fourth, Beck calls Peter Flannery's office.

All of this was puzzling. None of it was good.

Eric Wu hung up the phone and said, "You're not going to like this."

"What?"

"Our source with the FBI says that they suspect Beck killed his wife."

Gandle nearly fell over. "Explain."

"That's all the source knows. Somehow, they've tied the two dead bodies by the lake to Beck."

Very puzzling.

"Let me see those emails again," Gandle said.

Eric Wu handed them to him. When Gandle thought about who could have sent them, the creeping feeling in the pit of his stomach started to claw and grow. He tried to add the pieces together. He'd always wondered how Beck had survived that night. Now he wondered something else.

Had anyone else survived it?

"What time is it?" Gandle asked.

"Six-thirty."

"Beck still hasn't looked up that Bat-whatever address?"

"Bat Street. And no, he hasn't."

"Anything more on Rebecca Schayes?"

"Just what we already know. Close friend of Elizabeth Parker's. They shared an apartment before Parker
married Beck. I checked old phone records. Beck hasn't
called her in years."

"So why would he contact her now?"

Wu shrugged. "Ms. Schayes must know something."

Griffin Scope had been very clear. Learn what you
can, then bury it.

And use Wu.

"We need to have a chat with her," Gandle said.

16

Shauna met me on the ground floor of a high-rise at 462 Park Avenue in Manhattan.

"Come on," she said without preamble. "I have something to show you upstairs."

I checked my watch. A little under two hours until the Bat Street message came in. We entered an elevator. Shauna hit the button for the twenty-third floor. The lights climbed and the blind-person-counter beeped.

"Hester got me thinking," Shauna said.

"What about?"

"She said the feds would be desperate. That they'd do anything to get you."

"So?"

The elevator sounded its final ding.

"Hang on, you'll see."

The door slid open on a massive cubicle-divided floor. The norm in the city nowadays. Rip off the ceiling and view from above and you'd have a very hard time telling the difference between this floor and a rat maze. From down here too, when you thought about it.

Shauna marched between countless cloth-lined dividers. I trailed in her wake. Halfway down she turned left and then right and then left again.

"Maybe I should drop bread crumbs," I said.

Her voice was flat. "Good one."

"Thank you, I'm here all week."

She wasn't laughing.

"What is this place anyway?" I asked.

"A company called DigiCom. The agency works with them sometimes."

"Doing what?"

"You'll see."

We made a final turn into a cluttered cubbyhole occupied by a young man with a long head and the slender fingers of a concert pianist.

"This is Farrell Lynch. Farrell, this is David Beck."

I shook the slender hand briefly. Farrell said, "Hi."

I nodded.

"Okay," Shauna said. "Key it up."

Farrell Lynch swiveled his chair so that he was facing the computer. Shauna and I watched over his shoulders. He started typing with those slender fingers.

"Keyed up," he said.

"Run it."

He hit the return button. The screen went black and then Humphrey Bogart appeared. He wore a fedora and a trench coat. I recognized the scene right away. The fog, the plane in the background. The finale of *Casablanca*.

I looked at Shauna.

"Wait," she said.

The camera was on Bogie. He was telling Ingrid Bergman that she was getting on that plane with Laszlo and that the problems of three little people didn't amount to a hill of beans in this world. And then, when the camera went back to Ingrid Bergman . . .

. . . it wasn't Ingrid Bergman.

I blinked. There, beneath the famed hat, gazing up at Bogie and bathed in the gray glow, was Shauna.

"I can't go with you, Rick," the computer Shauna

said dramatically, "because I'm madly in love with Ava Gardner."

I turned to Shauna. My eyes asked the question. She nodded yes. I said it anyway.

"You think . . ." I stammered. "You think I was fooled by trick photography?"

Farrell took that one. "Digital photography," he corrected me. "Far simpler to manipulate." He spun his chair toward me. "See, computer images aren't film. They're really just pixels in files. Not unlike your word processing document. You know how easy it is to change a word processing document, right? To alter content or fonts or spacing?"

I nodded.

"Well, for someone with even a rudimentary understanding of digital imaging, that's how easy it is to manipulate a computer's streaming images. These aren't pictures, nor are they films or tapes. Computer video streams are simply a bunch of pixels. Anyone can manipulate them. Simply cut and paste and then you run a blend program."

I looked at Shauna. "But she looked older in the video," I insisted. "Different."

Shauna said, "Farrell?"

He hit another button. Bogie returned. When they went to Ingrid Bergman this time, Shauna looked seventy years old.

"Age progression software," Farrell explained. "It's mostly used to age missing children, but nowadays they sell a home version at any software store. I can also change any part of Shauna's image—her hairstyle, her eye color, the size of her nose. I can make her lips thinner or thicker, give her a tattoo, whatever."

"Thank you, Farrell," Shauna said.

She gave him a look of dismissal a blind man could

read. "Excuse me," Farrell said before making himself scarce.

I couldn't think.

When Farrell was out of earshot, Shauna said, "I remembered a photo shoot I did last month. One picture came out perfectly—the sponsor loved it—except my earring had slipped down. We brought the image over here. Farrell did a quick cut-and-paste and voilà, my earring was back in the right place."

I shook my head.

"Think about it, Beck. The feds think you killed Elizabeth, but they have no way to prove it. Hester explained how desperate they've become. I started thinking: Maybe they'd play mind games with you. What better mind game than sending you these emails?"

"But kiss time . . . ?"

"What about it?"

"How would they know about kiss time?"

"I know about it. Linda knows about it. I bet Rebecca knows too, maybe Elizabeth's parents. They could have found out."

I felt tears rush up to the surface. I tried to work my voice and managed to croak out, "It's a hoax?"

"I don't know, Beck. I really don't. But let's be rational here. If Elizabeth was alive, where has she been for eight years? Why choose now of all times to come back from the grave—the same time, by coincidence, that the FBI starts suspecting you of killing her? And come on, do you really believe she's still alive? I know you want to. Hell, I want to. But let's try to look at this rationally. When you really think about it, which scenario makes more sense?"

I stumbled back and fell into a chair. My heart started crumbling. I felt the hope start to shrivel up.

A hoax. Has this all been nothing but a hoax?

17

Once he was settled inside Rebecca Schayes's studio, Larry Gandle called his wife on the cell phone. "I'll be home late," he said.

"Don't forget to take your pill," Patty told him.

Gandle had a mild case of diabetes, controlled through diet and a pill. No insulin.

"I will."

Eric Wu, still plugged into his Walkman, carefully laid down a vinyl drop cloth near the door.

Gandle hung up the phone and snapped on a pair of latex gloves. The search was both thorough and time-consuming. Like most photographers, Rebecca Schayes saved tons of negatives. There were four metal file cabinets jammed full of them. They'd checked Rebecca Schayes's schedule. She was finishing up a shoot. She'd be back here to work the darkroom in about an hour. Not enough time.

"You know what would help," Wu said.

"What?"

"Having some idea what the hell we're looking for."

"Beck gets these cryptic emails," Gandle said. "And what does he do? For the first time in eight years, he rushes over to see his wife's oldest friend. We need to know why."

Wu looked through him some more. "Why don't we just wait and ask her?"

"We will, Eric."

Wu nodded slowly and turned away.

Gandle spotted a long metal desk in the darkroom. He tested it. Strong. The size was about right too. You could lay someone on it and tape a limb to each table leg.

"How much duct tape did we bring?"

"Enough," Wu said.

"Do me a favor, then," Gandle said. "Move the drop cloth under the table."

Half an hour until I picked up the Bat Street message.

Shauna's demonstration had hit me like a surprise left hook. I felt groggy, and I took the full count. But a funny thing happened. I got my ass off the canvas. I stood back up and shook off the cobwebs and started circling.

We were in my car. Shauna had insisted on coming back to the house with me. A limousine would take her back in a few hours. I know that she wanted to comfort me, but it was equally clear that she didn't want to go home yet.

"Something I don't get," I said.

Shauna turned to me.

"The feds think I killed Elizabeth, right?"

"Right."

"So why would they send me emails pretending she's alive?"

Shauna had no quick answer.

"Think about it," I said. "You claim that this is some sort of elaborate plot to get me to reveal my guilt. But if I killed Elizabeth, I'd know that it was a trick."

"It's a mind game," Shauna said.

"But that doesn't make sense. If you want to play a mind game with me, send me emails and pretend to be—I don't know—someone who witnessed the murder or something."

Shauna thought about it. "I think they're just trying to keep you off balance, Beck."

"Yeah, but still. It doesn't add up."

"Okay, how long until the next message comes in?"

I checked the clock. "Twenty minutes."

Shauna sat back in her seat. "We'll wait and see what it says."

Eric Wu set up his laptop on the floor in a corner of Rebecca Schayes's studio.

He checked Beck's office computer first. Still idle. The clock read a little past eight o'clock. The clinic was long closed. He switched over to the home computer. For a few seconds there was nothing. And then:

"Beck just signed on," Wu said.

Larry Gandle hurried over. "Can we get on and see the message before him?"

"It wouldn't be a good idea."

"Why not?"

"If we sign in and then he tries to, it will tell him that someone is currently using that screen name."

"He'll know he's being watched?"

"Yes. But it doesn't matter. We're watching him in real time. The moment he reads the message, we'll see it too."

"Okay, let me know when."

Wu squinted at the screen. "He just brought up the Bigfoot site. It should be any second now."

I typed in bigfoot.com and hit the return button.

My right leg started jackhammering. It does that when I'm nervous. Shauna put her hand on my knee.

My knee slowed to a stop. She took the hand off. My knee stayed still for a minute, and then it started up again. Shauna put her hand back on my knee. The cycle began again.

Shauna was playing it cool, but I know that she kept sneaking glances at me. She was my best friend. She'd support me to the end. But only an idiot wouldn't be wondering at this juncture if my elevator was stopping at every floor. They say that insanity, like heart disease or intelligence, is hereditary. The thought had been running through my mind since I'd first seen Elizabeth on the street cam. It wasn't a comforting one.

My father died in a car crash when I was twenty. His car toppled over an embankment. According to an eyewitness—a truck driver from Wyoming—my father's Buick drove straight off it. It had been a cold night. The road, while well plowed, was slick.

Many suggested—well, suggested in whispers anyway—that he committed suicide. I don't believe it. Yes, he had been more withdrawn and quiet in his last few months. And yes, I often wonder if all that made him more susceptible to an accident. But suicide? No way.

My mother, always a fragile person of seemingly gentle neuroses, reacted by slowly losing her mind. She literally shrank into herself. Linda tried to nurse her for three years, until even she agreed that Mom needed to be committed. Linda visits her all the time. I don't.

After a few more moments, the Bigfoot home page came up. I found the user name box and typed in Bat Street.

I hit the tab key and in the password text box I typed Teenage. I hit return.

Nothing happened.

"You forgot to click the Sign In icon," Shauna said.

I looked at her. She shrugged. I clicked the icon.

The screen went white. Then an ad for a CD store came up. The bar on the bottom went back and forth in a slow wave. The percentage climbed slowly. When it hit about eighteen percent, it vanished and then several seconds later a message appeared.

ERROR—Either the user name or password you entered is not in our database.

"Try again," Shauna said.

I did. The same error message came up. The computer was telling me the account didn't even exist.

What did that mean?

I had no idea. I tried to think of a reason that the account wouldn't exist.

I checked the time: 8:13.34 p.m.

Kiss Time

Could that be the answer? Could it be that the account, like the link yesterday, simply didn't exist yet? I mulled that one over. It was possible, of course, but unlikely.

As though reading my mind, Shauna said, "Maybe we should wait until eight-fifteen."

So I tried again at eight-fifteen. At eight-eighteen. At eight-twenty.

Nothing but the same error message.

"The feds must have pulled the plug," Shauna said.

I shook my head, not willing yet to give up.

My leg started shaking again. Shauna used one hand to stop it and one hand to answer her cell phone. She started barking at someone on the other end. I checked the clock. I tried again. Nothing. Twice more. Nothing.

It was after eight-thirty now.

"She, uh, could be late," Shauna said.

I frowned.

"When you saw her yesterday," Shauna tried, "you didn't know where she was, right?"

"Right."

"So maybe she's in a different time zone," Shauna said. "Maybe that's why she's late."

"A different time zone?" I frowned some more. Shauna shrugged.

We waited another hour. Shauna, to her credit, never said I told you so. After a while she put a hand on my back and said, "Hey, I got an idea."

I turned to her.

"I'm going to wait in the other room," Shauna said. "I think that might help."

"How do you figure?"

"See, if this were a movie, this would be the part where I get all fed up by your craziness and storm out and then bingo, the message appears, you know, so only you see it and everyone still thinks you're crazy. Like on Scooby-Doo when only he and Shaggy see the ghost and no one believes them?"

I thought about it. "Worth a try," I said.

"Good. So why don't I go wait in the kitchen for a while? Take your time. When the message comes in, just give a little shout."

She stood.

"You're just humoring me, aren't you?" I said.

Shauna thought about it. "Yeah, probably."

She left then. I turned and faced the screen. And I waited.

18

Nothing's happening," Eric Wu said. "Beck keeps trying to sign on, but all he gets is an error message."

Larry Gandle was about to ask a follow-up question, when he heard the elevator rev up. He checked the clock.

Rebecca Schayes was right on time.

Eric Wu turned away from his computer. He looked at Larry Gandle with the kind of eyes that make a man take a step back. Gandle took out his gun—a nine-millimeter this time. Just in case. Wu frowned. He moved his bulk to the door and flipped off the light.

They waited in the dark.

Twenty seconds later, the elevator stopped on their floor.

Rebecca Schayes rarely thought about Elizabeth and Beck anymore. It had, after all, been eight years. But this morning events had stirred up some long-dormant sensations. Nagging sensations.

About the "car accident."

After all these years, Beck had finally asked her about it.

Eight years ago, Rebecca had been prepared to tell him all about it. But Beck hadn't returned her calls. As time went by—and after an arrest had been made—she saw no point in dredging up the past. It would only hurt Beck. And after KillRoy's arrest, it seemed irrelevant.

But the nagging sensation—the sensation that Elizabeth's bruises from the "car accident" were somehow a precursor to her murder—lingered, even though it made no sense. More than that, the nagging sensation taunted her, making her wonder if she, Rebecca, had insisted, *really* insisted, on finding out the truth about the "car accident," maybe, just maybe, she could have saved her friend.

The lingering, however, faded away over time. At the end of the day, Elizabeth had been her friend, and no matter how close you are, you get over a friend's death. Gary Lamont had come into her life three years ago and changed everything. Yes, Rebecca Schayes, the bohemian photographer from Greenwich Village, had fallen in love with a money-grubbing Wall Street bond trader. They'd gotten married and moved into a trendy highrise on the Upper West Side.

Funny how life worked.

Rebecca stepped into the freight elevator and slid the gate down. The lights were out, which was hardly unusual in this building. The elevator started heading up to her floor, the churning sound reverberating off the stone. Sometimes at night, she could hear the horses whinny, but they were silent now. The smell of hay and something probably fouler mingled in the air.

She liked being here at night. The way the solitude blended with the city's night noises made her feel her most "artsy."

Her mind started drifting back to the conversation she'd had last night with Gary. He wanted to move out of New York City, preferably to a spacious home on Long Island, at Sands Point, where he'd been raised. The idea of moving to the 'burbs horrified her. More than her love of the city, she knew that it would be the final betrayal of her bohemian roots. She would become what she swore she would never become: her mother and her mother's mother.

The elevator stopped. She lifted the gate and stepped down the corridor. All the lights were off up here. She pulled back her hair and tied it into a thick ponytail. She peered at her watch. Almost nine o'clock. The building would be empty. Of human beings at least.

Her shoes clacked against the cool cement. The truth was—and Rebecca was having a hard time accepting it, she being a bohemian and all—that the more she thought about it, the more she realized that yes, she wanted children, and that the city was a lousy place to raise them. Children need a backyard and swings and fresh air and . . .

Rebecca Schayes was just reaching a decision—a decision that would have no doubt thrilled her broker husband, Gary—when she stuck her key in the door and opened her studio. She went inside and flipped the light switch.

That was when she saw the weirdly shaped Asian man.

For a moment or two the man simply stared at her. Rebecca stood frozen in his gaze. Then the Asian man stepped to the side, almost behind her, and blasted a fist into the small of her back.

It was like a sledgehammer hit her kidney.

Rebecca crumbled to her knees. The man grabbed her neck with two fingers. He squeezed a pressure point. Rebecca saw bright lights. With his free hand, the man dug with fingers like ice picks under her rib cage. When they reached her liver, her eyes bulged. The pain was beyond anything she'd ever imagined. She tried to scream, but only a choking grunt escaped her mouth.

From across the room, a man's voice sliced through the haze.

"Where is Elizabeth?" the voice asked.

For the first time.

But not the last.

19

I stayed in front of that damn computer and started drinking pretty heavily. I tried logging onto the site a dozen different ways. I used Explorer and then I used Netscape. I cleared my cache and reloaded the pages and signed off my provider and signed back on again.

It didn't matter. I still got the error message.

At ten o'clock, Shauna headed back into the den. Her cheeks were glowing from drink. Mine too, I imagined. "No luck?"

"Go home," I said.

She nodded. "Yeah, I think I'd better."

The limousine was there in five minutes. Shauna wobbled to the curb, fairly wasted on bourbon and Rolling Rock. Me too.

Shauna opened the door and turned back to me. "Were you ever tempted to cheat? I mean, when you two were married."

"No," I said.

Shauna shook her head, disappointed. "You know nothing about how to mess up your life."

I kissed her good-bye and went back inside. I continued to gaze at the screen as though it were something holy. Nothing changed.

Chloe slowly approached a few minutes later. She nudged my hand with her wet nose. Through her forest of hair, our eyes met and I swear that Chloe understood what I was feeling. I'm not one of those who give human characteristics to dogs—for one thing, I think that it might demean them—but I do believe they have a base understanding of what their anthropological counterparts are feeling. They say that dogs can smell fear. Is it such a stretch to believe that they also smell joy or anger or sadness?

I smiled down at Chloe and petted her head. She put a paw on my arm in a comforting gesture. "You want to go for a walk, girl?" I said.

Chloe's reply was to bound about like a circus freak on speed. Like I told you before, it's the little things.

The night air tingled in my lungs. I tried to concentrate on Chloe—her frolicking step, her wagging tail—but I was, well, crestfallen. Crestfallen. That is not a word I use very often. But I thought it fit.

I hadn't fully bought Shauna's too-neat digital-trick hypothesis. Yes, someone could manipulate a photograph and make it part of a video. And yes, someone could have known about kiss time. And yes, someone could have even made the lips whisper "I'm sorry." And yes, my hunger probably helped make the illusion real and made me susceptible to such trickery.

And the biggest yes: Shauna's hypothesis made a hell of a lot more sense than a return from the grave.

But there were two things that overrode a lot of that. First off, I'm not one for flights of fancy. I'm frighteningly boring and more grounded than most. Second, the hunger could have clouded my reasoning, and digital photography could do a lot of things.

But not those eyes . . .

Her eyes. Elizabeth's eyes. There was no way, I thought, that they could be old photographs manipulated into a digital video. Those eyes belonged to my wife. Was my rational mind sure of it? No, of course not. I'm not a fool. But between what I saw and all the questions I'd raised, I had semi-dismissed Shauna's video demonstration. I had come home still believing that I was to receive a message from Elizabeth.

Now I didn't know what to think. The booze was probably helping in that respect.

Chloe stopped to do some prolonged sniffing. I waited under a streetlight and stared at my elongated shadow.

Kiss time.

Chloe barked at a movement in the bush. A squirrel sprinted across the street. Chloe growled and feigned a chase. The squirrel stopped and turned back toward us. Chloe barked a boy-you're-lucky-I'm-on-a-leash sound. She didn't mean it. Chloe was a pure thoroughbred wimp.

Kiss time.

I tilted my head the way Chloe does when she hears a strange sound. I thought again about what I had seen yesterday on my computer—and I thought about the pains someone had gone through to keep this whole thing secret. The unsigned email telling me to click the hyperlink at "kiss time." The second email setting up a new account in my name.

They're watching . . .

Someone was working hard to keep these communications under wraps.

Kiss time . . .

If someone—okay, if Elizabeth—had simply wanted to give me a message, why hadn't she just called or written it in an email? Why make me jump through all these hoops?

The answer was obvious: secrecy. Someone—I won't say Elizabeth again—wanted to keep it all a secret.

And if you have a secret, it naturally follows that you have someone you want to keep it secret from. And maybe that someone is watching or searching or trying to find you. Either that or you're paranoid. Normally I'd side with paranoid but ...

They're watching ...

What did that mean exactly? Who was watching? The feds? And if the feds were behind the emails in the first place, why would they warn me that way? The feds wanted me to act.

Kiss time ...

I froze. Chloe's head snapped in my direction.

Oh my God, how could I have been so stupid?

They hadn't bothered to use the duct tape.

Rebecca Schayes lay upon the table now, whimpering like a dying dog on the side of the road. Sometimes, she uttered words, two or even three at a time, but they never formed a coherent chain. She was too far gone to cry anymore. The begging had stopped. Her eyes were still wide and uncomprehending; they saw nothing now. Her mind had shattered mid-scream fifteen minutes ago.

Amazingly, Wu had left no marks. No marks, but she looked twenty years older.

Rebecca Schayes had known nothing. Dr. Beck had visited her because of an old car accident that wasn't really a car accident. There were pictures too. Beck had assumed she had taken them. She hadn't.

The creeping feeling in his stomach—the one that had started as a mere tickle when Larry Gandle first heard about the bodies being found at the lake—kept growing. Something had gone wrong that night. That much was certain. But now Larry Gandle feared that maybe everything had gone wrong.

It was time to flush out the truth.

He had checked with his surveillance man. Beck was taking his dog for a walk. Alone. In light of the evidence Wu would plant, that would be a terrible alibi. The feds would shred it for laughs.

Larry Gandle approached the table. Rebecca Schayes looked up and made an unearthly noise, a cross between a high-pitched groan and a wounded laugh.

He pressed the gun against her forehead. She made that sound again. He fired twice and all the world fell silent.

I started heading back to the house, but I thought about the warning.

They're watching.

Why take the chance? There was a Kinko's three blocks away. They stay open twenty-four hours a day. When I reached the door, I saw why. It was midnight, and the place was packed. Lots of exhausted business-people carrying papers and slides and poster boards.

I stood in a maze line formed by crushed-velvet ropes and waited my turn. It reminded me of visiting a bank in the days before ATMs. The woman in front of me sported a business suit—at midnight—and big enough bags under her eyes to be mistaken for a bellhop. Behind me, a man with curly hair and dark sweats whipped out a cell phone and started pressing buttons.

"Sir?"

Someone with a Kinko's smock pointed at Chloe.

"You can't come in here with a dog."

I was about to tell him I already had but thought better of it. The woman in the business suit didn't react. The curly-haired guy with the dark sweats gave me a what-are-you-gonna-do shrug. I rushed outside, tied

Chloe to a parking meter, headed back inside. The curly-haired man let me have my place back in line. Manners.

Ten minutes later, I was at the front of the line. This Kinko's clerk was young and overly exuberant. He showed me to a computer terminal and explained too slowly their per-minute pricing plan.

I nodded through his little speech and signed on to the Web.

Kiss time.

That, I realized, was the key. The first email had said kiss time, not 6:15 p.m. Why? The answer was obvious. That had been code—in case the wrong people got their hands on the email. Whoever had sent it had realized that the possibility of interception existed. Whoever had sent it had known that only I would know what kiss time meant.

That was when it came to me.

First off, the account name Bat Street. When Elizabeth and I were growing up, we used to ride our bikes down Morewood Street on the way to the Little League field. There was this creepy old woman who lived in a faded yellow house. She lived alone and scowled at passing kids. Every town has one of those creepy old ladies. She usually has a nickname. In our case, we'd called her:

Bat Lady.

I brought up Bigfoot again. I typed Morewood into the user name box.

Next to me, the young and exuberant Kinko's clerk was repeating his Web spiel to the curly-haired man with the dark sweat suit. I hit the tab button and moved into the text box for the password.

The clue Teenage was easier. In our junior year of

high school, we'd gone to Jordan Goldman's house late one Friday night. There were maybe ten of us. Jordan had found out where his father hid a porn video. None of us had ever seen one before. We all watched, laughing uncomfortably, making the usual snide remarks and feeling deliciously naughty. When we needed a name for our intramural softball team, Jordan suggested we use the movie's stupid title:

Teenage Sex Poodles.

I typed in Sex Poodles under the password. I swallowed hard and clicked the Sign In icon.

I glanced over at the curly-haired man. He was focused on a Yahoo! search. I looked back toward the front desk. The woman in the business suit was frowning at another too-happy-at-midnight Kinko's staff member.

I waited for the error message. But that didn't happen this time. A welcome screen rolled into view. On the top, it read: Hi, Morewood!

Underneath that it said: You have 1 email in your box.

My heart felt like a bird banging against my rib cage.

I clicked on the New Mail icon and did the leg shake again. No Shauna around to stop it. Through the store window I could see my tethered Chloe. She spotted me and started barking. I put a finger to my lips and signaled for her to hush up.

The email message appeared:

Washington Square Park. Meet me at the southeast corner
Five o'clock tomorrow.
You'll be followed.

And on the bottom:

No matter what, I love you.

Hope, that caged bird that just won't die, broke free. I leaned back. Tears flooded my eyes, but for the first time in a long while, I let loose a real smile.

Elizabeth. She was still the smartest person I knew.

20

At two a.m., I crawled into bed and rolled onto my back. The ceiling started doing the too-many-drinks spins. I grabbed the sides of the bed and hung on.

Shauna had earlier asked if I had ever been tempted to cheat after getting married. She'd added that last part—the "after getting married" part—because she already knew about the other incident.

Technically, I did cheat on Elizabeth once, though cheating doesn't really fit. Cheating denotes doing harm to another. It didn't harm Elizabeth—I'm sure of that— but during my freshman year of college, I partook in a rather pitiful rite of passage known as the collegiate one-night stand. Out of curiosity, I guess. Purely experimental and strictly physical. I didn't like it much. I'll spare you the corny sex-without-love-is-meaningless cliché. It's not. But while I think it's fairly easy to have sex with someone you don't particularly know or like, it's hard to stay the night. The attraction, as it were, was strictly hormonal. Once the, uh, release took place, I wanted out. Sex is for anyone; the aftermath is for lovers.

Pretty nice rationalization, don't you think?

If it matters, I suspect Elizabeth probably did something similar. We both agreed that we would try to "see"—"see" being such a vague, all-encompassing term—other people when we first got to college. Any indiscretion could thus be chalked up to yet another commitment test. Whenever the subject was raised, Elizabeth denied that there had ever been anyone else. But then again, so did I.

The bed continued to spin as I wondered: What do I do now?

For one thing, I wait for five o'clock tomorrow. But I couldn't just sit back until then. I'd done enough of that already, thank you very much. The truth was—a truth I didn't like to admit even to myself—I hesitated at the lake. Because I was scared. I climbed out of the water and paused. That gave whomever a chance to hit me. And I didn't fight back after that first strike. I didn't dive for my assailant. I didn't tackle him or even make a fist. I simply went down. I covered up and surrendered and let the stronger man take away my wife.

Not again.

I considered approaching my father-in-law again—it hadn't escaped my attention that Hoyt might have been less than forthcoming during my previous visit—but what good would that do? Hoyt was either lying or ... or I don't know what. But the message had been clear. *Tell no one.* The only way I could maybe get him to talk would be by telling him what I saw on that street cam. But I wasn't ready to do that yet.

I got out of bed and hopped on the computer. I started surfing again. By morning, I had something of a plan.

Gary Lamont, Rebecca Schayes's husband, didn't panic right away. His wife often worked late, very late, sometimes spending the night on an old cot in the far right corner of her studio. So when four in the morning rolled around and Rebecca still wasn't home, he grew only concerned, not panicked.

At least, that's what he told himself.

Gary called her studio, but the answering machine picked up. Again that wasn't rare. When Rebecca was working, she hated interruptions. She didn't even keep a phone extension in the darkroom. He left a message and settled back into their bed.

Sleep came in fits and spurts. Gary contemplated doing something more, but that would only piss off Rebecca. She was a free spirit, and if there was a tension in their otherwise fulfilling relationship, it had to do with his relatively "traditional" lifestyle "clipping" her creative wings. Her terms.

So he gave her space. To unclip her wings or whatever.

By seven in the morning, concern had segued into something closer to genuine fear. Gary's call woke up Arturo Ramirez, Rebecca's gaunt, black-clad assistant.

"I just got in," Arturo complained groggily.

Gary explained the situation. Arturo, who had fallen asleep in his clothes, did not bother changing. He ran out the door. Gary promised to meet him at the studio. He hopped on the downtown A.

Arturo arrived first and found the studio door ajar. He pushed it open.

"Rebecca?"

No answer. Arturo called her name again. Still no answer. He entered and scanned the studio. She wasn't there. He opened the darkroom door. The usual harsh smell of film-development acids still dominated, but there was something else, something faint and below the surface that still had the ability to make his hair stand on end.

Something distinctly human.

Gary rounded the corner in time to hear the scream.

21

In the morning, I grabbed a bagel and headed west on Route 80 for forty-five minutes. Route 80 in New Jersey is a fairly nondescript strip of pavement. Once you get past Saddle Brook or so, the buildings pretty much vanish and you're faced with identical lines of trees on either side of the road. Only the interstate signs break up the monotony.

As I veered off exit 163 at a town called Gardensville, I slowed the car and looked out at the high grass. My heart started thumping. I had never been here before—I'd purposely avoided this stretch of interstate for the past eight years—but it was here, less than a hundred yards from where I now drove, that they found Elizabeth's body.

I checked the directions I'd printed off last night. The Sussex County coroner's office was on Mapquest.com, so I knew to the tenth of a kilometer how to get there. The building was a blinds-closed storefront with no sign or window lettering, a plain brick rectangle with no frills, but then again, did you want any at a morgue? I arrived a few minutes before eight-thirty and pulled around back. The office was still locked up. Good.

A canary-yellow Cadillac Seville pulled into a spot marked Timothy Harper, County Medical Examiner. The man in the car stubbed out a cigarette—it never ceases to amaze me how many M.E.'s smoke—before he stepped out. Harper was my height, a shade under six feet, with olive skin and wispy gray hair. He saw me standing by the door and set his face. People didn't visit morgues first thing in the morning to hear good news.

He took his time approaching me. "Can I help you?" he said.

"Dr. Harper?"

"Yes, that's right."

"I'm Dr. David Beck." Doctor. So we were colleagues. "I'd like a moment of your time."

He didn't react to the name. He took out a key and unlocked the door. "Why don't we sit in my office?"

"Thank you."

I followed him down a corridor. Harper flicked light switches. The ceiling fluorescents popped on grudgingly and one at a time. The floor was scratched linoleum. The place looked less like a house of death than a faceless DMV office, but maybe that was the point. Our footsteps echoed, mixing with the buzzing from the lights as though keeping the beat. Harper picked up a stack of mail and quick-sorted it as we walked.

Harper's private office, too, was no-frills. There was the same metal desk you might find a teacher using in an elementary school. The chairs were overvarnished wood, strictly functional. Several diplomas spotted one wall. He'd gone to medical school at Columbia, too, I saw, though he'd graduated almost twenty years before me. No family photographs, no golf trophy, no Lucite announcements, nothing personal. Visitors to this office were not in for pleasant chitchat. The last thing they needed to see was someone's smiling grandkids.

Harper folded his hands and put them on the desk. "What can I do for you, Dr. Beck?"

"Eight years ago," I began, "my wife was brought here. She was the victim of a serial killer known as KillRoy."

I'm not particularly good at reading faces. Eye contact has never been my forte. Body language means little to me. But as I watched Harper, I couldn't help but wonder what would make a practiced medical examiner, a man who oft dwelled in the world of the dead, blanch so.

"I remember," he said softly.

"You did the autopsy?"

"Yes. Well, in part."

"In part?"

"Yes. The federal authorities were involved too. We worked on the case in tandem, though the FBI doesn't have coroners, so we took the lead."

"Back up a minute," I said. "Tell me what you saw when they first brought the body in."

Harper shifted in his seat. "May I ask why you want to know this?"

"I'm a grieving husband."

"It was eight years ago."

"We all grieve in our own way, Doctor."

"Yes, I'm sure that's true, but—"

"But what?"

"But I'd like to know what you want here."

I decided to take the direct route. "You take pictures of every corpse brought in here, right?"

He hesitated. I saw it. He saw me seeing it and cleared his throat. "Yes. Currently, we use digital technology. A digital camera, in other words. It allows us to store photographs and various images on a computer. We find it helpful for both diagnosis and cataloguing."

I nodded, not caring. He was chattering. When he didn't continue, I said, "Did you take pictures of my wife's autopsy?"

"Yes, of course. But—how long ago did you say again?"

"Eight years."

"We would have taken Polaroids."

"And where would those Polaroids be right now, Doctor?"

"In the file."

I looked at the tall filing cabinet standing in the corner like a sentinel.

"Not in there," he added quickly. "Your wife's case is closed. Her killer was caught and convicted. Plus it was more than five years ago."

"So where would it be?"

"In a storage facility. In Layton."

"I'd like to see the photographs, if I could."

He jotted something down and nodded at the scrap of paper. "I'll look into it."

"Doctor?"

He looked up.

"You said you remember my wife."

"Well, yes, I mean, somewhat. We don't have many murders here, especially ones so high profile."

"Do you remember the condition of her body?"

"Not really. I mean, not details or anything."

"Do you remember who identified her?"

"You didn't?"

"No."

Harper scratched his temple. "Her father, wasn't it?"

"Do you remember how long it took for him to make an identification?"

"How long?"

"Was it immediate? Did it take a few minutes? Five minutes, ten minutes?"

"I really couldn't say."

"You don't remember if it was immediate or not?"

"I'm sorry, I don't."

"You just said this was a big case."

"Yes."

"Maybe your biggest?"

"We had that pizza delivery thrill kill a few years ago," he said. "But, yes, I'd say it was one of the biggest."

"And yet you don't remember if her father had trouble identifying the body?"

He didn't like that. "Dr. Beck, with all due respect, I don't see what you're getting at."

"I'm a grieving husband. I'm asking some simple questions."

"Your tone," he said. "It seems hostile."

"Should it be?"

"What on earth does that mean?"

"How did you know she was a victim of KillRoy's?"

"I didn't."

"So how did the feds get involved?"

"There were identifying marks—"

"You mean that she was branded with the letter K?"

"Yes."

I was on a roll now, and it felt oddly right. "So the police brought her in. You started examining her. You spotted the letter K—"

"No, they were here right away. The federal authorities, I mean."

"Before the body got here?"

He looked up, either remembering or fabricating. "Or immediately thereafter. I don't remember."

"How did they know about the body so quickly?"

"I don't know."

"You have no idea?"

Harper folded his arms across his chest. "I might surmise that one of the officers on the scene spotted the branding and called the FBI. But that would only be an educated guess."

My beeper vibrated against my hip. I checked it. The clinic with an emergency.

"I'm sorry for your loss," he said in a practiced tone. "I understand the pain you must be going through, but I have a very busy schedule today. Perhaps you can make an appointment at a later date—"

"How long will it take you to get my wife's file?" I asked.

"I'm not even sure I can do that. I mean, I'll have to check—"

"The Freedom of Information Act."

"Pardon me?"

"I looked it up this morning. My wife's case is closed now. I have the right to view her file."

Harper had to know that—I wasn't the first person to ask for an autopsy file—and he started nodding a little too vigorously. "Still, there are proper channels you have to go through, forms to fill out."

"Are you stalling?" I said.

"Excuse me?"

"My wife was the victim of a terrible crime."

"I understand that."

"And I have the right to view my wife's file. If you drag your feet on this, I'm going to wonder why. I've never spoken to the media about my wife or her killer. I'll gladly do so now. And we'll all be wondering why the local M.E. gave me such a hard time over such a simple request."

"That sounds like a threat, Dr. Beck."

I got to my feet. "I'll be back here tomorrow morning," I said. "Please have my wife's file ready."

I was taking action. It felt damn good.

22

Detectives Roland Dimonte and Kevin Krinsky of the NYPD's homicide division arrived first on the scene, even before the uniforms. Dimonte, a greasy-haired man who favored hideous snakeskin boots and an over-chewed toothpick, took the lead. He barked orders. The crime scene was immediately sealed. A few minutes later, lab technicians from the Crime Scene Unit skulked in and spread out.

"Isolate the witnesses," Dimonte said.

There were only two: the husband and the fey weirdo in black. Dimonte noted that the husband appeared distraught, though that could be an act. But first things first.

Dimonte, still chewing on the toothpick, took the fey weirdo—his name, figures, was Arturo—to the side. The kid looked pale. Normally, Dimonte would guess drugs, but the guy had tossed his cookies when he found the body.

"You okay?" Dimonte asked. Like he cared.

Arturo nodded.

Dimonte asked him if anything unusual had happened involving the victim lately. Yes, Arturo replied. What would that be? Rebecca got a phone call yesterday that disturbed her. Who called? Arturo was not sure, but an hour later—maybe less, Arturo couldn't be sure—a man stopped by to see Rebecca. When the man left, Rebecca was a wreck.

Do you remember the man's name?

"Beck," Arturo said. "She called the guy Beck."

Shauna put Mark's sheets in the dryer. Linda came up behind her.

"He's wetting his bed again," Linda said.

"God, you're perceptive."

"Don't be mean." Linda walked away. Shauna opened her mouth to apologize, but nothing came out. When she had moved out the first time—the only time—Mark had reacted badly. It started with bed-wetting. When she and Linda reunited, the bed-wetting stopped. Until now.

"He knows what's going on," Linda said. "He can feel the tension."

"What do you want me to do about that, Linda?"

"Whatever we have to."

"I'm not moving out again. I promised."

"Clearly, that's not enough."

Shauna tossed a sheet of fabric softener into the dryer. Exhaustion lined her face. She didn't need this. She was a big-money model. She couldn't arrive at work with bags under her eyes or a lack of sheen in her hair. She didn't need this shit.

She was tired of it all. Tired of a domesticity that didn't sit well with her. Tired of the pressure from damn do-gooders. Forget the bigotry, that was easy. But the pressure on a lesbian couple with a child—applied by supposedly well-meaning supporters—was beyond suffocating. If the relationship failed, it was a failure for all lesbianism or some such crap, as though hetero couples never break up. Shauna was not a crusader. She knew that. Selfish or not, her happiness would not be sacrificed on the altar of "greater good."

She wondered if Linda felt the same way.

"I love you," Linda said.

"I love you too."

They looked at each other. Mark was wetting his bed again. Shauna wouldn't sacrifice herself for the greater good. But she would for Mark.

"So what do we do?" Linda asked.

"We work it out."

"You think we can?"

"You love me?"

"You know I do," Linda said.

"Do you still think I'm the most exciting, wonderful creature on God's green earth?"

"Oh, yeah," Linda said.

"Me too." Shauna smiled at her. "I'm a narcissistic pain in the ass."

"Oh, yeah."

"But I'm your narcissistic pain in the ass."

"Damn straight."

Shauna moved closer. "I'm not destined for a life of easy relationships. I'm volatile."

"You're sexy as hell when you're volatile," Linda said.

"And even when I'm not."

"Shut up and kiss me."

The downstairs door buzzer sounded. Linda looked at Shauna. Shauna shrugged. Linda pressed the intercom and said, "Yes?"

"Is this Linda Beck?"

"Who is this?"

"I'm Special Agent Kimberly Green with the Federal Bureau of Investigation. I'm with my partner, Special Agent Rick Peck. We'd like to come up and ask you some questions."

Shauna leaned over before Linda could respond. "Our attorney's name is Hester Crimstein," she shouted into the intercom. "You can call her."

"You're not suspects in any crime. We just want to ask you some questions—"

"Hester Crimstein," Shauna interrupted. "I'm sure you have her number. Have a really special day."

Shauna released the button. Linda looked at her. "What the hell was that?"

"Your brother's in trouble."

"What?"

"Sit down," Shauna said. "We need to talk."

Raisa Markov, a nurse who cared for Dr. Beck's grandfather, answered the firm knock. Special agents Carlson and Stone, now working in conjunction with NYPD detectives Dimonte and Krinsky, handed her the document.

"Federal warrant," Carlson announced.

Raisa stepped aside without reacting. She had grown up in the Soviet Union. Police aggression did not faze her.

Eight of Carlson's men flooded into the Beck abode and fanned out.

"I want everything videotaped," Carlson called out. "No mistakes."

They were moving fast in the hope of staying a half-step ahead of Hester Crimstein. Carlson knew that Crimstein, like many a natty defense attorney in this post-OJ era, clung to the claims of police incompetence and/or misconduct like a desperate suitor. Carlson, a rather natty law enforcement officer in his own right, would not let that happen here. Every step/movement/breath would be documented and corroborated.

When Carlson and Stone first burst into Rebecca Schayes's studio, Dimonte had not been happy to see him. There had been the usual local-cops-versus-feds macho-turf posturing. Few things unify the FBI and the local authorities, especially in a big city like New York.

But Hester Crimstein was one of those things.

Both sides knew that Crimstein was a master obscurer and publicity hound. The world would be watching. No one wanted to screw up. That was the driving force here. So they forged an alliance with all the trust of a Palestinian-Israeli handshake, because in the end, both sides knew that they needed to gather and nail down the evidence fast—before Crimstein mucked up the waters.

The feds had gotten the search warrant. For them, it was a simple matter of walking across Federal Plaza to the southern district federal court. If Dimonte and the NYPD had wanted to get one, they'd have had to go to the county courthouse in New Jersey—too much time with Hester Crimstein lurking at their heels.

"Agent Carlson!"

The shout came from the street corner. Carlson sprinted outside, Stone waddling behind him. Dimonte and Krinsky followed. At the curb, a young federal agent stood next to an open trash canister.

"What is it?" Carlson asked.

"Might be nothing, sir, but . . ." The young federal agent pointed down to what looked like a hastily discarded pair of latex gloves.

"Bag them," Carlson said. "I want a gun residue test done right away." Carlson looked over to Dimonte. Time for more cooperation—this time, via competition. "How long will it take to get done at your lab?"

"A day," Dimonte said. He had a fresh toothpick in his mouth now and was working it over pretty well.

"Maybe two."

"No good. We'll have to fly the samples down to our lab at Quantico."

"Like hell you will," Dimonte snapped.

"We agreed to go with what's fastest."

"Staying here is fastest," Dimonte said. "I'll see to that."

Carlson nodded. It was as he expected. If you wanted the local cops to make the case a big-time priority, threaten to take it away from them. Competition. It was a good thing.

Half an hour later, they heard another cry, this time coming from the garage. Again they sprinted in that direction.

Stone whistled low. Dimonte stared. Carlson bent down for a better look.

There, under the newspapers in a recycle bin, sat a nine-millimeter handgun. A quick sniff told them the gun had recently been fired.

Stone turned to Carlson. He made sure that his smile was off camera.

"Got him," Stone said softly.

Carlson said nothing. He watched the technician bag the weapon. Then, thinking it all through, he began to frown.

23

The emergency call on my beeper involved TJ. He scraped his arm on a doorjamb. For most kids, that meant a stinging spray of Bactine; for TJ, it meant a night in the hospital. By the time I got there, they had already hooked him up to an IV. You treat hemophilia by administering blood products such as cryoprecipitate or frozen plasma. I had a nurse start him up right away.

As I mentioned earlier, I first met Tyrese six years ago when he was in handcuffs and screaming obscenities. An hour earlier, he had rushed his then nine-month-old son, TJ, into the emergency room. I was there, but I wasn't working the acute side. The attending physician handled TJ.

TJ was unresponsive and lethargic. His breathing was shallow. Tyrese, who behaved, according to the chart, "erratically" (how, I wondered, was a father who rushes an infant to an emergency room supposed to act?), told the attending physician that the boy had been getting worse all day. The attending physician gave his nurse a knowing glance. The nurse nodded and went to make the call. Just in case.

A fundoscopic examination revealed that the infant had multiple retinal hemorrhages bilaterally—that is, the blood vessels in the back of both eyes had exploded. When the physician put the pieces together—retinal bleeding, heavy lethargy, and, well, the father—he made a diagnosis:

Shaken baby syndrome.

Armed security guards arrived in force. They hand-cuffed Tyrese, and that was when I heard the screamed obscenities. I rounded the corner to see what was up. Two uniformed members of the NYPD arrived. So did a weary woman from ACS—aka the Administration for Children Services. Tyrese tried to plead his case. Everybody shook their heads in that what's-this-world-coming-to way.

I'd witnessed scenes like this a dozen times at the hospital. In fact, I'd seen a lot worse. I'd treated three-year-old girls with venereal diseases. I once ran a rape kit on a four-year-old boy with internal bleeding. In both cases—and in all similar abuse cases I'd been involved with—the perpetrator was either a family member or the mother's most recent boyfriend.

The Bad Man isn't lurking in playgrounds, kiddies. He lives in your house.

I also knew—and this statistic never failed to stagger me—that more than ninety-five percent of serious intracranial injuries in infants were due to child abuse. That made it pretty damn good—or bad, depending on your vantage point—odds that Tyrese had abused his son.

In this emergency room, we've heard all the excuses. The baby fell off the couch. The oven door landed on the baby's head. His older brother dropped a toy on him. You work here long enough, you grow more cynical than the most weathered city cop. The truth is, healthy children tolerate those sorts of accidental blows well. It is very rare that, say, a fall off a couch alone causes retinal hemorrhaging.

I had no problem with the child abuse diagnosis. Not at first blush anyway.

But something about the way Tyrese pleaded his case struck me odd. It was not that I thought he was innocent. I'm not above making quick judgments based on appearance—or, to use a more politically current term, racial profiling. We all do it. If you cross the street to avoid a gang of black teens, you're racial profiling; if you don't cross because you're afraid you'll look like a racist, you're racial profiling; if you see the gang and think nothing whatsoever, you're from some planet I've never visited.

What made me pause here was the pure dichotomy. I had seen a frighteningly similar case during my recent rotation out in the wealthy suburb of Short Hills, New Jersey. A white mother and father, both impeccably dressed and driving a well-equipped Range Rover, rushed their six-month-old daughter into the emergency room. The daughter, their third child, presented the same as TJ.

Nobody shackled the father.

So I moved toward Tyrese. He gave me the ghetto glare. On the street, it fazed me; in here, it was like the big bad wolf blowing at the brick house. "Was your son born at this hospital?" I asked.

Tyrese didn't reply.

"Was your son born here, yes or no?"

He calmed down enough to say "Yeah."

"Is he circumcised?"

Tyrese relit the glare. "You some kind of faggot?"

"You mean there's more than one kind?' I countered. "Was he circumcised here, yes or no?"

Grudgingly, Tyrese said, "Yeah."

I found TJ's social security number and plugged it into the computer. His records came up. I checked under the circumcision. Normal. Damn. But then I saw another entry. This was not TJ's first visit to the hospital. At the age of two weeks, his father brought him in because of a bleeding umbilicus—bleeding from the umbilical cord.

Curious.

We ran some blood tests then, though the police insisted on keeping Tyrese in custody. Tyrese didn't argue. He just wanted the tests done. I tried to have them rushed, but I have no power in this bureaucracy. Few do. Still the lab was able to ascertain through the blood samples that the partial thromboplastin time was prolonged, yet both the prothrombin time and platelet count were normal. Yeah, yeah, but bear with me.

The best—and worst—was confirmed. The boy had not been abused by his ghetto-garbed father. Hemophilia caused the retinal hemorrhages. They had also left the boy blind.

The security guards sighed and uncuffed Tyrese and walked away without a word. Tyrese rubbed his wrists. Nobody apologized or offered a word of sympathy to this man who had been falsely accused of abusing his now-blind son.

Imagine that in the wealthy 'burbs.

TJ has been my patient ever since.

Now, in his hospital room, I stroked TJ's head and looked into his unseeing eyes. Kids usually look at me with undiluted awe, a heady cross between fear and worship. My colleagues believe that children have a deeper understanding than adults of what is happening to them. I think the answer is probably simpler. Children view their parents as both intrepid and omnipotent—yet here their parents are, gazing up at me, the doctor, with a fear-filled longing normally reserved for religious rapture.

What could be more terrifying to a small child?

A few minutes later, TJ's eyes closed. He drifted off to sleep.

"He just bumped into the side of the door," Tyrese said. "That was all. He's blind. Gonna happen, right?"

"We'll need to keep him overnight," I said. "But he'll be fine."

"How?" Tyrese looked at me. "How will he ever be all right when he can't stop bleeding?"

I had no answer.

"I gotta get him out of here."

He didn't mean the hospital.

Tyrese reached into his pocket and started peeling off bills. I wasn't in the mood. I held up a hand and said, "I'll check back later."

"Thanks for coming, Doc. I appreciate it."

I was about to remind him that I had come for his son, not him, but I opted for silence.

Careful, Carlson thought, while his pulse raced. Be oh so careful.

The four of them—Carlson, Stone, Krinsky, and Dimonte—sat at a conference table with Assistant District Attorney Lance Fein. Fein, an ambitious weasel with constantly undulating eyebrows and a face so waxy that it looked ready to melt in extreme heat, strapped on his game face.

Dimonte said, "Let's bust his sorry ass."

"One more time," Lance Fein said. "Put it together for me so that even Alan Dershowitz would want him locked up."

Dimonte nodded at his partner. "Go ahead, Krinsky. Make me wet."

Krinsky took out his pad and started reading:

"Rebecca Schayes was shot twice in the head at very close range with a nine-millimeter automatic pistol. Under a federally issued warrant, a nine-millimeter was located in Dr. David Beck's garage."

"Fingerprints on the gun?" Fein asked.

"None. But a ballistic test confirmed that the nine-millimeter found in Dr. Beck's garage is the murder weapon."

Dimonte smiled and raised his eyebrows. "Anybody else getting hard nipples?"

Fein's eyebrows knitted and dropped. "Please continue," he said.

"Under the same federally issued warrant, a pair of latex gloves was retrieved from a trash canister at Dr. David Beck's residence. Gunpowder residue was found on the right glove. Dr. Beck is right-handed."

Dimonte put up his snakeskin boots and moved the toothpick across his mouth. "Oh, yeah, baby, harder, harder. I like it like that."

Fein frowned. Krinsky, his eyes never leaving the pad, licked a finger and turned the page.

"On the same right-hand latex glove, the lab discovered a hair that has been positively color matched to Rebecca Schayes."

"Oh God! Oh God!" Dimonte started screaming in fake orgasm. Or maybe it was real.

"A conclusive DNA test will take more time," Krinsky went on. "Moreover, fingerprints belonging to Dr. David Beck were found at the murder scene, though not in the darkroom where her body was found."

Krinsky closed up his notebook. All eyes turned to Lance Fein.

Fein stood and rubbed his chin. Dimonte's behavior notwithstanding, they were all suppressing a bit of giddiness. The room crackled with pre-arrest sparks, that heady, addictive high that came with the really infamous cases. There would be press conferences and calls from politicians and pictures in the paper.

Only Nick Carlson remained the tiniest bit apprehensive. He sat twisting and untwisting and retwisting a paper clip. He couldn't stop. Something had crawled into his periphery, hanging on the edges, still out of sight, but there, and irksome as all hell. For one thing, there were the listening devices in Dr. Beck's home. Someone had been bugging him. Tapping his phone too. Nobody seemed to know or care why.

"Lance?" It was Dimonte.

Lance Fein cleared his throat. "Do you know where Dr. Beck is right now?" he asked.

"At his clinic," Dimonte said. "I got two uniforms keeping an eye on him."

Fein nodded.

"Come on, Lance," Dimonte said. "Give it to me, big boy."

"Let's call Ms. Crimstein first," Fein said. "As a courtesy."

Shauna told Linda most of it. She left out the part about Beck's "seeing" Elizabeth on the computer. Not because she gave the story any credence. She'd pretty much proven that it was a digital hoax. But Beck had been adamant. Tell no one. She didn't like having secrets from Linda, but that was preferable to betraying Beck's confidence.

Linda watched Shauna's eyes the whole time. She didn't nod or speak or even move. When Shauna finished, Linda asked, "Did you see the pictures?"

"No."

"Where did the police get them?"

"I don't know."

Linda stood. "David would never hurt Elizabeth."

"I know that."

Linda wrapped her arms around herself. She started sucking in deep breaths. Her face drained of color.

"You okay?" Shauna said.

"What aren't you telling me?"

"What makes you think I'm not telling you something?"

Linda just looked at her.

"Ask your brother," Shauna said.

"Why?"

"It's not my place to tell."

The door buzzed again. Shauna took it this time.

"Yeah?"

Through the speaker: "It's Hester Crimstein."

Shauna hit the release button and left their door open. Two minutes later, Hester hurried into the room.

"Do you two know a photographer named Rebecca Schayes?"

"Sure," Shauna said. "I mean, I haven't seen her in a long time. Linda?"

"It's been years," Linda agreed. "She and Elizabeth shared an apartment downtown. Why?"

"She was murdered last night," Hester said. "They think Beck killed her."

Both women froze as though someone had just slapped them. Shauna recovered first.

"But I was with Beck last night," she said. "At his house."

"Till what time?"

"Till what time do you need?"

Hester frowned. "Don't play games with me, Shauna.

What time did you leave the house?"

"Ten, ten-thirty. What time was she killed?"

"I don't know yet. But I have a source inside. He said they have a very solid case against him."

"That's nuts."

A cell phone sounded. Hester Crimstein snatched hers up and pressed it against her ear. "What?"

The person on the other end spoke for what seemed a long time. Hester listened in silence. Her features started softening in something like defeat. A minute or two later, without saying good-bye, she closed the phone with a vicious snap.

"A courtesy call," she mumbled.

"What?"

"They're arresting your brother. We have an hour to surrender him to authorities."

24

All I could think about was Washington Square Park. True, I wasn't supposed to be there for another four hours. But emergencies notwithstanding, today was my day off. Free as a bird, as Lynyrd Skynyrd would sing— and this bird wanted to flock down to Washington Square Park.

I was on my way out of the clinic when my beeper once again sang its miserable song. I sighed and checked the number. It was Hester Crimstein's cell phone. And it was coded for an emergency.

This couldn't be good news.

For a moment or two, I debated not calling back— just continuing to flock—but what would be the point in that? I backpedaled to my examining room. The door was closed, and the red lever was slid into place. That meant another doctor was using the room.

I headed down the corridor, turned left, and found an empty room in the ob-gyn section of the clinic. I felt like a spy in enemy camp. The room gleamed with too much metal. Surrounded by stirrups and other devices that looked frighteningly medieval, I dialed the number.

Hester Crimstein did not bother with hello: "Beck, we got a big problem. Where are you?"

"I'm at the clinic. What's going on?"

"Answer a question for me," Hester Crimstein said. "When was the last time you saw Rebecca Schayes?"

My heart started doing a deep, slow thud. "Yesterday. Why?"

"And before that?"

"Eight years ago."

Crimstein let loose a low curse.

"What's going on?" I asked.

"Rebecca Schayes was murdered last night in her studio. Somebody shot her twice in the head."

A plunging feeling, the one you get moments before you fall asleep. My legs wobbled. I landed with a thump on a stool. "Oh Christ . . ."

"Beck, listen to me. Listen closely."

I remembered how Rebecca looked yesterday.

"Where were you last night?"

I pulled the phone away and sucked in some air. Dead. Rebecca was dead. Oddly I kept flashing to the sheen in her beautiful hair. I thought about her husband. I thought about what the nights would bring, lying in that bed, thinking about how that hair used to fan across the pillow.

"Beck?"

"Home," I said. "I was home with Shauna."

"And after that?"

"I took a walk."

"Where?"

"Around."

"Where around?"

I did not reply.

"Listen to me, Beck, okay? They found the murder weapon at your house."

I heard the words, but their meaning was having trouble reaching the cerebrum. The room suddenly felt cramped. There were no windows. It was hard to breathe.

"Do you hear me?"

"Yes," I said. Then, sort of understanding, I said, "That's not possible."

"Look, we don't have time for that now. You're about to be arrested. I spoke to the D.A. in charge. He's a prick and a half, but he agreed to let you surrender."

"Arrested?"

"Stay with me here, Beck."

"I didn't do anything."

"That's irrelevant right now. They're going to arrest you. They're going to arraign you. Then we're going to get you bail. I'm on my way over to the clinic now. To pick you up. Sit tight. Don't say anything to anyone, you hear me? Not to the cops, not to the feds, not to your new buddy in lockup. You understand?"

My gaze got snagged on the clock above the examining table. It was a few minutes after two. Washington Square. I thought about Washington Square. "I can't be arrested, Hester."

"It'll be all right."

"How long?" I said.

"How long what?"

"Until I get bail."

"Can't say for sure. I don't think bail per se will be a problem. You have no record. You're an upstanding member of the community with roots and ties. You'll probably have to surrender your passport—"

"But how long?"

"How long until what, Beck? I don't understand."

"Until I get out."

"Look, I'll try to push them, okay? But even if they rush it—and I'm not saying they will—they still have to send your fingerprints to Albany. That's the rule. If we're lucky—I mean very lucky—we can get you arraigned by midnight."

Midnight?

Fear wrapped itself around my chest like steel bands. Jail meant missing the meet at Washington Square Park. My connection with Elizabeth was so damn fragile, like strands of Venetian glass. If I'm not at Washington Square at five o'clock . . .

"No good," I said.

"What?"

"You have to stall them, Hester. Have them arrest me tomorrow."

"You're kidding, right? Look, they're probably there already, watching you."

I leaned my head out the door and looked down the corridor. I could see only part of the reception desk from my angle, the corner near the right, but it was enough.

There were two cops, maybe more.

"Oh Christ," I said, falling back into the room.

"Beck?"

"I can't go to jail," I said again. "Not today."

"Don't freak out on me here, Beck, okay? Just stay there. Don't move, don't talk, don't do anything. Sit in your office and wait. I'm on my way."

She hung up.

Rebecca was dead. They thought I killed her. Ridiculous, of course, but there had to be a connection. I visited her yesterday for the first time in eight years. That very night she ended up dead.

What the hell was going on here?

I opened the door and peeked my head out. The cops weren't looking my way. I slid out and started down the corridor. There was a back emergency exit. I could sneak out that way. I could make my way down to Washington Square Park.

Was this for real? Was I really going to run away

from the police?

I didn't know. But when I reached the door, I risked a look behind me. One of the cops spotted me. He pointed and hurried toward me.

I pushed open the door and ran.

I couldn't believe this. I was running from the police.

The exit door banged into a dark street directly behind the clinic. The street was unfamiliar to me. That might sound strange, but this neighborhood was not mine. I came, I worked, I left. I stayed locked inside a windowless environment, sickened by the lack of sunshine like some dour owl. One parallel block from where I worked and I was in totally alien territory.

I veered right for no particular reason. Behind me I heard the door fling open.

"Stop! Police!"

They actually yelled that. I didn't let up. Would they shoot? I doubted it. Not with all the repercussions in shooting an unarmed man who was in the midst of fleeing. Not impossible—not in this neighborhood anyway—but unlikely.

There weren't many people on this block, but those who were there regarded me with little more than passing, channel-surfing interest. I kept running. The world passed by in a blur. I sprinted past a dangerous-looking man with a dangerous-looking rottweiler. Old men sat at the corner and whined about the day. Women carried too many bags. Kids who probably should have been in school leaned against whatever was available, one cooler than the next.

Me, I was running away from the police.

My mind was having difficulty wrapping itself around that one. My legs were already feeling tingly, but the image of Elizabeth looking into that camera kept shoving me forward, pumping me up.

I was breathing too fast.

You hear about adrenaline, how it spurs you on and gives you uncanny strength, but there's a flip side. The feeling is heady, out of control. It heightens your senses to the point of paralysis. You have to harness the power or it'll choke you down.

I dove down an alleyway—that was what they always do on TV—but it dead-ended into a group of the foulest Dumpsters on the planet. The stench made me draw up like a horse. At one time, maybe when LaGuardia was mayor, the Dumpsters might have been green. All that remained was rust. In many places the rust ate through the metal, facilitating the many rats that poured through like sludge through a pipe.

I looked for some outlet, a door or something, but there was nothing. No back exit at all. I considered smashing a window to gain access, but all the lower ones were barred.

The only way out was the way I'd come in—where the police undoubtedly would see me.

I was trapped.

I looked left, right, and then, oddly enough, I looked up.

Fire escapes.

There were several above my head. Still mining my internal adrenaline drip, I leapt with all my might, stretched high with both hands, and fell flat on my ass. I tried again. Not even close. The ladders were far too high.

Now what?

Maybe I could somehow drag over a Dumpster, stand on it, and leap again. But the tops of the Dumpsters had been totally eaten away. Even if I could get footing on the piles of trash, it would still be too low.

I sucked in air and tried to think. The stench was getting to me; it crawled into my nose and seemed to nest there. I moved back toward the mouth of the alley.

Radio static. Like something you might hear coming from a police radio.

I threw my back against the wall and listened.

Hide. Had to hide.

The static grew louder. I heard voices. The cops were coming closer. I was totally exposed. I flattened myself closer to the wall, like that would help. Like they might turn the corner and mistake me for a mural.

Sirens shattered the still air.

Sirens for me.

Footsteps. They were definitely coming closer. There was only one place to hide.

I quickly discerned which Dumpster might be the least foul, closed my eyes, and dove in.

Sour milk. Very sour milk. That was the first smell that hit me. But it wasn't the only one. Something approaching vomit and worse. I was sitting in it. Something wet and putrid. It was sticking to me. My throat decided to do the gag reflex. My stomach heaved.

I heard someone run by the mouth of the alley. I stayed low.

A rat scrambled over my leg.

I almost screamed, but something in the subconscious kept it in the voice box. God, this was surreal. I held my breath. That lasted only so long. I tried to breathe through my mouth, but I started gagging again. I pressed my shirt against my nose and mouth. That helped, but not much.

The radio static was gone. So, too, were the footsteps. Did I fool them? If so, not for long. More police sirens joined in, harmonizing with the others, a true rhapsody in blue. The cops would have backup now. Someone would return soon. They would check the alley. Then what?

I grabbed hold of the Dumpster's edge to hoist myself out. The rust cut my palm. My hand flew toward my mouth. Bleeding. The pediatrician in me immediately scolded about the dangers of tetanus; the rest of me noted that tetanus would be the least of my worries.

I listened.

No footsteps. No blasts of radio static. Sirens wailed, but what had I expected? More backup. A murderer was on the loose in our fair city. The good guys would come out in force. They'd seal the area and throw a dragnet around it.

How far had I run?

I couldn't say. But I knew one thing. I had to keep moving. I had to put distance between the clinic and my person.

That meant getting out of this alley.

I crept toward the mouth again. Still no footsteps or radio. Good sign. I tried to think for a moment. Fleeing was a great plan, but a destination would make it even better. Keep heading east, I decided, even though it meant less safe neighborhoods. I remember seeing train tracks aboveground.

The subway.

That would get me out of here. All I had to do was get on a train, make a few sudden switches, and I could probably manage to disappear. But where was the closest entrance?

I was trying to conjure up my internal subway map, when a policeman turned into the alley.

He looked so young, so clean-cut and fresh-scrubbed and pink-faced. His blue shirtsleeves were neatly rolled up, two tourniquets on his bloated biceps. He started when he saw me—as surprised to see me as I was to see him.

We both froze. But he froze for a split second longer.

If I had approached him like a boxer or kung-fu expert, I'd probably have ended up picking my teeth out of my skull like so many splinters. But I didn't. I panicked. I worked on pure fear.

I launched myself straight at him.

With my chin tucked tight, I lowered my head and aimed for his center, rocketlike. Elizabeth played tennis. She told me once that when your opponent was at the net, it was often best to slam the ball right at their gut because he or she wouldn't know which way to move. You slow down their reaction time.

That was what happened here.

My body slammed into his. I grabbed hold of his shoulders like a monkey hanging on to a fence. We toppled over. I scrunched up my knees and dug them into his chest. My chin stayed tucked, the top of my head under the young cop's jaw.

We landed with an awful thud.

I heard a cracking noise. A shooting pain ricocheted down from where my skull had connected with his jaw. The young cop made a quiet "pluuu" noise. The air went out of his lungs. His jaw, I think, was broken. The flee panic took total control now. I scrambled off him as though he were a stun gun.

I had assaulted a police officer.

No time to dwell on it. I just wanted to be away from him. I managed to get to my feet and was about to turn and run, when I felt his hand on my ankle. I looked down and our eyes met.

He was in pain. Pain I had caused.

I kept my balance and unleashed a kick. It connected with his ribs. He made a wet "pluuu" sound this time. Blood trickled from his mouth. I couldn't believe what I was doing. I kicked him again. Just hard enough to loosen his grip. I pulled free.

And then I ran.

25

Hester and Shauna took a taxi to the clinic. Linda had taken the number 1 train down to their financial consultant at the World Financial Center to see about liquidating assets for bail.

A dozen police cars were angled in front of Beck's clinic, all pointing in various directions like darts thrown by a drunk. Their lights whirled at full red-blue alert. Sirens whined. More police cars pulled up.

"What the hell is going on?" Shauna asked.

Hester spotted Assistant District Attorney Lance Fein, but not before he spotted her. He stormed toward them. His face was scarlet and the vein in his forehead was pulsing.

"The son of a bitch ran," Fein spat out without preamble.

Hester took the hit and countered: "Your men must have spooked him."

Two more police cars pulled up. So did the Channel 7 news van. Fein cursed under his breath. "The press. Goddammit, Hester. You know how this is going to make me look?"

"Look, Lance—"

"Like a goddamn hack who gives special treatment to the rich, that's how. How could you do this to me, Hester? You know what the mayor is going to do to me? He's going to chew on my ass for jollies. And Tucker"— Tucker was the Manhattan district attorney—"Jesus

Christ, can you imagine what he'll do?"

"Mr. Fein!"

One of the police officers was calling him. Fein eyed both of them one more time before turning away with a snap.

Hester quickly spun on Shauna. "Is Beck out of his mind?"

"He's scared," Shauna said.

"He's running away from the police," Hester shouted. "Do you get that? Do you get what that means?" She pointed toward the news van. "The media is here, for Chrissake. They're going to talk about the killer on the run. It's dangerous. It makes him look guilty. Taints the jury pool."

"Calm down," Shauna said.

"Calm down? Do you understand what he's done?"

"He's run away. That's all. Like OJ, right? Didn't seem to hurt him with the jury."

"We're not talking about OJ here, Shauna. We're talking about a rich white doctor."

"Beck's not rich."

"That's not the point, dammit. Everyone is going to want to nail his ass to a wall after this. Forget bail. Forget a fair trial." She took a breath, crossed her arms. "And Fein isn't the only one whose reputation is going to be compromised."

"Meaning?"

"Meaning me!" Hester shrieked. "In one bold stroke, Beck's destroyed my credibility with the D.A.'s office. If I promise to deliver a guy, I have to deliver him."

"Hester?"

"What?"

"I don't give a rat's ass about your reputation right now."

178

A sudden eruption of noise jolted them both. They turned and saw an ambulance hurry down the block. Somebody cried out. Then another cry. Cops started bouncing around like too many balls released at the same time into a pinball machine.

The ambulance skidded to a stop. The EMTs—one male, one female—jumped out of the cab. Fast. Too fast. They unsnapped the back door and pulled out a stretcher.

"This way!" someone shouted. "He's over here!"

Shauna felt her heart skip a beat. She ran over to Lance Fein. Hester followed. "What's wrong?" Hester asked. "What's happened?"

Fein ignored her.

"Lance?"

He finally faced them. The muscles in his face quaked in rage. "Your client."

"What about him? Is he hurt?"

"He just assaulted a police officer."

This was nuts.

I had crossed a line by running, but attacking that young cop . . . No going back now. So I ran. I sprinted with all I had.

"Officer down!"

Someone actually shouted that. More shouts followed. More radio static. More sirens. They all swirled toward me. My heart leapt into my throat. I kept pumping my legs. They started feeling stiff and heavy, as though the muscles and ligaments were hardening to stone. I was out of shape. Mucus started flowing out of my nose. It mixed with whatever dirt I'd accumulated on my upper lip and snaked into my mouth.

I kept veering from block to block as though that

would fool the police. I didn't turn around to see if they were following. I knew they were. The sirens and radio static told me so.

I had no chance.

I dashed through neighborhoods I wouldn't even drive through. I hopped a fence and sprinted through the high grass of what might have once been a playground. People talked about the rising price of Manhattan real estate. But here, not far from the Harlem River Drive, there were vacant lots littered with broken glass and rusted ruins of what might have once been swing sets and jungle gyms and probably cars.

In front of a cluster of low-income high-rises, a group of black teens, all with the gangsta strut and coordinated ensemble, eyed me like a tasty leftover. They were about to do something—I didn't know what—when they realized that the police were chasing me.

They started cheering me on.

"Go, white boy!"

I sort of nodded as I dashed past them, a marathoner grateful for the little boost from the crowd. One of them yelled out, "Diallo!" I kept running, but I knew, of course, who Amadou Diallo was. Everyone in New York did. He'd been shot forty-one times by police officers—and he'd been unarmed. For a moment, I thought it was some kind of warning that the police might fire upon me.

But that wasn't it at all.

The defense in the Amadou Diallo trial claimed that when Diallo reached for his wallet, the officers thought it was a gun. Since then, people had been protesting by quickly reaching into their pockets, withdrawing their wallets, and yelling "Diallo!" Street officers reported that every time someone's hand went into their pockets like that, they still felt the thump of fear.

It happened now. My new allies—allies built on the fact that they probably thought I was a murderer—whipped out their wallets. The two cops on my tail hesitated. It was enough to increase my lead.

But so what?

My throat burned. I was sucking in way too much air. My hightops felt like lead boots. I got lazy. My toe dragged, tripping me up. I lost my balance, skidding across the pavement, scraping my palms and my face and my knees.

I managed to get back up, but my legs were trembling.

Closing in now.

Sweat pasted my shirt to my skin. My ears had that surf rush whooshing through them. I'd always hated running. Born-again joggers described how they got addicted to the rapture of running, how they achieved a nirvana known as runner's high. Right. I'd always firmly believed that—much like the high of auto-asphyxiation—the bliss came more from a lack of oxygen to the brain than any sort of endorphin rush.

Trust me, this was not blissful.

Tired. Too tired. I couldn't keep running forever. I glanced behind me. No cops. The street was abandoned. I tried a door. No go. I tried another. The radio crackle started up again. I ran. Toward the end of the block I spotted a street cellar door slightly ajar. Also rusted. Everything was rusted in this place.

I bent down and pulled at the metal handle. The door gave with an unhappy creak. I peered down into the blackness.

A cop shouted, "Cut him off the other side!"

I didn't bother looking back. I stepped down quickly

into the hole. I reached the first step. Shaky. I put my foot out for the second step. But there was none.

I stayed suspended for a second, like Wile E. Coyote after running off a cliff, before I plunged helplessly into the dark pit.

The fall was probably no more than ten feet, but I seemed to take a long time to hit ground. I flailed my arms. It didn't help. My body landed on cement, the impact rattling my teeth.

I was on my back now, looking up. The door slammed closed above me. A good thing, I suppose, but the darkness was now pretty much total. I did a quick survey of my being, the doctor doing an internal exam. Everything hurt.

I heard the cops again. The sirens had not let up, or maybe now the sound was just ringing in my ears. Lots of voices. Lots of radio static.

They were closing in on me.

I rolled onto my side. My right hand pressed down, stinging the cuts in my palms, and my body started to rise. I let the head trail; it screamed in protest when I got to my feet. I almost fell down again.

Now what?

Should I just hide here? No, that wouldn't work. Eventually, they'd start going house to house. I'd be caught. And even if they didn't, I hadn't run with the intention of hiding in a dank basement. I ran so that I could keep my appointment with Elizabeth in Washington Square.

Had to move.

But where?

My eyes started adjusting to the dark, enough to see shadowy shapes anyway. Boxes were stacked haphazardly. There were piles of rags, a few barstools, a broken mirror. I caught my reflection in the glass and almost jumped back at the sight. There was a gash on my forehead. My pants were ripped in both knees. My shirt was tattered like the Incredible Hulk's. I was smeared with enough soot to work as a chimney sweep.

Where to go?

A staircase. There had to be a staircase down here somewhere. I felt my way forward, moving in a sort of spastic dance, leading with my left leg as though it were a white cane. My foot crunched over some broken glass. I kept moving.

I heard what I thought was a mumbling noise, and a giant rag pile rose in my path. What could have been a hand reached out to me like something from a grave. I bit back a scream.

"Himmler likes tuna steaks!" he shouted at me.

The man—yes, I could see now it was clearly a man—started to stand. He was tall and black and he had a beard so white-gray and woolly it looked as though he might be eating a sheep.

"You hear me?" the man shouted. "You hear what I'm telling you?"

He stepped toward me. I shrunk back.

"Himmler! He likes tuna steaks!"

The bearded man was clearly displeased about something. He made a fist and aimed it at me. I stepped to the side without thought. His fist traveled past me with enough momentum—or maybe enough drink—to make him topple over. He fell on his face. I didn't bother to wait. I found the staircase and ran up.

The door was locked.

"Himmler!"

He was loud, too loud. I pressed against the door. No go.

"You hear me? You hear what I'm saying?"

I heard a creak. I glanced behind me and saw something that struck fear straight into my heart.

Sunlight.

Someone had pulled open the same storm door I'd come in from.

"Who's down there?"

A voice of authority. A flashlight started dancing around the floor. It reached the bearded man.

"Himmler likes tuna steaks!"

"That you yelling, old man?"

"You hear me?"

I used my shoulder against the door, putting everything I had behind it. The doorjamb started to crack. Elizabeth's image popped up—the one I'd seen on the computer—her arm raised, her eyes beckoning. I pushed a little harder.

The door gave way.

I fell out onto the ground floor, not far from the building's front door.

Now what?

Other cops were close by—I could still hear the radio static—and one of them was still interviewing Himmler's biographer. I didn't have much time. I needed help.

But from where?

I couldn't call Shauna. The police would be all over her. Same with Linda. Hester would insist I surrender.

Someone was opening the front door.

I ran down the corridor. The floor was linoleum and filthy. The doors were all metal and closed. The motif was chipped paint. I banged open a fire door and headed up the stairwell. At the third floor, I got out.

An old woman stood in the corridor.

She was, I was surprised to see, white. My guess was

that she'd probably heard the commotion and stepped out to see what was going on. I stopped short. She stood far enough away from her open door that I could get past her ...

Would I? Would I go that length to get away?

I looked at her. She looked at me. Then she took out a gun.

Oh, Christ ...

"What do you want?" she asked.

And I found myself answering: "May I please use your phone?"

She didn't miss a beat. "Twenty bucks."

I reached into my wallet and plucked out the cash. The old lady nodded and let me in. The apartment was tiny and well kept. There was lace on all the upholstery and on the dark wood tables.

"Over there," she said.

The phone was rotary dial. I jammed my finger into the little holes. Funny thing. I had never called this number before—had never wanted to—but I knew it by heart. Psychiatrists would probably have a field day with that one. I finished dialing and waited.

Two rings later, a voice said, "Yo."

"Tyrese? It's Dr. Beck. I need your help."

26

Shauna shook her head. "Beck hurt someone? That's not possible."

Assistant D.A. Fein's vein started fluttering again. He stepped toward her until his face was right up against hers. "He attacked a police officer in an alley. He probably broke the man's jaw and a couple of ribs." Fein leaned a little closer, his spittle landing on Shauna's cheeks. "You hear what I'm telling you?"

"I hear you," Shauna said. "Now step back, Breath Boy, or I'll knee your balls into your throat."

Fein stayed in place for a screw-you second before turning away. Hester Crimstein did likewise. She started heading back toward Broadway. Shauna chased her.

"Where are you going?"

"I quit," Hester said.

"What?"

"Find him another lawyer, Shauna."

"You can't be serious."

"I am."

"You can't just walk out on him."

"Watch me."

"It's prejudicial."

"I gave them my word he'd surrender," she said.

"Screw your word. Beck's the priority here, not you."

"To you maybe."

"You're putting yourself before a client?"

"I won't work with a man who'd do something like that."

"Who are you kidding? You've defended serial rapists."

She waved a hand. "I'm out of here."

"You're just a goddamn media-hound hypocrite."

"Ouch, Shauna."

"I'll go to them."

"What?"

"I'll go to the media."

Hester stopped. "And say what? That I walked away from a dishonest murderer? Great, go ahead. I'll leak so much shit about Beck, he'll make Jeffrey Dahmer look like a good dating prospect."

"You have nothing to leak," Shauna said.

Hester shrugged. "Never stopped me before."

The two women glared. Neither looked away.

"You may think my reputation is irrelevant," Hester said, her voice suddenly soft. "But it's not. If the D.A.'s office can't rely on my word, I'm useless to my other clients. I'm also useless to Beck. It's that simple. I won't let my practice—and my clients—go down the tubes because your boy acted erratically."

Shauna shook her head. "Just get out my face."

"One more thing."

"What?"

"Innocent men don't run, Shauna. Your boy Beck? Hundred to one he killed Rebecca Schayes."

"You're on," Shauna said. "And one more thing for you too, Hester. You say one word against Beck, and they'll need a soup ladle to bury your remains. We clear?"

Hester didn't reply. She took another step away from Shauna. And that was when the gunfire ripped through the air.

I was in mid-crouch, crawling down a rusted fire escape, when the sound of the gunfire nearly made me topple over. I flattened myself on the grated walk and waited.

More gunfire.

I heard shouts. I should have expected this, but it still packed a wallop. Tyrese told me to climb out here and wait for him. I had wondered how he planned on getting me out. Now I was getting some idea.

A diversion.

In the distance, I heard someone shouting, "White boy shooting up the place!" Then another voice: "White boy with a gun! White boy with a gun!"

More gunfire. But—and I strained my ears—no more police radio static. I stayed low and tried not to think much. My brain, it seemed, had short-circuited. Three days ago, I was a dedicated doctor sleepwalking through my own life. Since then, I had seen a ghost, gotten emails from the dead, had become a suspect in not one but two murders, was on the run from the law, had assaulted a police officer, and had enlisted the aid of a known drug dealer.

Heck of a seventy-two hours.

I almost laughed.

"Yo, Doc."

I looked down. Tyrese was there. So was another black man, early twenties, only slightly smaller than this building. The big man peered up at me with those sleek up-yours sunglasses that fit perfectly with his deadened facial expression.

"Come on, Doc. Let's roll."

I ran down the fire escape stairs. Tyrese kept glancing left and right. The big guy stood perfectly still, his arms folded across his chest in what we used to call the buffalo stance. I hesitated before the last ladder, trying to figure out how to release it so I could reach the ground.

"Yo, Doc, lever on the left."

I found it, pulled, and the ladder slid down. When I reached the bottom, Tyrese made a face and waved his hand in front of his nose. "You ripe, Doc."

"I didn't have a chance to shower, sorry."

"This way."

Tyrese did a quick-walk through the back lot. I followed, having to do a little run to keep up. The big man glided behind us in silence. He never moved his head left or right, but I still got the impression he didn't miss much.

A black BMW with tinted windows, a complicated antenna, and a chain frame on the back license plate was running. The doors were all closed, but I could feel the rap music. The bass vibrated in my chest like a tuning fork.

"The car," I said with a frown. "Isn't it kind of conspicuous?"

"If you five-oh and you looking for a lily-white doctor, where would be the last place you look?"

He had a point.

The big guy opened the back door. The music blared at the volume of a Black Sabbath concert. Tyrese extended his arm doorman-style. I got in. He slid next to me. The big guy bent into the driver's seat.

I couldn't understand much of what the rapper on the CD was saying, but he was clearly pissed off with "da man." I suddenly understood.

"This here is Brutus," Tyrese said.

He meant the big-guy driver. I tried to catch his eye

in the rearview mirror, but I couldn't see them through the sunglasses.

"Nice to meet you," I said.

Brutus didn't respond.

I turned my attention back to Tyrese. "How did you pull this off?"

"Coupla my boys are doing some shooting down a Hundred Forty-seventh Street."

"Won't the cops find them?"

Tyrese snorted. "Yeah, right."

"It's that easy?"

"From there, yeah, it's easy. We got this place, see, in Building Five at Hobart Houses. I give the tenants ten bucks a month to stick their garbage in front of the back doors. Blocks it up, see. Cops can't get through. Good place to conduct bidness. So my boys, they pop off some shots from the windows, you know what I'm saying. By the time the cops get through, poof, they gone."

"And who was yelling about a white man with a gun?"

"Couple other of my boys. They just running down the street yelling about a crazy white man."

"Theoretically, me," I said.

"Theoretically," Tyrese repeated with a smile. "That's a nice big word, Doc."

I laid my head back. Fatigue settled down hard on my bones. Brutus drove east. He crossed that blue bridge by Yankee Stadium—I'd never learned the bridge's name— and that meant we were in the Bronx. For a while I slumped down in case someone peered into the car, but then I remembered that the windows were tinted. I looked out.

The area was ugly as all hell, like one of those scenes you see in apocalyptic movies after the bomb detonates.

There were patches of what might have once been buildings, all in various states of decay. Structures had crumbled, yes, but as though from within, as though the supporting innards had been eaten away.

We drove a little while. I tried to get a grip on what was going on, but my brain kept throwing up roadblocks. Part of me recognized that I was in something approaching shock; the rest of me wouldn't allow me even to consider it. I concentrated on my surroundings. As we drove a little more—as we dove deeper into the decay—the habitable dwellings dwindled. Though we were probably less than a couple of miles from the clinic, I had no idea where we were. Still the Bronx, I guessed. South Bronx probably.

Worn tires and ripped mattresses lay like war wounded in the middle of the road. Big chunks of cement peeked out from the high grass. There were stripped cars and while there were no fires burning, maybe there should have been.

"You come here much, Doc?" Tyrese said with a small chuckle.

I didn't bother responding.

Brutus pulled the car to a stop in front of yet another condemned building. A chain-link fence encircled the sad edifice. The windows had been boarded over with plywood. I could see a piece of paper glued to the door, probably a demolition warning. The door, too, was plywood. I saw it open. A man stumbled out, raising both hands to shield his eyes from the sun, staggering like Dracula under its onslaught.

My world kept swirling.

"Let's go," Tyrese said.

Brutus was out of the car first. He opened the door for me. I thanked him. Brutus stuck with the stoic. He had the kind of cigar-store-Indian face you couldn't imagine—and probably wouldn't ever want to see—smiling.

On the right, the chain-link had been clipped and pulled back. We crouched through. The stumbling man approached Tyrese. Brutus stiffened, but Tyrese waved him down. The stumbling man and Tyrese greeted each other warmly and performed a complicated handshake. Then they went their separate ways.

"Come in," Tyrese said to me.

I ducked inside, my mind still numb. The stench came first, the acid smells of urine and the never-mistaken stink of fecal matter. Something was burning—I think I knew what—and the damp yellow odor of sweat seemed to be coming from the walls. But there was something else here. The smell, not of death, but of pre-death, like gangrene, like something dying and decomposing while still breathing.

The stifling heat was of the blast furnace variety. Human beings—maybe fifty of them, maybe a hundred—littered the floor like losing stubs at an OTB. It was dark inside. There seemed to be no electricity, no running water, no furniture of any sort. Wood planks blocked out most of the sun, the only illumination coming through cracks where the sun sliced through like a reaper's scythe. You could make out shadows and shapes and little more.

I admit to being naïve about the drug scene. In the emergency room, I'd seen the results plenty of times. But drugs never interested me personally. Booze was my poison of choice, I guess. Still, enough stimuli were getting through that even I could deduce that we were in a crack house.

"This way," Tyrese said.

We started walking through the wounded. Brutus led. The dearly reclined parted for him as though he were Moses. I fell in behind Tyrese. The ends of pipes would light up, popping through the darkness. It reminded me of going to the Barnum and Bailey circus as a kid and twirling those tiny flashlights around in the dark. That was what this looked liked. I saw dark. I saw shadows. I saw the flashes of light.

No music played. No one seemed to talk much either. I heard a hum. I heard the wet sucking sound of the pipes. Shrieks pierced the air every once in a while, the sound not quite human.

I also heard groaning. People were performing the lewdest of sex acts, out in the open, no shame, no attempt at privacy.

One particular sight—I'll spare you the details— made me pull up in horror. Tyrese watched my expression with something close to amusement.

"They run out of money, they trade this"—Tyrese pointed—"for hits."

The bile worked its way into my mouth. I turned to him. He shrugged.

"Commerce, Doc. Makes the world go round."

Tyrese and Brutus kept walking. I staggered alongside. Most of the interior walls had crumbled to the ground. People—old, young, black, white, men, women—hung everywhere, spineless, flopped over like Dali clocks.

"Are you a crackhead, Tyrese?" I said.

"Used to be. Got hooked when I was sixteen."

"How did you stop?"

Tyrese smiled. "You see my man Brutus?"

"Hard to miss him."

"I told him I'd give him a thousand dollars for every

week I stayed clean. Brutus moved in with me."

I nodded. That sounded far more effective than a week with Betty Ford.

Brutus opened a door. This room, while not exactly well appointed, at least had tables and chairs, even lights and a refrigerator. I noticed a portable generator in the corner.

Tyrese and I stepped inside. Brutus closed the door and stayed in the corridor. We were left alone.

"Welcome to my office," Tyrese said.

"Does Brutus still help you stay off the junk?"

He shook his head. "Nah, TJ does that now. You know what I'm saying?"

I did. "And you don't have a problem with what you do here?"

"I got lots of problems, Doc." Tyrese sat down and invited me to do the same. His eyes flashed at me, and I didn't like what I saw in them. "I ain't one of the good guys."

I didn't know what to say to that, so I changed subjects. "I have to get down to Washington Square Park by five o'clock."

He leaned back. "Tell me what's up."

"It's a long story."

Tyrese took out a blunt blade and started cleaning his nails. "My kid gets sick, I go to the expert, right?"

I nodded.

"You in trouble with the law, you should do likewise."

"That's some analogy."

"Something bad's happening with you, Doc." He spread his arms. "Bad is my world. I'm the best tour guide there is."

So I told him the story. Almost all of it. He nodded a

lot, but I doubted he believed me when I said I had nothing to do with the murders. I doubted he cared either.

"Okay," he said when I finished, "let's get you ready. Then we need to talk about something else."

"What?"

Tyrese did not answer. He moved to what looked like a reinforced metal locker in the corner. He unlocked it with a key, leaned inside, and withdrew a gun.

"Glock, baby, Glock," he said, handing me the gun. I stiffened. An image of black and blood flashed in my mind and quickly fled; I didn't chase it. It had been a long time. I reached out and plucked the gun with two fingers, as though it might be hot. "Gun of champions," he added.

I was going to refuse it, but that would be stupid. They already had me on suspicion of two murders, assaulting a police officer, resisting arrest, and probably a bunch of stuff for fleeing from the law. What's a concealed-weapon charge on top of all that?

"It's loaded," he said.

"Is there a safety or something?"

"Not anymore."

"Oh," I said. I slowly turned it over and over, remembering the last time I held a weapon in my hand. It felt good, holding a gun again. Something about the weight, I guessed. I liked the texture, the cold of the steel, the way it fit perfectly in my palm, the heft. I didn't like that I liked it.

"Take this too." He handed me what looked like a cell phone.

"What's this?" I asked.

Tyrese frowned. "What it look like? A cell phone. But it's got a stolen number. Can't be traced back to you, see?"

I nodded, feeling very much out of my element.

"Got a bathroom behind that door," Tyrese said, gesturing to my right. "No shower but there's a bath. Wash your smelly ass off. I'll get you some fresh clothes. Then Brutus and me, we'll get you down to Washington Square."

"You said you had something you wanted to talk to me about."

"After you get dressed," Tyrese said. "We'll talk then."

27

Eric Wu stared at the sprawling tree. His face was serene, his chin tilted up slightly.

"Eric?" The voice belonged to Larry Gandle.

Wu did not turn around. "Do you know what this tree is called?" he asked.

"No."

"The Hangman's Elm."

"Charming."

Wu smiled. "Some historians believe that during the eighteenth century, this park was used for public executions."

"That's great, Eric."

"Yeah."

Two shirtless men whipped by on Rollerblades. A boom box played Jefferson Airplane. Washington Square Park—named, not surprisingly, for George Washington—was one of those places that tried to cling to the sixties though the grip kept slipping. There were usually protestors of some sort, but they looked more like actors in a nostalgic revival than genuine revolutionaries. Street performers took the stage with a little too much finesse. The homeless were the type of colorful that felt somehow contrived.

"You sure we have this place covered?" Gandle asked.

Wu nodded, still facing the tree. "Six men. Plus the two in the van."

Gandle looked behind him. The van was white with

a magnetic sign reading B&T Paint and a phone number and a cute logo of a guy who looked a lot like the Monopoly man holding a ladder and a paintbrush. If asked to describe the van, witnesses would remember, if anything at all, the name of the paint company and maybe the phone number.

Neither existed.

The van was double-parked. In Manhattan, a legally parked work van would be more apt to draw suspicion than one that was double-parked. Still, they kept their eye out. If a police officer approached, they would drive away. They would take the van to a lot on Lafayette Street. They would change license plates and magnetic signs. They would then return.

"You should go back to the van," Wu said.

"Do you think Beck will even make it?"

"Doubt it," Wu said.

"I figured getting him arrested would draw her out," Gandle said. "I didn't figure that he'd have a meet set up."

One of their operatives—the curly-haired man who'd worn sweat pants at Kinko's last night—had seen the message pop up on the Kinko's computer. But by the time he relayed the message, Wu had already planted the evidence at Beck's house.

No matter. It would work out.

"We have to grab them both, but she's the priority," Gandle said. "Worse comes to worst, we kill them. But it would be best to have them alive. So we can find out what they know."

Wu did not respond. He was still staring at the tree.

"Eric?"

"They hung my mother from a tree like this," Wu said.

Gandle wasn't sure how to respond, so he settled for "I'm sorry."

"They thought she was a spy. Six men stripped her naked and took a bullwhip to her. They lashed her for hours. Everywhere. Even the flesh on her face was ripped open. She was conscious the whole time. She kept screaming. It took a long time for her to die."

"Jesus Christ," Gandle said softly.

"When they were done, they hung her on a huge tree." He pointed to the Hangman's Elm. "One just like this. It was supposed to be a lesson, of course. So no one else would spy. But birds and animals got to her. Two days later, there were only bones left on that tree."

Wu put the Walkman back on his ears. He turned away from the tree. "You really should get out of sight," he told Gandle.

Larry had trouble wresting his eyes from the massive elm, but he managed to nod and go on his way.

28

I put on a pair of black jeans with a waist the approximate circumference of a truck tire. I folded over the slack and tightened the belt. The black White Sox's uniform shirt fit like a muumuu. The black baseball cap—it had some logo on it I didn't recognize—already had the bill broken in for me. Tyrese also gave me a pair of the same up-yours sunglasses Brutus favored.

Tyrese almost laughed when I came out of the bathroom. "You look good, Doc."

"I think the word you're looking for is phat."

He chuckled and shook his head. "White people." Then his face grew serious. He slid some stapled sheets of paper toward me. I picked it up. On top it read Last Will and Testament. I looked the question at him.

"Been meaning to talk to you about this," Tyrese said.

"About your will?"

"I got two more years on my plan."

"What plan?"

"I do this two more years, I got enough money to get TJ out of here. I figure I got maybe sixty-forty chance of making it."

"What do you mean, making it?"

Tyrese's eyes locked on mine. "You know."

I did know. He meant surviving. "Where will you go?"

He handed me a postcard. The scene was sun, blue

water, palm trees. The postcard was crinkled from too much handling. "Down in Florida," he said with a soft lilt in his voice. "I know this place. It's quiet. Gotta pool and good schools. Nobody to start wondering where I got my money, you know what I'm saying?"

I handed him back the picture. "I don't understand what I have to do with this."

"This"—he held up the photograph—"is the plan if the sixty percent happens. That"—he pointed to the will—"that's if the forty plays out."

I told him that I still didn't understand.

"I went downtown six months ago, you know what I'm saying. Got a fancy lawyer. Cost me two grand for a coupla hours with him. His name is Joel Marcus. If I die, you have to go see him. You the executor of my will. I got some papers locked up. They'll tell you where the money is."

"Why me?"

"You care about my boy."

"What about Latisha?"

He scoffed. "She a woman, Doc. Soon as I hit the pavement, she be looking for another cock, you know what I'm saying? Probably get knocked up again. Maybe get back on the stuff." He sat back and folded his arms. "Can't trust women, Doc. You should know that."

"She's TJ's mother."

"Right."

"She loves him."

"Yeah, I know that. But she just a woman, you know what I'm saying? You give her this kind of cash, she'll blow it in a day. That's why I set up some trust funds and shit. You the executor. She want money for TJ, you have to approve it. You and this Joel Marcus."

I would have argued that it was sexist and that he was a Neanderthal, but this hardly seemed the time. I shifted in the chair and looked at him. Tyrese was maybe twenty-five years old. I had seen so many like him. I had always lumped them into a single entity, blurring their faces into a dark mass of bad. "Tyrese?"

He looked at me.

"Leave now."

He frowned.

"Use the money you have. Get a job down in Florida. I'll lend you more if you need it. But take your family and go now."

He shook his head.

"Tyrese?"

He stood up. "Come on, Doc. We best get going."

"We're still looking for him."

Lance Fein fumed, his waxy face almost dripping. Dimonte chewed. Krinsky took notes. Stone hitched up his pants.

Carlson was distracted, bent over a fax that had just come through in the car.

"What about the gunshots?" Lance Fein snapped.

The uniformed officer—Agent Carlson hadn't bothered learning his name—shrugged. "Nobody knows anything. I think they were probably unrelated."

"Unrelated?" Fein shrieked. "What kind of incompetent idiot are you, Benny? They were running down the street yelling about a white guy."

"Well, no one knows nothing now."

"Lean on them," Fein said. "Lean on them hard. I mean, for crying out loud, how the hell does a guy like this escape, huh?"

"We'll get him."

Stone tapped Carlson on the shoulder. "What's up, Nick?"

Carlson frowned at the printout. He didn't speak. He was a neat man, orderly to the point of obsessive-compulsive. He washed his hands too much. He often locked and unlocked his door a dozen times before leaving the house. He stared some more because something here just did not mesh.

"Nick?"

Carlson turned toward him. "The thirty-eight we found in Sarah Goodhart's safety-deposit box."

"The one the key on the body led us to?"

"Right."

"What about it?" Stone asked.

Carlson kept frowning. "There's lots of holes here."

"Holes?"

"First off," Carlson continued, "we assume the Sarah Goodhart safety-deposit box was Elizabeth Beck's, right?"

"Right."

"But someone's paid the bill for the box every year for the past eight years," Carlson said. "Elizabeth Beck is dead. Dead women pay no tabs."

"Her father maybe. I think he knows more than he's letting on."

Carlson didn't like it. "How about those listening devices we found at Beck's house? What's the deal there?"

"I don't know," Stone replied with a shrug. "Maybe someone else in the department suspected him too."

"We'd have heard by now. And this report on that thirty-eight we found in the box." He motioned toward it. "You see what the ATF came back with?"

"No."

"Bulletproof had no hits, but that's not surprising since the data doesn't go back eight years anyway." Bulletproof, a bullet-analyzing module used by the Bureau of Alcohol, Tobacco and Firearms, was used to link data from past crimes with more recently discovered firearms. "But the NTC got a hit." NTC stood for the National Tracing Center. "Guess who the last registered owner was."

He handed Stone the printout. Stone scanned down and found it. "Stephen Beck?"

"David Beck's father."

"He died, right?"

"Right."

Stone handed it back to him. "So his son probably inherited the weapon," he said. "It was Beck's gun."

"So why would his wife keep it locked in a safety-deposit box with those photographs?"

Stone considered that one a minute. "Maybe she feared he'd use it on her."

Carlson frowned some more. "We're missing something."

"Look, Nick, let's not make this more complicated than we have to. We got Beck nailed good on the Schayes murder. It'll be a righteous collar. Let's just forget about Elizabeth Beck, okay?"

Carlson looked at him. "Forget about her?"

Stone cleared his throat and spread his hands. "Let's face it. Nailing Beck on Schayes, that'll be a piece of pie. But his wife—Christ, that case is eight years old. We got some scraps, okay, but we're not going to get him for it. It's too late. Maybe"—he gave too dramatic a shrug—"maybe it's best to let sleeping dogs lie."

"What the hell are you talking about?"

Stone moved closer and beckoned Carlson to bend

down. "Some people at the Bureau would rather we didn't dig this all up."

"Who doesn't want us digging what up?"

"It's not important, Nick. We're all on the same side, right? If we find out KillRoy didn't kill Elizabeth Beck, it just opens a can of worms, right? His lawyer will probably ask for a new trial—"

"They never tried him for Elizabeth Beck."

"But we wrote her off as KillRoy's handiwork. It would add doubt, that's all. It's neater this way."

"I don't want neat," Carlson said. "I want the truth."

"We all want that, Nick. But we want justice even more, right? Beck will get a life sentence for Rebecca Schayes. KillRoy will stay in jail. That's how it should be."

"There are holes, Tom."

"You keep saying that, but I don't see any. You were the one who first came up with Beck being good for his wife's murder."

"Exactly," Carlson said. "For his wife's murder. Not Rebecca Schayes's."

"I don't get what you mean."

"The Schayes murder doesn't fit."

"You kidding me? It makes it more solid. Schayes knew something. We started closing in. Beck had to shut her up."

Carlson frowned again.

"What?" Stone continued. "You think Beck's visit to her studio yesterday—right after we pressured him—was just a coincidence?"

"No," Carlson said.

"Then what, Nick? Don't you see? Schayes's murder fits in beautifully."

"A little too beautifully," Carlson said.

"Ah, don't start with that crap."

"Let me ask you something, Tom. How well did Beck plan and execute his wife's murder?"

"Pretty damn well."

"Exactly. He killed every witness. He got rid of the bodies. If it wasn't for the rainfall and that bear, we'd have nothing. And let's face it. Even with that, we still don't have enough to indict, much less convict."

"So?"

"So why is Beck suddenly so stupid? He knows we're after him. He knows that Schayes's assistant will be able to testify that he saw Rebecca Schayes the day of the murder. So why would he be stupid enough to keep the gun in his garage? Why would he be stupid enough to leave those gloves in his own trash can?"

"Easy," Stone said. "He rushed this time. With his wife, he had plenty of time to plan."

"Did you see this?"

He handed Stone the surveillance report.

"Beck visited the medical examiner this morning," Carlson said. "Why?"

"I don't know. Maybe he wanted to know if there was anything incriminating in the autopsy file."

Carlson frowned yet again. His hands were itching for another wash. "We're missing something, Tom."

"I don't see what, but hey, either way, we got to get him into custody. Then we can sort it out, okay?"

Stone headed over to Fein. Carlson let the doubts sink in. He thought again about Beck's visit to the medical examiner's office. He took out his phone, wiped it down with a handkerchief, and pressed the digits. When someone answered, he said, "Get me the Sussex County medical examiner."

29

In the old days—ten years ago anyway—she had friends living at the Chelsea Hotel on West Twenty-third Street. The hotel was half tourist, half residential, all-around kooky. Artists, writers, students, methadone addicts of every stripe and persuasion. Black fingernails, goth-white face paint, bloodred lipstick, hair without a trace of curl—all in the days before it was mainstream.

Little had changed. It was a good place to remain anonymous.

After grabbing a slice of pizza across the street, she'd checked in and had not ventured out of her room. New York. She'd once called this city home, but this was only her second visit in the past eight years.

She missed it.

With too practiced a hand, she tucked her hair under the wig. Today's color would be blond with dark roots. She put on a pair of wire-rim glasses and jammed the implants into her mouth. They changed the shape of her face.

Her hands were shaking.

Two airplane tickets sat on the kitchen table. Tonight, they would take British Airways Flight 174 from JFK to London's Heathrow Airport, where her contact would meet them with new identities. Then they would take the train to Gatwick and take the afternoon flight to Nairobi, Kenya. A jeep would take them near the foothills of Mount Meru in Tanzania, and a three-day hike would follow.

Once they were there—in one of the few spots on this planet with no radio, no television, no electricity—they would be free.

The names on the tickets were Lisa Sherman. And David Beck.

She gave her wig one more tug and stared at her reflection. Her eyes blurred, and for a moment, she was back at the lake. Hope ignited in her chest, and for once she did nothing to extinguish it. She managed a smile and turned away.

She took the elevator to the lobby and made a right on Twenty-third Street.

Washington Square Park was a nice walk from here.

Tyrese and Brutus dropped me on the corner of West Fourth and Lafayette streets, about four blocks east of the park. I knew the area well enough. Elizabeth and Rebecca had shared an apartment on Washington Square, feeling deliciously avant garde in their West Village digs—the photographer and the social-working attorney, striving for Bohemia as they mingled with their fellow suburban-raised wannabes and trust-fund revolutionaries. Frankly I never quite bought it, but that was okay.

I was attending Columbia Medical School at the time, and technically, I lived uptown on Haven Avenue near the hospital now known as NewYork-Presbyterian. But naturally I spent a lot of time down here.

Those were good years.

Half an hour until the meet time.

I headed down West Fourth Street past the Tower Records and into a region of the city heavily occupied by New York University. NYU wanted you to know this. They staked claim to this land with garish purple NYU-logo flags everywhere. Ugly as hell, this garish purple set against Greenwich Village's subdued brick. Very possessive and territorial too, thought I, for such a liberal enclave. But there you go.

My heart pounded on my chest wall as though it wanted to break free.

Would she be there already?

I didn't run. I kept cool and tried to distract myself from what the next hour or so could bring. The wounds from my recent ordeal were in that state between burn and itch. I caught my reflection in a building window and couldn't help but notice that I looked utterly ridiculous in my borrowed garb. Gangsta Prep. Yo, word.

My pants kept sliding down. I hitched them up with one hand and tried to keep pace.

Elizabeth might be at the park.

I could see the square now. The southeast corner was only a block away. There seemed to be a rustle in the air, the onset of a storm maybe, but that was probably my imagination shifting into high gear. I kept my head lowered. Had my picture reached the television yet? Had the anchors broken in with a be-on-the-lookout announcement? I doubted it. But my eyes still stayed on the pavement.

I hurried my step. Washington Square had always been too intense for me during the summer months. It was trying too hard—too much happening with just a little too much desperation. Manufactured edge, I called it. My favorite spot was the large clutter of humanity near the cement game tables. I played chess there sometimes. I was pretty good, but in this park, chess was the great equalizer. Rich, poor, white, black, homeless, highrised, rental, co-oped—all harmonized over the age-old black and white figurines. The best player I'd ever seen down here was a black man who spent most of his pre-Giuliani afternoons harassing motorists for change with his squeegee.

Elizabeth wasn't there yet.

I took a seat on a bench.

Fifteen more minutes.

The tightness in my chest increased fourfold. I had never been so scared in my entire life. I thought about Shauna's technological demonstration. A hoax? I wondered again. What if this was all a hoax? What if Elizabeth was indeed dead? What would I do then?

Useless speculation, I told myself. A waste of energy. She had to be alive. There was no other choice.

I sat back and waited.

"He's here," Eric Wu said into his cell phone.

Larry Gandle looked out the van's tinted window. David Beck was indeed where he was supposed to be, dressed like a street punk. His face was covered with scrapes and flowering bruises.

Gandle shook his head. "How the hell did he pull it off?"

"Well," Eric Wu said in that singsong voice, "we can always ask him."

"We need this to go smoothly, Eric."

"Yes indeed."

"Is everybody in place?"

"Of course."

Gandle checked his watch. "She should be here any minute now."

* * *

Located between Sullivan and Thompson streets, Washington Square's most striking edifice was a high tower of washed-brown brick on the south side of the park. Most believed that the tower was still part of the Judson Memorial Church. It wasn't. For the past two decades, the tower held NYU student dorm rooms and offices. The top of the tower was easily accessible to anyone who looked as though she knew where she was going.

From up here, she could look down at the whole park. And when she did, she started to cry.

Beck had come. He wore the most bizarre disguise, but then again, the email had warned him that he might be followed. She could see him sitting on that bench, all alone, waiting, his right leg shaking up and down. His leg always did that when he was nervous.

"Ah, Beck ..."

She could hear the pain, the bitter agony, in her own voice. She kept staring at him.

What had she done?

So stupid.

She forced herself to turn away. Her legs folded and she slid with her back against the wall until she reached the floor. Beck had come for her.

But so had they.

She was sure of it. She had spotted three of them, at the very least. Probably more. She had also spotted the B&T Paint van. She'd dialed the number on the van's sign, but it was out of service. She checked with directory assistance. There was no B&T Paint.

They'd found them. Despite all her precautions, they were here.

She closed her eyes. Stupid. So stupid. To think that she could pull this off. How could she have allowed it to happen? Yearning had clouded her judgment. She knew that now. Somehow, she had fooled herself into believing that she could turn a devastating catastrophe—the two bodies being discovered near the lake—into some sort of divine windfall.

Stupid.

She sat up and risked another look at Beck. Her heart plummeted like a stone down a well. He looked so alone down there, so small and fragile and helpless. Had Beck adjusted to her death? Probably. Had he fought through what happened and made a life for himself? Again probably. Had he recovered from the blow only to have her stupidity whack him over the head again?

Definitely.

The tears returned.

She took out the two airplane tickets. Preparation. That had always been the key to her survival. Prepare for every eventuality. That was why she had planned the meet here, at a public park she knew so well, where she would have this advantage. She hadn't admitted it to herself, but she'd known that this possibility—no, this likelihood—existed.

It was over.

The small opening, if there had ever been one, had been slammed shut.

Time to go. By herself. And this time for good.

She wondered how he'd react to her not showing up. Would he keep scouring his computer for emails that would never come? Would he search the faces of strangers and imagine he saw hers? Would he just forget and go on—and, when she really mined her true feelings, did she want him to?

No matter. Survival first. His anyway. She had no choice. She had to go.

With great effort, she tore her gaze away and hurried

down the stairs. There was a back exit that led out to West Third Street, so she'd never even had to enter the park. She pushed the heavy metal door and stepped outside. Down Sullivan Street, she found a taxi on the corner of Bleecker.

She leaned back and closed her eyes.

"Where to?" the driver asked.

"JFK Airport," she said.

Too much time passed.

I stayed on the bench and waited. In the distance I could see the park's famed marble arch. Stanford White, the famous turn-of-the-century architect who murdered a man in a jealous fit over a fifteen-year-old girl, had purportedly "designed" it. I didn't get that. How do you design something that is a replica of someone else's work? The fact that the Washington Arch was a direct rip-off of the Arc de Triomphe in Paris was no secret. New Yorkers got excited over what was in effect a facsimile. I had no idea why.

You couldn't touch the arch anymore. A chain-link fence, not unlike the ones I'd just seen in the South Bronx, encircled it so as to discourage "graffiti artists." The park was big on fences. Almost all grassy areas were lined with loose fencing—double fencing in most places.

Where was she?

Pigeons waddled with the type of possessiveness usually associated with politicians. Many flocked in my direction. They pecked my sneakers and then looked up as though disappointed they weren't edible.

"Ty usually sits there."

The voice came from a homeless guy wearing a pinwheel hat and Spock ears. He sat across from me.

"Oh," I said.

"Ty feeds them. They like Ty."

"Oh," I said again.

"That's why they're all over you like that. They don't like you or nothing. They think maybe you're Ty. Or a friend of Ty's."

"Uh-huh."

I checked my watch. I had been sitting here the better part of two hours. She wasn't coming. Something had gone wrong. Again I wondered if it had all been a hoax, but I quickly pushed it away. Better to continue assuming that the messages were from Elizabeth. If it's all a hoax, well, I'd learn that eventually.

No matter what, I love you . . .

That was what the message said. No matter what. As though something might go wrong. As though something could happen. As though I should just forget about it and go on.

To hell with that.

It felt strange. Yes, I was crushed. The police were after me. I was exhausted and beaten up and near the edge sanity-wise. And yet I felt stronger than I had in years. I didn't know why. But I knew I was not going to let it go. Only Elizabeth knew all those things—kiss time, the Bat Lady, the Teenage Sex Poodles. Ergo, it was Elizabeth who had sent the emails. Or someone who was making Elizabeth send them. Either way, she was alive. I had to pursue this. There was no other way.

So, what next?

I took out my new cell phone. I rubbed my chin for a minute and then came up with an idea. I pressed in the digits. A man sitting across the way—he'd been reading a newspaper for a very long time there—sneaked a glance at me. I didn't like that. Better safe than sorry. I stood and moved out of hearing distance.

Shauna answered the phone. "Hello?"

"Old man Teddy's phone," I said.

"Beck? What the hell—?"

"Three minutes."

I hung up. I figured that Shauna and Linda's phone would be tapped. The police would be able to hear every word we said. But one floor below them lived an old widower named Theodore Malone. Shauna and Linda looked in on him from time to time. They had a key to his apartment. I'd call there. The feds or cops or whoever wouldn't have a tap on that phone. Not in time anyway.

I pressed the number.

Shauna sounded out of breath. "Hello?"

"I need your help."

"Do you have any idea what's going on?"

"I assume there's a massive manhunt for me." I still felt oddly calm—in the eye, I guess.

"Beck, you have to turn yourself in."

"I didn't kill anyone."

"I know that, but if you stay out there—"

"Do you want to help me or not?" I interrupted.

"Tell me," she said.

"Have they established a time for the murder yet?"

"Around midnight. Their timetable is a little tight, but they figure you took off right after I left."

"Okay," I said. "I need you to do something for me."

"Name it."

"First off, you have to pick up Chloe."

"Your dog?"

"Yes."

"Why?"

"For one thing," I said, "she needs a walk."

* * *

Eric Wu spoke on his cell phone. "He's on the phone, but my man can't get close enough."

"Did he make your guy?"

"Possibly."

"Maybe he's calling off the meet then."

Wu did not reply. He watched as Dr. Beck pocketed his cell phone and started crossing through the park.

"We have a problem," Wu said.

"What?"

"It appears as though he's leaving the park."

There was silence on the other end of the line. Wu waited.

"We lost him before," Gandle said.

Wu did not reply.

"We can't risk it, Eric. Grab him. Grab him now, find out what he knows, and end it."

Eric nodded a signal in the direction of the van. He started walking toward Beck. "Done."

I headed past the park's statue of Garibaldi unsheathing his sword. Strangely enough, I had a destination in mind. Forget visiting KillRoy, that was out for now. But the PF from Elizabeth's diary, aka Peter Flannery, ambulance-chaser-at-law, was another matter. I could still get to his office and have a chat with him. I had no idea what I would learn. But I'd be doing something. That would be a start.

A playground was nestled up on my right, but there were fewer than a dozen children in there. On my left, "George's Dog Park," a glorified doggy run, was chock-full of bandanna-clad canines and their parental alternatives. On the park's stage, two men juggled. I walked past a group of poncho-sheathed students sitting in a semi-circle. A dyed-blond Asian man built like the

Thing from the Fantastic Four glided to my right. I glanced behind me. The man who'd been reading the newspaper was gone.

I wondered about that.

He had been there almost the whole time I was. Now, after several hours, he decided to leave at the exact time I did. Coincidence? Probably.

You'll be followed ...

That was what the email had said. It didn't say maybe. It seemed, in hindsight, pretty sure of itself. I kept walking and thought about it a little more. No way. The best tail in the world wouldn't have stuck with me after what I'd just been through today.

The guy with the newspaper couldn't have been following me. At least, I couldn't imagine it.

Could they have intercepted the email?

I couldn't see how. I'd erased it. It had never even been on my own computer.

I crossed Washington Square West. When I reached the curb, I felt a hand on my shoulder. Gentle at first. Like an old friend sneaking up behind me. I turned and had enough time to see it was the Asian guy with the dyed hair.

Then he squeezed my shoulder.

31

His fingers bore into the joint's crevice like spearheads.

Pain—crippling pain—slashed down my left side. My legs gave out. I tried to scream or fight, but I couldn't move. A white van swung up next to us. The side door slid open. The Asian guy moved his hand onto my neck. He squeezed the pressure points on either side, and my eyes started rolling back. With his other hand, he toyed with my spine and I bent forward. I felt myself folding up.

He shoved me toward the van. Hands reached from inside the back and dragged me in. I landed on the cool metal floor. No seats in here. The door closed. The van pulled back into the traffic.

The whole episode—from the hand touching my shoulder to the van starting up—took maybe five seconds.

The Glock, I thought.

I tried to reach for it, but someone leapt on my back. My hands were pinned down. I heard a snap, and my right arm was cuffed at the wrist to the floorboard. They flipped me over, nearly ripping my shoulder out of the socket. Two of them. I could see them now. Two men, both white, maybe thirty years old. I could see them clearly. Too clearly. I could identify them. They would have to know that.

This wasn't good.

They cuffed my other hand so I was spread-eagle on

the floorboard. Then they sat on my legs. I was chained down now and totally exposed.

"What do you want?" I asked.

No one answered. The van pulled to a quick stop around the corner. The big Asian guy slid in, and the van started up again. He bent down, gazing at me with what looked like mild curiosity.

"Why were you at the park?" he asked me.

His voice threw me. I had expected something growling or menacing, but his tone was gentle, high-pitched, and creepily childlike.

"Who are you?" I asked.

He slammed his fist in my gut. He punched me so hard, I was sure his knuckles scraped the van floor. I tried to bend or crumple into a ball, but the restraints and the men sitting on my legs made that impossible. Air. All I wanted was air. I thought that I might throw up.

You'll be followed . . .

All the precautions—the unsigned emails, the code words, the warnings—they all made sense now. Elizabeth was afraid. I didn't have all the answers yet— hell, I barely had any of them—but I finally understood that her cryptic communications were a result of fear. Fear of being found.

Found by these guys.

I was suffocating. Every cell in my body craved oxygen. Finally, the Asian nodded at the other two men. They got off my legs. I snapped my knees toward my chest. I tried to gather some air, thrashing around like an epileptic. After a while, my breath came back. The Asian man slowly kneeled closer to me. I kept my eyes steady on his. Or, at least, I tried to. It wasn't like staring into the eyes of a fellow human being or even an animal. These were the eyes of something inanimate. If you could look into the eyes of a file cabinet, this would be what it felt like.

But I did not blink.

He was young too, my captor—no more than twenty, twenty-five tops. He put his hand on the inside of my arm, right above the elbow. "Why were you in the park?" he asked again in his singsong way.

"I like the park," I said.

He pressed down hard. With just two fingers. I gasped. The fingers knifed through my flesh and into a bundle of nerves. My eyes started to bulge. I had never known pain like this. It shut down everything. I flailed like a dying fish on the end of a hook. I tried to kick, but my legs landed like rubber bands. I couldn't breathe.

He wouldn't let go.

I kept expecting him to release the grip or let up a bit. He didn't. I started making small whimpering sounds. But he held on, his expression one of boredom.

The van kept going. I tried to ride out the pain, to break it down into intervals or something. But that didn't work. I needed relief. Just for a second. I needed him to let go. But he remained stonelike. He kept looking at me with those empty eyes. The pressure built in my head. I couldn't speak—even if I wanted to tell him what he wanted to know, my throat had shut down. And he knew that.

Escape the pain. That was all I could think about. How could I escape the pain? My entire being seemed to focus and converge on that nerve bundle in my arm. My body felt on fire, the pressure in my skull building.

With my head seconds from exploding, he suddenly released his grip. I gasped again, this time in relief. But it was short-lived. His hand began to snake down to my lower abdomen and stopped.

"Why were you in the park?"

I tried to think, to conjure up a decent lie. But he didn't give me time. He pinched deeply, and the pain was back, somehow worse than before. His finger pierced my liver like a bayonet. I started bucking against the restraints. My mouth opened in a silent scream.

I whipped my head back and forth. And there, in mid-whip, I saw the back of the driver's head. The van had stopped, probably for a traffic light. The driver was looking straight ahead—at the road, I guess. Then everything happened very fast.

I saw the driver's head swivel toward his door window as though he'd heard a noise. But he was too late. Something hit him in the side of the skull. He went down like a shooting gallery mallard. The van's front doors opened.

"Hands up now!"

Guns appeared. Two of them. Aimed in the back. The Asian guy let go. I flopped back, unable to move.

Behind the guns I saw two familiar faces, and I almost cried out in joy.

Tyrese and Brutus.

One of the white guys made a move. Tyrese casually fired his weapon. The man's chest exploded. He fell back with his eyes open. Dead. No doubt about that. In the front, the driver groaned, starting to come to. Brutus elbowed him hard in the face. The driver went quiet again.

The other white guy had his hands up. My Asian tormenter never changed his expression. He looked on as though from a distance, and he didn't raise or lower his hands. Brutus took the driver's seat and shifted into gear. Tyrese kept his weapon pointed straight at the Asian guy.

"Uncuff him," Tyrese said.

The white guy looked at the Asian. The Asian nodded his consent. The white guy uncuffed me. I tried to sit up. It felt as if something inside me had shattered and the shards were digging into tissue.

"You okay?" Tyrese asked.

I managed a nod.

"You want me to waste them?"

I turned to the still-breathing white guy. "Who hired you?"

The white guy slid his eyes toward the young Asian. I did the same.

"Who hired you?" I asked him.

The Asian finally smiled, but it didn't change his eyes. And then, once again, everything happened too fast.

I never saw his hand shoot out, but next thing I knew the Asian guy had me by the scruff of my neck. He hurled me effortlessly at Tyrese. I was actually airborne, my legs kicking out as though that might slow me down. Tyrese saw me coming, but he couldn't duck out of the way. I landed on him. I tried to roll off quickly, but by the time we righted ourselves, the Asian had gotten out via the van's side door.

He was gone.

"Fucking Bruce Lee on steroids," Tyrese said.

I nodded.

The driver was stirring again. Brutus prepared a fist, but Tyrese shook him off. "These two won't know dick," he said to me.

"I know."

"We can kill them or let them go." Like it was no big deal either way, a coin toss.

"Let them go," I said.

Brutus found a quiet block, probably someplace in

the Bronx, I can't be sure. The still-breathing white guy got out on his own. Brutus heaved the driver and the dead guy out like yesterday's refuse. We started driving again. For a few minutes, nobody spoke.

Tyrese laced his hands behind his neck and settled back. "Good thing we hung around, huh, Doc?"

I nodded at what I thought might be the understatement of the millennium.

32

The old autopsy files were kept in a U-Store-'Em in Layton, New Jersey, not far from the Pennsylvania border. Special Agent Nick Carlson arrived on his own. He didn't like storage facilities much. They gave him the black-cat creeps. Open twenty-four hours a day, no guard, a token security camera at the entrance ... God only knows what lay padlocked in these houses of cement. Carlson knew that many were loaded with drugs, money, and contraband of all sorts. That didn't bother him much. But he remembered a few years back when an oil executive had been kidnapped and crate-stored in one. The executive had suffocated to death. Carlson had been there when they found him. Ever since, he imagined *living* people in here too, right now, the inexplicably missing, just yards from where he stood, chained in the dark, straining against mouth gags.

People often note that it's a sick world. They had no idea.

Timothy Harper, the county medical examiner, came out of a garagelike facility, holding a large manila envelope closed with a wrap-around string. He handed Carlson an autopsy file with Elizabeth Beck's name on it.

"You have to sign for it," Harper said.

Carlson signed the form.

"Beck never told you why he wanted to see it?" Carlson asked.

"He talked about being a grieving husband and something about closure, but outside of that ..." Harper shrugged.

"Did he ask you anything else about the case?"

"Nothing that sticks out."

"How about something that doesn't stick out?"

Harper thought about it a moment. "He asked if I remembered who identified the body."

"Did you?"

"Not at first, no."

"Who did identify her?"

"Her father. Then he asked me how long it took."

"How long what took?"

"The identification."

"I don't understand."

"Neither did I, quite frankly. He wanted to know if her father had made the ID immediately or if it took a few minutes."

"Why would he want to know that?"

"I have no idea."

Carlson tried to find an angle on that one, but nothing came to him. "How did you answer him?"

"With the truth actually. I don't remember. I assume he did it in a timely fashion or I'd remember it better."

"Anything else?"

"Not really, no," he said. "Look, if we're done here, I got two kids who smashed a Civic into a telephone pole waiting for me."

Carlson gripped the file in his hand. "Yeah," he said. "We're done. But if I need to reach you?"

"I'll be at the office."

Peter Flannery, Attorney-at-Law was stenciled in faded gold into the door's pebbled glass. There was a hole in the glass the size of a fist. Someone had patched it up with gray duct tape. The tape looked old.

I kept the brim of my cap low. My insides ached from my ordeal with the big Asian guy. We had heard my name on the radio station that promises the world in exchange for twenty-two minutes. I was officially a wanted man.

Hard to wrap ye olde brain around that one. I was in huge trouble and yet that all seemed strangely remote, as though that were happening to someone with whom I was vaguely acquainted. I, me, the guy right here, didn't care much. I had a single focus: finding Elizabeth. The rest felt like scenery.

Tyrese was with me. Half a dozen people were scattered about the waiting room. Two wore elaborate neck braces. One had a bird in a cage. I had no idea why. No one bothered to glance up at us, as though they'd weighed the effort of sliding their eyes in our direction against the possible benefits and decided, hey, it isn't worth it.

The receptionist wore a hideous wig and looked at us as though we'd just plopped out of a dog's behind.

I asked to see Peter Flannery.

"He's with a client." She wasn't clacking gum, but it was close.

Tyrese took over then. Like a magician with a great sleight of hand, he flourished a roll of cash thicker than my wrist. "Tell him we be offering a retainer." Then, grinning, he added, "One for you too, we get in to see him right away."

Two minutes later, we were ushered into Mr. Flannery's inner sanctum. The office smelled of cigar smoke and Lemon Pledge. Snap-together furniture, the kind you might find at K-mart or Bradlees, had been stained dark, feigning rich oak and mahogany and working about as well as a Las Vegas toupee. There were no school diplomas on the wall, just that phony nonsense people put up to impress the easily impressed. One commemorated Flannery's membership in the "International Wine-tasting Association." Another ornately noted that he attended a "Long Island Legal Conference" in 1996. Big wow. There were sun-faded photos of a younger Flannery with what I guessed were either celebrities or local politicians, but nobody I recognized. The office staple of a golf foursome photo mounted wood-plaque-like adorned a prize spot behind the desk.

"Please," Flannery said with a big wave of his hand. "Have a seat, gentlemen."

I sat. Tyrese stayed standing, crossed his arms, and leaned against the back wall.

"So," Flannery said, stretching the word out like a wad of chaw, "what can I do for you?"

Peter Flannery had that athlete-gone-to-seed look. His once-golden locks had thinned and fled. His features were malleable. He wore a rayon three-piece suit—I hadn't seen one in a while—and the vest even had the pocket watch attached to a faux gold chain.

"I need to ask you about an old case," I said.

His eyes still had the ice blue of youth, and he aimed them my way. On the desk, I spotted a photograph of Flannery with a plump woman and a girl of maybe fourteen who was definitely in the throes of awkward adolescence. They were all smiling, but I saw a wince there too, as though they were bracing for a blow.

"An old case?" he repeated.

"My wife visited you eight years ago. I need to know what it was about."

Flannery's eyes flicked toward Tyrese. Tyrese still had the folded arms and showed him nothing more than the sunglasses. "I don't understand. Was this a divorce case?"

"No," I said.

"Then . . . ?" He put his hands up and gave me the I'd-like-to-help shrug. "Attorney-client confidentiality. I don't see how I can help you."

"I don't think she was a client."

"You're confusing me, Mr.—" He waited for me to fill in the blank.

"Beck," I said. "And it's doctor, not mister."

His double chin went slack at my name. I wondered if maybe he had heard the news reports. But I didn't think that was it.

"My wife's name is Elizabeth."

Flannery said nothing.

"You remember her, don't you?"

Again he flipped a glance at Tyrese.

"Was she a client, Mr. Flannery?"

He cleared his throat. "No," he said. "No, she wasn't a client."

"But you remember meeting her?"

Flannery shifted in his chair. "Yes."

"What did you discuss?"

"It's been a long time, Dr. Beck."

"Are you saying you don't remember?"

He didn't answer that one directly. "Your wife," he said. "She was murdered, wasn't she? I remember seeing something about it on the news."

I tried to keep us on track. "Why did she come here, Mr. Flannery?"

"I'm an attorney," he said, and he almost puffed out his chest.

"But not hers."

"Still," he said, trying to gain some sort of leverage, "I need to be compensated for my time." He coughed into his fist. "You mentioned something about a retainer."

I looked over my shoulder, but Tyrese was already on the move. The cash roll was out and he was peeling bills. He tossed three Ben Franklins on the desk, gave Flannery a hard sunglass glare, and then stepped back to his spot.

Flannery looked at the money but didn't touch it. He bounced his fingertips together and then flattened his palms against each other. "Suppose I refuse to tell you."

"I can't see why you would," I said. "Your communications with her don't fall under privilege, do they?"

"I'm not talking about that," Flannery said. His eyes pierced mine and he hesitated. "Did you love your wife, Dr. Beck?"

"Very much."

"Have you remarried?"

"No," I said. Then: "What does that have to do with anything?"

He settled back. "Go," he said. "Take your money and just go."

"This is important, Mr. Flannery."

"I can't imagine how. She's been dead for eight years. Her killer is on death row."

"What are you afraid to tell me?"

Flannery didn't answer right away. Tyrese again peeled himself off the wall. He moved closer to the desk. Flannery watched him and surprised me with a tired sigh. "Do me a favor," he said to Tyrese. "Stop with the posturing, okay? I've repped psychos who make you look like Mary Poppins."

Tyrese looked as though he might react, but that

230

wouldn't help. I said his name. He looked at me. I shook my head. Tyrese backed off. Flannery was plucking at his lower lip. I let him. I could wait.

"You don't want to know," he said to me after a while.

"Yeah, I do."

"It can't bring your wife back."

"Maybe it can," I said.

That got his attention. He frowned at me, but something there softened.

"Please," I said.

He swiveled his seat to the side and tilted way back, staring up at window blinds that had turned yellow and crusty sometime during the Watergate hearings. He folded his hands and rested them on his paunch. I watched the hands rise and fall as he breathed.

"I was a public defender back then," he began. "You know what that is?"

"You defended the indigent," I said.

"Something like that. The Miranda rights—they talk about having the right to counsel if you can afford one. I'm the guy you get when you can't."

I nodded, but he was still looking at the blinds.

"Anyway, I was assigned one of the most prominent murder trials in the state."

Something cold wormed into my stomach. "Whose?" I asked.

"Brandon Scope's. The billionaire's son. Do you remember the case?"

I froze, terrified. I could barely breathe. Little wonder Flannery's name had seemed familiar. Brandon Scope. I almost shook my head, not because I didn't remember the case, but because I wanted him to say anything but that name.

For the sake of clarity, let me give you the newspaper account: Brandon Scope, age thirty-three, was robbed and murdered eight years ago. Yes, eight years ago. Maybe two months before Elizabeth's murder. He was shot twice and dumped near a housing project in Harlem. His money was gone. The media played all the violins on this one. They made much of Brandon Scope's charitable work. They talked about how he helped street kids, how he preferred working with the poor to running Daddy's multinational conglomerate, that kind of spin. It was one of those murders that "shock a nation" and lead to plenty of finger-pointing and hand-wringing. A charitable foundation had been set up in young Scope's name. My sister, Linda, runs it. You wouldn't believe the good she does there.

"I remember it," I said softly.

"Do you remember that an arrest was made?"

"A street kid," I said. "One of the kids he helped, right?"

"Yes. They arrested Helio Gonzalez, then age twenty-two. A resident of Barker House in Harlem. Had a felony sheet that read like a Hall of Famer's career stats. Armed robbery, arson, assault, a real sunshine, our Mr. Gonzalez."

My mouth was dry. "Weren't the charges eventually dropped?" I asked.

"Yes. They didn't have much really. His fingerprints were found at the scene, but so were plenty of others. There were strands of Scope's hair and even a speck of matching blood found where Gonzalez lived. But Scope had been to the building before. We could have easily claimed that was how that material got there. Nonetheless, they had enough for an arrest, and the cops were sure something more would break."

"So what happened?" I asked.

Flannery still wouldn't look at me. I didn't like that. Flannery was the kind of guy who lived for the Willy Loman world of shined shoes and eye contact. I knew the type. I didn't want anything to do with them, but I knew them.

"The police had a solid time of death," he continued. "The M.E. got a good liver temperature reading. Scope was killed at eleven. You might be able to stretch it a half hour in either direction, but that was about it."

"I don't understand," I said. "What does this have to do with my wife?"

He bounced the fingertips again. "I understand that your wife worked with the poor as well," he said. "In the same office with the victim, as a matter of fact."

I didn't know where this was going, but I knew I wasn't going to like it. For the most fleeting of seconds, I wondered if Flannery was right, if I really didn't want to hear what he had to say, if I should just pick myself out of the chair and forget all about this. But I said, "So?"

"That's noble," he said with a small nod. "Working with the downtrodden."

"Glad you think so."

"It's why I originally went into law. To help the poor."

I swallowed down the bile and sat a little straighter. "Do you mind telling me what my wife has to do with any of this?"

"She freed him."

"Who?"

"My client. Helio Gonzalez. Your wife freed him."

I frowned. "How?"

"She gave him an alibi."

233

My heart stopped. So did my lungs. I almost pounded on my chest to get the inner workings started up again.

"How?" I asked.

"How did she give him an alibi?"

I nodded numbly, but he still wasn't looking. I croaked out a yes.

"Simple," he said. "She and Helio had been together during the time in question."

My mind started to flail, adrift in the ocean, no life preserver in reach. "I never saw anything about this in the papers," I said.

"It was kept quiet."

"Why?"

"Your wife's request, for one. And the D.A.'s office didn't want their wrongful arrest made more public. So it was all done as quietly as possible. Plus there were, uh, problems with your wife's testimony."

"What problems?"

"She sort of lied at first."

More flailing. Sinking under. Coming to the surface. Flailing. "What are you talking about?"

"Your wife claimed that she was doing some career counseling with Gonzalez at the charity office at the time of the murder. Nobody really bought that."

"Why not?"

He cocked a skeptical eyebrow. "Career counseling at eleven at night?"

I nodded numbly.

"So as Mr. Gonzalez's attorney, I reminded your wife that the police would investigate her alibi. That, for example, the counseling offices had security cameras and there would be tapes of the comings and goings. That was when she came clean."

He stopped.

"Go on," I said.

"It's obvious, isn't it?"

"Tell me anyway."

Flannery shrugged. "She wanted to spare herself— and you, I guess—the embarrassment. That was why she insisted on secrecy. She was at Gonzalez's place, Dr. Beck. They'd been sleeping together for two months."

I didn't react. No one spoke. In the distance, I heard a bird squawk. Probably the one in the waiting room. I got to my feet. Tyrese took a step back.

"Thank you for your time," I said in the calmest voice you ever heard.

Flannery nodded at the window blinds.

"It's not true," I said to him.

He didn't respond. But then again, I hadn't expected him to.

33

Carlson sat in the car. His tie was still knotted meticulously. His suit jacket was off, hung on a wooden hanger on the backseat hook. The air-conditioning blew loud and hard. Carlson read the autopsy envelope: Elizabeth Beck, Case File 94-87002. His fingers started unwinding the string. The envelope opened. Carlson extracted the contents and spread them out on the passenger seat.

What had Dr. Beck wanted to see?

Stone had already given him the obvious answer: Beck wanted to know if there was anything that might incriminate him. That fit into their early theories, and it had, after all, been Carlson who'd first started questioning the accepted scenario on Elizabeth Beck's murder. He had been the first to believe that the killing was not what it appeared to be—that indeed it was Dr. David Beck, the husband, who had planned the murder of his wife.

So why had he stopped buying it?

He had carefully reviewed the holes now poking through that theory, but Stone had been equally convincing in patching them back up. Every case has holes. Carlson knew that. Every case has inconsistencies. If it doesn't, ten to one you've missed something.

So why did he now have doubts about Beck's guilt?

Perhaps it had something to do with the case becoming too neat, all the evidence suddenly lining up and cooperating with their theory. Or maybe his doubts were based on something as unreliable as "intuition," though Carlson had never been a big fan of that particular aspect of investigative work. Intuition was often a way of cutting corners, a nifty technique of replacing hard evidence and facts with something far more elusive and capricious. The worst investigators Carlson knew relied on so-called intuition.

He picked up the top sheet. General information. Elizabeth Parker Beck. Her address, her birth date (she'd been twenty-five when she died), Caucasian female, height five seven, weight 98 pounds. Thin. The external examination revealed that rigor mortis had resolved. There were blisters on the skin and fluid leaks from the orifices. That placed the time of death at more than three days. The cause of death was a knife wound to the chest. The mechanism of death was loss of blood and dramatic hemorrhaging of the right aorta. There were also cut wounds on her hands and fingers, theoretically because she tried to defend herself against a knife attack.

Carlson took out his notebook and Mont Blanc pen. He wrote Defensive knife wounds?!?! and then he underlined it several times. Defensive wounds. That wasn't KillRoy's style. KillRoy tortured his victims. He bound them with rope, did whatever, and once they were too far gone to care, he killed them.

Why would there be defensive knife wounds on her hands?

Carlson kept reading. He scanned through hair and eye color, and then, halfway down the second page, he found another shocker.

Elizabeth Beck had been branded postmortem.

Carlson reread that. He took out his notebook and

scratched down the word postmortem. That didn't add up. KillRoy had always branded his victims while they were alive. Much was made at trial about how he liked the smell of sizzling flesh, how he enjoyed the screams of his victims while he seared them.

First, the defensive wounds. Now this. Something wasn't meshing.

Carlson took off his glasses and closed his eyes. Mess, he thought to himself. Mess upset him. Logic holes were expected, yes, but these were turning into gaping wounds. On the one hand, the autopsy supported his original hypothesis that Elizabeth Beck's murder had been staged to look like the work of KillRoy. But now, if that were true, the theory was coming unglued from the other side.

He tried to take it step by step. First, why would Beck be so eager to see this file? On the surface, the answer was now obvious. Anybody who scrutinized these results would realize that there was an excellent chance that KillRoy had not murdered Elizabeth Beck. It was not a given, however. Serial killers, despite what you might read, are not creatures of habit. KillRoy could have changed his M.O. or sought some diversity. Still, with what Carlson was reading here, there was enough to make one ponder.

But all of this just begged what had become the big question: Why hadn't anybody noticed these evidentiary inconsistencies back then?

Carlson sorted through possibilities. KillRoy had never been prosecuted for Elizabeth Beck's murder. The reasons were now pretty clear. Perhaps the investigators suspected the truth. Perhaps they realized that Elizabeth Beck didn't fit, but publicizing that fact would only aid KillRoy's defense. The problem with prosecuting a serial killer is that you cast a net so wide, something is bound to slither out. All the defense has to do is pick apart one case, find discrepancies with one murder, and bang, the other cases are tainted by association. So without a confession, you rarely try him for all the murders at once. You do it step by step. The investigators, realizing this, probably just wanted the murder of Elizabeth Beck to go away.

But there were big problems with that scenario too.

Elizabeth Beck's father and uncle—two men in law enforcement—had seen the body. They had in all likelihood seen this autopsy report. Wouldn't they have wondered about the inconsistencies? Would they have let her murderer go free just to secure a conviction on KillRoy? Carlson doubted it.

So where did that leave him?

He continued through the file and stumbled across yet another stunner. The car's air-conditioning was seriously chilling him now, reaching bone. Carlson slid down a window and pulled the key out of the ignition. The top of the sheet read: Toxicology Report. According to the tests, cocaine and heroin had been found in Elizabeth Beck's bloodstream; moreover, traces were found in the hair and tissues, indicating that her use was more than casual.

Did that fit?

He was thinking about it, when his cell phone rang. He picked it up. "Carlson."

"We got something," Stone said.

Carlson put down the file. "What?"

"Beck. He's booked on a flight to London out of JFK. It leaves in two hours."

"I'm on my way."

* * *

Tyrese put a hand on my shoulder as we walked. "Bitches," he said for the umpteenth time. "You can't trust them."

I didn't bother replying.

It surprised me at first that Tyrese would be able to track down Helio Gonzalez so quickly, but the street network was as developed as any other. Ask a trader at Morgan Stanley to locate a counterpart at Goldman Sachs and it would be done in minutes. Ask me to refer a patient to pretty much any other doctor in the state, and it takes one phone call. Why should street felons be different?

Helio was fresh off a four-year stint upstate for armed robbery. He looked it too. Sunglasses, a doo-rag on his head, white T-shirt under a flannel shirt that had only the top button buttoned so that it looked like a cape or bat wings. The sleeves were rolled up, revealing crude prison tattoos etched onto his forearm and the prison muscles coiling thereunder. There is an unmistakable look to prison muscles, a smooth, marblelike quality as opposed to their puffier health club counterparts.

We sat on a stoop somewhere in Queens. I couldn't tell you where exactly. A Latin rhythm tah-tah-tahhed, the beat driving into my chest. Dark-haired women sauntered by in too-clingy spaghetti-strap tops. Tyrese nodded at me. I turned to Helio. He had a smirk on his face. I took in the whole package and one word kept popping into my brain: scum. Unreachable, unfeeling scum. You looked at him, and you knew that he would continue to leave serious destruction in his wake. The question was how much. I realized that this view was not charitable. I realized, too, that based on surfaces, the very same could be said for Tyrese. That didn't matter. Elizabeth may have believed in the redemption for the street-hardened or morally anesthetized. I was still working on it.

"Several years ago, you were arrested for the murder of Brandon Scope," I began. "I know you were released, and I don't want to cause you any trouble. But I need to know the truth."

Helio took off his sunglasses. He flicked a glance at Tyrese. "You bring me a cop?"

"I'm not a cop," I said. "I'm Elizabeth Beck's husband."

I wanted a reaction. I didn't get one.

"She's the woman who gave you the alibi."

"I know who she is."

"Was she with you that night?"

Helio took his time. "Yeah," he said slowly, smiling at me with yellow teeth. "She was with me all night."

"You're lying," I said.

Helio looked back over at Tyrese. "What is this, man?"

"I need to know the truth," I said.

"You think I killed that Scope guy?"

"I know you didn't."

That surprised him.

"What the hell is going on here?" he said.

"I need you to confirm something for me."

Helio waited.

"Were you with my wife that night, yes or no?"

"What you want me to say, man?"

"The truth."

"And if the truth is she was with me all night?"

"It's not the truth," I said.

"What makes you so sure?"

Tyrese joined in. "Tell the man what he wants to know."

Helio took his time again. "It's like she said. I did her, all right? Sorry, man, but that's what happened. We were doing it all night."

I looked at Tyrese. "Leave us alone a second, okay?"

Tyrese nodded. He got up and walked to his car. He leaned against the side door, arms folded, Brutus by his side. I turned my gaze back to Helio.

"Where did you first meet my wife?"

"At the center."

"She tried to help you?"

He shrugged, but he wouldn't look at me.

"Did you know Brandon Scope?"

A flicker of what might have been fear crossed his face. "I'm going, man."

"It's just you and me, Helio. You can frisk me for a wire."

"You want me to give up my alibi?"

"Yeah."

"Why would I do that?"

"Because someone is killing everyone connected with what happened to Brandon Scope. Last night, my wife's friend was murdered in her studio. They grabbed me today, but Tyrese intervened. They also want to kill my wife."

"I thought she was dead already."

"It's a long story, Helio. But it's all coming back. If I don't find out what really happened, we're all going to end up dead."

I didn't know if this was true or hyperbole. I didn't much care either.

"Where were you that night?" I pressed.

"With her."

"I can prove you weren't," I said.

"What?"

"My wife was in Atlantic City. I have her old charge records. I can prove it. I can blow your alibi right out of the water, Helio. And I'll do it. I know you didn't kill Brandon Scope. But so help me, I'll let them execute you for it if you don't tell me the truth."

A bluff. A great big bluff. But I could see that I'd drawn blood.

"Tell me the truth, and you stay free," I said.

"I didn't kill that dude, I swear it, man."

"I know that," I said again.

He thought about it. "I don't know why she did it, all right?"

I nodded, trying to keep him talking.

"I robbed a house out in Fort Lee that night. So I had no alibi. I thought I was going down for it. She saved my ass."

"Did you ask her why?"

He shook his head. "I just went along. My lawyer told me what she said. I backed her up. Next thing I knew, I was out."

"Did you ever see my wife again?"

"No." He looked up at me. "How come you so sure your wife wasn't doing me?"

"I know my wife."

He smiled. "You think she'd never cheat?"

I didn't reply.

Helio stood up. "Tell Tyrese he owes me one."

He chuckled, turned, walked away.

No luggage. An e-ticket so she could check in by machine rather than with a person. She waited in a neighboring terminal, keeping her eye on the departure screen, waiting for the On Time next to her flight to evolve into Boarding.

She sat in a chair of molded plastic and looked out onto the tarmac. A TV blared CNN. "Next up *Headline Sports*." She made her mind blank. Five years ago, she had spent time in a small village outside Goa, India. Though a true hellhole, the village had something of a buzz about it because of the one-hundred-year-old yogi who lived there. She had spent time with the yogi. He had tried to teach her meditation techniques, pranayama breathing, mind cleansing. But none of it ever really stuck. There were moments when she could sink away into blackness. More often, though, wherever she sank, Beck was there.

She wondered about her next move. There was no choice really. This was about preservation. Preservation meant fleeing. She had made a mess and now she was running away again, leaving others to clean it up. But what other option was there? They were onto her. She had been careful as hell, but they had still been watching. Eight years later.

A toddler scrambled toward the plate-glass window, his palms hitting it with a happy splat. His harried father chased him down and scooped him up with a giggle. She watched and her mind scrambled to the obvious what-could-have-beens. An old couple sat to her right, chatting amiably about nothing. As teenagers, she and Beck would watch Mr. and Mrs. Steinberg stroll up Downing Place arm in arm, every night without fail, long after their children had grown and fled the nest. That would be their lives, Beck had promised. Mrs. Steinberg died when she was eighty-two. Mr. Steinberg, who had been in amazingly robust health, followed four months later. They say that happens a lot with the elderly, that—to paraphrase Springsteen—two hearts become one. When one dies, the other follows. Was that how it was with her and David? They had not been together sixty-one years like the Steinbergs, but when you think about it in relative terms, when you consider that you barely have any memories of your life before age five, when you figure that she and Beck had been inseparable since they were seven, that they could barely unearth any memory that didn't include the other, when you think of the time spent together not just in terms of years but in life percentages, they had more vested in each other than even the Steinbergs.

She turned and checked the screen. Next to British Airways Flight 174, the word Boarding started to flash.

Her flight was being called.

Carlson and Stone, along with their local buddies Dimonte and Krinsky, stood with the British Airways reservation manager.

"He's a no-show," the reservation manager, a blue-and-white-uniformed woman with a kerchief, a beautiful accent, and a name tag reading Emily told them.

Dimonte cursed. Krinsky shrugged. This was not unexpected. Beck had been successfully eluding a manhunt all day. It was a long shot that he would be dumb enough to try to board a flight using his real name.

"Dead end," Dimonte said.

Carlson, who still had the autopsy file clutched against his hip, asked Emily, "Who is your most computer-literate employee?"

"That would be me," she said with a competent smile.

"Please bring up the reservation," Carlson said.

Emily did as he requested.

"Can you tell me when he booked the flight?"

"Three days ago."

Dimonte leapt on that one. "Beck planned to run. Son of a bitch."

Carlson shook his head. "No."

"How do you figure?"

"We've been assuming that he killed Rebecca Schayes to shut her up," Carlson explained. "But if you're going to leave the country, why bother? Why take the risk of waiting three days and trying to get away with another murder?"

Stone shook his head. "You're overthinking this one, Nick."

"We're missing something," Carlson insisted. "Why did he all of a sudden decide to run in the first place?"

"Because we were onto him."

"We weren't onto him three days ago."

"Maybe he knew it was a matter of time."

Carlson frowned some more.

Dimonte turned to Krinsky. "This is a waste of time. Let's get the hell out of here." He looked at Carlson. "We'll leave a couple of uniforms around just in case."

Carlson nodded, only half listening. When they left, he asked Emily, "Was he traveling with anyone?"

Emily hit some keys. "It was a solo booking."

"How did he book it? In person? On the phone? Did he go through a travel agency?"

She clicked the keys again. "It wasn't through a travel agency. That much I can tell you because we'd have a marking to pay a commission. The reservation was made directly with British Airways."

No help there. "How did he pay?"

"Credit card."

"May I have the number, please?"

She gave it to him. He passed it over to Stone. Stone shook his head. "Not one of his cards. At least, not one we know about."

"Check it out," Carlson said.

Stone's cell phone was already in his hand. He nodded and pressed the keypad.

Carlson rubbed his chin. "You said he booked his flight three days ago."

"That's correct."

"Do you know what time he booked it?"

"Actually yes. The computer stamps it in. Six-fourteen in the p.m."

Carlson nodded. "Okay, great. Can you tell me if anyone else booked at around the same time?"

Emily thought about it. "I've never tried that," she said. "Hold on a moment, let me see something." She typed. She waited. She typed some more. She waited. "The computer won't sort by booking date."

"But the information is in there?"

"Yes. Wait, hold up." Her fingers started clacking again. "I can paste the information onto a spreadsheet. We can put fifty bookings per screen. It will make it faster."

The first group of fifty had a married couple who

booked the same day but hours earlier. Useless. The second group had none. In the third group, however, they hit bingo.

"Lisa Sherman," Emily pronounced. "Her flight was booked the same day, eight minutes later."

It didn't mean anything on its own, of course, but Carlson felt the hair on the back of his neck stand up.

"Oh, this is interesting," Emily added.

"What?"

"Her seat assignment."

"What about it?"

"She was scheduled to sit next to David Beck. Row sixteen, seats E and F."

He felt the jolt. "Has she checked in?"

More typing. The screen cleared. Another came up. "As a matter of fact, she has. She's probably boarding as we speak."

She adjusted her purse strap and stood. Her step was brisk, her head high. She still had the glasses and the wig and implants. So did the photograph of Lisa Sherman in her passport.

She was four gates away when she heard a snippet of the CNN report. She stopped short. A man wheeling an industrial-size piece of carry-on ran into her. He made a rude hand gesture as though she'd cut him off on a freeway. She ignored him and kept her eyes on the screen.

The anchorwoman was doing the report. In the right-hand corner of the screen was a photograph of her old friend Rebecca Schayes side by side with an image of . . . of Beck.

She hurried closer to the screen. Under the images in a bloodred font were the words *Death in the Darkroom.*

"... David Beck, suspected in the slaying. But is that the only crime they believe he's committed? CNN's Jack Turner has more."

The anchorwoman disappeared. In her place, two men with NYPD windbreakers rolled out a black body bag on a stretcher. She recognized the building at once and almost gasped. Eight years. Eight years had passed, but Rebecca still had her studio in the same location.

A man's voice, presumably Jack Turner's, began his report: "It's a twisted tale, this murder of one of New York's hottest fashion photographers. Rebecca Schayes was found dead in her darkroom, shot twice in the head at close range." They flashed a photograph of Rebecca smiling brightly. "The suspect is her longtime friend, Dr. David Beck, an uptown pediatrician." Now Beck's image, no smile, lit up the screen. She almost fell over.

"Dr. Beck narrowly escaped arrest earlier today after assaulting a police officer. He is still at large and assumed armed and dangerous. If you have any information on his whereabouts ..." A phone number appeared in yellow. Jack Turner read out the number before continuing.

"But what has given this story an added twist are the leaks coming out of Manhattan's Federal Building. Presumably, Dr. Beck has been linked to the murder of two men whose bodies were recently unearthed in Pennsylvania, not far from where Dr. Beck's family has a summer residence. And the biggest shocker of all: Dr. David Beck is also a suspect in the eight-year-old slaying of his wife, Elizabeth."

A photograph of a woman she barely recognized popped up. She suddenly felt naked, cornered. Her image vanished as they went back to the anchorwoman, who said, "Jack, wasn't it believed that Elizabeth Beck

249

was the victim of serial killer Elroy 'KillRoy' Kellerton?"

"That's correct, Terese. Authorities aren't doing much talking right now, and officials deny the reports. But the leaks are coming to us from very reliable sources."

"Do the police have a motive, Jack?"

"We haven't heard one yet. There has been some speculation that there may have been a love triangle here. Ms. Schayes was married to a Gary Lamont, who remains in seclusion. But that's little more than conjecture at this point."

Still staring at the TV screen, she felt the tears start welling up.

"And Dr. Beck is still at large tonight?"

"Yes, Terese. The police are asking for the public's cooperation, but they stress that no one should approach him on their own."

Chatter followed. Meaningless chatter.

She turned away. Rebecca. Oh God, not Rebecca. And she'd gotten married. Had probably picked out dresses and china patterns and done all those things they used to mock. How? How had Rebecca gotten tangled up in all this? Rebecca hadn't known anything.

Why had they killed her?

Then the thought hit her anew: What have I done?

She had come back. They had started looking for her. How would they have gone about that? Simple. Watch the people she was closest to. Stupid. Her coming back had put everyone she cared about in danger. She had messed up. And now her friend was dead.

"British Airways Flight 174, departing for London. All rows may now board."

There was no time to beat herself up. Think. What should she do? Her loved ones were in danger. Beck—

she suddenly remembered his silly disguise—was on the run. He was up against powerful people. If they were trying to frame him for murder—and that seemed pretty obvious right now—he'd have no chance.

She couldn't just leave. Not yet. Not until she knew that Beck was safe.

She turned and headed for an exit.

When Peter Flannery finally saw the news reports on the David Beck manhunt, he picked up the phone and dialed a friend at the D.A.'s office.

"Who's running the Beck case?" Flannery asked.

"Fein."

A true ass, Flannery thought. "I saw your boy today."

"David Beck?"

"Yeah," Flannery said. "He paid me a visit."

"Why?"

Flannery kicked back his BarcaLounger. "Maybe you should put me through to Fein."

35

When night fell, Tyrese found me a room at the apartment of Latisha's cousin. We couldn't imagine that the police would unearth my connection with Tyrese, but why take the chance?

Tyrese had a laptop. We hooked it up. I checked my email, hoping for a message from my mysterious mailer. Nothing under my work account. Nothing under my home account. I tried the new one at bigfoot.com. Nothing there either.

Tyrese had been looking at me funny since we'd left Flannery's office. "I ask you something, Doc?"

"Go ahead," I said.

"When that mouthpiece said about that guy being murdered—"

"Brandon Scope," I added.

"Yeah, him. You look like someone hit you with a stun gun."

It had felt it. "You're wondering why?"

Tyrese shrugged.

"I knew Brandon Scope. He and my wife shared an office at a charitable foundation in the city. And my father grew up with and worked for his father. In fact, my father was in charge of teaching Brandon about the family holdings."

"Uh-huh," Tyrese said. "What else?"

"That's not enough?"

Tyrese waited. I turned to face him. He kept his eyes

steady and for a moment I thought he could see all the way to the blackest corners of my soul. Thankfully, the moment passed. Tyrese said, "So what do you want to do next?"

"Make a few phone calls," I said. "You sure they can't be traced back here?"

"Can't see how. Tell you what, though. We'll do it with a conference call to another cell phone. Make it that much harder."

I nodded. Tyrese set it up. I had to dial another number and tell somebody I didn't know what numbers to dial. Tyrese headed for the door. "I'm gonna check on TJ. I'll be back in an hour."

"Tyrese?"

He looked back. I wanted to say thanks, but somehow it didn't feel right. Tyrese understood. "Need you to stay alive, Doc. For my kid, see?"

I nodded. He left. I checked my watch before dialing Shauna's cell phone. She answered on the first ring. "Hello?"

"How's Chloe?" I asked.

"Great," she said.

"How many miles did you walk?"

"At least three. More like four or five." Relief coursed through me. "So what's our next—"

I smiled and disconnected the phone. I dialed up my forwarding buddy and gave him another number. He mumbled something about not being a goddamn operator, but he did as I asked.

Hester Crimstein answered as though she were taking a bite out of the receiver. "What?"

"It's Beck," I said quickly. "Can they listen in, or do we have some kind of attorney-client protection here?"

There was a strange hesitation. "It's safe," she said.

"I had a reason for running," I began.

"Like guilt?"

"What?"

Another hesitation. "I'm sorry, Beck. I screwed up. When you ran like that, I freaked out. I said some stupid things to Shauna, and I quit as your attorney."

"Never told me," I said. "I need you, Hester."

"I won't help you run."

"I don't want to run anymore. I want to surrender. But on our terms."

"You're not in any position to dictate terms, Beck. They're going to lock you up tight. You can forget bail."

"Suppose I offer proof I didn't kill Rebecca Schayes."

Another hesitation. "You can do that?"

"Yes."

"What sort of proof?"

"A solid alibi."

"Provided by?"

"Well," I said, "that's where it gets interesting."

Special Agent Carlson picked up his cell phone. "Yeah."

"Got something else," his partner Stone said.

"What?"

"Beck visited a cheap mouthpiece named Flannery a few hours ago. A black street kid was with him."

Carlson frowned. "I thought Hester Crimstein was his attorney."

"He wasn't looking for legal representation. He wanted to know about a past case."

"What case?"

"Some all-purpose perp named Gonzalez was arrested for killing Brandon Scope eight years ago. Elizabeth Beck gave the guy a hell of an alibi. Beck wanted to know all about it."

Carlson felt his head doing a double spin. How the hell . . . ?

"Anything else?"

"That's it," Stone said. "Say, where are you?"

"I'll talk to you later, Tom." Carlson hung up the phone and pressed in another number.

A voice answered, "National Tracing Center."

"Working late, Donna?"

"And I'm trying to get out of here, Nick. What do you want?"

"A really big favor."

"No," she said. Then with a big sigh, "What?"

"You still have that thirty-eight we found in the Sarah Goodhart safety-deposit box?"

"What about it?"

He told her what he wanted. When he finished, she said, "You're kidding, right?"

"You know me, Donna. No sense of humor."

"Ain't that truth." She sighed. "I'll put in a request, but there's no way it'll get done tonight."

"Thanks, Donna. You're the best."

When Shauna entered the building's foyer, a voice called out to her.

"Excuse me. Miss Shauna?"

She looked at the man with the gelled hair and expensive suit. "And you are?"

"Special Agent Nick Carlson."

"Nighty-night, Mr. Agent."

"We know he called you."

Shauna patted her mouth in a fake yawn. "You must be proud."

"Ever hear the terms aiding and abetting and accessory after the fact?"

"Stop scaring me," she said in an exaggerated monotone, "or I might just make wee-wee right here on the cheap carpeting."

"You think I'm bluffing?"

She put out her hands, wrists together. "Arrest me, handsome." She glanced behind him. "Don't you guys usually travel in pairs?"

"I'm here alone."

"So I gather. Can I go up now?"

Carlson carefully adjusted his glasses. "I don't think Dr. Beck killed anyone."

That stopped her.

"Don't get me wrong. There's plenty of evidence he did it. My colleagues are all convinced he's guilty. There is still a massive manhunt going on."

"Uh-huh," Shauna said with more than a hint of suspicion in her voice. "But somehow you see through all that?"

"I just think something else is going on here."

"Like what?"

"I was hoping you could tell me."

"And if I suspect that this is a trick?"

Carlson shrugged. "Not much I can do about that."

She mulled it over. "It doesn't matter," she said. "I don't know anything."

"You know where he's hiding."

"I don't."

"And if you did?"

"I wouldn't tell you. But you already know that."

"I do," Carlson said. "So I guess you won't tell me what all that talk about walking his dog was about."

She shook her head. "But you'll find out soon enough."

"He'll get hurt out there, you know. Your friend

assaulted a cop. That makes it open season on him."

Shauna kept her gaze steady. "Not much I can do about that."

"No, I guess not."

"Can I ask you something?"

"Shoot," Carlson said.

"Why don't you think he's guilty?"

"I'm not sure. Lots of little things, I guess." Carlson tilted his head. "Did you know that Beck was booked on a flight to London?"

Shauna let her eyes take in the lobby, trying to buy a second or two. A man entered and smiled appreciatively at Shauna. She ignored him. "Bull," she said at last.

"I just came from the airport," Carlson continued. "The flight was booked three days ago. He was a no-show, of course. But what was really odd was that the credit card used to purchase the ticket was in the name of Laura Mills. That name mean anything to you?"

"Should it?"

"Probably not. We're still working on it, but apparently it's a pseudonym."

"For whom?"

Carlson shrugged. "Do you know a Lisa Sherman?"

"No. How does she fit in?"

"She was booked on the same flight to London. In fact, she was supposed to sit next to our boy."

"Another no-show?"

"Not exactly. She checked in. But when they called the flight, she never boarded. Weird, don't you think?"

"I don't know what to think," Shauna said.

"Unfortunately, nobody could give us an ID on Lisa Sherman. She didn't check any luggage and she used an e-ticket machine. So we started running a background check. Any guess what we found?"

Shauna shook her head.

"Nothing," Carlson replied. "It looks like another pseudonym. Do you know the name Brandon Scope?"

Shauna stiffened. "What the hell is this?"

"Dr. Beck, accompanied by a black man, visited an attorney named Peter Flannery today. Flannery defended a suspect in the murder of Brandon Scope. Dr. Beck asked him about that and about Elizabeth's role in his release. Any clue why?"

Shauna started fumbling in her purse.

"Looking for something?"

"A cigarette," she said. "You have one?"

"Sorry, no."

"Damn." She stopped, met his eye. "Why are you telling me all this?"

"I have four dead bodies. I want to know what's going on."

"Four?"

"Rebecca Schayes, Melvin Bartola, Robert Wolf—those are the two men we found at the lake. And Elizabeth Beck."

"KillRoy killed Elizabeth."

Carlson shook his head.

"What makes you so sure?"

He held up the manila folder. "This, for one."

"What is it?"

"Her autopsy file."

Shauna swallowed. Fear coursed through her, tingling her fingers. The final proof, one way or the other. She tried very hard to keep her voice steady. "Can I take a look?"

"Why?"

She didn't reply.

"And more important, why was Beck so eager to see it?"

"I don't know what you mean," she said, but the words rang hollow in her own ears and, she was sure, his.

"Was Elizabeth Beck a drug user?" Carlson asked.

The question was a total surprise. "Elizabeth? Never."

"You're sure?"

"Of course. She worked with drug addicts. That was part of her training."

"I know a lot of vice cops who enjoy a few hours with a prostitute."

"She wasn't like that. Elizabeth was no Goody Two-shoes, but drugs? Not a chance."

He held up the manila envelope again. "The tox report showed both cocaine and heroin in her system."

"Then Kellerton forced them into her."

"No," Carlson said.

"What makes you so sure?"

"There are other tests, Shauna. Tissue and hair tests. They show a pattern of use going back several months at the least."

Shauna felt her legs weaken. She slumped against a wall. "Look, Carlson, stop playing games with me. Let me see the report, okay?"

Carlson seemed to consider it. "How about this?" he said. "I'll let you see any one sheet in here. Any one piece of information. How about that?"

"What the hell is this, Carlson?"

"Good night, Shauna."

"Whoa, whoa, hold up a sec." She licked her lips. She thought about the strange emails. She thought about Beck's running from the cops. She thought about the murder of Rebecca Schayes and the toxicology report that couldn't be. All of a sudden, her convincing demonstration on digital imaging manipulation didn't seem so convincing.

"A photograph," she said. "Let me see a photograph of the victim."

Carlson smiled. "Now, that's very interesting."

"Why's that?"

"There are none in here."

"But I thought—"

"I don't understand it either," Carlson interrupted. "I've called Dr. Harper. He was the M.E. on this one. I'm seeing if he can find out who else has signed out for this file. He's checking as we speak."

"Are you saying someone stole the photographs?"

Carlson shrugged. "Come on, Shauna. Tell me what's going on."

She almost did. She almost told him about the emails and the street cam link. But Beck had been firm. This man, for all his fancy talk, could still be the enemy. "Can I see the rest of the file?"

He moved it toward her slowly. The hell with blasé, she thought. She stepped forward and grabbed it from his hand. She tore it open and found the first sheet. As her eyes traveled down the page, a block of ice hardened in her stomach. She saw the body's height and the weight and stifled a scream.

"What?" Carlson asked.

She didn't reply.

A cell phone rang. Carlson scooped it out of his pants pocket. "Carlson."

"It's Tim Harper."

"Did you find the old logs?"

"Yes."

"Did someone else sign out Elizabeth Beck's autopsy?"

"Three years ago," Harper said. "Right after it was

placed into cold storage. One person signed it out."

"Who?"

"The deceased's father. He's also a police officer. His name is Hoyt Parker."

36

Larry Gandle sat across from Griffin Scope. They were outside in the garden portico behind Scope's mansion. Night had taken serious hold, blanketing the manicured grounds. The crickets hummed an almost pretty melody, as though the super-rich could even manipulate that. Tinkling piano music spilled from the sliding glass doors. Lights from inside the house provided a modicum of illumination, casting shadows of burnt red and yellow.

Both men wore khakis. Larry wore a blue Polo shirt. Griffin had on a silk button-down from his tailor in Hong Kong. Larry waited, a beer cooling his hand. He watched the older man sitting in perfect copper-penny silhouette, facing his vast backyard, his nose tilted up slightly, his legs crossed. His right hand dangled over the arm of the chair, amber liquor swirling in his snifter.

"You have no idea where he is?" Griffin asked.

"None."

"And these two black men who rescued him?"

"I have no idea how they're involved. But Wu is working on it."

Griffin took a sip of his drink. Time trudged by, hot and sticky. "Do you really believe she's still alive?"

Larry was about to launch into a long narrative, offering evidence for and against, showing all the options and possibilities. But when he opened his mouth, he simply said, "I do."

Griffin closed his eyes. "Do you remember the day your first child was born?"

"Yes."

"Did you attend the birth?"

"I did."

"We didn't do that in our day," Griffin said. "We fathers paced in a waiting room with old magazines. I remember the nurse coming out to get me. She brought me down the hall and I still remember turning the corner and seeing Allison holding Brandon. It was the strangest feeling, Larry. Something welled up inside me so that I thought I might burst. The feeling was almost too intense, too overwhelming. You couldn't sort through or comprehend it. I assume that all fathers experience something similar."

He stopped. Larry looked over. Tears ran down the old man's cheeks, sparkling off the low light. Larry remained still.

"Perhaps the most obvious feelings on that day are joy and apprehension—apprehension in the sense that you are now responsible for this little person. But there was something else there too. I couldn't put my finger on it exactly. Not then anyway. Not until Brandon's first day of school."

Something caught in the old man's throat. He coughed a bit and now Larry could see more tears. The piano music seemed softer now. The crickets hushed as though they were listening too.

"We waited together for the school bus. I held his hand. Brandon was five years old. He looked up at me in that way children do at that age. He wore brown pants that already had a grass stain on the knee. I remember the yellow bus pulling up and the sound the door made when it opened. Then Brandon let go of my hand and started climbing up the steps. I wanted to reach out and snatch him back and take him home, but I stood there, frozen. He moved inside the bus and I heard that noise again and the door slid closed. Brandon sat by a window. I could see his face. He waved to me. I waved back and as the bus pulled away, I said to myself, 'There goes my whole world.' That yellow bus with its flimsy metal sides and its driver I didn't know from Adam chariotted away what was in effect everything to me. And at that moment, I realized what I had felt the day of his birth. Terror. Not just apprehension. Cold, stark terror. You can fear illness or old age or death. But there's nothing like that small stone of terror that sat in my belly as I watched that bus pull away. Do you understand what I'm saying?"

Larry nodded. "I think I do."

"I knew then, at that moment, that despite my best efforts, something bad could happen to him. I wouldn't always be there to take the blow. I thought about it constantly. We all do, I guess. But when it happened, when—" He stopped and finally faced Larry Gandle. "I still try to bring him back," he said. "I try to bargain with God, offering him anything and everything if he'll somehow make Brandon alive. That won't happen, of course. I understand that. But now you come here and tell me that while my son, my whole world, rots in the ground ... she lives." He started shaking his head. "I can't have that, Larry. Do you understand?"

"I do," he said.

"I failed to protect him once. I won't fail again."

Griffin Scope turned back to his garden. He took another sip of his drink. Larry Gandle understood. He rose and walked back into the night.

* * *

At ten o'clock, Carlson approached the front door of 28 Goodhart Road. He didn't worry much about the late hour. He had seen downstairs lights on and the flicker of a television, but even without that, Carlson had more important worries than someone's beauty sleep.

He was about to reach for the bell when the door opened. Hoyt Parker was there. For a moment they both stood, two boxers meeting at center ring, staring each other down as the referee reiterated meaningless instructions about low blows and not punching on the break.

Carlson didn't wait for the bell. "Did your daughter take drugs?"

Hoyt Parker took it with little more than a twitch. "Why do you want to know?"

"May I come in?"

"My wife is sleeping," Hoyt said, slipping outside and closing the door behind him. "You mind if we talk out here?"

"Suit yourself."

Hoyt crossed his arms and bounced on his toes a bit. He was a burly guy in blue jeans and a T-shirt that fit less snugly ten pounds ago. Carlson knew that Hoyt Parker was a veteran cop. Cute traps and subtlety would not work here.

"Are you going to answer my question?" Carlson asked.

"Are you going to tell me why you want to know?" Hoyt replied.

Carlson decided to change tactics. "Why did you take the autopsy pictures from your daughter's file?"

"What makes you think I took them?" There was no outrage, no loud, phony denials.

"I looked at the autopsy report today," Carlson said.

"Why?"

"Pardon me?"

"My daughter has been dead for eight years. Her killer is in jail. Yet you decide to look at her autopsy report today. I'd like to know why."

This was going nowhere and going there fast. Carlson decided to give a little, put down his guard, let him wade in, see what happened. "Your son-in-law visited the county M.E. yesterday. He demanded to see his wife's file. I was hoping to find out why."

"Did he see the autopsy report?"

"No," Carlson said. "Do you know why he'd be so eager to see it?"

"No idea."

"But you seemed concerned."

"Like you, I find the behavior suspicious."

"More than that," Carlson said. "You wanted to know if he'd actually gotten his hands on it. Why?"

Hoyt shrugged.

"Are you going to tell me what you did with the autopsy pictures?"

"I don't know what you're talking about," he replied in a flat voice.

"You were the only person to sign out this report."

"And that proves what?"

"Were the photographs there when you viewed the file?"

Hoyt's eyes flickered, but there was little delay. "Yes," he said. "Yes, they were."

Carlson couldn't help but smile. "Good answer." It had been a trap, and Hoyt had avoided it. "Because if you answered no, I'd have to wonder why you didn't report it then and there, wouldn't I?"

"You have a suspicious mind, Agent Carlson."

"Uh-huh. Any thoughts on where those photos might be?"

"Probably misfiled."

"Right, sure. You don't seem very upset over it."

"My daughter's dead. Her case is closed. What's to get upset about?"

This was a waste of time. Or maybe it wasn't. Carlson wasn't getting much information, but Hoyt's demeanor spoke volumes.

"So you still think KillRoy murdered your daughter?"

"Without question."

Carlson held up the autopsy report. "Even after reading this?"

"Yes."

"The fact that so many of the wounds were postmortem doesn't trouble you?"

"It gives me comfort," he said. "It means my daughter suffered less."

"That's not what I mean. I'm talking in terms of the evidence against Kellerton."

"I don't see anything in that file that contradicts that conclusion."

"It's not consistent with the other murders."

"I disagree," Hoyt said. "What was not consistent was the strength of my daughter."

"I'm not sure I follow."

"I know that Kellerton enjoyed torturing his victims," Hoyt said. "And I know that he usually branded them while they were still alive. But we theorized that Elizabeth had tried to escape or, at the very least, fought back. The way we saw it, she forced his hand. He had to subdue her and in doing so, he ended up killing her. That explains the knife wounds on her hands. That explains why the branding was postmortem."

"I see." A surprise left hook. Carlson tried to keep on his feet. It was a good answer—a hell of a good answer. It made sense. Even the smallest victims can make plenty of trouble. His explanation made all the apparent inconsistencies wonderfully consistent. But there were still problems. "So how do you explain the tox report?"

"Irrelevant," Hoyt said. "It's like asking a rape victim about her sexual history. It doesn't matter if my daughter was a teetotaler or a crack fiend."

"Which was she?"

"Irrelevant," he repeated.

"Nothing's irrelevant in a murder investigation. You know that."

Hoyt took a step closer. "Be careful," he said.

"You threatening me?"

"Not at all. I'm just warning you that you shouldn't be so quick to victimize my daughter a second time."

They stood there. The final bell had sounded. They were now waiting for a decision that would be unsatisfactory no matter how the judges leaned.

"If that's all," Hoyt said.

Carlson nodded and took a step back. Parker reached for the doorknob.

"Hoyt?"

Hoyt turned back around.

"So there's no misunderstanding," Carlson said. "I don't believe a word you just said. We clear?"

"Crystal," Hoyt said.

37

When Shauna arrived at the apartment, she collapsed onto her favorite spot on the couch. Linda sat next to her and patted her lap. Shauna laid her head down. She closed her eyes as Linda caressed her hair.

"Is Mark okay?" Shauna asked.

"Yes," Linda said. "Do you mind telling me where you were?"

"Long story."

"I'm only sitting here waiting to hear about my brother."

"He called me," Shauna said.

"What?"

"He's safe."

"Thank God."

"And he didn't kill Rebecca."

"I know that."

Shauna turned her head to look up. Linda was blinking her eyes. "He's going to be okay," Shauna said.

Linda nodded, turned away.

"What is it?"

"I took those pictures," Linda said.

Shauna sat up.

"Elizabeth came to my office. She was hurt pretty badly. I wanted her to go to a hospital. She said no. She just wanted to make a record of it."

"It wasn't a car accident?"

Linda shook her head.

"Who hurt her?"

"She made me promise not to tell."

"Eight years ago," Shauna said. "Tell me."

"It's not that simple."

"Like hell it's not." Shauna hesitated. "Why would she go to you anyway? And how can you think of protecting …" Her voice faded away. She looked at Linda hard. Linda didn't flinch, but Shauna thought about what Carlson had told her downstairs.

"Brandon Scope," Shauna said softly.

Linda didn't reply.

"He's the one who beat her up. Oh Christ, no wonder she came to you. She wanted to keep it a secret. Me or Rebecca, we would have made her go to the police. But not you."

"She made me promise," Linda said.

"And you just accepted that?"

"What was I supposed to do?"

"Drag her ass down to the police station."

"Well, we can't all be as brave and strong as you, Shauna."

"Don't give me that crap."

"She didn't want to go," Linda insisted. "She said that she needed more time. That she didn't have enough proof yet."

"Proof of what?"

"That he assaulted her, I guess. I don't know. She wouldn't listen to me. I couldn't just force her."

"Oh right—and that was likely."

"What the hell does that mean?"

"You were involved in a charity financed by his family with his face at the helm," Shauna said. "What would happen if it got out that he beat up a woman?"

"Elizabeth made me promise."

"And you were only too happy to keep your mouth shut, right? You wanted to protect your damn charity."

"That's not fair—"

"You put it over her well-being."

"Do you know how much good we do?" Linda shouted. "Do you know how many people we help?"

"On the blood of Elizabeth Beck," Shauna said.

Linda slapped her across the face. The slap stung. They stared at each other, breathing hard. "I wanted to tell," Linda said. "She wouldn't let me. Maybe I was weak, I don't know. But don't you dare say something like that."

"And when Elizabeth was kidnapped at the lake— what did you think, for crying out loud?"

"I thought it might be connected. I went to Elizabeth's father. I told him what I knew."

"What did he say?"

"He thanked me and said he knew about it. He also told me not to say anything because the situation was delicate. And then when it became clear that KillRoy was the murderer—"

"You decided to keep silent."

"Brandon Scope was dead. What good would dragging his name through the mud do?"

The phone rang. Linda reached for it. She said hello, paused, and then she handed the phone to Shauna. "For you."

Shauna didn't look at her as she took the receiver. "Hello?"

"Meet me down at my office," Hester Crimstein told her.

"Why the hell should I?"

"I'm not big on apologies, Shauna. So let's just agree that I'm a big fat idiot and move on. Grab a taxi and come down here. We've got an innocent man to rescue."

Assistant District Attorney Lance Fein stormed into Crimstein's conference room looking like a sleep-deprived weasel on too many amphetamines. The two homicide detectives Dimonte and Krinsky followed in his wake. All three had faces taut as piano wire.

Hester and Shauna stood on the other side of the table. "Gentlemen," Hester said with a sweep of her hand, "please have a seat."

Fein eyed her, then shot a look of pure disgust at Shauna. "I'm not here for you to jerk me around."

"No, I'm sure you do enough of that in the privacy of your own home," Hester said. "Sit."

"If you know where he is—"

"Sit, Lance. You're giving me a headache."

Everyone sat. Dimonte put his snakeskin boots up on the table. Hester took both hands and knocked them off, never letting her smile falter. "We are here, gentlemen, with one aim: saving your careers. So let's get to it, shall we?"

"I want to know—"

"Shh, Lance. I'm talking here. Your job is to listen and maybe nod and say things like 'Yes, ma'am' and 'Thank you, ma'am.' Otherwise, well, you're toast."

Lance Fein gave her the eye. "You're the one helping a fugitive escape justice, Hester."

"You're sexy when you talk tough, Lance. Actually, you're not. Listen up, okay, because I don't want to have to repeat myself. I'm going to do you a favor, Lance. I'm not going to let you look like a total idiot on this. An idiot, okay, nothing to be done about that, but maybe, if you listen carefully, not a total idiot. You with me? Good. First off, I understand you have a definitive time of death on Rebecca Schayes now. Midnight, give or take a half hour. We pretty clear on that?"

"So?"

Hester looked at Shauna. "You want to tell him?"

"No, that's okay."

"But you're the one who did all the hard work."

Fein said, "Cut the crap, Crimstein."

The door behind them opened. Hester's secretary brought the sheets of paper over to her boss along with a small cassette tape. "Thank you, Cheryl."

"No problem."

"You can go home now. Come in late tomorrow."

"Thanks."

Cheryl left. Hester took out her half-moon reading glasses. She slipped them on and started reading the pages.

"I'm getting tired of this, Hester."

"You like dogs, Lance?"

"What?"

"Dogs. I'm not a big fan of them myself. But this one ... Shauna, you have that photograph?"

"Right here." Shauna held up a large photograph of Chloe for all to see. "She's a bearded collie."

"Isn't she cute, Lance?"

Lance Fein stood. Krinsky stood too. Dimonte didn't budge. "I've had enough."

"You leave now," Hester said, "and this dog will piss all over your career like it's a fire hydrant."

"What the hell are you talking about?"

She handed two of the sheets to Fein. "That dog proves Beck didn't do it. He was at Kinko's last night. He entered with the dog. Caused quite a ruckus, I understand. Here are four statements from independent

273

witnesses positively IDing Beck. He rented some computer time while there—more precisely, from four past midnight to twelve twenty-three a.m., according to their billing records." She grinned. "Here, fellas. Copies for all of you."

"You expect me to take these at face value?"

"Not all. Please, by all means, follow up."

Hester tossed a copy at Krinsky and another at Dimonte. Krinsky gathered it up and asked if he could use a phone.

"Sure," Crimstein said. "But if you're going to make any toll calls, kindly charge it to the department." She gave him a sickly sweet smile. "Thanks so much."

Fein read the sheet, his complexion turning to something in the ash-gray family.

"Thinking about expanding the time of death a bit?" Hester asked. "Feel free, but guess what? There was bridge construction that night. He's covered."

Fein was actually quaking. He muttered something under his breath that might have rhymed with "witch."

"Now, now, Lance." Hester Crimstein made a tsk-tsk noise. "You should be thanking me."

"What?"

"Just think of how I could have sandbagged you. There you are, all those cameras, all that delightful media coverage, ready to announce the big arrest of this vicious murderer. You put on your best power tie, make that big speech about keeping the streets safe, about what a team effort the capture of this animal was, though really you should be getting all the credit. The flashbulbs start going off. You smile and call the reporters by their first names, all the while imagining your big oak desk in the governor's mansion—and then bam, I lower the boom. I give the media this airtight alibi. Imagine, Lance. Man, oh, man, do you owe me, or what?"

Fein shot daggers with his eyes. "He still assaulted a police officer."

"No, Lance, he didn't. Think spin, my friend. Fact: You, Assistant District Attorney Lance Fein, jumped to the wrong conclusion. You hunted down an innocent man with your storm troopers—and not just an innocent man, but a doctor who chooses to work for lower pay with the poor instead of in the lucrative private sector." She sat back, smiling. "Oh, this is good, let me see. So while using dozens of city cops at Lord-knows-what expense, all with guns drawn and chasing down this innocent man, one officer, young and beefy and gung-ho, traps him in an alleyway and starts pounding on him. Nobody else is in sight, so this young cop takes it upon himself to make this scared man pay. Poor, persecuted Dr. David Beck, a widower I might add, did nothing but lash out in self-defense."

"That'll never sell."

"Sure it will, Lance. I don't want to sound immodest, but who's better at spin than yours truly? And wait, you haven't heard me wax philosophical on the comparisons between this case and Richard Jewell, or on the overzealousness of the D.A.'s office, or how they were so eager to pin this on Dr. David Beck, hero to the downtrodden, that they obviously planted evidence at his residence."

"Planted?" Fein was apoplectic. "Are you out of your mind?"

"Come on, Lance, we know Dr. David Beck couldn't have done it. We have a proof-positive alibi in the testimony of four—ah, hell, we'll dig up more than four before this is through—independent, unbiased witnesses that he didn't do it. So how did all that evidence get there? You, Mr. Fein, and your storm troopers. Mark Fuhrman will look like Mahatma Gandhi by the time I'm through with you."

Fein's hands tightened into fists. He gulped down a few breaths and made himself lean back. "Okay," he began slowly. "Assuming this alibi checks out—"

"Oh it will."

"Assuming it does, what do you want?"

"Well now, that's an awfully good question. You're in a bind, Lance. You arrest him, you look like an idiot. You call off the arrest, you look like an idiot. I'm not sure I see any way around it." Hester Crimstein stood, started pacing as though working a closing. "I've looked into this and I've thought about it and I think I've found a way to minimize the damage. Care to hear it?"

Fein glared some more. "I'm listening."

"You've done one thing smart in all this. Just one, but maybe it's enough. You've kept your mug away from the media. That's because, I imagine, it would be a tad embarrassing trying to explain how this doctor escaped your dragnet. But that's good. Everything that has been reported can be blamed on anonymous leaks. So here's what you do, Lance. You call a press conference. You tell them that the leaks are false, that Dr. Beck is being sought as a material witness, nothing more than that. You do not suspect him in this crime—in fact, you're certain he didn't commit it—but you learned that he was one of the last people to see the victim alive and wanted to speak with him."

"That'll never fly."

"Oh it'll fly. Maybe not straight and true, but it'll stay aloft. The key will be me, Lance. I owe you one because my boy ran. So I, the enemy of the D.A.'s office, will back you up. I'll tell the media how you cooperated with us, how you made sure that my client's rights were not abused, that Dr. Beck and I wholeheartedly support your investigation and look forward to working with you."

Fein kept still.

"It's like I said before, Lance. I can spin for you or I can spin against you."

"And in return?"

"You drop all these silly assault and resisting charges."

"No way."

Hester motioned him toward the door. "See you in the funny pages."

Fein's shoulders slumped ever so slightly. His voice, when he spoke, was soft. "If we agree," he said, "your boy will cooperate? He'll answer all my questions?"

"Please, Lance, don't try to pretend you're in any condition to negotiate. I've laid out the deal. Take it— or take your chances with the press. Your choice. The clock is ticking." She bounced her index finger back and forth and made a tick-tock sound.

Fein looked at Dimonte. Dimonte chewed his toothpick some more. Krinsky got off the phone and nodded at Fein. Fein in turn nodded at Hester. "So how do we handle this?"

38

I woke up and lifted my head and almost screamed. My muscles were two steps beyond stiff and sore; I ached in parts of my body I didn't know I had. I tried to swing my legs out of bed. Swing was a bad idea. A very bad idea. Slow. That was the ticket this morning.

My legs hurt most, reminding me that despite my quasi-marathon of yesterday, I was pathetically out of shape. I tried to roll over. The tender spots where the Asian guy had attacked felt as though I'd ripped sutures. My body longed for a couple of Percodans, but I knew that they would put me on Queer Street, and that's not where I wanted to be right now.

I checked my watch. Six a.m. It was time for me to call Hester back. She picked up on the first ring.

"It worked," she said. "You're free."

I felt only mild relief.

"What are you going to do?" she asked.

A hell of a question. "I'm not sure."

"Hold on a sec." I heard another voice in the background. "Shauna wants to talk to you."

There was a fumbling sound as the phone changed hands, and then Shauna said, "We need to talk."

Shauna, never one for idle pleasantries or subtleties, still sounded uncharacteristically strained and maybe even—hard to imagine—scared. My heart started doing a little giddyap.

"What is it?"

"This isn't for the phone," she said.

"I can be at your place in an hour."

"I haven't told Linda about, uh, you know."

"Maybe it's time to," I said.

"Yeah, okay." Then she added with surprising tenderness, "Love you, Beck."

"Love you too."

I half crouched, half crawled toward the shower. Furniture helped support my stiff-legged stumble and keep me upright. I stayed under the spray until the hot water ran out. It helped ease the soreness, but not a lot.

Tyrese found me a purple velour sweat suit from the Eighties Al Sharpton collection. I almost asked for a big gold medallion.

"Where you gonna go?" he asked me.

"To my sister's for now."

"And then?"

"To work, I guess."

Tyrese shook his head.

"What?" I asked.

"You up against some bad dudes, Doc."

"Yeah, I kinda put that together."

"Bruce Lee ain't gonna let this slide."

I thought about that. He was right. Even if I wanted to, I couldn't just go home and wait for Elizabeth to make contact again. In the first place, I'd had enough with the passive; gentle repose simply was not on the Beck agenda anymore. But equally important, the men in that van were not about to forget the matter and let me go merrily on my way.

"I watch your back, Doc. Brutus too. Till this is over."

I was about to say something brave like "I can't ask you to do that" or "You have your own life to lead," but when you thought about it, they could either do this or deal drugs. Tyrese wanted to help—perhaps even needed to help—and let's face it, I needed him. I could warn him off, remind him of the danger, but he understood these particular perils far better than I did. So in the end, I just accepted with a nod.

Carlson got the call from the National Tracing Center earlier than he expected.

"We were able to run it already," Donna said.

"How?"

"Heard of IBIS?"

"Yeah, a little." He knew that IBIS stood for Integrated Ballistic Identification System, a new computer program that the Bureau of Alcohol, Tobacco and Firearms used to store bullet and shell casings. Part of the ATF's new Ceasefire program.

"We don't even need the original bullet anymore," she went on. "They just had to send us the scanned images. We can digitize and match them right on the screen."

"And?"

"You were right, Nick," she said. "It's a match."

Carlson disconnected and placed another call. When the man on the other end picked up, he asked, "Where's Dr. Beck?"

39

Brutus hooked up with us on the sidewalk. I said, "Good morning." He said nothing. I still hadn't heard the man speak. I slid into the backseat. Tyrese sat next to me and grinned. Last night he had killed a man. True, he had done so in defense of my life, but from his casual demeanor, I wasn't even sure he remembered pulling the trigger. I more than anyone should understand what he was going through, but I didn't. I'm not big on moral absolutes. I see the grays. I make the calls. Elizabeth had a clearer view of her moral compass. She would be horrified that a life had been lost. It wouldn't have mattered to her that the man was trying to kidnap, torture, and probably kill me. Or maybe it would. I don't really know anymore. The hard truth is, I didn't know everything about her. And she certainly didn't know everything about me.

My medical training insists that I never make that sort of moral call. It's a simple rule of triage: The most seriously injured gets treated first. It doesn't matter who they are or what they've done. You treat the most grievously wounded. That's a nice theory, and I understand the need for such thinking. But if, say, my nephew Mark were rushed in with a stab wound and some serial pedophile who stabbed him came in at the same time with a life-threatening bullet in the brain, well, come on. You make the call, and in your heart of hearts, you know that the call is an easy one.

You might argue that I'm nesting myself on an awfully slippery slope. I would agree with you, though I might counter that most of life is lived out there. The problem was, there were repercussions when you lived in the grays—not just theoretical ones that taint your soul, but the brick-and-mortar ones, the unforeseeable destruction that such choices leave behind. I wondered what would have happened if I had told the truth right from the get-go. And it scared the hell out of me.

"Kinda quiet, Doc."

"Yeah," I said.

Brutus dropped me off in front of Linda and Shauna's apartment on Riverside Drive.

"We'll be around the corner," Tyrese said. "You need anything, you know my number."

"Right."

"You got the Glock?"

"Yes."

Tyrese put a hand on my shoulder. "Them or you, Doc," he said. "Just keep pulling the trigger."

No grays there.

I stepped out of the car. Mothers and nannies ambled by, pushing complicated baby strollers that fold and shift and rock and play songs and lean back and lean forward and hold more than one kid, plus an assortment of diapers, wipes, Gerber snacks, juice boxes (for the older sibling), change of clothing, bottles, even car first-aid kits. I knew all this from my own practice (being on Medicaid did not preclude one from affording the high-end Peg Perego strollers), and I found this spectacle of bland normalcy cohabiting in the same realm as my recent ordeal to be something of an elixir.

I turned back toward the building. Linda and Shauna were already running toward me. Linda got there first.

She wrapped her arms around me. I hugged her back. It felt nice.

"You're okay?" Linda said.

"I'm fine," I said.

My assurances did not stop Linda from repeating the question several more times in several different ways. Shauna stopped a few feet away. I caught her eye over my sister's shoulder. Shauna wiped tears from her eyes. I smiled at her.

We continued the hugs and kisses through the elevator ride. Shauna was less effusive than usual, staying a bit out of the mix. An outsider might claim that this made sense, that Shauna was giving the sister and brother some space during this tender reunion. That outsider wouldn't know Shauna from Cher. Shauna was wonderfully consistent. She was prickly, demanding, funny, bighearted, and loyal beyond all reason. She never put on masks or pretenses. If your thesaurus had an antonym section and you looked up the phrase "shrinking violet," her lush image would stare back at you. Shauna lived life in your face. She wouldn't take a step back if smacked across the mouth with a lead pipe.

Something inside me started to tingle.

When we reached the apartment, Linda and Shauna exchanged a glance. Linda's arm slipped off me. "Shauna wants to talk to you alone first," she said. "I'll be in the kitchen. You want a sandwich?"

"Thanks," I said.

Linda kissed me and gave me one more squeeze, as though making sure I was still there and of substance. She hurried out of the room. I looked over at Shauna. She kept her distance. I put out my hands in a "Well?" gesture.

"Why did you run?" Shauna asked.

"I got another email," I said.

"At that Bigfoot account?"

"Yes."

"Why did it come in so late?"

"She was using code," I said. "It just took me time to figure it out."

"What kind of code?"

I explained about the Bat Lady and the Teenage Sex Poodles.

When I finished, she said, "That's why you were using the computer at Kinko's? You figured it out during your walk with Chloe?"

"Yes."

"What did the email say exactly?"

I couldn't figure out why Shauna was asking all these questions. On top of what I've already said, Shauna was strictly a big-picture person. Details were not her forte; they just muddied and confused. "She wanted me to meet her at Washington Square Park at five yesterday," I said. "She warned me that I'd be followed. And then she told me that no matter what, she loved me."

"And that's why you ran?" she asked. "So you wouldn't miss the meeting?"

I nodded. "Hester said I wouldn't get bail until midnight at the earliest."

"Did you get to the park in time?"

"Yes."

Shauna took a step closer to me. "And?"

"She never showed."

"And yet you're still convinced that Elizabeth sent you that email?"

"There's no other explanation," I said.

She smiled when I said that.

"What?" I asked.

"You remember my friend Wendy Petino?"

"Fellow model," I said. "Flaky as a Greek pastry."

Shauna smiled at the description. "She took me to dinner once with her"—she made quote marks with her fingers—"spiritual guru. She claimed that he could read minds and tell the future and all that. He was helping her communicate with her dead mother. Wendy's mother had committed suicide when she was six."

I let her go on, not interrupting with the obvious "what's the point?" Shauna was taking her time here, but I knew that she'd get to it eventually.

"So we finish dinner. The waiter serves us coffee. Wendy's guru—he had some name like Omay—he's staring at me with these bright, inquisitive eyes, you know the type, and he hands me the bit about how he senses—that's how he says it, senses—that maybe I'm a skeptic and that I should speak my mind. You know me. I tell him he's full of shit and I'm tired of him stealing my friend's money. Omay doesn't get angry, of course, which really pisses me off. Anyway, he hands me a little card and tells me to write anything I want on it—something significant about my life, a date, a lover's initials, whatever I wanted. I check the card. It looks like a normal white card, but I still ask if I can use one of my own. He tells me to suit myself. I take out a business card and flip it over. He hands me a pen, but again I decide to use my own—in case it's a trick pen or something, what do I know, right? He has no problem with that either. So I write down your name. Just Beck. He takes the card. I'm watching his hand for a switch or whatever, but he just passes the card to Wendy. He tells her to hold it. He grabs my hand. He closes his eyes and starts shaking like he's having a seizure and I swear I feel something course through me. Then Omay opens his eyes and says,

285

'Who's Beck?' "

She sat down on the couch. I did likewise.

"Now, I know people have good sleight of hand and all that, but I was there. I watched him up close. And I almost bought it. Omay had special abilities. Like you said, there was no other explanation. Wendy sat there with this satisfied smile plastered on her face. I couldn't figure it out."

"He did research on you," I said. "He knew about our friendship."

"No offense, but wouldn't he guess I'd put my own son's name or maybe Linda's? How would he know I'd pick you?"

She had a point. "So you're a believer now?"

"Almost, Beck. I said I almost bought it. Ol' Omay was right. I'm a skeptic. Maybe it all pointed to him being psychic, except I knew he wasn't. Because there are no such things as psychics—just like there are no such things as ghosts." She stopped. Not exactly subtle, my dear Shauna.

"So I did some research," she went on. "The good thing about being a famous model is that you can call anyone and they'll talk to you. So I called this illusionist I'd seen on Broadway a couple of years ago. He heard the story and then he laughed. I said what's so funny. He asked me a question: Did this guru do this after dinner? I was surprised. What the hell could that have to do with it? But I said yes, how did you know? He asked if we had coffee. Again I said yes. Did he take his black? One more time I said yes." Shauna was smiling now. "Do you know how he did it, Beck?"

I shook my head. "No clue."

"When he passed the card to Wendy, it went over his coffee cup. Black coffee, Beck. It reflects like a mirror.

That's how he saw what I'd written. It was just a dumb parlor trick. Simple, right? Pass the card over your cup of black coffee and it's like passing it over a mirror. And I almost believed him. You understand what I'm saying here?"

"Sure," I said. "You think I'm as gullible as Flaky Wendy."

"Yes and no. See, part of Omay's con is the want, Beck. Wendy falls for it because she wants to believe in all that mumbo-jumbo."

"And I want to believe Elizabeth is alive?"

"More than any dying man in a desert wants to find an oasis," she said. "But that's not really my point either."

"Then what is?"

"I learned that just because you can't see any other explanation doesn't mean that one doesn't exist. It just means you can't see it."

I leaned back and crossed my legs. I watched her. She turned away from my gaze, something she never does. "What's going on here, Shauna?"

She wouldn't face me.

"You're not making any sense," I said.

"I think I was pretty damn clear—"

"You know what I mean. This isn't like you. On the phone you said you needed to talk to me. Alone. And for what? To tell me that my dead wife is, after all, still dead?" I shook my head. "I don't buy it."

Shauna didn't react.

"Tell me," I said.

She turned back. "I'm scared," she said in a tone that made the hair on the back of my neck stand up.

"Of what?"

The answer didn't come right away. I could hear

287

Linda rustling around in the kitchen, the tinkling of plates and glasses, the sucking pop when she opened the refrigerator. "That long warning I just gave you," Shauna finally continued. "That was as much for me as for you."

"I don't understand."

"I've seen something." Her voice died out. She took a deep breath and tried again. "I've seen something that my rational mind can't explain away. Just like in my story about Omay. I know there has to be another explanation, but I can't find it." Her hands started moving, her fingers fidgeting with buttons, pulling imaginary threads off her suit. Then she said it: "I'm starting to believe you, Beck. I think maybe Elizabeth is still alive."

My heart leapt into my throat.

She rose quickly. "I'm going to mix a mimosa. Join me?"

I shook my head.

She looked surprised. "You sure you don't want—"

"Tell me what you saw, Shauna."

"Her autopsy file."

I almost fell over. It took me a little time to find my voice. "How?"

"Do you know Nick Carlson from the FBI?"

"He questioned me," I said.

"He thinks you're innocent."

"Didn't sound that way to me."

"He does now. When all that evidence started pointing at you, he thought it was all too neat."

"He told you that?"

"Yes."

"And you believed him?"

"I know it sounds naïve, but yeah, I believed him."

I trusted Shauna's judgment. If she said that Carlson was on the level, he was either a wonderful liar or he'd seen through the frame-up. "I still don't understand," I said. "What does that have to do with the autopsy?"

"Carlson came to me. He wanted to know what you were up to. I wouldn't tell him. But he was tracking your movements. He knew that you asked to see Elizabeth's autopsy file. He wondered why. So he called the coroner's office and got the file. He brought it with him. To see if I could help him out on that."

"He showed it to you?"

She nodded.

My throat was dry. "Did you see the autopsy photos?"

"There weren't any, Beck."

"What?"

"Carlson thinks someone stole them."

"Who?"

She shrugged. "The only other person to sign out the file was Elizabeth's father."

Hoyt. It all circled back to him. I looked at her. "Did you see any of the report?"

Her nod was more tentative this time.

"And?"

"It said Elizabeth had a drug problem, Beck. Not just that there were drugs in her system. He said that the reports showed the abuse was long-term."

"Impossible," I said.

"Maybe, maybe not. That alone wouldn't be enough to convince me. People can hide drug abuse. It's not likely, but neither is her being alive. Maybe the tests were wrong or inconclusive. Something. There are explanations, right? It can somehow be explained away."

289

I licked my lips. "So what couldn't be?" I asked.

"Her height and weight," Shauna said. "Elizabeth was listed as five seven and under a hundred pounds."

Another sock in the gut. My wife was five four and closer to a hundred fifteen pounds. "Not even close," I said.

"Not even."

"She's alive, Shauna."

"Maybe," she allowed, and her gaze flicked toward the kitchen. "But there's something more."

Shauna turned and called out Linda's name. Linda stepped into the doorway and stayed there. She looked suddenly small in her apron. She wrung her hands and wiped them on the apron front. I watched my sister, puzzled.

"What's going on?" I said.

Linda started speaking. She told me about the photographs, how Elizabeth had come to her to take them, how she'd been only too happy to keep her secret about Brandon Scope. She didn't sugarcoat or offer explanations, but then again, maybe she didn't have to. She stood there and poured it all out and waited for the inevitable blow. I listened with my head down. I couldn't face her, but I easily forgave. We all have our blind spots. All of us.

I wanted to hug her and tell her that I understood, but I couldn't quite pull it off. When she'd finished, I merely nodded and said, "Thanks for telling me."

My words were meant to be a dismissal. Linda understood. Shauna and I sat there in silence for almost a full minute.

"Beck?"

"Elizabeth's father has been lying to me," I said.

She nodded.

"I've got to talk to him."

"He didn't tell you anything before."

True enough, I thought.

"Do you think it'll be different this time?"

I absentmindedly patted the Glock in my waistband. "Maybe," I said.

Carlson greeted me in the corridor. "Dr. Beck?" he said.

Across town at the same time, the district attorney's office held a press conference. The reporters were naturally skeptical of Fein's convoluted explanation (vis-à-vis me), and there was a lot of backpedaling and finger-pointing and that sort of thing. But all that seemed to do was confuse the issue. Confusion helps. Confusion leads to lengthy reconstruction and clarification and exposition and several other "tions." The press and their public prefer a simpler narrative.

It probably would have been a rougher ride for Mr. Fein, but by coincidence, the D.A.'s office used this very same press conference to release indictments against several high-ranking members of the mayor's administration along with a hint that the "tentacles of corruption"—their phrase—may even reach the big man's office. The media, an entity with the collective attention span of a Twinkie-filled two-year-old, immediately focused on this shiny new toy, kicking the old one under the bed.

Carlson stepped toward me. "I'd like to ask you a few questions."

"Not now," I said.

"Your father owned a gun," he said.

His words rooted me to the floor. "What?"

"Stephen Beck, your father, purchased a Smith and Wesson thirty-eight. The registration showed that he bought it several months before he died."

"What does that have to do with anything?"

"I assume you inherited the weapon. Am I correct?"

"I'm not talking to you." I pressed the elevator button.

"We have it," he said. I turned, stunned. "It was in Sarah Goodhart's safety-deposit box. With the pictures."

I couldn't believe what I was hearing. "Why didn't you tell me this before?"

Carlson gave me a crooked smile.

"Oh right, I was the bad guy back then," I said. Then, making a point of turning away, I added, "I don't see the relevance."

"Sure you do."

I pressed the elevator button again.

"You went to see Peter Flannery," Carlson continued. "You asked him about the murder of Brandon Scope. I'd like to know why."

I pressed the call button and held it down. "Did you do something to the elevators?"

"Yes. Why did you see Peter Flannery?"

My mind made a few quick deductions. An idea—a dangerous thing under the best of circumstances—came to me. Shauna trusted this man. Maybe I could too. A little anyway. Enough. "Because you and I have the same suspicions," I said.

"What's that?"

"We're both wondering if KillRoy murdered my wife."

Carlson folded his arms. "And what does Peter Flannery have to do with that?"

"You were tracking down my movements, right?"

"Yes."

"I decided to do the same with Elizabeth's. From

eight years ago. Flannery's initials and phone number were in her day planner."

"I see," Carlson said. "And what did you learn from Mr. Flannery?"

"Nothing," I lied. "It was a dead end."

"Oh, I don't think so," Carlson said.

"What makes you say that?"

"Are you familiar with how ballistic tests work?"

"I've seen them on TV."

"Put simply, every gun makes a unique imprint on the bullet it fires. Scratches, grooves—unique to that weapon. Like fingerprints."

"That much I know."

"After your visit to Flannery's office, I had our people run a specific ballistic match on the thirty-eight we found in Sarah Goodhart's safety-deposit box. Know what I found?"

I shook my head, but I knew.

Carlson took his time before he said, "Your father's gun, the one you inherited, killed Brandon Scope."

A door opened and a mother and her teen son stepped into the hall. The teen was in mid-whine, his shoulder slumped in adolescent defiance. His mother's lips were pursed, her head held high in the don't-wanna-hear-it position. They came toward the elevator. Carlson said something into a walkie-talkie. We both stepped away from the elevator bank, our eyes locked in a silent challenge.

"Agent Carlson, do you think I'm a killer?"

"Truth?" he said. "I'm not sure anymore."

I found his response curious. "You're aware, of course, that I'm not obligated to speak to you. In fact, I can call Hester Crimstein right now and nix everything you're trying to do here."

He bristled, but he didn't bother denying it. "What's your point?"

"Give me two hours."

"To what?"

"Two hours," I repeated.

He thought about it. "Under one condition."

"What?"

"Tell me who Lisa Sherman is."

That genuinely puzzled me. "I don't know the name."

"You and she were supposed to fly out of the country last night."

Elizabeth.

"I don't know what you're talking about," I said. The elevator dinged. The door slid open. The pursed-lips mom and her slumped adolescent stepped inside. She looked back at us. I signaled for her to hold the door.

"Two hours," I said.

Carlson nodded grudgingly. I hopped into the elevator.

40

You're late!" the photographer, a tiny man with a fake French accent, shouted at Shauna. "And you look like— *comment dit-on?*—like something flushed through the *toilette.*"

"Up yours, Frédéric," Shauna snapped back, not knowing or caring if that was his name. "Where you from anyway, Brooklyn?"

He threw his hands up. "I cannot work like this!"

Aretha Feldman, Shauna's agent, hurried over. "Don't worry, François. Our makeup man will work magic on her. She always looks like hell when she arrives. We'll be right back." Aretha grabbed Shauna's elbow hard but never let up the smile. To Shauna, sotto voce, she said, "What the hell is wrong with you?"

"I don't need this crap."

"Don't play prima donna with me."

"I had a rough night, okay?"

"Not okay. Get in that makeup chair."

The makeup artist gasped in horror when he saw Shauna. "What are those bags under your eyes?" he cried. "Are we doing a shoot for Samsonite luggage now?"

"Ha-ha." Shauna moved toward the chair.

"Oh," Aretha said. "This came for you." She held an envelope in her hand.

Shauna squinted. "What is it?"

"Beats me. A messenger service dropped it off ten minutes ago. Said it was urgent."

She handed the envelope to Shauna. Shauna took it in one hand and flipped it over. She looked at the familiar scrawl on the front of the envelope—just the word "Shauna"—and felt her stomach clench.

Still staring at the handwriting, Shauna said, "Give me a second."

"Now's not the time—"

"A second."

The makeup artist and agent stepped away. Shauna slit open the seal. A blank white card with the same familiar handwriting fell out. Shauna picked it up. The note was brief: "Go to the ladies' room."

Shauna tried to keep her breath even. She stood.

"What's wrong?" Aretha said.

"I have to pee," she said, the calmness in her voice surprising even her. "Where's the head?"

"Down the hall on the left."

"I'll be right back."

Two minutes later, Shauna pushed the bathroom door. It didn't budge. She knocked. "It's me," she said. And waited.

A few seconds later, she heard the bolt slide back. More silence. Shauna took a deep breath and pushed again. The door swung open. She stepped onto the tile and stopped cold. There, across the room, standing in front of the near stall, was a ghost.

Shauna choked back a cry.

The brunette wig, the weight loss, the wire-framed spectacles—none of it altered the obvious.

"Elizabeth . . ."

"Lock the door, Shauna."

Shauna obeyed without thought. When she turned around, she took a step toward her old friend. Elizabeth shrunk back.

"Please, we don't have much time."

For perhaps the first time in her life, Shauna was at a loss for words.

"You have to convince Beck I'm dead," Elizabeth said.

"A little late for that."

Her gaze swept the room as though looking for an escape route. "I made a mistake coming back. A stupid, stupid mistake. I can't stay. You have to tell him—"

"We saw the autopsy, Elizabeth," Shauna said. "There's no putting this genie back in the bottle."

Elizabeth's eyes closed.

Shauna said, "What the hell happened?"

"It was a mistake to come here."

"Yeah, you said that already."

Elizabeth started chewing on her lower lip. Then: "I have to go."

"You can't," Shauna said.

"What?"

"You can't run away again."

"If I stay, he'll die."

"He's already dead," Shauna said.

"You don't understand."

"Don't have to. If you leave him again, he won't survive. I've been waiting eight years for him to get over you. That's what's supposed to happen, you know. Wounds heal. Life goes on. But not for Beck." She took a step toward Elizabeth. "I can't let you run away again."

There were tears in all four eyes.

"I don't care why you left," Shauna said, inching closer. "I just care that you're back."

"I can't stay," she said weakly.

"You have to."

"Even if it means his death?"

"Yeah," Shauna said without hesitation. "Even if. And you know what I'm saying is true. That's why you're here. You know you can't leave again. And you know I won't let you."

Shauna took another step.

"I'm so tired of running," Elizabeth said softly.

"I know."

"I don't know what to do anymore."

"Me neither. But running isn't an option this time. Explain it to him, Elizabeth. Make him understand."

Elizabeth lifted her head. "You know how much I love him?"

"Yeah," Shauna said, "I do."

"I can't let him get hurt."

Shauna said, "Too late."

They stood now, a foot apart. Shauna wanted to reach out and hold her, but she stayed still.

"Do you have a number to reach him?" Elizabeth said.

"Yeah, he gave me a cell—"

"Tell him Dolphin. I'll meet him there tonight."

"I don't know what the hell that means."

Elizabeth quickly slid past her, peeked out the bathroom door, slithered through it. "He'll understand," she said. And then she was gone.

41

As usual, Tyrese and I sat in the backseat. The morning sky was a charcoal ash, the color of tombstone. I directed Brutus where to turn off after we crossed the George Washington Bridge. Behind his sunglasses, Tyrese studied my face. Finally he asked, "Where we going?"

"My in-laws'."

Tyrese waited for me to say more.

"He's a city cop," I added.

"What's his name?"

"Hoyt Parker."

Brutus smiled. Tyrese did likewise.

"You know him?"

"Never worked with the man myself, but, yeah, I heard the name."

"What do you mean, worked with the man?"

Tyrese waved me off. We hit the town border. I had gone through several surreal experiences over the past three days—chalk "driving through my old neighborhood with two drug dealers in a car with tinted windows" as another. I gave Brutus a few more directions before we pulled up to the memory-laden split-level on Goodhart.

I stepped out. Brutus and Tyrese sped off. I made it to the door and listened to the long chime. The clouds grew darker. A lightning bolt ripped the sky at the seam. I pressed the chime again. Pain traveled down my arm. I still ached all over hell from yesterday's combination of torture and overexertion. For a moment, I let myself wonder what would have happened if Tyrese and Brutus hadn't shown up. Then I shoved that thought away hard.

Finally I heard Hoyt say, "Who is it?"

"Beck," I said.

"It's open."

I reached for the knob. My hand stopped an inch before touching the brass. Weird. I had visited here countless times in my life, but I never remembered Hoyt asking who it was at the door. He was one of the guys who preferred direct confrontation. No hiding in the bushes for Hoyt Parker. He feared nothing, and dammit, he would prove it every step of the way. You ring his bell, he opens the door and faces you full.

I looked behind me. Tyrese and Brutus were gone— no smarts in loitering in front of a cop's house in a white suburb.

"Beck?"

No choice. I thought about the Glock. As I put my left hand on the knob, I put my right closer to my hip. Just in case. I turned the knob and pushed the door. My head leaned through the crack.

"I'm in the kitchen," Hoyt called out.

I stepped all the way inside and closed the door behind me. The room smelled of a lemon disinfectant, one of those plug-in-a-socket cover-up brands. I found the odor cloying.

"You want something to eat?" Hoyt asked.

I still couldn't see him. "No, thanks."

I waded across the semi-shag toward the kitchen. I spotted the old photographs on the mantel, but this time I didn't wince. When my feet reached linoleum, I let my eyes take in the room. Empty. I was about to turn back when I felt the cold metal against my temple. A hand suddenly snaked around my neck and jerked back hard.

"You armed, Beck?"

I didn't move or speak.

With the gun still in place, Hoyt dropped the arm from my neck and patted me down. He found the Glock, pulled it out, skidded it across the linoleum.

"Who dropped you off?"

"A couple of friends," I managed to say.

"What sort of friends?"

"What the hell is this, Hoyt?"

He backed off. I turned around. The gun was pointed at my chest. The muzzle looked enormous to me, widening like a giant mouth readying to swallow me whole. It was hard to wrest my gaze from that cold, dark tunnel.

"You come here to kill me?" Hoyt asked.

"What? No." I forced myself to look up. Hoyt was unshaven. His eyes were red-tinged, his body was swaying. Drinking. Drinking a lot.

"Where's Mrs. Parker?" I asked.

"She's safe." An odd reply. "I sent her away."

"Why?"

"I think you know."

Maybe I did. Or was starting to.

"Why would I want to hurt you, Hoyt?"

He kept the gun pointed at my chest. "Do you always carry a concealed weapon, Beck? I could have you thrown in jail for that."

"You've done worse to me," I replied.

His face fell. A low groan escaped his lips.

"Whose body did we cremate, Hoyt?"

"You don't know shit."

"I know that Elizabeth is still alive," I said.

His shoulders slumped, but the weapon stayed right in place. I saw his gun hand tense, and for a moment, I was sure he was going to shoot. I debated jumping away, but it wasn't as though he couldn't nail me with the second round.

"Sit down," he said softly.

"Shauna saw the autopsy report. We know it wasn't Elizabeth in that morgue."

"Sit down," he repeated, raising the gun a bit, and I believe that he might have shot me if I didn't obey. He led me back to the living room. I sat on the hideous couch that had witnessed so many memorable moments, but I had the feeling that they would be pretty much Bic flicks next to the bonfire about to engulf this room.

Hoyt sat across from me. The weapon was still up and centered at my middle. He never let his hand rest. Part of his training, I supposed. Exhaustion bled from him. He looked like a balloon with a slow leak, deflating almost imperceptibly.

"What happened?" I asked.

He didn't answer my question. "What makes you think she's alive?"

I stopped. Could I have been wrong here? Was there any way he didn't know? No, I decided quickly. He had seen the body at the morgue. He had been the one who identified her. He had to be involved. But then I remembered the email.

Tell no one ...

Had it been a mistake to come here?

Again no. That message had been sent before all this—in practically another era. I had to make a decision here. I had to push, take some action.

"Have you seen her?" he asked me.

"No."

"Where is she?"

"I don't know," I said.

Hoyt suddenly cocked his head. He signaled me to silence with a finger to his lips. He stood and crept toward the window. The shades were all drawn. He peeked through the side.

I stood.

"Sit down."

"Shoot me, Hoyt."

He looked at me.

"She's in trouble," I said.

"And you think you can help her?" He made a sneering noise. "I saved both your lives that night. What did you do?"

I felt something in my chest contract. "I got knocked unconscious," I said.

"Right."

"You . . ." I was having trouble articulating. "You saved us?"

"Sit down."

"If you know where she is—"

"We wouldn't be having this conversation," he finished.

I took another step toward him. Then another. He aimed the gun at me. I did not stop. I walked until the muzzle pressed against my sternum. "You're going to tell me," I said. "Or you're going to kill me."

"You're willing to take that gamble?"

I looked him straight in the eye and really held the stare for perhaps the first time in our long relationship. Something passed between us, though I'm not sure what. Resignation on his part maybe, I don't know. But I stayed put. "Do you have any idea how much I miss your daughter?"

"Sit down, David."

"Not until—"

"I'll tell you," he said softly. "Sit down."

I kept my eyes on his as I backed up to the couch. I lowered myself onto the cushion. He put the gun down on the side table. "You want a drink?"

"No."

"You better have one."

"Not now."

He shrugged and walked over to one of those chintzy pull-down bars. It was old and loose. The glasses were in disarray, tinkling against one another, and I was more certain than ever that this had not been his first foray into the liquor cabinet today. He took his time pouring the drink. I wanted to hurry him, but I had done enough pushing for the time being. He needed this, I figured. He was gathering his thoughts, sorting through them, checking the angles. I expected as much.

He cupped the glass in both hands and sank into the chair. "I never much liked you," he said. "It was nothing personal. You come from a good family. Your father was a fine man, and your mother, well, she tried, didn't she." One hand held the drink while the other ran through his hair. "But I thought your relationship with my daughter was"—he looked up, searching the ceiling for the words—"a hindrance to her growth. Now ... well, now I realize how incredibly lucky you both were."

The room chilled a few degrees. I tried not to move, to quiet my breath, anything so as not to disturb him.

"I'll start with the night at the lake," he said. "When they grabbed her."

"Who grabbed her?"

He stared down into his glass. "Don't interrupt," he said. "Just listen."

304

I nodded, but he didn't see. He was still staring down at his drink, literally looking for answers in the bottom of a glass.

"You know who grabbed her," he said, "or you should by now. The two men they found buried up there." His gaze suddenly swept the room. He snatched up his weapon and stood, checking the window again. I wanted to ask what he expected to see out there, but I didn't want to throw off his rhythm.

"My brother and I got to the lake late. Almost too late. We set up to stop them midway down the dirt road. You know where those two boulders are?"

He glanced toward the window, then back at me. I knew the two boulders. They sat about half a mile down the dirt road from Lake Charmaine. Both huge, both round, both almost the exact same size, both perfectly placed on either side of the road. There were all kinds of legends about how they got there.

"We hid behind them, Ken and me. When they came close, I shot out a tire. They stopped to check it. When they got out of the car, I shot them both in the head."

With one more look out the window, Hoyt moved back to his chair. He put down the weapon and stared at his drink some more. I held my tongue and waited.

"Griffin Scope hired those two men," he said. "They were supposed to interrogate Elizabeth and then kill her. Ken and I got wind of the plan and headed up to the lake to stop them." He put up his hand as if to silence a question, though I hadn't dared open my mouth. "The hows and whys aren't important. Griffin Scope wanted Elizabeth dead. That's all you need to know. And he wouldn't stop because a couple of his boys got killed. Plenty more where they came from. He's like one of those mythical beasts where you cut off the head and it grows two more." He looked at me. "You can't fight that kind of power, Beck."

He took a deep sip. I kept still.

"I want you to go back to that night and put yourself in our position," he continued, moving closer, trying to engage me. "Two men are lying dead on that dirt road. One of the most powerful men in the world sent them to kill you. He has no qualms about taking out the innocent to get to you. What can you do? Suppose we decided to go to the police. What would we tell them? A man like Scope doesn't leave any evidence behind—and even if he did, he has more cops and judges in his pocket than I have hairs on my head. We'd be dead. So I ask you, Beck. You're there. You have two men dead on the ground. You know it won't end there. What do you do?"

I took the question as rhetorical.

"So I presented these facts to Elizabeth, just like I'm presenting them to you now. I told her that Scope would wipe us out to get to her. If she ran away—if she went into hiding, for example—he'd just torture us until we gave her up. Or he'd go after my wife. Or your sister. He'd do whatever it took to make sure Elizabeth was found and killed." He leaned closer to me. "Do you see now? Do you see the only answer?"

I nodded because it was all suddenly transparent. "You had to make them think she was dead."

He smiled, and new goose bumps surfaced all over me. "I had some money saved up. My brother Ken had more. We also had the contacts. Elizabeth went underground. We got her out of the country. She cut her hair, learned to wear disguises, but that was probably overkill. No one was really looking for her. For the past eight years she's been bouncing around third world countries, working for the Red Cross or UNICEF or whatever organization she could hook up with."

I waited. There was so much he hadn't yet told me, but I sat still. I let the implications seep in and shake me at the core. Elizabeth. She was alive. She had been alive for the past eight years. She had been breathing and living and working. . . . It was too much to compute, one of those incomprehensible math problems that make the computer shut down.

"You're probably wondering about the body in the morgue."

I allowed myself a nod.

"It was pretty simple really. We get Jane Does in all the time. They get stored in pathology until somebody gets bored with them. Then we stick them in a potter's field out on Roosevelt Island. I just waited for the next Caucasian Jane Doe who'd be a near enough match to pop up. It took longer than I expected. The girl was probably a runaway stabbed by her pimp, but, of course, we'll never know for sure. We also couldn't leave Elizabeth's murder open. You need a fall guy, Beck. For closure. We chose KillRoy. It was common knowledge that KillRoy branded the faces with the letter K. So we did that to the corpse. That only left the problem of identification. We toyed around with the idea of burning her beyond recognition, but that would have meant dental records and all that. So we took a chance. The hair matched. The skin tone and age were about right. We dumped her body in a town with a small coroner's office. We made the anonymous call to the police ourselves. We made sure we arrived at the medical examiner's office at the same time as the body. Then all I had to do was make a tearful ID. That's how the large majority of murder victims are identified. A family member IDs them. So I did, and Ken backed me up. Who would question that? Why on earth would a father and uncle lie?"

"You took a hell of a risk," I said.

"But what choice did we have?"

"There had to be other ways."

He leaned closer. I smelled his breath. The loose folds of skin by his eyes drooped low. "Again, Beck, you're on that dirt road with those two bodies—hell, you're sitting here right now with the benefit of hindsight. So tell me: What should we have done?"

I didn't have an answer.

"There were other problems too," Hoyt added, sitting back a bit. "We were never totally sure that Scope's people would buy the whole setup. Luckily for us, the two lowlifes were supposed to leave the country after the murder. We found plane tickets to Buenos Aires on them. They were both drifters, unreliable types. That all helped. Scope's people bought it, but they kept tabs on us—not so much because they thought she was still alive, but they worried that maybe she had given one of us some incriminating material."

"What incriminating material?"

He ignored the question. "Your house, your phone, probably your office. They've been bugged for the past eight years. Mine too."

That explained the careful emails. I let my eyes wander around the room.

"I swept for them yesterday," he said. "The house is clean."

When he was silent for a few moments, I risked a question. "Why did Elizabeth choose to come back now?"

"Because she's foolish," he said, and for the first time, I heard anger in his voice. I gave him some time.

He calmed, the red swells in his face ebbing away. "The two bodies we buried," he said quietly.

"What about them?"

"Elizabeth followed the news on the Internet. When she read that they'd been discovered, she figured, same as me, that the Scopes might realize the truth."

"That she was still alive?"

"Yes."

"But if she were overseas, it would still take a hell of a lot to find her."

"That's what I told her. But she said that wouldn't stop them. They'd come after me. Or her mother. Or you. But"—again he stopped, dropped his head—"I don't know how important all that was."

"What do you mean?"

"Sometimes I think she wanted it to happen." He fiddled with the drink, jiggled the ice. "She wanted to come back to you, David. I think the bodies were just an excuse."

I waited again. He drank some more. He took another peek out the window.

"It's your turn," he said to me.

"What?"

"I want some answers now," he said. "Like how did she contact you. How did you get away from the police. Where you think she is."

I hesitated, but not very long. What choice did I really have here? "Elizabeth contacted me by anonymous emails. She spoke in code only I'd understand."

"What kind of code?"

"She made references to things in our past."

Hoyt nodded. "She knew they might be watching."

"Yes." I shifted in my seat. "How much do you know about Griffin Scope's personnel?" I asked.

He looked confused. "Personnel?"

"Does he have a muscular Asian guy working for him?"

Whatever color was left on Hoyt's face flowed out as though through an open wound. He looked at me in awe, almost as though he wanted to cross himself. "Eric Wu," he said in a hushed tone.

"I ran into Mr. Wu yesterday."

"Impossible," he said.

"Why?"

"You wouldn't be alive."

"I got lucky." I told him the story. He looked near tears.

"If Wu found her, if he got to her before he got to you ..." He closed his eyes, wishing the image away.

"He didn't," I said.

"How can you be so sure?"

"Wu wanted to know why I was in the park. If he had her already, why bother with that?"

He nodded slowly. He finished his drink and poured himself another. "But they know she's alive now," he said. "That means they're going to come after us."

"Then we'll fight back," I said, with far more bravery than I felt.

"You didn't hear me before. The mystical beast keeps growing more heads."

"But in the end, the hero always defeats the beast."

He scoffed at that one. Deservedly, I might add. I kept my eyes on him. The grandfather clock ding-donged. I thought about it some more.

"You have to tell me the rest," I said.

"Unimportant."

"It's connected with Brandon Scope's murder, isn't it?"

He shook his head without conviction.

"I know that Elizabeth gave an alibi to Helio Gonzalez," I said.

"It's not important, Beck. Trust me."

"Been there, done that, got screwed," I said.

He took another swig.

"Elizabeth kept a safety-deposit box under the name Sarah Goodhart," I said. "That's where they found those pictures."

"I know," Hoyt said. "We were in a rush that night. I didn't know she'd already given the key to them. We emptied their pockets, but I never checked their shoes. Shouldn't have mattered, though. I had no intention of them ever being found."

"She left more in that box than just the photographs," I continued.

Hoyt carefully set down his drink.

"My father's old gun was in there too. A thirty-eight. You remember it?"

Hoyt looked away and his voice was suddenly soft. "Smith and Wesson. I helped him pick it out."

I felt myself start shaking again. "Did you know that Brandon Scope was killed with that gun?"

His eyes shut tight, like a child wishing away a bad dream.

"Tell me what happened, Hoyt."

"You know what happened."

I couldn't stop quaking. "Tell me anyway."

Each word came out like body blows. "Elizabeth shot Brandon Scope."

I shook my head. I knew it wasn't true.

"She was working side by side with him, doing that charity work. It was just a question of time before she stumbled across the truth. That Brandon was running all this penny-ante crap, playing at being a tough street guy. Drugs, prostitution, I don't even know what."

"She never told me."

"She didn't tell anyone, Beck. But Brandon found out. He beat the hell out of her to warn her off. I didn't know it then, of course. She gave me the same story about a bad fender-bender."

"She didn't kill him," I insisted.

"It was self-defense. When she didn't stop investigating, Brandon broke into your home, and this time he had a knife. He came at her . . . and she shot him. Total self-defense."

I couldn't stop shaking my head.

"She called me, crying. I drove over to your place. When I got there"—he paused, his breath caught—"he was already dead. Elizabeth had that gun. She wanted me to call the police. I talked her out of it. Self-defense or not, Griffin Scope would kill her and worse. I told her to give me a few hours. She was shaky, but she finally agreed."

"You moved the body," I said.

He nodded. "I knew about Gonzalez. The punk was on his way to a fulfilling life of crime. I've seen the type enough to know. He'd already gotten off on a technicality for one murder. Who better to frame?"

It was becoming so clear. "But Elizabeth wouldn't let that happen."

"I didn't count on that," he said. "She heard on the news about the arrest, and that was when she decided to make up that alibi. To save Gonzalez from"—sarcastic finger-quote marks—"a grave injustice." He shook his head. "Worthless. If she'd just let that scumbag take the fall, it would have been all over."

I said, "Scope's people found out about her making up that alibi."

312

"Someone inside leaked it to them, yeah. Then they started sending their own people around, and they found out about her investigation. The rest became obvious."

"So that night at the lake," I said. "It was about revenge."

He mulled that over. "In part, yes. And in part it was about covering up the truth about Brandon Scope. He was a dead hero. Maintaining that legacy meant a lot to his father."

And, I thought, to my sister.

"I still don't get why she kept that stuff in a safety-deposit box," I said.

"Evidence," he said.

"Of what?"

"That she killed Brandon Scope. And that she did it in self-defense. No matter what else happened, Elizabeth didn't want someone else to take the blame for what she did. Naïve, wouldn't you say?"

No, I wouldn't. I sat there and let the truth try to settle in. Not happening. Not yet anyway. Because this wasn't the full truth. I knew that better than anyone. I looked at my father-in-law, the sagging skin, the thinning hair, the softening gut, the still-impressive but eroding frame. Hoyt thought that he knew what had really happened with his daughter. But he had no idea how wrong he was.

I heard a thunderclap. Rain pounded the windows like tiny fists.

"You could have told me," I said.

He shook his head, this time putting more into it. "And what would you have done, Beck? Follow her? Run away together? They would have learned the truth and killed us all. They were watching you. They still are.

We told no one. Not even Elizabeth's mother. And if you need proof we did the right thing, look around you. It's eight years later. All she did was send you a few anonymous emails. And look what happened."

A car door slammed. Hoyt pounced toward the window like a big cat. He peered out again. "Same car you arrived in. Two black men inside."

"They're here for me."

"You sure they don't work for Scope?"

"Positive." On cue, my new cell phone rang. I picked it up.

"Everything okay?" Tyrese asked.

"Yes."

"Step outside."

"Why?"

"You trust that cop?"

"I'm not sure."

"Step outside."

I told Hoyt that I had to go. He seemed too drained to care. I retrieved the Glock and hurried for the door. Tyrese and Brutus were waiting for me. The rain had let up a bit, but none of us seemed to care.

"Got a call for you. Stand over there."

"Why?"

"Personal," Tyrese said. "I don't want to hear it."

"I trust you."

"Just do what I say, man."

I moved out of hearing distance. Behind me I saw the shade open up. Hoyt peered out. I looked back at Tyrese. He gestured for me to put the phone to my ear. I did. There was silence and then Tyrese said, "Line clear, go ahead."

The next voice I heard was Shauna's. "I saw her."

I remained perfectly still.

"She said for you to meet her tonight at the Dolphin."

I understood. The line went dead. I walked back to Tyrese and Brutus. "I need to go somewhere on my own," I said. "Where I can't be followed."

Tyrese glanced at Brutus. "Get in," Tyrese said.

42

Brutus drove like a madman. He took one-way streets in the wrong direction. He made sudden U-turns. From the right lane, he'd cut across traffic and make a left through a red light. We were making excellent time.

The MetroPark in Iselin had a train heading toward Port Jervis that left in twenty minutes. I could rent a car from there. When they dropped me off, Brutus stayed in the car. Tyrese walked me to the ticket counter.

"You told me to run away and not come back," Tyrese said.

"That's right."

"Maybe," he said, "you should do the same."

I put my hand out for him to shake. Tyrese ignored it and hugged me fiercely. "Thank you," I said softly.

He released his grip, adjusted his shoulders so that his jacket relaxed down, fixed his sunglasses. "Yeah, whatever." He didn't wait for me to say anything more before heading back to the car.

The train arrived and departed on schedule. I found a seat and collapsed into it. I tried to make my mind go blank. It wouldn't happen. I glanced around. The car was fairly empty. Two college girls with bulky backpacks jabbered in the language of "like" and "you know." My eyes drifted off. I spotted a newspaper—more specifically, a city tabloid—that someone had left on a seat.

I moved over and picked it up. The coveted cover featured a young starlet who'd been arrested for-

shoplifting. I flipped pages, hoping to read the comics or catch up on sports—anything mindless would do. But my eyes got snagged on a picture of, well, me. The wanted man. Amazing how sinister I looked in the darkened photo, like a Mideast terrorist.

That was when I saw it. And my world, already off kilter, lurched again.

I wasn't actually reading the article. My eyes were just wandering down the page. But I saw the names. For the first time. The names of the men who'd been found dead at the lake. One was familiar.

Melvin Bartola.

It couldn't be.

I dropped the paper and ran, opening those sliding doors until I found a conductor two cars away. "Where's the next stop?" I asked him.

"Ridgemont, New Jersey."

"Is there a library near the station?"

"I wouldn't know."

I got off there anyway.

Eric Wu flexed his fingers. With a small, tight push, he forced the door.

It hadn't taken him long to track down the two black men who'd helped Dr. Beck escape. Larry Gandle had friends in the police department. Wu had described the men to them, and then he went through the proper mug books. Several hours later, Wu spotted the image of a thug named Brutus Cornwall. They made a few calls and learned that Brutus worked for a drug dealer named Tyrese Barton.

Simple.

The chain lock snapped. The door flew open, the knob banging against the wall. Latisha looked up, startled. She was about to scream, but Wu moved fast. He clamped his hand over her mouth and lowered his lips to her ear. Another man, someone Gandle had hired, came in behind him.

"Shh," Wu said almost gently.

On the floor, TJ played with his Hot Wheels. He tilted his head at the noise and said, "Mama?"

Eric Wu smiled down at him. He let Latisha go and knelt to the floor. Latisha tried to stop him, but the other man held her back. Wu rested his enormous hand on the boy's head. He stroked TJ's hair as he turned to Latisha.

"Do you know how I can find Tyrese?" he asked her.

Once off the train, I took a taxi to the rent-a-car place. The green-jacketed agent behind the counter gave me directions to the library. It took maybe three minutes to get there. The Ridgemont library was a modern facility, nouveau colonial brick, picture windows, beech-wood shelves, balconies, turrets, coffee bar. At the reference desk on the second floor, I found a librarian and asked if I could use the Internet.

"Do you have ID?" she asked.

I did. She looked at it. "You have to be a county resident."

"Please," I said. "It's very important."

I expected to see a no-yield, but she softened. "How long do you think you'll be?"

"No more than a few minutes."

"That computer over there"—she pointed to a terminal behind me—"it's our express terminal. Anyone can use it for ten minutes."

I thanked her and hurried over. Yahoo! found me the site for the *New Jersey Journal*, the major newspaper of

Bergen and Passaic counties. I knew the exact date I needed. Twelve years ago on January twelfth. I found the search archive and typed in the information.

The Web site went back only six years.

Damn.

I hurried back over to the librarian. "I need to find a twelve-year-old article from the *New Jersey Journal*," I said.

"It wasn't in their Web archive?"

I shook my head.

"Microfiche," she said, slapping the sides of her chair to rise. "What month?"

"January."

She was a large woman and her walk was labored. She found the roll in a file drawer and then helped me thread the tape through the machine. I sat down. "Good luck," she said.

I fiddled with the knob, as if it were a throttle on a new motorcycle. The microfiche shrieked through the mechanism. I stopped every few seconds to see where I was. It took me less than two minutes to find the right date. The article was on page three.

As soon as I saw the headline, I felt the lump in my throat.

Sometimes I swear that I actually heard the screech of tires, though I was asleep in my bed many miles away from where it happened. It still hurt—maybe not as much as the night I lost Elizabeth, but this was my first experience with mortality and tragedy and you never really get over that. Twelve years later, I still remember every detail of that night, though it comes back to me in a tornado blur—the predawn doorbell, the solemn-faced police officers at the door, Hoyt standing with them, their soft, careful words, our denials, the slow

319

realization, Linda's drawn face, my own steady tears, my mother still not accepting, hushing me, telling me to stop crying, her already frayed sanity giving way, her telling me to stop acting like a baby, insisting that everything was fine, then suddenly, coming close to me, marveling at how big my tears were, too big, she said, tears that big belonged on the face of a child, not a grown-up, touching one, rubbing it between her forefinger and her thumb, stop crying David!, growing angrier because I couldn't stop, her screams then, screaming at me to stop crying, until Linda and Hoyt stepped in and shushed her and someone gave her a sedative, not for the first or last time. It all came back to me in an awful gush. And then I read the article and felt the impact jar me in a whole new direction:

CAR DRIVES OVER RAVINE
ONE DEAD, CAUSE UNKNOWN

Last night at approximately 3:00 AM, a Ford Taurus driven by Stephen Beck of Green River, New Jersey, ran off a bridge in Mahwah, not far from the New York state border. Road conditions were slick due to the snowstorm, but officials have not yet made a ruling on what caused the accident. The sole witness to the accident, Melvin Bartola, a truck driver from Cheyenne, Wyoming—

I stopped reading. Suicide or accident. People had wondered which. Now I knew it was neither.

Brutus said, "What's wrong?"

"I don't know, man." Then, thinking about it, Tyrese added, "I don't want to go back."

Brutus didn't reply. Tyrese sneaked a glance at his old

friend. They had started hanging out together in third grade. Brutus hadn't been much of a talker back then either. Probably too busy getting his ass whipped twice a day—home and school—until Brutus figured out the only way he was going to survive was to become the meanest son of a bitch on the block. He started taking a gun to school when he was eleven. He killed for the first time when he was fourteen.

"Ain't you tired of it, Brutus?"

Brutus shrugged. "All we know."

The truth sat there, heavy, unmoving, unblinking.

Tyrese's cell phone trilled. He picked it up and said, "Yo."

"Hello, Tyrese."

Tyrese didn't recognize the strange voice. "Who is this?"

"We met yesterday. In a white van."

His blood turned to ice. Bruce Lee, Tyrese thought. Oh, damn ... "What do you want?"

"I have somebody here who wants to say hi."

There was a brief silence and then TJ said, "Daddy?"

Tyrese whipped off his sunglasses. His body went rigid. "TJ? You okay?"

But Eric Wu was back on the line. "I'm looking for Dr. Beck, Tyrese. TJ and I were hoping you could help me find him."

"I don't know where he is."

"Oh, that's a shame."

"Swear to God, I don't know."

"I see," Wu said. Then: "Hold on a moment, Tyrese, would you? I'd like you to hear something."

43

The wind blew, the trees danced, the purple-orange of sunset was starting to give way to a polished pewter. It frightened me how much the night air felt exactly the same as it had eight years ago, the last time I'd ventured near these hallowed grounds.

I wondered if Griffin Scope's people would think to keep an eye on Lake Charmaine. It didn't matter really. Elizabeth was too clever for that. I mentioned earlier that there used to be a summer camp here before Grandpa purchased the property. Elizabeth's clue—Dolphin—was the name of a cabin, the one where the oldest kids had slept, the one deepest in the woods, the one we rarely dared to visit.

The rental car climbed what had once been the camp's service entrance, though it barely existed anymore. From the main road you couldn't make it out, the high grass hiding it like the entrance to the Batcave. We still kept a chain across it, just in case, with a sign that read No Trespassing. The chain and sign were both still there, but the years of neglect showed. I stopped the car, unhooked the chain, wrapped it around the tree.

I slid back into the driver's seat and headed up to the old camp mess hall. Little of it remained. You could still see the rusted, overturned remnants of what had once been ovens and stoves. Some pots and pans littered the ground, but most had been buried over the years. I got out and smelled the sweet of the green. I tried not to think about my father, but in the clearing, when I was able to look down at the lake, at the way the moon's silver sparkled on the crisp surface, I heard the old ghost again and wondered, this time, if it wasn't crying out for revenge.

I hiked up the path, though that, too, was pretty much nonexistent. Odd that Elizabeth would pick here to meet. I mentioned before that she never liked to play in the ruins of the old summer camp. Linda and I, on the other hand, would marvel when we stumbled over sleeping bags or freshly emptied tin cans, wondering what sort of drifter had left them behind and if, maybe, the drifter was still nearby. Elizabeth, far smarter than either of us, didn't care for that game. Strange places and uncertainty scared her.

It took ten minutes to get there. The cabin was in remarkably good shape. The ceiling and walls were all still standing, though the wooden steps leading to the door were little more than splinters. The Dolphin sign was still there, hanging vertically on one nail. Vines and moss and a mélange of vegetation I couldn't name had not been dissuaded by the structure; they burrowed in, surrounded it, slithered through holes and windows, consumed the cabin so that it now looked like a natural part of the landscape.

"You're back," a voice said, startling me.

A male voice.

I reacted without thought. I jumped to the side, fell on the ground, rolled, pulled out the Glock, and took aim. The man merely put his hands up in the air. I looked at him, keeping the Glock on him. He was not what I expected. His thick beard looked like a robin's nest after a crow attack. His hair was long and matted. His clothes were tattered camouflage. For a moment, I thought I was back in the city, faced with another home-less panhandler. But the bearings weren't right. The man stood straight and steady. He looked me dead in the eye.

"Who the hell are you?" I said.

"It's been a long time, David."

"I don't know you."

"Not really, no. But I know you." He gestured with his head toward the bunk behind me. "You and your sister. I used to watch you play up here."

"I don't understand."

He smiled. His teeth, all there, were blindingly white against the beard. "I'm the Boogeyman."

In the distance, I heard a family of geese squawk as they glided to a landing on the lake's surface. "What do you want?" I asked.

"Not a damn thing," he said, still smiling. "Can I put my hands down?"

I nodded. He dropped his hands. I lowered my weapon but kept it at the ready. I thought about what he'd said and asked, "How long have you been hiding up here?"

"On and off for"—he seemed to be doing some kind of calculation with his fingers—"thirty years." He grinned at the dumbstruck expression on my face. "Yeah, I've watched you since you were this high." He put his hand at knee level. "Saw you grow up and—" He paused. "Been a long time since you been up here, David."

"Who are you?"

"My name is Jeremiah Renway," he said.

I couldn't place the name.

"I've been hiding from the law."

"So why are you showing yourself now?"

He shrugged. "Guess I'm glad to see you."

"How do you know I won't tell the authorities on you?"

"I figure you owe me one."

"How's that?"

"I saved your life."

I felt the ground beneath me shift. "What?"

"Who do you think pulled you out of the water?" he asked.

I was dumbstruck.

"Who do you think dragged you into the house? Who do you think called the ambulance?"

My mouth opened, but no words came out.

"And"—his smile spread—"who do you think dug up those bodies so someone would find them?"

It took me a while to find my voice. "Why?" I managed to ask.

"Can't say for sure," he said. "See, I did something bad a long time ago. Guess I thought this was a chance at redemption or something."

"You mean you saw . . . ?"

"Everything," Renway finished for me. "I saw them grab your missus. I saw them hit you with the bat. I saw them promise to pull you out if she told them where something was. I saw your missus hand them a key. I saw them laugh and force her into the car while you stayed underwater."

I swallowed. "Did you see them get shot?"

Renway smiled again. "We've chatted long enough, son. She's waiting for you now."

"I don't understand."

"She's waiting for you," he repeated, turning away from me. "By the tree." Without warning, he sprinted into the woods, darting through the brush like a deer. I stood there and watched him vanish in the thicket.

The tree.

I ran then. Branches whipped my face. I didn't care. My legs begged me to let up. I paid them no heed. My lungs protested. I told them to toughen up. When I finally made the right at the semi-phallic rock and rounded the path's corner, the tree was still there. I moved closer and felt my eyes start to well up.

Our carved initials—E.P. + D.B.—had darkened with age. So, too, had the thirteen lines we had carved out. I stared for a moment, and then I reached out and tentatively touched the grooves. Not of the initials. Not of the thirteen lines. My fingers traced down the eight fresh lines, still white and still sticky from sap.

Then I heard her say, "I know you think it's goofy."

My heart exploded. I turned behind me. And there she was.

I couldn't move. I couldn't speak. I just stared at her face. That beautiful face. And those eyes. I felt as though I were falling, plummeting down a dark shaft. Her face was thinner, her Yankee cheekbones more pronounced, and I don't think I had ever seen anything so perfect in all my life.

I reminded myself of the teasing dreams then—the nocturnal moments of escape when I would hold her in my arms and stroke her face and all the while feel myself being pulled away, knowing even as I had been bathing in the bliss that it was not real, that soon I'd be flung back into the waking world. The fear that this might be more of the same engulfed me, crushing the wind out of my lungs.

Elizabeth seemed to read what I was thinking and nodded as if to say "Yeah, this is real." She took a tentative step toward me. I could barely breathe, but I managed to shake my head and point at the carved lines and say, "I think it's romantic."

She muffled a sob with her hand and sprinted toward me. I opened my arms and she jumped in. I held her. I held her as tight as I could. My eyes squeezed shut. I smelled the lilac and cinnamon in her hair. She buried her face into my chest and sobbed. We gripped and regripped. She still ... fit. The contours, the grooves of our bodies needed no adjusting. I cupped the back of her head. Her hair was shorter, but the texture hadn't changed. I could feel her shaking and I'm sure she could feel the same emanating from me.

Our first kiss was exquisite and familiar and frighteningly desperate, two people who'd finally reached the surface after misjudging the depth of the water. The years began to melt away, winter giving way to spring. So many emotions ricocheted through me. I didn't sort through them or try to figure them out. I just let it all happen.

She lifted her head and looked into my eyes and I couldn't move. "I'm sorry," she said, and I thought my heart would shatter all over again.

I held her. I held her, and I wondered if I would ever risk letting her go. "Just don't leave me again," I said.

"Never."

"Promise?"

"Promise," she said.

We kept the embrace. I pressed against the wonder of her skin. I touched the muscles in her back. I kissed the swan neck. I even looked up to the heavens as I just held on. How? I wondered. How could this not be another cruel joke? How could she still be alive and back with me?

I didn't care. I just wanted it to be real. I wanted it to last.

But even as I held her against me, the sound of the cell phone, like something from my teasing dreams, started pulling me away. For a moment, I debated not answering it, but with all that had happened, that wasn't really an option. Loved ones had been left lying in our wake. We couldn't just abandon them. We both knew that. Still keeping one arm around Elizabeth—I'd be damned if I was ever going to let her go—I put the phone to my ear and said hello.

It was Tyrese. And as he spoke, I could feel it all start to slip away.

44

We parked in the abandoned lot at Riker Hill Elementary School and cut across the grounds, holding hands. Even in the dark, I could see that very little had changed from the days when Elizabeth and I had frolicked here. The pediatrician in me couldn't help but notice the new safety features. The swing set had stronger chains and harnessed seats now. Soft mulch was spread thickly under the jungle gyms in case a kid fell. But the kickball field, the soccer field, the blacktop with its painted-on hopscotch and four-square courts—they were all the same as when we were kids.

We walked past the window of Miss Sobel's second-grade class, but it was so long ago now that I think neither of us felt more than a ripple of nostalgia. We ducked into the woods, still hand in hand. Neither one of us had taken the path in twenty years, but we still knew the way. Ten minutes later, we were in Elizabeth's backyard on Goodhart Road. I turned to her. She stared at her childhood house with moist eyes.

"Your mother never knew?" I asked her.

She shook her head. She turned to me. I nodded and slowly let go of her hand.

"Are you sure about this?" she asked.

"No choice," I said.

I didn't give her a chance to argue. I stepped away and headed for the house. When I reached the sliding glass door, I cupped my hands around my eyes and peered in. No sign of Hoyt. I tried the back door. It was unlocked. I turned the knob and went inside. No one was there. I was about to head out when I saw a light snap on in the garage. I went through the kitchen and into the laundry room. I opened the door to the garage slowly.

Hoyt Parker sat in the front seat of his Buick Skylark. The engine was off. He had a drink in his hand. When I opened the door, he lifted his gun. Then, seeing me, he lowered it back to his side. I took the two steps down to the cement and reached for the passenger door handle. The car was unlocked. I opened the door and slid in next to him.

"What do you want, Beck?" There was the slur of drink in his speech.

I made a production of settling back in the seat. "Tell Griffin Scope to release the boy," I said.

"I don't know what you're talking about," he replied without an iota of conviction.

"Graft, payola, on the take. Choose your own term, Hoyt. I know the truth now."

"You don't know shit."

"That night at the lake," I said. "When you helped convince Elizabeth not to go to the police."

"We talked about that already."

"But now I'm curious, Hoyt. What were you really afraid of—that they'd kill her or that you'd be arrested too?"

His eyes lazily drifted toward me. "She'd be dead if I hadn't convinced her to run."

"I don't doubt that," I said. "But still it was lucky for you, Hoyt—shooting down two birds with one stone like that. You were able to save her life—and you were able to stay out of jail."

"And why exactly would I go to jail?"

"Are you denying you were on Scope's payroll?"

He shrugged. "You think I'm the only one who took their money?"

"No," I said.

"So why would I be more worried than the next cop?"

"Because of what you'd done."

He finished his drink, looked around for the bottle, poured himself some more. "I don't know what the hell you're talking about."

"Do you know what Elizabeth was investigating?"

"Brandon Scope's illegal activities," he said. "Prostitution. Underage girls. Drugs. The guy was playing at being Mr. Bad."

"What else?" I said, trying to stop quivering.

"What are you talking about?"

"If she kept digging, she might have stumbled across a bigger crime." I took a deep breath. "Am I right, Hoyt?"

His face sagged when I said that. He turned and stared straight out the front windshield.

"A murder," I said.

I tried to follow his gaze, but all I saw were Sears Craftsman tools hanging neatly on a pegboard. The screwdrivers with their yellow-and-black handles were lined up in perfect size order, flat-tops on the left, Phillips head on the right. Three wrenches and a hammer separated them.

I said, "Elizabeth wasn't the first one who wanted to bring Brandon Scope down." Then I stopped and waited, waited until he looked at me. It took some time, but eventually he did. And I saw it in his eyes. He didn't blink or try to hide it. I saw it. And he knew that I saw it.

"Did you kill my father, Hoyt?"

He took a deep swig from the glass, swished it around his mouth, and swallowed hard. Some of the whiskey spilled onto his face. He didn't bother to wipe it away. "Worse," he said, closing his eyes. "I betrayed him."

The rage boiled up in my chest, but my voice stayed surprisingly even. "Why?"

"Come on, David. You must have figured that out by now."

Another flash of fury shot across me. "My father worked with Brandon Scope," I began.

"More than that," he interjected. "Griffin Scope had your dad mentor him. They worked very closely together."

"Like with Elizabeth."

"Yes."

"And while working with him, my father discovered what a monster Brandon really was. Am I right?"

Hoyt just drank.

"He didn't know what to do," I continued. "He was afraid to tell, but he couldn't just let it go. The guilt ate at him. That was why he was so quiet the months before his death." I stopped and thought about my father, scared, alone, nowhere to turn. Why hadn't I seen it? Why hadn't I looked past my own world and seen his pain? Why hadn't I reached out to him? Why hadn't I done something to help him?

I looked at Hoyt. I had a gun in my pocket. How simple it would be. Just take out the gun and pull the trigger. Bam. Gone. Except I knew from personal experience that it wouldn't solve a damn thing. Just the opposite, in fact.

"Go on," Hoyt said.

"Somewhere along the line, Dad decided to tell a

friend. But not just any friend. A cop, a cop who worked in the city where the crimes were being committed." My blood started boiling, threatening again to erupt. "You, Hoyt."

Something in his face shifted.

"I got it right so far?"

"Pretty much," he replied.

"You told the Scopes, didn't you?"

He nodded. "I thought they'd transfer him or something. Keep him away from Brandon. I never thought ..." He made a face, clearly hating the self-justification in his own voice. "How did you know?"

"The name Melvin Bartola, for starters. He was the witness to the supposed accident that killed my father, but, of course, he worked for Scope too." My father's smile flashed in front of me. I tightened my hands into fists. "And then there was the lie you told about saving my life," I continued. "You did go back to the lake after you shot Bartola and Wolf. But not to save me. You looked, you saw no movement, and you figured I was dead."

"Figured you were dead," he repeated. "Not wanted you dead."

"Semantics," I said.

"I never wanted you to get hurt."

"But you weren't very broken up about it either," I said. "You went back to the car and told Elizabeth that I had drowned."

"I was just trying to convince her to disappear," he said. "It helped too."

"You must have been surprised when you heard I was still alive."

"More like shocked. How did you survive anyway?"

"It's not important."

Hoyt settled back as though from exhaustion. "Guess not," he said. His expression veered again and I was surprised when he said, "So what else do you want to know?"

"You're not denying any of this?"

"Nope."

"And you knew Melvin Bartola, right?"

"That's right."

"Bartola tipped you off about the hit on Elizabeth," I said. "I can't figure out what happened exactly. Maybe he had a conscience. Maybe he didn't want her to die."

"Bartola a conscience?" He chuckled. "Please. He was a low-life murdering scum. He came to me because he thought he could double-dip. Collect from the Scopes and from me. I told him I'd double his money and help him out of the country if he helped me fake her death."

I nodded, seeing it now. "So Bartola and Wolf told Scope's people that they were going to lie low after the killing. I wondered why their disappearance didn't raise more eyebrows, but thanks to you, Bartola and Wolf were supposed to go away."

"Yes."

"So what happened? Did you double-cross them?"

"Men like Bartola and Wolf—their word means nothing. No matter how much I paid them, I knew that they'd come back for more. They'd get bored living out of the country or maybe they'd get drunk and boast about it in a bar. I've dealt with this type of garbage my whole life. I couldn't risk that."

"So you killed them."

"Yep," he said without an ounce of regret.

I knew it all now. I just didn't know how it was all going to play out. "They're holding a little boy," I said to him. "I promised I'd turn myself in if they let him go.

You call them. You help make the trade."

"They don't trust me anymore."

"You've worked for Scope for a long time," I said. "Come up with something."

Hoyt sat there and thought about it. He looked at his tool wall again, and I wondered what he was seeing. Then slowly, he lifted the gun and pointed it at my face. "I think I got an idea," he said.

I didn't blink. "Open the garage door, Hoyt."

He didn't move.

I reached across him to the visor and pressed the garage's remote. The door came to life with a whir. Hoyt watched it rise. Elizabeth stood there, not moving. When it was open all the way, her gaze settled hard on her father's.

He flinched.

"Hoyt?" I said.

His head snapped toward me. With one hand he grabbed my hair. He pressed the gun against my eye. "Tell her to move out of the way."

I stayed still.

"Do it or you die."

"You wouldn't. Not in front of her."

He leaned closer to me. "Just do it, dammit." His voice was more like an urgent plea than a hostile command. I looked at him and felt something strange course through me. Hoyt turned on the ignition. I faced the front and gestured for her to move out of the way. She hesitated, but eventually she stepped to the side. Hoyt waited until she was clear of his path. Then he hit the gas. We flew past her with a jerk. As we hurtled away, I turned and watched out the back window as Elizabeth grew dimmer, fainter, until finally she was gone.

Again.

I sat back and wondered if I would ever see her again. I had feigned confidence before, but I knew the odds. She fought me on it. I explained that I had to do this. I needed to be the one doing the protecting this time. Elizabeth hadn't liked it, but she understood.

In the past few days I'd learned that she was alive. Would I trade my life for that? Gladly. I understood that going in. A strange, peaceful feeling came over me as I drove with the man who betrayed my father. The guilt that had weighed me down for so long finally lifted its hold. I knew now what I had to do—what I had to sacrifice—and I wondered if there was ever any choice, if it had been preordained to end like this.

I turned to Hoyt and said, "Elizabeth didn't kill Brandon Scope."

"I know," he interrupted, and then he said something that shook me to the core: "I did."

I froze.

"Brandon beat up Elizabeth," he went on quickly. "He was going to kill her. So I shot him when he got to the house. Then I framed Gonzalez, just like I said before. Elizabeth knew what I had done. She wouldn't let an innocent man take the fall. So she made up that alibi. Scope's people heard about it and it made them wonder. When they then began to suspect that maybe Elizabeth was the killer"—he stopped, kept his eyes on the road, summoned something from deep inside— "God help me, I let them."

I handed him the cell phone. "Call," I said.

He did. He called a man named Larry Gandle. I had met Gandle several times over the years. His father had gone to high school with mine. "I have Beck," Hoyt told him. "We'll meet you at the stables, but you have to release the kid."

Larry Gandle said something I couldn't make out.

"As soon as we know the kid is safe, we'll be there," I heard Hoyt say. "And tell Griffin I have what he wants. We can end this without hurting me or my family."

Gandle spoke again and then I heard him click off the line. Hoyt handed me back the phone.

"Am I part of your family, Hoyt?"

He aimed the gun at my head again. "Slowly take out your Glock, Beck. Two fingers."

I did as he asked. He hit the electric window slide.

"Toss it out the window."

I hesitated. He pushed the muzzle into my eye. I flipped the gun out of the car. I never heard it land.

We drove in silence now, waiting for the phone to ring again. When it did, I was the one who answered it. Tyrese said in a soft voice, "He's okay."

I hung up, relieved.

"Where are you taking me, Hoyt?"

"You know where."

"Griffin Scope will kill us both."

"No," he said, still pointing the gun at me. "Not both."

45

We turned off the highway and headed into the rural. The number of streetlights dwindled until the only illumination came from the car's headlights. Hoyt reached into the backseat and pulled out a manila envelope.

"I have it here, Beck. All of it."

"All of what?"

"What your father had on Brandon. What Elizabeth had on Brandon."

I was puzzled for a second. He'd had it with him the whole time. And then I wondered. The car. Why had Hoyt gone to the car?

"Where are the copies?" I asked.

He grinned as though happy I had asked. "There aren't any. It's all here."

"I still don't understand."

"You will, David. I'm sorry, but you're my fall guy now. It's the only way."

"Scope won't buy it," I said.

"Yeah, he will. Like you said, I've worked for him a long time. I know what he wants to hear. Tonight it ends."

"With my death?" I asked.

He didn't reply.

"How are you going to explain it to Elizabeth?"

"She might end up hating me," he said. "But at least she'll be alive."

Up ahead, I could see the estate's gated back entrance.

Endgame, I thought. The uniformed security guard waved us through. Hoyt kept the gun on me. We started up the drive and then, without warning, Hoyt slammed on the brake.

He spun toward me. "You wearing a wire, Beck?"

"What? No."

"Bullshit, let me see." He reached for my chest. I leaned away. He lifted the gun higher, closed the gap between us, and then started patting me down. Satisfied, he sat back.

"You're lucky," he said with a sneer.

He shifted back into drive. Even in the dark, you could get a feel for the lushness of the grounds. Trees stood silhouetted against the moon, swaying even though there seemed to be no wind. In the distance, I saw a burst of lights. Hoyt followed the road toward them. A faded gray sign told us we'd arrived at the Freedom Trails Stables. We parked in the first spot on the left. I looked out the window. I don't know much about the housing of horses, but this sprawl was impressive. There was one hangar-shaped building large enough to house a dozen tennis courts. The stables themselves were V-shaped and stretched as far as I could see. There was a sprouting fountain in the middle of the grounds. There were tracks and jumps and obstacle courses.

They were also men waiting for us.

With the weapon still on me, Hoyt said, "Get out."

I did. When I closed the door, the slam echoed in the stillness. Hoyt came around to my side of the car and jammed the gun into the small of my back. The smells brought on a quick spell of 4-H-fair déjà vu. But when I saw the four men in front of me, two of whom I recognized, the image fled.

le other two—the two I had never seen before—
both armed with some sort of semiautomatic rifle.
ney pointed them at us. I barely shuddered. I guess that
I was getting used to weapons aimed in my direction.
One of the men stood on the far right near the stable
entrance. The other was leaning against a car on the left.

The two men I had recognized were huddled together under a light. One was Larry Gandle. The other was
Griffin Scope. Hoyt nudged me forward with the gun.
As we moved toward them, I saw the door to the big
building open.

Eric Wu stepped out.

My heart thumped against my rib cage. I could hear
my breath in my ears. My legs tingled. I might be
immune to weapon intimidation, but my body remembered Wu's fingers. I involuntarily slowed a step. Wu
hardly glanced at me. He walked straight to Griffin
Scope and handed him something.

Hoyt made me stop when we were still a dozen yards
away. "Good news," he called out.

All eyes turned to Griffin Scope. I knew the man, of
course. I was, after all, the son of an old friend and the
brother of a trusted employee. Like most everyone else,
I'd been in awe of the burly man with the twinkle in his
eye. He was the guy you wanted to notice you—a back-
slap buy-you-a-drink compadre who had the rare ability to walk the tightrope between friend and employer. It
was a mix that rarely worked. The boss either lost
respect when he became a friend, or the friend was
resented when he suddenly had to be the boss. That
wasn't a problem for a dynamo like Griffin Scope. He'd
always known how to lead.

Griffin Scope looked puzzled. "Good news, Hoyt?"

Hoyt tried a smile. "Very good news, I think."

"Wonderful," Scope said. He glanced at Wu. Wu nodded but stayed where he was. Scope said, "So tell me this good news, Hoyt. I'm all a-twitter."

Hoyt cleared his throat. "First of all, you have to understand. I never meant to harm you. In fact, I went to great lengths to make sure nothing incriminating ever got out. But I also needed to save my daughter. You can understand that, can't you?"

A shadow flickered across Scope's face. "Do I understand the desire to protect a child?" he asked, his voice a quiet rumble. "Yes, Hoyt, I think I do."

A horse neighed in the distance. All else was silence. Hoyt licked his lips and held up the manila envelope.

"What's that, Hoyt?"

"Everything," he replied. "Photographs, statements, tapes. Everything that my daughter and Stephen Beck had on your son."

"Are there copies?"

"Only one," Hoyt said.

"Where?"

"In a safe place. An attorney has it. If I don't call him in an hour and give him the code, he releases them. I don't mean this as a threat, Mr. Scope. I would never reveal what I know. I have as much to lose as anyone."

"Yes," Scope said. "You do at that."

"But now you can leave us alone. You have it all. I'll send the rest. There is no need to hurt me or my family."

Griffin Scope looked at Larry Gandle, then at Eric Wu. The two perimeter men with the weapons seemed to tense. "What about my son, Hoyt? Someone shot him down like a dog. Do you expect me to just let that go?"

"That's just it," Hoyt said. "Elizabeth didn't do it."

arrowed his eyes in what was supposed to be interest, but I thought I saw something else , something akin to bemusement. "Pray tell," he id. "Then who did?"

I heard Hoyt swallow hard. He turned and looked at me. "David Beck."

I wasn't surprised. I wasn't angry either.

"He killed your son," he continued quickly. "He found out what was going on and he took vengeance."

Scope made a production of gasping and putting his hand on his chest. Then he finally looked at me. Wu and Gandle turned my way too. Scope met my eyes and said, "What do you have to say in your defense, Dr. Beck?"

I thought about it. "Would it do any good to tell you he's lying?"

Scope didn't reply to me directly. He turned to Wu and said, "Please bring me that envelope."

Wu had the walk of a panther. He headed toward us, smiling at me, and I felt a few of my muscles contract instinctively. He stopped in front of Hoyt and put out his hand. Hoyt handed him the envelope. Wu took the envelope with one hand. With the other—I've never seen anyone move so fast—he snatched away Hoyt's gun as though from a child, and tossed it behind him.

Hoyt said, "What the—?"

Wu punched him deep in the solar plexus. Hoyt fell to his knees. We all stood and watched as he dropped to all fours, retching. Wu circled, took his time, and placed his kick squarely on Hoyt's rib cage. I heard something snap. Hoyt rolled onto his back, blinking, his arms and legs splayed.

Griffin Scope approached, smiling down at my father-in-law. Then he held up something in the air. I squinted. It was small and black.

Hoyt looked up, spitting out blood. "I don't unde
stand," he managed.

I could see what was in Scope's hand now. It was a
microcassette player. Scope pressed the play button. I
heard first my own voice, then Hoyt's:

"Elizabeth didn't kill Brandon Scope."

"I know. I did."

Scope snapped off the tape recorder. Nobody spoke.
Scope glared down at my father-in-law. As he did, I realized a number of things. I realized that if Hoyt Parker
knew that his house was bugged, he'd also know that it
was more than likely that the same would be true of his
car. That was why he left the house when he spotted us
in the backyard. That was why he waited for me in the
car. That was why he interrupted me when I said that
Elizabeth didn't kill Brandon Scope. That was why he
confessed to the murder in a place where he knew they'd
be listening. I realized that when he patted me down, he
did indeed feel the wire that Carlson had put on my
chest, that he wanted to make sure that the feds, too,
would hear everything and that Scope wouldn't bother
frisking me. I realized that Hoyt Parker was taking the
fall, that while he had done many terrible things, including betraying my father, this had all been a ruse, a last
chance at redemption, that in the end, he, not I, would
sacrifice himself to save us all. I also realized that for his
plan to work, he had to do one more thing. So I stepped
away. And even as I heard the FBI helicopters start to
descend, even as I heard Carlson's voice through a
megaphone shout for everyone to freeze, I watched
Hoyt Parker reach into his ankle holster, pull out a gun,
and fire it three times at Griffin Scope. Then I watched
him turn the gun around.

I shouted "No!" but the final blast smothered it out.

We buried Hoyt four days later. Thousands of uniformed cops showed up to pay their respects. The
details of what had happened at the Scope estate weren't
out yet, and I wasn't sure they ever would be. Even
Elizabeth's mother hadn't pushed for answers, but perhaps that had more to do with the fact that she was
delirious with joy over her daughter's return from the
dead. It made her not want to ask too many questions
or look at the cracks too closely. I could relate.

For now, Hoyt Parker had died a hero. And maybe
that was true. I'm not the best judge.

Hoyt had written a long confession, basically restating
what he had told me in the car. Carlson showed it to me.

"Does this end it?" I asked.

"We still have to make a case against Gandle and Wu
and some of the others," he said. "But with Griffin
Scope dead, everyone's cutting deals now."

The mythical beast, I thought. You don't chop off its
head. You stab it in the heart.

"You were smart to come to me when they kidnapped that little boy," Carlson said to me.

"What was my alternative?"

"Good point." Carlson shook my hand. "Take care
of yourself, Dr. Beck."

"You too," I said.

You may want to know if Tyrese ever goes down to
Florida and what happens to TJ and Latisha. You may

be wondering if Shauna and Linda stay together
what that means to Mark. But I can't tell any of
because I don't know.

This story ends now, four days after the death of
Hoyt Parker and Griffin Scope. It is late. Very late. I am
lying in bed with Elizabeth, watching her body rise and
fall in sleep. I watch her all the time. I don't close my
eyes much. My dreams have perversely reversed themselves. It is in my dreams now that I lose her—where she
is dead again and I am alone. So I hold her a lot. I am
clingy and needy. So is she. But we'll work that out.

As though she feels my eyes on her, Elizabeth rolls
over. I smile at her. She smiles back and I feel my heart
soar. I remember the day at the lake. I remember drifting on that raft. And I remember my decision to tell her
the truth.

"We need to talk," I say.

"I don't think so."

"We're not good at keeping secrets from each other,
Elizabeth. It's what caused this mess in the first place. If
we had just told each other everything ..." I didn't
finish.

She nods. And I realize that she knows. That she's
always known.

"Your father," I say. "He always thought you killed
Brandon Scope."

"That's what I told him."

"But in the end—" I stop, start again. "When I said
in the car that you didn't kill him, do you think he realized the truth?"

"I don't know," Elizabeth says. "I like to think that
maybe he did."

"So he sacrificed himself for us."

"Or he tried to stop you from doing it," she says.

died still thinking I killed Brandon Scope.
...ly know. And it doesn't matter."
...ch other.

...ew," I say, my chest hitching. "From the
...ning. You—"

She hushes me with a finger on my lips. "It's okay."

"You put all that stuff in the safety-deposit box," I
say, "for me."

"I wanted to protect you," she says.

"It was in self-defense," I say, again remembering the
feel of the gun in my hand, the sickening backfire when
I pulled the trigger.

"I know," she says, wrapping her arms around my
neck and pulling me close. "I know."

You see, I was the one who was home when Brandon
Scope broke into our house eight years ago. I was the
one lying alone in the bed when he sneaked up with the
knife. We struggled. I fumbled for my father's gun. He
lunged again. I shot and killed him. And then, in a
panic, I ran. I tried to gather my thoughts, figure out
what to do. When I came to my senses, when I returned
to the house, the body was gone. So was the gun. I
wanted to tell her. I was going to at the lake. But in the
end, I never said anything about it. Until now.

Like I told you earlier, if I had just told the truth from
the get-go ...

She pulls me closer.

"I'm here," Elizabeth whispers.

Here. With me. It would take a while to accept that.
But I would. We hold each other and drift off to sleep.
Tomorrow morning we would wake up together. And
the morning after that too. Her face would be the first
I'd see every day. Her voice would be the first I'd hear.

And that, I knew, would always be enough.